FOUR GREAT MYSTERY NOVELS

From the lorry leapt two pencils of flame

[See page 297

FOUR
GREAT MYSTERY
NOVELS

THE CASK
by Freeman Wills Crofts

THE TERROR
by Edgar Wallace

THE W PLAN
by Graham Seton

THE SECRET OF TANGLES
by Leonard R. Gribble

ODHAMS PRESS LIMITED
LONG ACRE, LONDON, W.C.2

Reprinted 1948
Copyright
T648.1R.S.

Made in Great Britain
Printed at the St Ann's Press, Altrincham

CONTENTS

THE CASK
by *Freeman Wills Crofts*

PART I — LONDON

PART II — PARIS

5

CONTENTS

PART III — LONDON AND PARIS

THE TERROR
by Edgar Wallace

THE W PLAN
by Graham Seton

THE SECRET OF TANGLES
by Leonard R. Gribble

"Look out, there! Look out!"

[See page 29

The figure within became revealed

[See page 93

"I stepped close to her"

[See page 278

The detective could see his assistant lying motionless

[See page 287

He was swung from his feet

[See page 315

He descended a flight of stone stairs

[See page 353

He . . . came stealthily towards her

[See page 355

The tank burst with a loud explosion:

flames mounted with renewed violence

[See page 433

He . . . saw the bright red lights of an engine

[See page 462

He struck Grant savagely across the face

[See page 190

A tremendous roar engulfed his ears and senses

[See page 529

She gave a piercing cry

[See page 553

" Suddenly the other lunged at him "

[See page 612

Slade slunk back against the doorway

[See page 660

The man being pursued took a flying jump

[See page 697

THE CASK

By

FREEMAN WILLS CROFTS

THE CASK

PART I—LONDON

CHAPTER I

A STRANGE CONSIGNMENT

MR. AVERY, managing director of the Insular and Continental Steam Navigation Company, had just arrived at his office. He glanced at his inward letters, ran his eye over his list of engagements for the day, and inspected the return of the movements of his company's steamers. Then, after spending a few moments in thought, he called his chief clerk, Wilcox.

"I see the *Bullfinch* is in this morning from Rouen," he said. "I take it she'll have that consignment of wines for Norton and Banks?"

"She has," replied the chief clerk, "I've just rung up the dock office to inquire."

"I think we ought to have it specially checked from here. You remember all the trouble they gave us about the last lot. Will you send some reliable man down? Whom can you spare?"

"Broughton could go. He has done it before."

"Well, see to it, will you, and then send in Miss Johnson, and I shall go through the mail."

The office was the headquarters of the Insular and Continental Steam Navigation Company, colloquially known as the I. and C., and occupied the second floor of a large block of buildings at the western end of Fenchurch Street. The company was an important concern, and owned a fleet of some thirty steamers ranging from three hundred to one thousand tons burden, which traded between London and the smaller continental ports. Low freights was their speciality, but they did not drive their boats, and no attempt was made to compete with the more expensive routes in the matter of speed. Under these circumstances they did a large trade in all kinds of goods other than perishables.

Mr. Wilcox picked up some papers and stepped over to the desk at which Tom Broughton was working.

"Broughton," he said, "Mr. Avery wants you to go down at once to the docks and check a consignment of wines for Norton and Banks. It came in last night from Rouen in the *Bullfinch*. These people gave us a lot of trouble about their last lot, disputing our figures, so you will have to be very careful. Here are the invoices, and don't take the men's figures but see each cask yourself."

"Right, sir," replied Broughton, a young fellow of three-and-twenty, with a frank, boyish face and an alert manner. Nothing loath to exchange the monotony of the office for the life and bustle of the quays, he put away his books, stowed the invoices carefully in his pocket, took his hat and went quickly down the stairs and out into Fenchurch Street.

It was a brilliant morning in early April. After a spell of cold, showery weather, there was at last a foretaste of summer in the air, and the contrast made it seem good to be alive. The sun shone with that clear freshness seen only after rain. Broughton's spirits rose as he hurried through the busy streets, and watched the ceaseless flow of traffic pouring along the arteries leading to the shipping.

His goal was St. Katherine's Docks, where the *Bullfinch* was berthed, and, passing across Tower Hill and round two sides of the grim old fortress, he pushed on till he reached the basin in which the steamer was lying. She was a long and rather low vessel of some eight hundred tons burden, with engines amidships, and a single black funnel ornamented with the two green bands that marked the company's boats. Recently out from her annual overhaul, she looked trim and clean in her new coat of black paint. Unloading was in progress, and Broughton hurried on board, anxious to be present before any of the consignment of wine was set ashore.

He was just in time, for the hatches of the lower forehold, in which the casks were stowed, had been cleared and were being lifted off as he arrived. As he stood on the bridge deck waiting for the work to be completed he looked around.

Several steamers were lying in the basin. Immediately behind, with her high bluff bows showing over the *Bullfinch's* counter, was the *Thrush,* his company's largest vessel, due to sail that afternoon for Corunna and Vigo. In the berth in front lay a Clyde Shipping Company's boat bound for Belfast and Glasgow and also due out that afternoon, the smoke from her black funnel circling lazily up into the clear sky. Opposite was the *Arcturus,* belonging to the I. and C.'s rivals, Messrs. Babcock and Millman, and commanded by "Black Mac," so called to distinguish him from the Captain M'Tavish of differently coloured hair, "Red Mac," who was master of the same company's *Sirius.* To Broughton these boats represented links with the mysterious, far-off world of romance, and he never saw one put to sea without longing to go with her to Copenhagen, Bordeaux, Lisbon, Spezzia, or to whatever other delightful-sounding place she was bound.

The fore-hatch being open, Broughton climbed down into the hold armed with his notebook, and the unloading of the casks began. They were swung out in lots of four fastened together by rope slings. As each lot was dealt with, the clerk noted the contents in his book, from which he would afterwards check the invoices.

The work progressed rapidly, the men straining and pushing to get the heavy barrels in place for the slings. Gradually the space under and around the hatch was cleared, the casks then having to be rolled forward from the farther parts of the hold.

A quartet of casks had just been hoisted and Broughton was turning to examine the next lot when he heard a sudden shout of "Look out, there! Look out!" and felt himself seized roughly and pulled backwards. He swung round and was in time to see the four casks turning over out of the sling and falling heavily to the floor of the hold. Fortunately they had only been lifted some four or five feet, but they were heavy things and came down solidly. The two under were damaged slightly and the wine began to ooze out between the staves. The others had had their fall broken and neither seemed the worse. The men had all jumped clear and no one was hurt.

"Up-end those casks, boys," called the foreman, when the damage had been briefly examined, "and let's save the wine."

The leaking casks were turned damaged end up and lifted aside for temporary repairs. The third barrel was found to be uninjured, but when they came to the fourth it was seen that it had not entirely escaped.

This fourth cask was different in appearance from the rest, and Broughton had noted it as not belonging to Messrs. Norton and Banks's consignment. It was more strongly made and better finished, and was stained a light oak colour and varnished. Evidently, also, it did not contain wine, for what had called their attention to its injury was a little heap of sawdust which had escaped from a crack at the end of one of the staves.

"Strange looking cask this. Did you ever see one like it before?" said Broughton to the I. and C. foreman who had pulled him back, a man named Harkness. He was a tall, strongly built man with prominent cheekbones, a square chin and a sandy moustache. Broughton had known him for some time and had a high opinion of his intelligence and ability.

"Never saw nothin' like it," returned Harkness. "I tell you, sir, that there cask 'as been made to stand some knocking about."

"Looks like it. Let's get it rolled back out of the way and turned up, so as to see the damage."

Harkness seized the cask and with some difficulty rolled it close to the ship's side out of the way of the unloading, but when he tried to up-end it he found it too heavy to lift.

"There's something more than sawdust in there," he said. "It's the 'eaviest cask ever I struck. I guess it was its weight shifted the other casks in the sling and spilled the lot."

He called over another man and they turned the cask damaged end up. Broughton stepped over to the charge-hand and asked him to check the tally for a few seconds while he examined the injury.

As he was returning across the half-dozen yards to join the foreman, his eye fell on the little heap of sawdust that had fallen out of the crack, and the glitter of some bright object showing through it caught his attention. He stooped and picked it up. His amazement as he looked at it may be imagined, for it was a sovereign!

He glanced quickly round. Only Harkness of all the men present had seen it.

"Turn the 'eap over, sir," said the foreman, evidently as surprised as the younger man, "see if there are any more."

Broughton sifted the sawdust through his fingers and his astonishment was not lessened when he discovered two others hidden in the little pile.

He gazed at the three gold coins lying in his palm. As he did so Harkness gave a smothered exclamation and, stooping rapidly, picked something out from between two of the boards of the hold's bottom.

"Another, by gum!" cried the foreman in low tones, "and another!" He bent down again and lifted a second object from behind where the cask was standing. "Blest if it ain't a blooming gold mine we've struck."

Broughton put the five sovereigns in his pocket, as he and Harkness unostentatiously scrutinized the deck. They searched carefully, but found no other coins.

"Did you drop them when I dragged you back?" asked Harkness.

"I? No, I wish I had, but I had no gold about me."

"Some of the other chaps must 'ave then. Maybe Peters or Wilson. Both jumped just at this place."

"Well, don't say anything for a moment. I believe they came out of the cask."

"Out o' the cask? Why, sir, 'oo would send sovereigns in a cask?"

"No one, I should have said; but how would they get among the sawdust if they didn't come out through the crack with it?"

"That's so," said Harkness thoughtfully, continuing, "I tell you, Mr. Broughton, you say the word and I'll open that crack a bit more and we'll 'ave a look into the cask."

The clerk recognized that this would be irregular, but his curiosity was keenly aroused and he hesitated.

"I'll do it without leaving any mark that won't be put down to the fall," continued the tempter, and Broughton fell.

"I think we should know," he replied. "This gold may have been stolen and inquiries should be made."

The foreman smiled and disappeared, returning with a hammer and cold chisel. The broken piece at the end of the stave was entirely separated from the remainder by the crack, but was held in position by one of the iron rings. This piece Harkness with some difficulty drove upwards, thus widening the crack. As he did so, a little shower of sawdust fell out and the astonishment of the two men was not lessened when with it came a number of sovereigns, which went rolling here and there over the planks.

It happened that at the same moment the attention of the other men was concentrated on a quartet of casks which was being slung up through the hatches, the nervousness caused by the slip not having yet subsided. None of them therefore saw what had taken place, and Broughton and Harkness had picked up the coins before any of them turned round. Six sovereigns had come out, and the clerk added them to the five he already had, while he and his companion unostentatiously searched for others. Not finding any, they turned back to the cask deeply mystified.

"Open that crack a bit more," said Broughton. "What do you think about it?"

"Blest if I know what to think," replied the foreman. "We're on to something mighty queer anyway. 'Old my cap under the crack till I prize out that there bit of wood altogether."

With some difficulty the loose piece of the stave was hammered up, leaving a hole in the side of the barrel some six inches deep by nearly four wide. Half a capful of sawdust fell out, and the clerk added to it by clearing the broken edge of the wood. Then he placed the cap on the top of the cask and they eagerly felt through the sawdust.

"By Jehoshaphat!" whispered Harkness excitedly, "it's just full of gold!"

It seemed to be so, indeed, for in it were no fewer than seven sovereigns.

"That's eighteen in all," said Broughton, in an awed tone, as he slipped them into his pocket. "If the whole cask's full of them it must be worth thousands and thousands of pounds."

They stood gazing at the prosaic looking barrel, outwardly remarkable only in its strong design and good finish, marvelling if beneath that commonplace exterior there was indeed hidden what to them seemed a fortune. Then Harkness crouched down and looked into the cask through the hole he had made. Hardly had he done so when he sprang back with a sudden oath.

"Look in there, Mr. Broughton!" he cried in a suppressed tone. "Look in there!"

Broughton stooped in turn and peered in. Then he also recoiled, for there, sticking up out of the sawdust, were the fingers of a hand.

"This is terrible," he whispered, convinced at last they were in the presence of tragedy, and then he could have kicked himself for being such a fool.

"Why, it's only a statue," he cried.

"Statue?" replied Harkness sharply. "Statue? That ain't no statue. That's part of a dead body, that is. And don't you make no mistake."

"It's too dark to see properly. Get a light, will you, till we make sure."

When the foreman had procured a hand-lamp Broughton looked in again and speedily saw that his first impression was correct. The fingers were undoubtedly those of a woman's hand, small, pointed, delicate, and bearing rings which glinted in the light.

"Clear away some more of the sawdust, Harkness," said the young man as he stood up again. "We must find out all we can now."

He held the cap as before, and the foreman carefully picked out with the cold chisel the sawdust surrounding the fingers. As its level lowered, the remainder of the hand and the wrist gradually became revealed. The sight of the whole only accentuated the first impression of dainty beauty and elegance.

Broughton emptied the cap on to the top of the cask. Three more sovereigns were found hidden in it, and these he pocketed with the others. Then he turned to re-examine the cask.

It was rather larger than the wine barrels, being some three feet six high by nearly two feet six in diameter. As already mentioned, it was of unusually strong construction, the sides, as shown by the broken stave, being quite two inches thick. Owing possibly to the difficulty of bending such heavy stuff, it was more cylindrical than barrel shaped, the result being that the ends were unusually large, and this no doubt partly accounted for Harkness's difficulty in up-ending it. In place of the usual thin metal bands, heavy iron rings clamped it together.

On one side was a card label, tacked round the edges and addressed in a foreign handwriting: "M. Léon Felix, 141 West Jubb Street, Tottenham Court Road, London, W., via Rouen and long sea," with the words "Statuary only" printed with a rubber stamp. The label bore also the sender's name: "Dupierre et Cie, Fabricants de la Sculpture Monumentale, Rue Provence, Rue de la Convention, Grenelle, Paris." Stencilled in black letters on the woodwork was "Return to" in French, English, and German, and the name of the same firm. Broughton examined the label with care, in the half-unconscious hope of discovering something from the handwriting. In this he was disappointed, but, as he held the hand-lamp close, he saw something else which interested him.

The label was divided into two parts, an ornamental border containing the sender's advertisement and a central portion for the address. These two were separated by a thick black line. What had caught Broughton's eye was an unevenness along this line, and closer examination showed that the central portion had been cut out, and a piece of paper pasted on the back of the card to cover the hole. Felix's address was therefore written on this paper, and not on the original label. The alteration had been neatly done, and was almost unnoticeable. Broughton was puzzled at first, then it occurred to him that the firm must have run out of labels and made an old one do duty a second time.

"A cask containing money and a human hand—probably a body," he mused. "It's a queer business and something has got to be done about it." He stood looking at the cask while he thought out his course of action.

That a serious crime had been committed he felt sure, and that it was his duty to report his discovery immediately he was no less certain. But there was the question of the consignment of wines. He had been sent specially to the docks to check it, and he wondered if he would be right to leave the work undone. He thought so. The matter was serious enough to justify him. And it was not as if the wine would not be checked. The ordinary tallyman was there, and Broughton knew him to be careful and accurate. Besides, he could probably get a clerk from the dock office to help. His mind was made up. He would go straight to Fenchurch Street and report to Mr. Avery, the managing director.

"Harkness," he said, "I'm going up to the head office to report this. You'd better close up the hole as best you can and then stay here and watch the cask. Don't let it out of your sight on any pretext until you get instructions from Mr. Avery."

"Right, Mr. Broughton," replied the foreman, "I think you're doing the proper thing."

They replaced as much of the sawdust as they could, and Harkness fitted the broken piece of stave into the space and drove it home, nailing it fast.

"Well, I'm off," said Broughton, but as he turned to go a gentleman stepped down into the hold and spoke to him. He was a man of medium height, foreign looking, with a dark complexion and a black, pointed beard, and dressed in a well-cut suit of blue clothes, with white spats and a Homburg hat. He bowed and smiled.

"Pardon me, but you are, I presume, an I. and C. official?" he asked, speaking perfect English, but with a foreign accent.

"I am a clerk in the head office, sir," replied Broughton.

"Ah, quite so. Perhaps then you can oblige me with some information? I am expecting from Paris by this boat a cask containing a group of statuary from Messrs. Dupierre of that city. Can you tell me if it has arrived? This is my name." He handed Broughton a card on which was printed: "M. Léon Felix, 141 West Jubb Street, Tottenham Court Road, W."

Though the clerk saw at a glance the name was the same as that on the label on the cask, he pretended to read it with care while considering his reply. This man clearly was the consignee, and if he were told the cask was there he would doubtless claim immediate possession. Broughton could think of no excuse for refusing him, but he was determined all the same not to let it go. He had just decided to reply that it had not yet come to light, but that they would keep a look out for it, when another point struck him.

The damaged cask had been moved to the side of the hold next the dock, and it occurred to the clerk that any one standing on the wharf beside the hatch could see it. For all he knew to the contrary, this man Felix might have watched their whole proceedings, including the making of the hole in the cask and the taking out of the sovereigns. If he had recognized his property, as was possible, a couple of steps from where he was standing would enable him to put his finger on the label and so convict Broughton of a falsehood. The clerk decided that in this case honesty would be the best policy.

"Yes, sir," he answered, "your cask has arrived. By a curious coincidence it is this one beside us. We had just separated it out from the wine-barrels owing to its being differently consigned."

M. Felix looked at the young man suspiciously, but he only said: "Thank you. I am a collector of *objets d'art,* and am anxious to see the statue. I have a cart here and I presume I can get it away at once?"

This was what Broughton had expected, but he thought he saw his way.

"Well, sir," he responded civilly, "that is outside my job and I fear I cannot help you. But I am sure you can get it now if you will come over to the office on the quay and go through the usual formalities. I am going there now and will be pleased to show you the way."

"Oh, thank you. Certainly," agreed the stranger.

As they walked off, a doubt arose in Broughton's mind that Harkness might misunderstand his replies to Felix, and if the latter returned with a plausible story might let the cask go. He therefore called out :—

"You understand then, Harkness, you are to do nothing till you hear from Mr. Avery," to which the foreman replied by a wave of the hand.

The problem the young clerk had to solve was threefold. First, he had to go to Fenchurch Street to report the matter to his managing director. Next, he must ensure that the cask was kept in the company's possession until that gentleman had decided his course of action, and lastly, he wished to accomplish both of these things without raising the suspicions either of Felix or the clerks in the quay office. It was not an easy matter, and at first Broughton was somewhat at a loss. But as they entered the office a plan occurred to him. He turned to his companion.

"If you will wait here a moment, sir," he said, "I'll find the clerk who deals with your business and send him to you."

"I thank you."

He passed through the door in the screen dividing the outer and inner offices and, crossing to the manager's room, spoke in a low tone to that official.

"Mr. Huston, there's a man outside named Felix for whom a cask has come from Paris on the *Bullfinch* and he wants possession now. The cask is there, but Mr. Avery suspects there is something not quite right about it, and he sent me to tell you to please delay delivery until you hear further from him. He said to make any excuse, but under no circumstances to give the thing up. He will ring you up in an hour or so when he has made some further inquiries."

Mr. Huston looked queerly at the young man, but he only said, "That will be all right," and the latter took him out and introduced him to Mr. Felix.

Broughton delayed a few moments in the inner office to arrange with one of the clerks to take up his work on the *Bullfinch* during his absence. As he passed out by the counter at which the manager and Mr. Felix were talking, he heard the latter say in an angry tone :—

"Very well, I will go now and see your Mr. Avery, and I feel sure he will make it up to me for this obstruction and annoyance."

"It's up to me to be there first," thought Broughton, as he hurried out of the dock gates in search of a taxi. None was in sight and he stopped and considered the situation. If Felix had a car waiting he would get to Fenchurch Street while he, Broughton, was looking round. Something else must be done.

Stepping into the Little Tower Hill Post Office, he rang up the head office, getting through to Mr. Avery's private room. In a few words he explained that he had accidentally come on evidence which pointed to the commission of a serious crime, that a man named Felix appeared to know something about it, and that this man was about to call on Mr. Avery, continuing :—

"Now, sir, if you'll let me make a suggestion, it is that you don't see this Mr. Felix immediately he calls, but that you let me into your private office by the landing door, so that I don't need to pass through the outer office. Then you can hear my story in detail and decide what to do."

"It all sounds rather vague and mysterious," replied the distant voice, "can you not tell me what you found?"

"Not from here, sir, if you please. If you'll trust me this time, I think you'll be satisfied that I am right when you hear my story."

"All right. Come along."

Broughton left the post office and, now when it no longer mattered, found an empty taxi. Jumping in, he drove to Fenchurch Street and, passing up the staircase, knocked at his chief's private door.

"Well, Broughton," said Mr. Avery, "sit down there." Going to the door leading to the outer office he spoke to Wilcox.

"I've just had a telephone call and I want to send some other messages. I'll be engaged for half an hour." Then he closed the door and slipped the bolt.

"You see I have done as you asked and I shall now hear your story. I trust you haven't put me to all this inconvenience without a good cause."

"I think not, sir, and I thank you for the way you have met me. What happened was this," and Broughton related in detail his visit to the docks, the mishap to the casks, the discovery of the sovereigns and the woman's hand, the coming of Mr. Felix and the interview in the quay office, ending up by placing the twenty-one sovereigns in a little pile on the chief's desk.

When he ceased speaking there was silence for several minutes, while Mr. Avery thought over what he had heard. The tale was a strange one, but both from his knowledge of Broughton's character as well as from the young man's manner he implicitly believed every word he had heard. He considered the firm's position in the matter. In one way it did not concern them if a sealed casket, delivered to them for conveyance, contained marble, gold, or road metal, so long as the freight was paid. Their contract was to carry what was handed over to them from one point to another and give it up in the condition they received it. If any one chose to send sovereigns under the guise of statuary, any objection that might be raised concerned the Customs Department, not them.

On the other hand, if evidence pointing to a serious crime came to the firm's notice, it would be the duty of the firm to acquaint the police. The woman's hand in the cask might or might not indicate a murder, but the suspicion was too strong to justify them in hiding the matter. He came to a decision.

"Broughton," he said, "I think you have acted very wisely all through. We will go now to Scotland Yard, and you may repeat your tale to the authorities. After that I think we will be clear of it. Will you go out the way you came in, get a taxi, and wait for me in Fenchurch Street at the end of Mark Lane?"

Mr. Avery locked the private door after the young man, put on his coat and hat, and went into the outer office.

"I am going out for a couple of hours, Wilcox," he said.

The head clerk approached with a letter in his hand.

"Very good, sir. A gentleman named Mr. Felix called about 11.30 to see you. When I said you were engaged, he would not wait, but asked for a sheet of paper and an envelope to write you a note. This is it."

The managing director took the note and turned back into his private office to read it. He was puzzled. He had said at 11.15 he would be engaged for half an hour. Therefore Mr. Felix would only have had fifteen minutes to wait. As he opened the envelope he wondered why that gentleman could not have spared this moderate time, after coming all the way from the docks to see him. And then he was puzzled again, for the envelope was empty!

He stood in thought. Had something occurred to startle Mr. Felix when writing his note, so that in his agitation he omitted to enclose it? Or had he simply made a mistake? Or was there some deep-laid plot? Well, he would see what Scotland Yard thought.

He put the envelope away in his pocket-book and going down to the street, joined Broughton in the taxi. They rattled along the crowded thoroughfares while Mr. Avery told the clerk about the envelope.

" I say, sir," said the latter, " but that's a strange business. When I saw him, Mr. Felix was not at all agitated. He seemed to me a very cool, clear-headed man."

It happened that about a year previously the shipping company had been the victim of a series of cleverly-planned robberies, and, in following up the matter, Mr. Avery had become rather well acquainted with two or three of the Yard inspectors. One of these in particular he had found a shrewd and capable officer, as well as a kindly and pleasant man to work with. On arrival at the Yard he asked for this man, and was pleased to find he was not engaged.

" Good morning, Mr. Avery," said the inspector, as they entered his office, " what good wind blows you our way today?"

" Good morning, inspector. This is Mr. Broughton, one of my clerks, and he has got a rather singular story that I think will interest you to hear."

Inspector Burnley shook hands, closed the door, and drew up a couple of chairs.

" Sit down, gentlemen," he said. " I am always interested in a good story."

" Now, Broughton, repeat your adventures over again to Inspector Burnley."

Broughton started off and, for the second time, told of his visit to the docks, the damage to the heavily-built cask, the finding of the sovereigns and the woman's hand, and the interview with Mr. Felix. The inspector listened gravely and took a note or two, but did not speak till the clerk had finished, when he said:—

" Let me congratulate you, Mr. Broughton, on your very clear statement."

" To which I might add a word," said Mr. Avery, and he told of the visit of Mr. Felix to the office and handed over the envelope he had left.

" That envelope was written at 11.30," said the inspector, " and it is now nearly 12.30. I am afraid this is a serious matter, Mr. Avery. Can you come to the docks at once?"

" Certainly."

" Well, don't let us lose any time." He threw a London directory down before Broughton. " Just look up this Felix, will you, while I make some arrangements."

Broughton looked for West Jubb Street, but there was no such street near Tottenham Court Road.

"I thought as much," said Inspector Burnley, who had been telephoning. "Let us proceed."

As they reached the courtyard a taxi drew up, containing two plain-clothes men as well as the driver. Burnley threw open the door, they all got in, and the vehicle slid quickly out into the street.

Burnley turned to Broughton. "Describe the man Felix as minutely as you can."

"He was a man of about middle height, rather slightly and elegantly built. He was foreign-looking, French, I should say, or even Spanish, with dark eyes and complexion, and black hair. He wore a short, pointed beard. He was dressed in blue clothes of good quality, with a dark green or brown Homburg hat, and black shoes with light spats. I did not observe his collar and tie specially, but he gave me the impression of being well dressed in such matters of detail. He wore a ring with some kind of stone on the little finger of his left hand."

The two plain-clothes men had listened attentively to the description, and they and the inspector conversed in low tones for a few moments, when silence fell on the party.

They stopped opposite the *Bullfinch's* berth and Broughton led the way down.

"There she is," he pointed, "if we go to that gangway we can get down direct to the forehold."

The two plain-clothes men had also alighted and the five walked in the direction indicated. They crossed the gangway and, approaching the hatchway, looked down into the hold.

"There's where it is," began Broughton, pointing down, and then suddenly stopped.

The others stepped forward and looked down. The hold was empty. Harkness and the cask were gone!

CHAPTER II

INSPECTOR BURNLEY ON THE TRACK

THE immediate suggestion was, of course, that Harkness had had the cask moved to some other place for safety, and this they set themselves to find out.

" Get hold of the gang that were unloading this hold," said the inspector.

Broughton darted off and brought up a stevedore's foreman, from whom they learned that the forehold had been emptied some ten minutes earlier, the men having waited to complete it and then gone for dinner.

" Where do they get their dinner? Can we get hold of them now?" asked Mr. Avery.

" Some of them, sir, I think. Most of them go out into the city, but some use the night watchman's room where there is a fire."

" Let's go and see," said the inspector, and headed by the foreman they walked some hundred yards along the quay to a small brick building set apart from the warehouses, inside and in front of which sat a number of men, some eating from steaming cans, others smoking short pipes.

" Any o' you boys on the *Bullfinch's* lower forehold?" asked the foreman, " if so, boss wants you 'alf a sec."

Three of the men got up slowly and came forward.

" We want to know, men," said the managing director, " if you can tell us anything about Harkness and a damaged cask. He was to wait with it till we got down."

" Well, he's gone with it," said one of the men, " less'n 'alf an hour ago."

" Gone with it?"

" Yes. Some toff in blue clothes an' a black beard came up an' give 'im a paper, an' when 'e'd read it 'e calls out an' sez, sez 'e, ' 'Elp me swing out this 'ere cask.' 'e says. We 'elps 'im, an' 'e puts it on a 'orse dray—a four-wheeler. An' then they all goes off, 'im an' the cove in the blue togs walkin' together after the dray."

" Any name on the dray?" asked Mr. Avery.

" There was," replied the spokesman, "but I'm blessed if I knows what it was. 'Ere Bill, you was talking about that there name. Where was it?"

Another man spoke.

" It was Tottenham Court Road, it was. But I didn't know the street, and I thought that a strange thing, for I've lived off the Tottenham Court Road all my life."

" Was it East John Street?" asked Inspector Burnley.

" Ay, it was something like that. East or West. West, I think. An' it was something like John. Not John, but something like it."

" What colour was the dray?"

" Blue, very fresh and clean."

" Any one notice the colour of the horse?"

But this was beyond them. The horse was out of their line. Its colour had not been observed.

"Well," said Mr. Avery, as the inspector signed that was all he wanted, "we are much obliged to you. Here's something for you."

Inspector Burnley beckoned to Broughton.

"You might describe this man Harkness."

"He was a tall chap with a sandy moustache, very high cheek-bones, and a big jaw. He was dressed in brown dungarees and a cloth cap."

"You hear that," said the inspector, turning to the plain-clothes men. "They have half an hour's start. Try to get on their track. Try north and east first, as it is unlikely they'd go west for fear of meeting us. Report to headquarters."

The men hurried away.

"Now, a telephone," continued the inspector. "Perhaps you'd let me use your quay office one."

They walked to the office, and Mr. Avery arranged for him to get the private instrument in the manager's room. He rejoined the others in a few minutes.

"Well," he said, "that's all we can do in the meantime. A description of the man and cart will be wired round to all the stations immediately, and every constable in London will be on the look-out for them before very much longer."

"Very good that," said the managing director.

The inspector looked surprised.

"Oh no," he said, "that's the merest routine. But now I'm here I would like to make some other inquiries. Perhaps you would tell your people that I'm acting with your approval, as it might make them give their information more willingly."

Mr. Avery called over Huston, the manager.

"Huston, this is Inspector Burnley of Scotland Yard. He is making some inquiries about that cask you already heard of. I'll be glad if you see that he is given every facility." He turned to the inspector. "I suppose there's nothing further I can do to help you? I should be glad to get back to the City again, if possible."

"Thank you, Mr. Avery, there's nothing more. I'll cruise round here a bit. I'll let you know how things develop."

"Right. Good-bye then, in the meantime."

The inspector, left to his own devices, called Broughton and, going on board the *Bullfinch,* had the clerk's story repeated in great detail, the actual place where each incident happened being pointed out. He made a search for any object that might have been dropped, but without success, visited the wharf and other points from which

G.M.N.—B*

the work at the cask might have been overlooked, and generally made himself thoroughly familiar with the circumstances. By the time this was done the other men who had been unloading the forehold had returned from dinner and he interviewed them, questioning each individually. No additional information was received.

The inspector then returned to the quay office.

" I want you," he asked Mr. Huston, " to be so good as to show me all the papers you have referring to that cask, waybills, forward notes, everything."

Mr. Huston disappeared, returning in a few seconds with some papers which he handed to Burnley. The latter examined them and then said :—

" These seem to show that the cask was handed over to the French State Railway at their rue Cardinet goods station, near the Gare St. Lazare, in Paris, by MM. Dupierre et Cie, carriage being paid forward. They ran it by rail to Rouen, when it was loaded on to your *Bullfinch*."

" That is so."

" I suppose you cannot say whether the Paris collection was made by a railway vehicle?"

" No, but I should think not, as otherwise the cartage charges would probably show."

" I think I am right in saying that these papers are complete and correct in every detail?"

" Oh yes, they are perfectly in order."

" How do you account for the cask being passed through by the Customs officials without examination?"

" There was nothing suspicious about it. It bore the label of a well-known and reputable firm, and was invoiced as well as stencilled, ' Statuary only.' It was a receptacle obviously suitable for transporting such goods, and its weight was also in accordance. Unless in the event of some suspicious circumstance, cases of this kind are seldom opened."

" Thank you, Mr. Huston, that is all I want at present. Now, can I see the captain of the *Bullfinch*?"

" Certainly. Come over and I'll introduce you."

Captain M'Nabb was a big, rawboned Ulsterman, with a hooked nose and sandy hair. He was engaged in writing up some notes in his cabin.

" Come in, sir, come in," he said, as Huston made the inspector known. " What can I do for you?"

Burnley stated his business. He had but few questions to ask.

"How is the trans-shipment done from the railway to your boat at Rouen?"

"The wagons come down on the wharf right alongside. The Rouen stevedores load them, either with the harbour travelling crane or our own winches."

"Would it be at all possible for a barrel to be tampered with after it was once aboard?"

"How do you mean tampered with? A barrel of wine might be tapped, but that's all could be done."

"Could a barrel be changed, or completely emptied and filled with something else?"

"It could not. The thing's altogether impossible."

"I'm much obliged to you, captain. Good day."

Inspector Burnley was nothing if not thorough. He questioned in turn the winch drivers, the engineers, even the cook, and before six o'clock had interviewed every man that had sailed on the *Bullfinch* from Rouen. The results were unfortunately entirely negative. No information about the cask was forthcoming. No question had been raised about it. Nothing had happened to call attention to it, or that was in any way out of the common.

Puzzled but not disheartened, Inspector Burnley drove back to Scotland Yard, his mind full of the mysterious happenings, and his pocket-book stored with all kinds of facts about the *Bullfinch*, her cargo, and crew.

Two messages were waiting for him. The first was from Ralston, the plain-clothes man that he had sent from the docks in a northerly direction. It read:—

"Traced parties as far as north end of Leman Street. Trail lost there."

The second was from a police station in Upper Head Street:—

"Parties seen turning from Great Eastern Street into Curtain Road about 1.20 p.m."

"H'm, going north-west, are they?" mused the inspector, taking down a large scale map of the district. "Let's see. Here's Leman Street. That is, say, due north from St. Katherine's Docks, and half a mile or more away. Now, what's the other one?"—he referred to the wire—"Curtain Road should be somewhere here. Yes, here it is. Just a continuation of the same line, only more west, say, a mile and a half from the docks. So they're going straight, are they, and using the main streets. H'm. H'm. Now I wonder where they're heading to. Let's see."

The inspector pondered. "Ah, well," he murmured at last, putting the map back, "we must wait till tomorrow," and, sending instructions recalling his two plain-clothes assistants. he went home.

But his day's work was not done. Hardly had he finished his meal and lit one of the strong, black cigars he favoured, when he was summoned back to Scotland Yard. There waiting for him was Broughton, and with him the tall, heavy-jawed foreman, Harkness.

The inspector pulled forward two chairs.

" Sit down, gentlemen," he said, when the clerk had introduced his companion, " and let me hear your story."

" You'll be surprised to see me so soon again, Mr. Burnley," answered Broughton, " but, after leaving you, I went back to the office to see if there were any instructions for me, and found our friend here had just turned up. He was asking for the chief, Mr. Avery, but he had gone home. Then he told me his adventures, and as I felt sure Mr. Avery would have sent him to you, I thought my best plan was to bring him along without delay."

" And right you were, Mr. Broughton. Now, Mr. Harkness, I would be obliged if you would tell me what happened to you."

The foreman settled himself comfortably in his chair.

" Well, sir," he began, " I think you're listening to the biggest fool between this and St. Paul's. I 'ave been done this afternoon, fairly diddled, an' not once only, but two separate times. 'Owever, I'd better tell you from the beginning.

" When Mr. Broughton an' Felix left, I stayed an' kept an eye on the cask. I got some bits of 'oop iron by way o' mending it, so that none o' the boys would wonder why I was 'anging around. I waited the best part of an hour, an' then Felix came back.

" ' Mr. 'Arkness, I believe?' 'e said.

" ' That's my name, sir,' I answered.

" ' I 'ave a letter for you from Mr. Avery. P'raps you would kindly read it now,' 'e said.

" It was a note from the 'ead office, signed by Mr. Avery, an' it said that 'e 'ad seen Mr. Broughton an' that it was all right about the cask, an' for me to give it up to Felix at once. It said, too, that we 'ad to deliver the cask at the address that was on it, an' for me to go there along with it and Felix, an' to report if it was safely delivered.

" ' That's all right, sir,' said I, an' I called to some o' the boys an' we got the cask swung ashore an' on to a four-wheeled dray Felix 'ad waiting. 'E 'ad two men with it, a big, strong fellow with red 'air an' a smaller dark chap that drove. We turned east at the dock gates, an' then went up Leman Street an' on into a part o' the city I didn't know.

" When we 'ad gone a mile or more, the red-'aired man said

'e could do with a drink. Felix wanted 'im to carry on at first, but
'e gave in after a bit an' we stopped in front o' a bar. The small
man's name was Watty, an' Felix asked 'im could 'e leave the 'orse,
but Watty said 'No,' an' then Felix told 'im to mind it while the
rest of us went in, an' 'e would come out soon an' look after it, so's
Watty could go in an' get 'is drink. So Felix an' I an' Ginger went
in, an' Felix ordered four bottles o' beer an' paid for them. Felix
drank 'is off, an' then 'e told us to wait till 'e would send Watty in
for 'is, an' went out. As soon as 'e 'ad gone Ginger leant over an'
whispered to me, 'Say, mate, wot's 'is game with the blooming
cask? I lay you five to one 'e 'as something crooked on.'

"'Why,' said I, 'I don't know about that.' You see, sir, I 'ad
thought the same myself, but then Mr. Avery wouldn't 'ave written
wot it was all right if it wasn't.

"'Well, see 'ere,' said Ginger, 'maybe if you an' I was to keep
our eyes skinned, it might put a few quid in our pockets.'

"''Ow's that?' said I.

"''Ow's it yourself?' said 'e. 'If 'e 'as some game on wi' the
cask 'e'll not be wanting for to let any outsiders in. If you an' me
was to offer for to let them in for 'im, 'e'd maybe think we was
worth something.'

"Well, gentlemen, I thought over that, an' first I wondered if
this chap knew there was a body in the cask, an' I was going to
see if I couldn't find out without giving myself away. Then I
thought maybe 'e was on the same lay, an' was pumping me. So
I thought I would pass it off a while, an' I said :—

"'Would Watty come in?'

"Ginger said 'No,' that three was too many for a job o' that
kind, an' we talked on a while. Then I 'appened to look at Watty's
beer standing there, an' I wondered 'e 'adn't been in for it.

"'That beer won't keep,' I said. 'If that blighter wants it 'e'd
better come an' get it.'

"Ginger sat up when 'e 'card that.

"'Wot's wrong with 'im?' 'e said. 'I'll drop out an' see.'

"I don't know why, gentlemen, but I got a kind o' notion there
was something in the air, an' I followed 'im out. The dray was
gone. We looked up an' down the street, but there wasn't a sign
of it nor Felix nor Watty.

"'Blow me, if they 'aven't given us the slip,' shouted Ginger.
'Get a move on. You go that way an' I'll go this, an' one of us
is bound to see them at the corner.'

"I guessed I was on to the game then. These three were wrong
'uns, an' they were out to get rid o' the body, an' they didn't want

me around to see the grave. All that about the drinks was a plant to get me away from the dray, an' Ginger's talk was only to keep me quiet till the others got clear. Well, two o' them 'ad got quit o' me right enough, but I was blessed if the third would.

"'No, you don't, ol' pal,' I said. 'I guess you an' me'll stay together.' I took 'is arm an' 'urried 'im on the way 'e 'ad wanted to go 'imself. But when we got to the corner there wasn't a sign o' the dray. They 'ad given us the slip about proper.

"Ginger cursed an' raved, an' wanted to know 'oo was going to pay 'im for 'is day. I tried to get out of 'im 'oo 'e was an' 'oo 'ad 'ired 'im, but 'e wasn't giving anything away. I kept close beside 'im, for I knew 'e'd 'ave to go 'ome some time, an' I thought if I saw where 'e lived it would be easy to find out where 'e worked, an' so likely get 'old o' Felix. 'E tried different times to juke away from me, an' 'e got real mad when 'e found 'e couldn't.

"We walked about for more than three hours till it was near five o'clock, an' then we 'ad some more beer, an' when we came out o' the bar we stood at the corner o' two streets an' thought wot we'd do next. An' then suddenly Ginger lurched up against me, an' I drove fair into an old woman that was passing, an' nearly knocked 'er over. I caught 'er to keep 'er from falling—I couldn't do no less—but when I looked round, I'm blessed if Ginger wasn't gone. I ran down one street first, an' then down the other, an' then I went back into the bar, but never a sight of 'im did I get. I cursed myself for every kind of a fool, an' then I thought I'd better go back an' tell Mr. Avery anyway. So I went to Fenchurch Street, an' Mr. Broughton brought me along 'ere."

There was silence when the foreman ceased speaking, while Inspector Burnley, in his painstaking way, considered the statement he had heard, as well as that made by Broughton earlier in the day. He reviewed the chain of events in detail, endeavouring to separate the undoubted facts from what might be only the narrators' opinions. If the two men were to be believed, and Burnley had no reason for doubting either, the facts about the discovery and removal of the cask were clear, with one exception. There seemed to be no adequate proof that the cask really did contain a corpse.

"Mr. Broughton tells me he thought there was a body in the cask. Do you agree with that, Mr. Harkness?"

"Yes, sir, there's no doubt of it. We both saw a woman's hand."

"But might it not have been a statue? The cask was labelled 'Statuary,' I understand."

"No, sir, it wasn't no statue. Mr. Broughton thought that at first, but when 'e looked at it again 'e gave in I was right. It was a body, sure enough."

Further questions showed that both men were convinced the hand was real, though neither could advance any grounds for their belief other than that he " knew from the look of it." The inspector was not satisfied that their opinion was correct, though he thought it probable. He also noted the possibility of the cask containing a hand only or perhaps an arm, and it passed through his mind that such a thing might be packed by a medical student as a somewhat gruesome practical joke. Then he turned to Harkness again.

" Have you the letter Felix gave you on the *Bullfinch*?"

" Yes, sir," replied the foreman, handing it over.

It was written in what looked like a junior clerk's handwriting on a small-sized sheet of business letter paper. It bore the I. and C.'s ordinary printed heading, and read:—

5th April, 1912.

Mr. HARKNESS,
 on S.S. *Bullfinch*,
  St. Katherine's Docks.

Re Mr. Broughton's conversation with you about cask for Mr. Felix.

I have seen Mr. Broughton and Mr. Felix on this matter, and am satisfied the cask is for Mr. Felix and should be delivered immediately.

On receipt of this letter please hand it over to Mr. Felix without further delay.

As the company is liable for its delivery at the address it bears, please accompany it as the representative of the company, and report to me of its safe arrival in due course.

 For the I. and C. S. N. Co., Ltd.,
  X. AVERY,
   per X. X.,
    Managing Director.

The initials shown " X " were undecipherable and were apparently written by a person in authority, though curiously the word " Avery " in the same hand was quite clear.

" It's written on your company's paper anyway," said the inspector to Broughton. " I suppose that heading is yours and not a fake?"

" It's ours right enough," returned the clerk, " but I'm certain the letter's a forgery for all that."

" I should imagine so, but just how do you know?"

" For several reasons, sir. Firstly, we do not use that quality of paper for writing our own servants; we have a cheaper form of memorandum for that. Secondly, all our stuff is typewritten; and thirdly, that is not the signature of any of our clerks."

" Pretty conclusive. It is evident that the forger did not know either your managing director's or your clerks' initials. His knowledge was confined to the name Avery, and from your statement we can conceive Felix having just that amount of information."

" But how on earth did he get our paper?"

Burnley smiled.

" Oh, well, that's not so difficult. Didn't your head clerk give it to him?"

" By Jove! sir, I see it now. He got a sheet of paper and an envelope to write to Mr. Avery. He left the envelope and vanished with the sheet."

" Of course. It occurred to me when Mr. Avery told me of the empty envelope. I guessed what he was going to do, and therefore I hurried to the docks in the hope of being before him. And now about that label on the cask. You might describe it again as fully as you can."

" It was a card about six inches long by four high, fastened on by tacks all round the edge. Along the top was Dupierre's name and advertisement, and in the bottom right-hand corner was a space about three inches by two for the address. There was a thick, black line round this space, and the card had been cut along this line so as to remove the enclosed portion and leave a hole three inches by two. The hole had been filled by pasting a sheet of paper or card behind the label. Felix's address was therefore written on this paper, and not on the original card."

" A curious arrangement. How do you explain it?"

" I thought perhaps Dupierre's people had temporarily run out of labels and were making an old one do again."

Burnley replied absently, as he turned the matter over in his mind. The clerk's suggestion was of course possible, in fact, if the cask really contained a statue, it was the likely one. On the other hand, if it held a body, he imagined the reason was further to seek. In this case he thought it improbable that the cask had come from Dupierre's at all and, if not, what had happened? A possible explanation occurred to him. Suppose some unknown person had received a statue from Dupierre's in the cask and, before returning the latter, had committed a murder. Suppose he wanted to get rid of the body by sending it somewhere in the cask. What would he do with the label? Why, what had been done. He would wish to retain Dupierre's printed matter in order to facilitate the passage of the cask through the Customs, but he would have to change the written address. The inspector could think of no better way of doing this than by the alteration that had been made. He turned again to his visitors.

"Well, gentlemen, I'm greatly obliged to you for your prompt call and information, and if you will give me your addresses, I think that is all we can do tonight."

Inspector Burnley again made his way home. But it was not his lucky night. About half-past nine he was again sent for from the Yard. Someone wanted to speak to him urgently on the telephone.

CHAPTER III

THE WATCHER ON THE WALL

At the same time that Inspector Burnley was interviewing Broughton and Harkness in his office, another series of events centring round the cask was in progress in a different part of London.

Police Constable Z 76, John Walker in private life, was a newly-joined member of the force. A young man of ideas and of promise, he took himself and his work seriously. He had ambitions, the chief of which was to become a detective officer, and he dreamed of the day when he would have climbed to the giddy eminence of an inspector of the Yard. He had read Conan Doyle, Austin Freeman, and other masters of detective fiction, and their tales had stimulated his imagination. His efforts to emulate their heroes added to the interest of life and, if they did not do him very much good, at least did him no harm.

About half-past six that evening, Constable Walker, attired in plain clothes, was strolling slowly along the Holloway Road. He had come off duty shortly before, had had his tea, and was now killing time until he could go to see the second instalment of that thrilling drama, "Lured by Love," at the Islington Picture House. Though on pleasure bent, as he walked he kept on practising observation and deduction. He had made a habit of noting the appearance of the people he saw and trying to deduce their histories and, if he did not succeed in this so well as Sherlock Holmes, he hoped he would some day.

He looked at the people on the pathway beside him, but none of them seemed a good subject for study. But as his gaze swept over the vehicles in the roadway it fell on one which held his attention.

Coming along the street to meet him was a four-wheeled dray drawn by a light brown horse. On the dray, up-ended, was a large cask. Two men sat in front. One, a thin-faced wiry fellow, was driving. The other, a rather small-sized man, was leaning as if wearied out against the cask. This man had a black beard.

Constable Walker's heart beat fast. He had always made it a point to memorize thoroughly the descriptions of wanted men, and only that afternoon he had seen a wire from Headquarters containing the description of just such an equipage. It was wanted, and wanted badly. Had *he* found it? Constable Walker's excitement grew as he wondered.

Unostentatiously he turned and strolled in the direction in which the dray was going, while he laboured to recall in its every detail the description he had read. A four-wheeled dray—that was right; a single horse—right also. A heavily made, iron-clamped cask with one stave broken at the end and roughly repaired by nailing. He glanced at the vehicle which had now drawn level with him. Yes, the cask was well and heavily made and iron clamped, but whether it had a broken stave he could not tell. The dray was painted a brilliant blue and had a Tottenham Court Road address. Here Constable Walker had a blow. This dray was a muddy brown colour and bore the name, John Lyons and Son, 127 Maddox Street, Lower Beechwood Road. He suffered a keen disappointment. He had been getting so sure, and yet—— It certainly looked very like what was wanted except for the colour.

Constable Walker took another look at the reddish brown paint. Curiously patchy it looked. Some parts were fresh and more or less glossy, others dull and drab. And then his excitement rose again to fever heat. He knew what that meant.

As a boy he had had the run of the small painting establishment in the village in which he had been brought up, and he had learnt a thing or two about paint. He knew that if you want paint to dry very quickly you flat it—you use turpentine or some other flatting instead of oil. Paint so made will dry in an hour, but it will have a dull, flat surface instead of a glossy one. But if you paint over with flat colour a surface recently painted in oil it will not dry so quickly, and when it does it dries in patches, the dry parts being dull, the wetter ones glossy. It was clear to Constable Walker that the dray had been recently painted with flat brown, and that it was only partly dry.

A thought struck him and he looked keenly at the mottled side. Yes, he was not mistaken. He could see dimly under the flat coat, faint traces of white lettering showing out lighter than the old blue ground. And then his heart leaped for he was sure! There was no possible chance of error!

He let the vehicle draw ahead, keeping his eye carefully on it while he thought of his great luck. And then he recollected that there should have been four men with it. There was a tall man with a sandy moustache, prominent cheekbones, and a strong chin; a small, lightly made, foreign looking man with a black beard, and two others whose descriptions had not been given. The man with the beard was on the dray, but the tall, red-haired man was not to be seen. Presumably the driver was one of the undescribed men.

It occurred to Constable Walker that perhaps the other two were walking. He therefore let the vehicle draw still farther ahead, and devoted himself to a careful examination of all the male foot-passengers going in the same direction. He crossed and recrossed the road, but nowhere could he see anyone answering to the red-haired man's description.

The quarry led steadily on in a north-westerly direction, Constable Walker following at a considerable distance behind. At the end of the Holloway Road it passed through Highgate, and continued out along the Great North Road. By this time it was growing dusk, and the constable drew slightly closer so as not to miss it if it made a sudden turn.

For nearly four miles the chase continued. It was now nearly eight, and Constable Walker reflected with a transient feeling of regret that "Lured by Love" would then be in full swing. All immediate indications of the city had been left behind. The country was now suburban, the road being lined by detached and semi-detached villas, with an occasional field bearing a "Building Ground to Let" notice. The night was warm and very quiet. There was still light in the west, but an occasional star was appearing eastwards. Soon it would be quite dark.

Suddenly the dray stopped and a man got down and opened the gate of a drive on the right-hand side of the road. The constable melted into the hedge some fifty yards behind and remained motionless. Soon he heard the dray move off again and the hard, rattling noise of the road gave place to the softer, slightly grating sound of gravel. As the constable crept up along the hedge he could see the light of the dray moving towards the right.

A narrow lane branched off in the same direction immediately before reaching the property into which the dray had gone. The drive, in fact, was only some thirty feet beyond the lane and, so far as the constable could see, both lane and drive turned at right angles to the road and ran parallel, one outside and the other inside the property. The constable slipped down the lane, thus leaving the thick boundary hedge between himself and the others.

It was nearly though not quite dark, and the constable could make out the rather low outline of the house, showing black against the sky. The door was in the end gable facing the lane and was open, though the house was entirely in darkness. Behind the house, from the end of the gable and parallel to the lane, ran a wall about eight feet high, evidently the yard wall, in which was a gate. The drive passed the hall door and gable and led up to this gate. The buildings were close to the lane, not more than forty feet from where the constable crouched. Immediately inside the hedge was a row of small trees.

Standing in front of the yard gate was the dray, with one man at the horse's head. As the constable crept closer he heard sounds of unbarring, and the gate swung open. In silence the man outside led the dray within and the gate swung to.

The spirit of adventure had risen high in Constable Walker, and he felt impelled to get still closer to see what was going on. Opposite the hall door he had noticed a little gate in the hedge, and he retraced his steps to this and with infinite care opened it and passed silently through. Keeping well in the shadow of the hedge and under the trees, he crept down again opposite the yard door and reconnoitred.

Beyond the gate, that is on the side away from the house, the yard wall ran on for some fifty feet, at the end of which a cross hedge ran between it and the one under which he was standing. The constable moved warily along to this cross hedge, which he followed until he stood beside the wall.

In the corner between the hedge and the wall, unobserved till he reached it in the growing darkness, stood a small, openwork, rustic summer-house. As the constable looked at it an idea occurred to him.

With the utmost care he began to climb the side of the summer-house, testing every foothold before trusting his weight on it. Slowly he worked his way up until, cautiously raising his head, he was able to peep over the wall.

The yard was of fair length, stretching from where he crouched to the house, a distance of seventy or eighty feet, but was not more than about thirty feet wide. Along the opposite side it was bounded by a row of out-offices. The large double doors of one of these, apparently a coach-house, were open, and a light shone out from the interior. In front of the doorway and with its back to it stood the dray.

The coach-house being near the far end of the yard, Constable Walker was unable to see what was taking place within. He therefore raised himself upon the wall and slowly and silently crawled along the coping in the direction of the house. He was aware his strategic position was bad, but he reflected that, being on the south-east side of the yard, he had dark sky behind him, while the row of trees would still further blacken his background. He felt safe from observation, and continued till he was nearly opposite the coach-house. Then he stretched himself flat on the coping, hid his face, which he feared might show white if the lantern shone on it, behind the dark sleeve of his reddish brown coat, and waited.

He could now see into the coach-house. It was an empty room of fair size with whitewashed walls and a cement floor. On a peg in the wall hung a hurricane lamp, and by its light he saw the bearded man descending a pair of steps which was placed in the centre of the floor. The wiry man stood close by.

"That hook's all right," said the bearded man, "I have it over the tie beam. Now for the differential."

He disappeared into an adjoining room, returning in a moment with a small set of chain blocks. Taking the end of this up the steps, he made it fast to something above. The steps were then removed, and Constable Walker could just see below the lintel of the door, the hook of the block with a thin chain sling hanging over it.

"Now back in," said the bearded man.

The dray was backed in until the cask stood beneath the blocks. Both men with some apparent difficulty got the sling fixed, and then pulling on the chain loop, slowly raised the cask.

"That'll do," said the bearded man when it was some six inches up. "Draw out now."

The wiry man came to the horse's head and brought the dray out of the building, stopping in front of the yard gate. Taking the lantern from its hook and leaving the cask swinging in mid-air, the bearded man followed. He closed the coach-house doors and secured them with a running bolt and padlock, then crossed to the yard gates and began unfastening them. Both men were now within fifteen feet of Constable Walker, and he lay scarcely daring to breathe.

The wiry man spoke for the first time.

" 'Arf a mo', mister," he said, " what abaht that there money?"

"Well," said the other, "I'll give you yours now, and the other fellow can have his any time he comes for it."

"I don't think," the wiry man replied aggressively. "I'll take my pal's now along o' my own. When would 'e 'ave time to come around 'ere looking for it?"

"If I give it to you, what guarantee have I that he won't deny getting it and come and ask for more?"

"You'll 'ave no guarantee at all abaht it, only that I just tells yer. Come on, mister, 'and it over an' let me get away. And don't yer go for to think two quid's goin' for to settle it up. This ain't the job wot we expected when we was 'ired, this ain't. If you want us for to carry your little game through on the strict q.t., why, you'll 'ave to pay for it, that's wot."

"Confound your impertinence! What the devil do you mean?"

The other leered.

"There ain't no cause for you to swear at a poor workin' man. Come now, mister, you an' me understands each other well enough. You don't want no questions asked. Ten quid apiece an' me an' my pal we don't know nothin' abaht it."

"My good man, you've gone out of your senses. I have nothing to keep quiet. This business is quite correct."

The wiry man winked deliberately.

"That's orl right, mister. I know it's quite c'rrect. And ten quid apiece'll keep it that way."

There was silence for a moment, and the bearded man spoke :—

"You suspect there is something wrong about the cask? Well, you're wrong, for there isn't. But I admit that if you talk before Thursday next I'll lose my bet. See here, I'll give you five pounds apiece and you may have your mate's." He counted out some coins, chinking them in his hands. "You may take it or leave it. You won't get any more, for then it would be cheaper for me to lose the bet."

The wiry man paused, eyeing the gold greedily. He opened his mouth to reply, then a sudden thought seemed to strike him. Irresolutely he stood, glancing questioningly at the other. Constable Walker could see his face clearly in the light of the lantern, with an evil, sardonic smile curling his lips. Then, like a man who, after weighing a problem, comes to a decision, he took the money and turned to the horse's head.

"Well, mister," he said, as he put his vehicle in motion, "that's straight enough. I'll stand by it."

The bearded man closed and bolted the yard gates and disappeared with his lantern into the house. In a few seconds the sounds of the receding wheels on the gravel ceased and everything was still.

After waiting a few minutes motionless, Constable Walker slipped off the coping of the wall and dropped noiselessly to the ground. Tiptoeing across to the hedge, he passed silently out of the little gate and regained the lane.

CHAPTER IV

A MIDNIGHT INTERVIEW

THE constable paused in the lane and considered. Up to the present he felt he had done splendidly, and he congratulated himself on his luck. But his next step he did not see clearly at all. Should he find the nearest police station and advise the head constable, or should he telephone, or even go to Scotland Yard? Or more difficult still, should he remain where he was and look out for fresh developments?

He paused irresolutely for some fifteen minutes pondering the situation, and had almost made up his mind to telephone for instructions to his own station, when he heard a footstep slowly approaching along the lane. Anxious to remain unseen, he rapidly regained the small gate in the hedge, passed inside, and took up a position behind the trunk of one of the small trees. The sounds drew gradually nearer. Whoever was approaching was doing so exceedingly slowly, and seemed to be coming on tiptoe. The steps passed the place where the constable waited, and he could make out dimly the form of what seemed to be a man of medium height. In a few seconds they stopped, and then returned slowly past the constable, finally coming to a stand close by the little gate. It was intensely still, and the constable could hear the unknown yawning and softly clearing his throat.

The last trace of light had gone from the sky and the stars were showing brightly. There was no wind, but a sharpness began to creep into the air. At intervals came the disconnected sounds of night, the bark of a dog, the rustle of some small animal in the grass, the rush of a motor passing on the high road.

The constable's problem was settled for him for the moment. He could not move while the other watcher remained. He gave a gentle little shiver and settled down to wait.

He began reckoning the time. It must, he thought, be about half-past eight o'clock. It was about eight when the dray had turned into the drive and he was sure half an hour at least must have passed since then. He had leave until ten and he did not want to be late without authority, though surely, under the circumstances, an excuse would be made for him. He began to picture the scene if he were late, the cold anger of the sergeant, the threat to report him, then his explanation, the sudden change of manner. . . .

A faint click of what seemed to be the entrance gate of the drive recalled him with a start to his present position. Footsteps sounded on the gravel, firm, heavy footsteps, walking quickly. A man was approaching the house.

Constable Walker edged round the tree trunk so as to get it between himself and any light that might come from the hall door. The man reached the door and rang.

In a few seconds a light appeared through the fanlight, and the door was opened by the bearded man. A big, broad-shouldered man in a dark overcoat and soft hat stood on the steps.

"Hallo, Felix!" cried the newcomer heartily. "Glad to see you're at home. When did you get back?"

"That you, Martin? Come in. I got back on Sunday night."

"I'll not go in, thanks, but I want you to come round and make up a four at bridge. Tom Brice is with us, and he has brought along a friend of his, a young solicitor from Liverpool. You'll come, won't you?"

The man addressed as Felix hesitated a moment before replying. "Thanks, yes. I'll go, certainly. But I'm all alone and I haven't changed. Come in a minute till I do so."

"And, if it's a fair question, where did you get your dinner if you're all alone?"

"In town. I'm only just home."

They went in and the door was closed. Some few minutes later they emerged again and, pulling the door behind them, disappeared down the drive, the distant click of the gate signifying their arrival at the road. As soon as this sounded, the watcher in the lane moved rapidly, though silently, after them, and Constable Walker was left in undisputed possession.

On the coast becoming clear he slipped out on to the lane, walked down it to the road and turned back in the direction of London. As he did so a clock struck nine.

Entering the first inn he came to, he called for a glass of ale and, getting into conversation with the landlord, learnt that he was near the hamlet of Brent, on the Great North Road, and that

Mr. Felix's house was named St. Malo. He also inquired his way to the nearest public telephone, which, fortunately, was close by.

A few minutes later he was speaking to Scotland Yard. He had to wait for a little time while Inspector Burnley, who had gone home, was being fetched, but in fifteen minutes he had made his report and was awaiting instructions.

The inspector questioned him closely about the position of the house, finally instructing him to return to his post behind the tree and await developments.

"I will go out with some men now, and will look for you by the little gate in the hedge."

Constable Walker walked rapidly back, and as he did so the same clock struck ten. He had been gone exactly an hour. In the meantime, Inspector Burnley got a taxi and, after a careful examination of his route and the district on a large-scale map, started for St. Malo with three other men. He called on his way at Walpole Terrace, Queen Mary Road, where Tom Broughton lived, and delighted that young man by inviting him to join the party. On the way, he explained in detail the lie of the house and grounds, where he wanted each man to stand, and what was to be done in various eventualities. The streets were full of people and motoring was slow, but it was still considerably before eleven when they entered the Great North Road.

They ran on till the inspector judged they were not far from the house, when the car was run up a side road and the engine stopped. The five men then walked on in silence.

"Wait here," whispered Burnley, when they had gone some distance, and slipped away into the dark. He found the lane, walked softly down it until he came to the little gate, slipped inside and came up to Constable Walker standing behind his tree.

"I'm Inspector Burnley," he whispered. "Has anyone come in or out yet?"

"No, sir."

"Well, wait here until I post my men."

He returned to the others and, speaking in a whisper, gave his directions.

"You men take up the positions I explained to you. Listen out for a whistle to close in. Mr. Broughton, you come with me and keep silent."

The inspector and his young acquaintance walked down the lane, stopping outside the little gate. The other three men posted themselves at various points in the grounds. And then they waited.

It seemed to Broughton that several hours must have passed

when a clock in the distance struck twelve. He and the inspector were standing beside each other concealed under the hedge. Once or twice he had attempted whispered remarks, but Burnley was not responsive. It was rather cold and the stars were bright. A light breeze had risen and it rustled gently through the hedge and stirred the branches of the trees. An insistent dog was barking somewhere away to the right. A cart passed on the road, the wheels knocking on their axles annoyingly. It took ages to get out of earshot, the sounds coming in rotation through nearly a quarter of the compass. Then a car followed with a swift rush, the glare of the headlights glancing along through the trees. And still nothing happened.

After further ages the clock struck again—one. A second dog began barking. The breeze freshened, and Broughton wished he had brought a heavier coat. He longed to stamp up and down and ease his cramped limbs. And then the latch of the road gate clicked and footsteps sounded on the gravel.

They waited motionless as the steps came nearer. Soon a black shadow came into view and moved to the hall door. There was a jingling of keys, the rattling of a lock, the outline of the door became still darker, the shadow disappeared within and the door was closed.

Immediately Burnley whispered to Broughton :—

" I am going now to ring at the door, and when he opens it I will flash my light in his face. Take a good look at him and if you are sure—absolutely positive—it is Felix, say ' yes,' just the one word ' yes.' Do you understand?"

They went in through the small gate, no longer taking any precautions against noise, walked to the door, and Burnley knocked loudly.

" Now, remember, don't speak unless you are sure," he whispered.

A light flickered through the fanlight and the door was opened. A beam from the inspector's dark lantern flashed on the face of the man within, revealing the same dark complexion and black beard that had attracted Constable Walker's attention. The word " Yes " came from Broughton and the inspector said :—

" Mr. Léon Felix, I am Inspector Burnley from Scotland Yard. I have called on rather urgent business, and would be glad of a few minutes' conversation."

The black-bearded man started.

" Oh, certainly," he said, after a momentary pause, " though I don't know that it is quite the hour I would have suggested for a chat. Will you come in?"

"Thanks. I'm sorry it's late, but I have been waiting for you for a considerable time. Perhaps my man might sit in the hall out of the cold?"

Burnley called over one of his men who had been stationed near the summer-house.

"Wait here till I speak to Mr. Felix, Hastings," he said, giving him a sign to be ready if called on. Then, leaving Broughton outside with Constable Walker and the other men, he followed Felix into a room on the left of the hall.

It was fitted up comfortably though not luxuriously as a study. In the middle of the room stood a flat-topped desk of modern design. Two deep, leather-covered arm-chairs were drawn up on each side of the fireplace, in which the embers still glowed. A tantalus stood on a small side table with a box of cigars. The walls were lined with bookshelves with here and there a good print. Felix lighted a reading-lamp which stood on the desk. He turned to Burnley.

"Is it a sitting down matter?" he said, indicating one of the arm-chairs. The inspector took it while Felix dropped into the other.

"I want, Mr. Felix," began the detective, "to make some inquiries about a cask which you got from the steamer *Bullfinch* this morning—or rather yesterday, for this is really Tuesday—and which I have reason to believe is still in your possession."

"Yes?"

"The steamboat people think that a mistake has been made and that the cask that you received was not the one consigned to you, and which you expected."

"The cask I received is my own property. It was invoiced to me and the freight was paid. What more do the shipping company want?"

"But the cask you received was not addressed to you. It was invoiced to a Mr. Felix of West Jubb Street, Tottenham Court Road."

"The cask was addressed to me. I admit the friend who sent it made a mistake in the address, but it was for me all the same."

"But if we bring the other Mr. Felix—the West Jubb Street Mr. Felix—here, and he also claims it, you will not then, I take it, persist in your claim?"

The black-bearded man moved uneasily. He opened his mouth to reply, and then hesitated. The inspector felt sure he had seen the little pitfall only just in time.

"If you produce such a man," he said at last, "I am sure I can easily convince him that the cask was really sent to me and not to him."

"Well, we shall see about that later. Meantime, another question. What was in the cask you were expecting?"

"Statuary."

"You are sure of that?"

"Why, of course I'm sure. Really, Mr. Inspector, I'd like to know by what right I am being subjected to this examination."

"I shall tell you, Mr. Felix. Scotland Yard has reason to believe there is something wrong about that cask, and an investigation has been ordered. You were naturally the first person to approach, but since the cask turns out not to be yours, we shall——"

"Not to be mine? What do you mean? Who says it is not mine?"

"Pardon me, you yourself said so. You have just told me the cask you expected contained statuary. We know the one you received does not contain statuary. Therefore you have got the wrong one."

Felix paled suddenly, and a look of alarm crept into his eyes. Burnley leant forward and touched him on the knee.

"You will see for yourself, Mr. Felix, that if this matter is to blow over we must have an explanation of these discrepancies. I am not suggesting you can't give one. I am sure you can. But if you refuse to do so you will undoubtedly arouse unpleasant suspicions."

Felix remained silent, and the inspector did not interrupt his train of thought.

"Well," he said at length, "I have really nothing to hide, only one does not like being bluffed. I will tell you, if I can, what you want to know. Satisfy me that you are from Scotland Yard."

Burnley showed his credentials, and the other said:—

"Very good. Then I may admit I misled you about the contents of the cask, though I told you the literal and absolute truth. The cask is full of plaques—plaques of kings and queens. Isn't that statuary? And if the plaques should be small and made of gold and called sovereigns, aren't they still statuary? That is what the cask contains, Mr. Inspector. Sovereigns. £988 in gold."

"What else?"

"Nothing else."

"Oh, come now, Mr. Felix. We knew there was money in the cask. We also know there is something else. Think again."

"Oh, well, there will be packing, of course. I haven't opened it and I don't know. But £988 in gold would go a small way towards filling it. There will be sand or perhaps alabaster or some other packing."

"I don't mean packing. Do you distinctly tell me no other special object was included?"

"Certainly, but I suppose I'd better explain the whole thing."

He stirred the embers of the fire together, threw on a couple of logs and settled himself more comfortably in his chair.

CHAPTER V

FELIX TELLS A STORY

"I AM a Frenchman, as you know," began Felix, "but I have lived in London for some years, and I run over to Paris frequently on both business and pleasure. About three weeks ago on one of these visits I dropped into the Café Toisson d'Or in the rue Royale, where I joined a group of acquaintances. The conversation turned on the French Government lotteries, and one of the men, a M. Le Gautier, who had been defending the system, said to me, 'Why not join in a little flutter?' I refused at first, but afterwards changed my mind and said I would sport five hundred francs if he did the same. He agreed, and I gave him £20 odd as my share. He was to carry the business through in his name, letting me know the result and halving the profits, if any. I thought no more about the matter till last Friday, when, on my return home in the evening, I found a letter from Le Gautier, which surprised, pleased, and annoyed me in equal measure."

Mr. Felix drew a letter from a drawer of his writing-table and passed it to the inspector. It was in French, and though the latter had a fair knowledge of the language, he was not quite equal to the task, and Mr. Felix translated. The letter ran as follows:—

Rue de Vallorbes, 997,
Avenue Friedland,
Paris.
Thursday, 1st April, 1912.

MY DEAR FELIX,—I have just had the most wonderful news! *We have won!* The lottery has drawn trumps and our 1,000 francs has become 50,000—25,000 francs each! I shake both your hands!

The money I have already received, and I am sending your share at once. And now, old chap, do not be very annoyed when I tell you I am playing a little trick on you. I apologize.

You remember Dumarchez? Well, he and I had an argument about you last week. We were discussing the ingenuity and resource of criminals in evading the police. Your name happened to be mentioned, and I remarked what a splendid criminal a man of your inventive talents would make. He said " No," that you were too transparently honest to deceive the police. We got hot about it and finally arranged a little test. I have packed your money in a cask, in English sovereigns—there are 988 of them—and am booking it to you, carriage paid, by the Insular and Continental Steam Navigation Company's boat from Rouen, due in London about Monday, 5th April. But I am addressing it to " M. Léon Felix, 141 West Jubb Street, Tottenham Court Road, London, W.," and labelling it " Statuary only," from Dupierre et Cie, the monumental sculptors of Grenelle. It will take some ingenuity to get a falsely addressed and falsely described cask away from the steamer officials without being suspected of theft. That is the test. I have bet Dumarchez an even 5,000 francs that you will do it. He says you will certainly be caught.

I send you my best congratulations on the greatness of your coup, of which the visible evidence goes to you in the cask, and my only regret is that I shall be unable to be present to see you open it.

With profound apologies,

Yours very truly,

ALPHONSE LE GAUTIER.

PS.—Please excuse the typewriter, but I have hurt my hand.

" I don't know whether pleasure at the unexpected windfall of nearly £1,000, or annoyance at Le Gautier's test with the cask was my strongest emotion. The more I thought of this part of it, the more angry I became. It was one thing that my friends should amuse themselves by backing their silly theories, it was quite another that I should be the victim and scapegoat of their nonsense. Two things obviously might lead to complications. If it came out that a cask labelled ' Statuary ' contained gold, suspicion would be aroused, and the same thing would happen if anyone discovered the address to be false. The contents of the cask might be questioned owing to the weight—that I did not know; the false address might come to light if an advice note of the cask's arrival was sent out, while there was always the fear of unforeseen accidents. I was highly incensed, and I determined to wire early next morning to Le Gautier asking him not to send the cask, and saying I would go over and get the money. But to my further annoyance I had a card by the first post which said that the cask had already been dispatched.

"It was clear to me then that I must make arrangements to get it away as soon as possible after the boat came in, and before inquiries began to be made. I accordingly made my plans and, as I did so, my annoyance passed away and I got interested in the sporting side of the affair. First, I had a few cards of the false address printed. Then I found an obscure carting contractor, from whom I hired a four-wheeled dray and two men, together with the use of an empty shed for three days.

"I had found out that the Steam Navigation boat would be due on the following Monday, and on the preceding Saturday I brought the men and the dray to the shed and prepared them for what I wanted done. To enlist their help and prevent them becoming suspicious, I gave the former a qualified version of Le Gautier's story. I told them I had made a bet and said I wanted their help to pull it off. A certain cask was coming in by the Rouen boat, addressed to a friend of mine, and he had bet me a large sum that I could not get this cask from the steamer people and take it to my house, while I held that I could. The point was to test the effectiveness of the ordinary business precautions. In order, I told the men, that no real trouble should arise and that I should not, in the event of failure, be charged with theft, my friend had given me a written authorization to take the cask. This I had written out previously and I showed it to them. Finally, I promised them two pounds each if we succeeded.

"I had got a couple of pots of quick-drying blue and white paint, and I altered the lettering on the dray to that of the address my Paris friend had put on the cask. I am skilful at this kind of work and I did it myself.

"On Monday morning we drove to the docks, and I found the *Bullfinch* had just come in with the Paris goods aboard. She was discharging casks from the forehold, and I strolled along the wharf and had a look at the work. The casks coming ashore were wine-casks, but I noticed one at the side of the hold, over which one of the dockers and a young man who looked like a clerk were bending. They seemed very engrossed, and of course I wondered, 'Is this my cask, and have they discovered the gold?' I spoke to the young man, found that the cask was mine, and asked him if I could get it away at once.

" He was quite polite, but would not help me, referring me to the quay office and offering to take me there and find a clerk to attend to me. As we were leaving he called out to the man at the cask, ' You understand, Harkness, to do nothing till you hear from Mr. Avery.'

" At the wharf office the young man left me in the outer office while he went, as he said, to get the proper clerk for my work. But he returned with a man who was evidently the manager, and I knew at once that something was wrong. This opinion was confirmed when the manager began raising objection after objection to letting the cask go.

" Some judicious questions elicited the fact that ' Mr. Avery ' was the managing director in the head office in Fenchurch Street. I left the wharf office, sat down on some boxes, and thought out the situation.

" It was clear that something had aroused the suspicions of the clerk and the docker, Harkness, and the former's remark to the latter to do nothing without instructions from Mr. Avery seemed to mean that the matter was to be laid before that gentleman. To ' do nothing ' evidently meant to hold on to the cask. If I were to get my property it was clear I must see to the supplying of those instructions myself.

" I went to Fenchurch Street and asked for Mr. Avery. Fortunately for me he was engaged. I said I could not wait, and asked for a sheet of paper and envelope on which to write him a note. By the simple expedient of sealing and addressing the empty envelope, I thus provided myself with a sheet of paper bearing the firm's heading.

" I dropped into a bar and, ordering some ale, borrowed a pen and ink. Then I composed a letter from Mr. Avery to Harkness, instructing him to hand over the cask at once to me.

" While I was writing this it occurred to me that if this man's suspicions were really seriously aroused, he would probably follow the cask and thus trace me to my house. I lost another quarter of an hour pondering this problem. Then an idea occurred to me, and I added a paragraph saying that as the Navigation Company had contracted to deliver the cask at an address in the city, he, Harkness, was to accompany it and see that it reached its destination safely.

" I wrote the letter in the round hand of a junior clerk, signing it ' The I. and C. S. N. Co., Ltd., per ' in the same hand, and

'Avery' with an undecipherable initial in another kind of writing, with another 'per,' and then two not very clear initials. I hoped in this way to mislead Harkness, if he happened to know the genuine signature.

"It was my design to get Harkness away from the ship with the cask and my own men, when I hoped to find some way of giving him the slip. This I eventually did by instructing one of the men to clamour for a drink, and the other, a man named Watty, to refuse to leave the horse when I invited the party to a bar for some beer. On the plea of relieving Watty, I left Harkness and the other man drinking in the bar, and slipped away with Watty and the dray. Then he and I went back to the shed and I ran a coat of paint over the dray, restoring it to its original brown and painting out the fictitious name. In the evening we brought the dray home, timing ourselves to arrive here after dark, and unloaded the cask in one of the outhouses, where it now is."

When Felix ceased speaking, the two men sat in silence for several minutes while Burnley turned the statement over in his mind. The sequence of events was unusual, but the story hung together, and, as he went over it in detail, he could see no reason why it should not, from Felix's point of view, be true. If Felix believed his friend's letter, as he appeared to, his actions were accounted for, and if the cask really contained a statue, the letter might explain the whole thing. On the other hand, if it held a corpse, the letter was a fraud, to which Felix might or might not be party.

Gradually, as he pondered, the matter shaped itself into three main considerations.

First, there was Felix's general bearing and manner. The inspector had a long and varied experience of men who told the truth and of men who lied, and all his instincts led him to believe this man. He was aware that such instincts are liable to error—he had himself erred on more than one occasion in the past—yet he could not overlook the fact that Felix's bearing, as far as his impression went, was that of a sincere and honest man. Such a consideration would not be a decisive factor in his conclusion, but it would undoubtedly weigh.

Secondly, there was Felix's account of his actions in London. Of the truth of this the inspector had already received considerable independent testimony. He reviewed the chain of events and was surprised to find how few statements of Felix were unsupported. His first visit to the *Bullfinch* had been described in almost similar terms by Broughton and by Huston in the wharf office. His call at the Fenchurch Street office and the ruse by which he obtained the shipping company's headed notepaper had been testified to by Mr. Avery and his chief clerk, Wilcox. His description of the letter he had written to Harkness was certainly accurate from the inspector's own knowledge. His account of the removal of the cask and the shaking off of Harkness was in agreement with the statement of the latter and finally, Felix's description of the removal of the cask to its present resting place was completely corroborated by Constable Walker.

There was practically no part of the statement unsupported by outside evidence. In fact, Inspector Burnley could not recall any case where so much confirmation of a suspect's story was forthcoming. Weighing the matter point by point, he came to the deliberate conclusion that he must unreservedly believe it.

So much for Felix's actions in London. But there was a third point—his actions in Paris, culminating in the letter of his friend. The letter. That was the kernel of the nut. Was it really written under the circumstances described? Had Le Gautier written it? Was there even such a man as Le Gautier? All this, he thought, it should not be difficult to find out. He would get some more information from Felix and if necessary slip across to Paris and put the statements to the test. He broke the silence.

" Who is M. Le Gautier? "

" Junior partner in the firm of Le Gautier, Fils, wine merchants, in the rue Henri Quatre."

" And M. Dumarchez? "

" A stockbroker."

" Can you give me his address? "

" I don't know his home address. His office is, I think, in the Boulevard Poissonière. But I could get you the address from M. Le Gautier."

" Please give me an account of your relations with these gentlemen."

" Well, I have known them both for years and we are good friends, but I cannot recall ever having had any money transactions with either until this matter of the lottery."

" The details of that mentioned in the letter are correct? "

" Oh, perfectly."

" Can you remember where precisely the conversation about the lottery took place? "

" It was in the ground floor room of the café, at the window to the right of the entrance, looking inwards."

" You say other gentlemen were present? "

"Yes, a group of us were there and the conversation was general."

"Was your arrangement to enter the lottery heard by the group?"

"Yes, we had quite a lot of good-natured chaff about it."

"And can you remember who were present?"

Mr. Felix hesitated.

"I'm not sure that I can," he said at last. "The group was quite a casual one and I only joined it for a few moments. Le Gautier was there, of course, and a man called Daubigny, and Henri Boisson, and, I think, Jaques Rôget, but of him I'm not sure. There were a number of others also."

Felix answered the questions readily and the inspector noted his replies. He felt inclined to believe the lottery business was genuine. At all events inquiries in Paris would speedily establish the point. But even if it was all true, that did not prove that Le Gautier had written the letter. A number of people had heard the conversation, and anyone could have written it, even Felix himself. Ah, that was an idea! Could Felix be the writer? Was there any way of finding that out? The inspector considered and then spoke again.

"Have you the envelope this letter came in?"

"Eh?" said Felix, "the envelope? Why, no, I'm sure I haven't. I never keep them."

"Or the card?"

Felix turned over the papers on his desk and rummaged in the drawers.

"No," he answered, "I can't find it. I must have destroyed it too."

There was then no proof that these communications had been received by Felix. On the other hand there was no reason to doubt it. The inspector kept an open mind as he turned again to the letter.

It was typewritten on rather thin, matt surfaced paper and, though Burnley was not an expert, he believed the type was foreign. Some signs of wear were present which he thought might identify the typewriter. The n's and the r's were leaning slightly to the right, the t's and the e's were below alignment, and the l's had lost the horizontal bar at the top of the downstroke. He held the paper up to the light. The watermark was somewhat obscured by the type, but after a time he made it out. It was undoubtedly French paper. This, of course, would not weigh much, as Felix, by his own statement, was frequently in Paris, but still it did weigh.

The inspector read the letter again. It was divided into four paragraphs and he pondered each in turn. The first was about the lottery. He did not know much about French lotteries, but the statements made could at least be verified. With the help of the French police it would be easy to find out if any drawings and payments had recently been made, and he could surely get a list of the winners. A winner of fifty thousand francs, living in or near Paris, should be easily traced.

The second and third paragraphs were about the bet and the sending of the cask. Burnley turned the details over in his mind. Was the whole story a likely one? It certainly did not strike him as such. Even if such an unusual bet had been made, the test was an extremely poor one. He could hardly believe that a man who could invent the plan of the cask would not have done better. And yet it was undoubtedly possible.

Another idea entered the inspector's mind. He had, perhaps, been thinking too much of the £988, and too little of the woman's hand. Suppose there really was a corpse in the cask. What then?

Such an assumption made all the circumstances more serious and explained partly the sending of the cask, but it did not, so far as the inspector could see, throw light on the method of doing so. But when he came to the fourth paragraph he saw that it might easily bear two meanings. He read it again:—

> I send you my best congratulations on the greatness of your coup, of which the visible evidence goes to you in the cask, and my only regret is that I shall be unable to be present to see you open it.

This seemed at first sight obviously to mean congratulations on winning the lottery, the "visible evidence" of which, namely £988 in gold, was in the cask. But did it really mean this? Did a more sinister interpretation not also offer itself? Suppose the body was the "visible evidence"? Suppose the death was the result, possibly indirect, of something that Felix had done. If money only was being sent, why should Le Gautier experience regret that he could not see the cask opened? But if a corpse was unexpectedly hidden there, would not that statement be clarified? It certainly looked so. One thing at least seemed clear. If a corpse had been sent to Felix, he must know something of the circumstances leading up to it. The inspector spoke again:—

"I am obliged for your statement, Mr. Felix, which, I may be allowed to say, I fully accept so far as it goes. But I fear you have not told me everything?"

"I have told you everything material."

"Then I am afraid we are not in agreement as to what is material. At all events, it all goes back to my original question, 'What is in the cask?'"

"Do you not accept my statement that it is money?"

"I accept your statement that you believe it to be money. I do not necessarily accept your authority for that belief."

"Well," said Felix, jumping up, "the cask's in the coach-house and I see there is nothing for it but to go and open it now. I did not want to do so tonight, as I did not want to have all that gold lying loose about the house, but it's clear nothing else will satisfy you."

"Thank you, Mr. Felix, I wanted you to make the suggestion. It is, as you say, the only way to settle the matter. I'll call Sergeant Hastings here as a witness and we'll go now."

In silence, Felix got a lantern and led the way. They passed through a back-door into the yard and paused at the coach-house door.

"Hold the light, will you, while I get the keys."

Burnley threw a beam on the long running bolt that closed the two halves of the door. A padlock held the handle down on the staple. Felix inserted a key, but at his first touch the lock fell open.

"Why, the thing's not fastened!" he cried, "and I locked it myself a few hours ago!"

He removed the padlock and withdrew the running bolt, swinging the large door open. Burnley flashed in the lantern.

"Is the cask here?" he said.

"Yes, swinging there from the ceiling," answered Felix, as he came over from fastening back the door. Then his jaw dropped and he stared fixedly.

"My heavens!" he gasped, in a strangled tone, "it's gone! The cask's gone!"

CHAPTER VI

THE ART OF DETECTION

Astonished as Burnley was himself at this unexpected development, he did not forget to keep a keen watch on Felix. That the latter was genuinely amazed and dumbfounded he could not doubt. Not only was his surprise too obviously real to be questioned, but his anger and annoyance at losing his money was clearly heartfelt.

"I locked it myself. I locked it myself," he kept on repeating. "It was there at eight o'clock, and who could get at it since then? Why, no one but myself knew about it. How could anyone else have known?"

"That's what we have to find out," returned the inspector. "Come back to the house, Mr. Felix, and let us talk it over. We cannot do anything outside until it gets light."

"You may not know," he continued, "that you were followed here with your cask by one of our men, who watched you unloading it in the coach-house. He waited till you left with your friend Martin, a few minutes before nine. He then had to leave to advise me of the matter, but he was back at the house by ten. From ten till after eleven he watched alone, but since then the house has been surrounded by my men, as I rather expected to find a gang instead of a single man. Whoever took the cask must therefore have done so between nine and ten."

Felix stared at his companion open-mouthed.

"By Jove!" he said. "You amaze me. How in thunder did you get on my track?"

Burnley smiled.

"It is our business to know these things," he answered. "I knew all about how you got the cask away from the docks also."

"Well, thank heaven! I told you the truth."

"It was the wise thing, Mr. Felix. I was able to check your statements as you went along, and I may say I felt really glad when I heard you were going to be straight. At the same time, sir, you will realize that my orders prevent me being satisfied until I have seen the contents of the cask."

"You cannot be more anxious to recover it than I am, for I want my money."

"Naturally," said Burnley, "but before we discuss the matter excuse me a moment. I want to give my fellows some instructions."

He went out and called the men together. Sergeant Hastings and Constable Walker he retained, the rest he sent home in the car with instructions to return at eight o'clock in the morning. To Broughton he bade "Good night," thanking him for his presence and help.

When he re-entered the study Felix made up the fire and drew forward the whisky and cigars.

"Thank you, I don't mind if I do," said the detective, sinking back into his chair. "Now, Mr. Felix, let us go over every one who knew about the cask being there."

"No one but myself and the carter, I assure you."

"Yourself, the carter, myself, and my man Walker—four to start with."

Felix smiled.

"As far as I am concerned," he said, "I left here, as you appear to know, almost immediately after the arrival of the cask and did not return till after one o'clock. All of that time I was in the company of Dr. William Martin and a number of mutual friends. So I can prove an alibi."

Burnley smiled also.

"For me," he said, "I am afraid you will have to take my word. The house was watched by Walker from ten o'clock, and we may take it as quite impossible that anything could have been done after that hour."

"There remains therefore the carter."

"There remains therefore the carter, and, as we must neglect no possibilities, I will ask you to give me the address of the cartage firm and any information about the man that you may have."

"John Lyons and Son, 127 Maddox Street, Lower Beechwood Road, was the contractor. The carter's name, beyond Watty, I don't know. He was a rather short, wiry chap, with a dark complexion and small black moustache."

"And now, Mr. Felix, can you not think of any others who may have known about the cask."

"There was no one," replied the other with decision.

"I'm afraid we can't assume that Mr. Felix. We certainly can't be sure."

"Who could there be?"

"Well, your French friend. How do you know he didn't write to others besides you?"

Felix sat up as if he had been shot.

"By Jove!" he cried, "it never entered my head. But it's most unlikely—most unlikely."

"The whole thing's most unlikely as far as that goes. Perhaps you are not aware that someone else was watching the house last evening?"

"Good God, inspector! What do you mean?"

"Someone came to the lane shortly after your arrival with the cask. He waited and heard your conversation with your friend Martin. When you and your friend left, he followed you."

Felix passed his hand over his forehead. His face was pale.

"This business is too much for me," he said. "I wish to heaven I was out of it."

"Then help me to get you out of it. Think. Is there anyone your friend knows to whom he might have written?"

Felix remained silent for some moments.

"There is only one man," he said at length in a hesitating voice, "with whom I know he is friendly—a Mr. Percy Murgatroyd, a mining engineer who has an office in Westminster. But I don't for one moment believe he had anything to say to it."

"Let me have his name and address, anyway."

"4 St. John's Mansions, Victoria Street," said Felix, on referring to an address book.

"You might write it down, if you please, and sign it."

Felix looked up with a smile.

"You generally write notes yourself, I should have thought?"

Burnley laughed.

"You're very quick, Mr. Felix. Of course it's your handwriting I want also. But I assure you it's only routine. Now please, think. Is there anyone else?"

"Not a living soul that I know of."

"Very well, Mr. Felix. I want to ask just one other question. Where did you stay in Paris?"

"At the Hotel Continental."

"Thanks, that's everything. And now, if you will allow me, I will take a few winks here in the chair till it gets light, and if you take my advice you will turn in."

Felix looked at his watch.

"Quarter-past three. Well, perhaps I shall. I'm only sorry I cannot offer you a bed as the house is absolutely empty, but if you will take a shakedown in the spare room——?"

"No, no, thanks very much, I shall be all right here."

"As you wish. Good night."

When Felix had left, the inspector sat on in his chair, smoking his strong black cigars and thinking. He did not sleep, though he remained almost motionless, only at long intervals rousing up to light another cigar, and it was not until five had struck that he got up and looked out of the window.

"Light at last," he muttered, as he let himself quietly out of the back door into the yard.

His first care was to make a thorough search in the yard and all the outhouses to ensure that the cask was really gone and not merely hidden in some other room. He was speedily satisfied on this point.

Since it was gone it was obvious that it must have been removed on a vehicle. His next point was to see how that vehicle got in, and if it had left any traces. And first as to the coach-house door.

He picked up the padlock and examined it carefully. It was an ordinary old-fashioned four-inch one. The ring had been forced open while locked, the hole in the opening end through which the bolt passes being torn away. Marks showed that this had been done by inserting some kind of lever between the body of the lock and the staple on the door, through which the ring had been passed. The inspector looked round for the lever, but could not find it. He therefore made a note to search for such a tool, as if it bore marks which would fit those on the door, its evidence might be important.

There was next the question of the yard gate. This opened inwards in two halves, and was fastened by a wooden beam hinged through the centre to the edge of one of the half gates. When it was turned vertically the gates were free, but when horizontally it engaged with brackets, one on each half gate, thus holding them closed. It could be fastened by a padlock, but none was fitted. The gate now stood closed and with the beam lying in the brackets.

The inspector took another note to find out if Mr. Felix had locked the beam, and then stood considering. It was clear the gate must have been closed from the inside after the vehicle had gone out. It must have been opened similarly on the latter's arrival. Who had done this? Was Felix lying, and was there someone else in the house?

At first it seemed likely, and then the inspector thought of another way. Constable Walker had climbed the wall. Why should not the person who opened and shut the gate have also done so? The inspector moved slowly along the wall scrutinizing it and the ground alongside it.

At first he saw nothing out of the common, but on retracing his steps he noticed, about three yards from the gate, two faint marks of mud or dust on the plaster. These were some six feet from the ground and about fifteen inches apart. On the soft soil which had filled in between the cobble stones in this disused part of the yard, about a foot from the wall and immediately under these marks, were two sharp-edged depressions, about two inches long by half an inch wide, arranged with their longer dimensions in line. Someone had clearly used a short ladder.

Inspector Burnley stood gazing at the marks. It struck him they were very far apart for a ladder. He measured the distance between them and found it was fifteen inches. Ladders, he knew, are about twelve.

G.M.N.—C*

Opening the gate he went to the outside of the wall. A grass plot ran alongside it here and the inspector, stooping down, searched for corresponding marks. He was not disappointed. Two much deeper depressions showed where the ends of the ladder-like apparatus had sunk into the softer ground. These were not narrow like those in the yard, but rectangular and of heavier stuff, three inches by two, he estimated. He looked at the plaster on the wall above, but it was not till he examined it through his lens that he was satisfied it bore two faint scratches, corresponding in position to the muddy marks on the opposite side.

A further thought struck him. Scooping up a little soil from the grass, he went again into the yard and compared with his lens the soil and the dry mud of the marks on the plaster. As he had anticipated, they were identical.

He could now dimly reconstruct what had happened. Someone had placed a peculiar kind of ladder against the outside of the wall and presumably crossed it and opened the gate. The ladder had then been carried round and placed against the inside of the wall, but, probably by accident, *opposite end up*. The outside plaster was therefore clean but scraped, while that on the inside bore traces of the soil from the ends that had stood on the grass. In going out after barring the gate, he imagined the thief had pulled the ladder after him with a cord and passed it over the wall.

The inspector returned to the grass and made a further search. Here he found confirmation of his theory in a single impression of one of the legs of the ladder some two feet six out from the wall. That, he decided, had been caused by the climber throwing down the ladder when leaving the yard. He also found three footmarks, but, unfortunately, they were so blurred as to be valueless.

He took out his notebook and made a sketch with accurate dimensions showing what he had learnt of the ladder—its length, width, and the shape of the legs at each end. Then, bringing out the steps Felix had used to hang the chain blocks, he got on the wall. He examined the cement coping carefully, but without finding any further traces.

The yard, being paved, no wheel or foot marks were visible, but Burnley spent quite a long time crossing and recrossing it, examining every foot of ground in the hope of finding some object that had been dropped. Once before, in just such another case, he had had the luck to discover a trouser button concealed under some leaves, a find which had led to penal servitude for two men. On this occasion he was disappointed, his search being entirely unsuccessful.

He went out on the drive. Here were plenty of marks, but try as he would he could make nothing of them. The surface was covered thickly with fine gravel and only showed vague disturbances with no clear outlines. He began methodically to search the drive as he had done the yard. Every foot was examined in turn, Burnley gradually working down towards the gate. After he left the immediate neighbourhood of the house the gravel became much thinner, but the surface below was hard and bore no marks. He continued perseveringly until he got near the gate, and then he had some luck.

In the lawn between the house and the road some work was in progress. It seemed to Burnley that a tennis or croquet ground was being made. From the corner of this ground a recently filled in cut ran across the drive and out to the hedge adjoining the lane. Evidently a drain had just been laid.

Where this drain passed under the drive the newly filled ground had slightly sunk. The hollow had been made up in the middle with gravel, but it happened that a small space on the lane side which had not gone down much was almost uncovered, the clay showing through. On this space were two clearly defined foot-marks, pointing in the direction of the house.

I have said two, but that is not strictly correct. One, that of a workman's right boot with heavy hobnails, was complete in every detail, the clay holding the impression like plaster of paris. The other, some distance in front and to the left, and apparently the next step forward, was on the edge of the clay patch and showed the heel only, the sole having borne on the hard.

Inspector Burnley's eyes brightened. Never had he seen better impressions. Here was something tangible at last. He bent down to examine them more closely, then suddenly sprang to his feet with a gesture of annoyance.

"Fool that I am," he growled, "that's only Watty bringing up the cask."

All the same he made a careful sketch of the marks, showing the distance between them and the size of the clay patch. Watty, he felt sure, would be easy to find through the carting establishment, when he could ascertain if the footsteps were his. If it should chance they were not, he had probably found a useful clue to the identity of the thief. For the convenience of the reader I reproduce the sketch.

Burnley turned to go on, but his habit of thinking things out reasserted itself, and he stood gazing at the marks and slowly pondering. He was puzzled that the steps were so close together.

He took out his rule and re-measured the distance between them. Nineteen inches from heel to heel. That was surely very close. A man of Watty's size would normally take a step of at least thirty inches, and carters were generally long-stepping men. If he had

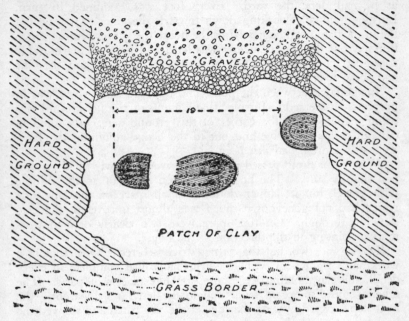

put it at thirty-two or thirty-three inches he would probably be nearer the thing. Why, then, this short step?

He looked and pondered. Then suddenly a new excitement came into his eyes and he bent swiftly down again.

"Jove!" he murmured. "Jove! I nearly missed that! It makes it more like Watty and, if so, it is conclusive! Absolutely conclusive!" His cheek was flushed and his eyes shone.

"That probably settles that hash," said the evidently delighted inspector. He, nevertheless, continued his methodical search down the remainder of the drive and out on to the road, but without further result.

He looked at his watch. It was seven o'clock.

"Two more points and I'm through," he said to himself in a satisfied tone.

He turned into the lane and walked slowly down it, scrutinizing the roadway as he had done the drive. Three separate times he stopped to examine and measure footmarks, the third occasion being close by the little gate in the hedge.

"Number one point done. Now for number two," he muttered, and returning to the entrance gate stood for a moment looking up and down the road. Choosing the direction of London he walked for a quarter of a mile examining the gateways at either side, particularly those that led into fields. Apparently he did not find what he was in search of, for he retraced his steps to where a cross road led off to the left and continued his investigations along it. No better luck rewarding him, he tried a second cross road with the same result. There being no other cross roads, he returned to the lane and set out again, this time with his back to London. At the third gateway, one leading into a field on the left-hand side of the road, he stopped.

It was an ordinary iron farm gate set in the rather high and thick hedge that bounded the road. The field was in grass and bore the usual building ground notice. Immediately inside the gate was a patch of low and swampy looking ground, and it was a number of fresh wheel marks crossing this patch that caught the inspector's eye.

The gate was not padlocked, and Burnley slipped the bolt back and entered the field. He examined the wheel marks with great care. They turned sharply at right angles on passing through the gate and led for a short distance along the side of the fence, stopping beside a tree which grew in the hedge. The hoof marks of a horse and the prints of a man's hobnailed boots leading over the same ground also came in for a close scrutiny.

It was a contented looking Burnley who turned out of the field and walked back to St. Malo. He was well satisfied with his night's work. He had firstly succeeded in getting a lot of information out of Felix, and had further turned the latter into a friend anxious to help in the clearing up of the mystery. And though an unexpected check had arisen in the disappearance of the cask, he felt that with the information he had gained in the last three hours it would not be long before he had his hands on it again.

As he approached the door Felix hailed him.

"I saw you coming up," he said. "What luck?"

"Oh, not so bad, not so bad," returned the other. "I'm just going back to the city."

"But the cask? What about it?"

"I'll start some inquiries that may lead to something."

"Oh, come now, inspector, don't be so infernally close. You might tell me, for I can see you have something on your mind."

Burnley laughed.

" Oh, well," he said, " I don't mind. I'll tell you what I found; you see what you make of it.

" First, I found your coach-house padlock had been forced with a lever. There was nothing of the kind lying about, therefore whatever theory we adopt must account for this lever's production and disposal. It may quite likely bear marks corresponding to those on the padlock, which evidence might be valuable.

" I then found that your visitor had arrived at the yard gate with a vehicle and had climbed the wall with the aid of a very peculiar ladder. He had, presumably, opened the gate and, after loading up the cask and drawing his vehicle out on to the drive, had closed the gate, leaving by the same means. There is evidence to show that he lifted the ladder over after him, probably pulling it up by a cord.

" I have said the ladder was a peculiar one. Here is a sketch of its shape so far as I could learn it. You will see that it is short and wide with the ends shaped differently.

" I may remind you, in passing, how easy it would have been to load up the cask in spite of its weight. All that was necessary was to back the vehicle under it and lower out the differential pulley, a thing a man could do with one hand.

" I examined the drive, but could find nothing except at one place where there was a most interesting pair of footmarks. You must really see these for yourself, and if you will stroll down now I will point them out. There is reason to believe they were made by Watty when he was approaching the house with the dray, but I cannot be positive as yet.

" I then examined the lane and I found in three places other footmarks by the same man. Finally, about two hundred yards along the main road to the north, I found wheel marks leading into a grass field beside which he had walked.

" Now, Mr. Felix, put all these things together. You will find them suggestive, but the footmarks on the drive are very nearly conclusive."

They had by this time reached the marks.

" Here we are," said Burnley. " What do you think of these?"

" I don't see anything very remarkable about them."

" Look again."

Felix shook his head.

" See here, Mr. Felix. Stand out here on the gravel and put your right foot in line with this first print. Right. Now take a step forward as if you were walking to the house. Right. Does anything occur to you now?"

"I can't say that it does, unless it is that I have taken a very much longer step."

"But your step was of normal length."

"Well then, conversely, the unknown must have taken a short one."

"But did he? Assume it was Watty, as I think it must have been. You were with him and you saw him walking."

"Oh, come now, inspector. How could I tell that? He didn't normally take very short steps or I should have noticed it, but I couldn't possibly say that he never took one."

"The point is not essential except that it calls attention to a peculiarity in the steps. But you must admit that while possible, it is quite unlikely he would take a step of that length—nineteen inches as against a probable thirty-three—without stumbling or making a false step."

"But how do you know he didn't stumble?"

"The impression, my dear sir, the impression. A false step or a stumble would have made a blurred mark or shown heavier on one side than the other. This print shows no slip and is evenly marked all over. It was clearly made quite normally."

"That seems reasonable, but I don't see how it matters."

"To me it seems exceedingly suggestive though, I agree, not conclusive. But there is a nearly conclusive point, Mr. Felix. Look at those prints again."

"They convey nothing to me."

"Compare them."

"Well, I can only compare the heels and there is not much difference between them, just as you would expect between the heels of a pair of boots." Felix hesitated. "By Jove! inspector," he went on, "I've got you at last. They're the same marks. They were both made by the same foot."

"I think so, Mr. Felix; you have it now. Look here." The inspector stooped. "The fourth nail on the left-hand side is gone. That alone might be a coincidence, but if you compare the wear of the other nails and of the leather you will see they are the same beyond doubt."

He pointed to several little inequalities and inaccuracies in the outline, each of which appeared in both the marks.

"But even if they are the same, I don't know that I see what you get from that."

"Don't you? Well, look here. How could Watty, if it was he, have produced them? Surely only in one of two ways. Firstly, he could have hopped on one foot. But there are three reasons why it is unlikely he did that. One is that he could hardly have done it without your noticing it. Another, that he could never have left so clear an impression in that way. The third, why should he hop? He simply wouldn't do it. Therefore they were made in the second way. What was that, Mr. Felix?"

"I see what you're after at last," Felix said. "He walked up the drive twice."

"Of course he did. He walked up first with you to leave the cask. He walked up the second time with the empty dray to get it. If the impressions were really made by Watty that seems quite certain."

"But what on earth would Watty want with the cask? He could not know there was money in it."

"Probably not, but he must have guessed it held something valuable."

"Inspector, you overwhelm me with delight. If he took the cask it will surely be easy to trace it."

"It may or it may not. Question is: Are we sure he was acting for himself."

"Who else?"

"What about your French friend? You don't know whom he may have written to. You don't know that all your actions with the cask may not have been watched."

"Oh, don't make things worse than they are. Trace this Watty, won't you?"

"Of course we will, but it may not be so easy as you seem to think. At the same time there are two other points, both of which seem to show he was at least alone."

"Yes?"

"The first is the watcher in the lane. That was almost certainly the man who walked twice up your drive. I told you I found his footmarks at three points along it. One was near your little gate, close beside and pointing to the hedge, showing he was standing there. That was at the very point my man saw the watcher.

"The second point concerns the horse and dray, and this is what leads me to believe the watcher was really Watty. If Watty was listening up the lane where were these? If he had a companion the latter would doubtless have walked them up and down the road. But if he was alone they must have been hidden somewhere while he made his investigations. I've been over most of the roads immediately surrounding, and on my fourth shot—towards the north, as I already told you—I found the place. It is fairly clear what took place. On leaving the cask he had evidently driven along the road until he found a gate that did not lead to a house. It was, as I said, that of a field. The marks there are unmistakable. He led the dray in behind the hedge and tied the horse to a tree. Then he came back to reconnoitre and heard you going out. He must have immediately returned and brought the dray, got the cask, and cleared out, and I imagine he was not many minutes gone before my man Walker returned. What do you think of that for a working theory?"

"I think it's conclusive. Absolutely conclusive. And that explains the queer shaped ladder."

"Eh, what? What's that you say?"

"It must have been the gangway business for loading barrels on the dray. I saw one hooked on below the deck."

Burnley smote his thigh a mighty slap.

"One for you, Mr. Felix," he cried, "one for you, sir. I never thought of it. That points to Watty again."

"Inspector, let me congratulate you. You have got evidence that makes the thing a practical certainty."

"I think it's a true bill. And now, sir, I must be getting back to the Yard." Burnley hesitated and then went on : "I am extremely sorry and I'm afraid you won't like it, but I shall be straight with you and tell you I cannot—I simply dare not—leave you without some kind of police supervision until this cask business is cleared up. But I give you my word you shall not be annoyed."

"That's all right. You do your duty. The only thing I ask you is to let me know how you get on."

"I hope we'll have some news for you later in the day."

It was now shortly after eight, and the car had arrived with the two men sent back the previous evening. Burnley gave them instructions about keeping a watch on Felix, then with Sergeant Hastings and Constable Walker he was driven towards London.

CHAPTER VII

THE CASK AT LAST

INSPECTOR BURNLEY reached Scotland Yard, after dropping Constable Walker at his station with remarks which made the heart of that observer glow with triumph and conjure up pictures of the day when he, Inspector Walker, would be one of the Yard's most skilled and trusted officers. During the run citywards Burnley had thought out his plan of campaign, and he began operations by taking Sergeant Hastings to his office and getting down the large scale map.

"Look here, Hastings," he said, when he had explained his theories and found what he wanted. "Here's John Lyons and Son's, the carriers where Watty is employed, and from where the dray was hired. You see it's quite a small place. Here close by is Goole Street, and here is the Goole Street Post Office. Got the lie of those? Very well. I want you, when you've had your breakfast, to go out there and get on the track of Watty. Find out first his full name and address, and wire or phone it at once. Then shadow him. I expect he has the cask, either at his own house or hidden somewhere, and he'll lead you to it if you're there to follow. Probably he won't be able to do anything till night, but of that we can't be certain. Don't interfere or let him see you if possible, but of course don't let him open the cask if he has not already done so, and under no circumstances allow him to take anything out of it. I will follow you out and we can settle further details. The Goole Street Post Office will be our headquarters, and you can advise me there at, say, the even hours of your whereabouts. Make yourself up as you think best and get to work as quickly as you can."

The sergeant saluted and withdrew.

"That's everything in the meantime, I think," said Burnley to himself, as with a yawn he went home to breakfast.

When some time later Inspector Burnley emerged from his house, a change had come over his appearance. He seemed to have dropped his individuality as an alert and efficient representative of Scotland Yard and taken on that of a small shopkeeper or contractor in a small way of business. He was dressed in a rather shabby suit of checks, with baggy knees and draggled coat. His tie was woefully behind the fashion, his hat required brushing, and his boots were soiled and down at heel. A slight stoop and a slouching walk added to his almost slovenly appearance.

He returned to the Yard and asked for messages. Already a telephone had come through from Sergeant Hastings: "Party's name, Walter Palmer, 71 Fennell Street, Lower Beechwood Road." Having had a warrant made out for the "party's" arrest, he got a police motor with plain-clothes driver, and left for the scene of operations.

It was another glorious day. The sun shone out of a cloudless sky of clearest blue. The air had the delightful freshness of early spring. Even the inspector, with his mind full of casks and corpses, could not remain insensible of its charm. With a half sigh he thought of that garden in the country which it was one of his dearest dreams some day to achieve. The daffodils would now be in fine show and the primroses would be on, and such a lot of fascinating work would be waiting to be done among the later plants. . . .

The car drew up as he had arranged at the end of Goole Street and the inspector proceeded on foot. After a short walk he reached his objective, an archway at the end of a block of buildings, above which was a faded signboard bearing the legend, "John Lyons and Son, Carriers." Passing under the arch and following a short lane, he emerged into a yard with an open-fronted shed along one side and a stable big enough for eight or nine horses on the other. Four or five carts of different kinds were ranged under the shed roof. In the middle of the open space, with a horse yoked in, was a dray with brown sides, and Burnley, walking close to it, saw that under the paint the faint outline of white letters could be traced. A youngish man stood by the stable door and watched Burnley curiously, but without speaking.

" Boss about?" shouted Burnley.

The youngish man pointed to the entrance.

" In the office," he replied.

The inspector turned and entered a small wooden building immediately inside the gate. A stout, elderly man with a grey beard, who was posting entries in a ledger, got up and came forward as he did so.

" 'Morning," said Burnley, " have you a dray for hire?"

" Why, yes," answered the stout man. " When do you want it and for how long?"

" It's this way," returned Burnley. " I'm a painter, and I have always stuff to get to and from jobs. My own dray has broken down and I want one while it's being repaired. I've asked a friend for the loan of his, but he may not be able to supply. It will take about four days to put it right."

" Then you wouldn't want a horse and man?"

" No, I should use my own."

" In that case, sir, I couldn't agree, I fear. I never let my vehicles out without a man in charge."

" You're right in that, of course, but I don't want the man. I'll tell you. If you let me have it I'll make you a deposit of its full value. That will guarantee its safe return."

The stout man rubbed his cheek.

"I might do that," he said. "I've never done anything like it before, but I don't see why I shouldn't."

"Let's have a look at it, anyway," said Burnley.

They went into the yard and approached the dray, Burnley going through the form of examining it thoroughly.

"I have a lot of small kegs to handle," he said, "as well as drums of paint. I should like to have that barrel loader fixed till I see if it's narrow enough to carry them."

The stout man unhooked the loader and fixed it in position.

"Too wide, I'm afraid," said the inspector, producing his rule. "I'll just measure it."

It was fifteen inches wide and six feet six long. The sides were of six by two material, with iron-shod ends. One pair of ends, that resting on the ground, was chisel-pointed, the other carried the irons for hooking it on to the cart. The ends of these irons made rectangles about three inches by two. Burnley looked at the rectangles. Both were marked with soil. He was satisfied. The loader was what Watty had used to cross the wall.

"That'll do all right," he said. "Let's see, do you carry a box for hay or tools?" He opened it and rapidly scanned its contents. There was a halter, a nosebag, a small coil of rope, a cranked spanner, and some other small objects. He picked up the spanner. "This, I suppose, is for the axle caps?" he said, bending down and trying it. "I see it fits the nuts." As he replaced it in the box he took a quick look at the handle. It bore two sets of scratches on opposite sides, and the inspector felt positive these would fit the marks on the padlock and staple of the coach-house door, had he been able to try them.

The stout man was regarding him with some displeasure.

"You weren't thinking of buying it?" he said.

"No, thanks, but if you want a deposit before you let me take it, I want to be sure it won't sit down with me."

They returned to the office, discussing rates. Finally these were arranged, and it was settled that when Burnley had seen his friend he was to telephone the result.

The inspector left the yard well pleased. He had now complete proof that his theories were correct and that Watty with that dray had really stolen the cask.

Returning to Goole Street he called at the Post Office. It was ten minutes to twelve, and there being no message for him he stood waiting at the door. Five minutes had not elapsed before a street arab appeared, looked him up and down several times, and then said :—

"Name o' Burnley?"

"That's me," returned the inspector. "Got a note for me?"

"The other cove said as 'ow you'ld give me a tanner."

"Here you are, sonny," said Burnley, and the sixpence and the note changed owners. The latter read:—

"Party just about to go home for dinner. Am waiting on road south of carrier's yard."

Burnley walked to where he had left the motor and getting in, was driven to the place mentioned. At a sign from him the driver drew the car to the side of the road, stopping his engine at the same time. Jumping down, he opened the bonnet and bent over the engine. Anyone looking on would have seen that a small breakdown had taken place.

A tall, untidy looking man, in threadbare clothes and smoking a short clay, lounged up to the car with his hands in his pockets. Burnley spoke softly without looking round:—

"I want to arrest him, Hastings. Point him out when you see him."

"He'll pass this way going for his dinner in less than five minutes."

"Right."

The loafer moved forward and idly watched the repairs to the engine. Suddenly he stepped back.

"That's him," he whispered.

Burnley looked out through the back window of the car and saw a rather short, wiry man coming down the street, dressed in blue dungarees and wearing a grey woollen muffler. As he reached the car, the inspector stepped quickly out and touched him on the shoulder, while the loafer and the driver closed round.

"Walter Palmer, I am an inspector from Scotland Yard. I arrest you on a charge of stealing a cask. I warn you anything you say may be used against you. Better come quietly, you see there are three of us."

Before the dumbfounded man could realize what was happening, a pair of handcuffs had snapped on his wrists and he was being pushed in the direction of the car.

"All right, boss, I'll come," he said as he got in, followed by Burnley and Hastings. The driver started his engine and the car slipped quietly down the road. The whole affair had not occupied twenty seconds and hardly one of the passers-by had realized what was taking place.

"I'm afraid, Palmer, this is a serious matter," began Burnley. "Stealing the cask is one thing, but breaking into a man's yard at night is another. That's burglary and it will mean seven years at least."

"I don't know what you're talking abaht, boss," answered the prisoner hoarsely, licking his dry lips. "I don't know of no cask."

"Now, man, don't make things worse by lying. We know the whole thing already. Your only chance is to make a clean breast of it."

Palmer's face grew paler but he did not reply.

"We know how you brought out the cask to Mr. Felix's about eight o'clock last night, and how, when you had left it there, you thought you'd go back and see what chances there were of getting hold of it again. We know how you hid the dray in a field close by, and then went back down the lane and waited to see if anything would turn up. We know how you learnt the house was empty and that after Mr. Felix left you brought the dray back. We know all about your getting over the wall with the barrel loader, and forcing the coach-house door with the wheel-cap wrench. You see, we know the whole thing, so there's not the slightest use in your pretending ignorance."

During this recital the prisoner's face had grown paler and paler until it was now ghastly. His jaw had dropped and great drops of sweat rolled down his forehead. Still he said nothing.

Burnley saw he had produced his impression and leant forward and tapped him on the shoulder.

"Look here, Palmer," he said. "If you go into court nothing on earth can save you. It'll be penal servitude for at least five, and probably seven, years. But I'm going to offer you a sporting chance if you like to take it." The man's eyes fixed themselves with painful intentness on the speaker's face. "The police can only act if Mr. Felix prosecutes. But what Mr. Felix wants is the cask. If you return the cask at once, unopened, Mr. Felix might—I don't say he will—but he might be induced to let you off. What do you say?"

At last the prisoner's self-control went. He threw up his manacled hands with a gesture of despair.

"My Gawd!" he cried hoarsely. "I can't."

The inspector jumped.

"Can't?" he cried sharply. "What's that? Can't? What do you mean?"

"I don't know where it is. I don't, I swear. See 'ere, boss," the words now poured out of his mouth in a rapid stream, "I'll tell you the truth, I will, swelp me Gawd. Listen to me."

They had reached the City and were rapidly approaching

Scotland Yard. The inspector gave instructions for the car to be turned and run slowly through the quieter streets. Then he bent over to the now almost frantic man.

"Pull yourself together and tell me your story. Let's have the whole of it without keeping anything back, and remember the truth is your only chance."

Palmer's statement, divested of its cockney slang and picturesque embellishments was as follows:—

"I suppose you know all about the way Mr. Felix hired the dray," began Palmer, "and painted it in the shed, and about my mate Jim Brown and me?" The inspector nodded, and he continued: "Then I don't need to tell you all that part of it, only that Jim and I from the first were suspicious that there was something crooked about the whole business. Mr. Felix told us he had a bet on that he could get the cask away without being caught, but we didn't believe that, we thought he was out to steal it. Then when he told us that stevedore fellow was to be fixed so he couldn't follow us, we were both quite sure it was a do. Then you know how Felix and I left Jim and him in the bar and went back to the shed and repainted the dray? You know all that?"

"I know," said Burnley.

"We waited in the shed till it was getting on towards dusk, and then we got the cask out to Felix's, and left it swinging in a set of chain blocks in an outhouse. Well, sir, I asked more than twice the pay he'd promised, and when he gave it without a word I was certain he was afraid of me. I thought, 'There's some secret about that cask and he'd be willing to pay to have it kept quiet.' And then it occurred to me that if I could get hold of it, I could charge him my own price for its return. I didn't mean to steal it. I didn't, sir, honest. I only meant to keep it a day or two till he'd be willing to pay a reward."

The man paused.

"Well, you know, Palmer, blackmail is not much better than theft," said Burnley.

"I'm only telling you the truth, sir; that's the way it was. I thought I'd try and find out what part of the house Felix slept in and if there were others about, so as to see what chances there'd be of getting the dray up again without being heard, so I hid it in a field as you know, and went up the lane. I don't think I would have done anything only for Felix going away and saying the house was empty. Then it came over me so strongly how easy everything would be with the coast clear and the cask swinging in the chain blocks. The temptation was too strong for me, and I went back and got in as you said. I suppose you must have been there all the time watching me?"

The inspector did not reply, and Palmer went on :—

"It happened that for some time I had been going to change my house. There was an empty one close by I thought would suit. I'd got the key on Saturday and looked over it on Sunday. The key was still in my pocket, for I hadn't had time to return it.

"I intended to drive the dray down the lane behind this house and get the cask off it, then run round and get in from the front, open the yard door, roll the cask in, lock up again and return the dray to the yard. I would make an excuse with the landlord to keep the key for a day or two till I could get the money out of Felix.

"Well, sir, I drove down the lane to the back of the house, and then a thing happened that I'd never foreseen. I couldn't get the cask down. It was too heavy. I put my shoulder to it, and tried my utmost to get it over on its side, but I couldn't budge it.

"I worked till the sweat was running down me, using anything I could find for a lever, but it was no good, it wouldn't move. I went over all my friends in my mind to see if there was anyone I could get to help, but there was no one close by that I thought would come in, and I was afraid to put myself in anyone's power that I wasn't sure of. I believed Jim would be all right, but he lived two miles away and I did not want to go for him for I was late enough as it was.

"In the end I could think of no other way, and I locked the house and drove the dray to Jim's. Here I met with another disappointment. Jim had gone out about an hour before, and his wife didn't know where he was or when he'd be in.

"I cursed my luck. I was ten times more anxious now to get rid of the cask than I had been before to get hold of it. And then I thought I saw a way out. I would drive back to the yard, leave the cask there on the dray all night, get hold of Jim early in the morning, and with his help take the cask back to the empty house. If any questions were asked I would say Felix had given me instructions to leave it overnight in the yard and deliver it next morning to a certain address. I should hand over ten shillings and say he had sent this for the job.

"I drove to the yard, and then everything went wrong. First, the boss was there himself, and in a vile temper. I didn't know till afterwards, but one of our carts had been run into by a motor lorry earlier in the evening and a lot of damage done and that had upset him.

"'What's this thing you've got?' he said, when he saw the cask.

"I told him, and added that Felix had asked me to take it on in the morning, handing him the ten shillings.

"'Where is it to go?' he asked.

"Now this was a puzzler, for I hadn't expected there'd be anyone there to ask questions and I had no answer ready. So I made up an address. I chose a big street of shops and warehouses about four miles away—too far for the boss to know much about it, and I tacked on an imaginary number.

"'133 Little George Street,' I answered.

"The boss took a bit of chalk and wrote the address on the blackboard we have for such notes. Then he turned back to the broken cart, and I unyoked the horse from the dray and went home.

"I was very annoyed by the turn things had taken, but I thought that after all it would not make much difference having given the address. I could go to the empty house in the morning as I had arranged.

"I was early over at Jim's next morning and told him the story. He was real mad at first and cursed me for all kinds of a fool. I kept on explaining how safe it was, for we were both sure Felix couldn't call in the police or make a fuss. At last he agreed to stand in with me, and it was arranged that he would go direct to the empty house, while I followed with the cask. He would explain his not turning up at the yard by saying he was ill.

"The boss was seldom in when we arrived, but he was there this morning, and his temper was no better.

"'Here, you,' he called, when he saw me, 'I thought you were never coming. Get the big grey yoked into the box cart and get away to this address'—he handed me a paper—'to shift a piano.'

"'But the cask,' I stammered.

"'You mind your own business and do what you're told. I've settled about that.'

"I looked round. The dray was gone, and whether he'd sent it back to Felix or to the address I'd given, I didn't know.

"I cursed the whole affair bitterly, particularly when I thought of Jim waiting at the house. But there was nothing I could do, and I yoked the box cart and left. I went round by the house and told Jim, and I never saw a madder man in all my life. I could make nothing of him, so I left him and did the piano job. I just got back to the yard and was going for dinner when you nabbed me."

When the prisoner had mentioned the address in Little George

Street, Burnley had given a rapid order to the driver, and the statement had only just been finished when the car turned into the street.

"No. 133, you said?"

"That's it, sir."

No. 133 was a large hardware shop. Burnley saw the proprietor.

"Yes," the latter said, "we have the cask, and I may say I was very annoyed with my foreman for taking it in without an advice note or something in writing. You can have it at once on your satisfying me you really are from Scotland Yard."

His doubts were quickly set at rest, and he led the party to his yard.

"Is that it, Palmer?" asked Burnley.

"That's it, sir, right enough."

"Good. Hastings, you remain here with it till I send a dray. Get it loaded up and see it yourself to the Yard. You can then go off duty. You, Palmer, come with me."

Re-entering the car, Burnley and his prisoner were driven to the same destination, where the latter was handed over to another official.

"If Mr. Felix will consent not to prosecute," said Burnley as the man was being led off, "you'll get out at once."

The inspector waited about till the dray arrived, and, when he had seen with his own eyes that the cask was really there, he walked to his accustomed restaurant and sat down to enjoy a long deferred meal.

CHAPTER VIII

THE OPENING OF THE CASK

IT was getting on towards five when Inspector Burnley, like a giant refreshed with wine, emerged once more upon the street. Calling a taxi, he gave the address of St. Malo, Great North Road.

"Now for friend Felix," he thought, as he lit a cigar. He was tired and he lay back on the cushions, enjoying the relaxation as the car slipped dexterously through the traffic. Familiar as he was with every phase of London life, he never wearied of the panorama of the streets, the ceaseless movement, the kaleidoscopic colours. The sights of the pavement, the sound of pneus upon asphalt, the very smell of burnt petrol—each appealed to him as part of the alluring whole he loved.

They passed through the Haymarket and along Shaftesbury Avenue, turned up Tottenham Court Road, and through Kentish Town out on the Great North Road. Here the traffic was less dense and they made better speed. Burnley removed his hat and allowed the cool air to blow on his head. His case was going well. He was content.

Nearly an hour had passed before he rang the bell at St. Malo. Felix opened the door, the visage of Sergeant Kelvin, his watchdog, appearing in the gloom at the back of the hall

"What luck, inspector?" he cried, when he recognized his visitor.

"We've got it, Mr. Felix. Found it a couple of hours ago. I've got a taxi here, and, if convenient for you, we'll go right in and open the thing at once."

"Right. I'm sure I am ready."

"You come along too, Kelvin," said the inspector to his subordinate, and when Felix had got his hat and coat the three men walked up to the taxi.

"Scotland Yard," called Burnley, and the car swung round and started citywards.

As they sped swiftly along, the inspector gave an account of his day to his companion. The latter was restless and excited, and admitted he would be glad to get the business over. He was anxious about the money, as it happened that a sum of £1,000 would just enable him to meet a mortgage, which otherwise would press rather heavily upon him. Burnley looked up sharply when he heard this.

"Did your French friend know that?" he asked.

"Le Gautier? No, I'm sure he did not."

"If you take my advice, Mr. Felix, you won't count too much on the cask. Indeed, you should prepare yourself for something unpleasant."

"What do you mean?" exclaimed Felix. "You hinted that you thought the cask contained something besides the money. What was it?"

"I'm sorry I can't answer you. The thing was only a suspicion, and we shall learn the truth in so short a time it's not worth discussion."

Burnley having to make a call on some other business, they returned by a different route, coming down to the river near London Bridge. Already the day was drawing in, and yellow spots of light began to gleam in the windows of the palace hotels, and from the murky buildings on the south side. On the comparatively deserted Embankment they made good speed, and Big Ben was chiming the quarter after seven as they swung into the Yard.

"I'll see if the Chief's in," said Burnley, as they reached his office. "He wanted to see the cask opened."

The great man was just getting ready to go home, but decided to wait on seeing the inspector. He greeted Felix politely.

"Singular set of circumstances, Mr. Felix," he said, as they shook hands. "I trust they will remain only that."

"You're all very mysterious about it," returned Felix. "I have been trying to get a hint of the inspector's suspicions but he won't commit himself."

"We shall see now in a moment."

Headed by Burnley, they passed along a corridor, down some steps and through other passages, until they emerged in a small open yard entirely surrounded by a high, window-pierced building. Apparently in the daytime it acted as a light well, but now in the growing dusk it was itself illuminated by a powerful arc lamp which threw an intense beam over every part of the granolithic floor. In the centre stood the cask, on end, with the damaged stave up.

The little group numbered five. There were the Chief, Felix, Burnley, Sergeant Kelvin, and another nondescript looking man. Burnley stepped forward.

"This cask is so exceedingly strongly made," he said, "I've got a carpenter to open it. I suppose he may begin?"

The Chief nodded, and the nondescript man advancing set to work and soon lifted out the pieces of wood from the top. He held one up.

"You see, gentlemen, it's nearly two inches thick, more than twice as heavy as an ordinary wine cask."

"That'll do, carpenter. I'll call you if I want you again," said Burnley, and the man, putting away his tools, and touching his cap, promptly disappeared.

The four men drew closer. The cask was filled up to the top with sawdust. Burnley began removing it, sifting it carefully through his fingers.

"Here's the first," he said, as he laid a sovereign on the floor to one side. "And another! And another!"

The sovereigns began to grow into a tiny pile.

"There's some very uneven-shaped thing here," he said again. "About the centre the sawdust is not half an inch thick, but it goes down deep round the sides. Lend a hand, Kelvin, but be careful and don't use force."

The unpacking continued. Handful after handful of dust was taken out and, after being sifted, was placed in a heap beside the sovereigns. As they got deeper the operation became slower, the spaces from which the tightly packed dust was removed growing narrower and harder to get at. Fewer sovereigns were found, suggesting that these had been placed at the top of the cask after the remainder of the contents had been packed.

"All the sawdust we can get at is out now," Burnley said presently, and then, in a lower tone, "I'm afraid it's a body. I've come on a hand."

"A hand? A body?" cried Felix, his face paling and an expression of fear growing in his eyes. The Chief moved closer to him as the others bent over the cask.

The two men worked silently for some moments and then Burnley spoke again :—

"Lift now. Carefully does it."

They stooped again over the cask and, with a sudden effort lifted out a paper-covered object and laid it reverently on the ground. A sharp "My God!" burst from Felix, and even the case-hardened Chief drew in his breath quickly.

It was the body of a woman, the head and shoulders being wrapped round with sheets of brown paper. It lay all bunched together as it had done in the cask. One dainty hand, with slim, tapered fingers protruded from the paper, and stuck stiffly upwards beside the rounded shoulder.

The men stopped and stood motionless, looking down at the still form. Felix was standing rigid, his face blanched, his eyes protruding, horror stamped on his features. The Chief spoke in a low tone :—

"Take off the paper."

Burnley caught the loose corner and gently removed it. As it came away the figure within became revealed to the onlookers.

The body was that of a youngish woman, elegantly clad in an evening gown of pale pink cut low round the throat and shoulders, and trimmed with old lace. Masses of dark hair were coiled round the small head. On the fingers the glint of precious stones caught the light. The feet were cased in silk stockings, but no shoes. Pinned to the dress was an envelope.

But it was on the face and neck the gaze of the men was riveted. Once she had clearly been beautiful, but now the face was terribly black and swollen. The dark eyes were open and protruding, and held an expression of deadly horror and fear. The lips were drawn back showing the white, even teeth. And below, on the throat were two discoloured bruises, side by side, round marks close to the windpipe, thumb-prints of the animal who had squeezed out that life with relentless and merciless hands.

When the paper was removed from the dead face, the eyes of Felix seemed to start literally out of his head.

"God!" he shrieked in a thin, shrill tone. "It's Annette!" He stood for a moment, waved his hands convulsively, and then, slowly turning, pitched forward insensible on the floor.

The Chief caught him before his head touched the ground.

"Lend a hand here," he called.

Burnley and the sergeant sprang forward and, lifting the inanimate form, bore it into an adjoining room and laid it gently on the floor.

"Doctor," said the Chief shortly, and the sergeant hurried off.

"Bad business, this," resumed the Chief. "He didn't know what was coming?"

"I don't think so, sir. My impression has been all through that he was being fooled by this Frenchman, whoever he is."

"It's murder now, anyway. You'll have to go to Paris, Burnley, and look into it."

"Yes, sir, very good." He looked at his watch. "It's eight o'clock. I shall hardly be able to go tonight. I shall have to take the cask and the clothing, and get some photos and measurements of the corpse and hear the result of the medical examination."

"Tomorrow will be time enough, but I'd go by the nine o'clock train. I'll give you a personal note to Chauvet, the chief of the Paris police. You speak French, I think?"

"Enough to get on, sir."

"You shouldn't have much difficulty, I think. The Paris men are bound to know if there are any recent disappearances, and if not you have the cask and the clothing to fall back on."

"Yes, sir, they should be a help."

Footsteps in the corridor announced the arrival of the doctor. With a hasty greeting to the Chief, he turned to the unconscious man.

"What happened to him?" he asked.

"He has had a shock," answered the Chief, explaining in a few words what had occurred.

"He'll have to be removed to hospital at once. Better get a stretcher."

The sergeant disappeared again and in a few seconds returned with the apparatus and another man. Felix was lifted on to it and borne off.

"Doctor," said the Chief, as the former was about to follow, "as soon as you are through with him I wish you'd make an examination of the woman's body. It seems fairly clear what happened to her, but it would be better to have a post-mortem. Poison may have been used also. Burnley, here, is going to Paris by the nine o'clock in the morning to make inquiries, and he will want a copy of your report with him."

"I shall have it ready," said the doctor as, with a bow, he hurried after his patient.

"Now, let's have a look at that letter."

They returned to the courtyard and Burnley unpinned the envelope from the dead woman's gown. It was unaddressed, but the Chief slit it open and drew out a sheet of folded paper. It bore a single line of typing:—

"Your £50 loan returned herewith with £2 10s. od. interest."

That was all. No date, address, salutation, or signature. Nothing to indicate who had sent it, or whose was the body that had accompanied it.

He took the paper and scrutinized it carefully. Then he held it up to the light.

"This is from Le Gautier also," he continued. "See the watermark. It is the same paper as Felix's letter. Look also at the typing. Here are the crooked n's and r's, the defective l's and the t's and e's below alignment. It was typed on the same machine."

"Looks like it certainly." Then, after a pause: "Come to my room for the letter to M. Chauvet."

They traversed the corridors and the inspector got his introduction to the Paris police. Then, returning to the little yard, he began the preparations for his journey.

First he picked up and counted the money. There was £31 10s. in English gold and, having made a note of the amount, he slipped it into his pocket as a precaution against chance passers-by. With the £21 handed by Broughton to Mr. Avery, this made the £52 10s. referred to in the typewritten slip. Then he had the body moved to the dissecting-room and photographed from several points of view, after which it was stripped by a female assistant. The clothes he went through with great care, examining every inch of the material for makers' names, initials, or other marks. Only on the delicate cambric handkerchief was his search rewarded, a small A. B. being embroidered amid the tracery of one corner. Having attached a label to each garment separately, as well as to the rings from the fingers and a diamond comb from the luxuriant hair, he packed them carefully in a small portmanteau, ready for transport to France.

Sending for the carpenter, he had the end boards of the cask replaced, and the whole thing wrapped in sacking and corded. Labelling it to himself at the Gare du Nord, he had it dispatched to Charing Cross with instructions to get it away without delay.

It was past ten when his preparations were complete, and he was not sorry when he was free to go home to supper and bed.

PART II—PARIS

CHAPTER IX

M. LE CHEF DE LA SÛRETÉ

AT nine o'clock next morning the continental express moved slowly out of Charing Cross station, bearing in the corner of a first-class smoking compartment, Inspector Burnley. The glorious weather of the past few days had not held, and the sky was clouded over, giving a promise of rain. The river showed dark and gloomy as they drew over it, and the houses on the south side had resumed their normal dull and grimy appearance. A gentle breeze blew from the south-west, and Burnley, who was a bad sailor, hoped it would not be much worse at Dover. He lit one of his strong-smelling cigars and puffed at it thoughtfully as the train ran with ever-increasing speed through the tangle of lines south of London Bridge.

He was glad to be taking this journey. He liked Paris and he had not been there for four years, not indeed since the great Marcelle murder case, which attracted so much attention in both countries. M. Lefarge, the genial French detective with whom he had then collaborated had become a real friend and he hoped to run across him again.

They had reached the outer suburbs and occasional fields began to replace the lines of little villas which lie closer to the city. He watched the flying objects idly for a few minutes, and then with a little sigh turned his attention to his case, as a barrister makes up his brief before going into court.

He considered first his object in making the journey. He had to find out who the murdered woman was, if she was murdered, though there appeared little doubt about that. He had to discover and get convicting evidence against the murderer, and lastly, he had to learn the explanation of the strange business of the cask.

He then reviewed the data he already had, turning first to the medical report which up till then he had not had an opportunity of reading. There was first a note about Felix. That unhappy man was entirely prostrated from the shock and his life was in serious danger.

The inspector had already known this, for he had gone to the ward before seven that morning in the hope of getting a statement from the sick man, only to find him semi-conscious and delirious. The identity of the dead woman could not, therefore, be ascertained from him. He, Burnley, must rely on his own efforts.

The report then dealt with the woman. She was aged about five-and-twenty, five feet seven in height and apparently gracefully built, and weighing a little over eight stone. She had dark hair of great length and luxuriance, and eyes with long lashes and delicately pencilled brows. Her mouth was small and regular, her nose slightly *retroussée* and her face a true oval. She had a broad, low forehead, and her complexion appeared to have been very clear, though dark. There was no distinguishing mark on the body.

"Surely," thought Burnley, "with such a description it should be easy to identify her."

The report continued :—

"There are ten marks about her neck, apparently finger marks. Of these eight are together at the back of the neck and not strongly marked. The remaining two are situated in front of the throat, close together and one on each side of the windpipe. The skin at these points is much bruised and blackened, and the pressure must therefore have been very great.

"It seems clear the marks were caused by some individual standing in front of her and squeezing her throat with both hands, the thumbs on the windpipe and the fingers round the neck. From the strength necessary to produce such bruises, it looks as if this individual were a man.

"An autopsy revealed the fact that all the organs were sound, and there was no trace of poison or other cause of death. The conclusion is therefore unavoidable that the woman was murdered by strangulation. She appears to have been dead about a week or slightly longer."

"That's definite, anyway," mused Burnley. "Let's see what else we have."

There was the woman's rank in life. She was clearly well off if not rich, and probably well born. Her fingers suggested culture, they were those of the artist or musician. The wedding ring on her right hand showed that she was married, and living in France. "Surely," thought the inspector again, "the Chief is right. It would be impossible for a woman of this kind to disappear without the knowledge of the French police. My job will be done when I have seen them."

But supposing they did not know. What then?

There was first of all the letter to Felix. The signatory, M. Le Gautier, assuming such a man existed, should be able to give a clue. The waiters in the Toisson d'Or Café might know something. The typewriter with the defective letters was surely traceable.

The clothes in which the corpse was dressed suggested another line of attack. Inquiry at the leading Paris shops could hardly fail to produce information. And if not there were the rings and the diamond comb. These would surely lead to something.

Then there was the cask. It was a specially made one, and must surely have been used for a very special purpose. Inquiry from the firm whose label it had borne could hardly be fruitless.

And lastly, if all these failed, there was left advertisement. A judiciously worded notice with a reward for information of identity would almost certainly draw. Burnley felt he was well supplied with clues. Many and many a thorny problem he had solved with far less to go on.

He continued turning the matter over in his mind in his slow, painstaking way, until a sudden plunge into a tunnel and a grinding of brakes warned him they were coming into Dover.

The crossing was calm and uneventful. Before they passed between the twin piers at Calais the sun had burst out, the clouds were thinning, and blue sky showing in the distance.

They made a good run to Paris, stopping only at Amiens, and at 5.45 precisely drew slowly into the vast, echoing vault of the Gare du Nord. Calling a taxi, the inspector drove to a small private hotel he usually patronized in the rue Castiglione. Having secured his room, he re-entered the taxi and went to the Sûreté, the Scotland Yard of Paris.

He inquired for M. Chauvet, sending in his letter of introduction. The Chief was in and disengaged, and after a few minutes' delay Inspector Burnley was ushered into his presence.

M. Chauvet, Chef de la Sûreté, was a small, elderly man with a dark, pointed beard, gold-rimmed glasses, and an exceedingly polite manner.

"Sit down, Mr. Burnley," he said in excellent English, as they shook hands. "I think we have had the pleasure of co-operating with you before?"

Burnley reminded him of the Marcelle murder case.

"Ah, of course, I remember. And now you are bringing us another of the same kind. Is it not so?"

"Yes, sir, and a rather puzzling one also. But I am in hopes we have enough information to clear it up quickly."

"Good, I hope you have. Please let me have, in a word or two, the briefest outline, then I shall ask you to go over it again in detail."

Burnley explained in half a dozen sentences the gist of the case.

"The circumstances are certainly singular," said the Chief. "Let me think who I shall put in charge of it with you. Dupont is perhaps the best man, but he is engaged on that burglary at Chartres." He looked up a card index. "Of those disengaged, the best perhaps are Cambon, Lefarge, and Bontemps. All good men."

He stretched out his hand to the desk telephone.

"Pardon me, sir," said Burnley. "I don't want to make suggestions or interfere in what is not my business, but I had the pleasure of co-operating with M. Lefarge in the Marcelle case, and if it was quite the same I should like to work with him again."

"But excellent, monsieur. I hear you say that with much pleasure."

He lifted his desk telephone, pressing one of the many buttons on its stand.

"Ask M. Lefarge to come here at once."

In a few seconds a tall, clean-shaven, rather English looking man entered.

"Ah, Lefarge," said the Chief. "Here is a friend of yours." The two detectives shook hands warmly.

"He has brought us another murder mystery and very interesting it sounds. Now, Mr. Burnley, perhaps you would let us hear your story in detail."

The inspector nodded, and beginning at the sending of the clerk Tom Broughton to check the consignment of wine at the Rouen steamer, he related all the strange events that had taken place, the discovery of the cask, and the suspicions aroused, the forged note, the removal of the cask, the getting rid of Harkness, the tracing and second disappearance of the cask, its ultimate recovery, its sinister contents, and finally, a list of the points which might yield clues if followed up. The two men listened intently, but without interrupting. After he had finished they sat silently in thought.

"In one point I do not quite follow you, Mr. Burnley," said the Chief at last. "You appear to assume that this murdered woman was a Parisienne. But what are your reasons for that?"

"The cask came from Paris. That is certain, as you will see from the steamship's documents. Then the letter to Felix purports to be from a Parisian, a M. Le Gautier, and both it and the note pinned to the body were typed on French paper. Further, the label on the cask bore the name of a Paris firm."

"It does not seem to me very conclusive. The cask admittedly came from Paris, but might not Paris have been only the last stage of a longer journey? How, for example, do we know that it was not sent from London, or Brussels, or Berlin, in the first instance, and rebooked at Paris with the object of laying a false scent? With regard to the letter, I understand you did not see the envelope. Therefore it does not seem to be evidence. As for the French paper, Felix had been frequently in France, and he might be responsible for that. The label, again, was a re-addressed old one. Might it not therefore have been taken off some quite different package and put on the cask?"

"I admit the evidence is far from conclusive, though it might be said in answer to your first point about the re-addressing of the cask in Paris that such would involve a confederate here. In any case it seemed to both our Chief and myself that Paris should be our first point of inquiry."

"But yes, monsieur, in that I entirely agree. I only wished to make the point that you have no real evidence that the solution of the problem lies here."

"I'm afraid we have not."

"Well, to proceed. As you have suggested, the first point is to ascertain if anyone resembling the dead woman has disappeared recently. Your doctor says that she has been dead for a week or longer, but I do not think that we can confine our inquiries to that period only. She might have been kidnapped and held a prisoner for a considerable time previous to her death. I should say that it is not likely, but it may have happened."

He lifted his telephone, pressing another button.

"Bring me the list of disappearances of persons in the Paris area during the last four weeks, or rather "—he stopped and looked at the others—"the disappearances in all France for the same period."

In a few seconds a clerk entered with some papers.

"Here are all the disappearances reported during March, monsieur," he said, "and here those for April up to the present date. I haven't a return for the last four weeks only, but can get one out at once if you wish."

"No. These are all right."

The Chief examined the documents.

"Last month," he said, "seven persons disappeared of whom six were women, four being in the Paris area. This month two people have disappeared, both women and both in the Paris area. That is six women in Paris in the last five weeks. Let's see, now," he ran his fingers down the column, "Suzanne Lemaître, aged seventeen, last seen—well, it could not be she. Lucille Marquet, aged twenty—no good either. All these are girls under twenty-one, except one. Here, what is this? Marie Lachaise, aged thirty-four, height 172 centimetres—that is about five feet eight in English measure—dark hair and eyes and clear complexion, wife of M. Henri Lachaise, the avocat, of 41 rue Tinques, Boulevard Arago. Left home on the twenty-ninth ultimo, that is about ten days ago, at three o'clock, ostensibly for shopping. Has not been heard of since. Better take a note of that."

M. Lefarge did so, and spoke for the first time.

"We shall try it, of course, monsieur, but I don't expect much result. If that woman went out to shop she would hardly be wearing evening dress, as was the corpse."

"Also," said Burnley, "I think we may take it the dead woman's name was Annette B."

"Probably you are both right. Still, you had better make sure." The Chief tossed away the papers and looked at Burnley.

"No other disappearances have been reported, nor have we any further information here that would seem to help. I am afraid we must fall back on our other clues. Let us consider, therefore, where we should start."

He paused for a few moments and then resumed.

"We may begin, I think, by checking the part of Felix's statement which you, Mr. Burnley, have not yet been able to inquire into, and to do so we must interview M. Le Gautier and try to ascertain if he wrote the letter. If he admits it we will be a step farther on, if not, we must find out how far the story of the lottery and the bet is true, and whether the conversation described by Felix actually took place. In this case we must ascertain precisely who were present and overheard that conversation, and would therefore have the knowledge necessary to write that letter. If this does not give us what we want, it may be necessary to follow up each of these persons and try for our man by elimination. A part of that inquiry would be a search for the typewriter used, which, as Mr. Burnley points out, is identifiable. Simultaneously, I think we should endeavour to trace the wearing apparel and the cask. What do you think of that, gentlemen, for a rough programme?"

"I don't think we could do better, sir," returned Burnley as the Chief looked at him, while Lefarge nodded his approval.

"Very well, I would suggest that you and Lefarge go into the matter of the letter tomorrow. Arrange your programme as you think best for yourselves and keep me advised of how you get on. And now as to the clothes. Let me see exactly what you have."

Burnley spread out the dead woman's clothes and jewellery on a table. The Chief examined them for some minutes in silence.

"Better separate them into three lots," he said at length, "the dress, the underclothes, and the trinkets. It will take three to work it properly." He consulted his card index and picked up the telephone.

"Send Mme. Furnier and Mlles. Lecoq and Blaise here."

In a few seconds three stylishly dressed women entered. The Chief introduced Burnley and briefly explained the case.

"I want you three ladies," he said, "to take one each of these three lots of clothes and trinkets, and find the purchaser. Their quality will give you an idea of the shops to try. Get at it first thing tomorrow, and keep yourselves in constant touch with headquarters."

When the women had withdrawn he turned to Burnley:—

"In an inquiry of this sort I like a report in the evenings of progress during the day. Perhaps you and Lefarge wouldn't mind calling about nine tomorrow evening, when we shall have a further discussion. And now it is nearly eight o'clock, so you cannot do anything tonight. You, Mr. Burnley, are doubtless tired from your journey and will be glad to get to your hotel. So good night, gentlemen."

The detectives bowed themselves out. After an exchange of further greetings and compliments, Lefarge said:—

"Are you really very tired? Are you game for a short inquiry tonight?"

"Why, certainly. What do you propose?"

"This. Let us cross and get some dinner at Jules's in the Boule Miche. It's on the way to that address the Chief gave us. Then we could go on and see whether the body you found in the cask can be identified as that of Madame Marie Lachaise."

They strolled leisurely over the Pont St. Michael and crossed the Quai into the Boulevard. When Burnley was in London he swore there was no place like that city, but in Paris he never felt so sure. Jove! he was glad to be back. And what luck to have met this good fellow Lefarge again! He felt that in the intervals of business he was going to enjoy himself.

They dined inexpensively but well, sitting over their cigars and liqueur coffee until nine o'clock. Then Lefarge made a move.

"I don't like to go to this place too late," he said. "Do you mind coming now?"

They took a taxi and, leaving the Luxembourg behind on the left, quickly ran the mile or so to the Boulevard Arago. M. Lachaise received them at once and they stated their melancholy business, showing the photograph of the body. The avocat took it to the light and examined it earnestly. Then he returned it with a gesture of relief.

"Thank God," he said at length, "it's not she."

"The body was clothed in a light pink evening dress, with several diamond rings on the fingers and a diamond comb in her hair."

"It is not she at all. My wife had no pink dress, nor did she wear a diamond comb. Besides, she left here in an out-of-door walking dress and all her evening things were in her wardrobe."

"It is conclusive," said M. Lefarge, and with thanks and compliments they took their leave.

"I thought that would be no good," said Lefarge, "but we must do what the Chief says."

"Of course. Besides, you never know. Look here, old man," he added, "I am tired after all. I think, if you don't mind, I'll get away to the hotel."

"But, of course. Whatever you feel like. Let's stroll to the end of the Boulevard. We can get the Metro across the street at the Avenue d'Orleans."

They changed at Chatelet and, having arranged to meet next morning, the inspector took the Maillot train for Concorde, while Lefarge went in the opposite direction to his home near the Place de la Bastille.

CHAPTER X

WHO WROTE THE LETTER?

AT ten o'clock next morning Lefarge called for Burnley at the latter's hotel in the rue Castiglione.

"Now for M. Alphonse Le Gautier, the wine merchant," said the former as he hailed a taxi.

A short drive brought them to the rue de Vallorbes, off the Avenue Friedland, and there they discovered that the gentleman they were in search of was no myth, but a creature of real flesh and blood. He occupied a flat on the first floor of a big corner house, and the spacious approach and elegant furnishing indicated that he was a man of culture and comparative wealth. He had gone, they were told, to his office in the rue Henri Quatre, and thither the two friends followed him. He was a man of about five-and-thirty, with jet black hair and a pale, hawk-like face, and his manner was nervous and alert.

" We have called, monsieur," said Lefarge, when the detectives had introduced themselves, " at the instance of M. le Chef de la Sûreté, to ask your assistance in a small inquiry we are making. We want to trace the movements of a gentleman who is perhaps not unknown to you, a M. Léon Felix, of London."

" Léon Felix? Why, of course I know him. And what has he been up to?"

" Nothing contrary to the law, monsieur," returned Lefarge with a smile, " or, at least, we believe not. But unfortunately, in the course of another inquiry a point has arisen which makes it necessary for us to check some statements he has made about his recent actions. It is in this we want your help."

" I don't think I can tell you much about him, but any questions you ask I'll try to answer."

" Thank you, M. Le Gautier. Not to waste your time, then, I'll begin without further preface. When did you last meet M. Felix?"

" Well, it happens I can tell you that, for I had a special reason to note the date." He referred to a small pocket diary. " It was on Sunday the 14th of March, four weeks ago next Sunday."

" And what was the special reason to which you refer?"

" This. On that day M. Felix and I made an arrangement to purchase coupons in the Government lotteries. He handed me five hundred francs as his share, and I was to add another five hundred francs and put the business through. Naturally I noted the transaction in my engagement book."

" Can you tell me under what circumstances this arrangement came to be made?"

" Certainly. It was the result of an otherwise idle conversation on the lottery system, which took place that afternoon between a number of men, of whom I was one, at the Café Toisson d'Or, in the rue Royale. At the close of the discussion I said I would try my luck. I asked Felix to join me, and he did so."

" And did you purchase the bonds?"

"I did. I wrote enclosing a cheque that same evening."

"And I hope your speculation turned out successful?"

M. Le Gautier smiled.

"Well, I can hardly tell you that, you know. The drawing will not be made till next Thursday."

"Next Thursday? Then I can only hope you will have luck. Did you write M. Felix that you had actually moved in the matter?"

"No, I took it, that went without saying."

"So that you have not communicated with M. Felix in any way since last Sunday three weeks?"

"That is so."

"I see. Now, another point, M. Le Gautier. Are you acquainted with a M. Dumarchez, a stockbroker, whose office is in the Boulevard Poissonière?"

"I am. As a matter of fact he also was present at the discussion about the lotteries."

"And since that discussion you made a certain bet with him?"

"A bet?" M. Le Gautier looked up sharply. "I don't understand you. I made no bet."

"Do you remember having a discussion with M. Dumarchez about criminals pitting their wits against the police?"

"No, I recollect nothing of the kind."

"Are you prepared, monsieur, to say that no such conversation took place?"

"Certainly, I do say it. And I should very much like to know the purport of all these questions."

"I am sorry, monsieur, for troubling you with them, and I can assure you they are not idle. The matter is a serious one, though I am not at liberty to explain it fully at present. But if you will bear with me I would like to ask one or two other things. Can you let me have the names of those present at the Toisson d'Or when the conversation about the lotteries took place?"

M. Le Gautier remained silent for some moments.

"I hardly think I can," he said at last. "You see, there was quite a fair sized group. Besides Felix, Dumarchez, and myself, I can recollect M. Henri Briant and M. Henri Boisson. I think there were others, but I cannot recall who they were."

"Was a M. Daubigny one of them?"

"You are right. I had forgotten him. He was there."

"And M. Jaques Rôget?"

"I'm not sure." M. Le Gautier hesitated again. "I think so, but I'm not really sure."

"Can you let me have the addresses of these gentlemen?"

G.M.N.—D*

" Some of them. M. Dumarchez lives five doors from me in the rue de Vallorbes. M. Briant lives near the end of the rue Washington, where it turns into the Champs Elysées. The other addresses I cannot tell you off-hand, but I can help you to find them in a directory."

" Many thanks. Now, please excuse me for going back a moment. You gave me to understand you did not write to M. Felix on the subject of the lottery?"

" Yes, I said so, I think, quite clearly."

" But M. Felix states the very opposite. He says he received a letter from you, dated Thursday, 1st April, that is, this day week."

M. Le Gautier stared.

" What's that you say? He says he heard from me? There must be a mistake there, monsieur, for I did not write to him."

" But he showed me the letter."

" Impossible, monsieur. He could not have shown you what did not exist. Whatever letter he may have shown you was not from me. I should like to see it. Have you got it there?"

For answer Lefarge held out the sheet which Felix had given to Burnley during their midnight conversation at the villa of St. Malo. As M. Le Gautier read it the look of wonder on his expressive face deepened.

" Extraordinary!" he cried, " but here is a mystery! I never wrote, or sent, or had any knowledge of such a letter. It's not only a forgery, but it's a pure invention. There's not a word of truth in that story of the bet and the cask from beginning to end. Tell me something more about it. Where did you get it?"

" From M. Felix himself. He gave it to Mr. Burnley here, saying it was from you."

" But, good heavens!" the young man sprang to his feet and began pacing up and down the room. " I can't understand that. Felix is a decent fellow, and he wouldn't say it was from me if he didn't believe it. But how could he believe it? The thing is absurd." He paused and then continued. " You say, monsieur, that Felix said this note was from me. But what made him think so? There's not a scrap of writing about it. It isn't even signed. He must have known anyone could write a letter and type my name below it. And then, how could he suppose that I should write such a tissue of falsehoods?"

" But that is just the difficulty," returned Lefarge. " It's not so false as you seem to imagine. The description of the conversation about the lottery and your arrangement with Felix to purchase bonds is, by your own admission, true."

"Yes, that part is, but the rest, all that about a bet and a cask, is wholly false."

"But there I fear you are mistaken also, monsieur. The part about the cask is apparently true. At least the cask arrived, addressed as described, and on the day mentioned."

Again the young merchant gave an involuntary exclamation of astonishment.

"The cask arrived?" he cried. "Then there really was a cask?" He paused again. "Well, I cannot understand it, but I can only repeat that I never wrote that letter, nor have I the slightest idea what it is all about."

"It is, of course, obvious, monsieur, as you point out, that anyone could have typed a letter ending with your name. But you will admit it is equally obvious that only a person who knew of your entering the lottery could have written it. You tell us you are not that person, and we fully accept your statement. Who else then, M. Le Gautier, had this information?"

"As far as that goes, anyone who was present at the discussion at the Toisson d'Or."

"Quite so. Hence you will see the importance of my questions as to whom these were."

M. Le Gautier paced slowly up and down the room, evidently thinking deeply.

"I don't know that I do," he said at last. "Suppose everything in that letter was true. Suppose, for argument's sake, I had written it. What then? What business of the police is it? I can't see that the law has been broken."

Lefarge smiled.

"That ought to be clear enough, anyway. Look at the facts. A cask arrives in London by the I. and C. boat from Rouen, labelled to a man named Felix at a certain address. Inquiries show that no one of that name lives at that address. Further, the cask is labelled 'Statuary,' but examination shows that it does not contain statuary, but money, sovereigns. Then a man representing himself as Felix appears, states he lives at the false address, which is untrue, says he is expecting by that boat a cask of statuary, which is also untrue, and claims the one in question. The steamer people, being naturally suspicious, will not give it up, but by a trick Felix gets hold of it, and takes it to quite another address. When questioned by the police he produces this letter to account for his actions. I do not think it surprising that we are anxious to learn who wrote the letter, and if its contents are true."

"No, no, of course it is reasonable. I did not understand the sequence of events. All the same, it is the most extraordinary business I ever heard of."

"It is strange, certainly. Tell me, M. Le Gautier, have you ever had any disagreement with Mr. Felix? Can you imagine him having, or thinking he had, any cause of offence against you?"

"Nothing of the kind."

"You never gave him cause, however innocently, to feel jealousy?"

"Never. But why do you ask?"

"I was wondering whether he might not have played a trick on you, and have written the letter himself."

"No, no. I'm sure it's not that. Felix is a very straight, decent fellow. He would not do a thing like that."

"Well, can you think of anyone who might be glad to give you annoyance? What about the men who were present when you discussed the lottery? Or anyone else at all?"

"I cannot think of a single person."

"Did you tell anyone about this matter of the lottery?"

"No. I never mentioned it."

"One other question, monsieur, and I have done. Did you at any time borrow £50 or the equivalent of French money from M. Felix?"

"I never borrowed from him at all."

"Or do you know anyone who borrowed such a sum from him?"

"No one, monsieur."

"Then, monsieur, allow me to express my regret for the annoyance given, and my thanks for your courteous replies to my questions." He flashed a glance at Burnley, "If we might still further inflict ourselves on you, I should like, with your permission, to ask M. Dumarchez to join us here so that we may talk the matter over together."

"An excellent idea, monsieur. Do so by all means."

One of the eventualities the colleagues had discussed before starting their morning's work was the possible denial by M. Le Gautier of any bet with M. Dumarchez. They had decided that in such a case the latter must be interrogated before a communication could reach him from Le Gautier. It was with this in view that Lefarge left his friend with the wine-merchant, while going himself to interview his neighbour.

As the detective reached the door of the stockbroker's office in the Boulevard Poissonière it opened and a middle-aged gentleman with a long, fair beard emerged.

"Pardon, but are you M. Dumarchez?" asked Lefarge.

"My name, monsieur. Did you wish to see me?"

The detective introduced himself, and briefly stated his business.

"Come in, monsieur," said the other. "I have an appointment in another part of Paris shortly, but I can give you ten minutes." He led the way into his private room and waved his visitor to a chair.

"It is the matter of the bet, monsieur," began Lefarge. "The test has failed, and the police have therefore to satisfy themselves that the cask was really sent with the object stated."

M. Dumarchez stared.

"I do not understand," he replied. "To what bet are you referring?"

"To the bet between you and M. Le Gautier. You see, M. Felix's dealings with the cask are the result of the bet, and it must be obvious to you that confirmation of his statement is required."

The stockbroker shook his head with decision as if to close the conversation.

"You have made some mistake, monsieur. I made no bet with M. Le Gautier and, for the rest, I have no idea what you are speaking of."

"But, monsieur, M. Felix stated directly that you had bet M. Le Gautier he could not get the cask away. If that is not true, it may be serious for him."

"I know nothing of any cask. What Felix are you referring to?"

"M. Léon Felix, of St. Malo, London."

A look of interest passed over the stockbroker's face.

"Léon Felix? I certainly know him. A decent fellow he is too. And you mean to say he told you I was mixed up with some matter connected with a cask?"

"Certainly. At least he told my colleague, Mr. Burnley, of the London police."

"My dear monsieur, your colleague must be dreaming. Felix must have been speaking of some one else."

"I assure you not, monsieur. There is no mistake. M. Felix states the bet arose out of a conversation on the State lotteries, which took place in the Café Toisson d'Or, three weeks ago last Sunday, at which you were present."

"He is right about the conversation, anyway. I recollect that quite well, but I know nothing whatever of any bet. Certainly, I made none."

"In that case, monsieur, I have to offer my apologies for having troubled you. I can see a mistake has been made. But before I leave, perhaps you would have the kindness to tell me who else were present on that occasion. Probably I should have gone to one of them."

After some consideration M. Dumarchez mentioned three names, all of which Lefarge already had in his notebook. Then excusing himself on the ground of his appointment, the stockbroker hurried away, while Lefarge returned to report to Burnley and M. Le Gautier.

During the afternoon the colleagues called on each of the men whose names they had been given as having been present at the Café Toisson d'Or when the lottery discussion took place. M. Briant had gone to Italy, but they saw the others, and in each case the result was the same. All remembered the conversation, but none knew anything of the bet or the cask. Inquiries from the waiters at the Toisson d'Or likewise were without result.

"We don't seem to get much forrader," remarked Burnley, as the two friends sat over their coffee after dinner that evening. "I am inclined to believe that these men we have seen really don't know anything about the cask."

"I agree with you," returned Lefarge. "At any rate it shouldn't be difficult to test at least part of their statements. We can find out from the lottery people whether Le Gautier did purchase one thousand francs worth of bonds on Sunday three weeks. If he did, I think we must take it that the story of the conversation in the Toisson d'Or is true, and that he and Felix did agree to go in for it jointly."

"There can be no reasonable doubt of that."

"Further, we can find out if the drawing takes place next Thursday. If it does, it follows that all that part of the letter about the winning of the money and the test with the cask is false. If, on the other hand, it has already been made, the letter may conceivably be true, and Le Gautier is lying. But I don't think that likely."

"Nor I. But I don't quite agree with you about the letter. We already know the letter is false. It said £988 would be sent in the cask, whereas there was a body and £52 10s. But the question of the test is not so clear to me. The cask *did* come as described in the letter, bearing the false address and description, and if it was not so sent for the reason mentioned, what other reason can you suggest?"

"None, I admit."

"Let us see, then, just what we do know about the writer of

the letter. Firstly, he must have known of the conversation about the lottery, and of the arrangement made by Felix and Le Gautier to enter for it. That is to say, he must either have been present in the Toisson d'Or when it took place, or some one who was there must have repeated it to him. Secondly, he must have known all the circumstances of the sending out of the cask, at least as far as the false address and description were concerned. Thirdly, he must have had access to a rather worn typewriter, which we believe could be identified, and fourthly, he must have possessed, or been able to procure French note paper. So much is certain. We may also assume, though it has neither been proved, nor is it very important, that he could use the typewriter himself, as it is unlikely that such a letter would be done by a typist from dictation."

"That's true, and so far as I can see, the only man that fills the bill so far is Felix himself."

"I don't think it was Felix. I believe he was telling the truth all right. But we haven't enough information yet to judge. Perhaps when we follow up the cask we shall be able to connect some of these men we saw today with it."

"Possibly enough," answered Lefarge, rising. "If we are to get to the Sûreté by nine, we had better go."

"Is it your Chief's habit to hold meetings at nine o'clock? It seems a curious time to me."

"And he's a curious man, too. First rate at his job, you know, and decent, and all that. But peculiar. He goes away in the afternoons, and comes back after dinner and works half the night. He says he gets more peace then?"

"I dare say he does, but it's a rum notion for all that."

M. Chauvet listened with close attention to the report of the day's proceedings and, after Lefarge ceased speaking, sat motionless for several seconds, buried in thought. Then, like a man who arrives at a decision he spoke :—

"The matter, so far as we have gone, seems to resolve itself into these points. First, did a conversation about the lotteries take place in the Café Toisson d'Or about four weeks ago? I think we may assume that it did. Second, did Felix and Le Gautier agree to enter, and if so, did Le Gautier send a cheque that day? Here we can get confirmation by making inquiries at the lottery offices, and I will send a man there tomorrow. Third, has the drawing taken place? This can be ascertained in the same way. Beyond that, I do not think we can go at present, and I am of opinion our next move should be to try and trace the cask. That line of inquiry may lead us back to one of these gentlemen you have seen today, or may point to some one else whom we may find was present at the Toisson d'Or. What do you think, gentlemen?"

"We had both arrived at the same conclusion, monsieur," answered Lefarge.

"Well then, you will make inquiries about the cask tomorrow, will you? Good. I will look out for you in the evening."

Having arranged eight o'clock at the Gare du Nord for the rendezvous next day, the detectives bid each other good night and went their ways.

CHAPTER XI

MM. DUPIERRE ET CIE

THE hands of the large clock at the Gare du Nord were pointing to three minutes before eight next morning as Inspector Burnley walked up the steps of the entrance. Lefarge was there before him and the two men greeted each other warmly.

"I have a police box cart here," said Lefarge. "Give me your papers and we'll have the cask out in a brace of shakes."

Burnley handed them over and they went to the luggage bureau. Lefarge's card had a magical effect, and in a very few minutes the sacking-covered barrel had been found and loaded on to the cart. Lefarge instructed the driver.

"I want that taken to a street off the rue de la Convention at Grenelle. You might start now and stop at the Grenelle end of the Pont Mirabeau. Wait there until I come for you. I suppose it will take you an hour or more?"

"It'll take more than an hour and a half, monsieur," replied the man. "It is a long way and this cart is very heavy."

"Very well, just do the best you can."

The man touched his cap and moved off with his load.

"Are we in any hurry?" asked Burnley.

"No, we have to kill time until he gets there. Why do you ask?"

"Nothing, except that if we have time enough, let's go down directly to the river and take a boat. I always thoroughly enjoy the Seine boats."

"As a matter of fact so do I," replied Lefarge. "You get the air and the motion is pleasanter and more silent than a bus. They are not so slow either when you consider the stops."

They took a bus which brought them southwards through the Louvre, and, alighting at the Pont des Arts, caught a steamer going to Suresnes. The morning was fresh and exquisitely clear. The sun, immediately behind them at first, crept slowly round to the left as they followed the curve of the river. Burnley sat admiring perhaps for the fiftieth time the graceful architecture of the bridges, justly celebrated as the finest of any city in the world. He gazed with fresh interest and pleasure also on the buildings they were carried past, from the huge pile of the Louvre on the right bank to the great terrace of the Quai d'Orsay on the left, and from the Trocadero and the palaces of the Champs Elysées back to the thin tapering shaft of the Eiffel Tower. How well he remembered a visit that he and Lefarge had paid to the restaurant on the lower stage of this latter when they lunched at the next table to Madame Marcelle, the young and attractive looking woman who had murdered her English husband by repeated doses of a slow and irritant poison. He had just turned to remind his companion of the circumstance when the latter's pleasant voice broke in on his thoughts.

"I went back to the Sûreté after we parted last night. I thought it better to make sure of the cart this morning, and I also looked up our records about this firm of monumental sculptors. It seems that it is not a very large concern, and all the power is vested in the hands of M. Paul Thévenet, the managing director. It is an old establishment and apparently eminently respectable, and has a perfectly clean record so far as we are concerned."

"Well, that's so much to the good."

They disembarked at the Pont Mirabeau and, crossing to the south side and finding a tolerably decent looking café, sat down at one of the little tables on the pavement behind a screen of shrubs in pots.

"We can see the end of the bridge from here, so we may wait comfortably until the cart appears," said Lefarge, when he had ordered a couple of bocks.

They sat on in the pleasant sun, smoking, and reading the morning papers. Nearly an hour passed before the cart came into view slowly crossing the bridge. Then they left their places at the café and, signing to the driver to follow, walked down the rue de la Convention, and turned into the rue Provence. Nearly opposite, a little way down the street, was the place of which they were in search.

Its frontage ran the whole length of the second block, and consisted partly of a rather ancient looking four-story factory or warehouse and partly of a high wall, evidently surrounding a yard. At the end of the building this wall was pierced by a gateway leading into the yard, and just inside was a door in the end wall of the building labelled " Bureau."

Having instructed the driver to wait outside the gate, they pushed open the small door and asked to see M. Thévenet on private business. After a delay of a few minutes a clerk ushered them into his room.

The managing director was an elderly man, small and rather wizened, with a white moustache, and a dry but courteous manner. He rose as the detectives entered, wished them good morning, and asked what he could do for them.

" I must apologize for not sending in my card, M. Thévenet," began Lefarge, presenting it, " but, as the matter in question is somewhat delicate, I preferred that your staff should not know my profession."

M. Thévenet bowed.

" This, sir," went on Lefarge, " is my colleague, Mr. Burnley of the London police, and he is anxious for some information, if you would be so kind as to let him have it."

" I will be pleased to answer any questions I can. I speak English if Mr. Burnley would prefer it."

" I thank you," said Burnley. " The matter is rather a serious one. It is briefly this. On Monday last—four days ago—a cask arrived in London from Paris. Some circumstances with which I need not trouble you aroused the suspicions of the police, with the result that the cask was seized and opened. In it were found, packed in sawdust, two things, firstly, £52 10s. in English gold, and secondly, the body of a youngish woman, evidently of good position, and evidently murdered by being throttled by a pair of human hands."

" Horrible!" ejaculated the little man.

" The cask was of very peculiar construction, the woodwork being at least twice as heavy as that of an ordinary wine cask and secured by strong iron bands. And, sir, the point that has brought us to you is that your firm's name was stencilled on it after the words ' Return to,' and it was addressed on one of your firm's labels."

The little man sprang to his feet.

" Our cask? Our label?" he cried in evident astonishment. " Do I understand you to say, sir, that the cask containing this body was sent out by us?"

" No, sir," returned Burnley, " I did not say that. I simply say that it arrived bearing your name and label. I am in total ignorance of how or when the body was put in. That is what I am over from London to investigate."

"But the thing is utterly incredible," said M. Thévenet, pacing up and down the room. "No, no," he added, with a wave of his hand as Burnley would have spoken, "I don't mean that I doubt your word. But I cannot but feel that there must be a terrible mistake."

"It is only right to add, sir," continued Burnley, "that I did not myself see the label. But it was seen by the men of the carrying company, and especially by one of their clerks who examined it carefully after suspicion had been aroused. The label was afterwards destroyed by Felix, to whom the cask was addressed."

"Felix, Felix, the name seems familiar. What was the full name and address?"

"M. Léon Felix, 141 West Jubb Street, Tottenham Court Road, London, W.C."

"Ah, of course," rejoined M. Thévenet. "There is, then, really such a man? I rather doubted it at the time, you know, for our advice card of the despatch of the cask was returned marked 'Not known,' and I then looked him up in the London directory and could not find him. Of course, as far as we were concerned, we had the money and it did not matter to us."

Burnley and his colleague sat up sharply.

"I beg your pardon, M. Thévenet," said Burnley. "What's that you say? At the time? At what time, if you please?"

"Why, when we sent out the cask. When else?" returned the director, looking keenly at his questioner.

"But, I don't understand. You *did* send out a cask, then, addressed to Felix at Tottenham Court Road?"

"Of course we did. We had the money, and why should we not do so?"

"Look here, M. Thévenet," continued Burnley, "we are evidently talking at cross purposes. Let me first explain more fully about the label. According to our information, which we have no reason to doubt, the address space had been neatly cut out and another piece of paper pasted behind, bearing the address in question. It seemed to us therefore, that some person had received the cask from you and, having altered the label, packed the body in it and sent it on. Now we are to understand that the cask was sent out by you. That being so why then should the label have been altered?"

"I'm sure I cannot tell."

" May I ask what was in the cask when it left here?"

" Certainly. It was a small group of statuary by a good man and rather valuable."

" I'm afraid, M. Thévenet, I haven't got the matter clear yet. It would oblige us both very much if you would be kind enough to tell us all you know about the sending out of that cask."

" With pleasure." He touched a bell and a clerk entered.

" Bring me," he said, " all the papers about the sale of that group of Le Mareschal's to M. Felix of London." He turned again to his visitors.

" Perhaps I had better begin by explaining our business to you. It is in reality three businesses carried on simultaneously by one firm. First, we make plaster casts of well-known pieces. They are not valuable and sell for very little. Secondly, we make monuments, tombstones, decorative stone panels and the like for buildings, rough work, but fairly good. Lastly we trade in really fine sculpture, acting as agents between the artists and the public. We have usually a considerable number of such good pieces in our showroom. It was one of these latter, a one thousand four hundred franc group, that was ordered by M. Felix."

" Felix ordered it?" burst in Burnley, " but there, pardon me. I must not interrupt."

The clerk returned at this moment and laid some papers on his principal's desk. The latter turned them over, selected one, and handed it to Burnley.

" Here is his letter, you see, received by us on the morning of the 30th of March, and enclosing notes for one thousand five hundred francs. The envelope bore the London postmark."

The letter was written by hand on one side of a single sheet of paper and was as follows :—

141 West Jubb Street,
Tottenham Court Road,
London, W.C.,
29th March, 1912.

Messrs. Dupierre et Cie,
   Rue Provence,
     Rue de la Convention,
       Grenelle, Paris.

GENTLEMEN.—I am anxious to purchase the group of statuary in the left-hand corner back of your Boulevard des Capucines showroom, looking from the street. The group is of three female figures, two seated and one standing. There can be no doubt about the one I mean, as it is the only such in the left of the window.

Please forward immediately to the above address.

I do not know the exact price, but understand it is about one thousand five hundred francs. I therefore enclose notes for that sum, and if a balance remains on either side it can be adjusted by letter.

I may say that an unexpected call to England prevented me ordering this in person.

Yours, etc.

LÉON FELIX.

Inspector Burnley examined the letter.

"You will allow us to keep this in the meantime, I presume?" he asked.

"Certainly."

"You said the money was in notes. You mean, I take it, ordinary State paper money whose source could not be traced; not any kind of cheque or draft payable through a bank?"

"Precisely."

"Well, sir, pardon my interruption."

"There is little more to add. The group was packed and despatched on the day we received the letter. Its price was, as a matter of fact, only one thousand four hundred francs, and the balance of one hundred francs was therefore enclosed with it. This was considered as safe as any other way of sending it, as the cask was insured for its full value."

"The cask? You packed it then in a cask?"

"Yes. We make a special kind of cask in two sizes, very heavy and strong, for sending out such pieces. It is our own idea, and we are rather proud of it. We find it simpler and safer than a crate."

"We have the cask in a cart outside. Perhaps, if we brought it in, you would be good enough to see if it could be identified, firstly if it is yours, and secondly, if so, if it is the particular one you sent to Felix."

"Well, you see, unfortunately it was sent from our showrooms in the Boulevard des Capucines. If you have time to take it there I will instruct the manager to assist you in every way in his power. Indeed, I will go with you myself. I shall not be able to rest until the matter is cleared up."

The detectives thanked him and, while Lefarge was instructing the carter, M. Thévenet procured a taxi and they drove to the Boulevard des Capucines.

CHAPTER XII

AT THE GARE ST. LAZARE

THE showrooms consisted of a small but luxuriously fitted up shop, containing many objects of excellence and value. M. Thévenet introduced the manager, M. Thomas, a young and capable looking man, who invited them into his office. He did not speak English, and Lefarge carried on the conversation.

"These gentlemen," said M. Thévenet, "are making some inquiries about the sale of Le Mareschal's group to Mr. Felix of London last week. I want you to tell them all you can, Thomas."

The young man bowed. "With pleasure, monsieur."

In a few words Lefarge put him in possession of the main facts. "Perhaps," he continued, "if you would tell me all that you know, I could then ask questions on any point I did not understand."

"But certainly, monsieur. There is not much to tell." He looked up some memoranda. "On Tuesday week, March 30, we had a phone from the head office saying that M. Le Mareschal's last group, which we had on exhibition in our window, was sold. We were to send it at once to M. Léon Felix, at the London address you know. Also we were to enclose one hundred francs, refund of an overpayment of the cost. This was done. The group and the money were duly packed and despatched. Everything was perfectly in order and in accordance with our usual custom. The only remarkable feature in the whole transaction was the absence of a receipt from Felix. I do not think I can recall another instance in which we were not advised of our goods' safe arrival, and in this case it was doubly to be expected, owing to the enclosure of money. I might perhaps mention also that on that same Tuesday we had a telephone call from M. Felix, through from London, asking when and by what route we were sending the cask, to which I replied in person."

Lefarge asked how the group was packed.

"In a number A cask, our usual practice."

"We have a cask coming along. It will be here presently. Could you identify it?"

"Possibly I or the foreman might."

"Well, M. Thévenet, I do not think we can get any further till it arrives. There would just be time for *déjeuner*. We hope you and M. Thomas will give us the pleasure of your company."

This was agreed to, and they lunched at one of the comfortable restaurants on the Boulevard. When they returned to the shop the cart was waiting.

"We had better have him round to the yard," said M. Thomas. "If you will go through I shall show him the way."

The yard was a small open area surrounded by sheds. Into one of these the cart was backed and the cask unpacked. M. Thomas examined it.

"That's certainly one of our casks," he said. "They are our own design and, so far as I am aware, I can say they are used by no one else."

"But M. Thomas," said Lefarge, "can you identify it in any special manner? We do not, of course, doubt what you have said, but if it could be established that this particular cask had passed through your yard it would be important. Otherwise, if you judge only by likeness to type, we cannot be sure that some one has not copied your design to try and start a false scent."

"I see what you mean, but I fear I cannot certify what you want. But I'll call the foreman and packers. Possibly some of them can help you."

He went into another of the sheds, returning immediately with four men.

"Look at that cask, men," he said. "Have any of you ever seen it before?"

The men advanced and inspected the cask minutely, looking at it from all sides. Two of them retreated, shaking their heads, but the third, an elderly man with white hair, spoke up.

"Yes," he said. "I packed this cask not a fortnight ago."

"How are you so certain of that?" asked Lefarge.

"By this, monsieur," said the man, pointing to the broken stave. "That stave was split. I remember quite well the shape of the crack. I noticed it, and wondered if I should report it to the foreman, and then I thought it was safe enough and didn't. But I told my mate about it. See here, Jean," he called to the fourth man, "is that the crack I showed you some days ago, or is it only like it?"

The fourth man advanced and inspected it in his turn.

"It's the same one," he said confidently. "I know, because I thought that split was the shape of my hand, and so it is."

He placed his hand on the adjoining stave, and there certainly was a rude resemblance in shape.

"I suppose neither of you men remember what you packed in it, or whom it was for?"

"As far as I remember," said the third man, "it was a statue of three or four women, but I don't remember who it was for."

"It wasn't for a man c^ ''d Felix, of London?"

"I remember the name, but I can't say if it was for him."

"Thank you. Would you tell me how it was packed? What steadied the group?"

"Sawdust, monsieur, simply sawdust, carefully rammed."

"Can you tell me if the railway cart took it from here, or how did it go?"

"No, monsieur, it was taken by one of our own motor lorries from the Grenelle works."

"Did you know the driver?"

"Yes, monsieur, it was Jules Fouchard."

"I suppose, monsieur," Lefarge turned to the managing director, "we could interview this man Fouchard?"

"Why, certainly. M. Thomas will find out where he is."

"Pardon, messieurs," interposed the elderly packer, "but he's here now. Or at least I saw him not ten minutes ago."

"Good. Then try and find him, and tell him not to go away till we have seen him."

In a few moments the driver was found and, having asked him to wait outside, Lefarge continued his questions to the packer.

"At what o'clock did the cask leave here?"

"About four. I had it packed and ready by two, but the lorry did not come for a couple of hours after that."

"Did you see it loaded up?"

"I helped to load it up."

"Now tell me," continued Lefarge, "where was the cask between the time you put the group in and the arrival of the motor?"

"Here, monsieur, in this shed where I packed it."

"And did you leave it during that time?"

"No, monsieur, I was here all the time."

"So that—please be very careful about this—no one could have tampered with it in any way up till the time it left the yard?"

"Absolutely impossible, monsieur. It is quite out of the question."

"Thank you, we are exceedingly obliged to you," said Lefarge, slipping a couple of francs into the man's hand as he withdrew. "Now, could I see the lorry driver?"

Jules Fouchard proved to be a small, energetic looking man, with sharp features and intelligent eyes. He was sure of his facts, and gave his answers clearly and without hesitation.

"M. Fouchard," began Lefarge, "this gentleman and I are

trying to trace the movements of one of your casks, which I am informed left here by your lorry about four o'clock on Tuesday, the thirtieth of March last. Can you recall the occasion?"

"Permit me to get my delivery book, monsieur."

He disappeared for a moment, returning with a small cloth-covered book. Rapidly turning over the pages, he found what he was looking for.

"For M. Léon Felix, 141 West Jubb Street, Tottenham Court Road, London? Yes, monsieur. It was the only cask which left here that day. I took it to the Gare St. Lazare, and handed it to the railway officials. Here is their signature for it."

He passed the book over and Lefarge read the name.

"Thank you. Who is this Jean Duval? I shall probably want to see him and would like to know where to find him."

"He is a clerk in the departure passenger cloak-room."

"You left here with the cask, I understand, about four o'clock?"

"About that, monsieur."

"And what time did you arrive at the Gare St. Lazare?"

"Just a few minutes later. I went direct."

"You didn't stop on the way?"

"No, monsieur."

"Well now, monsieur, please don't answer till you have considered carefully. Was there any way in which the cask could have been tampered with between the time it was loaded up here and your handing it over to Jean Duval at the Gare St. Lazare?"

"None, monsieur. No one could have got on the lorry without my knowledge, much less have done anything to the cask."

"And I take it from that, it would have been equally impossible to remove it entirely and substitute another?"

"It would have been absolutely out of the question, monsieur."

After thanking and dismissing the driver, they returned to the manager's room.

"The position, then, seems to be this," said Lefarge, as they sat down. "The cask left your yard containing a group of statuary, and it arrived in London containing the dead body of a woman. The change must therefore have been effected along the route, and the evidence of the steamer people seems to narrow it down to between here and Rouen."

"Why Rouen?" asked both gentlemen in a breath.

"Well, I should have said, perhaps, between here and the time of loading on to the steamer at Rouen wharf."

"But I am afraid you are making a mistake there," said M. Thomas, "the cask went by Havre. All our stuff does."

"Pardon me, M. Thomas, for seeming to contradict you," said Burnley, in his somewhat halting French, "but I am as certain of it as of my presence here now, however the cask may have been sent, it certainly arrived in the London Docks by the Insular and Continental Steam Navigation Company's boat from Rouen."

"But that is most mysterious," rejoined Thomas. He struck a bell and a clerk appeared.

"Bring me the railway papers about the sending of that cask to Felix, London, on the thirtieth ultimo."

"Here you are," he said to Burnley, when the clerk returned. "Look at that. That is the receipt from the St. Lazare people for the freight on the cask between this and the address in London, per passenger train via Havre and Southampton."

"Well," said Burnley, "this gets me altogether. Tell me," he added after a pause, "when Felix telephoned you from London asking when and by what route you were sending the cask, what did you reply?"

"I told him it was crossing on Tuesday night, the 30th March, by Havre and Southampton."

"We'd better go to St. Lazare," said Lefarge. "Perhaps M. Thomas will kindly lend us that receipt?"

"Certainly, but you must please sign for it, as I shall want it for my audit."

They parted with expressions of thanks on the part of the detectives, who promised to keep the others advised of the progress of the inquiry.

A taxi brought them to St. Lazare where, at the office of the superintendent of the line, Lefarge's card had the usual magical effect.

"Please be seated, gentlemen," said the superintendent, "and let me know what I can do for you."

Lefarge showed him the receipt.

"The matter is somewhat puzzling," he said. "That cask, as you see, was invoiced out via Havre and Southampton on the 30th ultimo, and yet it turned up in London on Monday, the 5th instant, by the Insular and Continental Steam Navigation Company's boat *Bullfinch* from Rouen. The contents of the cask when it left Messrs. Dupierre's showroom was a group of statuary, but when it arrived at St. Katharine Docks—well, I may tell you, monsieur, in confidence—it contained the body of a woman—murdered."

The superintendent gave an exclamation of surprise.

"You see, therefore, monsieur, the necessity of our tracing the cask as privately as possible."

"I certainly do. If you will wait a few minutes, gentlemen, I can get you part at least of the information you want."

The few minutes had expanded into nearly an hour before the superintendent returned.

"Sorry to have kept you so long," he apologized. "I find that your cask was delivered at our outward passenger cloak-room at about 4.15 p.m. on the 30th ultimo. It remained there until about 7.0 p.m., and during all this time it was under the personal supervision of one of the clerks named Duval, a most conscientious and reliable man. He states it stood in full view of his desk, and it would have been quite impossible for any one to have tampered with it. He particularly remembers it from its peculiar shape and its weight, as well as because it was an unusual object to send by passenger train. At about 7.0 p.m. it was taken charge of by two porters and placed in the van of the 7.47 p.m. English boat train. The guard of the train was present when they put it into the van, and he should have been there till the train left. The guard is unfortunately off duty at present, but I have sent for him and will get his statement. Once the train left, the cask would simply be bound to go to Havre. If it had not done so with that insurance on it, we should have heard about it. However, I will communicate with our agent at Havre, and I should be able to get definite information in the morning."

"But my dear sir," cried Burnley helplessly, "I know of my own knowledge that it came by long sea from Rouen. I don't for one moment doubt your word, but there must be a mistake somewhere."

"Ah," returned the superintendent, smiling, "now I come to something that will interest you. The cask we have just spoken of was sent out on the evening of the 30th ult. But I find another cask was despatched three days later, on the 1st instant. It also was addressed to M. Felix at the same London address and sent in by Messrs. Dupierre. It was labelled via Rouen and the I. and C. Company's boat. It went by goods train that night, and I will get our Rouen agent to try and trace it, though, as he would have had no reason to remark it, I doubt if he will be able to do so."

Burnley swore. "I beg your pardon, sir, but this gets deeper and deeper. Two casks!" He groaned.

"At least," said the superintendent, "it has cleared up your difficulty about how a cask that left by one route arrived by another."

"It has done that, monsieur, and we are really extremely obliged for all your kindness and trouble."

"If there is anything else I can do I shall be very pleased."

"Thank you again. The only other point is to trace the cart that brought the second cask."

"Ah," the superintendent shook his head, "I can't do that for you, you know."

"Of course not. But perhaps you could get hold of, or put us in a position to get hold of your men who received the cask? We might get some information from them."

"I shall do what I can. Now, gentlemen, if you will call any time in the morning, I shall let you have any further information I receive."

The detectives, having thanked him again, bowed themselves out and, strolling up and down the vast concourse, discussed their plans.

"I should like to wire to London now, and also to write by tonight's post," said Burnley. "They'll want to get on to tracing that second cask from Waterloo as soon as possible."

"Well, the ordinary letter-boxes are cleared at half-past six, but if you are late you can post in the van of the English mail at the Gare du Nord up till 9.10 p.m., so you have plenty of time for that later. What about sending your wire from here now, and then take a taxi to the Hotel Continental to look up your friend Felix?"

Burnley agreed, and when the telegram had been sent they took another taxi and drove to the Continental. Lefarge's card produced immediately a polite and agreeable manager, anxious to assist.

"We are trying to trace a man whom we believe stayed here recently," explained Lefarge. "His name was Léon Felix."

"A rather short and slight man with a black beard and a pleasing manner?" replied the manager. "Oh, yes, I know M. Felix very well, and very pleasant I have always found him. He was here recently. I will inquire the exact dates."

He disappeared for a few seconds.

"He was here from Saturday, the 13th of March till Monday, the 15th. Then he returned on Friday, the 26th, and left again on the morning of Sunday, the 28th, to catch the 8.20 train for England at the Gare du Nord."

The two detectives exchanged glances of surprise.

"Could you let me compare his signature in your register with one I have here?" asked Burnley. "I am anxious to make sure it is the same man."

"Certainly," replied the manager, leading the way.

The signature was the same, and, after thanking the manager, they took their departure.

"That's an unexpected find," Burnley remarked. "Felix said nothing to me about being here ten days ago."

"It's a bit suggestive, you know," returned his companion. "We'll have to find out what he was doing during the visit."

Burnley nodded.

"Now for my report, anyway," he said.

"I think I'll go to the Sûreté and do the same," answered Lefarge.

They parted, having arranged to meet later in the evening. Burnley wrote a detailed account of his day to his Chief, asking him to have inquiries made at Waterloo about the second cask. Having posted it, he gave himself up to a study of Felix's letter ordering the group of statuary.

It was written on a sheet of the same kind of paper as those of the two typewritten letters received by Felix. Burnley carefully compared the watermarks and satisfied himself on the point. Then, drawing from his pocket the address he had got Felix to write in the house on the Great North Road, he spent some time very carefully comparing them.

The handwriting was the same in each, at least that was his first impression, but on a closer examination he felt somewhat less certain. He was not a handwriting expert, but he had come across a good many of these men, and was aware of some of their methods. He applied those he knew and at last came to the conclusion that Felix had written the order, though a certain doubt remained. He wrote another note to his Chief and enclosed the two letters, asking him to have them compared.

Then he went out to spend the evening with Lefarge.

CHAPTER XIII

THE OWNER OF THE DRESS

WHEN some time later the two friends met, Lefarge said:—
"I saw the Chief, and he's not very satisfied with the way things are going. None of those women have done anything with the clothes. He's got a notion we ought to advertise and he wants us to go there at nine tonight and talk it over."

Accordingly, at the hour named, they presented themselves at the office in the Sûreté.

"Sit down, gentlemen," began the Chief. "I wanted to consult with you about this case. In our efforts to identify the dead woman, which we agreed was our first essential, we have unfortunately had no success. Our three women have done exceedingly well as far as covering ground goes, but they have had no luck. You, gentlemen, have found out some important facts, but they have not led in this particular direction. Now, I am inclined to think we ought to advertise and I'd like to hear your views."

"What particular advertisements do you suggest, sir?" asked Burnley.

"For everything. Advertise, in each case with one hundred francs reward, for information about the dress, the underclothes if singular in any way, the rings, the comb, and the body itself."

There was silence for a few moments, and then Burnley replied hesitatingly :—

"We have a bit of prejudice at Scotland Yard about advertising except in special cases. I think the idea is that it puts people on their guard who might otherwise give themselves away. But in this case it would probably be the quickest way to a result."

"To me it would seem," said Lefarge, "that even if there was a band of persons anxious to hush this murder up, there would also be enough outside that band to answer every one of the advertisements."

"That is rather my view," agreed the Chief. "Take the servants, for example. A woman wearing such clothes is certain to have lived in a house with several servants. Some one of them is bound to read the advertisement and recognize the description. If he or she intends to try for the reward we get the information, if not, he will certainly show the paper to the others, one of whom is almost certain to come. The same thing applies to shop assistants, none of whom could conceivably wish to keep the thing a secret. Yes, I think we'll try it. Will you draft out some forms, something like this, I should imagine : 'One hundred francs reward will be paid for information leading to the identification of the body of a lady, believed to have died about the 30th March '—say ' died,' of course, not ' was murdered '—then the description, and ' Apply at any Police Station.' The others would be for information leading to the identification of the purchaser of the various clothes."

"I shall have to see the three ladies for a proper description of the clothes," said Lefarge.

"Of course. I'll send for them."

M. Chauvet telephoned to the department in question, and, after a delay of a few minutes, the three female detectives came in. With their help the advertisements were drawn up, and when the Chief had read and approved they were telephoned to the principal papers for insertion next day. Special trade journals relating to the millinery and jewellery trades were also supplied with copies for their next issues.

"By the way," observed M. Chauvet, when the women had left, "I have had a report about the lottery business. M. Le Gautier is correct on both points. He paid in the cheque on the date stated, and the drawing does not take place till next Thursday. The probabilities seem therefore to point to his being an honest man and having had nothing to do with the letter. And now, with regard to tomorrow. What do you propose?"

"First, monsieur, we thought of going to the Gare St. Lazare to see if the superintendent has any further information for us. I thought we should then try and trace back the cask that went via Rouen."

"Very good. I think I shall try another scent also, though not a very promising one. I shall put on a couple of men to go round the fashionable photographers with that photo of yours, and try if they can find a portrait of the woman. I had rather you could have done it"—he looked at Burnley—"because you have seen the body, but they may get something. That's all, then, is it not? Good night."

"Hard lines being done out of our evening," said Lefarge, when they had left the great man's room. "I was going to propose the Folies Bergères. It's not too late yet, though. What do you say?"

"I'm on," answered Burnley, "but I don't want to stay more than an hour or so. I can always work better on plenty of sleep."

"Right," returned Lefarge, and, calling a taxi, the two friends were driven to the famous music-hall.

Lefarge called for Burnley the next morning at the latter's hotel, and they made their way to the superintendent's office at the Gare St. Lazare.

"Well, gentlemen," said their friend of the previous afternoon, motioning them to be seated, "I think I've got the information you want." He took up some papers. "I have here the receipt of the Southampton boat people for what we may call number one cask, which was handed them on the arrival of the 7.47 from this station on the night of the 30th ult. Here," he took up a similar paper, "I have the receipt of the I. and C. Steam Navigation Co. at Rouen for cask number two, which left here by goods train on the 1st inst., and was got on board on the 3rd. Finally, our agent at the goods station at the rue Cardinet informs me he has found the porters who assisted to unload this number two cask when it arrived. You can see them by going down there now."

"I can hardly find words to thank you, sir," said Lefarge, "your help has been of the utmost value."

"Delighted, I am sure."

They parted with mutual compliments, and the detectives took a Ceinture train to Batignoles, and walked down the rue Cardinet to the vast goods station.

They introduced themselves to the agent, who was expecting them, and brought them through long passages and across wide yards alive with traffic to a dock in the side of one of the huge goods sheds for outward bound traffic. Calling up two blue-bloused porters and instructing them to answer the detectives' questions, he excused himself and took his leave.

"Now, men," said Lefarge, "we'll be much obliged for some information and there'll be a few francs going if you can give it."

The men expressed anxiety to supply whatever was needed.

"Do you remember on Thursday week, the 1st instant, unloading a cask labelled for Felix, London, via Rouen and long sea?"

"But yes, monsieur, we remember it," said the men in chorus.

"You must unload hundreds of casks. How did you come to notice this one so specially?"

"Ah, monsieur," replied one of the men, "had monsieur had to lift it himself he also would have noticed it. The weight was remarkable, extraordinary. The shape also was peculiar. In the middle there was no bulge."

"At what time did it arrive here?"

"Just after six in the evening, monsieur, between five and ten minutes past."

"It is a good while since then. How do you come to remember the time so exactly?"

"Because, monsieur," the man smiled, "we were going off duty at half-past six, and we were watching the time."

"Can you tell me who brought it to the yard?"

The men shrugged their shoulders.

"Alas! monsieur, we do not know," the spokesman answered. "The carter we would recognize if we saw him again, but neither of us know where he lives nor the name of his employers."

"Can you describe him?"

"But certainly, monsieur. He was a small man, thin and sickly-looking, with white hair and a clean shaven face."

"Well, keep a good look out, and if you see him again find out who he is and let me know. Here is my address. If you do that there will be fifty francs for you."

Lefarge handed over a couple of five franc pieces and the detectives left, followed by the promises and thanks of the men.

"I suppose an advertisement for the carter is the next scheme," said Burnley, as they walked back in the Clichy direction.

"We had better report to headquarters, I think," replied Lefarge, "and see what the Chief advises. If he approves, we might get our advertisement into tonight's papers."

Burnley agreed, and when they had had some lunch they rang up the Sûreté from the nearest call office.

"That Lefarge?" was the answer. "The Chief wants you to return immediately. He's got some news."

They took the Metro from Clichy to Chatelet and reached the Sûreté as the clocks were striking two. M. Chauvet was in.

"Ah," he said, as they entered, "we've had a reply to the dress advertisement. Madame Clothilde's people near the Palais Royal rang up about eleven saying they believed they had supplied the dress. We got hold of Mlle. Lecoq, who was working it, and sent her over, and she returned here about an hour ago. The dress was sold in February to Madame Annette Boirac, at the corner of Avenue de l'Alma and rue St. Jean, not far from the American Church. You'd better go round there now and make some inquiries."

"Yes, monsieur," said Lefarge, "but before we go there is this question of the cask," and he told what they had learned, and suggested the advertisement about the carter.

M. Chauvet had just begun his reply when a knock came to the door and a boy entered with a card.

"The gentleman's waiting to see you on urgent business, monsieur," he said.

"Hallo!" said the Chief, with a gesture of surprise. "Listen to this." He read out the words, "'M. Raoul Boirac, rue St. Jean, 1 Avenue de l'Alma.' This will be Mme. Annette B.'s husband, I presume. These advertisements are doing well. You had better stop, both of you," and then to the boy: "Wait a moment."

He picked up the telephone, pressing one of the buttons on its stand.

"Send Mlle. Joubert here immediately."

In a few moments a girl stenographer entered. M. Chauvet pointed to a corner of the room where Burnley had noticed a screen, set back as if to be out of the way.

"I want every word of this conversation, mademoiselle," said

G.M.N.—E

the Chief. "Please be careful to miss none of it, and also to keep quiet."

The girl bowed and, having seen her settled behind the screen, the Chief turned to the messenger.

"I'll see him now."

In a few seconds M. Boirac entered the room. He was a strongly built man of rather under middle age, with thick black hair and a large moustache. On his face was an expression of strain, as if he was passing through a period of acute bodily or mental pain. He was dressed entirely in black and his manner was quiet and repressed.

He looked round the room and then, as M. Chauvet rose to greet him, he bowed ceremoniously.

"M. le Chef de la Sûreté?" he asked, and, as M. Chauvet bowed him to a chair, continued,—

"I have called to see you, monsieur, on a very painful matter. I had hoped to have been able to do so alone," he paused slightly, "but these gentlemen, I presume, are completely in your confidence?" He spoke slowly with a deliberate pronunciation of each word, as if he had thought out whether that was the best possible he could use and had come to the conclusion that it was.

"If, monsieur," returned M. Chauvet, "your business is in connection with the recent unfortunate disappearance of your wife, these gentlemen are the officers who are in charge of the case, and their presence would be, I think, to the advantage of all of us."

M. Boirac sprang from his chair, deep emotion showing under his iron control.

"Then it is she?" he asked, in a suppressed voice. "You know? It seemed possible from the advertisement, but I wasn't sure. I hoped—that perhaps—— There is no doubt, I suppose?"

"I shall tell you all we know, M. Boirac, and you can form your own conclusions. First, here is a photograph of the body found."

M. Boirac took the slip of card and looked at it earnestly.

"It is she," he murmured hoarsely, "it is she without a doubt."

He paused, overcome, and, the others respecting his feelings, there was silence for some moments. Then with a strenuous effort he continued, speaking hardly above a whisper—

"Tell me," his voice shook as he pronounced the words with difficulty, "what makes her look so terrible? And those awful marks at her throat? What are they?"

"It is with the utmost regret I have to tell you, M. Boirac, that your wife was undoubtedly murdered by strangulation.

Further, you must know that she had been dead several days when that photograph was taken."

M. Boirac dropped into his chair, and sank his head in his hands. "My God!" he panted. "My poor Annette! Though I had no cause to love her, I did, God help me, in spite of everything, I did. I know it now when I have lost her. Tell me," he continued in a low tone after another pause, "tell me the details."

"I fear they are rather harrowing, monsieur," said the Chief, with sympathetic sorrow in his tone. "A certain cask was noticed by the London police, a detail, with which I need hardly trouble you, having aroused their suspicions. The cask was seized and opened, and the body was found inside."

The visitor remained with his face buried in his hands. After a few seconds he raised himself and looked at M. Chauvet.

"Any clue?" he asked, in a choking tone. "Have you any clue to the villain who has done this?"

"We have a number of clues," returned the Chief, "but have not yet had time to work them. I have no doubt that we will have our hands on the murderer shortly. In the meantime, M. Boirac, to make assurance doubly sure, I would be glad if you would see if you can identify these clothes."

"Her clothes? Oh, spare me that. But there, I understand it is necessary."

M. Chauvet picked up his telephone and gave directions for the clothes to be sent in. The jewellery was not available, as Mlle. Blaise had taken it in her round of the shops.

"Alas! Yes," cried M. Boirac sadly, when he saw the dress, "it is hers, it is hers. She wore it the evening she left. There can be no further doubt. My poor, mistaken Annette!"

"I am afraid, M. Boirac, at the risk of giving you pain, I must ask you to be good enough to tell us all you can about the circumstances of your wife's disappearance. These gentlemen are Mr. Burnley of the London police, and M. Lefarge of our own staff, and they are collaborating in the matter. You may speak before them with complete freedom."

M. Boirac bowed.

"I will tell you everything, monsieur, but you must pardon me if I seem a little incoherent. I am not myself."

M. Chauvet stepped to a press and took from it a flask of brandy. "Monsieur," he said, "you have our fullest sympathy. Allow me to offer you a little of this." He poured out a stiff glass.

"I thank you, monsieur," returned the visitor, as he drank the cordial. It pulled him together, and he became once more the unemotional man of business. He kept himself well in hand and did not, during the telling of his story, allow his emotion to overcome him, though at times it was clear all his powers of self-control were needed. In a stronger voice he began his statement, and his three companions settled themselves more comfortably in their chairs to listen.

CHAPTER XIV

M. BOIRAC MAKES A STATEMENT

"MY name and address you know," began M. Boirac. "In business I am the managing director of the Avrotte Pump Construction Co., whose works are situated off the rue Championnet, not far from the Omnibus Co.'s depot. I am fairly well off, and we lived comfortably, my wife going a good deal into society.

"On Saturday, the 27th ult., this day fortnight, we had a dinner party at the Avenue de l'Alma. Our principal guest was the Spanish ambassador, at whose house my wife had visited when in Madrid the previous year. Among the others was a M. Léon Felix, an old friend of my wife's who lived in London, and was in some business there. The guests arrived and we sat down to dinner, but unfortunately before the meal was concluded a telephone message came for me from the works to say that a serious accident had happened, and requiring my immediate presence. There was nothing for it but to apologize to my guests and go off at once, which I did, though I promised to return at the earliest possible moment.

"When I reached the works I found that the main bed casting of a new two-hundred horse-power engine which was being put in during the week-end, had slipped and slewed sideways while being got into place, killing one man and seriously injuring two others. One of the cylinders was fractured, and the whole casting had jammed between the wall and the flywheel pit and could not be got out.

"As soon as I saw how serious things were, I telephoned home to say I would be very late, and that there would be no chance of my returning in time to see my guests. However, we got on much better than I expected, and it was barely eleven when I turned out of the works. Not seeing a taxi, I walked to the Simplon station of the Metro. My route, as you will understand, involved a change of trains at Chatelet and I accordingly alighted there. I had hardly done so when I was clapped on the back by some one, and turning, found an American acquaintance called Myron H. Burton, with whom I had stayed in the same hotel in New York and with whom I had become friendly. We stood in talk for some time, and then I asked him where he was staying, inviting him to put up at my house instead of returning to his hotel. He declined, saying he was going to Orleans by the 12.35 from the Quai d'Orsay, and asked me to go and see him off and have a drink at the station. I hesitated, but remembering I was not expected at home, I agreed and we set off. The night being mild and pleasant we walked along the quais, but when we reached the Pont Royal it was barely a quarter to twelve. Burton suggested continuing our stroll, which we did, going round the Place de la Concorde and the end of the Champs Elysées. Interested in our talk, we forgot the passage of time, and arrived at the Gare Quai d'Orsay with only a minute to spare for my friend to catch his train and, therefore, to his apparent great chagrin, missing the drinks to which he had wished to treat me. I felt wakeful, and began to walk home, but when I had gone about half-way, rain began to fall. I looked for a taxi, but could not see one, and therefore continued my journey on foot, arriving home about one o'clock.

"François, the butler, met me in the hall. He seemed uneasy.

"'I heard the front door bang not ten minutes ago, monsieur,' he said, as I took off my wet coat. 'I got up to see if anything was wrong.'

"'Got up?' I said. 'How had you come to go to bed before I returned?'

"'Madame told me to, monsieur, about half-past eleven. She said you would be very late and that she would be sitting up.'

"'All right,' I said, 'where is madame?'

"He hesitated.

"'I don't know, monsieur,' he said at length.

"'Don't know?' I said. I was growing angry. 'Has she gone to bed?'

"'She has not gone to bed, monsieur,' he answered.

"I am not, M. le Chef, an imaginative man, but suddenly a feeling of foreboding swept over me. I hurried into the drawing-room and from that to my wife's small sitting-room. They were both empty. I ran to her bedroom. There was no one there. Then I recollected she had frequently waited for me in my study. I went there to find it also untenanted, and I was just about to withdraw when I saw on my desk a letter which had not been there earlier in the evening. It was addressed to me in my wife's handwriting, and, with a terrible sinking of the heart, I opened it. Here, M. le Chef, it is."

It was a short note, written on a sheet of cream-laid notepaper in a woman's hand and without date or address. It read:—

I do not ask you to forgive me for what I am doing tonight, Raoul, for I feel it would be quite too much to expect, but I do ask you to believe that the thought of the pain and annoyance it will be bound to give you cuts me to the heart. You have always been just and kind according to your lights, but you know, Raoul, as well as I do, that we have never loved each other. You have loved your business and your art collection, and I have loved—Léon Felix, and now I am going to him. I shall just disappear, and you will never hear of me again. You, I hope, will get your divorce, and be happy with some more worthy woman.

Good-bye, Raoul, and do not think worse of me than you can help.   ANNETTE.

M. Boirac bowed his head while the others read this unhappy note. He seemed overcome with emotion, and there was silence in the Chief's room for a few seconds. The sun shone gaily in with never a hint of tragedy, lighting up that bent figure in the arm-chair, and bringing into pitiless prominence details that should have been cloaked decently in shadow, from the drops of moisture on the drawn brow to the hands clenched white beneath the edge of the desk. Then, as they waited, he pulled himself together with an effort and continued:—

"I was almost beside myself from the blow, and yet I instinctively felt I must act as if nothing had happened. I steadied myself and called to François, who was still in the hall:—

"'It's all right, François. I've had a note from madame. She was obliged to go out at a moment's notice to catch the Swiss train. She had a message that her mother is dying.'

"He replied in his ordinary tone, but I could see that he did not believe one word. The understanding and the pity in his eyes almost drove me frantic. I spoke again as casually and as carelessly as I could,—

"'I wonder had she time to call Suzanne and get properly dressed. You might send her here and then you can get back to bed.'

"Suzanne was my wife's maid, and when she came into the

study I saw from her startled and embarrassed manner that she knew.

"'Suzanne,' I said, 'madame has had to go to Switzerland suddenly and unexpectedly. She had to rush off to catch the train without proper time for packing, still, I hope she was able to take enough for the journey?'

"The girl answered at once in a nervous, frightened tone. 'I have just been to her room, monsieur. She has taken her fur coat and hat and a pair of walking shoes. The evening shoes she was wearing tonight are there where she changed them. She did not ring for me and I did not hear her go to her room.'

"I had become somewhat calmer by this time, and I was thinking rapidly while she spoke.

"'Ah, well,' I answered, 'you had better pack some of her things tomorrow so that I can send them after her. She will be staying with her mother, and will no doubt be able to borrow what she wants till her own things arrive.'

"François was still hanging about the corridor. I sent them both to bed and then I sat down to try and realize all that had taken place.

"I need hardly trouble you with my thoughts. For some days I was half crazed, then I pulled myself together. Suzanne I sent home, saying I had heard from madame that she was employing one of her mother's maids."

M. Boirac paused.

"That," he said at length, "I think is all I have to tell you, M. le Chef. From that awful evening until I saw your advertisement in the *Figaro* a couple of hours ago, I have not heard a syllable from either my wife or Felix."

M. Boirac had told his story simply and directly, and his manner seemed to bear the impress of truth. The statement carried conviction to his hearers, who felt their sympathy going out to this man who had acted so loyally to the wife who had betrayed him. M. Chauvet spoke,—

"Permit me to express to you, M. Boirac, our deep regret for what has happened and particularly for your having had to come here and make this painful statement. Still more we regret that the terrible *dénouement* should make it almost impossible to keep the matter hushed up. Our search for the murderer has, of course, begun. We shall not detain you any longer, except to ask you to repeat a few names and hours so that we may note them to make your statement complete."

M. Boirac bowed.

"I thank you for your courtesy, M. le Chef."

The Chief continued,—

"There is first of all your address. That we have on your card. Next—I shall put it in question form—What time was dinner?"

"Quarter to eight."

"And what time did the message come for you from your works?"

"About a quarter to nine."

"And you arrived there?"

"About nine-fifteen, I should think, I did not look. I walked to the Champs Elysées and took a taxi."

"You said, I think, that you telephoned home then informing your wife that you could not return until very late?"

"I believe I did say that, but it is not strictly correct. I went to see the damage immediately on arrival, and was occupied there for quite some time. I should say I telephoned at about ten o'clock."

"But you unexpectedly got away about eleven?"

"That is so."

"So that you must have met your friend at Chatelet about twenty past eleven?"

"About that, I should think."

"Now your friend. I should like a note of his name and address."

"His name I have already given you, Myron H. Burton. His address I unfortunately cannot, as I do not know it."

"His home address, then?"

"I don't know that, either. I met him in an hotel in New York. We played billiards together a few times and became friendly enough, but not to the extent of exchanging our family histories."

"When was that, M. Boirac?"

"In the summer of 1908, no, 1909, three years ago."

"And the hotel?"

"The Hudson View. If you remember, it was burnt out last Christmas."

"I remember, a terrible business, that. Your friend went by the 12.35 to Orleans. He was staying there I suppose?"

"No, he was changing there and going on, though where he was going to I do not know. He told me this because I remarked on his choosing such a train—it does not get in until about 4.30—instead of sleeping in Paris and going by an early express that would do the journey in two hours."

"Oh, well, it is not of much importance. The only other thing, I think, is the name and address of your wife's maid."

M. Boirac shook his head.

"I'm sorry I can't give you that either. I only know her as Suzanne. But I dare say François or some of the other servants would know it."

"I shall have, with your permission, to send a man to look over the house, and he can make inquiries. I am sure, M. Boirac, we are extremely obliged to you for your information. And now, what about the formal identification of the body? I have no doubt from what you say it is indeed that of your wife, but I fear the law will require a personal identification from you. Would it be convenient for you to run over to London and see it? Interment has not yet, I understand, taken place."

M. Boirac moved uneasily. The suggestion was clearly most unwelcome to him.

"I needn't say I would infinitely prefer not to go. However, if you assure me it is necessary, I can have no choice in the matter."

"I am exceedingly sorry, but I fear it is quite necessary. A personal examination is required in evidence of identification. And if I might make a suggestion, I think that the visit should be made as soon as convenient to you."

The visitor shrugged his shoulders.

"If I have to go, I may as well do it at once. I will cross tonight and be at Scotland Yard at, say, 11.0 tomorrow. It is Scotland Yard, I suppose?"

"It is, monsieur. Very good. I will telephone to the authorities there to expect you."

The Chief rose and shook hands, and M. Boirac took his leave. When he had gone, M. Chauvet jumped up and went over to the screen.

"Get half a dozen copies of that statement and the questions and answers typed at once, mademoiselle. You can get a couple of the other girls to help you."

He turned to the two detectives.

"Well, gentlemen, we have heard an interesting story, and, whatever we may think of it, our first business will be to check it as far as we can. I think you had better get away immediately to the Avenue de l'Alma and see this François, if possible before Boirac gets back. Go through the house and get anything you can, especially a sample of the wife's handwriting. Try also and trace the maid. In the meantime, I will set some other inquiries on foot. You might call in about nine tonight to report progress."

CHAPTER XV

THE HOUSE IN THE AVENUE DE L'ALMA

Burnley and Lefarge took the tram along the quais and, dismounting at the Pont Alma, proceeded up the Avenue on foot. The house was a corner one fronting on the Avenue, but with the entrance in the side street. It was set a few feet back from the footpath, and was a Renaissance building of grey rubble masonry, with moulded architraves and enrichments of red sandstone and the usual mansard roof.

The two men mounted the steps leading to the ornate porch. On their right were the windows of a large room which formed the angle between the two streets.

"You can see into that room rather too clearly for my taste," said Burnley. "Why, if that's the drawing-room, as it looks to be by the furniture, every caller can see just who's visiting there as they come up to the door."

"And conversely, I expect," returned Lefarge, "the hostess can see her visitors coming and be prepared for them."

The door was opened by an elderly butler of typical appearance, respectability and propriety oozing out of every pore of his sleek face. Lefarge showed his card.

"I regret M. Boirac is not at home, monsieur," said the man politely, "but you will probably find him at the works in the rue Championnet."

"Thanks," returned Lefarge, "we have just had an interview with M. Boirac, and it is really you we wish to see."

The butler ushered them into a small sitting-room.

"Yes, messieurs?" he said.

"Did you see an advertisement in this morning's papers for the identification of a lady's body?"

"I saw it, monsieur."

"I am sorry to say it was that of your mistress."

François shook his head sadly.

"I feared as much, monsieur," he said in a low tone.

"M. Boirac saw the advertisement also. He came just now to the Sûreté and identified the remains beyond any doubt. It is a painful case, for I regret to tell you she has been murdered in a rather brutal way, and now we are here with M. Boirac's approval to make some inquiries."

The old butler's face paled.

"Murdered!" he repeated in a horrified whisper. "It couldn't be. No one that knew her could do that. Every one, messieurs, loved madame. She was just an angel of goodness."

The man spoke with feeling and seemed overcome with emotion.

"Well, messieurs," he continued, after a pause, "any help I can give you to get your hands on the murderer I'll give with real delight, and I only hope you'll succeed soon."

"I hope so too, François. We'll do our best anyway. Now, please, will you answer some questions. You remember M. Boirac being called to the works on Saturday the 27th of March, the evening of the dinner party, at about a quarter to nine. That was about the time, wasn't it?"

"Yes, monsieur."

"He went out at once?"

"He did, monsieur."

"Then he telephoned at about half-past ten that he could not return until later. Was that about the time?"

"Rather earlier than that, I should think, monsieur. I don't remember exactly, but I think it was very little, if at all past ten."

"About ten, you think? Can you tell me what words he used in that message?"

"He said the accident was serious, and that he would be very late, and possibly might not get back before the morning."

"You told your mistress, I suppose? Did the guests hear you?"

"No, monsieur, but madame immediately repeated the message aloud."

"What happened then?"

"Shortly after that, about 11.0 or 11.15, the guests began to leave."

"All of them?"

The butler hesitated.

"There was one, a M. Felix, who waited after the others. He was differently situated to them, being a friend of the family. The others were merely acquaintances."

"And how long did he wait after the others?"

François looked confused and did not immediately reply.

"Well, I don't know, monsieur," he said slowly. "You see, it was this way. I happened to have a rather bad headache that evening, and madame asked me if I was not well—it was just like her to notice such a thing—and she told me to go to bed and not to sit up for monsieur. She said M. Felix was waiting to get some books and would let himself out."

" So you went to bed?"

" Yes, monsieur. I thanked her, and went after a little time."

" About how long?"

" Perhaps half an hour."

" And had M. Felix gone then?"

" No, monsieur, not at that time."

" And what happened then?"

" I fell asleep, but woke up suddenly again after about an hour. I felt better and I thought I would see if monsieur was in and if everything was properly locked up. I got up and went towards the hall, but just as I came to the staircase I heard the front door close. I thought, ' That's monsieur coming in,' but there was no sound of any one moving in the hall and I went down to see."

" Yes?"

" There was no one there, so I looked into the different rooms. They were all empty, though lighted up. I thought to myself, ' This is strange,' and I went to find Suzanne, madame's maid, who was sitting up for her. I asked her had madame gone to bed, but she said not. ' Well,' I said, ' she's not downstairs. Better go up and see if she's in her room.' She went and came down in a moment looking frightened, and said the room was empty, but that madame's hat and fur coat and a pair of walking shoes were gone. Her evening shoes that she had been wearing were lying on the floor, where she had changed them. I went up myself and we searched around, and then I heard the latch of the front door again and went down. Monsieur was just coming in and, as I took his coat and hat, I told him about hearing the door close. He asked where madame was, and I answered I did not know. He looked himself, and in the study he found a note which I suppose was from her, for after he had read it he asked no more questions, but told me she had had to go to Switzerland to her mother, who was ill. But I knew when he got rid of Suzanne two days later that she wasn't coming back."

" What time did M. Boirac come in?"

" About one o'clock, or a few minutes after."

" Were his hat and coat wet?"

" Not very wet, monsieur, but he had been evidently walking through rain."

" You didn't make any further search to see if anything else had been taken, I suppose?"

" Yes, monsieur. Suzanne and I searched the entire house most thoroughly on Sunday."

" With no result?"

" None, monsieur."

" I suppose the body could not have been concealed anywhere in the house?"

The butler started as this new idea struck him.

" Why, no, monsieur," he said, " it would have been absolutely impossible. I myself looked in every spot and opened everything large enough to contain it."

" Thank you, I think that's about all I want to know. Can you put me in touch with Suzanne?"

" I believe I can get you her address, monsieur, from one of the parlourmaids with whom she was friends."

" Please do, and in the meantime we shall have a look through the house."

" You will not require me, monsieur?"

" No, thanks."

The plan of the downstairs rooms was simple. The hall, which was long and rather narrow, stretched back from the entrance door in the rue St. Jean to the staircase in a direction parallel to the Avenue de l'Alma. On the right was the drawing-room, a large apartment in the angle between the two streets, with windows looking out on both. Across the hall, with its door facing that of the drawing-room, was the study, another fine room facing on to the rue St. Jean. A small sitting-room, used chiefly by the late Madame Boirac, and the dining-room were situated behind the study and the drawing-room respectively. To the rear of the doors of these latter rooms were the staircase and servants' quarters.

The detectives examined these respective rooms in detail. The furnishing was luxurious and artistic. The drawing-room furniture was Louis Quatorze, with an Ambusson carpet and some cabinets and tables of buhl. There was just enough of good Sèvres and Ormolu, the whole selection and arrangement reflecting the taste of the connoisseur. The dining-room and boudoir gave the same impression of wealth and culture, and the detectives as they passed from room to room were impressed by the excellent taste everywhere exhibited. Though their search was exhaustive it was unfortunately without result.

The study was a typical man's room, except in one respect. There was the usual thick carpet on the floor, the customary book-lined walls, the elaborate desk in the window, and the huge leather arm-chairs. But there was also what almost amounted to a collection of statuary—figures, groups, friezes, plaques, and reliefs, in marble and bronze. A valuable lot, numerous enough and of sufficient excellence not to have disgraced the art galleries of a city. M.

Boirac had clearly the knowledge, as well as the means, to indulge his hobby to a very full extent.

Burnley took his stand inside the door and looked slowly round the room, taking in its every detail in the rather despairing hope that he would see something helpful to his quest. Twice he looked at the various objects before him, observing in the slow, methodical way in which he had trained himself, making sure that he had a clear mental conception of each before going on to the next. And then his gaze became riveted on an object standing on one of the shelves.

It was a white marble group about two feet high of three garlanded women, two standing and one sitting.

"I say," he said to Lefarge, in a voice of something approaching triumph, "have you heard of anything like that lately?"

There was no reply, and Burnley, who had not been observing his companion, looked round. Lefarge was on his knees examining with a lens something hidden among the thick pile of the carpet. He was entirely engrossed, and did not appear to have heard Burnley's remark, but as the latter moved over he rose to his feet with a satisfied little laugh.

"Look here!" he cried. "Look at this!"

Stepping back to the cross wall adjoining the door, he crouched down with his head close to the floor and his eyes fixed on a point on the carpet in a line between himself and the window.

"Do you see anything?" he asked.

Burnley got into the same position, and looked at the carpet.

"No," he answered slowly, "I do not."

"You're not far enough this way. Come here. Now look."

"Jove!" Burnley cried, with excitement in his tones. "The cask!"

On the carpet, showing up faintly where the light struck it, was a ring-shaped mark about two feet four inches diameter. The pile was slightly depressed below the general surface, as might have been caused by the rim of a heavy cask.

"I thought so too," said Lefarge, "but this makes it quite certain."

He held out his lens, and indicated the part of the floor he had been scrutinizing.

Burnley knelt down and, using the lens, began to push open the interstices of the pile. They were full of a curious kind of dust. He picked out some and examined it on his hand.

"Sawdust!" he exclaimed.

"Sawdust," returned the other, in a pleased and important tone.

"See here"—he traced a circle on the floor—"sawdust has been spilled over all this, and there's where the cask stood beside it. I tell you, Burnley, mark my words, we are on to it now. That's where the cask stood while Felix, or Boirac, or both of them together, packed the body into it."

"By Jove!" Burnley cried again, as he turned over this new idea in his mind. "I shouldn't wonder if you are right!"

"Of course I'm right. The thing's as plain as a pikestaff. A woman disappears and her body is found packed in sawdust in a cask, and here, in the very house where she vanishes, is the mark of the same cask—a very unusual size, mind you—as well as traces of the sawdust."

"Ay, it's likely enough. But I don't see the way of it for all that. If Felix did it, how could he have got the cask here and away again?"

"It was probably Boirac."

"But the alibi? Boirac's alibi is complete."

"It's complete enough, so far as that goes. But how do we know it's true? We have had no real confirmation of it so far."

"Except from François. If either Boirac or Felix did it, François must have been in it too, and that doesn't strike me as likely."

"No, I admit the old chap seems all right. But if they didn't do it, how do you account for the cask being here?"

"Maybe that had something to do with it," answered Burnley, pointing to the marble group.

Lefarge started.

"But that's what was sent to Felix, surely?" he cried, in surprise.

"It looks like it, but don't say anything. Here's François. Let us ask him."

The butler entered the room holding a slip of paper which he gave to Lefarge.

"Suzanne's address, messieurs." Lefarge read:—

Mlle. Suzanne Daudet,
rue Popeau, 14B,
Dijon.

"Look here, François," said the detective, pointing to the marble group. "When did that come here?"

"Quite recently, monsieur. As you see, monsieur is a collector of such things, and that is, I think, the latest addition."

"Can you remember the exact day it arrived?"

"It was about the time of the dinner-party, in fact, I remember now distinctly. It was that very day."

" How was it packed?"

" It was in a cask, monsieur. It was left in here that Saturday morning with the top boards loosened for monsieur to unpack. He never would trust any one to do that for him."

" Was he, then, in the habit of getting these casks?"

" Yes, monsieur, a good many of the statues came in casks."

" I see. And when was this one unpacked?"

" Two days later, monsieur, on Monday evening.'

" And what happened to the cask?"

" It was returned to the shop. Their cart called for it two or three days later."

" You don't remember exactly when?"

The butler paused in thought.

" I do not, monsieur. It was on the Wednesday or Thursday following, I believe, but I'm not positive."

" Thank you, François. There is one other thing I should be greatly obliged if you could do for me. Get me a sample of madame's writing."

François shook his head.

" I haven't such a thing, monsieur," he replied, " but I can show you her desk, if you would care to look over it."

They went into the boudoir, and François pointed out a small davenport finished with some delicate carving and with inlaid panels, a beautiful example of the cabinetmaker's art. Lefarge seated himself before it and began to go through the papers it contained.

" Somebody's been before us," he said. " There's precious little here."

He produced a number of old receipted bills and circulars, with some unimportant letters and printed papers, but not a scrap in madame's handwriting could he discover.

Suddenly François gave an exclamation.

" I believe I can get you what you want, messieurs, if you will wait a moment."

" Yes," he said, as he returned a few seconds later, " this will perhaps do. It was framed in the servants' hall."

It was a short document giving the work of the different servants, their hours of duty, and other similar information, and was written in the hand, so far as the detectives could recollect, of the letter of farewell to M. Boirac. Lefarge put it away very carefully in his notebook.

" Now let us see madame's room."

They examined the bedroom, looking particularly for old letters, but without success. Next they interviewed the other servants, also fruitlessly.

"All we want now," said Lefarge to the old butler, "is a list of the guests at that dinner, or at least some of them."

"I can tell you, I think, all of them, monsieur," returned François, and Lefarge noted the names in his book.

"What time is M. Boirac likely to return?" asked Burnley, when they had finished.

"He should have been here before this, monsieur. He generally gets back by half-past six."

It was now nearly seven, and, as they waited, they heard his latchkey in the door.

"Ah, messieurs," he greeted them, "so you are here already. Any luck?"

"No luck so far, M. Boirac," replied Lefarge, continuing after a pause: "There is a point on which we should be obliged for some information, monsieur. It is about this marble group."

"Yes?"

"Could you tell us the circumstances under which you got it, and of its arrival here?"

"Certainly. I am a collector of such articles, as you must have noticed. Some time ago, in passing Dupierre's in the Boulevard des Capucines, I saw that group and admired it greatly. After some hesitation I ordered it and it arrived—I believe it was the very day of—of the dinner-party, either that or the day before—I am not positive. I had the cask containing it brought into the study to unpack myself—I always enjoy unpacking a new purchase—but I was so upset by what had happened I hadn't much heart in doing so. However, on the following Monday evening, to try and distract my thoughts, I did unpack it, and there you see the result."

"Can you tell me, monsieur," asked Burnley, "was M. Felix also interested in such things?"

"He was. He is an artist and painting is therefore his speciality, but he had a good knowledge of sculpture also."

"He wasn't interested in that particular group, I suppose?"

"Well, I can hardly tell you that. I told him about it and described it to him, but, of course, so far as I am aware he had not seen it."

"Did you happen to mention the price?"

"I did, fourteen hundred francs. That was the thing he specially asked. That, and the shop at which I had bought it. He said he could not afford it then, but that at some time he might try and get another."

"Well, I think that's all we want to know. Our best thanks, M. Boirac."

"Good evening, messieurs."

They bowed themselves out, and, walking to the top of the Avenue, took the Metro to Concorde, from which they passed up the rue Castiglione to the Grands Boulevards to dine and spend the time until they were due back at the Sûreté.

CHAPTER XVI

INSPECTOR BURNLEY UP AGAINST IT

At nine o'clock that evening the usual meeting was held in the Chief's room at the Sûreté.

"I also have had some news," said M. Chauvet, when he had heard Burnley's and Lefarge's reports. "I sent a man up to that pump manufactory and he found out enough to substantiate entirely Boirac's statement of the hours at which he arrived there and left on the night of the accident. There is also a despatch from Scotland Yard. On receipt of Mr. Burnley's wire immediate inquiries were made about the cask sent by Havre and Southampton. It appears it arrived all right at Waterloo on the morning after it was despatched from here. It was booked through, as you know, to an address near Tottenham Court Road, and the railway people would in the ordinary course have delivered it by one of their lorries. But just as it was being removed from the van of the train, a man stepped forward and claimed it, saying he was the consignee, that he wished to take it to another address, and that he had a cart and man there for the purpose. He was a man of about medium height, with dark hair and beard, and the clerk thought he was a foreigner, probably French. He gave his name as Léon Felix and produced several envelopes addressed to himself at the Tottenham Court Road address as identification. He signed for, and was handed over the cask, and took it away. His movements after that were completely lost sight of, and no further traces of him have been discovered. A photo of Felix was shown to the Waterloo people, but while the clerk said it was like the man, neither he nor any of the others would swear to it.

"Inquiries have also been made about Felix. It turns out he is an artist or designer in Messrs. Greer and Hood's the advertisement poster people of Fleet Street. He is not married, but keeps an elderly servant-housekeeper. This woman was on a fortnight's holiday from the 25th of March to the 8th of this month.

"So much for London," continued M. Chauvet. "Now let us see what we have still to do. First, that lady's maid at Dijon must be interviewed. I think, Lefarge, you might do that. Tomorrow is Sunday. Suppose you go tomorrow. You could sleep at Dijon, and get back as early as possible on Monday. Then Mr. Burnley, that matter of the statue sent to M. Boirac must be gone into. Perhaps you would be good enough to make inquiries at Dupierre's on Monday morning, and please keep in touch with me by phone. I will look into some other points, and we shall meet here at the same time that evening."

The detectives took the Metro at Chatelet, Burnley going west to his hotel in the rue Castiglione, and Lefarge east to the Gare de Lyons.

On Monday morning Burnley called to see M. Thomas at the showroom in the Boulevard des Capucines.

"I'm back again, M. Thomas," he said, as they greeted one another. He explained what had been learned about the casks at the Gare St. Lazare, continuing, "So you see, two must have been sent out. Now, can you give me any information about the sending out of the second cask?"

"Absolutely none, monsieur," returned Thomas, who was evidently amazed at this new development, "I am quite positive we only sent one."

"I suppose it's impossible that Felix's order could have been dealt with twice in error, once by you here, and once by the head office in the rue Provence?"

"I should say quite, because they do not stock the good work there, it is all stored and dealt with here. But if you like I'll phone the head office now, and make quite sure."

In a few minutes there was a reply from M. Thévenet. No cask of any kind had been sent out from the rue Provence establishment on or about the date mentioned, and none at any time to Felix.

"Well, M. Thomas, it's certain, is it not, that one of your casks was sent by Rouen and long sea about the 1st instant. Do you think you could let me have a list of all the casks of that size that were out of your yard on that date? It must surely have been one of them."

"Yes, I suppose it must. I think I can give you that information, but it will take some time to get out."

"I'm sorry for giving you the trouble, but I see no other way.

We shall have to follow up each of these casks until we find the right one."

M. Thomas promised to put the work in hand without delay, and Burnley continued :—

"There is another point. Could you tell me something about your dealings with M. Raoul Boirac, of the Avenue de l'Alma, and particularly of any recent sales you made him?"

"M. Boirac? Certainly. He is a very good customer of ours and a really well-informed amateur. For the last six years, since I was appointed manager here, we must have sold him thirty or forty thousand francs' worth of stuff. Every month or two he would drop in, take a look round, and select some really good piece. We always advised him of anything new we came across and as often as not he became a purchaser. Of recent sales," M. Thomas consulted some papers, "the last thing we sold him was, curiously enough, the companion piece of that ordered by Felix. It was a marble group of three female figures, two standing and one seated. It was ordered on the 25th of March, and sent out on the 27th."

"Was it sent in a cask?"

"It was. We always use the same packing."

"And has the cask been returned?"

M. Thomas rang for a clerk and asked for some other papers.

"Yes," he said, when he had looked over them, "the cask sent to M. Boirac on the 27th of last month was returned here on the 1st instant."

"One other point, M. Thomas. How can one distinguish between the two groups, that sent to M. Felix, and that to M. Boirac?"

"Very easily. Both consist of three female figures, but in M. Felix's two were seated and one standing, while in M. Boirac's two were standing and one seated."

"Thank you very much. That's all I want."

"Not at all. Where shall I send that list of casks?"

"To the Sûreté, if you please," and with a further exchange of compliments the two men parted.

Burnley was both mystified and somewhat disappointed by the information M. Thomas had given him. He had been really impressed by Lefarge's discovery that a cask containing sawdust had recently been opened in M. Boirac's study, though he had not admitted it at the time. His friend's strongly expressed opinion that either Felix or Boirac, or both, had at that time packed the body in the cask had seemed more and more likely, the longer he had thought it over. There were, however, difficulties in the theory.

First, as he had pointed out to Lefarge, there was the personality of François. He felt he would stake his reputation on François's innocence, and without the butler's co-operation he did not see how the murder could have been carried through. Then, what possible motive could either of the men named have had for desiring the death of the lady? These and other difficulties he had foreseen, but he had not considered them insuperable. Possibly, in spite of them, they were on the right track. But now all hopes of that were dashed. The explanation of M. Boirac of the presence of the cask was complete, and it had been confirmed by François. This perhaps was not conclusive, but M. Thomas had confirmed it also, and Burnley felt the evidence of its truth was overwhelming. The body could not therefore have been packed in the cask, because it had been returned direct from M. Boirac's to the showrooms. Reluctantly he felt Lefarge's theory must be abandoned, and, what was much worse, he had no other to substitute.

Another point struck him. If he could find out the hour at which Felix had reached his hotel on the fatal evening, and his condition on arrival, it might confirm or disprove some of the statements they had heard. Therefore, having phoned to the Sûreté and finding he was not required there, he turned his steps again to the Hotel Continental and asked for the manager.

"I'm afraid I am back to give more trouble, monsieur," he said, as they met, "but one point has arisen upon which we want some information."

"I shall be pleased to assist you as far as I can."

"We want to know at what hour M. Felix returned to the hotel on the night of Saturday fortnight, the 27th March, and his condition on arrival. Can you get us that?"

"I'll make enquiries. Excuse me a moment."

The manager was gone a considerable time. When he returned after more than half an hour he shook his head.

"I can't find out," he said. "I've asked every one I can think of, but no one knows. One of the hall porters was on duty that evening up till midnight, and he is positive he did not come in before that hour. This is a very reliable man and I think you may take what he says as accurate. The man who relieved him is off duty at present, as is also the night lift boy, and the chambermaid on late duty in M. Felix's corridor, but I will interview them later and let you know the result. I presume that will be time enough?"

"Certainly," and with thanks Burnley withdrew.

He lunched alone, greatly regretting M. Lefarge's absence, and then called up the Sûreté again. M. Chauvet wanted to speak to him, he was told, and soon he was switched through to the great man's private room.

"There has been another wire from London," said the distant voice, "and it seems a cask was sent by passenger train from Charing Cross to Paris via Dover and Calais on Thursday week, the 1st of April, consigned to M. Jaques de Belleville, from Raymond Lemaitre. I think you had better go to the Gare du Nord and find out something about it."

"How many more casks are we going to find?" thought the puzzled Burnley, as he drove in the direction of the station. As the taxi slipped through the crowded streets he again took stock of his position, and had to admit himself completely at sea. The information they gained—and there was certainly plenty coming in—did not work into a connected whole, but each fresh piece of evidence seemed, if not actually to conflict with some other, at least to add to the tangle to be straightened out. When in England he had thought Felix innocent. Now he was beginning to doubt that conclusion.

He had not Lefarge's card to show to the clerk in the parcels office, but fortunately the latter remembered him as having been with the French detective on their previous call.

"Yes," he said, when Burnley had explained, in his somewhat halting French, what he wanted, "I can tell you about that cask." He turned up some papers.

"Here we are," he said. "The cask came off the Calais boat train at 5.45 p.m. on Thursday week, the 1st instant. It was consigned from Charing Cross to M. Jaques de Belleville, to be kept here until called for. He claimed it personally almost immediately after, and removed it on a cart he had brought."

"Can you describe M. de Belleville?"

"He was of medium height and dark, with a black beard. I did not take special notice of him."

Burnley produced a photograph of Felix he had received from London.

"Is that the man?" he asked, handing it over.

The clerk scrutinized it carefully.

"I could hardly say," he replied, hesitatingly, "it's certainly like my recollection of him, but I am not sure. Remember, I only saw him once, and that about ten days ago."

"Of course, you could hardly be expected to remember. Can you tell me another thing? At what time did he take the cask away?"

"I can tell you that because I book off duty at 5.15, and I waited five minutes after that to finish the business. He left at 5.20 exactly."

"I suppose there was nothing that attracted your attention about the cask, nothing to differentiate it from other casks?"

"As a matter of fact," returned the clerk, "there were two things. First, it was exceedingly well and strongly made and bound with thicker iron hoops than any I had previously seen, and secondly, it was very heavy. It took two men to get it from here to the cart that M. de Belleville had brought."

"You didn't notice any lettering on it, other than the labels?"

"I did," he answered, "there was 'Return to' in French, English, and German, and the name of a Paris firm."

"Do you recollect the name?"

The young man paused in thought.

"No, monsieur," he replied, after a few seconds, "I regret to say I have quite forgotten it."

"I suppose you wouldn't recognize it if you heard it? It was not, for example, Messrs. Dupierre, the monumental sculptors, of Grenelle?"

The clerk hesitated again.

"Possibly it was, monsieur, but I fear I could not say definitely."

"Well, I am greatly obliged for what you have told me, anyway. Just one other question. What was in the cask?"

"It was invoiced *Statuary*, but of course I did not see it opened, and don't know if the description was correct."

Burnley thanked the young man and turned out of the great station. Certainly it sounded as if this was a similar cask to that he had taken to Scotland Yard, if it was not the same one. Of course, he had to remember that even if it were one of Messrs. Dupierre's, which was not proven, there was a large number of these casks in circulation, and it did not follow that this one was connected with his quest. But the whole circumstances gave him to think, and he felt that his bewilderment was not lessened by the new development. As he walked slowly down the rue de Lafayette towards his hotel, he racked his brains in the endeavour to piece together into a connected whole the various facts he had learnt. He strolled on into the Tuileries and, choosing a quiet spot under a tree, sat down to think the matter out.

And first, as to these mysterious journeyings of casks. He went over the three in his mind. First, there was the cask sent out by Messrs. Dupierre on the Tuesday evening after the dinner-party, which travelled via Havre and Southampton, and which was received at Waterloo on the following morning by a black-bearded man, believed to have been Felix. That cask was addressed to Felix and it contained a statue. Then there was the second cask, sent out from Paris two days later—on the Thursday evening—which went via Rouen and long sea, and which was undoubtedly received at St. Katharine Docks by Felix. This number two cask contained the body of Madame Annette Boirac. And finally, there was what he might call number three cask, which was sent from London to Paris on that same Thursday, and which was claimed on arrival at the Gare du Nord by a M. Jaques de Belleville. This cask, like both the others, was labelled "Statuary," but whether that was really its contents was not known.

The inspector lit one of his strong cigars and puffed thoughtfully, as he turned these journeys over in his mind. He could not but think there was some connection between them, though at first he could not trace it. Then it occurred to him that if they were considered, not in the order of their discovery, but chronologically, some light might be gained. He went over them anew. The first journey was still that from Paris to London via Havre and Southampton, leaving Paris on Tuesday night and arriving at Waterloo on Wednesday morning. The second was now that leaving London on Thursday morning and reaching Paris that afternoon, via Dover and Calais, and the third that from Paris to London via Rouen, leaving on that same Thursday evening, and arriving at St. Katharine Docks on the following Monday. That is, from Paris to London, back from London to Paris, and back again from Paris to London. This seemed to show an element of design. And then a possible connection flashed across his mind. Instead of three casks might there not have been only one? Did the same cask not travel in each case?

The more Burnley thought over this, the more likely it seemed. This would explain M. Thomas's statement that only one cask had been sent out. It would make clear how the cask containing the body had been obtained. It would account for the astonishing coincidence that three casks of this unusual kind had made three such journeys almost at the same time.

Yes, it seemed probable. But if so, at some point in that triple journey the cask must have been opened, the statue removed, and the body substituted. The evidence was overwhelming that the cask had contained a statue when it left the Boulevard des Capucines yard, and that it had not been tampered with till it reached the van of the 7.47 p.m. from the Gare St. Lazare to Havre. Further, it had contained the body on arrival at St. Katharine Docks, and here again there was evidence that it could not have been opened in the hold of the *Bullfinch*. Therefore, at some point along the route, Gare St. Lazare, Havre, Southampton, Waterloo, Charing Cross, Dover, Calais, Gare du Nord, rue Cardinet goods station, Rouen, the change must have been made. Burnley made a mental note that every part of that journey must be the subject of the closest inquiry.

He went a step further. At the end of each of the three journeys it was met by a middle-sized, black-bearded, French-looking man. In the case of the third journey that man was Felix. In the two earlier, his identity was not definitely known, but he was like Felix. Suppose it was Felix in each case, would not this also tend to prove there was only one cask, and that Felix was sending it backwards and forwards with some design of his own? The inspector felt sure that he was right so far.

But if Felix had acted in this way, it followed that either he was the murderer and wished to get the body to his house to dispose of it there, or else he was an innocent man upon whom the real criminal wished to plant the corpse. This latter idea had been growing in the inspector's mind for some time. It seemed to hinge very much on the question : Did Felix know what was in the cask when he met it at St. Katharine Docks? Burnley recalled the scene at Scotland Yard when it was opened. Either Felix was an incomparable actor, or else he did not know. Burnley doubted even whether any acting could have been so realistic. He remembered also that Felix's illness from the shock was genuine. No, he rather believed Felix knew nothing of the corpse and, if so, he must be innocent. The point was one Burnley felt he could not settle alone. They must have medical evidence.

But if Felix was innocent, who was likely to be guilty? Who else could have had any motive to kill this lady? What could that motive have been, in any case? He could not tell. No evidence had yet come to light to suggest the motive.

His thoughts turned from the motive to the manner of the crime. Strangulation was an unusual method. It was, moreover, a horrible method, ghastly to witness and comparatively slow in accomplishment. Burnley could not imagine anyone, no matter how brutal, deliberately adopting it and carrying it out in cold blood. No, this was a crime of passion. Some of the elemental forces of love and hate were involved. Jealousy, most probably. He considered it in his careful, methodical way. Yes, jealousy certainly seemed the most likely motive.

And then another point struck him. Surely strangulation would only be adopted, even in the heat of passion, if no other method was available. If a man about to commit a murder had a weapon in his hand, he would use it. Therefore, thought Burnley, in this case the murderer could have had no weapon. And if he had no weapon, what followed from that? Why, that the crime was unpremeditated. If the affair had been planned, a weapon would have been provided.

It seemed, therefore, probable that the crime was not deliberate and cold-blooded. Someone, when alone with madame, had been suddenly and unexpectedly roused to a pitch of furious, over-mastering passion. And here again, what more likely to cause this passion than acute jealousy?

The inspector lit another cigar, as he continued his train of thought. If the motive was what he suspected, who would be a likely person to feel jealousy in reference to madame? A former lover, he thought. So far they knew of none, and Burnley took a mental note that inquiries must be made to ascertain if such existed. Failing a former lover, the husband immediately came into his mind, and here he seemed on firmer ground. If madame had had an understanding with Felix, and Boirac had come to know of it, there was the motive at once. Jealousy was what one would naturally expect Boirac to feel under such circumstances. There was no doubt that, so far as the facts had as yet come to light, Boirac's guilt was a possibility they must not overlook.

The inspector then turned his thoughts to a general review of the whole case. He was a great believer in getting things on paper. Taking out his notebook, he proceeded to make a list of the facts so far as they were known, in the order of their occurrence, irrespective of when they were discovered.

First of all was the dinner party at M. Boirac's, which took place on Saturday evening the 27th March. At this Felix was present, and, when Boirac was called away to his works, he remained behind, alone with Madame Boirac, after the other guests had left. He was alone with her from 11.0 p.m. till at least 11.30, on the evidence of François. About one in the morning, François heard the front door close, and, coming down, found that both Felix and madame had disappeared. Madame had changed her shoes and taken a coat and hat. On Boirac's return, a few minutes later, he found a note from his wife stating that she had eloped with Felix. Felix was believed to have gone to London next day, this having been stated by the manager of the Hotel Continental, as well as by Felix to his friend Martin outside his house when Constable Walker was listening in the lane. On that Sunday or the Monday following, a letter, apparently written by Felix, was posted in London. It contained an order on Messrs. Dupierre to send a certain group of statuary to that city. This letter was received by the firm on Tuesday. On the same day, Tuesday, the statue was packed in a cask and dispatched to London via Havre and Southampton. It reached Waterloo on the following morning, and was removed from there by a man who claimed to be Felix, and probably was. The next morning, Thursday, a similar cask was dispatched from Charing Cross to the Gare du Nord in Paris, being met by a man giving his name as Jaques de Belleville, but who was probably Felix. The same evening, some fifty minutes later, a similar cask was delivered at the goods station of the State Railway in the rue Cardinet, for dispatch to London via Rouen and long sea. Next day, Friday, Felix stated he received a typewritten letter purporting to be from Le Gautier, telling about the lottery and the bet, stating the cask was being sent by long sea, and asking him to get it to his house. On the following morning, Saturday, he had a card from the same source, saying the cask had left, and on Monday, the 5th of April, he got the cask from the *Bullfinch* at St. Katharine Docks, and took it home. Burnley's list then read as follows :—

Saturday, March 27.—Dinner at M. Boirac's. Madame disappears.

Sunday, March 28.—Felix believed to cross to London.

Monday, March 29.—Felix writes to Dupierre, ordering statue.

Tuesday, March 30.—Order received by Dupierre. Statue dispatched via Havre and Southampton.

Wednesday, March 31.—Cask claimed at Waterloo, apparently by Felix.

Thursday, April 1.—Cask sent from Charing Cross. Cask met at Gare du Nord. Cask delivered at rue Cardinct goods station for dispatch to London.

Friday, April 2.—Felix receives Le Gautier's letter.

Saturday, April 3.—Felix receives Le Gautier's card.

Monday, April 5.—Felix meets cask at docks.

Some other points he added below, which did not fall into the chronological scheme.

1. The typescript letter produced by Felix purporting to be from Le Gautier about the lottery, the bet, and the test with the cask, and the typescript slip in the cask about the return of a £50 loan, were done by the same machine, on the same paper.

2. The letter from Felix to Dupierre, ordering the statue was written on the same paper as the above, pointing to a common origin for the three.

Pleased with the progress he had made, Burnley left his seat under the tree and strolled back to his hotel in the rue Castiglione to write his daily report to Scotland Yard.

CHAPTER XVII

A COUNCIL OF WAR

At nine that evening, Inspector Burnley knocked at the door of the Chief's room in the Sûreté. Lefarge was already there, and, as Burnley sat down, M. Chauvet said:—

"Lefarge is just going to tell his adventures. Now, Lefarge, if you please."

"As arranged on Saturday," began the detective, "I went to Dijon yesterday and called on Mlle. Daudet in the rue Popeau. She seems a quiet, reliable girl, and, I think, truthful. She corroborated M. Boirac's and the butler's statements on every point, but added three details they omitted. The first was that Mme. Boirac took a wide-brimmed hat but no hatpins. This seemed to strike the girl as very strange, and I asked why. She said because the hat was useless without the pins, as it would not stay on. I suggested the lady must have been so hurried she forgot them, but the girl did not think that possible. She said it would have taken no appreciable time to get the pins, as they were stuck in the cushion at madame's hand, and that a lady would put in hatpins quite automatically and as a matter of habit. In fact, had they been forgotten, the loose feel of the hat, even in the slight air caused by descending the stairs, would have at once called attention to the omission. She could offer no explanation of the circumstance. The second detail was that madame took no luggage—not even a hand-bag with immediate necessaries for the night. The third seems more important still. On the morning of the dinner-party madame sent Suzanne to the Hotel Continental with a note for Felix. Felix came out and instructed her to tell madame he had her note and would come."

"A curious point, that about the pins," said the Chief, and, after a few moments' silence, he turned to Burnley and asked for his report. When this had been delivered and discussed he went on:—

"I also have some news. There has been a telephone call from the manager of the Hotel Continental. He says it can be established beyond doubt that Felix returned to the hotel at 1.30 on Sunday morning. He was seen by the hall porter, the lift boy, and the chamber-maid, all of whom are agreed on the time. All three also agree that he was in a quite normal condition, except that he was in a specially good humour and seemed pleased about something. The manager points out, however, that he was habitually good-humoured, so that there may be nothing remarkable about this."

M. Chauvet took some cigars from a drawer and, having selected one, passed the box to the others.

"Help yourselves, gentlemen. It seems to me that at this stage we should stop and see just where we stand, what we have learnt, if we have any tenable theory, and what still remains to be done. I am sure each of us has already done this, but three minds are better together than separate. What do you say, Mr. Burnley?"

"An excellent idea, monsieur," returned the inspector, congratulating himself on his cogitations earlier in the day.

"Perhaps you would tell us how you approached the problem, and we shall add our ideas as you go on?"

"I started, monsieur, with the assumption that the murder was the central factor of the whole affair, and the other incidents merely parts of a design to get rid of the body and divert suspicion."

"I fancy we are all agreed there, eh, Lefarge?"

The Frenchman bowed, and Burnley continued:—

"I thought then of the method of the murder. Strangulation is such a brutal way of killing that it seemed the work either of a maniac, or a man virtually mad from passion. Even then it would hardly have been used if other means had been available. From that I argued the crime must have been unpremeditated. If it had been planned, a weapon would have been provided."

"A good point, Mr. Burnley. I also had come to the same conclusion. Please continue."

"If this was so, it followed that some person, when alone with Mme. Boirac, had suddenly been overcome with absolute, blind passion. What, I asked myself, could have aroused this?

"A love affair, causing hate or jealousy, naturally suggested itself, but I could not fit it in. Who could have felt these passions?

"Considering Felix first, I did not see how he could experience either hate or jealousy against a woman who had eloped with him. It is true, a lover's quarrel might have taken place, resulting in something approaching temporary hatred, but it was inconceivable this would be bitter enough to lead to such a climax. Jealousy, I did not believe could be aroused at all. It seemed to me that Felix would be the last man in the world to commit the crime.

"Then it occurred to me that hate and jealousy would be just what one might expect to find in Boirac's case. If he were guilty, the motive would be obvious. And then, when M. Lefarge discovered yesterday that a cask similar to that in which the body was found had been unpacked in Boirac's study, I felt sure this was the solution. However, since hearing the explanation of that cask, I admit I am again in doubt."

"I agree with all you say, Mr. Burnley, except that we should remember that the passions of hate and jealousy could only arise in Boirac's mind in a certain circumstance, namely, that he was aware his wife had eloped or was about to elope, with Felix. If he were in ignorance of that, it is obvious he could have had no such feelings."

"That is so, sir. Yes, it would only be if he knew."

"And then, again, it would only be if he really loved his wife. If not, he might be vastly annoyed and upset, but not enough to throttle her in the blind passion we have spoken of. If they were not on good terms, or if there was some other woman in Boirac's life, he might even view her action with delight, as a welcome relief, particularly as there were no children to complicate the question of a divorce." The Chief looked inquiringly at his companions.

"I agree with that too, sir," said Burnley, answering the look.

"And I, monsieur," added Lefarge.

"So then, we have reached this point. If Boirac was in love with his wife, and if he knew she had eloped or was about to do so, he would have had a motive for the crime. Otherwise, we can suggest no motive at all, either for him, or Felix, or anybody else."

"Your last words, monsieur, open up possibilities," observed Lefarge. "Might it not have been some other person altogether? I do not see that we are limited to Felix or Boirac. What about Le Gautier, for instance, or some one we have not yet heard of?"

"Quite so, Lefarge. That is undoubtedly a possibility. There are others, François, the butler, for example, into whose actions we must inquire. The possibility of madame's having had some former lover must not be forgotten either. But I think we should make up our minds about these two men before we go farther afield."

"There is another point," resumed Burnley. "The medical evidence shows that only a short time can have elapsed between the time madame left her house and the murder. We assume, on the hotel manager's testimony, Felix went to London the morning after the dinner-party. If so, did madame accompany him?

If it is the former, it points to Felix, and if the latter, to Boirac."

"I think we can deduce that," said Lefarge.

"And how?"

"In this way, monsieur. Leave aside for a moment the question of the identity of the murderer, and consider how he got the body into the cask. This cask we have traced fairly well. It was packed in the showrooms in the Boulevard des Capucines, and in it was placed a statue. Then it travelled to Waterloo, and the evidence that it was not tampered with *en route* is overwhelming. Therefore the body was not in it when it arrived at Waterloo. Then, for twenty-two hours, it disappeared. It reappeared at Charing Cross, for it is too much to suppose there are really two casks in question, and travelled back to Paris, and again it is quite impossible that it could have been interfered with on the journey. At Paris it left the Gare du Nord at 5.20, and disappeared again, but it turned up at the State Railway goods station at 6.10 p.m. the same evening, and returned to London by long sea. On arrival in London it contained the body. It is certain the change was not made during any of the three journeys, therefore it must have been done during those disappearances in London or Paris.

"Of these disappearances, take that in Paris first. It lasted fifty minutes, and, during that time, the cask was conveyed between the Gare du Nord and the rue Cardinet goods station on a horse cart. How long, monsieur, should that journey have taken?"

"About fifty minutes, I should think," returned the Chief.

"I thought so too. That is to say, the whole time of the disappearance is accounted for. We may reckon, also, it would take some considerable time to open, unpack, repack, and close the cask, and it seems to me it would have been utterly impossible for it to have *both* been opened and to have made that journey in the time. It made the journey, therefore it wasn't opened. Therefore the body must have been put into it in London."

"Excellent, Lefarge. I believe you are right."

"There is a further point, monsieur. If my suggestion is correct, it definitely proves Madame Boirac went to London while alive, because her dead body obviously could not have been brought there. If we consider this in relation to the point about the medical evidence raised by Mr. Burnley, I think we shall be forced to conclude she crossed with Felix on Sunday."

"It certainly sounds probable."

"If she crossed with Felix, it seems almost certain that he is the guilty man. But there are a good many other things that point to Felix. Suppose for a moment he is guilty, and picture him faced with the question of how to dispose of the body. He wants a receptacle to remove it in. It suddenly occurs to him that only a few hours before he has seen the very thing. A cask for statuary. And, fortunately for him, he has not only seen it, but he has learned where to get a similar cask. What does he do? He proceeds to get that similar cask. He writes to the firm who use them, and he orders just such a piece of statuary as will ensure his getting the kind of cask he wants."

"What about the false address?"

"Of that, monsieur, I cannot suggest the explanation, but I presume it was with some idea of covering his tracks."

"Please continue."

"I suggest, then, that he got the cask on arrival in London, brought it to St. Malo, unpacked and probably destroyed the statue, packed the body, took the cask to Charing Cross and sent it to Paris, travelling over in the same train himself. In Paris he got a cart, and took it from the Gare du Nord to the rue Cardinet goods station, travelled back to London, and met the cask at St. Katharine Docks on the following Monday."

"But what was the object of all these journeys? If his purpose was to get rid of the body, why would he first get rid of it, and then arrange an elaborate scheme to bring it back again?"

"I saw that difficulty, monsieur," admitted Lefarge, "and I cannot explain it, though I would suggest it was for the same purpose as the false address—in some way to divert suspicion. But more than that, monsieur. We have evidence that the black-bearded man who met the cask on its various journeys was like Felix. But we have so far found no other black-bearded man in the entire case. It seems to me, therefore, it must have been Felix."

"If M. Lefarge's theory is correct," interposed Burnley, "the letter about the bet must have been written by Felix. In this case, could this letter and the journeys of the cask not have been devised with the object of throwing suspicion on Le Gautier?"

"Or of Boirac?" suggested the Chief.

"Boirac!" cried Lefarge, with a rapid gesture of satisfaction. "That was it, of course! I see it now. The whole of the business of the letter and the cask was a plant designed by Felix to throw suspicion on Boirac. What do you think, monsieur?"

"It certainly presents a working theory."

"But why," queried the Englishman, "should Le Gautier's name be brought in? Why did he not use Boirac's?"

"It would have been too obvious," returned Lefarge, delighted with the rapid strides his theory was making. "It would have been crude. Felix would argue that if Boirac had written that letter, he would never have signed it himself. It was a subtle idea introducing Le Gautier's name."

"If Felix did it," Burnley continued, "it would certainly clear up the difficulty of the authorship of the letter. He is the only man we have discovered so far that would have had the necessary knowledge to write it. He was present at the Café Toisson d'Or, and had joined with Le Gautier in the lottery, and therefore knew that part of it. The discussion about criminals evading the police and the bet between Le Gautier and Dumarchez, neither of which we believe took place, he could have invented to account for the receipt of the cask, and finally, he would naturally know the details about the last journey of the cask, since he himself arranged them."

"Quite so," cried Lefarge eagerly, "it all works in. I believe we are beginning to see light. And we must not forget Suzanne's evidence about the note. It is clear madame and Felix had an understanding for that night. At least, we know of messages passing between them and the reply of Felix points to an assignation."

"An important point, certainly. And yet," the Chief objected, "there are difficulties. That singular point about the hatpins, for example. What do you make of that, Lefarge?"

"Agitation, monsieur. I would suggest that this lady was so excited at the action she was about to take that she hardly knew what she was doing."

The Chief shook his head.

"I don't know that that is very satisfactory," he said. "Might it not, as also the fact that she took no luggage, mean that she never left the house at all? That she was murdered that same evening of the dinner-party, and the hat and coat removed to make a false scent? I suppose you have considered that?"

Burnley answered at once.

"I thought of that first of all, monsieur, but I dismissed it as impossible for the following reasons. First, if she was murdered on Saturday night, what was done with the body? It could not have been put into the cask in the study, as I had thought at first, for that was full. The statue was not unpacked till two nights later, on Monday. We know, indeed, it was not put into the cask, for that was returned direct to Messrs. Dupierre's and found to be empty. Secondly, it could not have been hidden anywhere else in the house, for François and Suzanne made a thorough search on the Sunday, and the corpse would have been too big a thing for them to have overlooked. Further, if she was murdered in the house, either Felix, Boirac, or some third person or persons must have done it. Felix could hardly be the man, as I do not see how he could have removed the body without a confederate, and we have not found such. Boirac would perhaps have had more chances of disposing of the body, though I do not see how, but he had a complete alibi. Lastly, I felt strongly that François, the butler, was to be believed. I could not imagine him party to the murder, and I did not see how it could have been done at the time you suggest without his knowledge."

"That certainly seems probable. In fact, when you add it to M. Lefarge's point that the body must have been put into the cask in London, it seems to me almost conclusive."

"I also feel sure it could not have been done then," observed Lefarge, "though I don't agree with Mr. Burnley that Boirac's alibi is good."

"Well now, I was rather inclined to accept the alibi," said M. Chauvet. "What part of it do you consider doubtful, Lefarge?"

"All of it from the time Boirac left the works. We don't know whether that American exists at all. As far as I can see, the whole thing may be an invention."

"That is quite true," admitted the Chief, "but it didn't seem to me so very important. The crucial point, to my mind, is the hour at which Boirac says he returned home—a few minutes past one. That is confirmed by François and by Suzanne, and I think we may accept their statement. But we have a further rather convincing incident. You may recollect Boirac stated that when he was half-way home from the Gare Quai d'Orsay it began to rain? You very properly tried to check even so small a point by asking François if his master's coat was wet. He replied that it was. Now, I made inquiries, and I find that night was perfectly fine till almost one o'clock, when a thick, wetting rain began to fall. We know, therefore, quite definitely that Boirac was out until the time he said. Therefore he could not have done the deed before 1.15. Also, we know that he could not have done it after that hour, because the lady was gone, and also the butler and maid were about. Therefore, if Boirac did it at all, it must have been after that night."

"That seems unquestionable, monsieur," said Lefarge, "and when you add to that the fact that we have, so far at any rate, been quite unable to connect Boirac with the letter or the cask, and that we are practically certain madame travelled to London, I think he may almost be eliminated from the inquiry. What do you say, Burnley?"

"Well, I think it's a little too soon to eliminate any one from the inquiry. I confess that point of motive struck me as being very strong against Boirac."

"That also, by the way, seems to show the deed was not done by Boirac that night," the Chief went on. "Your point is that he killed his wife because she had run away with Felix. But if he came home and found her there, she obviously *hadn't* run away. Hence the motive for that night at least, falls to the ground."

The three men laughed, and M. Chauvet resumed:—

"Now, to sum up our present position. We know that Mme. Boirac was murdered between 11.30 p.m. on the Saturday of the dinner party, and the following Monday evening, when the letter purporting to be from Felix and ordering the statue, was written. Obviously only Felix, Boirac, or some third person could be guilty. There is not, so far, a scintilla of evidence of any third person being involved, therefore it almost certainly was one of the other two. Taking Boirac first, we find that under certain circumstances he would have had a motive for the crime, but we have not yet been able to obtain any evidence that these circumstances existed. Apart from this, we can find nothing whatever against him. On the other hand, he has established a strong alibi for the only time during which so far as we can now see, he could have committed the crime.

"Against Felix there are several suspicious circumstances. Firstly, it is proved he received a note from madame, presumably arranging a meeting. Then we know he took advantage of the husband's absence on the night of the dinner to have a private interview with her. That went on from 11.0 till at least 11.30, and there is reason to believe, though not proof, till 1.0. Then we believe madame went to London, either actually with Felix, or at the same time. We conclude that for three reasons. First, she wrote to her husband that she had done so. The value of this evidence will, of course, depend on the opinion of our handwriting experts, whose report on the genuineness of this letter we have not yet received. Second, she could not have remained in the house, either alive or dead, as it was thoroughly searched by the servants, who found no trace of her. Neither could her body have been put in the cask in the study, for that contained the statue, and was not unpacked till the following Monday evening. Third, it is certain from the journeyings of the cask that the body was put into it in London, for the simple reason that it could not have been done anywhere else. Therefore she must have travelled to that city.

"Further, the letter presumed to be written to Felix by Le Gautier could be reasonably accounted for if Felix himself wrote it as a blind to cover his actions with the cask, should such be discovered. It is clear that it was written with some such purpose, as half of it—all about the bet and the test—is entirely untrue, and evidently invented to account for the arrival of the cask. Now, we may take it, Le Gautier did not write that letter. On the other hand, Felix is the only man we have yet found who had sufficient information to do so.

"Again, we know that a black-bearded man like Felix arranged the journeys of the cask. So far, Felix himself is the only black-bearded man we have found. On the other hand we have two strong points in Felix's favour. First, we have not been able to prove motive, and second, his surprise when the body was found in the cask appears to have been genuine. We have undoubtedly a good deal of evidence against Felix, but we must note that not only is this evidence circumstantial, but there is also evidence in his favour.

"The truth is, in my opinion, that we have not yet sufficient information to come to a conclusion, and I fear it will take a lot of work to get it. Firstly, we must definitely prove the authorship of that letter about the lottery and the bet. And here, it seems to me, the tracing of that typewriter is essential. This should not be so difficult, as I think we may take it that the author used the typewriter himself. Therefore, only machines to which the possible writers could have had access need be examined. I will send a man tomorrow to get samples from all the machines Boirac could have used, and if that produces nothing, he can do the same in connection with Le Gautier, Dumarchez, and the other gentlemen whose names we have. I presume, Mr. Burnley, your people will take similar action with regard to Felix?"

"I expect they have done so already, but I will write tonight and make sure."

"I consider that a vital point, and the next is almost equally important. We must trace Felix's movements from the Saturday night till the Thursday evening when the cask containing the body was despatched from Paris. Further, we must ascertain by direct evidence, if madame travelled with him to London.

"We must similarly trace the movements of Boirac for the same period. If none of these inquiries help us, other points would be the confronting of Felix and Boirac with the various luggage clerks that did business with the black-bearded man with the cask, in the hope that some of them might possibly identify him. The tracing of the carters who brought the cask to and from the various stations might or might not lead us to the men from whom they got their instructions. An exhaustive inquiry into the past life of Mme. Boirac and all the suspected men is also likely to be necessary. There are several other directions in which we can prosecute inquiries, but I fancy the above should give us all we want."

The discussion was carried on for some time longer, various points of detail being more fully gone into. Finally, it was arranged that on the following morning Burnley and Lefarge should begin the tracing of Felix's movements from the night of the dinner-party until he left French soil, after which Burnley would continue the quest alone, while Lefarge turned his attention to ascertaining Boirac's movements during the crucial period.

CHAPTER XVIII

LEFARGE HUNTS ALONE

At nine o'clock next morning the two colleagues met at the hotel in the rue Castiglione. They had discussed their plan of campaign before separating the previous evening, and did not waste time getting to work. Calling a taxi, they drove once more to the Hotel Continental and asked for their old friend the manager. They were quickly ushered into his office.

"We are exceedingly sorry to trouble you again, monsieur," apologized Lefarge, "but the fact is we find we require some more information about your recent visitor, M. Felix. If you can help us to obtain it, you will greatly add to our already large debt of gratitude."

The manager bowed.

"I shall be delighted to tell you anything I can. What is the point in question?"

"We want to trace M. Felix's movements after he left here. You have already told us he went to catch the 8.20 English boat train at the Gare du Nord. We wondered if he really did travel by it. Can you help us to find out?"

"Our bus meets all the incoming boat trains, but attends only those outward bound by which visitors are travelling. If you will pardon me a moment, I will ascertain if it ran that day. It was Sunday, I think?"

"Sunday, the 28th of March."

The manager was absent for a few moments, returning with a tall young man in the uniform of a porter.

"I find the bus did run on the day in question, and Karl, here, went with it. He may be able to answer your questions."

"Thank you, monsieur." Lefarge turned to the porter. "You went to the Gare du Nord on Sunday, the 28th March, with some passengers for the 8.20 English boat train?"

"Yes, monsieur."

"How many passengers had you?"

The porter considered.

"Three, monsieur," he replied at length.

"Did you know who they were?"

"Two of them I knew, monsieur. One was M. Leblanc, a gentleman who had stayed in the hotel for over a month. The second was M. Felix, who has been a constant visitor for years. The third was an English gentleman, but I do not know his name."

"Did these gentlemen converse together while in the bus?"

"I saw M. Felix speaking to the Englishman as they were leaving the bus, otherwise I cannot say."

"Did they go by the 8.20?"

"Yes, monsieur. I put their luggage into the carriages, and I saw all three in the train as it was starting."

"Was M. Felix alone?"

"He was, monsieur."

"Did he meet or speak with a lady at the station?"

"I do not think so, monsieur. Certainly I did not see a lady."

"Did he seem anxious or perturbed?"

"Not at all, monsieur. He was just as usual."

"Thank you, I am exceedingly obliged."

Some silver changed hands, and Karl withdrew.

"That is very satisfactory information, M. le Directeur. The only other point I want is the names and addresses of the two other occupants of the bus."

These were ascertained with some slight difficulty—M. Guillaume Leblanc, rue Verte, Marseilles, and Mr. Henry Gordon, 327 Angus Lane, Sauchiehall Street, Glasgow—and the detectives bowed themselves out with compliments and thanks.

"That's a piece of luck," remarked Lefarge, as they drove towards the Gare du Nord. "Those men may have seen Felix at other stages of the journey, and we may be able to trace him the whole way."

They spent the morning in the great station, interviewing ticket examiners and other officials, but without success. No one had seen either of the travellers.

"The boat is more likely," observed Burnley. "If he is a

constant traveller, some of the stewards will certainly know him."

Taking the 4.0 p.m. train, they reached Boulogne as dusk was falling, and began their inquiries at the pier. Finding the *Pas de Calais,* which had made the run in which they were interested, would not leave till noon next day, they turned their steps to the local police station. There they saw the men who had been on duty when the boat left on the Sunday in question, but here again without getting any information. Then they went on board the steamer and sought the chief steward.

"I know that gentleman, yes," he said when, after introducing themselves, Lefarge showed him Felix's photograph. "He crosses frequently, once or twice a month, I should say. He is a M. Felix, but I cannot say where he lives, nor do I know anything else about him."

"What we want to find out, monsieur, is when he last crossed. If you can tell us that, we shall be extremely obliged."

The official considered.

"I am afraid I could hardly be sure of that. He crossed both ways fairly lately. I should say about ten days or a fortnight ago, but I'm not sure of the exact date."

"We think he crossed on Sunday, the 28th of March. Can you think of anything that would confirm whether it was this date?"

"No, I cannot. You see there would be nothing to record it. We could not now trace the ticket he held, and there is no way in which the identity of our passengers is ascertained and noted. Speaking from memory, I should say that the date you mention is about correct, but I could not be sure."

"Is there any one on board who might be able to help us?"

"I'm really very sorry, monsieur, but I don't think there is. The captain, or one of the officers, might know him; I could not say."

"Well, just one other question, monsieur. Was he travelling alone?"

"I think so. No, wait a minute, was he? I believe, now that you mention it, there was a lady with him. You will understand I was not noticing particularly, as my mind was occupied with my work, but it's like a dream to me, I saw him talking to a lady on the promenade deck."

"You could not describe her?"

"I could not, monsieur. I cannot be even positive she was there at all."

Seeing there was nothing further to be learnt, they thanked the chief steward courteously. Then, remaining on board, they interviewed every one they could find, whom they thought might be able to give them information. Of all they spoke to, only one, a waiter, knew Felix, and he had not seen him on the occasion in question.

"That's no good, I'm afraid," said Burnley, as they walked to an hotel. "I believe that steward did see a woman, but he would be useless as a witness."

"Quite. I don't fancy you'll get much at Folkestone either."

"Most unlikely, I should say, but I can but try. I think I'll probably run up to Glasgow and see that man that travelled in the bus with him. He might know something."

"If not, I'll see the other—the one who lives in Marseilles."

A few minutes before twelve next day saw the detectives strolling along the wharf beside the English boat.

"Well," said Lefarge, "our ways part here. There is no use in my going to Folkestone, and I'll take the 2.12 back to Paris. We have had a pleasant inquiry, and I'm only sorry we have not had a more definite result."

"We're not done with it yet," returned the Englishman. "I expect we'll get it pretty square before we stop. But I'm really sorry to say 'Good-bye,' and I hope we may be working together again before long."

They parted with mutual assurances of goodwill, Burnley expressing his appreciation of the kindly treatment he had received in Paris, and Lefarge inviting him back to spend his next holidays in the gay capital.

We may accompany Lefarge on his return journey to Paris, and follow him as he endeavours to trace the movements of M. Boirac from the Saturday night of the dinner-party to the following Thursday evening, when the cask containing the body was despatched to London from the State Railway goods station in the rue Cardinet.

He reached the Gare du Nord at 5.45 p.m., and immediately drove to the Sûreté. M. Chauvet was in his office, and Lefarge reported his movements since they parted.

"I had a telephone call from Scotland Yard yesterday," said the Chief. "It seems Boirac turned up at eleven as arranged. He definitely identified the body as that of his wife, so that point is settled."

"Has he returned yet, do you know, monsieur?"

"I have not heard. Why do you ask?"

"I thought if he was still away I might take the opportunity of pumping François about his movements since the murder."

"A good idea. We can find out at once."

M. Chauvet turned over the pages of his telephone directory and, having found what he wanted, gave a call.

"Hallo! Is that M. Boirac's?—Is M. Boirac at home?—About seven o'clock? Ah, thank you. I'll ring up again later.—No, don't mind. It's of no consequence."

He replaced the receiver.

"He's crossing by the 11.0 from Charing Cross, and will be home about seven. If you were to call about half-past six, which is the hour at which he usually returns, your visit would not be suspicious, and you could have a chat with François."

"I shall do that, monsieur," and with a bow the detective withdrew.

The clocks had just finished chiming the half-hour after six when Lefarge presented himself at the house in the Avenue de l'Alma. François opened the door.

"Good evening, M. François. Is M. Boirac at home?"

"Not yet, monsieur. We expect him in about half an hour. Will you come in and wait?"

Lefarge seemed to consider, and then,—

"Thanks. I think I will."

The butler preceded him to the small sitting-room into which he had shown the two detectives on their first call.

"I heard at the Sûreté that M. Boirac had gone to London to identify the body. You don't know, I suppose, if he was able to do so?"

"No, monsieur. I knew he had gone to London, but I did not know for what purpose."

The detective settled himself in a comfortable chair and took out a cigarette case.

"Try one of these. They're special Brazilian cigarettes. I suppose we may smoke here?"

"Certainly, monsieur. I thank you."

"It's a long way over from London. I don't envy monsieur his journey. You've been, I suppose, monsieur?"

"Twice, monsieur."

"Once is all right to see the place, but after that—no, thank you. But I suppose M. Boirac is used to it? They say you can get used to anything."

"I should think he must be. He travels a lot. London, Brussels, Berlin, Vienna—he had been at them all to my knowledge in the last two years."

"I'm glad it's he and not I. But I should think this unhappy event would take away his love of travelling. I should imagine he

G.M.N.—F*

would want to stay quiet in his own home and see no one. What do you think, M. François?"

"Well, he hasn't anyway, or else he can't help himself. This is the second journey he's made since then."

"You surprise me. Or rather, no, you don't. I suppose we shouldn't be talking about what doesn't concern us, but I would be willing to lay a napoleon I could tell you where the first journey was to and what it was for. It was to see the Wilson Test. Am I not right?"

"The Wilson Test, monsieur? What is that?"

"Have you never heard of the Wilson Test? Wilson is the head of a great firm of English pump manufacturers, and each year a reward of over ten thousand francs is offered by them for any pump that can throw more water than theirs. A test is held every year, and the last one took place on Wednesday. M. Boirac would naturally be interested, being head of a pump manufactory himself. He would go to the Test."

"I'm afraid you would have lost your money, then, monsieur. He was away on Wednesday right enough, but I happen to know he went to Belgium."

"Well," said Lefarge, with a laugh, "I'm glad we didn't bet, anyway. But," he added, in a changed tone, "maybe I'm right after all. Maybe he went from Belgium to London, or vice versa. Was he long away?"

"He could not have done that, monsieur. He was only away two days, Wednesday and Thursday."

"It ought to be a lesson to me. I'm always too ready to bet on an unsupported opinion," and Lefarge led the conversation on to bets he had won and lost, till François excused himself to prepare for his master's arrival.

Shortly after seven M. Boirac came in. He saw Lefarge at once.

"I don't wish to trouble you after your journey, monsieur," said the latter, "but some further points have arisen in this unhappy business, and I would be obliged if you could kindly give me an appointment at whatever time would suit you."

"No time like the present. If you will excuse me for an hour till I change and get some dinner, I shall be at your service. You have dined, I suppose?"

"Yes, thank you. If, then, I may wait here for you, I would be glad to do so."

"Then come into the study. You'll perhaps find something to read in these book-cases."

"I thank you, monsieur."

The hands of the clock on the study chimney-piece were point-ing to half-past eight when M. Boirac re-entered. Sinking into an easy chair, he said :—

"Now, monsieur, I am at your service."

"The matter is a somewhat difficult one for me to approach, monsieur," began Lefarge, "in case it might seem to you that we had suspicions which we do not really entertain. But, as a man of the world, you will recognize that the position of the husband in unhappy affairs such as this must inevitably be made clear. It is a matter of necessary routine. My Chief, M. Chauvet, has there-fore placed on me the purely formal, but extremely unpleasant duty of asking you some questions about your own movements since the unhappy event."

"That's rather roundabout. Do you mean that you suspect me of murdering my wife?"

"Certainly not, monsieur. It is simply that the movements of *every one* in a case like this must be gone into. It is our ordinary routine, and we cannot consult our inclination in carrying it out."

"Oh, well, go ahead. You must, of course, do your duty."

"The information my Chief requires is a statement from you of how you passed your time from the night of the dinner-party until the evening of the following Thursday."

M. Boirac looked distressed. He paused before replying, and then said in an altered tone :—

"I don't like to think of that time. I passed through a rather terrible experience. I think I was temporarily insane."

"I still more regret that I must persevere in my questions."

"Oh, I will tell you. The seizure, or whatever it was is over and I am myself again. What happened to me was this.

"From the Saturday night, or rather Sunday morning, when I learnt that my wife had left me, I was in a kind of dream. My brain felt numb, and I had the curious feeling of existing in some way outside of and apart from myself. I went as usual to my office on Monday, returning home at my ordinary time in the evening. After dinner, in the hope of rousing myself, I unpacked the cask, but even that failed to excite my interest or lighten my depression. On the following morning, Tuesday, I again went to the office at my customary time, but after an hour of effort I found I could no longer concentrate my mind on my work. I felt that at all costs I must be alone so as to relax the strain of pretending nothing had happened. Still like a man in a dream, I left the office and, going down into the street, entered a Metro station. On the wall my eye caught sight of the notice, "Direction Vincennes," and it occurred to me that the Bois de Vincennes would be the very place for me to go. There I could walk without fear of meeting any of my acquaintances. I accordingly took the train there, and spent the morning pacing the more sequestered paths. The physical exercise helped me, but as I grew tired my mood changed. A great longing for human sympathy took possession of me, and I felt I must confide in some one, or go mad. I thought of my brother Armande, and felt sure I would get the sympathy I wanted from him. He lived not far from Malines, in Belgium, and I determined to go and see him at once. I lunched at a little café at Charenton, and from there telephoned to the office and to my house that I was going to Belgium for a couple of days. I instructed François to pack a handbag of necessaries and leave it immediately at the cloak room at the Gare du Nord, where I should call for it. While sitting at lunch it occurred to me that if I went by the 4.5 p.m. train—the first I could get— I would not arrive at my destination till the middle of the night, so I decided I would wait till the evening train and see my brother the following day. Accordingly, I went for a long walk up the Seine, returning by a local train to the Gare du Lyon. I dined at a café in the Place de la Bastille, and finally went to the Gare du Nord, got my bag, and left by the 11.20 for Brussels. I slept well in the train and breakfasted in one of the cafés off the Place du Nord. About eleven I left for Malines, walking the four miles to my brother's house for the sake of the exercise. But when I reached it I found it empty, and then I recollected, what had entirely slipped my memory, that my brother had spoken of a business trip to Stockholm, on which he was going to take his wife. I cursed my forgetfulness, but my mind was in such a state I hardly realized my loss of time and money. Walking slowly back to Malines, I considered returning to Paris that evening. Then I thought I had had enough travelling for one day. It was pleasant in the afternoon sun, and I let the time slip away, returning to Brussels about six. I dined at a café in the Boulevard Anspach, and then, thinking I would try and distract my thoughts, decided I would turn in for a couple of hours to a theatre. I telephoned to the Hotel Maximilian, where I usually stayed, to reserve a room, and then I went to Berlioz's *Les Troyens* at the Théâtre de la Monnaie, getting to my hotel about eleven. That night I slept well and next day my brain seemed saner and better. I left Brussels by the 12.50 from the Gare du Midi, arriving at Paris about five. Looking back on that abortive journey is like remembering a nightmare, but I think the solitude and the exercise really helped me."

When M. Boirac ceased speaking, there was silence for a few

moments, while Lefarge, in just the same painstaking way that Burnley would have adopted, went over in his mind what he had heard. He did not wish to question M. Boirac too closely lest, in the unlikely event of that gentleman proving guilty, he should put him on his guard; but he was anxious to miss no detail of the statement, so that he might as far as possible check it by independent testimony. On the whole, he thought the story reasonable, and, so far, he could see no internal reason for doubting it. He would, therefore, get a few details made clearer and take his leave.

"Thank you, M. Boirac. Might I ask a few supplementary questions? At what time did you leave your office on Tuesday?"

"About nine-thirty."

"What café did you lunch at in Charenton?"

"I don't remember. It was in a street about half-way between the station and the steamboat wharf, a rather poor place with an overhanging, half-timbered front."

"And what time was that?"

"About one-thirty, I think. I am not sure."

"And from where did you telephone to your house and office?"

"From the same café."

"About what time?"

"About an hour later, say half-past two."

"Now, the café in the Place de la Bastille. Which one was it?"

"I am not very certain. I think it was at the corner of the rue St. Antoine. At all events it faced up the rue de Lyon."

"And you were there about what time?"

"Eight-thirty, I should say."

"Did you get your bag at the Gare du Nord?"

"Yes, it was waiting for me at the left luggage office."

"Did you have a sleeping berth on the train?"

"No, I travelled in an ordinary first-class compartment."

"Was there any one else in it?"

"Three other men. I did not know any of them."

"Now, all that day, Tuesday, did you meet any one who knew you, or who could confirm your statement?"

"Not that I can remember, unless the waiters at the cafés could do so."

"On the next day, Wednesday, from where did you telephone to the Hotel Maximilian?"

"From the café where I dined. It was in the Boulevard Anspach, just before it opens into the Place Brouckère. I don't recall the name."

"What time was the message sent?"

" Just before dinner, about seven, I should say."

The detective stood up and bowed.

"Well, M. Boirac, accept my thanks for your courtesy. That is all I want to know. Good night, monsieur."

The night being fine, Lefarge walked slowly to his home near the Place de la Bastille. As he paced along he thought over the statement he had just listened to. If it was true, it appeared at first sight entirely to clear M. Boirac from suspicion. If he was in Paris on Monday he could not have sent the letter to Dupierre ordering the statue. That was received on Tuesday morning, and must therefore have been posted in London the previous day. If he was at Brussels and Malines, he obviously could not have met the cask in London. The first thing would therefore be to test the statement by independent inquiries. He reviewed it again in detail, taking a mental note of all the points on which confirmation should be obtainable.

First of all, it should be easy to find out whether he really was in Paris up till Tuesday evening. François and the other servants could tell him this with regard to Sunday, Sunday night, and Monday night, and the office staff at the pump manufactory could testify to Monday and Tuesday morning. The servants could also tell whether he unpacked the statue on Monday evening. There was then the question of the time he left his office on Tuesday; that could easily be ascertained. With regard to the restaurant at Charenton, M. Boirac would be a well-dressed and striking luncher at a place in such a locality, and would therefore undoubtedly have been specially noticed. If he really did lunch there, confirmation should be easily obtainable, particularly as the episode of the telephone would further call attention to the visit. The receipt of these telephone messages should also be easy to substantiate, as well as the leaving of the luggage at the Gare du Nord. Confirmation from the Gare du Nord cloak-room attendant, as well as from the waiters in the restaurant in the Place de la Bastille, could hardly be expected, owing to the larger numbers of strangers these men served, but both places would be worth trying. Inquiries at Malines might prove Boirac's visit, and certainly would show whether he had a brother there, as well as whether the house was locked up on the day in question. The staff in the Hotel Maximilian in Brussels would know whether or not he was there on the Wednesday night, and could tell about the receipt of the telephone message booking the room. Finally, it would be worth finding out if Berlioz's *Les Troyens* was really given on that evening at the Théâtre de la Monnaie.

As Lefarge thought over the matter, he saw that the statement was one which admitted of a good many tests, and he felt that, if it stood those he had enumerated, it might be fully accepted.

CHAPTER XIX

THE TESTING OF AN ALIBI

THE Seine was looking its best on the following morning, as Lefarge boarded an east-bound steamer at the Pont des Artes, behind the Louvre. The day was charming, the air having some of the warmth and colouring of summer, without having lost the clear freshness of spring. As the boat swung out into the current, the detective recalled the last occasion on which he had embarked at this same pier—that on which he and Burnley had gone downstream to Grenelle to call on M. Thévenet at the statuary works. This time the same quest took him in the opposite direction, and they passed round the Ile de la Cité, along the quais, whose walls are topped by the stalls of the book-vendors of the Latin Quarter, past the stately twin towers of Notre Dame, and under the bridge of the Metropolitaine opposite the Gare d'Austerlitz. As they steamed up the broad river the buildings became less and less imposing, till before they had covered the four miles to the suburb of Charenton, where the Marne pours its waters into the Seine, trees and patches of green had begun to appear.

Landing at Charenton, which was as far as the steamer went, Lefarge strolled up the street in the direction of the station, looking for a restaurant with an overhanging, half-timbered front. He had not to make a long search. The largest and most pretentious café in the street answered the description and, when he saw telephone wires leading to it, he felt it was indeed the one he sought. Entering, he sat down at one of the small marble-topped tables and called for a bock.

The room was fair sized, with a bar at one corner, and a small dancing stage facing the door. But for the detective, it was untenanted. An elderly, white-moustached waiter passed back and forward from some room in the rear.

"Pleasant day," said Lefarge, when this man came over with his bock. "I suppose you don't get busy till later on?"

The man admitted it.

"Well, I hear you give a very good lunch, anyway," continued the detective. "A friend of mine lunched here some days ago and was much pleased. And he's not so easy to satisfy either."

The waiter smiled and bowed.

"We try to do our best, monsieur. It is very gratifying to learn that your friend was satisfied."

"Did he not tell you so? He generally says what he thinks."

"I am not sure that I know your friend, monsieur. When was he here?"

"Oh, you'd remember him right enough if you saw him. There he is." Lefarge took a photograph of Boirac from his pocket and handed it over.

"But yes, monsieur. Quite well I remember your friend. But," he hesitated slightly, "he did not strike me as being so much pleased with the lunch as you suggest. I thought indeed he considered the restaurant not quite——" He shrugged his shoulders.

"He was not very well, but he was pleased right enough. It was last Thursday he was here, wasn't it?"

"Last Thursday, monsieur? No, I think it was earlier. Let me see, I think it was Monday."

"I made a mistake. It was not Thursday. I remember now it was Tuesday he said. Was it not Tuesday?"

"Perhaps it was, monsieur, I am not certain; though I rather think it was Monday."

"He telephoned to me that day from Charenton—I think he said from here. Did he telephone from here?"

"Yes, monsieur, he made two calls. See, there is the telephone. We allow all our patrons to use it."

"An excellent idea. I am sure it is much appreciated. But there was an unfortunate mistake about the message he sent me. It was making an appointment, and he did not turn up. I am afraid I misunderstood what he said. Could you hear the message? Perhaps, if so, you would tell me if he spoke of an appointment on last Tuesday?"

The waiter, who up to then had been all smiles and amiability, flashed a suspicious little glance at the detective. He continued to smile politely, but Lefarge felt he had closed up like an oyster in his shell, and when he replied: "I could not hear, monsieur. I was engaged with the service," the other suspected he was lying.

He determined to try a bluff. Changing his manner and speaking authoritatively, though in a lower tone, he said:—

"Now, look here, garçon. I am a detective officer. I want to find out about those telephone messages, and I don't want to have the trouble of taking you to the Sûreté to interrogate you." He took out a five-franc piece. "If you can tell me what he said, this will be yours."

A look of alarm came into the man's eyes.

"But, monsieur——" he began.

"Come now, I am certain you know, and you've got to tell. You may as well do it now and get your five francs, as later on at the Sûreté and for nothing. What do you say now? Which is it to be?"

The waiter remained silent, and it was obvious to Lefarge that he was weighing his course of action. His hesitation convinced the detective that he really did know the messages, and he determined to strike again.

"Perhaps you are doubtful whether I really am from the Sûreté," he suggested. "Look at that."

He displayed his detective's credentials, and the sight seemed to bring the other to a decision.

"I will tell you, monsieur. He first called up some one that I took to be his valet, and said he was going unexpectedly to Belgium, and that he wanted something left at the Gare du Nord for him—I did not catch what it was. Then he called up some other place and gave the same message, simply that he was going to Belgium for a couple of days. That was all, monsieur."

"That's all right, garçon. Here's your five francs."

"A good beginning," thought the detective, as he left the café and, turning his back on the river, passed on up the street. There could be no doubt that Boirac really had lunched at Charenton as he said. It was true the waiter thought he had been there on Monday, whereas Boirac had said Tuesday, but the waiter was not certain, and, in any case, the mistake would be a very easy one to make. Besides, the point could be checked. He could find out from M. Boirac's chief clerk and butler on what day they received their messages.

He walked to Charenton Station, and took a train to the Gare du Lyon. Hailing a taxi, he was driven to the end of the rue Championnet, the street in which was situated the pump factory of which M. Boirac was managing director. As he left the motor and began strolling down the footpath, he heard the clocks chiming the half hour after eleven.

The pump factory had not a very long frontage on the street, but, glancing in through an open gateway, Lefarge saw that it stretched a long way back. At one side of the gate was a four-story block of buildings, the door of which bore the legend, "Bureau au Deuxième Etage." The detective strolled past with his head averted, looking round only to make sure there was no other entrance to the works.

Some fifty yards or more beyond the factory, on the opposite side of the street, there stood a café. Entering in a leisurely way, Lefarge seated himself at a small marble-topped table in the window, from where he had a good view of the office door and yard gate of the works. Ordering another bock, he drew a newspaper from his pocket and, leaning back in his chair, began to read. He held it carefully at such a level that he could keep an eye over it on the works entrance, while at any moment raising it by a slight and natural movement would screen him from observation from without. So, for a considerable time he sipped his bock and waited.

Several persons entered and left the works, but it was not till the detective had sat there nearly an hour and had consumed two more bocks, that he saw what he had hoped for. M. Boirac stepped out of the office door and, turning in the opposite direction, walked down the street towards the city. Lefarge waited for five minutes longer, then, slowly folding up his paper and lighting a cigarette, he left the café.

He strolled a hundred yards farther from the works, then crossed and turning, retraced his steps and passed in through a door from which the managing director had emerged. Handing in his private card, he asked for M. Boirac.

"I'm sorry, monsieur," replied the clerk who had come forward, "but he has just gone out. I wonder you didn't meet him."

"No," said Lefarge, "I must have missed him. But if his confidential clerk is in, perhaps he could see me instead? Is he here at present?"

"I believe so, monsieur. If you will take a seat, I'll inquire."

In a few moments the clerk returned to say that M. Dufresne was in, and he was shown into the presence of a small, elderly man, who was evidently just about to leave for lunch.

"I rather wanted to see M. Boirac himself, monsieur," said Lefarge, when the customary greetings had passed. "It is on a private matter, but I think I need hardly wait for M. Boirac, as you can probably tell me what I want to know, if you will be so kind. I am, monsieur, a detective officer from the Sûreté "—here he produced his official card—"and my visit is in connection with some business about which we are in communication with M. Boirac. You will readily understand I am not at liberty to discuss its details, but in connection with it he called recently at the Sûreté and made a statement. There were, unfortunately, two points which he omitted to tell us and which we, not then understanding they were relevant, omitted to ask. The matter is in connection with his recent visit to Belgium, and the two points I wanted to ask him are, first, the hour he left the office here on that Tuesday, and second, the hour at which he telephoned to you from Charenton that he was making the journey. Perhaps you can tell me, or would you prefer I should wait and see M. Boirac himself?"

The chief clerk did not immediately reply, and Lefarge could see he was uncertain what line he should take. The detective therefore continued:—

"Pray do not answer me if you feel the slightest hesitation. I can easily wait, if you would rather."

This had the desired effect and the clerk answered:—

"Certainly not, monsieur, if you do not wish to do so yourself. I can answer your questions, or at least one of them. The other I am not so sure of. I received the telephone message from M. Boirac from Charenton at about quarter before three. That I am sure of as I particularly noted the time. As to when M. Boirac left here that morning, I cannot be so definite. He asked me at nine o'clock to draft a rather difficult reply to a letter and to take it in to him when ready. It took me half an hour to compose, as several figures had to be got out to make the matter clear. I took it in at 9.30 and he had then gone."

"That was on the Tuesday, wasn't it?"

"Yes, on the Tuesday."

"And it was on the Friday morning M. Boirac returned?"

"That is so, monsieur."

Lefarge rose.

"A thousand thanks, monsieur. I am very grateful to you for saving me a long wait."

He left the office and, walking to the Simplon station of the Metropolitaine, took the train for the centre of the town. He was pleased with his progress. As in the earlier stages of the inquiry, information was coming in rapidly. At first he was inclined to think he had already got enough to confirm the first portion of Boirac's statement, then his training re-asserted itself, and he decided to go back to the house in the Avenue de l'Alma, and if possible get François' corroboration. He therefore alighted at Chatelet and took the Maillot train to Alma, walking down the Avenue.

"Ah, M. François," he began, when the butler opened the door. "Here I am back to trouble you again. Can you spare me a couple of minutes?"

"Certainly, monsieur. Come in."

They went to the same small sitting-room and Lefarge produced his Brazilian cigarettes.

" How do you like them? " he asked, as the butler helped himself. " Some people think they're too strong, but they suit me down to the ground. Like strong whiffs, only without the cigar flavour. I won't keep you a moment. It's just about that bag of M. Boirac's you took to the Gare du Nord last Tuesday. Tell me, were you followed to the station? "

" Followed, monsieur? I? Why no, certainly not. At least not that I know of. "

" Well, did you observe at the left luggage office a rather tall man, dressed in grey and with a red beard? "

" No, " he answered, " I saw no one answering to the description. "

" At what hour did you leave the bag in? "

" About 3.30, monsieur. "

Lefarge affected to consider.

" Perhaps it's my mistake, " he said at last. " It was on Tuesday, wasn't it? "

" On Tuesday. Yes, monsieur. "

" And M. Boirac sent his telephone call about two, did he not? I think he said about two. "

" It was later, monsieur. It was nearer three. But, monsieur, you fill me with curiosity. How, if I may ask, did you know I took monsieur's bag to the station? "

" He told me last night. He happened to mention he had unexpectedly gone to Belgium, and that you had taken his bag to the left luggage office. "

" And the man with the red beard? "

Lefarge having got his information, was not much troubled to justify his little ruse.

" One of our detectives. He has been on a case of theft of valuable luggage. I wondered if you had seen him. By the way, did M. Boirac bring back the bag with him? *It* wasn't stolen? "

Lefarge smiled, and the butler, politely presuming this was meant for a joke, smiled also.

" It certainly was not stolen, monsieur. He brought it back all right. "

So far so good. M. Boirac had then, beyond any doubt or question, telephoned about 2.45 on Tuesday and had instructed the butler to take his bag to the Gare du Nord, as he had said. Further, he had called there himself and got the bag. So much was certain. But the statement he made of his movements on Sunday and

Monday, and the unpacking of the cask on Monday night still remained to be tested. Lefarge spoke again :—

"While I'm here, M. François, I wonder would you mind checking one or two dates for my report?" He pulled out his notebook. "I will read out and perhaps you would please say if the items are correct. Saturday, 27th March, the day of the dinner-party."

"Correct, monsieur."

"Sunday, 28th, nothing special occurred. M. Boirac unpacked the cask in the evening."

"That's not right, monsieur. It was on Monday the cask was unpacked."

"Ah, Monday." Lefarge pretended to correct his notes. "Monday evening, of course. M. Boirac was at home on Sunday night, but he did not unpack it till Monday. That's right, I think?"

"That's right."

"Then on Tuesday he went to Belgium, and returned home on Thursday evening?"

"Correct, monsieur."

"Thanks very much. I'm glad you noticed that slip. I've got it right now, I think."

He remained conversing for a few minutes, making himself agreeable to the old man and telling him some of the adventures he had met with during his career. The more he saw of François, the more he came to respect him, and he felt increasingly certain the old man's statement was to be believed and that he would not lend himself to anything dishonourable.

As if to balance the successes of the morning, during the whole of the afternoon Lefarge drew blank. After leaving the house in the Avenue de l'Alma, he questioned the clerks in the left luggage office at the Gare du Nord. Here he could get no information at all. No one remembered François putting in the bag, nor Boirac claiming it, nor could any record of the bag itself be turned up. Again, in the Place de la Bastille, where he spent some hours interviewing the waiters in the various restaurants, both in the Place itself and close by in the diverging streets, no better luck attended his efforts. He could find no trace of Boirac's having dined in any of them.

All the same, he was well satisfied with his day's work. The information he had got was definite and valuable, in fact, he thought it conclusively established the truth of Boirac's statement, at least in so far as Tuesday was concerned. If he could do as well in connection with the Wednesday and Thursday, he thought that the manufacturer's alibi would stand, and his innocence of the murder must then be admitted.

To carry on the inquiry, he would have to visit Brussels, and he accordingly telephoned to the Gare du Nord engaging a berth on the 11.20 p.m. sleeping car train that night. Then, after calling up the Sûreté, he turned his steps homewards to dine and have a rest till it was time to start.

He made a comfortable journey, and, having breakfasted in one of the cafés in the Place du Nord in Brussels, took an early train to Malines. He presented himself at the post office and asked if he could be directed to the residence of M. Armande Boirac. The clerk knew the name, though he was not certain of the address, but after inquiries at two or three of the principal shops, the detective found one at which M. Boirac dealt.

"Yes, monsieur, it's a good four miles out on the Louvain road. A large white house with a red roof, standing in trees on the right-hand side, immediately beyond a cross roads. But I think M. Boirac is from home, if you wanted to see him."

"I did wish to see him," returned Lefarge, "but I dare say Mme. Boirac would see me instead."

"I fear she is also away, monsieur. I least, I can only tell you what I know. She came in here about a fortnight ago, indeed, I remember now it was just this day fortnight, and said: 'Oh, Laroche,' she said, 'you need not send anything for two or three weeks, till you hear from me again. We are going away and are shutting up the house.' So, monsieur, I don't think you'll see either of them if you go out."

"I am greatly obliged to you, monsieur. I wonder if you could still further add to your kindness by informing me of M. Boirac's place of business, where I might get his address. He is in business, I suppose?"

"He is a banker, monsieur, and goes frequently to Brussels, but I don't know in which bank he is interested. But if you go across the street to M. Leblanc, the avocat, I expect he could tell you."

Lefarge thanked the polite shopman and, following his advice, called on the avocat. Here he learned that M. Boirac was one of the directors of a large private bank, the Crédit Mazières, in the Boulevard de la Senne, in Brussels.

He was half tempted to return at once to the capital, but a long experience had convinced him of the folly of accepting *any* statement without investigation. To be on the safe side, he felt he should go out and see for himself if the house was indeed empty.

He therefore hired a small car and drove out along the Louvain road.

The day was bright and sunny, though with a little sharpness in the air, and Lefarge enjoyed the run through the pleasant Belgian country. He hoped to get his work finished by the afternoon, and, in that case, he would go back to Paris by the night train.

About fifteen minutes brought them to the house, which Lefarge immediately recognized from the shopman's description. A glance showed it was empty. The gates of the avenue were fastened with a padlock and chain, and, through the surrounding trees, the window shutters could be seen to be closed. The detective looked about him.

Alongside the road close to the gates were three cottages, occupied apparently by peasants or farm labourers. Lefarge stepped up to the first of these and knocked.

"Good morning," he said, as a buxom, middle-aged woman came to the door. "I have just come from Brussels to see M. Boirac, and I find the house is locked up. Can you tell me if there is a caretaker, or anyone who could tell me where M. Boirac is to be found?"

"I am the caretaker, monsieur, but I do not know M. Boirac's address. All he told me before he left was that any letters sent to the Crédit Mazières in Brussels would be forwarded."

"He has not then been gone long, I suppose?"

"A fortnight today, monsieur. He said he would be away three weeks, so if you could call in about a week, you should see him then."

"By the way, a friend of mine was to call on him here last week. I am afraid he must have missed him also. You did not see my friend?" He showed her Boirac's photograph.

"No, monsieur, I did not see him."

Lefarge thanked the woman and, having walked round to two or three of the other neighbouring houses and asked the same questions without result, he re-entered the car and was driven back to Malines. From there he took the first train to Brussels.

It was close on two o'clock when he entered the ornate portal of the Crédit Mazières, of which M. Boirac was a director. The building was finished with extraordinary richness, no expense having been spared in its decoration. The walls of the vast public office were entirely covered with choice marbles—panels of delicate green separated by pilasters and cornice of pure white. The roof rose into a lofty dome of glass which filled the building with a mellow and pleasant light. "No want of money here," Lefarge thought, as he approached the counter and, handing in his card, asked to see the manager.

He had to wait for some minutes, then, following a clerk along a corridor decorated in the same style as the office, he was ushered into the presence of a tall, elderly gentleman with clean-shaven features and raven black hair, who was seated at a large roll-top desk.

Having exchanged greetings, Lefarge began:—

"I wonder, monsieur, if you would be so very kind as to tell me whether the M. Armande Boirac who is a member of your board, is the brother of M. Raoul Boirac, the managing director of the Avrotte Pump Construction Company of Paris? I went to Malines this morning to see M. Armande, but he was from home, and I do not wish to spend time in finding out his address and communicating with him, unless he really is the man I seek."

"Our director, monsieur," replied the manager, "is a brother of M. Raoul. Though I don't know the latter personally, I have heard our M. Boirac speak of him. I can also give you M. Armande's present address, if you require it."

"I am exceedingly obliged, monsieur, and should be most grateful for the address."

"It is Hotel Rydberg, Stockholm."

Lefarge noted it in his book and, with further thanks, left the bank.

"Now for the Théâtre de la Monnaie," he thought. "It is just round the corner."

He crossed the Place de Brouckère, and turned into the Place de la Monnaie. The box office of the theatre was open, and he interviewed the clerk, learning that Berlioz's *Les Troyens* was given on the Wednesday night in question, as stated by M. Boirac. But a search for that gentleman's name through the list of that evening's bookings was unproductive, though, as the clerk pointed out, this did not mean that he was not present, but only that he had not reserved a seat.

Lefarge's next visit was to the Hotel Maximilian. It was a large modern building occupying a complete block of the Boulevard Waterloo, not far from the Porte Louise. A polite clerk came to the bureau window to attend to him.

"I am expecting to meet a M. Boirac here," Lefarge began. "Can you tell me if he is in the hotel?"

"M. Boirac?" repeated the clerk, doubtfully, "I do not think we have anyone of that name here at present." He turned over a card index on the desk. "No, monsieur, he has not come yet."

Lefarge took out a photograph.

"That is he," he said, "a M. Raoul Boirac, of Paris."

"Oh, to be sure," returned the clerk, "I know that gentleman. He has frequently stayed with us, but he is not here at present."

The detective began to turn over the leaves of his pocket-book as if looking for something.

"I hope I haven't made a mistake in the date," he said. "He wasn't here recently by any chance, was he?"

"He was here, monsieur, quite lately—last week in fact. He spent one night."

Lefarge made a gesture of annoyance.

"I've missed him!" he exclaimed. "As sure as fate I've missed him. Can you tell me what night he was here?"

"Certainly, monsieur." He turned up some papers. "He was here on Wednesday night, the 31st March."

"I've missed him. Now, isn't that too bad? I must have mistaken the date." The detective stood apparently considering. "Did he mention my name—Pascal, Jules Pascal?"

The clerk shook his head.

"Not to me, monsieur."

Lefarge continued, as if to himself:—

"He must have come through from Paris that night." And then to the clerk: "You don't remember, I suppose, what time he arrived?"

"Yes, I do. It was late in the evening, about eleven, I should think."

"Rather a chance coming at that hour, wasn't it? He might easily have found you full?"

"Oh, he had reserved his room. Earlier in the evening he telephoned up from a restaurant in the Boulevard Anspach that he was coming."

"Was that before five? I was to meet him about five."

"Not so early, I think. More like half-past seven or even eight, as well as I can remember."

"Well, I can't understand it at all. But I mustn't be wasting your time. I'll write a note and, if he should turn up again, perhaps you would be kind enough to give it to him? I'm much obliged to you, I'm sure."

Lefarge was an artist in his profession. He never made an impersonation without carrying through the details in the most thorough manner possible. He therefore wrote a note to M. Boirac in an assumed hand, regretting having missed him and carefully explaining some quite imaginary business. Having signed it

" Jules Pascal " with a flourish, and left it with the clerk, he took his leave.

As he passed out of the Boulevard Waterloo to return to the old town, the clocks were striking six. He had completed his errand and he was tired, though well satisfied with its result. He would have a leisurely dinner and then catch the midnight train for Paris.

Sitting over his coffee in a quiet corner of one of the large restaurants in the Boulevard du Nord, he reviewed once more M. Boirac's statement, ticking off in his mind the various items he had been able to check. On Saturday night madame had disappeared. On Sunday and Sunday night Boirac was at his home. Monday he spent at his office, and that night he was again at home. On that same Monday evening he had unpacked the statue from the cask. Tuesday morning saw him in his office at the usual hour, but he had left again between nine o'clock and half-past. About 1.30 that same day he had lunched at Charenton, and shortly after 2.30 had telephoned to François and to his office. François had taken his bag to the Gare du Nord about 3.30, and Boirac had got it from there, as he had brought it back with him from Belgium. He had telephoned to the Hotel Maximilian about 7.30 or 8.0 on the Wednesday, and had slept there that night. Next day he had returned to Paris, reaching his house in the evening. Further, it was true that his brother lived at Malines and that his house had been shut up on the Wednesday in question, also that Berlioz's *Les Troyens* was given on the night he said.

So much was absolute bedrock fact, proved beyond any doubt or question. Lefarge then turned his mind to the portions of Boirac's statement which he had not been able to verify.

He could not tell whether the manufacturer had walked in the Bois de Vincennes before lunching at Charenton, or if he had gone up the Seine after it. He could not trace his having dined in any of the cafés of the Place de la Bastille. He had not proved that he went to Malines or called at his brother's house, nor did he know if he had been present at the opera in Brussels.

As he considered the matter, he came to the conclusion that in the nature of things he could hardly have expected to confirm these points, and he also decided they were not essential to the statement. All the essentials—Boirac's presence at Charenton and in Brussels— particularly in Brussels—he had proved up to the hilt. He therefore came to the deliberate conclusion that the pump manufacturer's statement was true. And if it was true M. Boirac was innocent of the murder, and if he was innocent—Felix. . . .

Next day he made his report to M. Chauvet at the Sûreté.

CHAPTER XX

SOME DAMNING EVIDENCE

WHEN Burnley left Lefarge on the pier at Boulogne, he felt as if he was losing a well-tried friend. Not only had the Frenchman, by his kindliness and cheerful companionship, made Burnley's stay in the French capital a pleasant one, but his skill and judgment had been a real asset in the inquiry.

And how rapidly the inquiry had progressed! Never before could Burnley recall having obtained so much information on any case in so short a time. And though his work was by no means complete, he was yet within reasonable distance of the end.

After an uneventful crossing he reached Folkestone and immediately went to the police station. There he saw the men who had been on duty when the *Pas de Calais* had berthed on the Sunday in question. But his inquiries were without result. No one resembling either Felix or Mme. Boirac had been observed.

He next tried the Customs officials, the porters who had taken the luggage from the boat, and the staff at the Pier Station. No information was forthcoming.

"H'm. Means going to Glasgow, I suppose," he thought and, turning into the telegraph office on the platform he sent a wire:—

"Henry Gordon, 327 Angus Lane, Sauchiehall Street, Glasgow. Could you see me if I called at ten tomorrow? Reply Burnley, Scotland Yard."

Then he set off to walk to the Town Station to catch the next train for London.

At New Scotland Yard he had an interview with his Chief, to whom he recounted the results of the consultation in the Sûreté, and his movements during the past two days, explaining that he proposed to go on to Glasgow that night if Mr. Gordon could see him the next morning. Then he went home for an hour's rest. Ten o'clock saw him back at the Yard, where a telegram from Mr. Gordon was awaiting him. "Can see you tomorrow at the hour named."

"So far, so good," he thought, as he called a taxi and was driven to Euston, where he caught the 11.50 express for the north. He usually slept well in trains, and on this occasion he surpassed himself, only waking when the attendant came round half an hour before they were due in Glasgow.

A bath and breakfast at the Central Hotel made him feel fresh and fit as he sallied forth to keep his appointment in Angus Lane, Sauchiehall Street. Ten o'clock was chiming from the city towers as he pushed open the office door of No. 327, which bore the legend, " Mr. Henry Gordon, Wholesale Tea Merchant." That gentleman was expecting him, and he was ushered into his private room without delay.

" Good morning, sir," he began, as Mr. Gordon, a tall man with small, fair, side whiskers, and two very keen blue eyes, rose to meet him. " I am an inspector from Scotland Yard, and I have taken the liberty of making this appointment to ask your help in an inquiry in which I am engaged."

Mr. Gordon bowed.

" Well, sir, and what do you wish me to do?"

" To answer a few questions, if you don't mind."

" I shall be pleased if I am able."

" Thank you. You were in Paris recently, I believe?"

" That is so."

" And you stayed at the Hotel Continental?"

" I did."

" Can you tell me what day you left to return to England?"

" Yes, it was Sunday the 28th of March."

" You drove, if I am not mistaken, from the hotel to the Gare du Nord in the hotel bus?"

" I did."

" Now, Mr. Gordon, can you recollect what, if any, other persons travelled with you in the bus?"

The tea merchant did not immediately reply.

" I did not specially observe, Mr. Inspector. I am not sure that I can tell you."

" My information, sir, is that three gentlemen travelled by that bus. You were one, and the man I am interested in was another. I am told that he conversed with you, or made at least one remark as you were leaving the bus at the station. Does this bring the circumstance to your mind?"

Mr. Gordon made a gesture of assent.

" You are correct. I recall the matter now, and the men too. One was small, stout, clean-shaven, and elderly, the other younger, with a black pointed beard and rather foppishly dressed. They were both French, I took it, but the black-bearded man spoke English excellently. He was talkative, but the other hadn't much to say. Is it the bearded man you mean?"

For answer Burnley held out one of Felix's photographs.

"Is that he?"

"Yes, that's the man sure enough. I remember him perfectly now."

"Did he travel with you to London?"

"He didn't travel with me, but he got to London all right, for I saw him twice again, once on the boat and once as I was leaving the station at Charing Cross."

Here was definite evidence anyway. Burnley congratulated himself and felt glad he had not delayed making this visit.

"Did he travel alone?"

"So far as I know. He certainly started alone from the hotel."

"And he didn't meet anyone *en route* that you saw?"

"When I saw him on the boat he was talking to a lady, but whether they were travelling together or merely chance acquaintances I couldn't say."

"Was this lady with him in London?"

"Not that I saw. He was talking to a man on the platform as I drove out. A tall young fellow, dark and rather good-looking."

"Would you know this young man again if you saw him?"

"Yes, I think so. I got a good look at his face."

"I should be obliged if you would describe him more fully."

"He was about five feet eleven or six feet in height, rather thin and athletic looking. He had a pale complexion, was clean-shaven except for a small black moustache, and was rather French looking. He was dressed in some dark clothes, a brown overcoat, I fancy, but of that I'm not sure. I imagined he was meeting your friend, but I had really no definite reason to think so."

"Now, the lady, Mr. Gordon. Can you describe her?"

"No, I'm afraid I can't. She was sitting beside him and I did not see her face."

"Can you tell how she was dressed?"

"She wore a reddish brown fur coat, sable, I fancy, though I'm not certain."

"And her hat? You didn't notice anything special about that."

"No, nothing."

"It hadn't, for example, a wide brim?"

"A wide brim? Not that I noticed. But it may have had."

"Was it windy where they were sitting?"

"Every place was windy that day. It was a bad crossing."

"So that if it had had a wide brim, the lady would have had difficulty in keeping it on?"

"Possibly," replied Mr. Gordon a trifle dryly, "but you probably can form an opinion on that as well as I."

Burnley smiled.

"We Scotland Yard people like to know everything," he said. "And now, Mr. Gordon, I have to express my thanks for your courtesy and help."

"That's all right. Would it be indiscreet to ask the reason of these queries?"

"Not at all, sir, but I fear I am not at liberty to give you much information. The man with the pointed beard is suspected of having decoyed a French lady over to England and murdered her. But, you will understand, it is so far only a matter of suspicion."

"Well, I should be interested to hear how it turns out."

"I am afraid you will hear, sir. If this man is tried, I expect your evidence will be required."

"Then for both our sakes I hope your case will not go on. Good day, Mr. Burnley. Glad to have met you."

There being nothing to keep him in Glasgow, the inspector returned to the Central and took the midday London express. As it thundered southwards across the smiling country, he thought over the interview he had just had. He could not help marvelling again at the luck that had pursued his efforts ever since the inquiry began. Nearly every one he had interviewed had known at least something, if not always exactly what he wanted. He thought how many thousands of persons crossed the Channel each week whose journey it would be absolutely impossible to trace, and here, in the one instance that mattered, he had found a man who had been able to give him the very information he needed. Had Felix not gone in the bus, had Mr. Gordon not been so observant, had the circumstances not fallen out precisely as they did, he might never have ascertained the knowledge of Felix's movements that day. And the same applied all through. Truly, if he did not get a complete case it would be his own fault.

And yet the evidence was unsatisfactory. It was never conclusive. It had a kind of thus-far-and-no-farther quality which always pointed to a certain thing, but stopped short of certainty. Here there was a strong presumption that Mme. Boirac had crossed with Felix, but no proof. It might, however unlikely, have been someone else. Nearly all the evidence he had got was circumstantial, and he wanted certainty.

His mind switched over to the case itself. He felt the probability of Felix's guilt had been somewhat strengthened. Mr. Gordon's statement was entirely consistent with that hypothesis. One would naturally expect the journey to be carried out just as it had been. In Paris, the lovers would be careful not to be seen together. At a station like the Gare du Nord, where acquaintances of both might easily be present, they would doubtless ignore each other's existence. On the boat they would probably risk a conversation, particularly as the deck was almost deserted owing to the weather, but in London, especially if Felix expected someone to meet him, they would follow their Paris plan and leave the station separately. Yes, it certainly worked in.

The inspector lit one of his strong cigars and gazed with unseeing eyes at the flying landscape as he continued his ruminations. On arrival in London what would be their next step? Felix, he expected, would shake off his friend, meet madame at some prearranged spot, and in all probability take her to St. Malo. Then he recalled that the housekeeper had been granted a holiday, and they would doubtless arrive to find a house without food or fire, empty and cheerless. Therefore would they not go to an hotel? He thought it likely, and began to plan a possible future step, a visit to all the probable hotels. But while speculating on the best to begin with, it occurred to him that if Felix had really committed the murder it must, almost certainly, have been done at St. Malo. He could not conceive it possible at an hotel. Therefore probably they did go to the villa after all.

He went a step further. If the murder had taken place at St. Malo, the cask must have been packed there. He recalled the traces this operation had left in Boirac's study. Surely some similar indications must have been left at the villa? If the cask had stood on a carpet or even possibly a linoleum, he might expect marks of the ring. And if not, there was the sawdust. He did not believe every trace of sawdust could have been removed.

It had been his intention in any case to search the house, and he took a mental note when doing so to look with special care for any such traces. This search, he decided, should be his next business.

On the following morning, therefore, he set out for St. Malo with his assistant, Sergeant Kelvin. As they drove, he explained his theory about the unpacking of the cask, and pointed out what, if this had been done, they might expect to find.

The house was empty as, owing to Felix still being in hospital, the housekeeper's leave had been extended. Burnley opened the door with a key from Felix's bunch and the two men entered.

Then took place a search of the most meticulous thoroughness. Burnley began in the yard and examined each of the out-houses in turn. These had concrete floors and marks of the cask itself were not to be expected, but they were carefully brushed and the sweepings examined with a powerful lens for traces of sawdust. All their contents were also inspected, Felix's two-seater, which was standing in the coach-house, receiving its full share of attention. Then the searchers moved to the house, one room after another being gone over in the same painstaking way, but it was not till they were doing Felix's dressing-room that Burnley made his first discovery.

Several of Felix's suits were hanging in a press, and in the right-hand side pocket of one of the coats—that of a blue lounge suit—there was a letter. It was crumpled and twisted, as if thrust carelessly into the pocket. Burnley did not at first notice anything interesting or important about it, till, reading it for the second time, it flashed across his mind that here, perhaps, was the very thing for which they had been searching—the link in that chain of evidence against Felix which up to then had been missing.

The letter was written on a sheet of rather poor quality note-paper in a woman's hand, rather uneducated both as to caligraphy and diction—such a letter, thought Burnley, as might be written by a barmaid or waitress or shopgirl. There was no water or other distinctive mark on it. It bore no address, and ran as follows:—

"Monday.

"My Dearest Léon.—It is with a heavy heart I take up my pen to write these few lines. What has happened to you, dearest? Are you ill? If you are, I will come out to you, no matter what happens. I can't go on without you. I waited in all yesterday hoping you would come, same as I waited in all the Sunday before, and every night of the week, but you didn't come. And the money is nearly done, and Mrs. Hopkins says if I can't pay next week I'll have to go. I've sometimes thought you were tired of me and weren't going to come back at all, and then I thought you weren't that sort, and that you were maybe ill or away. But do write or come, for I can't go on any longer without you.

"Your heartbroken

"Emmie."

When Burnley glanced over this melancholy epistle it seemed at first merely to indicate that Felix was no better than he might be, and it was not till he had read it again that its immense significance struck him. What if this paper supplied the motive of the murder? What if it had opened to Mme. Boirac a chapter in Felix's life which otherwise would have remained closed, and which he intended should remain closed? As Burnley thought over it he believed he could at least dimly reconstruct the scene. Felix and madame had arrived at St. Malo, and then in some way, by some act of extraordinary carelessness on Felix's part, she had got hold of the letter.

A quarrel would be inevitable. What would Felix do? Probably first snatch the letter from her and thrust it into his pocket out of sight. Then, perhaps, try to pacify the angry lady, and, finding this impossible, the quarrel would get worse and worse till finally in a paroxysm of passion he would seize her throat and choke out her life. The murder committed, he would be so upset that he would quite probably forget all about the letter. The oversights of criminals were notorious.

The more the inspector considered the matter, the more likely his theory seemed. But here again he had to recognize it was entirely surmise. No proof that this had taken place was forth coming. It was another case of the thus-far-and-no-farther evidence he had been deploring in the train. At all events it suggested another line of inquiry. This girl must be found and the relations between her and Felix gone into. Burnley foresaw much arduous work in front of him.

At length he put the letter away in his notebook, and the search continued. Finally, as it was beginning to get dusk, every room had been done except the study where Felix and the inspector had had their midnight discussion.

"I think we had better come back tomorrow," said Burnley. "There's no use in searching by lamplight."

Accordingly, the next morning saw them again at work. They crawled over the floor so as to get every part of the carpet between themselves and the light, but could find no impressions. They peered with their lenses in the pile of the carpet, they felt between the arms and seats of the padded leathern chairs, all to no purpose. And then Burnley made his second discovery.

Between the study and the dining-room adjoining there was a door, evidently unused, as it was locked and the key was gone. On the study side this door was covered by a heavy curtain of dark green plush. In front of the curtain, and standing with its back to it, was a small chair whose low, leather-padded back formed a half-circle with the arms. In his anxiety to leave no part of the carpet unexamined, Burnley had moved this chair aside.

As he stooped at the place where the chair had been a bright object sticking to the curtain caught his eye. He looked more closely. A small, slightly bent, gold safety-pin, bearing a tiny row of diamonds, was caught in the braid at the top of the hem. The point had not penetrated, and the pin fell to the floor when Burnley touched the plush.

He picked it up.

"That's rather a fine thing even for a natty boy like Felix," he said as he showed it to Kelvin. And then he stood quite still as it flashed across his mind that here, perhaps, was another link in the chain that was being forged about Felix—a link possibly even more important than any of the foregoing. What if it did not belong to Felix at all? It looked too dainty and delicate for a man's use. What if it was a lady's? And, most important question of all, what if that lady was Mme. Boirac? If this proved true, his case was complete.

Dropping into the arm-chair he had occupied on the occasion of his midnight interview with Felix, he considered the possibilities opened up by this new discovery, endeavouring to evolve some theory of how a pin or brooch belonging to the deceased lady could have been dropped where he found this one. As he did so, a picture of what might have happened gradually grew in his mind. Firstly, he thought it likely that a lady in evening dress would wear such a pin, and it might easily be at her neck or shoulder. And if she had sat in that chair with her back to the curtain, and anyone had caught her by the throat and forced her head backwards, what could be more likely than that the pin should be pulled out in the struggle? And if it were pulled out it almost certainly would drop where or whereabouts he found it.

The inspector recognized again that this was all surmise, but it was strengthened by the fact that the pin was undoubtedly bent as if it had been pulled out of something without being unhooked. The more he thought over it the more likely his idea seemed. At all events it would be easy to test it. Two points suggested themselves to his mind which would settle it conclusively. First, if the pin was madame's, the maid Suzanne would recognize it. The arrangement of the diamonds made it quite distinctive. The girl would also know if madame wore it on the night of the dinner-party. Secondly, if it was pulled out of madame's dress, the latter would probably be torn or at least marked. Both these points could easily be ascertained, and he decided he would write to Paris about them that night.

He put the brooch into a pocket case, and, getting up, resumed his search of the study. For a time he pursued his labours without result, and then he made another discovery which struck him as being of even greater importance than that of the pin. He had completed his examination of the furniture, and now, for over an hour, had been seated at Felix's desk going through drawer after drawer, reading old letters and examining the watermarks of paper and the alignment of typewritten documents. Felix evidently had some of the defects of the artistic temperament, for his paper

were jumbled together without any attempt at filing or classification
—accounts, receipts, invitations, engagements, business letters—all
were thrust higgledy-piggledy into the first drawer that came handy.
But Burnley had methodically gone through every one without
finding anything of interest. None of the papers had the watermark
of that ordering the statue from Dupierre, none of the typewriting
had the defective letters of that ostensibly from Le Gautier to Felix.
The inspector had just reflected that he had only to go through the
half-dozen shelves of books and his work would be done, when he
made his third find.

On the desk lay a number of sheets of blotting paper folded
pamphlet-wise, it being evidently Felix's custom to blot his wet
papers between two of the leaves. Following his usual routine, the
inspector fetched a mirror from the bathroom, and with its aid
examined the sheets from each edge in turn. At the fourth of these
sheets he stopped suddenly with a little gesture of triumph, for
there, clearly revealed in the mirror, were some words he had seen
before :—

.s ...s th. ..... s.c. .. ... l... .. t.. ......
.le... fo.wa.. ..med....ly to ..e ..ove .dd.ess.

I do ..t kn.w th. e.a.t pric., but ..der.t..d .t is about 1,500
francs. I therefore enclose notes for that

It was the bottom of the first page of the letter ordering the
statue from Dupierre! Here was certainty : here, at last, proofs of
the most complete kind! Felix had ordered the statue and like a
fool had blotted his letter and omitted to destroy the blotsheet!

The inspector chuckled with content at his find. Felix had
ordered the statue. That was now certain. And if he had done
so he was responsible for its first journey, and therefore undoubtedly
for its second and third. In fact, it was now evident he had arranged
all the movements of the cask, and, if so, he must unquestionably
have put in the body, and if he put in the body he must be the
murderer.

Then there was the further point about the paper. The paper
on which this letter had been written was the same as that on which
the letter about the lottery and the bet was typed. Felix had stated
he had received this letter by post, but at the discussion in M.
Chauvet's office the probability that he himself was the author had
been recognized. This probability was now strengthened by finding
he had had in his possession the peculiar French paper which had
been used.

Truly these three discoveries, the letter signed "Your heart-broken Emmie," the bent brooch on the curtain, and the tell-tale impression on the blotting paper seemed to the inspector entirely to settle the question of Felix's guilt.

On the other hand he had failed to find any trace of the unpacking of the cask, and his search had been so thorough that he almost felt impelled to the conclusion that it had not been there at all. And then a possible explanation struck him. Suppose Felix had got a cart and brought the cask to St. Malo intending to remove it again the following morning. Where would he put it for the night? It was too heavy to move by himself, and he would not want to have a helper. What then would he do? Why, leave it on the cart, of course! His obvious plan would be to stable the horse and open the cask where it stood—on the cart. And if he dropped some sawdust in the process, the wind would see to that. There would be none left now.

He felt sure he was on the right track, and then he had a further idea. If a horse was stabled at the villa all night, some traces should surely be visible. He went to the yard again and began a new quest. He went carefully and thoroughly over the ground. But this time he had no luck. He was forced to conclude no horse had been kept.

The possibility that the carter might have left his vehicle and taken the horse away with him for the night next occurred to him, but he thought that unlikely, and left the question undecided in the meantime.

On his return to Scotland Yard, the Chief heard his story with close attention, and was much impressed by his discoveries. He gave his views at some length, ending up:—

"We shall send the pin over to Paris and see if that girl identifies it. Indeed, whether or not, I think we have a sufficient case against Felix to go into court. By the way, I don't think I told you I sent a man to his firm, the poster people, and found that he was absent on holidays during the week the cask was travelling backwards and forwards to Paris. This, of course, is not evidence against him, but it works in with our theory."

Two days later a wire came from M. Chauvet:—

"Suzanne Daudet identifies pin as madame's property."

"That settles it," said the Chief, and a warrant was made out for Felix's arrest, so soon as he should be well enough to leave the hospital.

PART III—LONDON AND PARIS

CHAPTER XXI

A NEW POINT OF VIEW

OF the millions who unfolded their papers a few mornings after the events described in the last chapter, there were few but felt a thrill of excitement as their eyes fell on the headlines, " The Cask Mystery. Arrest of Léon Felix." Though by no means all the facts discovered by the police had become public, enough had leaked out to arouse a keen and general interest. The tragic circumstances of the case, no less than the baffling mystery in which it was shrouded, intrigued the popular imagination and, though the police were early credited with having the usual clue and the customary arrest was stated to be imminent, none outside the official ranks had any real idea in what direction suspicion was tending.

But to none of those millions did the news come with such a sense of personal shock and affront as to our old acquaintance, Dr. William Martin, of The Elms, near Brent village, on the Great North Road. Dr. Martin, it will be remembered, was the man who, on the night on which Constable Walker watched from behind his tree, called at St. Malo and insisted on Felix accompanying him home to play bridge. The two men were close friends. Many an afternoon they had spent together on the banks of a neighbouring trout stream, many an evening had slipped rapidly away round the doctor's billiard table. And with Martin's family also Felix was a favourite. No member of it but was pleased to welcome the Frenchman to the house, or but had some special confidence to share with him.

At first Dr. Martin could hardly believe his eyes as they rested on the fatal headlines. That Felix, his friend, his trusted companion, should be arrested! And for murder! The thought was so incredible, so utterly horrible, he could not take it in. But, unlike the nightmare to which he compared it, the idea had permanence. Though his thoughts might wander, it was always there, grim and terribly definite, for them to return to.

He began to think over his friend's circumstances. Felix had always been reticent about his life, but to the doctor he had seemed a lonely man. He lived alone, and Martin had never known him to have visitors staying in the house. Nor could the doctor recall the Frenchman's ever having spoken of relatives. "Who," he wondered, "will help him now?"

But with so kindly and warm-hearted a man as Dr. Martin, such a question could not long remain unanswered. "I must go and see him," he thought. "I must find out who is going to act for him. If he has no one, then I must do the best I can myself."

But a practical difficulty arose. How were orders to visit prisoners obtained? The doctor did not know. For a man of his age and standing he was singularly ignorant of legal matters. But when such came his way he invariably adopted the same simple expedient. He "saw Clifford." This difficulty he would meet in the same way. He would "see Clifford."

"Clifford"—otherwise John Wakefield Clifford, senior partner of Messrs. Clifford and Lewisham, Solicitors, Gray's Inn—was Martin's man of business, friend, and crony. The chance that they took the same weekly half-holiday had thrown them together on the links, and they had followed up the acquaintanceship by occasional visits at each other's houses. Mr. Clifford was an almost startling contrast to the breezy doctor. Small, elderly, and rather wizened, with white hair and moustache, and dressed always with meticulous care, he seemed the embodiment of conventional propriety. His manner generally speaking was precise and dry, but the fortunate gift of a sense of humour invariably saved him from becoming dull.

He was a fine lawyer. His admirers, who were many, held that an opinion from him was as good as counsel's any day, and knew that, beneath the keenness which made him so formidable and indomitable an opponent, there lay a deep vein of very real human kindness.

A press of unavoidable business kept Martin at work till the afternoon, but three o'clock saw him ascending the stairs of Messrs. Clifford and Lewisham's office.

"How are you, Martin?" the senior partner greeted him. "I am glad to see you. This is an unexpected pleasure."

"Thanks, old chap," returned the doctor, accepting the cigarette the other offered, and sinking back into a deep, leather-lined arm chair. "But I'm afraid there won't be much pleasure about my visit. It's business, and nasty business at that. Have you a few minutes to spare?"

The little man bowed gravely.

"Certainly," he said, "I am at your service."

"It's about that neighbour of mine, Léon Felix," went on the doctor, plunging without further preamble into his subject. "You saw he was arrested last night on a charge of murdering the woman whose body was found in the cask? You know about it?"

"I read the account in this morning's paper. And so Felix was a neighbour of yours?"

"Yes, and a close friend. He was in and out of the house like one of the family."

"Indeed? I am sorry to hear that."

"Yes. I thought a good deal of him and I'm naturally upset. We all are, as a matter of fact. I wanted your advice as to what could be done for him."

"You mean with regard to his defence?"

"Yes."

"Have you seen him since his arrest?"

"No. That's one of the things I wanted to ask you about. I am not quite sure how you get an order."

"That can be obtained where a sufficient reason for its application can be shown. I understand, then, that you are unaware of his own plans for his defence?"

"Yes. My idea was to see him and talk the thing over, and, unless he has made some other arrangement, to ask you to undertake it."

The lawyer nodded slowly. Martin's suggestion was eminently satisfactory to him. Apart from the mere money involved, this case, from its unusual and dramatic nature, promised to be at least one of the most famous of the year. He decided that if it came his way he would attend to it personally, and see that no stone was left unturned to secure an acquittal.

"If you put the case in our hands," he replied at length, "quite apart from our personal friendship, you may depend on our doing our utmost for your friend. But I am afraid it will be an expensive business. We shall have to retain counsel, perhaps two or even three men, and their fees are not negligible. Then, as you can imagine "—Mr. Clifford gave a wintry little smile—" we also have to live, or at all events we think so. There will unquestionably be expense in hunting up witnesses, a private detective may have to be employed, in short, the defence of a big case means heavy outlay. Now, can your friend meet this? What are his circumstances financially?"

"I think he is all right," answered Martin, "but, in any case, the money will be my affair. Felix may pay what he can. I shall be responsible for the rest."

Clifford looked at the speaker keenly.

"Very handsome of you, Martin, I'm sure." He hesitated a

moment as if about to continue the subject, then, with a change of manner, he went on :—

"I think, in that case, you should see Felix and ascertain his plans. If you can spare the time now, I shall go with you to Bow Street and try and procure for you an immediate visiting order. If, after your conversation, you find you require our assistance, we shall be very pleased to take up the case; if not, you are perfectly free to go elsewhere. Is that agreed?"

"Thank you, Clifford. That's all right. Nothing could be better."

After introducing his prospective client to the authorities at the famous police station, the lawyer excused himself on the ground of another engagement, while Martin sat down to await the order. The formalities as is usual took some time, and it was not till nearly half-past five that the door of Felix's cell opened to admit his friend.

"Martin!" cried the unhappy inmate, springing up and seizing his visitor's hand in both his own. "But this is good of you! I hardly dared to expect you."

"Couldn't see a pal in a hole without butting in," answered the doctor gruffly, somewhat affected by the warmth of the other's welcome. "You're a nice one, getting yourself into such a mess, eh? What have you been up to that's raised this dust?"

Felix passed his hand wearily over his forehead.

"My God, Martin," he groaned, "I don't know. I'm absolutely at sea. I know no more about the wretched business than you do. The proceedings today were purely formal, so that the evidence against me—whatever it can be—did not come out. I can't conceive or even guess what they have got hold of, that has made them suspect me."

"I've heard nothing about the case at all. I just came along to see you when I saw what had happened."

"Martin, I can never thank you! I can never repay you! I thought of writing to you today to ask your help, and I should probably have done it tomorrow. But you can't think what it means to me, your coming without being asked. It means, for one thing, that you don't believe this abominable charge? Doesn't it?"

"Well, naturally. You keep your heart up and don't get flustered. You've got some friends left still. All the family are upset about the thing. The mater's shocked, and so are the boys. They all say for you to cheer up, and that the mistake is sure to be put right soon."

"God bless them for that," cried Felix, rising and pacing the cell in evident emotion. "Tell them—how much I appreciate—what all their thought means to me."

"Rot!" said the doctor shortly. "What would you expect? But now, I have only a minute or two here, and what I want to ask you is this, what plans have you made for your defence?"

"Defence? None, I fear. I just haven't been able to think about it. I haven't an idea who to turn to, or what to do. What would you advise?"

"Clifford."

"Eh? What? I don't follow."

"Employ Clifford, of Clifford and Lewisham. He's a dry stick, but as clever as they're made, and a good sort. He's your man."

"I don't know him. Do you think he would take up the case?"

"Sure. Fact is, I went round to ask him how I could get an order to see you—I know him pretty well—and I pumped him. The firm would take it on if they were asked, but that means himself, and you couldn't have a better man."

"Martin, you put new life into me! God bless you for all you're doing! Will you arrange it with him? But, wait a minute, can I afford it? Are his fees very high?"

"What can you afford?"

"Oh, I don't know. Say a thousand pounds."

"More than enough. I shall arrange it with him at once."

The friends conversed for some minutes, and then a warder opened the door of the cell. Martin's time was up. He left Felix cheered by the promise of a further visit, and with tears of thankfulness glistening in his eyes.

Determined to lose no time in completing his work, Martin returned direct to the offices of Messrs. Clifford and Lewisham. But there the day's work was over, and all but one or two junior clerks had already left. The doctor therefore made an appointment for the next day and, with a glow of righteous self-satisfaction, went home to tell his family what he had done.

On the following afternoon he again found himself in the solicitor's office.

"Now," said Mr. Clifford, when it had been definitely agreed that his firm was to take up the case, "I have to warn you that proceedings will be slow. First, the prosecution will make up their case—get depositions of the evidence, you know, and so on—and that will take time. We, of course, shall also immediately start work, but it is improbable we shall make much headway till we learn the full evidence against us. Additional time will therefore be required for the preparation of the defence. If Felix is returned for trial—and I fear from what I have heard, he will be—weeks and months will probably elapse before both sides are ready. You and I shall therefore require to exercise patience."

"I can believe it," muttered the doctor. "You lawyers take the devil of a time over everything."

"We can't cover our mistakes like you, so we have to be careful," retorted the lawyer with his dry, wintry smile.

Martin smote his thigh.

"Ha! ha," he laughed. "That's good. You had me there. But I mustn't be wasting your time. There were some things you wanted to speak to me about?"

"Yes," admitted Clifford, "a couple of points. Firstly, I propose to retain Heppenstall—you know, Lucius Heppenstall, the K.C. He may want one or two juniors. I suppose that is all right?"

"Of course. You know what is best to be done."

"The other point is that I want you to tell me everything you possibly can about Felix."

"As a matter of fact," returned Martin, "I can't tell you very much. I was just thinking over what I knew of him, and I was amazed it was so little. We became acquainted about four years ago. Felix had just taken St. Malo, an empty house a couple of hundred yards from my own, and the first thing he did was to go and get pneumonia. I was called in, but the attack was bad, and for a time it was touch and go with him. However, he pulled through, and, during his convalescence, we became very good friends. When he came out of the hospital I invited him to my house for a week or two—he had only a not very satisfactory house-keeper at St. Malo—and the family took to him, till he became quite like one of ourselves. Since then he has been in and out like a pet dog. He dines quite often, and, in return, insists on taking the boys to the theatre, and the mater when she'll go."

"He lives quite alone, you say?"

"Quite, except for the housekeeper."

"And you haven't met any of his people?"

"None. I've never even heard of his people. I don't think he has any. If he has, he never speaks of them." Martin hesitated for a moment, then went on: "It may be my fancy, but it has struck me that he seems to avoid women, and the only cynical remarks I have heard him make have been at their expense. I have often wondered if he has had some love disappointment. But he has never hinted at such a thing."

"How does he live?"

"He is an artist. He designs for some poster firm in the city, and he draws for the better-class magazines. I do not know if he has private means, but he seems to do well enough."

"Do you know anything about this extraordinary business of the cask?"

"No, except this. On—let me see, what night was it? Monday, I think—yes, Monday, the 5th of April, a couple of friends turned in, and we wanted a rubber of bridge. I went round to St. Malo to see if Felix would make a fourth. That was about 8.30 o'clock. At first he hesitated, but afterwards he agreed to come. I went in and waited while he changed. The study fire had just been freshly lighted and the room, and indeed the whole house, was cold and cheerless. We played bridge till nearly one. The next thing we heard was that he was in St. Thomas's Hospital, prostrated from a mental shock. Not professionally, but as a friend, I went to see him, and then he told me about the cask."

"And what did he tell you?"

"He said he had had a letter saying a cask of money was being sent him—he will tell you the details himself—and that he had just got this cask from the steamer and brought it to St. Malo when I called on that Monday evening. The reason he hesitated about leaving home was that he was on tenterhooks to unpack the cask."

"Why did he not tell you about it?"

"I asked him that, and he said he had had trouble with the steamer people about getting it away, and he did not want any one to know where the cask was, lest it should get round to these steamer folk. But I would rather he would tell you about that himself."

"I shall ask him, but I want to hear from you anything you know personally about it."

"Well, there is nothing more than that."

"Can you tell me anything of his friends?"

"Nothing. I think only twice in all the years I have known him have I met acquaintances of his, in each case artists who were looking at the paintings in his studio, and who I know did not stay the night. Whom he met during the day I can't tell."

The lawyer sat silent for some minutes.

"Well," he said at length, "I think that is all we can do today. I'll let you know how things go on, but, as I warned you before, the business will be slow."

With a hearty handshake and a word of thanks the doctor took his leave, while Clifford sat down to write to Heppenstall, K.C., to know if he would take up the case.

CHAPTER XXII

FELIX TELLS A SECOND STORY

THE next day Mr. Clifford was occupied with various technical formalities, and in obtaining from the authorities such information as was then available about the case, and it was not till the following morning he set out to make the acquaintance of his client. He found him seated in his cell, his head on his hands, and an expression of deep gloom upon his face. The two men talked generalities for some time, and then the lawyer came to business.

"Now, Mr. Felix," he said, "I want you please to tell me everything you know of this unhappy affair—everything, no matter how seemingly minute or unimportant. Remember—I cannot impress it on you too strongly—for a man in your position it is suicidal to withhold information. Keep nothing back. Your confidence will be as safe as the confessional. If you have made mistakes, done foolish things, or criminal things, or even—forgive me—if you have committed the crime you are charged with, tell me the whole truth. Else I shall be a blind man leading the blind, and we shall both have our fall."

"I will do so, Mr. Clifford. I will keep nothing back. And first, before we go on to the details, one point must be settled." He raised his hand. "I swear to you, in the presence of Almighty God, in whom I believe, that I am innocent of this crime." He sat down and then continued : "I don't ask you if you believe me; I am willing to leave that till afterwards, but I want now, at the commencement of our intercourse, to put that fact as it were on record. I absolutely and categorically deny all knowledge of this hateful and ghastly crime. Now let us get on."

"I am glad you have made this statement and in this way, Mr. Felix," said the lawyer, who was impressed by his client's manner and earnestness. "Now, please, begin at the beginning and tell me with all the detail you can, what you know of the matter."

Felix had the gift of narration, and he held the lawyer enthralled as he related the strange story of his experiences.

"I hardly know where to begin," he said. "The first thing directly bearing on the affair was a meeting between myself and some friends at the Café Toisson d'Or in Paris, but before I come to that I think I ought to explain just who I am and how I, a Frenchman, come to be living in London. I think this is necessary, as the question of my previous knowledge of poor Annette Boirac is certain to come up. What do you say, Mr. Clifford?"

"Necessary to tell this?" thought the lawyer, to whom the fact that Felix had had knowledge of the dead woman came as an ugly discovery. "Why, my good fellow, no other point in the whole case is likely to be more important for you." But aloud he only said:—

"Yes, I consider it most necessary."

"Very good, then. As I said, I am a Frenchman, and I was born in Avignon in 1884. I was always keen on drawing, and, as my teachers thought there was promise in my work, I early moved to Paris and entered the *atelier* of M. Dauphin. I studied there for several years, living in a small hotel off the Boule Miche. My parents were both dead, and I had inherited a little money—not much, but enough to live on.

"Amongst those working at the art school was a young fellow called Pierre Bonchose. He was some four years my junior, and was an attractive and thoroughly decent chap. We became close friends, eventually sharing the same room. But he was not much good at his work. He lacked perseverance, and was too fond of supper parties and cards to settle down seriously to paint. I was not, therefore, surprised when one day he told me he was fed up with art, and was going into business. It seemed he had applied to an old friend of his father's, the senior partner of Messrs. Rôget, the wine exporters of Narbonne, and had been offered a position in that firm, which he had decided to accept.

"But a month or two before he left Paris he had introduced to the *atelier* a new pupil, his cousin, Mlle. Annette Humbert. They seemed more like brother and sister than cousins, and Bonchose told me that they had been brought up together, and had always been what you English call 'pals.' This, Mr. Clifford, was none other than the unfortunate young lady who afterwards became Mme. Boirac.

"She was one of the loveliest girls that ever breathed. From the first moment I saw her I admired her as I had never before admired any one. As fate would have it we were both making certain pastel studies and, being thus thrown together, we became interested in each other's work. The inevitable happened, and I fell deeply in love with her. She did not discourage me, but, as she was kind and gracious to everyone, I hardly dared to hope she could care for me. At last, to make a long story short, I took my courage in both hands and proposed, and I could hardly believe my good fortune when she accepted me.

"It then became necessary for me to approach her father. M. Humbert came of an old and distinguished family, endowed with much pride of birth. He was well off, though not rich, and lived almost in state in his old château at Laroche, occupying a leading position in the local society. To broach such a subject to him would have been an ordeal for any one, but for me, who lacked so many of the social advantages he possessed, it was a veritable nightmare. And my forebodings were not disappointed. He received me courteously, but scouted my proposal. Mlle. Humbert was too young, she did not yet know the world nor her own mind, he had other plans for her future, and so on. Also, he delicately indicated that my social standing and means hardly fitted me to enter a family of such age and traditions as his own.

"I need not try to describe the effect this decision had upon both of us, suffice it to say that Annette, after a stormy scene, submitted to her father's authority, leaving the art school and going for an indefinite visit to an aunt in the southern provinces. I, finding life without her insupportable in my old haunts, also left Paris, and, coming to London, obtained a position as artist with Messrs. Greer and Hood, the advertisement poster printers of Fleet Street. What with their salary and my spare time drawings for *Punch* and other papers, I soon found myself in receipt of over a thousand a year, and then realized one of my ambitions and moved to a small villa in the suburbs, buying at the same time a two-seater to take me to and from my work. This villa, St. Malo, was situated near Brent, on the Great North Road. Here I settled down, alone except for an elderly housekeeper. I fitted up a large attic as a studio where I began studies for a picture I had in mind.

"But before I had been a month in my new home, I developed a nasty attack of pneumonia. Martin, who was the nearest doctor, was called in, and so began the friendship from which your presence here today has resulted.

"I lived a somewhat humdrum existence for some two years, and then one morning I had a pleasant surprise in the shape of a visit from my old friend, Pierre Bonchose. He explained that, having done pretty well in business, he had been sent to represent permanently his firm in London. He also told me that after a year of what he called 'sulking,' his cousin Annette had, at her father's desire, married a M. Boirac, a wealthy manufacturer, that he had seen her coming through Paris, and that she appeared to be quite happy.

"Bonchose and I resumed our former intimacy, and, during the next summer, that is, two years ago, we had a walking tour through Cornwall. I mention this because of an incident which occurred near Penzance, and which profoundly modified our relations. While bathing in a deserted cove of that rocky coast, I was caught in an off-shore current and, in spite of all my efforts, found myself being carried out to sea. Bonchose, hearing my shouts, swam out after me and at the imminent risk of his own life assisted me back into still water. Though he made light of the matter, I could not forget the danger he had faced to save me, and I felt I had incurred a debt which I should be glad of an opportunity to pay.

"But though, as I have said, I had settled down in London, I did not by any means entirely desert Paris. First at long intervals, but afterwards more frequently, I ran over to see my friends and to keep myself in touch with artistic circles in France. About eight months ago, on one of these visits, it happened that I dropped into an exhibition of the work of a famous sculptor, and there I incidentally came across a man whose conversation interested me extremely. His hobby was statuary, and he was clearly an expert in his subject. He told me he had amassed one of the largest private collections in the world, and as we became more intimate he invited me to dine that evening and see it. I went, and on arrival he introduced me to his wife. You can imagine my feelings, Mr. Clifford, when I found she was none other than Annette. Acting on the impulse of the moment, we met as strangers, though I am sure that, had M. Boirac not been so full of his collection, he must have noticed our embarrassment. But as we sat at dinner I found that, after the first shock of recognition, her presence left me cold. Though I still profoundly admired her, my infatuation had passed away, and I realized that whatever love I might have had for her was dead. And from her manner I felt sure her feelings towards myself had undergone a similar change.

"M. Boirac and I became good friends over his collection, and, on his invitation, I several times repeated my call during subsequent visits to Paris.

"That, Mr. Clifford, is all of what I may call my preliminary history. I am afraid it is rather involved, but I have tried to make it as clear as I could."

The lawyer bowed gravely.

"Your statement is perfectly clear. Pray proceed."

"I come now," went on Felix, "to the events connected with the cask and therefore apparently with the tragedy. I think it will be better to tell you these in their chronological order, even though this makes my story seem a little disconnected?"

Again Mr. Clifford inclined his head and the other resumed :—

"On Saturday, 13th March, I crossed to Paris for the weekend, returning the following Monday morning. On the Sunday afternoon I happened to drop into the Café Toisson d'Or in the rue Royale and there found a group of men, with most of whom I was acquainted. They were talking about the French Government lotteries, and in the course of conversation one of them, a M. Alphonse Le Gautier, said to me, 'Why not have a little flutter with me?' I ridiculed the idea at first, but afterwards agreed to enter a thousand francs jointly with him. He undertook to arrange the matter, the profits, if any, being halved between us. I paid him over my five hundred francs and, believing it was the last I should hear of the affair, dismissed it from my mind.

"A week after my return to England I had a visit from Bonchose. I saw at once he was in trouble and after a while it all came out. It seemed he had been losing heavily at cards, and to meet his liabilities he had gone to moneylenders, who were now pressing him for repayment. In answer to my questions, he explained that he had paid off all his loans with the exception of one for £600. That sum he was utterly unable to raise, and if he failed to procure it before the 31st, that was, in about a week, he was a ruined man. I was much annoyed, for I had helped him out of similar scrapes twice before, on each of which occasions he had given me his word not to play again. I felt I could not go on throwing good money after bad, and yet because of our friendship and the debt I owed him for saving my life, I could not see him go to the wall. Divining what was in my mind, he assured me he had not come to beg, saying that he realized I had already done more for him than he deserved. Then he said he had written to Annette telling her the circumstances, and asking, not for a gift, but for a loan on which he would pay four per cent interest. I talked to him seriously, offering no help, but asking him to keep me advised of how things went on. But though I did not tell him, I decided I would pay the £600 rather than see him stuck.

"'I am going to Paris on Friday,' I ended up, 'and hope to dine at the Boirac's on Saturday. If Annette speaks to me on the subject, I shall tell her you are making an unholy mess of things.'

"'Don't put her against helping me,' he pleaded. I said I would not influence her at all, and then he asked me when I was returning, so that he could meet me and hear what had been said. I told him I would cross by Boulogne on Sunday.

"That weekend, a fortnight after the meeting in the Café Toisson d'Or, I was again in the French capital. On the Saturday

morning as I sat in the Hotel Continental meditating a visit to
M. Dauphin's *atelier,* a note was handed to me. It was from
Annette, and in it she said she wanted to speak to me in private,
asking if I could come at 7.30 that night, instead of the dinner
hour of 7.45, and requiring a verbal reply. I gave the necessary
assurance to the messenger, who proved to be Annette's maid,
Suzanne.

"I reached the Boirac's house at the appointed hour, but I did
not see Annette. As I entered, M. Boirac was passing through
the hall, and, seeing me, he invited me into his study to look at an
engraving which had been sent him on approval. Naturally, I
could not refuse. We went to the study and examined the picture.
But there was another object in the study which I also saw and
commented on. Standing on the carpet was a large cask, and, Mr.
Clifford, you will hardly believe me when I tell you it was either
the identical cask which was sent me containing poor Annette's
body, or else one so similar as to be indistinguishable!"

Felix paused to let this significant statement, as he evidently
considered it, sink into the lawyer's mind. But the latter only
bowed and said : —

"Pray proceed, Mr. Felix, with your statement."

"I was interested in the cask, as it seemed an unusual object
to find in a study. I asked Boirac about it, and he explained that
he had just purchased a piece of statuary, and that the cask was
simply the special kind of packing case in which it had been sent
home."

"Did he describe the statue?" asked the lawyer, interrupting
for the first time.

"No, except to say it was a fine group. He promised to show it
to me on my next visit."

"Did he tell you from whom he had purchased it, or what price
he had paid?"

"Neither; the matter was only referred to incidentally as we
were leaving the room."

"Thank you. Pray continue."

"We then went to the salon, but, as several visitors had already
arrived, I could not, at that time, get a private word with Annette.

"The dinner was an important social affair, the Spanish
Ambassador being the principal guest. Before it was over M. Boirac
was called from the house, owing to an accident having taken place
at his works. He apologized for leaving, promising to return
speedily, but after a time a telephone message came to say the
accident had been more serious than he had supposed, and he would

be detained till very late or even all night. The guests began to leave about eleven, but, in obedience to a sign from Annette, I remained till all had gone. Then she told me she had received a letter from Bonchose which had much upset her. She did not mind his having got into difficulties—indeed, she thought a fright would do him good; but she was really troubled lest he might become a confirmed gambler. She wished for my candid opinion of him.

"I told her exactly what I thought; that there wasn't a bit of real harm in him, but that he had got into a bad set and that his only chance was to break with it. She agreed with me, saying he should not be helped until this breach had actually been made. We then discussed where the money was to come from. She, it appeared, could lay her hands on only £300, and, as she felt M. Boirac would disapprove, she did not wish to ask him for the remainder. She therefore proposed to sell a couple of her jewels— her own private property—and she asked me to undertake the matter for her. But I could not bring myself to agree to this, and I said that if she would advance the £300 she had, I would find the balance. At first she would not hear of it, and we had quite a heated argument. Finally I carried my point, and she went upstairs and brought down the money. I took my leave immediately afterwards, promising to let her know how the matter ended. She was much affected, for she was sincerely attached to him. The next day, Sunday, I returned to London."

"I think you said, Mr. Felix," interrupted Clifford, "that the last of the guests left at eleven?"

"Yes, about then."

"And at what time did you yourself leave?"

"About quarter to twelve."

"Then your conversation lasted about three-quarters of an hour. Now, did anyone see you leave?"

"No one except Annette. She came to the door with me."

"You returned to your hotel, I suppose?"

"Yes."

"At what hour did you reach it?"

"About half-past one, I should say."

"From madame's house to the Hotel Continental is about fifteen minutes' walk. What, then did you do in the interval?"

"I felt wakeful, and thought a stroll would be pleasant. I walked across Paris; to the Place de la Bastille by the Rue de Rivoli, and back to the hotel by the Grands Boulevards."

"Did you meet any one you knew?"

"No, not that I can recall."

"I am afraid this is important, Mr. Felix. Think again. Is there no one that could testify to meeting you on this walk? No waiter or other official, for example?"

"No," said Felix, after a pause, "I don't think I spoke to a soul, and I certainly did not enter a café."

"You say you returned to London next day. Did you meet anyone on the journey you knew?"

"Yes, but it will be no help to me. I met Miss Gladys Devine on the Folkestone boat. But she cannot confirm this. As you must know, she died suddenly a week later."

"Miss Gladys Devine? Not the celebrated Miss Devine, the actress?"

"The same. I have met her at supper parties in Paris."

"But you must be able to get confirmation of that? So well known a lady would be recognized wherever she went. But perhaps you visited her private cabin?"

"No, I saw her on the boat deck. She was sitting in the shelter of one of the funnels. I joined her for about half an hour."

"But somebody must have seen you?"

"Possibly, but possibly not. You see, it was horribly rough. Almost everyone was sick. People, anyway, weren't walking about."

"What about her maids?"

"I did not see them."

"Now, Mr. Felix, what you must think over when I leave you is, first, what evidence can we get confirming your statement of how you spent your time between 11.0 and 1.30 on the Saturday night? and second, who saw you with Miss Devine on the Folkestone boat? In the meantime, please continue your statement."

"Bonchose met me at Charing Cross. He was keen to know how I had fared. We drove to his rooms, where I told him the whole thing. I said I would hand him the £600 on condition he broke finally with his gambling friends. He assured me the breach had already been effected, and I therefore gave him the money. We then drove to the Savoy and, after a rather early dinner, I left him and went home."

"At what hour?"

"About 8.30."

"How did you go?"

"I took a taxi."

"From where?"

"The Savoy commissionaire called it."

"Yes?"

"The next thing was I received an astonishing letter," and Felix went on to tell the lawyer about the typewritten letter signed "Le Gautier," his preparations to obtain the cask, his visit to St. Katharine Docks, his interviews with the clerk, Broughton, and the manager of the dock office, his ruse to get the I. and C.'s note-paper, the forging of the letter to Harkness, the removal of the cask to St. Malo, his dining at Dr. Martin's, the midnight interview with Burnley, the disappearance of the cask, its final recovery, its unpacking, and the discovery of its terrible contents. "That, Mr. Clifford," he ended up, "is every single thing I know about the affair, good, bad, or indifferent."

"I congratulate you on the clear way you have made your statement," returned the solicitor. "Now, excuse me while I think if there is anything further I want to ask you."

He slowly turned over the rather voluminous notes he had taken.

"The first point," he went on at length, "is the question of your intimacy with Madame Boirac. Can you tell me how many times you saw her since her marriage?"

Felix considered.

"About half a dozen, I should say, or perhaps eight or even nine. Not more than nine certainly."

"Excepting on the night of the dinner, was her husband present on all these occasions?"

"Not all. At least twice I called in the afternoon and saw her alone."

"I think I need hardly ask you, but answer me fully all the same. Were there at any time any tender or confidential passages between you and madame?"

"Absolutely none. I state most positively that nothing passed between us which Boirac might not have seen or heard."

Again Clifford paused in thought.

"I want you now to tell me, and with the utmost detail, exactly how you spent the time between your leaving Bonchose after dinner on the Sunday night of your return from Paris, and your meeting the cask at St. Katharine Docks on the following Monday week."

"I can do so easily. After leaving Bonchose I drove out to St. Malo, as I told you, arriving about 9.30. My housekeeper was on holidays, so I went straight over to Brent village and arranged with a charwoman to come in the mornings and make my breakfast. This woman had acted in a similar capacity before. I myself was taking a week's holidays, and each day I passed in the same manner. I got up about half-past seven, had breakfast, and went to my studio to paint. The charwoman went home after breakfast, and I got my own lunch. Then I painted again in the afternoon, and in the evening went into town for dinner and usually, but not always, a theatre. I generally got back between eleven and twelve. On Saturday, instead of painting all day, I went into town and arranged about meeting the cask."

"Then at ten o'clock on Wednesday you were painting in your studio?"

"That is so, but why that day and hour?"

"I will tell you later. Now, can you prove that? Did anyone call in the studio, or see you there?"

"No one, I'm afraid."

"What about the charwoman? What is her name, by the way?"

"Mrs. Bridget Murphy. No, I don't think she could tell where I was. You see, I practically did not see her at all. My breakfast was ready when I came down, and when I had finished I went direct to the studio. I don't know when she went home, but I should think it was fairly early."

"What time did you breakfast?"

"Eight nominally, but I wasn't always very punctual."

"Do you remember, and have you any way of proving what time you had breakfast on this particular Wednesday?"

Felix thought over the question.

"No," he answered, "I don't think so. There was nothing to distinguish that morning from the others."

"The point is important. Perhaps Mrs. Murphy would remember?"

"Possibly, but I hardly think so."

"No one else could prove it? Were there no callers? No tradesmen's messengers?"

"None. One or two people rang, but I didn't bother. I was expecting no one, and I just let them ring."

"An unfortunate omission. Now, tell me, where did you dine in town and spend the evenings?"

"I'm afraid a different restaurant each night, and naturally a different theatre."

By dint of further questions Clifford obtained a list of all the places his client had visited during the week, his intention being to go round them in turn in search of material to build up an alibi. He was very disappointed with all he had heard, and the difficulties of his task seemed to be growing. He continued his examination.

"Now, this typewritten letter, signed 'Le Gautier'. Did you believe it was genuine?"

"I did. I thought the whole thing absurd and annoying, but

I did not doubt it. You see, I had actually entered for the lottery with Le Gautier, and fifty thousand francs was the sum we would have made had we been lucky. I did think at first it was a practical joke on Le Gautier's part, but he is not that kind of man, and I at last concluded it was genuine."

" Did you write or wire to Le Gautier?"

" No. I got the letter late one evening on my return home. It was too late to do anything then, but I intended to wire next morning that I would go over, and not to send the cask. But next morning's post brought a card, also typewritten, and signed 'Le Gautier,' saying the cask had actually been dispatched. I forgot to mention that in my statement."

Clifford nodded and again referred to his notes.

" Did you write a letter to Messrs. Dupierre of Paris, ordering a statue to be sent to you, to the West Jubb Street address?"

" No."

" Do you recollect the blotter on your study desk at St. Malo?"

" Why, yes," returned Felix, with a look of surprise.

" Did you ever let that blotter out of your possession?"

" Not to my knowledge."

" Did you ever take it to France?"

" Never."

" Then how, Mr. Felix," asked the lawyer slowly, " how do you account for the fact that the blotted impression of such a letter, in your handwriting, was found on the blotter?"

Felix sprang to his feet.

" What?" he cried. " What's that you say? A letter in my handwriting? I don't believe it! It's impossible!"

" I have seen it."

" You have seen it?" The speaker moved excitedly about the cell, gesticulating freely. " Really, Mr. Clifford, this is too much. I tell you I wrote no such letter. You are making a mistake."

" I assure you, Mr. Felix, I am making no mistake. I saw not only the impression on your pad, but also the original letter itself, which had been received by Messrs. Dupierre."

Felix sat down and passed his hand across his brow, as if dazed.

" I cannot understand it. You can't have seen a letter from me, because no such exists. What you saw must have been a forgery."

" But the impression on the blotter?"

" Good Heavens, how do I know? I tell you I know nothing about it. See here," he added, with a change of tone, " there's some trick in it. When you say you've seen these things I'm bound to believe you. But there's a trick. There must be."

"Then," said Clifford, "if so, and I'm inclined to agree with you, who carried out the trick? Some one must have had access to your study, either to write the letter there, or to abstract your blotter or a page of it which could afterwards be replaced. Who could that have been?"

"I don't know. Nobody—or anybody. I can think of no one who would do such a thing. When was the letter written?"

"It was received by Dupierre on Tuesday morning, 30th March. It bore a London postmark, therefore it must have been posted on Sunday night or Monday. That would be either the day or the day after you returned to London, after the dinner."

"Anyone could have got into the house while I was away. If what you say is true, some one must have, but I saw no traces."

"Now, Mr. Felix, who is Emmie?"

Felix stared.

"Emmie?" he said. "I don't understand. Emmie what?"

Clifford watched the other keenly as he replied,—

"Your heartbroken Emmie."

"My dear Mr. Clifford, I haven't the slightest idea what you're talking about. 'Your heartbroken Emmie?' What under the sun do you mean?"

"It should be clear enough, Mr. Felix. Who was the girl that wrote to you recently imploring you not to desert her, and who signed herself, 'Your heartbroken Emmie'?"

Felix gazed at his visitor in amazement.

"Either you're mad or I'm mad," he said slowly. "I have had no letter from any girl asking me not to desert her, and I have had no letter on any subject from anyone signing herself Emmie. Really, I think you might explain yourself."

"Now tell me something else, Mr. Felix. You possess, I understand, two navy-blue suits?"

The astonishment on the artist's face did not lessen as he assented.

"I want to know now when you last wore each of those suits."

"As it happens, I can tell you. One of them I wore on my Paris trip and again on the following Saturday when I went to town to arrange about the cask, as well as on the Monday and following days till I went to hospital. I am wearing it today. The other blue suit is an old one, and I have not had it on for months."

"I'll tell you now why I ask. In the coat pocket of one of your blue suits, evidently, from what you tell me, the old one, was found a letter beginning, 'My dearest Léon,' and ending 'Your heartbroken Emmie,' and in it the writer said—but here, I have a copy of it, and you may read it."

The artist looked over the paper as if in a dream. Then he turned to the other.

"I can assure you, Mr. Clifford," he said earnestly, "that I am as much in the dark as you about this. It is not my letter. I never saw it before. I never heard of Emmie. The whole thing is an invention. How it got into my pocket I cannot explain, but I tell you positively I am absolutely ignorant of the whole thing."

Clifford nodded.

"Very good. Now there is only one other thing I want to ask you. Do you know the round-backed, leather-covered arm-chair which stood before the plush curtain in your study?"

"Yes."

"Think carefully, and tell me who was the last lady to occupy it."

"That doesn't require much thought. No lady has ever sat in it since I bought it. Very few ladies have been in St. Malo since I took it, and these without exception were interested in art and were in the studio only."

"Now, don't be annoyed, Mr. Felix, when I ask you once more, did Madame Boirac ever sit in that chair?"

"I give you my solemn word of honour she never did. She was never in the house, and I believe I am right in saying she was never in London."

The lawyer nodded.

"Now I have another unpleasant thing to tell you. Caught in the hem of that curtain and hidden by the chair, a pin was found—a diamond safety pin. That pin, Mr. Felix, was attached to the shoulder of Madame Boirac's dress on the night of the dinner party."

Felix, unable to speak, sat staring helplessly at the lawyer. His face had gone white, and an expression of horror dawned in his eyes. There was silence in the dull, cheerless cell, whose walls had heard so many tales of misery and suffering. Clifford, watching his client keenly, felt the doubts which had been partly lulled to rest, again rising. Was the man acting? If so, he was doing it extraordinarily well, but. . . . At last Felix moved.

"My God!" he whispered hoarsely. "It's a nightmare! I feel helpless. I am in a net, and it is drawing close round me. What does it mean, Mr. Clifford? Who has done this thing? I didn't know anyone hated me, but some one must." He made a gesture of despair. "I'm done for. What can help me after that? Can you see any hope, Mr. Clifford? Tell me."

But whatever doubts the lawyer felt he kept to himself.

"It is too soon to come to any conclusion," he answered in a matter-of-fact tone. "In cases of difficulty such as this, I have frequently known some small fact to come out, perhaps accidentally, which has cleared up the whole affair. You must not despair. We are only at the beginning. Wait for a week or two, and then I'll tell you what I think."

"Bless you, Mr. Clifford. You put heart into me. But this matter of the pin. What can it mean? There is some terrible conspiracy against me. Can it ever be unravelled?"

The lawyer rose.

"That's what we have to try and do, Mr. Felix. I'm afraid I must be off now. Do as I say, keep up your heart, and if you can think of any evidence supporting your statements, let me know."

Having shaken hands, Mr. Clifford withdrew.

CHAPTER XXIII

CLIFFORD GETS TO WORK

WHEN Clifford had finished dinner that evening, he went to his study, and, drawing a large arm-chair up to the fire, for the evenings were still cold, he lit a cigar and composed himself to master the details of his new case. To say that he was disappointed with Felix's statement would not be to give a true indication of his state of mind. He was woefully chagrined. He had hoped and expected that his client would tell him something that would instantly indicate the line the defence should take, and instead of that he was puzzled to know where any defence at all was to come from.

And the more he thought over it, the worse the outlook seemed. He went over the facts in order, marshalling them in his mind and weighing the bearing of each on the question of Felix's innocence or guilt.

There was first of all the fundamental question of what had taken place in the house in the Avenue de l'Alma between 11.0 p.m. and 1.15 a.m. on the night of the dinner party. At 11.0 Annette Boirac was alive and well; at 1.15 she had disappeared. Felix was the last person, so far as was known, to see her alive, and it was not unreasonable to have expected him to have thrown some light on her fate. But he hadn't.

It was true he had explained the motive for his interview with madame. Confirmation of the truth of this, Clifford thought, should be obtainable from an investigation of the affairs of Bonchose. But even if it was established, he did not see how it would help his client. It would not prove him innocent. Indeed, it might be argued that this very discussion had been the indirect cause of the elopement, if such took place. It had given Felix an opportunity to see madame alone which otherwise he might not have had. And who could tell what dormant passions that private interview might not have aroused? No. There was no help here.

And the remainder of Felix's statement was equally unfruitful. He had said that after conversing with the lady till 11.45 p.m., he had walked about Paris till half-past one. But by a singular coincidence he had not been seen leaving the house, he had not met anyone he knew, and he had not been anywhere he was known. Was this, Clifford wondered, so singular a coincidence? Might it not simply mean that Felix's story was untrue?

Then he remembered the closing of the front door. François had heard it shut at 1.0 a.m. If Felix left at 11.45, who shut it? As far as he could see, either Felix must be lying when he said he left at 11.45, or else madame must have gone out by herself at the later hour. But the lawyer did not know which of these had happened, and unfortunately there seemed no way of finding out.

Equally useless for the defence was Felix's identification of the fur-coated lady on the Folkestone boat. Even had this been Miss Devine, it did not prove Madame Boirac was not a traveller. Might not Felix, travelling with madame, have seen the actress on board, her subsequent death suggesting his story? No, even if he could prove all that the artist had said about the crossing, it would not help matters.

But Felix's failure to find an alibi for himself was much more serious. Clifford had confidently expected a defence along these lines, and he was more than disappointed. He ran over the facts. The location of the man or men who had arranged the journeys of the cask was known at two periods; on the Wednesday at 10.0 a.m. at Waterloo, and on the Thursday at 5.15 p.m. at the Gare du Nord. Clifford got out his Continental Bradshaw. To have been in Paris at the time named, a Londoner must have left by the 9.0 a.m. from Charing Cross on Thursday, and he could not have arrived back before 5.35 on Friday morning. Therefore Felix had only to prove an alibi at 10.0 on Wednesday morning, or between 9.0 on Thursday morning and 5.35 on Friday morning, and the greatest part of the case against him would be met. But this was just what he could not do.

Clifford turned to his notes of the artist's statement. According to it, at 10.0 a.m. on Wednesday, Felix had been painting in his studio. But the chance of the housekeeper's absence and the peculiar arrangement under which the charwoman got breakfast prevented this being proved. And like an idiot, Felix had heard people ringing at the door, and, because he did not wish to be disturbed, had not opened it. One of those callers might have saved him now.

And then, with regard to Thursday and Thursday night. To have caught the 9.0 a.m. from Charing Cross, Felix must have left St. Malo at not later than 8.5. According to his statement, his breakfast was left ready for him at 8.0, and there certainly would not have been time for him to eat it. But there was nothing to prevent him having in two or three minutes dirtied the plates and carried away some food, to give the impression he had had his meal. Here there was hope of help from the charwoman. Clifford could not decide the point till he had interviewed her.

He turned back to his notes. After breakfast, Felix, according to his statement, had painted without ceasing, except for a cup of cocoa at lunch time, until half-past six. He had then changed and gone to town, dining alone at the Gresham. Though he had seen no one he knew at the famous restaurant, there was a chance that a waiter or commissionaire or other official might have recognized him. He had left about nine and, feeling tired, he had returned straight home. There, no one could know of his presence till 7.30 the next morning, when Mrs. Murphy would expect to hear him answer her knock.

But if he had been to Paris, meeting the cask at the Gare du Nord, he could have been home equally at 7.30 a.m. Therefore the evidence of his answering the knock would be immaterial. Certainly if Felix were telling the truth, the manner in which confirmation was eluding him was most unfortunate. But was Felix telling the truth? . . .

Then there were those three discoveries of Burnley at St. Malo, the "Emmie" letter, the impression on the blotsheet, and the pin. Any one of these alone would have been highly damaging to Felix's case; the three together seemed overwhelming. And yet Felix had not attempted a word of explanation. He had simply denied knowledge of all three. If the accused man could not explain these damaging facts, how was Clifford to set about it?

But nothing in the whole affair depressed the lawyer so much as the admissions Felix had made about his previous relations with Madame Boirac. It was, of course, true that Felix, a stranger introduced into the Boirac household, might have fallen in love with madame and persuaded her to elope with him. But if Felix, instead of being a stranger, could be shown to have been not only desperately in love with, but actually formerly engaged to the mistress of the house, how tremendously the probabilities of such an elopement would be strengthened. What a picture a clever counsel could draw of this lady, tied to a man whom perhaps she detested, and with whom life in such case must have been an endless misery, brought unexpectedly in touch with the man of her real choice. . . . And her lover, his crushed-down feelings swelling up at the unlooked-for meeting, seeing her languishing in this bondage. . . . Why, the elopement would be amply accounted for. To Clifford it seemed that if the Crown got hold of the facts he had learnt, Felix was a doomed man. Indeed, the more he himself thought of the affair, the more doubtful of the artist's innocence he became. As far as he could see, Felix had only one uncontrovertible point in his favour—his surprise on seeing the cask opened. And this would prove a matter of medical testimony, and no doubt there would be contradictory evidence. . . . The lawyer could see very little light even here.

And then he reminded himself it was not his business to try Felix. Innocent or guilty, he, Clifford, was there to do the best he could for him. But what form was that best to take?

Till the morrow had dawned he sat smoking in his chair, turning the case over in his mind, looking at the problem from every point of view, still without much result. But though he could not yet see the line his defence should follow, he was clear enough about his immediate next step. Obviously he must first see Bonchose, Mrs. Murphy, and the other persons of whom Felix had spoken, not only to test the latter's story, but also in the hope of learning some new facts.

Accordingly, next morning saw the lawyer ascending the steps of the house in Kensington in which the apartments of Mr. Pierre Bonchose were situated. But here he met with a disappointment. Mr. Bonchose had gone to the south of France on business and would not be home for three or four days.

"That explains why he has made no attempt to see Felix since his arrest," said the lawyer to himself, as he turned away and hailed a taxi with the idea of a call on the charwoman.

An hour later he reached the small village of Brent, on the Great North Road, and was directed to Mrs. Murphy's cottage. The door was opened by a woman who had been tall, but was now shrunken, her sharp, careworn features and grey hair indicating that her life had been a struggle against odds.

"Good morning," began the lawyer, courteously raising his hat. "You are Mrs. Murphy?"

"I am, sir," returned the woman, "and would you come in?"

"Thank you." He followed her into the small, poorly-furnished living-room, and sat cautiously down on the somewhat dilapidated chair she pulled forward.

"You know, I suppose," he went on, "that your neighbour, Mr. Felix of St. Malo, has been arrested on a very serious charge?"

"'Deed then, I do, sir. And sorry I was to hear of it. A fine, decent man he was too."

"Well, Mrs. Murphy, my name is Clifford, and I am the lawyer who is going to defend Mr. Felix. I wondered if you would be good enough to answer some questions, to help me in his defence?"

"I would, sir, be glad to do it."

"You managed the house for him recently, while his housekeeper was away?"

"I did, sir."

"And when did Mr. Felix ask you to do that?"

"On Sunday evening, sir. I was just thinking of going to bed when he came to the door."

"Now tell me, please, exactly what you did each day at St. Malo."

"I went in the mornings, sir, and lit the fire and got his breakfast. Then I did out his room and washed up and left his lunch ready. He got his own lunch himself in the middle of the day, and went into London for dinner at night."

"I see. At what hour did you reach the house in the mornings?"

"About seven o'clock. I called him at half-past seven and he had his breakfast at eight."

"And about what hour did you leave?"

"I could hardly be sure, sir. About half-past ten or eleven, or maybe later."

"Can you remember the Wednesday of that week? I suppose you were at St. Malo at ten o'clock?"

"I was, sir. I was never left by ten any morning."

"Quite so. Now what I want to know is this: On that Wednesday morning was Mr. Felix in the house at ten o'clock?"

"So far as I know, he was, sir."

"Ah, but I want to be sure. Can you say positively he was there?"

"Well, not to be certain, sir, I couldn't."

"Now Thursday, Mrs. Murphy. Did you see Mr. Felix on Thursday?"

The woman hesitated.

" I saw him two or three mornings," she said at last, " but I couldn't be sure whether it was on Thursday. It might have been, though."

" You couldn't tell me at what hour he took his breakfast that morning?"

" Well, I could not, sir."

It was evident to Clifford that Mrs. Murphy, though an intelligent woman, would be no use to him as a witness. He remained at her house for a considerable time, and was very probing and painstaking in his questions. But all to no purpose. While she corroborated what Felix had stated about his household arrangements, she dashed any hope the lawyer might have had of establishing an alibi.

By the time he again reached the city it was one o'clock. He decided he would lunch at the Gresham, and pursue his investigations among the staff.

The head waiter, with whom he began, could not himself give any information, but he took Felix's photo round among his men, and at last found one who had seen the artist. Felix, it appeared from this man's statement, had dined there one evening some five or six weeks previously. The man, an Italian, remembered him because he had at first supposed him to be a compatriot. Unfortunately, he could not fix the date, and no one else, so far as Clifford could learn, had seen the artist at all. Clifford had regretfully to admit that this evidence, like Mrs. Murphy's was useless. In the lawyer's private judgment it undoubtedly tended to confirm Felix's statement, and he found himself more and more inclined to believe the Frenchman. But a personal impression was one thing, and evidence in a court of law another.

On reaching his office, he wrote to Bonchose, asking him to call on urgent business immediately on his return to London.

The next day saw him again at Brent village. Felix had stated he had gone by train to town each evening of the fateful week, and it had occurred to the lawyer that possibly some of the railway officials might have noticed him travelling. He made exhaustive inquiries and at last found a ticket-collector who volunteered some information. Felix, said this man, was a regular traveller. He went to town each morning by the 8.57 and returned at 6.5 each evening. But the collector had noticed that for some days he had not travelled by these trains, but had instead gone up by the evening trains leaving Brent at either 6.20 or 6.47. The collector went off duty at seven o'clock, so he could not tell anything about Felix's return. Nor could anyone else, so far as Clifford could ascertain.

But unfortunately the collector could not state how long it was since the artist had changed his habits, still less could he say if he travelled up to town on the Thursday evening in question.

Clifford then strolled to St. Malo in the hope of finding it was overlooked by some other house, the occupants of which might have seen the artist on the fateful Thursday. But here again he encountered disappointment. There was no house in the immediate vicinity.

Puzzled as to his next step, the lawyer returned to his office. He found pressing business of another kind awaiting him, and for the remainder of that day, as well as the next two, he was too fully occupied to turn his attention seriously to the murder case.

On the morning of the fourth day there was a letter from Mr. Lucius Heppenstall, K.C. It was written from Copenhagen, and the barrister explained that he was in Denmark on business and hoped to be back in about a week, when he and Clifford could meet and go into the case together.

Hardly had Clifford finished reading the letter when a young man was announced. He was tall and slight, with dark hair and eyes, a small black moustache and a short, hooked nose, which gave him something of the appearance of a hawk.

"Bonchose," said Clifford to himself, and he was not mistaken.

"You had not heard of Mr. Felix's arrest?" he asked, as he waved his visitor to an arm-chair and held out his cigarette case.

"Not a word," replied Bonchose, speaking good English, but with a foreign accent. He had a quick, vivacious manner, and moved sharply, as if on wires. "I cannot tell you how utterly surprised and shocked I was to get your note. But the thing is perfectly absurd—outrageous! Anyone that knew Felix would know he could not commit such a crime. It is surely a misunderstanding that a very short time will clear up?"

"I fear not, Mr. Bonchose; I very much fear not. Unfortunately, the case against your friend is strong. The evidence is admittedly circumstantial, but it is strong for all that. Indeed, to be perfectly candid with you, I do not for the moment see any good line of defence."

The young man made a gesture of amazement.

"You horrify me, sir," he cried; "absolutely horrify me. You surely do not mean to suggest there is any chance of a conviction?"

"I am sorry to say that I do. There is a very great chance—unless a good deal more comes to light than we know at present."

"But this is awful!" He wrung his hands. "Awful! First it was poor Annette and now Felix! But you don't mean that nothing can be done?" There was real concern and anxiety in the young man's tone.

Mr. Clifford was satisfied. This man's affection for and belief in his friend were genuine. Felix could not be altogether a villain to inspire such friendship. The lawyer changed his tone.

"No, Mr. Bonchose," he answered. "I do not mean that. All I mean is that the fight will not be easy. Mr. Felix's friends will have to put their backs into it. And it is to begin that fight I asked you to call here as soon as you returned."

"I got back early this morning, and I was here before your office opened. Take that as the measure of my willingness to help."

"I do not doubt it, Mr. Bonchose. And now I want you please to tell me everything you can about Mr. Felix, and your own life, where it has touched his. Also about your unhappy cousin, the late Madame Boirac."

"I shall do so, and if at any point I am not clear, please ask me questions."

Beginning by explaining who he and Annette really were—children of a younger daughter and the eldest son respectively of the late M. André Humbert of Laroche—he gave an account of their childhood, their early love of art, their moving to M. Dauphin's school in Paris, the meeting with Felix, and the latter's love for Annette. Then he told of his move to the wine merchant's firm at Narbonne, his being sent to London, his joy at again meeting Felix, his weakness for cards, the help Felix had given him, and the recent serious money difficulties into which he had fallen. He recounted his having written on the matter to Annette, the hope expressed to Felix that he would see her on the subject, his meeting the artist at Charing Cross on the Sunday evening of his return to London, their dinner together, the receipt of the £600, and finally Felix's departure in a taxi for St. Malo.

His whole statement, thought Clifford, was singularly like those of Mrs. Murphy, the Gresham waiter, and the ticket-collector at Brent station, in that, while it confirmed what Felix had said and strengthened the lawyer's growing belief in the artist's innocence, it was of very little use for the trial. It was true that he, Clifford, was now in a position to prove most of Felix's statement, but the worst of it was that most of Felix's statement might be proved without proving Felix's innocence. So much so, indeed, that Clifford could not yet quite banish the suspicion that the whole thing was pre-arranged.

He questioned Mr. Bonchose exhaustively, but without learning anything fresh. His visitor had not seen the artist on the Wednesday

r Thursday, and could not help towards the alibi. Finding that
nothing was to be gained by further conversation, Clifford bowed
he young man out, having promised to let him know how things
progressed.

CHAPTER XXIV

MR. GEORGES LA TOUCHE

SOME days later Mr. Clifford and Mr. Lucius Heppenstall, K.C.—
who were close personal friends—dined together at the former's
residence, intending afterwards to have a long chat over the case.
Mr. Heppenstall had returned from Denmark rather earlier than
was expected, and had already studied the documents received from
the prosecution, as well as Clifford's notes of what he had learnt.
The two men had together interviewed Felix and Bonchose and some
ther small inquiries had been made, the only point of importance
iscovered being that the late Miss Devine had crossed from Calais
to Folkestone on the Sunday in question and had been alone on
eck, both her maids having been helplessly ill. The meeting on
his evening was to formulate a policy, to decide on the exact line
hich the defence should take.

The difficulty of this decision was felt by both men to be con-
derable. In their previous cases there had nearly always been an
bvious defence. Frequently two distinct lines, or even three, had
een possible, the problem then being the selection of the best.
ut here their difficulty was to find any defence at all.

"The first thing we must settle," said Heppenstall, throwing
imself into an easy-chair, "is whether we are going to assume this
llow Felix innocent or guilty. What is your own private opinion?"

Clifford did not speak for a few moments.

"I hardly know what to think," he answered finally. "I must
dmit that Felix's manner and personality impresses me favourably.
e certainly told his story in a convincing way. Then these people
at we have recently seen confirm a great deal of what he said.
urther, they evidently like and believe in him. Look at Martin,
r example. He is a noisy, blustering fellow, but he is no fool.
e knows Felix well, and he believes in him to the extent of offering
guarantee our fees to get him off. All that must count for some-
ing. Then there is nothing inherently impossible in his story.

It all might have happened just as he says. And lastly, his admitted shock when the cask was opened seems strongly in his favour."

"But?"

"But? Well, there is all the rest of the case."

"Then you have no private opinion?"

"Not definitely. My opinion inclines towards innocence, but I am by no means sure."

"I rather agree with you," remarked the K.C. Then, after a pause, "I have been thinking this thing over and I don't for the life of me see a chance of clearing him on the evidence. It is too strong. Why, if it is true, it is overpowering. It seems to me our only hope is to deny the evidence."

"To deny it?"

"To deny it. You must admit that Felix is either guilty or the victim of a plot."

"Of course."

"Very well. Let us stick to that. The evidence is not genuine because Felix is the victim of a plot. How does that strike you?"

"Well, you know, I shouldn't be at all surprised if that was the actual fact. I've thought over it a good deal, and the more I think the more I begin to doubt those things that were found at St. Malo. That letter from Emmie, the marks on the blotting paper, and the diamond pin, they all strike me as being a little too conclusive to be natural. Their very comprehensiveness suggests selection. Then typewritten letters anyone can produce. No, I shouldn't wonder if you're on the right track."

"I think it's our best defence, anyway."

"I think it's our only defence. But, mind you, it's an easy theory to suggest, but a mighty hard one to establish."

"There's only one way," Heppenstall declared, pouring himself out some whisky from the jar at his elbow, "we must suggest the real murderer."

"If we must find the real murderer we may as well let the case alone. If Scotland Yard and the Sûreté couldn't get him, we are not likely to."

"You haven't quite got me. I don't say we must find him. It will be enough to suggest him. All we have to do is to show that some other person had a motive for madame's death, and could have murdered her and carried out the plot against Felix. A doubt would then arise as to which of the two was guilty, and, if that doubt was strong enough, Felix would get the benefit of it."

"But that makes our problem no easier. The difficulty still lies in the finding of this other person."

"We can only try; it may lead to something. Our first question then is: If Felix is innocent, who might be guilty?"

There was silence for several seconds, then Heppenstall spoke again.

"Who, perhaps I should say, is least unlikely to be guilty?"

"I think there can be only one answer to that," returned Clifford. "In the very nature of the case a certain suspicion must attach to Boirac. But the police were fully alive to that. From all we hear, they went into it thoroughly and came to the conclusion he was innocent."

"It depended on an alibi. But you know as well as I do alibis can be faked."

"Undoubtedly, but they concluded this one wasn't. We don't know the exact details, but it certainly seems to have been very fully tested."

"At all events, from the information available, I think we may assume that if Felix is innocent, Boirac is guilty. There is no suggestion of any third party being involved. If, then, we can show that Boirac had a motive for the crime, and that he could have committed it and made the plant, that's all we want. We have not to prove him guilty."

"I suppose that is so. Then our next point is: What might have been Boirac's motive?"

"That's not hard to find. If Boirac found his wife was carrying on with Felix, it might explain his desire to kill her."

"Yes, and it would give a two-fold reason for his working for Felix's conviction; first, self-defence by shifting over the suspicion, and, second, revenge on the man who had spoilt his home."

"Quite. I think a plausible motive might be built up. Next let us ask: When was the body put in the cask?"

"The police say in London, because there was no opportunity elsewhere."

"Yes, and to me it seems a quite sound deduction. Now, if that true, it follows that if Boirac killed his wife, he must have travelled here to do it."

"But the alibi?"

"Leave the alibi for a moment. Our defence must be that Boirac followed his wife to London and murdered her there. Now can we suggest possible details? He would arrive at his house on that Sunday morning and find his wife gone, and a letter from her saying she had eloped with Felix. What, then, would he do?"

Clifford leaned forward to stir the fire.

"I have thought over that," he said somewhat hesitatingly,

"and I have worked out a possible theory. It is, of course, pure guesswork, but it fits a number of the facts."

"Let's hear it. Naturally our theories at present can only be guesswork."

"I imagined Boirac, then, mad with his discovery on the Sunday morning, sitting down and working out a plan for vengeance. He perhaps goes on that morning to the Gare du Nord, and possibly sees them start. He follows them to London. Or, at least, he sees and follows Felix. Madame may have gone by another route. By the time he finds they have reached St. Malo his plan is worked out. He learns they are alone in the house, and he watches till he sees them go out. Then he enters by, say, an open window, and, sitting down at Felix's desk, he forges a letter to Dupierre, ordering the companion statue to that he has already purchased. He does this in order to obtain a cask in which to pack madame's body, as he intends to murder her. To throw suspicion on Felix, he copies the artist's handwriting and dries it on his blotting paper. For the same reason he signs it with Felix's name. But he does not give Felix's address, as he wants to get the cask himself."

"Good!" interjected Heppenstall.

"He then comes away with his letter, posts it, telephones to Paris to know when and by what route the cask is being sent, and arranges a carter to meet it and bring it near, but not to, St. Malo instructing the carter to await him. Meantime, by some letter or telegram or other trick, he gets Felix out of the way, leaving madame alone in the house. He rings, she opens the door, he forces his way in, and, in that little round-backed chair in the study, he throttles her. The pin falls out of the neck of the dress and lies unnoticed. Then he goes back to the carter and brings the cask into the yard. He sends the carter to the nearest inn for his dinner, unpacks and destroys the statue, and packs the body. By this time the carter has returned and Boirac has him remove the cask, giving him instructions to send it to Paris next morning. To compromise Felix still further he has prepared the Emmie note, and he shoves this into the pocket of Felix's clothes."

"Good," said Heppenstall again.

"He goes himself to Paris, gets hold of the cask at the Gare du Nord and sends it to Felix from the rue Cardinet goods station. He works out a tricky letter which will have the effect of making Felix claim the cask. Felix, as expected, does so, and the police get on his track."

"By George, Clifford, you haven't been idle. I shouldn't wonder if you are pretty near the thing. But if all that had taken place

St. Malo, do you think Felix wouldn't have said something about it?"

"I think he would have. On the other hand, he may have wanted to save madame's memory, and if so, he obviously couldn't mention it?"

"What about the charwoman?"

"Well, that is another difficulty. But I think a clever woman could have hidden her traces."

"The theory accounts for a great many things, and I think we must adopt it as a basis for investigation. Let us now see what it involves."

"It involves Boirac having been in London on the Sunday night or Monday after the dinner-party to learn what had taken place and to write his letter, and again on the Wednesday to commit the murder and arrange about the cask."

"Quite. It seems to me, then, our first business is definitely to find out where Boirac was on these dates."

"He satisfied the police he was in Paris and Belgium."

"I know, but we agreed alibis could be faked. We'd better have the thing gone into again."

"It will mean a detective."

"Yes, and what about La Touche?"

"La Touche is the best man we could have, of course, but he's fairly expensive."

Heppenstall shrugged his shoulders.

"Can't help that," he said. "We must have him."

"Very well. I'll ask him to meet us—shall I say at three tomorrow?"

"That will suit me."

The two men continued discussing the affair until the clock struck twelve, when Heppenstall made a move to return to town.

Mr. Georges La Touche was commonly regarded as the smartest private detective in London. Brought up in that city, where his father kept a small foreign book store, he learned till he was twelve the English language and ideas. Then, on the death of his English mother, the family moved to Paris, and Georges had to adjust himself to a new environment. At twenty, he entered Cook's office as a courier, and, learning successively Italian, German, and Spanish, he gradually acquired a first-hand acquaintanceship with Middle and South-Western Europe. After some ten years of this work he grew tired of the constant travelling, and, coming to London, he offered his services to a firm of well-known private detectives. Here he did so well that, on the death of the founder some fifteen years later, he stepped into his place. He soon began to specialize in foreign or international cases, for which his early training peculiarly fitted him.

But he was not much in appearance. Small, sallow, and slightly stooped, he would have looked insignificant only for the strength of the clear-cut features and the intelligence of the dark, flashing eyes. Years of training had enabled him to alter his expression and veil these tell-tale signs of power, and he had frequently found the weak and insipid impression thus produced, an asset in allaying the suspicions of his adversaries.

His delight in the uncommon and bizarre had caused him to read attentively the details of the cask mystery. When, therefore, he received Clifford's telephone asking him to act on behalf of the suspected man, he eagerly agreed, and cancelled some minor engagements in order to meet the lawyers at the time appointed.

The important question of fees having been settled, Clifford explained to the detective all that was known of the case, as well as the ideas he and Heppenstall evolved regarding the defence.

"What we want you to do for us, Mr. La Touche," he wound up, "is to go into the case on the assumption that Boirac is the guilty man. Settle definitely whether this is a possible theory. I think you will agree that this depends on the truth of his alibi. Therefore, test that first. If it cannot be broken down, Boirac cannot be guilty, and our line of defence won't work. And I need hardly say, the sooner you can give us some information the better."

"You have given me a congenial task, gentlemen, and if I don't succeed it won't be for want of trying. I suppose that is all today? I'll go over these papers and make the case up. Then I fancy I had best go to Paris. But I'll call in to see you, Mr. Clifford, before I start."

La Touche was as good as his word. In three days he was again in Clifford's room.

"I've been into this case as far as is possible this side of the Channel, Mr. Clifford," he announced. "I was thinking of crossing to Paris tonight."

"Good. And what do you think of it all?"

"Well, sir, it's rather soon to give an opinion, but I'm afraid we're up against a tough proposition."

"In what way?"

"The case against Felix, sir. It's pretty strong. Of course, I expect we'll meet it all right, but it'll take some doing. There's not much in his favour, if you think of it."

"What about the shock he got when the cask was opened? Have you seen the doctor about it?"

"Yes. He says the thing was genuine enough, but, sir, I'm afraid that won't carry us so far as you seem to think."

"To me it seems very strong. Look at it this way: the essence of a shock is surprise; the surprise could only have been at the contents of the cask; therefore Felix did not know the contents; therefore he could not have put the body in; therefore surely he must be innocent?"

"That sounds all right, sir, I admit. But I'm afraid a clever counsel could upset it. You see, there's more than surprise in a shock. There's horror. And it could be argued that Felix got both surprise and horror when the cask was opened."

"How, if he knew what was in it?"

"This way, sir. What was in it was hardly what he was expecting. It might be said that he put in the body as he had seen the lady alive. But she had been dead for a good many days when the cask was opened. She would look a very different object. He would be filled with horror when he saw her. That horror, together with the fact that he would be all keyed up to act surprise in any case, would produce the effect."

Clifford had not thought of this somewhat gruesome explanation, and the possibility of its truth made him uncomfortable. If the strongest point in Felix's favour could be met as easily as this, it was indeed a black look out for his client. But he did not voice his doubts to his visitor.

"If you can't get enough to support the defence we suggest," he said, "we must just try some other line."

"I may get what you want all right, sir. I'm only pointing out that the thing is not all plain sailing. I'll cross, then, tonight, and hope I may soon have some good news to send you."

"Thank you. I hope so."

The two men shook hands, and La Touche took his leave. That night he left Charing Cross for Paris.

CHAPTER XXV

DISAPPOINTMENT

LA TOUCHE was a good traveller, and usually slept well on a night journey. But not always. It sometimes happened that the rhythmic rush and roar through the darkness stimulated rather than lulled his brain, and on such occasions, lying in the wagon-lit of some long-distance express, more than one illuminating idea had had its birth. Tonight, as he sat in the corner of a first-class compartment in the Calais-Paris train, though outwardly a lounging and indolent figure, his mind was keenly alert, and he therefore took the opportunity to consider carefully the business which lay before him.

His first duty obviously was to re-test Boirac's alibi. He had learnt what the authorities had done in the matter, and he would begin his work by checking Lefarge's investigation. For the moment he did not see how to improve on his confrère's methods, and he could only hope that some clue would present itself during his researches, which his predecessor had missed.

So far he was in no doubt as to his proceedings, for this inquiry into Boirac's alibi had been directly asked for by his employers. But, after that, he had been given a free hand to do as he thought best.

He turned to what he considered the central feature of the case —the finding of the body in the cask—and began to separate in his mind those facts actually known about it from those assumed. Firstly, the body was in the cask when the latter reached St. Katharine Docks. Secondly, it could not have been put in during the journey from the rue Cardinet goods station. So much was certain. But the previous step in the cask's journey was surmise. It was assumed that it had been taken from the Gare du Nord to the rue Cardinet on a horse-cart. On what was this assumption founded? Three facts. First, that it left the Gare du Nord on a horse-cart; second, that it reached the rue Cardinet in the same manner; and third, that such a vehicle would have occupied about the time the trip had actually taken. The assumption seemed reasonable, and yet . . . He had to remember that they were up against a man of no ordinary ability, whoever he might be. Might not the cask have been taken by the first horse-cart to some adjoining house or shed where the body could have been put in, then sent by motor-lorry to some other shed near the goods station and there transferred to a horse-cart again? This undoubtedly seemed farfetched and unlikely, nevertheless, the facts were not known, and, he thought, they should be. He must find the carter who brought the cask to the goods station. Then he would be certain where the body was put in, and therefore whether the murder was committed in London or Paris.

He noted a third point. The various letters in the case—and there were several—might or might not be forgeries, and if the former, it was obviously impossible for him to say off-hand who had written them. But there was one letter which could not be a forgery—at least in a certain sense. The Le Gautier letter which Felix said he had received was done on a typewriter which could be identified. It was hardly too much to assume that the man who typed that letter was the murderer. Find the typewriter, thought La Touche, and the chances are it will eventually lead to the guilty man.

A further point struck him. If Boirac were guilty, might he not even yet give himself away? The detective recalled case after case in his own experience in which a criminal had, after the crime, done something or gone somewhere that had led to his arrest. Would it be worth while having Boirac shadowed? He considered the question carefully and finally decided to bring over two of his men for this purpose.

Here, then, were four directions in which inquiries might be made, of which the first three at least promised a certain and definite result. As the train slackened speed for the capital, he felt his work was cut out for him.

And then began a period of tedious and unprofitable work. He was very efficient, very thorough and very pertinacious, but the only result of all his painstaking labours was to establish more firmly than ever the truth of Boirac's statements.

He began with the waiter at Charenton. Very skilfully he approached the subject, and, painting a moving picture of an innocent man falsely accused of murder, he gradually enlisted the man's sympathy. Then he appealed to his cupidity, promising him a liberal reward for information that would save his client, and finally he soothed his fears by promising that in no case should any statement he might make get him into trouble. The waiter, who seemed a quiet, honest man, was perfectly open, and readily replied to all La Touche's questions, but except on one point he stoutly adhered to his previous statement to Lefarge. M. Boirac—whom he identified unhesitatingly from a photograph—had lunched in the café about 1.30, and had then telephoned to two separate places—he had heard the two numbers asked for. As before, he made the reservation that he was not certain of the day of the week, his impression having been that it was Monday and not Tuesday, but he stated that in this he might easily be mistaken. There was no shaking his evidence, and La Touche was strongly of the opinion that the man was speaking the truth.

But as well as repeating his statement to Lefarge, the waiter added one item of information that seemed important. Asked if he could not recall either of the numbers demanded, he now said he recollected the last two figures of one of them. They were 45. They caught his attention because they were the café's own telephone number—Charenton 45. He could not recall either the previous figures of the number nor yet the division. He had intended to tell this to Lefarge, but being somewhat upset by the detective's call, the point had slipped his memory, and it was only when thinking the matter over afterwards it had occurred to him.

For La Touche to look up the telephone directory was the work of a few seconds. The number of Boirac's house in the Avenue de l'Alma did not suit, but when he looked up the Pump Construction Office he found it was Nord 745.

Here was fresh confirmation. It was obvious the waiter could not have invented his tale, and La Touche left utterly convinced that Boirac had indeed lunched at the café and sent the messages.

As he was returning to the city it occurred to him that perhaps the waiter's impression was really correct and that Boirac had been in the café on Monday afternoon instead of Tuesday. How was this point to be ascertained?

He recollected how Lefarge had settled it. He had interviewed the persons to whom Boirac had spoken, the butler and the head clerk, and both were certain of the date. La Touche decided he must follow Lefarge's example.

Accordingly he called at the house in the Avenue de l'Alma and saw François. He was surprised to find the old man genuinely grieved at the news of Felix's arrest. Few though the occasions had been in which the two had met, something in the personality of the former had in this case, as in so many others, inspired attachment and respect. La Touche therefore adopted the same tactics as with the waiter, and, on his explaining that he was acting for the suspected man, he found François anxious to give all the help in his power.

But here again all that La Touche gained was confirmation of Boirac's statement. François recollected the telephone message, and he was sure Boirac had spoken. He positively recognized the voice and equally positively he remembered the day. It was Tuesday. He was able to connect it with a number of other small events which definitely fixed it.

"Lefarge was right," thought the detective, as he strolled up the Avenue de l'Alma. "Boirac telephoned from Charenton at 2.30 on Tuesday. However, I may as well go through with the business."

He turned his steps therefore towards the head office of the

Avrotte Pump Construction Company. Repeating Lefarge's tactics, he watched till he observed Boirac leave. Then he entered the office and asked if he could see M. Dufresne.

"I am afraid not, monsieur. I believe he has gone out," answered the clerk who had come over to attend him. "But if you will take a seat for a moment I shall ascertain."

La Touche did as he was asked, looking admiringly round the large office with its polished teak furniture, its rows of vertical file cabinets, its telephones, its clicking typewriters and its industrious and efficient-looking clerks. Now La Touche was not merely a thinking machine. He had his human side, and, except when on a hot scent, he had a remarkably quick eye for a pretty girl. Thus it was that as this eye roamed inquisitively over the room, it speedily halted at and became focused on the second row of typists, a girl of perhaps two- or three-and-twenty. She looked, it must be admitted, wholly charming. Small, dark, and evidently vivacious, she had a tiny, pouting mouth and an adorable dimple. Plainly dressed as became her business-like surroundings, there was, nevertheless, a daintiness and chicness about her whole appearance that would have delighted an even more critical observer than the detective. She flashed an instantaneous glance at him from her dark, sparkling eyes, and then, slightly elevating her pert little nose, became engrossed in her work.

"I am sorry, monsieur, but M. Dufresne has gone home slightly indisposed. He expects to be back in a couple of days, if you could conveniently call again."

La Touche hardly felt a proper appreciation of the clerk's promptness, but he thanked him politely and said he would return later. Then, with a final glance at an averted head of dark, luxuriant hair, he left the office.

The chief clerk's absence was a vexatious delay. But, though it would hold up his work on the alibi for a day or two, he might begin on one of the other points which had occurred to him during the journey to Paris. There was, for example, the tracing of the carter who brought the cask from the Gare du Nord to the rue Cardinet. He at once decided he would see what could be done on that.

Accordingly he went out to the great goods station and, introducing himself to the agent in charge, explained his errand. The official was exceedingly polite, and, after some delay, the two porters whom Burnley and Lefarge had interviewed some weeks before were ushered into the room. La Touche questioned them minutely, but without gaining any fresh information. They repeated their statement that they would recognize the carter who had brought the cask were they to see him again, but were unable to describe him more particularly than before.

La Touche then went to the Gare du Nord. Here he was fortunate in finding the clerk who had handed over the cask to the black-bearded Jaques de Belleville. But again he was disappointed. Neither the clerk nor any of the other officials he interviewed recollected the carter who had taken the cask, and none therefore could say if he was like the man who delivered it at the goods station.

Baffled on this point, La Touche turned into a café and, ordering a bock, sat down to consider his next step. Apparently Lefarge had been right to advertise. He recollected from the report he had had from the authorities that all the advertisements had appeared in, among other papers, *Le Journal*. He determined he would see those advertisements in the hope of discovering why they had failed.

He accordingly drove to the office of the paper and asked leave to look over the files. A slight research convinced him that the advertising had been thoroughly and skilfully done. He took copies of each fresh announcement—there were nearly a dozen. Then, returning to his hotel, he lay down on his bed and looked them over again.

The paragraphs varied in wording, type, and position in the columns, but necessarily they were similar in effect. All asked for information as to the identity of a carter who, about six o'clock on Thursday, the 1st of April, had delivered a cask at the rue Cardinet goods station. All offered a reward varying from 1,000 to 5,000 francs, and all undertook that the carter would not suffer from the information being divulged.

After a couple of hours hard thinking La Touche came to the conclusion that the advertising had been complete. He saw no way in which he could improve on what Lefarge had done, nor could he think of anything in the announcements themselves which might have militated against their success.

To clear his brain he determined to banish all thoughts of the case for the remainder of the day. He therefore went for a stroll along the boulevards, and, after a leisurely dinner, turned his steps towards the Folies Bergères, and there passed a very pleasant evening.

On his way home it occurred to him that while waiting to interview M. Dufresne at the office of the Pump Construction Company he might run over to Brussels and satisfy himself as to that part of Boirac's alibi. Accordingly, next morning saw him entrained for the Belgian capital, where he arrived about midday. He drove to the Hotel Maximilian, lunched, and afterwards made exhaustive inquiries at the office. Here he saw copies of the visitors' returns which every Belgian hotel must furnish to the police, and satisfied himself absolutely that Boirac had been there on the date in question. As a result of Lefarge's inquiries the clerk recollected the circumstances of the pump manufacturer's telephone, and adhered to his previous statement in every particular. La Touche took the afternoon train for Paris considerably disappointed with the results of his journey.

On the chance that the chief clerk might be back at work, he returned next day to the pump works. Again he watched till Boirac had left and again entered and asked for M. Dufresne. The same prompt clerk came forward to speak to him, and, saying that M. Dufresne had returned that morning, once more asked him to be seated while he took in his card. La Touche then suddenly remembered the girl he had so much admired, but whose existence he had forgotten since his last visit. He glanced across the room. She was there, but he could not see her face. Something had evidently gone wrong with the splendid-looking machine which she—La Touche whimsically wondered why you did not say " played " or " drove " —and she was bending over it, apparently adjusting some screw. But he had no time to pursue his studies of female beauty. The prompt clerk was back at his side almost immediately to say that M. Dufresne could see him. He accordingly followed his guide to the chief clerk's room.

M. Dufresne was quite as ready to assist him as had been his other informants, but he could tell him nothing the detective did not already know. He repeated his statement to Lefarge almost word for word. He was sure M. Boirac had telephoned about 2.30 on the Tuesday—he unmistakably recognized his voice, and he was equally certain of the date.

La Touche regained the street and walked slowly back to his hotel. It was beginning to look very much as if the alibi could not be broken, and he was unable for the moment to see his next step in the matter. Nor had any information resulted from the labours of Mallet and Farol, the two men he had brought over to shadow Boirac. Up to the present the latter had been most circumspect, not having been anywhere or done anything in the slightest degree suspicious. As La Touche wrote a detailed report of his proceedings to Clifford, he felt for the first time a distinct doubt as to the outcome of his investigations.

CHAPTER XXVI

A CLUE AT LAST

LA TOUCHE, having finished his report, put on his hat and sallied forth into the rue de la Fayette. He intended after posting his letter to cross to the south side and spend the evening with some friends. He was not in an agreeable frame of mind. The conclusion to which he was apparently being forced would be a disappointment to Clifford, and, if the theory of Boirac's guilt broke down, he saw no better than the solicitor what defence remained.

He sauntered slowly along the pavement, his mind brooding almost subconsciously on the case. Then, noticing a letter-box on the opposite side of the street, he turned to cross over. But as he stepped off the sidewalk an idea flashed into his mind and he stopped as if shot. That typewriter the pretty girl in Boirac's office had been using was *a new machine*. La Touche was an observant man, and he had noted the fact, as he habitually noted small details about the objects he saw. But not until this moment did he realize the tremendously suggestive deduction which might be made from that fact. Lefarge, in his search for the machine on which the Le Gautier letter had been typed, had obtained samples from all the typewriters to which Boirac, so far as he could ascertain, had access. But what if that new machine replaced an old? What if that old machine had typed the Le Gautier letter and had been then got rid of so that samples taken by suspicious detectives might be supplied from some other typewriter? Here was food for thought. He would delay the report till he could adjust himself to this new point of view.

And then he had a revulsion of feeling. After all, offices must necessarily procure new typewriters, and there was no reason in this case to suppose a machine had been purchased otherwise than in the ordinary course of business. And yet—the idea was attractive.

He decided he might as well make some inquiries before forwarding his report. It would be a simple matter to find out when the new machine was purchased, and, if the date was not suspicious, the matter could be dropped.

He considered the best way of ascertaining his information. His first idea was to meet the typist and ask her the direct question. Then he saw that if her answer supported his theory, not only would further inquiries be necessary, but no hint that these were being made must reach Boirac. It might be better to try diplomacy.

To La Touche diplomatic dealing was second nature, and he was not long in devising a plan. He looked at his watch. It was 5.15. If he hurried he might reach the pump works before the pretty typist left.

From the window of the café which had so often served in a similar capacity, he watched the office staff take their departure. For a long time his victim did not appear, and he had almost come to the conclusion she must have gone, when he saw her. She was with two other girls, and the three, after glancing round the street, tripped off daintily citywards.

When they had gone a fair distance La Touche followed. The girls stood for a moment at the Simplon Station of the Metro, then the pretty typist vanished down the steps, while the others moved on along the pavement. La Touche sprinted to the entrance and was in time to see the grey dress of the quarry disappearing down the passage labelled Port d'Orléans. He got his ticket and followed to the platform. There was a fairly dense crowd, and, after locating mademoiselle he mingled with it, keeping well back out of sight.

A train soon drew up and the girl got in. La Touche entered the next carriage. Standing at the end of his vehicle he could see her through the glass between the coaches without, he felt sure, being himself visible. One, two, five stations passed, and then she got up and moved towards the door ready to alight. La Touche did the same, observing from the map in the carriage that the next station was not a junction. As the train jerked and groaned to a standstill he leaped out and hurried to the street. Crossing rapidly, he stopped at a kiosk and asked for an evening paper. Bending over the counter of the stall, he saw her emerge up the steps and start off down the street. He remained on the opposite side, cautiously following until, after about two blocks, she entered a small, unpretentious restaurant.

" If she is going to dine alone," thought La Touche, " I am in luck."

He waited till she would have probably reached her second or third course and then entered the building.

The room was narrow, corresponding to the frontage, but stretched a long way back, the far end being lighted with electric lamps. A row of marble-topped tables stretched down each side, with six cane chairs at each. Mirrors framed in dingy white and gold lined the walls. At the extreme back was a tiny stage on which an orchestra of three girls was performing.

The place was about half full. As La Touche's quick eye took in the scene, he noticed the typist seated alone at a table three or four from the stage. He walked forward.

"If mademoiselle permits?" he murmured, bowing, but hardly looking at her, as he pulled out a chair nearly opposite her and sat down.

He gave his order and then, business being as it were off his mind, he relaxed so far as to look around. He glanced at the girl, seemed suddenly to recognize her, gave a mild start of surprise and leant forward with another bow.

"Mademoiselle will perhaps pardon if I presume," he said, in his best manner, "but I think we have met before or, if not quite, almost."

The girl raised her eyebrows but did not speak.

"In the office of M. Boirac," went on the detective. "You would not, of course, notice, but I saw you there busy with a fine typewriter."

Mademoiselle was not encouraging. She shrugged her shoulders, but made no reply. La Touche had another shot.

"I am perhaps impertinent in addressing mademoiselle, but I assure her no impertinence is meant. I am the inventor of a new device for typewriters, and I try to get opinion of every expert operator I can find on its utility. Perhaps mademoiselle would permit me to describe it and ask hers?"

"Why don't you take it to some of the agents?" She spoke frigidly.

"Because mademoiselle," answered La Touche, warming to his subject, "I am not quite certain if the device would be sufficiently valuable. It would be costly to attach and no firm would buy unless it could be shown that operators wanted it. That is what I am so anxious to learn."

She was listening, though not very graciously. La Touche did not wait for a reply, but began sketching on the back of the menu.

"Here," he said, "is my idea," and he proceeded to draw and describe the latest form of tabulator with which he was acquainted. The girl looked at him with scorn and suspicion.

"You're describing the Remington tabulator," she said coldly.

"Oh, but, pardon me, mademoiselle. You surely don't mean that? I have been told this is quite new."

"You have been told wrongly. I ought to know, for I have been using one the very same, as what you say is yours, for several weeks."

"You don't say so, mademoiselle? That means that I have been forestalled and all my work has been wasted."

La Touche's disappointment was so obvious that the girl thawed slightly.

"You'd better call at the Remington depot and ask to see one of their new machines. Then you can compare their tabulator with yours."

"Thank you, mademoiselle, I'll do so tomorrow. Then you use a Remington?"

"Yes, a No. 10."

"Is that an old machine? Pardon my questions, but have you had it long?"

"I can't tell you how long it has been at the office. I am only there myself six or seven weeks."

Six or seven weeks! And the murder took place just over six weeks before! Could there be a connection, or was this mere coincidence?

"It must be a satisfaction to a man of business," La Touche went on conversationally, as he helped himself to wine, "when his business grows to the extent of requiring an additional typist. I envy M. Boirac his feelings when he inserted his advertisement nearly as much as I envy him when you applied."

"You have wasted your envy then," returned the girl in chilly and contemptuous tones, "for you are wrong on both points. M. Boirac's business has not extended, for I replaced a girl who had just left, and no advertisement was inserted as I went to M. Boirac from the Michelin School in the rue Scribe."

La Touche had got his information; at least, all he had expected from this girl. He continued the somewhat one-sided conversation for some minutes, and then with a courteous bow left the restaurant. He reached his hotel determined to follow the matter up.

Accordingly, next morning saw him repeating his tactics of the previous evening. Taking up his position in the restaurant near the pump works shortly before midday, he watched the staff go for *déjeuner*. First came M. Boirac, then M. Dufresne, and then a crowd of lesser lights—clerks and typists. He saw his friend of the night before with the same two companions, closely followed by the prompt clerk. At last the stream ceased, and in about ten minutes the detective crossed the road and once more entered the office. It was empty except for a junior clerk.

"Good morning," said La Touche affably, "I called to ask whether you would be so good as to do me a favour. I want a piece of information for which, as it may give you some trouble to procure, I will pay twenty francs. Will you help me?"

"What is the information, monsieur?" asked the boy.

" I am manager of a paper works and I am looking for a typist for my office. I am told that a young lady typist left here about six weeks ago?"

" That is true, monsieur; Mlle. Lambert."

" Yes, that is the lady's name," returned La Touche, making a mental note of it.

" Now," he continued confidentially, " can you tell me why she left?"

" I think she was dismissed, monsieur, but I never really understood why."

" Dismissed?"

" Yes, monsieur. She had some row with M. Boirac, our managing director. I don't know—none of us know—what it was about."

" I had heard she was dismissed, and that is why I was interested in her. Unfortunately my business is not for the moment as flourishing as I should wish. It occurred to me that if I could find a typist who had some blot on her record, she might be willing to come to me for a smaller salary than she would otherwise expect. It would benefit her as well as me, as it would enable her to regain her position."

The clerk bowed without comment, and La Touche continued :—

" The information I want is this. Can you put me in touch with this young lady? Do you know her address?"

The other shook his head.

" I fear not, monsieur. I don't know where she lives."

La Touche affected to consider.

" Now, how am I to get hold of her?" he said. The clerk making no suggestion, he went on after a pause :—

" I think if you could tell me just when she left it might help me. Could you do that?"

" About six weeks ago. I can tell you the exact day by looking up the old wages sheets if you don't mind waiting. Will you take a seat?"

La Touche thanked him and sat down, trusting the search would be concluded before any of the other clerks returned. But he was not delayed long. In three or four minutes the boy returned.

" She left on Monday, the 5th of April, monsieur."

" And was she long with you?"

" About two years, monsieur."

" I am greatly obliged. And her Christian name was?"

" Eloise, monsieur. Eloise Lambert."

" A thousand thanks. And now I have just to beg of you not

to mention my visit, as it would injure me if it got out that my business was not too flourishing. Here is my debt to you." He handed over the twenty francs.

"It is too much, monsieur. I am glad to oblige you without payment."

"A bargain is a bargain," insisted the detective, and, followed by the profuse thanks of the young clerk, he left the office.

"This grows interesting," thought La Touche, as he once more emerged into the street. "Boirac dismisses a typist on the very day the cask reaches St. Katharine Docks. Now I wonder if that new typewriter made its appearance at the same time. I must get hold of that girl Lambert?"

But how was this to be done? No doubt there would be a record of her address somewhere in the office, but he was anxious that no idea of his suspicions should leak out, and he preferred to leave that source untapped. What, then, was left to him? He could see nothing for it but an advertisement.

Accordingly, he turned into a café and, calling for a bock, drafted out the following:—

"If Mlle. Eloise Lambert, stenographer and typist, will apply to M. Georges La Touche, Hotel Suisse, rue de La Fayette, she will hear something to her advantage."

He read over the words and then a thought struck him, and he took another sheet of paper and wrote:—

"If Mlle. Eloise Lambert, stenographer and typist, will apply to M. Guillaume Faneuil, Hotel St. Antoine, she will hear something to her advantage."

"If Boirac should see the thing, there's no use in my shoving into the limelight," he said to himself. "I'll drop Georges La Touche for a day or two and try the St. Antoine."

He sent his advertisement to several papers, then going to the Hotel St. Antoine, engaged a room in the name of M. Guillaume Faneuil.

"I shall not require it till tomorrow," he said to the clerk, and next day he moved in.

During the morning there was a knock at the door of his private sitting-room, and a tall, graceful girl of about five-and-twenty entered. She was not exactly pretty, but exceedingly pleasant and good-humoured looking. Her tasteful, though quiet, dress showed she was not in need as a result of losing her situation.

La Touche rose and bowed.

"Mlle. Lambert?" he said with a smile. "I am M. Faneuil. Won't you sit down?"

"I saw your advertisement in *Le Soir*, monsieur, and—here I am."

"I am much indebted to you for coming so promptly, mademoiselle," said La Touche, reseating himself, "and I shall not trespass long on your time. But before explaining the matter may I ask if you are the Mlle. Lambert who recently acted as typist at the Avrotte Works?"

"Yes, monsieur. I was there for nearly two years."

"Forgive me, but can you give any proof of that? A mere matter of form, of course, but in justice to my employers I am bound to ask the question."

An expression of surprise passed over the girl's face.

"I really don't know that I can," she answered. "You see, I was not expecting to be asked such a question."

It had occurred to La Touche that in spite of his precautions Boirac might have somehow discovered what he was engaged on, and sent this girl with a made up story. But her answer satisfied him. If she had been an impostor she would have come provided with proofs of her identity.

"Ah, well," he rejoined with a smile, "I think I may safely take the risk. May I ask you another question? Was a new typewriter purchased while you were at the office?"

The surprise on the pleasant face deepened.

"Why, yes, monsieur, a No. 10 Remington."

"And can you tell me just when?"

"Easily. I left the office on Monday, 5th April, and the new machine was sent three days earlier—on Friday, the 2nd."

Here was news indeed! La Touche was now in no doubt about following up the matter. He must get all the information possible out of this girl. And the need for secrecy would make him stick to diplomacy.

He smiled and bowed.

"You will forgive me, mademoiselle, but I had to satisfy myself you were the lady I wished to meet. I asked you these questions only to ensure that you knew the answers. And now I shall tell you who I am and what is the business at issue. But first, may I ask you to keep all I may tell you secret?"

His visitor looked more and more mystified as she replied:—

"I promise, monsieur."

"Then I may say that I am a private detective, employed on behalf of the typewriter company to investigate some very extraordinary—I can only call them frauds, which have recently been taking place. In some way, which up to the present we have been unable to fathom, several of our machines have developed faults which, you understand, do not prevent them working, but which prevent them being quite satisfactory. The altering of tensions and the slight twisting of type to put them out of alignment are the kind of things I mean. We hardly like to suspect rival firms of practising these frauds to get our machines into disfavour, and yet it is hard to account for it otherwise. Now, we think that you can possibly give us some information, and I am authorized by my company to hand you one hundred francs if you will be kind enough to do so."

The surprise had not left the girl's face as she answered:—

"I should have been very pleased, monsieur, to tell you all I knew without any payment, had I known anything to tell. But I am afraid I don't."

"I think, mademoiselle, you can help us if you will. May I ask you a few questions?"

"Certainly."

"The first is, can you describe the machine you used prior to the purchase of the new one?"

"Yes, it was a No. 7 Remington."

"I did not mean that," answered La Touche, eagerly noting this information, "I knew that, of course, as it is this No. 7 machine I am inquiring about. What I meant to ask was, had it any special marks or peculiarities by which it could be distinguished from other No. 7's?"

"Why, no, I don't think so," the girl answered thoughtfully. "And yet there were. The letter S on the S-key had got twisted round to the right and there were three scratches here"—she indicated the side plate of an imaginary typewriter.

"You would then be able to identify the machine if you saw it again?"

"Yes, I certainly should."

"Now, mademoiselle, had it any other peculiarities—defective letters or alignment or anything of that kind?"

"No, nothing really bad. It was old and out of date, but quite good enough. M. Boirac, of course, thought otherwise, but I maintain my opinion."

"What did M. Boirac say exactly?"

"He blamed me for it. But there wasn't anything wrong, and if there had been it wasn't my fault."

"I am sure of that, mademoiselle. But perhaps you would tell me about it from the beginning?"

"There's not much to tell. I had a big job to do—typing a long specification of a pumping plant for the Argentine, and when I had finished I left it as usual on M. Boirac's desk. A few minutes later he sent for me and asked how I came to put such an untidy document before him. I didn't see anything wrong with it and I asked him what he complained of. He pointed out some very small defects—principally uneven alignment, and one or two letters just a trifle blurred. You really would hardly have seen it. I said that wasn't my fault, and that the machine wanted adjustment. He said I had been striking while the shift key was partly moved, but, M. Faneuil, I had been doing nothing of the kind. I told M. Boirac so, and he then apologized and said I must have a new machine. He telephoned there and then to the Remington people, and a No. 10 came that afternoon."

"And what happened to the old No. 7?"

"The man that brought the new one took the old away."

"And was that all that was said?"

"That was all, monsieur?"

"But, pardon me, I understood you left owing to some misunderstanding with M. Boirac."

The girl shook her head.

"Oh, no," she said, "nothing of the sort. M. Boirac told me the following Monday, that is, two days after the typewriter business, that he was reorganizing his office and would do with a typist less. As I was the last arrival, I had to go. He said he wished to carry out the alterations immediately so that I might leave at once. He gave me a month's salary instead of notice, and a good testimonial which I have here. We parted quite friends."

The document read:—

"I have pleasure in certifying that Mlle. Eloise Lambert was engaged as a stenographer and typist in the head office of this company from August, 1910, till 5th April, 1912, during which time she gave every satisfaction to me and my chief clerk. She proved herself diligent and painstaking, thoroughly competent in her work, and of excellent manners and conduct. She leaves the firm through no fault of her own, but because we are reducing staff. I regret her loss and have every confidence in recommending her to those needing her services.

"(Signed) RAOUL BOIRAC, *Managing Director.*"

"An excellent testimonial, mademoiselle," La Touche commented. "Pray excuse me for just a moment."

He stepped into the adjoining bedroom and closed the door. Then taking a sample of Boirac's writing from his pocket-book, he compared the signature with that of the testimonial. After a careful scrutiny he was satisfied the latter was genuine. He returned to the girl and handed her the document.

"Thank you mademoiselle. Now, can you recall one other point? Did you, within the last three or four weeks, type a letter about some rather unusual matters—about someone winning a lot of money in the State Lottery and about sending this packed in a cask to England?"

"Never, monsieur," asserted the typist, evidently completely puzzled by the questions she was being asked. La Touche watched her keenly and was satisfied she had no suspicion that his business was other than he had said. But he was nothing if not thorough, and his thoroughness drove him to make provision for suspicions which might arise later. He therefore went on to question her about the No. 7 machine, asking whether she had ever noticed it had been tampered with, and finally saying that he believed there must have been a mistake and that the machine they had discussed was not that in which he was interested. Then, after obtaining her address, he handed her the hundred francs, which, after a protest, she finally accepted.

"Now, not a word to anyone, if you please, mademoiselle," he concluded, as they parted.

His discoveries, to say the least of it, were becoming interesting. If Mlle. Lambert's story was true—and he was strongly disposed to believe her—M. Boirac had acted in a way that required some explanation. His finding fault with the typist did not seem genuine. In fact, to La Touche it looked as if the whole episode had been arranged to provide an excuse for getting rid of the typewriter. Again, the manufacturer's dismissal of his typist at a day's notice was not explained by his statement that he was about to reorganize his office. Had that been true he would have allowed her to work her month's notice, and, even more obviously, he would not have immediately engaged her successor. As La Touche paid his bill at the hotel he decided that though there might be nothing in his suspicions, the matter was well worth further investigation. He therefore called a taxi and was driven to the Remington typewriter depot.

"I want," he said to the salesman who came forward, "to buy a second-hand machine. Can you let me see some?"

"Certainly, monsieur. Will you step this way?"

They went to a room at the back of the building where was stored a vast assemblage of typewriters of all sizes and in all states of repair. La Touche, inquiring as to prices and models, moved slowly about, running his quick eye over the machines, looking always for one with a twisted S-key. But, search as he would, he could not find what he wanted. Nor could he find any No. 7's. These machines were all more modern.

He turned at last to the shopman.

"These are all rather expensive for me. I should explain that I am the principal of a commercial school, and I merely want a machine on which beginners could learn the keys. Any old thing would do, if I could get it cheap. Have you any older machines?"

"Certainly, monsieur, we have several quite good No. 7's and a few No. 5's. Come this way, please."

They went to a room devoted to more antiquated specimens. Here La Touche continued his investigations, searching always for the twisted S.

At last he saw it. Not only was the letter turned to the right, but on the side plate were the three scratches mentioned by Mlle. Lambert.

"I think that one would suit," he said. "Could you get it down and let me have a look at it?"

He went through the pretence of examining it with care.

"Yes," he said, "this will do if it works all right. I should like to try it."

He put in a sheet of paper and typed a few words. Then, drawing out his work, he examined the letters and alignment.

As he looked at it even his long experience scarcely prevented him giving a cry of triumph. For, to the best of his belief, this was undoubtedly the machine on which the Le Gautier letter had been typed!

He turned again to the shopman.

"That seems all right," he said. "I'll take the machine, please."

He paid for it and obtained a receipt. Then he asked to see the manager.

"I'm going to ask you, monsieur," he said, when he had drawn that gentleman aside, "to do me a rather unusual favour. I have just bought this machine, and I want you to see it before I take it away, and, if you will be so kind, to give me some information about it. I shall tell you in confidence why I ask. I am a detective, employed on behalf of a man charged with a serious crime, but who I believe is innocent. A certain letter, on the authorship of which his guilt largely depends, was written, if I am not mistaken, on this machine. You will forgive me if I do not go into all the particulars. An adequate identification of the typewriter is obviously essential. I would therefore ask you if you would be kind enough to put a private mark on it. Also, if you would tell me how it came into your possession, I should be more than obliged."

" I shall do what you ask with pleasure, monsieur," returned the manager, " but I trust I shall not be required to give evidence."

" I do not think so, monsieur. I feel sure the identity of the machine will not be questioned. I make my request simply as a matter of precaution."

The manager, with a small centre punch, put a few " spots " on the main frame, noting the machine's number at the same time.

" Now you want to know where we got it," he went on to La Touche. " Excuse me a moment."

He disappeared to his office, returning in a few minutes with a slip of paper in his hand.

" The machine was received from the Avrotte Pump Construction office "—he referred to the paper—" on 2nd April last. It was supplied to the firm several years earlier, and on the date mentioned they exchanged it for a more up-to-date machine, a No. 10."

" I am extremely obliged, monsieur. You may trust me to keep you out of the business if at all possible."

Calling a taxi, La Touche took the machine to his hotel in the rue de La Fayette. There he typed another sample, and, using a powerful lens, compared the letters with the photographic enlargements he had obtained of the Le Gautier type. He was satisfied. The machine before him was that for which he had been in search.

He was delighted at his success. The more he thought of it, the more certain he felt that Boirac's fault-finding was merely an excuse to get rid of the typewriter. And the manufacturer had dismissed Mlle. Lambert simply because she knew too much. If inquiries were made in the office, he would be safer with her out of the way.

And as to Boirac's deeper object? So far as the detective could see, there could be only one explanation. Boirac knew the Le Gautier letter was done on that machine. And if he knew, did it not follow that he had sent the letter to Felix? And if he had sent the letter, must he not be guilty? To La Touche it began to look like it.

Then a further point struck him. If Boirac were guilty, what about the alibi? The alibi seemed so conclusive. And yet, if he were innocent, what about the typewriter? There seemed to be no escape from the dilemma, and La Touche was horribly puzzled.

But as he thought over the matter he began to see that the discovery of the typewriter did not so greatly help his client after all.

Though at first sight it had seemed to indicate Boirac's guilt, second thoughts showed him that the manufacturer could make a very good case for himself. He could stick to the story told by Mlle. Lambert —that the type was in point of fact not good enough for his work. He could say plausibly enough that for some time he had wanted a machine with a tabulator, and that the bad alignment had only brought the matter to a head. Then, with regard to the typist. Though the girl seemed quiet and truthful, goodness only knew what she might not be holding back. On her own showing she had had exchanges of opinion with her employer, and she might have been very impertinent. At all events, Boirac could give his own version of what took place and no one would know the truth. Further, he could account for his testimonial by saying that while he disliked the girl and wished to be rid of her, he did not want to injure her permanently. He might even admit falsely telling the girl he was going to reorganize his office in order to smooth over her leaving.

With regard to the Le Gautier letter, Boirac could simply deny knowledge, and La Touche did not see how he could be contradicted. It could even be argued that Felix might have bribed a clerk to copy the letter for him on that machine so as to throw suspicion on Boirac. If Felix were guilty, it would be a likely enough move.

At last La Touche came to the definite conclusion that he had not enough evidence either to convict Boirac or clear Felix. He *must* do better. He *must* break the alibi and find the carter.

CHAPTER XXVII
LA TOUCHE'S DILEMMA

THAT night La Touche could not sleep. The atmosphere was sultry and tense. Great masses of blue-black clouds climbing the south-western sky seemed to promise a storm. The detective tossed from side to side, his body restless, his mind intently awake and active. And then an idea suddenly occurred to him.

He had been mentally reviewing the wording of the various advertisements Lefarge had inserted for the carter. These, he recollected, were all to the effect that a reward would be paid for information as to the identity of the carter who had delivered the cask at the rue Cardinet goods station. Who, he thought, in the nature of things could answer that? Only, so far as he could see, two people—the carter himself and the man who engaged him. No one else would know anything about the matter. Of these, obviously the latter was not going to give the affair away. Nor would the carter if the other paid him well or had some hold over him. This, thought La Touche, may be why these advertisements have all failed.

So far he had got when his illuminating idea struck him. The fault of these advertisements was that they had appealed to the wrong people. Instead of appealing to the carter, could his associates not be approached? Or rather his employer, for it was obvious that neither Boirac nor Felix could be his employer, except in the case of this one job. He jumped out of bed, turned on the light, and began to draft a circular letter.

"Dear Sir," (he wrote) "An innocent man is in danger of conviction on a murder charge for want of certain evidence. This could be supplied by a carter—a clean-shaven, sharp-featured man with white hair. If you have (or had last March) such a man in your employment, or know of such, I most earnestly beg you to advise me. I am a private detective, working on behalf of the accused man. I guarantee no harm to the carter. On the contrary, I am willing to pay all men who answer the description five francs if they will call on me here any evening between 8.0 and 10.0, as well as five hundred francs to the man who can give me the information I require."

Repeating the manœuvre he had employed in the case of the advertisement for Mlle. Lambert, La Touche did not add his own name and address. He signed the note Charles Epée, and headed it Hotel d'Arles, rue de Lyon.

Next morning he took his draft to a manufactory of office supplies and arranged for copies to be made and posted to the managers of all the carting establishments in Paris, the envelopes being marked "confidential." Then he went on to the rue de Lyon, and, in the name of Charles Epée, engaged a room at the Hotel d'Arles.

Taking the Metro at the Place de la Bastille, he returned to the goods station in the rue Cardinet. There, after a considerable delay he found his two friends, the porters who had unloaded the cask on that Thursday nearly two months before. Explaining that he expected the carter he was in search of to call at his hotel on some evening in the early future, he offered them five francs a day to sit in his room between 8.0 and 10.0 p.m. to identify the man, should he arrive. To this the porters willingly agreed. That evening they had their first meeting, but without success. No clean-shaven, white-haired, sharp-featured carters turned up.

When La Touche returned to his rue de La Fayette hotel he found a letter from Clifford. The police had made two discoveries. The first La Touche had realized they were bound to make sooner or later. They had learnt of Felix's identity with the art school student who had been in love with the late Mme. Boirac, and of the short-lived engagement between the two. All the assistance which these facts gave the prosecution was therefore now at the disposal of the authorities.

The second piece of information was that Inspector Burnley had found the carter who had taken the cask from Waterloo on the Wednesday morning of the fateful week and delivered it at Charing Cross next morning, for, it seemed, both these jobs had been done by the same man.

It appeared that about 7.30 on the Tuesday evening of that week a dark, foreign-looking man with a pointed black beard had called at the office of Messrs. Johnson, the large carting agents in Waterloo Road, and had hired a dray and man for the two following days, as well as the use of an empty shed for the same period. He had instructed the carter to meet him at Waterloo Station at 10.0 next morning, Wednesday. There, on the arrival of the Southampton boat train, he had claimed the cask and had it loaded up on the dray, as was already known. The vehicle had been taken to the shed, where it had been left, the horse having been sent back to the stable. The black-bearded man had told the driver he might take the remainder of the day as a holiday, but that he wanted him to return on the following morning, Thursday, take the cask to Charing Cross, and there book it to Paris. He had handed him the amount of the freight as well as ten shillings for himself. Upon the man asking where in Paris the cask was to be sent, the other had told him he would leave it properly addressed. This he had done, for next morning the cask had a new label, bearing the name of Jaques de Belleville, Cloakroom, Gare du Nord. The carter had then left the black-bearded man in the shed with the cart and cask. Next morning he had booked the latter to Paris.

Asked if he could identify the black-bearded man, the carter said he believed he could. But he failed to do so. On being taken to see Felix, he stated the artist was like the dark foreigner, but he would not swear he was the same man.

This news interested La Touche greatly, and he sat smoking

into the small hours seeing how far he could work these new facts into the theories of the crime which he and Clifford had discussed. If the prosecution were correct, Felix must have been the man who called at the cartage establishment at 7.30 on Tuesday evening. He would therefore have had undisputed possession of the cask from about 11.0 a.m. on the Wednesday until, say, 7.0 on the following morning, and there were two obvious ways in which he could have put in the body. Either he could have procured another horse and taken the cask to St. Malo, where, in the privacy of the walled yard, he could have removed the statue and substituted the body, returning the cask to the shed by the same means, or he could have hidden the body in his two-seater and run it to the shed, making the exchange there. Unfortunately, La Touche saw, the facts he had just learnt would fit in only too well with the theory of Felix's guilt.

On the other hand they supplied another period for which an alibi might be found for the artist—7.30 on the Tuesday night. But, remembering his own and Clifford's researches into the manner in which Felix spent that week, La Touche was not hopeful of help here.

The detective then turned his thoughts to Clifford's theory of Boirac's guilt. And immediately he saw how the news crystallized the issue of the alibi. Up to the present the alibi had been considered as a whole, the portions which had been tested and those which had not, alike included. Generally speaking, it had been argued that if Boirac was in Paris and in Belgium during the fateful days, he could not have been in London. But now here was a direct issue between definite hours. At 7.30 on the Tuesday evening the bearded man was at Johnson's in the Waterloo Road. At 2.30 that same day Boirac was at Charenton. La Touche looked up his Continental Bradshaw. A train arrived at Victoria at 7.10, which would just enable a traveller from Paris to reach the carting contractor's at the hour named. But that train left Paris at 12.0 noon. Therefore it was utterly and absolutely out of the question that Boirac could be the man. But then there was the typewriter. . . .

La Touche was back on the horns of the old dilemma. If Boirac was guilty, how did he work the alibi? if innocent, why did he get rid of the typewriter? He almost writhed in his exasperation. But it only made him more determined than ever to reach a solution, cost him what it might of labour and trouble.

The next evening he set off to the Hotel d'Arles in the rue de Lyon, to await with the goods yard porters the coming of sharp-featured carters with white hair.

A number of replies to his circular had come in. Some were merely negative, the recipients having written to say that no carter answering to the description was known to them. Others stated they knew men of the type required, mentioning names and addresses. La Touche made lists of these, determining to call on any who did not come to see him at the hotel.

While he was engaged in this work his first visitor was announced. This man was clean-shaven and white-haired, but the sharpness of his features was not much in evidence. The porters immediately gave the pre-arranged sign that this was not the man, and La Touche, handing him his five francs, bowed him out, at the same time noting him " Seen " on his list.

After he left came another and another, till before ten o'clock they had interviewed no less than fourteen men. All these more or less completely answered the description, but all the porters instantly negatived. The following evening eleven men called and the next four, with the same result.

On the third day there was another letter from Clifford. The lawyer wrote that he had been greatly struck by the intelligence of the carter who had carried about the cask in London. Surprised at so superior a man holding such a position, he had brought him to his house in the hope of learning his history. And there he had made a discovery of the highest importance, and which, he thought, would lead them direct to the end of their quest. The carter, John Hill, had been quite ready to tell his story, which was as follows: Until four years previously Hill had been a constable in the Metropolitan police. He had a good record, and, he had believed, a future. Then he had had an unfortunate difference with his superior officer. Hill did not give the particulars, but Clifford understood it was a private matter and concerned a girl. But it led to a row during hours of duty, in which Hill admitted having entirely forgotten himself. He had been dismissed, and, after a long and weary search, could find no better job than that he now held.

" But," wrote Clifford, " it's an ill wind, etc. This curious history of Hill's is the thing that will settle our case. He has been trained in observation, and he observed something about the man with the cask that will definitely settle his identity. When he was paying him he noticed on the back of the first joint of his right forefinger, a small scar as if from a burn. He says he is sure of this mark and could swear to it. I asked him had he told the police. He said not, that he didn't love the police, and that he had answered what he had been asked and nothing more. When he understood I was acting against the police he volunteered the information, and

I could see that he would be glad to give evidence that would upset their conclusions."

Clifford had then done the obvious thing. He had gone to inspect Felix's finger, and he had found there was no mark on it.

At first to La Touche this seemed the end of the case. This man's evidence definitely proved Felix innocent. His next business would be to examine Boirac's hand, and, if the mark was there, the matter was at an end.

But as he thought over it he saw that this was indeed far from being the fact. There was still the alibi. As long as that stood, a clever counsel would insist on Boirac's innocence. To a jury the thing would be conclusive. And this ex-policeman's evidence could be discredited. In fact, the very thing that had enabled them to get hold of it—the man's dislike of the official force—would minimize its value. It would be argued that Hill had invented the scar to upset the police case. By itself, a jury might not accept this suggestion, but the alibi would give it weight, in fact, would make it the only acceptable theory.

However, the next step was clear. La Touche must see Boirac's hand, and, if there was a scar, Hill must see it too.

About eleven o'clock therefore, the detective hailed a taxi with an intelligent looking driver. Having reached the end of the rue Championnet he dismounted, explaining to the man what he wanted him to do. A few moments later found him once more seated in the window of the café, his eyes fixed on the Pump Construction office across the street. The taxi in accordance with orders, drove slowly about, ready to pick him up if required.

About quarter to twelve, Boirac came out and began walking slowly citywards. La Touche quietly followed, keeping at the other side of the street, the taxi hovering close behind. Then the detective congratulated himself on his foresight, for, on Boirac's reaching the end of the street, he hailed another taxi, and, getting in, was driven rapidly off.

It was the work of a couple of seconds for La Touche to leap into his car and to instruct his driver to follow the other vehicle.

The chase led down to the Grands Boulevards to Bellini's in the Avenue de l'Opera. Here Boirac entered, followed by his shadower.

The great restaurant was about three parts full, and La Touche from the door was able to see Boirac taking his seat in one of the windows. The detective dropped into a place close to the cash desk, and, ordering table d'hôte lunch, insisted on getting the bill at once, on the grounds that his time was limited and that he might have to leave before finishing. Then he ate a leisurely lunch, keeping an eye on the manufacturer.

That gentleman was in no hurry, and La Touche had spent a long time over his coffee before the other made a move. A number of people were leaving the restaurant and there was a very short queue at the cash desk. La Touche so arranged his departure that he was immediately behind Boirac in this queue. As the manufacturer put down his money La Touche saw his finger. The scar was there!

"Here at last is certainty," thought the detective, as he drew back out of the other's sight. "So Boirac is the man after all! My work is done!"

And then the annoying afterthought arose. Was his work done? Was the proof he had got of Boirac's guilt sufficient? There was still the alibi. Always that alibi loomed in the background, menacing his success.

Though La Touche had now no doubt Boirac was the man the carter saw, he felt it would be more satisfactory if the two could be brought together in the hope of getting direct evidence of identity. As time was of value he called up Clifford and rapidly discussed the point. It was agreed that, if possible, Hill should be sent to Paris by that evening's train. A couple of hours later there was a telegram from the solicitor that this had been arranged.

Accordingly, next morning La Touche met the English boat train at the Gare du Nord and welcomed a tall, dark man with a small, close-cut moustache. As they breakfasted, the detective explained what he wished done.

"The difficulty is that you must see Boirac without his seeing you," he ended up, "we do not want him to know we are on his trail."

"I understand that, sir," returned Hill. "Have you any plan arranged for me?"

"Not exactly, but I thought if you were to make up with a false beard and wear glasses he wouldn't spot you. You could dress differently also. Then I think you might lunch in the same restaurant and come out behind him and see his hand when he's paying same as I did."

"That would do, sir, but the worst of it is I don't know my way about either in Paris or in a restaurant of that class."

"You can't speak any French?"

"Not a word, sir."

"Then I think I had better ask my man, Mallet to go with you. He could keep you straight, and you needn't talk at all."

Hill nodded his head.

" A good idea, sir."

" Come, then, and let me get you a rig-out."

They drove to shop after shop till the ex-policeman was supplied with new clothes from head to foot. Then they went to a theatrical property maker, where a flowing black beard and long moustache were fitted on. A pair of clear glass pince-nez completed the purchases. When, an hour later, Hill stood in La Touche's room dressed up in his new disguise, no one who had known him before would have recognized the ex-policeman, still less the London carter.

" Capital, Hill," said La Touche. " Your own mother wouldn't know you."

The detective had sent a wire for his assistant, and Mallet was waiting for them. La Touche introduced the two men and explained his plans.

" We haven't much more than time," said Mallet, " so if you're ready, Hill, we'll go on."

In something under three hours they returned. The expedition had been a complete success. They had gone direct to Bellini's, preferring to take the risk that the manufacturer did not lunch at the same place each day, rather than that of following him again. And they were not disappointed. Towards twelve Boirac had entered and taken his seat at what was probably the same table in the window. On his rising to leave, they had repeated La Touche's manœuvre and Hill, just behind him when he was paying, had seen his finger. Instantly he had identified the scar. Indeed, before seeing it he had been sure from Boirac's build and way of moving he was the man they sought.

In the evening, La Touche gave Hill a good dinner, paid him well, and saw him off by the night train to London. Then he returned to his hotel, lit a cigar, and lay down on his bed to wrestle again with the problem of the alibi.

He now knew that the alibi was faked. Boirac, beyond question, had been in London at 7.30 on the Tuesday evening. Therefore he could not have been at Charenton at 2.0. That was the ever-recurring difficulty, and he could see no way out.

He took a piece of paper and wrote down the hours at which they definitely knew the manufacturer's whereabouts. At 7.30 on Tuesday evening he was in London at Johnson's carting establishment in Waterloo Road. From 10.0 till 11.0 next morning, Wednesday, he was with Hill, getting the cask from Waterloo to the shed. He could not have left London in the interval, so this meant that he must have been in the English capital from 7.30 o'clock on

Tuesday evening till 11.0 on Wednesday morning. Then he wa
at the Hotel Maximilian in Brussels at 11.0 on that same Wednesda
evening. So much was certain beyond doubt or question.

Did these hours work in? On Tuesday, frankly, they did no
What about Wednesday? Could a man who was in London a
11.0 in the morning be in Brussels at 11.0 the same evening? L
Touche got his Continental Bradshaw. Here it was. London depai
2.20 p.m.; Brussels arrive 10.25 p.m. That seemed all right. /
traveller arriving by that train would reach the Hotel Maximilia
"about 11.0." Then La Touche remembered that Boirac's accoun
of how he spent this day had not been substantiated. He had tol
Lefarge he had gone to his brother's house at Malines, havin
forgotten that the latter was in Sweden. No confirmation of tha
statement was forthcoming. Neither the caretaker nor anyon
else had seen the manufacturer. La Touche was not long in comin
to the conclusion he had never been there at all. No, he had crosse
from London by the 2.20.

Then the detective recalled the telephone. A message had bee
sent by Boirac from one of the cafés in the old town, asking th
hotel clerk to reserve a room. That call had been received abou
eight o'clock. But at eight o'clock Boirac was not in the old towr
He was on his journey from London.

La Touche took up his Bradshaw again. Where would
traveller by the 2.20 p.m. from Charing Cross be at eight o'clock
And then like a flash he understood. The boat arrived at Osten
at 7.30 p.m. and the Brussels train did not leave until 8.40. H
had telephoned from Ostend!

So that was it! A simple plan, but how ingenious! And the
La Touche remembered that Lefarge had been quite unable
confirm the statement that Boirac had dined at the café in th
Boulevard Anspach, or had been present at *Les Troyens* in th
Théâtre de la Monnaie. No. He was on the right track at las

The Wednesday was now accounted for, but there still remaine
the terrible difficulty of the Tuesday. What about the café
Charenton?

And then La Touche got another of his inspirations. He ha
solved the Wednesday telephone trick. Could that on Tuesda
be explained in the same way?

He had already noted that a traveller by the train leaving Par
at 12.0 noon and arriving at Victoria at 7.10 could just reac
Waterloo Road by 7.30. Thinking again over the point, he sudden
saw the significance of the hour of the call at the carting establisl
ment. It was late. A man wishing to do business there would ha

gone earlier, had he been able. But this man was not able. He had only reached the city at 7.10.

He turned back to the telephone calls. Where, he asked himself with growing excitement, would a passenger by the 12.0 noon from Paris be at 2.30? And then he was dashed with disappointment. That train did not reach Calais till 3.31 p.m., and at 2.30 it must have been running at full speed somewhere between Abbeville and Boulogne. Boirac could not have telephoned from the train. Therefore he could not have travelled by it.

La Touche had hoped to find that, adopting the same manœuvre on each day, the manufacturer had telephoned from some station en route, presumably Calais. But that apparently was not so. At the same time, the detective could not but feel he was getting near the truth.

He looked at the time table again. The train in question reached Calais at 3.31 and the boat left at 3.45. That was a delay of fourteen minutes. Would there be time, he wondered, to make two long-distance calls in fourteen minutes? Hardly, he thought. He considered what he himself would do if confronted with Boirac's problem.

And then suddenly he saw it. What could be more obvious than to go by an earlier train and to break the journey at Calais? How would this time table work?

Paris	dep.	9.50 a.m.
Calais	arr.	1.11 p.m.
Calais	dep.	3.45 p.m.
Victoria	arr.	7.10 p.m.

If Boirac had done that he would have had over two and a half hours in Calais, which would have given him the opportunity he required. La Touche believed he had reached the solution at last.

But Boirac had been actually seen telephoning from Charenton. For a moment the detective's spirits fell. But he felt he must be right so far. Some explanation of the difficulty would occur to him.

And it did. The waiter had believed Boirac was there on Monday. And he must have been! In some way he must have faked the telephoning. There could be nothing else for it.

Another point occurred to him. Surely, he thought, the telephone operator always mentions the name of the calling town in inter-urban calls? If Boirac had called up his office from Calais, would not the operator have said, "Calais wants you"? If so, how had the manufacturer been able to deceive his butler and chief clerk?

This was undoubtedly a difficulty. But he put it on one side as he began to think how this new theory could be tested.

First he would go again to the Charenton waiter and explain the importance of settling the day on which Boirac lunched. Perhaps the man would now be able to recall some circumstance which would make this clear. Next he would find out from François and Dufresne whether any phrase such as " Calais wants you " had been used by the telephone operator. This inquiry, he noted, must be made with great skill, so as to avoid rousing Boirac's suspicion should either man repeat the conversation. From the telephone central at Calais, if not at Paris, he could doubtless find if calls were made from the former town to the latter at the hour in question, and he might also find that someone answering to the description of Boirac had made those calls. Finally, it might be possible at Ostend to get information about the Brussels call.

Inquiries would either confirm or disprove his theory.

The next morning therefore saw La Touche again in the café at Charenton in conversation with the waiter.

" The point as to which day the gentleman was here has become important," he explained, " and I shall hand you another twenty francs if you can settle it."

The man was evidently anxious to earn the money. He thought earnestly for some time, but at last had to confess he could recall nothing fixing the date.

" Do you remember what he had to eat? Would that help you? " asked the detective.

The waiter shook his head after consideration.

" Or any little matter of a clean cloth or napkin or anything of that kind? No? Or any other person who was in at the same time, or to whom you may have spoken on the subject?"

Again the man shook his head. Then suddenly a look of satisfaction passed over his face.

" But yes, monsieur," he said eagerly, " I remember now. What you have just asked me brings it to my mind. M. Pascot lunched also when the gentleman was here, and he noticed him and asked me if I knew who he was. M. Pascot may be able to tell us."

" Who is M. Pascot?"

" The apothecary, monsieur. From a dozen doors up the street. He comes here sometimes when madame goes shopping to Paris. If you like, monsieur, I will go with you to him and we can inquire."

" I should be greatly obliged."

A walk of a few yards brought them to the chemist's shop. M. Pascot was a large, bald man, with a consequential manner.

" Good-day, M. Pascot," the waiter greeted him deferentially. " This gentleman is a friend of mine, a detective, and he is engaged on an inquiry of much importance. You remember that man with the black beard who was lunching in the café the last day you were in? He was sitting at the little table in the alcove and then he began telephoning. You remember? You asked me who he was."

"I remember," rumbled the apothecary in a deep bass voice, "and what of him?"

"My friend here wants to find out what day he was at the café, and I thought perhaps you would be able to tell him?"

"And how should I be able to tell him?"

"Well, M. Pascot, you see it was on the same day that you were with us, and I thought maybe you would be able to fix that date, the day madame was in Paris—you told me that."

The pompous man seemed slightly annoyed, as if the waiter was taking a liberty in mentioning his personal concerns before a stranger. La Touche broke in with his smooth suavity.

"If, M. Pascot, you could do anything to help me, I should be more than grateful. I should explain to you that I am acting on behalf of an innocent man," and he drew a pathetic picture of the evil case in which Felix found himself, ending up by delicately insinuating that a reward for suitable information was probable.

M. Pascot thawed.

"Permit me to consult madame, monsieur," he said, and with a bow he withdrew. In a few moments he reappeared.

"I can recollect the date now, monsieur. Madame had occasion to go to Paris to see her solicitor on business, and a note of the date was kept. It was Monday, the 29th of March last."

"I cannot say, monsieur, how obliged I am to you," said La Touche in heartfelt tones, and, by a sort of legerdemain, of which both participants remained profoundly unconscious, a twenty-franc bill passed from hand to hand. La Touche was extraordinarily pleased. He had broken the alibi.

Leaving the apothecary and waiter bowing and smiling as a result of their *douceurs,* La Touche turned his steps to the pier and took a river steamer to the Pont de l'Alma. Walking up the Avenue he rang at Boirac's, and was soon closeted with François in his little room.

"About that telephone message we were talking of the other day, M. François," he remarked casually, when they had conversed on general subjects for some minutes, "I wasn't quite certain where you said M. Boirac was speaking from. My first recollection was that you said Calais; then I wondered if it was not Charenton. I have to make a report on my proceedings and I would like to get it as correct as possible."

The butler looked surprised and interested.

"It is curious, monsieur, that you should ask me that, for I don't remember mentioning anything about it. I also thought at first it was Calais. I thought the operator said 'Calais wants you,' and I was surprised, for I did not know M. Boirac intended to leave Paris. But I was wrong, for when M. Boirac began to speak I asked him the direct question. 'You are speaking from Calais?' I said. 'No,' he answered, 'from Charenton.' I am sure now it was my mistake and that what I thought was Calais was really Charenton. I am not very quick and on the telephone these names sound very much alike. Strange your making the same mistake."

"It is curious," admitted La Touche, "almost like one of those extraordinary cases of thought transference you read of. However, I am obliged for your confirmation that it was Charenton," and he diverted the conversation into other channels.

His next visit was to the Telephone Central. Here at first they were not keen to give him any information, but on producing his card and confidentially explaining his business to the head of the department, he obtained what he wanted. Inquiries were made from Calais by wire, and after a considerable delay he was informed that at 2.32 and 2.44 on the Tuesday in question calls were made on Paris. The demand came from the public call office and were for the following numbers: Passy 386 and Nord 745. When La Touche found from the directory that these numbers were those of M. Boirac's house and office respectively, he could hardly refrain from laughing aloud.

"How, I wonder," he thought, "did Lefarge neglect so obvious a check on the Charenton messages?" Then it occurred to him that probably only inter-urban calls were so noted.

The proof of his theory seemed so complete he did not think it necessary to make inquiries at Ostend. Indeed, he believed his task was done, and began to consider an immediate return to London.

CHAPTER XXVIII

THE UNRAVELLING OF THE WEB

WHEN La Touche solved the problem of how Boirac had faked his alibi, his first impression was that his work was done. But as had happened so often before, second thoughts showed him that his was hardly the case. Though he had established Boirac's guilt o his own satisfaction, he doubted if he could prove it in court, and, indeed, the whole matter was still far from clear.

He felt that if he could only find the carter who had brought the cask to the rue Cardinet he would reach certainty on at least some of the points which were puzzling him. He therefore decided to concentrate once more on this problem.

Since the sending out of his circular to the managers of the various carting establishments in the city, he had interviewed no less than twenty-seven more or less clean-shaven, white-haired, and sharp-featured carters. But all to no purpose. The man he wanted was not among them. And as answers to practically all his circulars had been received, he had reluctantly come to the conclusion his plan had failed.

That evening, when Mallet called to make his customary report on Boirac's doings, the two men discussed the matter, and it was a remark dropped by his assistant that turned La Touche's thoughts to a point he had previously overlooked.

"Why do you think he was employed by a cartage contractor?" Mallet had asked, and La Touche had been going to reply with some asperity that cartage contractors were not uncommonly found to employ carters, when the pertinence of the other's question struck him. Why, indeed? Of the thousands of carters in Paris, only a small proportion were employed by cartage firms. By far the greater number worked for specific businesses. Might not the man who brought the cask to the goods station belong to this class, and if so, might not this account for the failure of the original advertisements? If a carter were bribed to use his employer's vehicle for his own gain he would not afterwards give the fact away. And to La Touche it seemed that such a move would be just what might be expected from a man of Boirac's mentality.

But if this theory were correct; if the carter had thus been bound over to silence, how was the man to be discovered and the truth wrung from him?

La Touche smoked two cigars over this problem, and then it occurred to him that the method he had already adopted was sound as far as it went. It merely did not go far enough.

The only way in which he could ensure finding his hypothetical carter would be to send a circular to every employer in Paris. But that was too large an order.

That night, he discussed the matter with the two porters, whom he found intelligent men and keenly interested in the inquiry. He made them describe the kind of cart the cask was brought in, then with a directory he marked off the trades in which the employment of such a vehicle was likely. When he had finished, though some thousands of names were included, he did not think the number overwhelming.

For a considerable time he pondered the question of advertising his circular in the press. At last he decided he could not do so, as if Boirac saw it he would doubtless take precautions to prevent the truth becoming known. La Touche therefore returned to the office of the Business Supplies Company and instructed them to send his circular to each of the thousands of employers in the selected trades, they tabulating the replies and giving him the summary. Though he was by no means sanguine of the success of this move, he felt it offered a chance.

For the next three evenings La Touche and the porters had a busy time. White-haired carters turned up at the Hotel d'Arles literally in dozens, till the management threatened an ejectment and talked of a claim for fresh carpets. But all was fruitless. The man they wanted did not appear.

On the third day, amongst other letters sent on from the Business Supplies Company, was one which immediately interested La Touche.

"In reply to your circular letter of the 18th inst," wrote Messrs. Corot, Fils, of the rue de Rivoli, "we have a man in our employment who, at the end of March, answered your description. His name is Jean Dubois, of 18b rue de Falaise, near Les Halles. About that time, however, he ceased shaving and has now grown a beard and moustache. We have asked him to call on you."

Was it, thought La Touche, merely a coincidence that this clean-shaven carter should begin to grow a beard immediately after the delivery of the cask? When two more days passed and the man did not turn up, La Touche determined to call on him.

Accordingly the next evening he arranged for Mallet and one of the porters to deal with the men at the Hotel d'Arles, while he himself in company with the other porter set out to find Dubois. The rue de Falaise turned out to be a narrow, dirty street of high sombre buildings, with the word slum writ large across their grimy frontages. At 18b, La Touche ascended and knocked at a ramshackle door on a dark stone landing. It was opened by a slatternly woman, who stood, silently waiting for him to speak, in the gloom of the threshold. La Touche addressed her in his usual bland manner.

"Good evening, madame. Is this where M. Jean Dubois of Messrs. Corot, Fils, lives?"

The woman signified assent, but without inviting her visitor in.

"I have a little job for him. Could I see him, please?"

"He's not in, monsieur."

"That's unfortunate for me and for him too, I fancy. Can you tell me where I should find him?"

The woman shrugged her shoulders.

"I cannot tell, monsieur." She spoke in a dull, toneless way, as if the struggle for existence had sapped away all her interest in life.

La Touche took out a five franc piece and pushed it into her hand.

"You get hold of him for me," he said. "I want this little job done and he could do it. It'll get him into no trouble, and I'll pay him well."

The woman hesitated. Then, after a few seconds, she said:—

"If I tell you where he is, will you give me away?"

"No, on my honour. We shall have found him by accident."

"Come this way, then, monsieur."

She led them down the stairs and out again into the dingy street. Passing along it like a furtive shadow she turned twice, then halted at the corner of a third street.

"Down there, monsieur," she pointed. "You see that café with the coloured glass windows? He'll be in there," and without waiting for an acknowledgment she slipped away, vanishing silently into the gloom.

The two men pushed open the café door and entered a fairly large room dotted with small marble tables, with a bar in one corner and a dancing stage at the back. Seating themselves unostentatiously at a table near the door they called for drinks.

There were some fifteen or twenty men and a few women in the place, some reading the papers, some playing dominoes, but most lounging in groups and talking. As La Touche's keen eye ran over the faces, he soon spotted his man.

"Is that he, Charcot?" he asked, pointing to a small, unhealthy looking fellow, with a short, untidy, white beard and moustache.

The porter looked cautiously. Then he assented eagerly.

"It's the man, monsieur, I believe. The beard changes him a bit, but I'm nearly sure it's he."

The suspect was one of those on the outskirts of a group, to whom a stout, fussy man with a large nose was holding forth on some socialistic subject. La Touche crossed over and touched the white-haired man on the arm.

"M. Jean Dubois?"

The man started and an expression of fear came into his eyes. But he answered civilly enough.

"Yes, monsieur. But I don't know you."

"My name is La Touche. I want a word or two with you. Will you have a drink with me and my friend here?"

He indicated the porter, Charcot, and they moved over. The fear had left Dubois's eyes, but he still looked uneasy. In silence they sat down.

"Now, Dubois, what will you take?"

When the carter's wants were supplied, La Touche bent towards him and began speaking in a low tone :—

"I dare say, Dubois, you already guess what I want and I wish to say before anything else that you have nothing to fear if you are straight with me. On the contrary, I will give you one hundred francs if you answer my questions truly. If not—well, I am connected with the police, and we'll become better acquainted."

Dubois moved uneasily as he stammered :—

"I don't know what you mean, monsieur."

"So that there shall be no mistake, I shall tell you. I want to know who it was engaged you to take the cask to the rue Cardinet goods station."

La Touche, who was watching the other intently, saw him start, while his face paled and the look of fear returned to his eyes. It was evident he understood the question. That involuntary motion had given him away.

"I assure you, monsieur, I don't know what you mean. What cask are you referring to?"

La Touche bent closer.

"Tell me, do you know what was in that cask? No? Well, I'll tell you. There was a body in it—the body of a woman—a murdered woman. Did you not guess that from the papers? Did you not realize that the cask you carried to the station was the one that all the papers have been full of? Now, do you want to be arrested as an accessory after the fact in a murder case?"

The man was ghastly, and beads of perspiration stood on his forehead. In a trembling voice he began again to protest his ignorance. La Touche cut him short.

"Chut, man! You needn't keep it up. Your part in the thing is known, and if it wasn't you would soon give it away. Dubois, you haven't red enough blood for this kind of thing! Be guided by me. Make a clean breast of it, and I'll give you the hundred francs, and, what's more, I'll do my best to help you out of your trouble with your employers. If you don't, you'll have to come along now to the Sûreté. Make up your mind quickly what you're going to do."

The man, evidently panic stricken, remained silent. La Touche took out his watch.

"I'll give you five minutes," he said, and, leaning back in his chair, he lit a cigar.

Before the time was up the man spoke.

"If I tell you everything will you not arrest me?" His fright was pitiable.

"Certainly not. I don't want to do you any harm. If you give me the information you go free with a hundred francs in your pocket. But if you try to deceive me, you can explain your position tomorrow to the examining magistrate."

The bluff had its effect.

"I'll tell you, monsieur. I'll tell you the whole truth."

"Good," said La Touche, "then we had better move to a more private place. We'll go to my hotel, and you, Charcot"—he turned to the porter—"get away back to the rue de Lyon and tell M. Mallet and your friend the man's found. Here's what I owe you and a trifle more."

Charcot bowed and vanished, while La Touche and the carter, getting out into one of the larger streets, drove to the rue de La Fayette.

"Now, Dubois," said the detective, when they were seated in his room.

"I'm going to tell you the gospel truth, monsieur," began the carter, and from his earnest, anxious manner La Touche believed him. "And I'm not going to deny that I was in the wrong, even if I do get the sack over it. But I was fair tempted, and I thought it was an easy way to earn a bit of money without doing anyone any harm. For that's the fact, monsieur. What I did, did no harm to anyone.

"It was on Monday, monsieur, Monday the 29th March, that I was out at Charenton delivering goods for Messrs. Corot. I stopped at a café there for a glass of beer. While I was drinking it a man came up to me and asked was that my cart? I said I was in charge of it, but it belonged to Messrs. Corot. 'I want a little job done with a cart,' he says, 'and it's not convenient for me to go into Paris to an agent's, and if you would save me the trouble by doing it for me I'll pay you well.' 'I couldn't do that, monsieur,' I says, 'for if my employers got to know they'd give me the sack.' 'But how would they know?' he asks, 'I wouldn't tell them, and I guess you wouldn't either.' Well, monsieur, we talked on, and first I refused, but afterwards I agreed to do it. I admit I was wrong using the cart like that, but he tempted me. He said it would only take about an hour, and he would give me ten francs. So I agreed."

" What was this man like?"

" He was a middle-sized man, monsieur, with a black pointed beard, and very well dressed."

" And what did he want you to do?"

" On the next Thursday afternoon at half-past four I was to go to an address he gave me and load up a cask, and bring it to the corner of the rue de La Fayette, close to the Gare du Nord. He said he would meet me there and tell me where to take it."

" And did he?"

" Yes. I got there first and waited about ten minutes, and then he came up. He took the old label off the cask and nailed on another he had with him. Then he told me to take the cask to the State Railway Goods Station in the rue Cardinet and book it to London. He gave me the freight as well as the ten francs for myself. He said he should know if the cask did not get to London, and threatened that if I played any tricks he would inform Messrs. Corot what I had done."

This statement was not at all what La Touche had expected, and he was considerably puzzled.

" What was the address he gave you at which you were to get the cask?"

" I forget the exact address. It was from a large corner house in the Avenue de l'Alma."

" What?" roared La Touche, springing excitedly to his feet. " The Avenue de l'Alma, do you say?" He laughed aloud.

So this was it! The cask that went to St. Katharine Docks— the cask containing the body—had gone, not from the Gare du Nord, but direct from Boirac's house! Fool that he was not to have thought of this! Light was at last dawning. Boirac had killed his wife—killed her in her own house—and had there packed her body in the cask, sending it direct to Felix. At long last La Touche had got the evidence he wanted, evidence that would clear Felix— evidence that would bring Boirac to the scaffold!

He was thrilled with his discovery. For a moment the whole affair seemed clear, but once again second thoughts showed him there was a good deal still to be explained. However, once he had got rid of this Dubois, he would see just where he stood.

He questioned the carter exhaustively, but without gaining much further information. That the man had no idea of the identity of his seducer was clear. The only name he had got hold of was that of Dupierre, for Boirac had instructed him to say at his house that he had called for Messrs. Dupierre's cask. Asked if he had not seen the advertisements of rewards for the information he had now given, the man said he had, but that he was afraid to come forward. First he feared he would lose his job if the matter came to his employer's ears, and then the very fact that so large a reward was offered had frightened him, as he assumed he had unwittingly helped with some crime. He had suspected the matter was one of robbery until he saw of the discovery of the cask in the papers. Then he had at once guessed that he had assisted a murderer to dispose of his victim's body, and he had lived in a veritable nightmare lest his share in the business should be discovered. Failing to get anything further out of him, La Touche finally dismissed him somewhat contemptuously with his hundred francs. Then he settled himself to try and puzzle out his problem.

And first as to the movements of the cask. It had started from Boirac's house; how did it get there? Clearly from Dupierre's. It must have been the cask in which Boirac's statue had been sent home. That cask, then, left Dupierre's on the Saturday of the dinner-party, reaching Boirac's house the same day. It lay there until the following Thursday. During that time the statue was taken out and the body substituted. The cask then travelled to London, was taken by Felix to St. Malo, and finally got into the hands of the police at Scotland Yard.

But then, what about the cask which was met at Waterloo and sent back from London to the Gare du Nord?

This, La Touche saw, must have been a different cask, and there must therefore have been two moving about, and not one as they had believed. He tried to follow the movements of this second cask. It left Dupierre's on the Tuesday evening, reached Waterloo on the following morning and on the next day, Thursday, was sent back to Paris, reaching the Gare du Nord at 4.45 p.m. It had always been assumed this cask went from there to the rue Cardinet goods station. This was now proved to have been an error. Where, then, did it go?

Like a flash La Touche saw. It had gone from the Gare du Nord to Dupierre's. He looked up his chronology of the case. Yes, a cask had been received by Dupierre on that Thursday evening, but they had believed it had come from Boirac's house. And then the whole diabolical plot began dimly to appear, as La Touche endeavoured to picture the scene which had probably taken place.

Boirac, he conjectured, must have discovered his wife has eloped with Felix. Mad with jealousy and hatred he kills her. Then, cooling down somewhat, he finds himself with the body on his hands. What is he to do with it? He thinks of the cask standing in the study. He sees that a better receptacle for getting the body out of the house could hardly be devised. He therefore unpacks the statue and puts in the body. The question then arises, where is he to send it? A horrible idea occurs to him. He will wreak his vengeance on Felix by sending it to him. And then a second idea strikes him. If he could arrange that the police would find the body in Felix's possession, would the artist not then be suspected and perhaps executed? Truly a ghastly vengeance! Boirac then types the Le Gautier letter, and sends it to Felix with the idea of making the artist act in so suspicious a way that the police will interfere and find him with the body.

So far La Touche felt his surmises had a ring of probability, but he was still puzzled about the second cask. But, as he turned the matter over in his mind, he gradually began to see light here too.

Boirac had received a cask from Dupierre with his statue. But as it had gone to Felix he had no empty cask to send back in its place to the sculptors. He must return them an empty cask, or else suspicion falls on him at once. Where is he to get it?

And then La Touche saw that the whole business of the second cask must have been arranged simply to meet this difficulty. Boirac must have ordered it, forging Felix's handwriting. La Touche recollected that order was written on the same paper as the Le Gautier letter, suggesting a common origin for both. Boirac met it in London, took it to the shed, there removed and destroyed the statue, and had the cask returned to Paris. At the Gare du Nord he doubtless changed the labels, so that when it reached Dupierre's it bore that with the address of his own house. The other label he must have altered from the Waterloo route to that of long sea. This would account for Dubois's statement that Boirac had changed the labels when he met him in the rue de La Fayette, as well as for the curious faking of that described by the clerk Broughton.

The more La Touche pondered over this theory, the more satisfied he became that he had at last reached the truth. But he had to admit that even yet there were several points he could not understand. When did the murder take place, and where? Did madame really elope with Felix, and, if so, did her husband bring her back alive or dead? How did the impression of the letter ordering the second statue come to be on Felix's blotting paper? If madame was murdered in Paris, how did the jewelled pin reach St. Malo?

But in spite of these and other difficulties, La Touche was more than pleased with his progress, and, as very late he went to his bedroom, he felt a short investigation should be sufficient to test his theory, as well as to clear up all that still remained doubtful.

CHAPTER XXIX

A DRAMATIC DENOUEMENT

THREE days after the finding of the carter, Dubois, and La Touche's discovery of what he believed was the true solution of the mystery, he received a letter which interested him considerably. It came by post to his hotel, and was as follows:—

RUE ST. JEAN 1,
AVENUE DE L'ALMA,
26th May, 1912.

DEAR MONSIEUR,—In connection with your calls here and inquiries into the death of my late mistress, I have just by accident hit on a piece of information which I am sure would be of value to you. It explains the closing of the front door which, you will recollect, I heard about 1.0 a.m. on the night of the dinner-party. I think it will have the effect of entirely clearing your client, though I am afraid it does not point to anyone else as the murderer. M. Boirac is dining out tonight and most of the servants are attending the marriage festivities of one of the housemaids; the house is therefore unprotected, and I cannot leave it to call on you, but if you could see your way to call here any time during the evening, I shall tell you what I have learnt.

Yours respectfully,
HENRI FRANÇOIS.

"Extraordinary," thought La Touche, "how, when you get some information about a case, more nearly always comes in. Here I worked for ages on this case without getting any forrader, and François made no discoveries to encourage me. Now, when I have almost solved it and it no longer matters, he comes forward with his help. I suppose it's the inverse of misfortunes never coming singly."

He looked at his watch. It was just five o'clock. M. Boirac

might not leave home till nearly eight. If he went a few minutes past that hour he could see François and hear his news.

He wondered what the butler could have discovered. If it really did what he claimed—explained the closing of the front door, that would necessarily clear up much that was still doubtful about the events of that tragic night.

Suddenly an idea flashed into his mind. Was the letter genuine? He had never seen the butler's handwriting, and therefore could form no opinion from its appearance. But was the whole thing *likely*? Could it possibly be the work of Boirac? Might not the manufacturer have discovered that he, La Touche, was on his trail, and might not this be a trap? Could it be an attempt to lure him into a house in which he and his information would be at the manufacturer's mercy?

This was a sinister idea, and he sat pondering its possibility for some minutes. On the whole, he was disposed to reject it. Any attempt on his life or liberty would be exceedingly risky for Boirac. If he really knew what had come out, his game would surely be to collect what money he could and disappear while there was yet time. All the same La Touche felt he should neglect no precaution for his own safety.

He went to the telephone and called up the house in the Avenue de l'Alma.

"Is M. François there?" he asked when he had got through.

"No, monsieur," was the reply. "He has gone out for the afternoon. He will be in about 7.30."

"Thank you. Who is speaking, please?"

"Jules, monsieur, the footman. I am in charge till M. François returns."

This was unsatisfactory, but quite natural and unsuspicious. La Touche felt fairly satisfied, and yet, almost against his will, a doubt remained. He thought he might be better with company, and made another call.

"That you, Mallet? Which of you is off duty? You? Well, I want your company tonight on a short excursion. Will you call round for dinner here at seven and we can go on afterwards?"

When Mallet arrived, La Touche showed him the letter. The subordinate took precisely the same view as his chief.

"I don't think it's a plant," he said, "but with Boirac you can't be too careful. I should bring your John Cockerill, or whatever you use, if I were you."

"I'll do so," said the other, slipping an automatic pistol into his pocket.

They reached the house in the Avenue de l'Alma about 8.15, and La Touche rang. To their surprise and disappointment the door was opened by no less a person than Boirac himself. He seemed to be on the point of going out, as he wore his hat and a dark, caped overcoat which, open at the front, showed his evening dress. Round his right hand was tied a blood-stained handkerchief. He appeared annoyed and as if his temper might give way at any minute. He looked inquiringly at the detectives.

"Could we see M. François, monsieur," asked La Touche politely.

"If you don't mind waiting a few minutes, certainly," answered Boirac. "I was just going out when I cut my hand and I had to send him for a doctor to stop the bleeding. He will be back in a moment. If you like to wait, you can do so in his room—the fourth door on the right."

La Touche hesitated a moment. What if it was a plant after all? Finding Boirac here alone was certainly suspicious. But the cut at least was genuine. La Touche could see the red stain slowly spreading across the handkerchief.

"Well, messieurs, I'm sorry I can't hold the door open. Kindly either come in and wait, or, if you prefer it, call back later on."

La Touche made up his mind. They were armed and on their guard. As he entered the hall his left hand in his overcoat pocket crept to the handle of his magazine pistol, and he quietly covered the manufacturer.

The latter closed the front door behind them and led the way to François's room. It was in darkness, but Boirac, entering before the others, turned on the light.

"Come in and be seated, gentlemen, if you please," he said. "I should like a word with you before François returns."

La Touche did not at all like the turn affairs were taking. Boirac's conduct seemed to him to grow more and more suspicious. Then he reflected again that they were two to one, were armed, and keenly on their guard, and that there could be no cause for uneasiness. Besides, there could be no trap. Boirac had preceded them into the room.

The manufacturer pulled together three chairs.

"If you would kindly be seated, gentlemen, I would tell you what I want you to know."

The detectives obeyed, La Touche still keeping his pistol turned on his host.

"Gentlemen," went on the latter, "I owe you both a very full apology for having played a trick on you, but I am sure, when I have explained the extraordinary circumstances in which I am placed, you will hold me, if not justified, at least excused. And first, I must tell you that I know who you are, and on what business you came to Paris."

He paused for a moment. Then, the others not replying, he continued :—

"I happened to notice your advertisement, M. La Touche, for Mlle. Lambert, and it set me thinking. And when I found, M. Mallet, that you and your friend were shadowing me, I thought still more. As a result of my cogitations I employed a private detective, and learnt from him the identity of both of you and what you were engaged on. When I learnt that you had found Mlle. Lambert, I guessed you would soon discover the typewriter, and sure enough, my detective soon after reported that you had purchased a second-hand No. 7 Remington. Then I had the carter, Dubois shadowed, and I thus learnt that you had discovered him also. I have to compliment you, M. La Touche, on the cleverness with which you found out these matters."

Again he paused, looking inquiringly and somewhat hesitatingly at the others.

"Pray proceed, M. Boirac," said La Touche at last.

"First, then, I offer you my apologies for the trick played you. I wrote the note which brought you here. I feared if I wrote in my own name you would suspect some trick on my part and refuse to come."

"Not unnaturally a suspicion of the kind did enter our minds," answered La Touche. "It is but fair to tell you, M. Boirac, that we are armed"—La Touche withdrew his automatic pistol from his pocket and laid it on a table at his hand—"and if you give either of us the slightest cause for anxiety, we shall fire without waiting to make inquiries."

The manufacturer smiled bitterly.

"I am not surprised at your suspicions. They are reasonable, though absolutely unfounded, and your precautions cannot therefore be offensive to me. As I try to do everything thoroughly, I may admit this cut on my hand was also faked. I simply squeezed a tube of liquid red paint on to the handkerchief. I did it to account for my being alone in the hall when you arrived, which I thought necessary, lest you might refuse to enter."

La Touche nodded.

"Pray proceed with your statement," he said again.

For a man of his years, Boirac looked strangely old and worn. His black hair was flecked with white, his face drawn and unhappy and his eyes weary and sombre. Though he had been speaking quietly enough, he seemed deeply moved and at a loss how to proceed. At last, with a gesture of despair, he went on :—

"What I have to say is not easy, but, alas, I deserve that. I may tell you at once without beating about the bush—I brought you here tonight to make my confession. Yes, gentlemen, you see before you the miserable, guilty man. I killed her, gentlemen. I did it that awful night of the dinner-party. And since then I have never known one moment's ease. What I have suffered no living being could describe. I have been in hell ever since. I have aged more in these last few weeks than in ten years of ordinary life. And now, when to the gnawings of remorse the certainty of the result of your researches is looming before me—I can bear it no longer. The suspense must end. Therefore, after much thought I have decided to make my confession."

That the man was in earnest and his emotion genuine La Touche could no longer doubt. But his suspicions still remained. He asked a question.

"Why have you brought us here to tell us, M. Boirac? Surely the obvious thing would have been for you to go to the Sûreté and see M. Chauvet."

"I know. I should have done that. But this was easier. I tell you, gentlemen, it is bad enough to have to say this to you here, sitting quietly in my own house. There—with several and perhaps stupid officials, with typists—I just couldn't face it. What I want you to do is this. I will tell you everything. Any questions you ask I will answer. Then I don't want to be bothered with it again. All I now hope for is that the end will come quickly. You do what is necessary and at the trial I will plead guilty. You will agree?"

"We will hear what you have to say."

"For that, at least, I am grateful." He pulled himself together with an obvious effort and continued in a low tone, without showing very evident traces of emotion.

"My statement, I fear, will be a long one, as I must tell you all that occurred from the beginning, so that you may understand what led up to this awful consummation. A great part of it you already know—how my wife and Felix fell in love at the art school, and how her father refused his consent to their marriage, then how I, too, fell a victim and asked her hand; how my suit was looked upon with favour and I was misled both by herself and her father about what had taken place at the art school, and how, in short, we were married. And you know, too, I imagine, that our marriage from the first was a failure. I loved Annette intensely, but she never cared for me. We needn't go into it, but I soon saw that she had only married me in a fit of despair at her engagement being broken off. She did me the gravest wrong, though I admit I don't think she meant or realized it. We drifted farther and farther apart, till life together became insupportable. And then I met Felix and asked him to the house, not knowing till weeks later that he was the man who had been in love with my wife at the art school. But you must not think I have anything to say against the honour of either of them. My wife spoiled my life it is true, but she did not elope with Felix, nor did he, so far as I know, ask her to. They were good friends, but, to the best of my belief, nothing more. That is the smallest and the only reparation I can make them, and I make it unreservedly.

"But with me, alas, it was different. Baulked of any chance of happiness in my home through my wife's wicked action—I say it advisedly—her wicked action in marrying me while she loved another, I succumbed to the temptation to look elsewhere for happiness. I met, quite by accident, some one with whom I could have been happy. You will never learn who she was or how I managed to meet her without being suspected—it is enough to say that things reached such a pass that this woman and I found we could no longer go on in the way we were, meeting by stealth, seeing each other only with carefully thought out precautions. The situation was intolerable and I determined to end it. And it was on the evening of the dinner-party that I first saw the way.

"But here, before I go on to tell you the events of that terrible night, lest you might try to find this woman and saddle her with a part of the responsibility for what followed, let me tell you that here again I lost. The week after I destroyed my soul with the ghastly crime of which I will tell you, she got a chill. It turned to pneumonia, and in four days she was dead. I saw the judgment of Heaven beginning. But that is for me alone. Her name, at any rate, is safe. You will never find it out."

Boirac's voice had fallen still lower. He spoke in a sort of toneless, numb way, as if mechanically, and yet his hearers could see that only his iron control prevented a breakdown.

"On that night of the dinner-party," he resumed, "I met Felix accidentally in the hall on his arrival, and brought him into my study to see an etching. It is true we there spoke of the cask which had just arrived with my group, but I gave him no information such as would have enabled him to obtain a similar one.

"All that has been found out of the events of that evening up to the time that I left the works is true. It is true I thought at first I would be kept till late, and afterwards got away comparatively early. I actually left the works about eleven, took the Metro and changed at Châtelet, as I said, but from there my statement to the police was false. No American friend clapped me on the back as I alighted there, nor did such a man exist at all. My walk with him to the Quai d'Orsay, our further stroll round the Place de la Concorde, his going by train to Orleans, and my walk home—all these were pure inventions on my part, made to account for my time between eleven-fifteen and one. What really happened during this time was as follows:—

"I changed at Châtelet, taking the Maillot train for Alma, and walked home down the Avenue. I must have reached my house about twenty minutes or a quarter to twelve.

"I took out my latchkey as I mounted the steps, and then I noticed that one of the slats of the venetian blind of the drawing room window looking out towards the porch had caught up at one end, and a long, thin, triangular block of light shone out into the night. It was just on the level of my eyes and involuntarily I glanced through. What I saw inside stiffened me suddenly and I stood looking. In an arm-chair in the farther part of the room sat my wife, and bending closely over her, with his back towards me, was Felix. They were alone, and, as I watched, a plan entered my mind, and I stood transfixed with my pulses throbbing. Was there something between my wife and Felix? And if not, would it not suit my purpose to assume there was? I continued looking in and presently Felix rose to his feet and they began talking earnestly, Felix gesticulating freely, as was his habit. Then my wife left the room, returning in a few moments and handing him a small object. I was too far off to see what it was, but it seemed like a roll of banknotes. Felix put it carefully in his pocket and then they turned and walked towards the hall. In a few seconds the door opened and I shrank down into the shadows below the window sill.

"'Oh, Léon,' I heard my wife's voice, and it seemed charged with emotion. 'Oh, Léon, how good you are! How glad I am you have been able to do this!'

"Felix's voice showed that he also was moved.

"'Dear lady, is it not such happiness to me? You know I am always at your service.'

"He moved down the steps.

"'You'll write?'

"'Immediately,' he answered, and was gone.

"As the door closed, a furious passion of hate burned up in me for this woman who had ruined my life—who had not only ruined it, but who was still blocking out any chance of happiness I might have had. And also I furiously and jealously hated Felix for being the cause, however innocent, of my loss. And then suddenly I felt as if—perhaps I should say I felt that—a devil had entered and taken possession of me. I became deadly cold and I had the strange feeling that I myself was not really there, but that I was watching someone else. I slipped out my key, noiselessly opened the door, and followed my wife into the drawing-room. Her calm, nonchalant walk across the room roused me to still wilder fury. How well I knew her every motion. This was the way she would have turned to greet me when I arrived from the works, with cold politeness—when it might have been so different. . . .

"She reached her chair in the corner of the room and turned to sit down. As she did so she saw me. She gave a little scream.

"'Raoul, how you startled me!' she cried. 'Have you just arrived?'

"I threw off my hat and she saw my face.

"'Raoul,' she cried again, 'what's the matter? Why do you look like that?'

"I stood and looked at her. Outwardly I was calm, inwardly my blood whirled like molten metal through my veins and my mind was a seething fire.

"'Nothing really,' I said, and someone else seemed to be speaking in a voice I had never heard before, a hoarse, horrible voice. 'Only a mere trifle. Only madame entertaining her lover after her husband has come home.'

"She staggered back as if from a blow and collapsed into her chair, and turned her now pallid face to me.

"'Oh!' she cried in a trembling, choking voice, 'Raoul, it's not true! It's not true, Raoul, I swear it! Don't you believe me, Raoul?'

"I stepped close to her. My hate swelled up in a blinding, numbing, overwhelming passion. It must have shown in my eyes, for a sudden fear leapt into hers.

"She tried to scream, but her dry throat produced only a piteous little cry. Her face had grown ghastly. Drops of sweat grew on her brow.

"I was close by her now. Instinctively my hands went out. I seemed to feel her slender neck between them, with my thumbs pressing. . . . She read my purpose, for a hideous terror shone in her eyes. Dimly I was conscious of her hands tearing at my face. . . .

"I stopped. My brain was numb. I seemed to see myself from

a great distance standing looking at her. She was dead. I hated her more than ever. I was glad to see her dead, to watch that horror still lingering in her eyes. And he? How I hated him, he who had lost me my love and spoilt my life. I would go now. I would follow him and I would kill him. Kill him as I had killed her. I stumbled blindly to find the door.

"And then the devil that possessed me suggested another plan. He had wanted her. Well, he would get her. If he couldn't have her alive, he could have the next best thing. He could have her dead."

M. Boirac paused. He had been speaking in a high-pitched voice and gesticulating as if overwhelmed with excitement. He seemed unconscious of his hearers, as if, carried away by his recollections, he was mentally living over again the awful scene, passing once more through the frenzy of that terrible time. Then, after a few moment's silence he pulled himself together and went on in a more normal tone.

"I determined to send the body to Felix, not only to satisfy my hate, but in the hope that his efforts to get rid of it would bring suspicion of the murder on him. Where, I wondered, could I get a receptacle in which to send it? And then it occurred to me that in the study adjoining was the cask that had just arrived with my statue. It was large, strongly made and bound with iron. It would suit my purpose admirably.

"I crossed to the study and unpacked the group. Then quite coolly I carried the body in and placed it in the cask. The idea that I must divert suspicion from myself grew in my mind, and I therefore took off my wife's evening shoes as their presence would tend to show she had not left the house. I filled up the cask with sawdust, ramming it tight. The body being so much larger than the group, there was a lot of sawdust over. This I swept up with the clothes brush from the hall and put in a handbag, which I locked. Finally I replaced the wooden top of the cask loosely as before, though still strongly enough not to come out if the cask was moved. When I had finished no one would have suspected that anything had been tampered with.

"It was my intention to create the impression that my wife had gone away with Felix. To this end two things appeared immediately necessary. Firstly, such of her outdoor clothes as she probably would have worn must disappear. I accordingly picked up the group and her shoes and went to her room. There I threw the shoes down carelessly before a chair, as if she had changed them. I took her fur coat, a hat, and a pair of walking shoes, and, with the group, carried them to my dressing-room. The only place I could think of for hiding them was in a couple of empty portmanteaux, so I packed the group in one and the clothes in another, carefully locking both.

"The second point was to produce a letter purporting to be from my wife to myself, in which she would say she loved Felix and had gone away with him. I had not time to write one then, but for temporary purposes I put an old letter of my own into a new envelope, addressing it to myself as best I could in my wife's hand. This I left on my desk.

"I had already spent over three-quarters of an hour and it was nearly one. I took a final look round to see that nothing had been forgotten, and was just leaving the drawing-room when my eye caught a glint of light from the carpet immediately behind the chair in which my wife had died. I stepped over and saw it was a brooch which had evidently been torn from her dress during the struggle. I broke out into a cold sweat as I thought how nearly I had missed it, and realized that its discovery by someone else might have disproved my story and brought me to the scaffold. With no clear idea except to hide it, I put it in my waistcoat pocket, took my hat, and, letting myself out, drew the door sharply behind me. After strolling as far as the Champs Elysées and back, I re-entered with my key. As I had hoped and intended, the shutting of the front door had been heard, and I found the butler obviously uneasy at my wife's disappearance. I endeavoured to confirm his suspicions that she had gone away with Felix, and, as you know, completely succeeded.

"Most of that night I spent in my study working out my plans. There was first of all the cask. A cask had been sent me by Dupierre, and it was obvious I must return them an empty one against it or I would give myself away. Where was this empty one to come from?

"It was clear to me that I must get a precisely similar cask to return, and the only way I could do so would be to order another group, in the hope that it would be sent packed in the same way. But obviously I could not have this group sent to me. The idea then occurred to me that I must write in some imaginary name ordering the statue to be delivered at some place such as a station cloak-room, to be kept till called for. There I could get it without letting my identity become known.

"But this plan did not please me. I was afraid the police would be able to trace me. I thought over it again, and then I saw that if I ordered it in Felix's name it would meet the case. It would account for his getting the cask I was sending him, and he would not be believed when he denied ordering it. But I couldn't give Felix's name and address, for then he might get both casks, and I would be as badly fixed as ever. Finally I worked out the plan you know. I forged an order in Felix's hand for the companion group to my own to be sent to Felix at an imaginary address, made a tracing of it, left the letter in Dupierre's letter-box on Monday night, telephoned them on Tuesday morning ascertaining by what route and train they were sending the group, went to London, met it and had it left in a shed there, all as you must have learnt."

"A moment, please," interrupted La Touche. "You are going a little too quickly for me. You say you made a tracing of your forged order for the companion group and left the letter in Dupierre's letter-box. I don't quite understand that."

"Oh, you hadn't found that out, had you not? I will explain. I was in Paris, you see, when I forged the letter. But Dupierre must believe it came to him from London, or his suspicions would be aroused. I met the difficulty by sticking on the envelope a cancelled stamp from a letter I had received from London, copying the remainder of the postmark with a little lampblack. Then I went down to Grenelle in the middle of Monday night and dropped the letter into Dupierre's box. He would find it next morning all correct with its English stamp, cancelled in a London office."

In spite of their loathing for this callous and cynical criminal, La Touche and Mallet could not but be impressed by the cleverness of the trick. All the detectives concerned had argued that as the order for the statue had been received apparently from London on Tuesday, it must have been posted there on Monday, and that as Felix was there and Boirac in Paris, the former must have posted it. But how simply they had been duped! Truly, thought the detectives with unwilling admiration, Boirac had deserved to succeed.

"But the tracing?" persisted La Touche.

"I thought that not only must Dupierre believe the letter came from London, but some definite proof that Felix had written it must be provided. I did it in this way. After I had written the letter I made a careful tracing of it on a bit of tracing paper. As you probably know, I visited St. Malo when in London, and there, with Felix's pen and ink, I retraced over the writing and blotted it. This gave the impression."

Again his hearers had to admit a rueful admiration for the ingenious ruse. The finding of the impression had seemed so conclusive, and—it was only a trick. And what a simple trick—when you knew it!

"That is quite clear, thank you," said La Touche.

"I met the cask in London and brought it to the shed," went on the manufacturer. "There, after dismissing the carter, I opened the cask, took out the statue, packed it in a portmanteau I had with me, took the label off the cask and put it carefully in my pocket, replacing it with one addressed to Jaques de Belleville at the Gare du Nord. As you probably know, this Jaques de Belleville was myself.

"As you found Dubois, the carter, you will have learnt the method by which I exchanged the casks, sending that containing the body from my house to Felix, while the other, which I had emptied in London, went back to Dupierre. You understand that part of it?"

"Perfectly."

"So much then for the getting of the body to Felix. But it was my desire not only to give him the shock of opening the cask and discovering it; I wished also to make the police suspicious so that he would be watched and his attempts to get rid of the corpse discovered. In this case I intended he should be charged with the murder, incidentally clearing me. To ensure this result I set myself to construct such evidence as would weave a net round him from which he would be unable to escape. Gradually the details of my plan arranged themselves in my mind.

"Firstly, it was necessary that I should really have the letter of farewell, the envelope of which I had prepared, and which I had pretended to find on going to my study. Collecting a number of specimens of my wife's handwriting from her davenport, I forged the letter I showed to the French police. Putting it away for future use, I burnt the specimens to prevent them from being compared with the forgery.

"The problem of getting Felix to meet the cask which I intended to send him, and while doing so to attract the attention of the police, then occupied my thoughts. After much consideration I decided on the plan you know. It happened that some three weeks previously I had been seated in the Café Toisson d'Or, when a bad neuralgic headache had come on, and I moved into an alcove to be as private as possible. While there I had seen Felix come in and begin talking to a group of men. I had not made myself known, as I was in considerable pain, but I had overheard their conversation and learnt the arrangement Felix and his friend Le Gautier had made about the lottery. This I now decided to use, and I drafted a letter to Felix purporting to come from Le Gautier, mentioning this matter of the lottery to make it seem genuine. I also drafted a slip about money I intended to send in the cask. The contents of this letter and slip you know. These I put away in my pocket-book, to be used later.

"The next evening, Monday, I pretended to unpack the cask. I brought the group I had taken out of it on the previous Saturday from the portmanteau in which I had hidden it, and placed it on the table in my study. On the floor, about the cask, I sprinkled some of the sawdust from the handbag. By this manœuvre I hoped if suspicion arose it would be argued that as the cask was not unpacked till Monday night, the body could not have been put into it on the night of the dinner. As you know, this ruse also succeeded. I also took the label off the cask and put it in my pocket.

"Opening the cask again, I put in £52 10s. in English gold, to correspond with my slip. I hoped that, if the police got hold of the cask, they would assume that Felix had put in this money in order to strengthen his story that the cask had been sent to him. I put in sovereigns instead of French gold with the intention of making this theory more likely, as I hoped it would be argued that Felix in his agitation had overreached himself, and forgotten from what country the cask was supposed to be coming.

"Calling François, I told him I had unpacked the statue, and when Messrs. Dupierre sent for the cask he was to give it to them. Then, informing him that I would be from home for a couple of nights, I left next morning by the early train for London.

"On the Monday I had purchased a false beard and arranged to get myself up to resemble Felix, and I wore this disguise all the time till my return. I brought with me on the journey the portmanteau containing my wife's clothes, and, on board the boat, from a quiet place on the lower deck, slipped these articles overboard without being observed. On arrival in London I arranged with a carting firm to carry about the cask on the next two days, as you already know. I then went out to St. Malo, Felix's house, which I found after some judicious inquiries. A careful reconnoitre showed me it was unoccupied. I tried round the windows and had the luck to find one unhasped. Opening it, I crept into the house and went to the study. There by the light of an electric torch I carefully inked over the tracing I had made of the forged letter ordering the cask, and blotted it on Felix's pad. This, I felt sure, would be found, and would seem to prove that he had written the order.

"I had foreseen that it would be argued that Felix must be innocent because not only would he have no motive to murder my wife, but also he would naturally be the last man in the world to do such a thing. It was necessary for me, therefore, to provide a motive. For this purpose I had written a letter purporting to be from a girl whom Felix had wronged. Having crumpled this letter I put it into the side pocket of one of Felix's coats. I hoped this would be found, and that it would be argued that my wife had got hold of it and that there had been a quarrel which led to her death. Crumpling it was to suggest Felix had snatched it from her, thrust it into his pocket and forgotten it.

"As I stood in the study a further idea occurred to me. I had thought of a use for a brooch that had dropped from my wife's clothes. It had fallen just behind the chair she had been sitting in, and I thought if I placed it on the floor behind a chair in this room, it would suggest she had been murdered here. My eye fell on a chair with a low back, standing in front of a curtain, and I saw at once it would suit my purpose. I dropped the brooch behind it and it caught on the braid at the bottom of the curtain. There it was hidden from casual inspection by the chair, but I knew the police would not overlook it. I withdrew without disturbing anything or leaving traces, closed the window, and returned to the city.

"Such was my plot, and, but for your cleverness, it would have succeeded. Is there any other point on which you are not clear?"

"Only one, I think," answered La Touche. "You were heard to telephone on the Monday from the café at Charenton to your butler and chief clerk. They received their messages on the Tuesday from Calais. How did you manage that?"

"Easily. I never telephoned on Monday at all. I slipped a tiny wooden wedge into the instrument to prevent the hook rising when I lifted off the receiver. No call was therefore made on the exchange, though I went through the form of speaking. Any other point?"

"I do not think so," returned La Touche, who again could but feel a kind of rueful admiration for this ingenious ruffian. "Your statement has been very complete."

"It is not quite complete," M. Boirac resumed. "There are two more points of which I wish to speak. Read that."

He took a letter from his pocket and handed it to La Touche. Both men leaned a little forward to look. As they did so there was a slight click and the light went out. What sounded like Boirac's chair was heard falling.

"Hold the door!" yelled La Touche, springing to his feet and fumbling for his electric torch. Mallet leaped for the door, but, tripping over the chair, missed it. As La Touche flashed on his light they could see it closing. There was a low, mocking laugh. Then the door slammed and they heard the key turn in the lock.

La Touche fired rapidly through the panels, but there was no sound from without. Then Mallet flung himself on the handle.

But at his first touch it came off. The holes for the screws had been enlarged so that they had no hold.

The door opened inwards, and presented to the imprisoned men a smooth, unbroken surface, with nothing on which to pull. To push it through towards the hall was impossible, as it shut solidly against the frame. Their only hope seemed to split it, but as they gazed at its solid oak timbers this hope died.

"The window," cried La Touche, and they swung round. The sashes opened readily, but outside were shutters of steel plate, closely fastened. Both men shoved and prised with all their might. But Boirac had done his work well. They were immovable.

As they stood panting and baffled, Mallet's eye caught the switch of the electric light. It was off. He clicked it on. Though no answering flood of light poured down, he noticed something that interested him.

"Your torch, La Touche!" he cried, and then he saw what it was. Tied to the switch was a length of fisherman's gut. Practically invisible, it passed down the wall and through a tiny hole in the floor. Anyone pulling it from below would switch off the light.

"I don't understand," said La Touche. "That means he had a confederate?"

"No!" cried Mallet, who had been looking about with the torch. "See here!"

He pointed to the chair Boirac had occupied and which now lay on its side on the floor. Fastened to the left arm was another end of gut which also entered a hole in the floor.

"I bet those are connected!"

Their curiosity temporarily overcame their fears. La Touche turned on the switch and Mallet, pulling the gut at the arm of the chair, heard it click off again.

"Ingenious devil," he muttered. "It must go round pulleys under the floor. And now he has cut off the current at the meter."

"Come on, Mallet," La Touche called. "Don't waste time. We must get out of this."

Together they threw themselves on the door with all the weight of their shoulders. Again they tried, and again, but to no purpose. It was too strong.

"What does it mean, do you think?" panted Mallet.

"Gas, I expect. Perhaps charcoal."

"Any use shouting at the window?"

"None. It's too closely shuttered, and it only opens into a courtyard."

And then suddenly they perceived a faint odour which, in spite of their hardened nerves, turned their blood cold and set them working with ten times more furious energy at the door. It was a very slight smell of burning wood.

"My God!" cried Mallet, "he's set the house on fire!"

It seemed impossible that any door could withstand so furious an onslaught. Had it opened outwards, hinges and lock must long since have given way, but the men could not make their strength tell. They worked till the sweat rolled in great drops down their foreheads. Meanwhile the smell increased. Smoke must be percolating into the room.

"The torch here," cried La Touche suddenly.

Taking his pistol, he fired a number of shots on the bolt of the lock.

"Don't use them all. How many have you?"

"Two more."

"Keep them."

The lock seemed shattered, but still the door held. The men's efforts were becoming frenzied when Mallet had an idea. Along the farther wall of the room stood a heavy, old-fashioned sofa.

"Let's use the couch as a battering-ram."

The room was now thick with smoke, biting and gripping the men's throats. Hampered by coughing and bad light, they could not work fast. But at last they got the couch across the room and planted end on to the door. Standing one at each side, they swung it back and then with all their strength drove it against the timber. A second time they drove, and a third, till at the fourth blow there was a sound of splitting wood, and the job was done.

Or so they thought. A moment later they found their mistake. The right bottom panel only was gone.

"The left panel! Then the bar between!"

Though the men worked feverishly, their operations took time. The smoke was now increasing rapidly. And then suddenly La Touche heard a terrible, ominous sound. Crackling was beginning somewhere not far off.

"We haven't much time, Mallet," he gasped, as the sweat poured down his face.

Desperately they drove the couch against the bar. Still it held. The terrible fear that the couch would come to pieces was in both their hearts.

"The torch!" cried Mallet hoarsely. "Quick, or we're done!"

Drawing his magazine pistol and holding it close to the door, he fired its full charge of seven shots at the vertical bar. La Touche instantly grasped his idea, and emptied his two remaining shots at the same place. The bar was thus perforated by a transverse line of nine holes.

There was a singing in the men's ears and a weight on their chests as, with the energy of despair, they literally hurled the heavy couch against the weakened bar. With a tearing sound it gave way. They could get through.

"You for it, Mallet! Quick!" yelled La Touche, as he staggered drunkenly back. But there was no answer. Through the swirling clouds the detective could see his assistant lying motionless. That last tremendous effort had finished him.

La Touche's own head was swimming. He could no longer think connectedly. Half unconsciously he pulled the other's arms to the hole. Then, passing through, he turned to draw his confrère out. But the terrible roaring was swelling in his ears, the weight on his chest was growing insupportable, and a black darkness was coming down over him like a pall. Insensible, he collapsed, half in and half out of the doorway.

As he fell there was a lurid flicker and a little dancing flame leaped lightly from the floor.

CHAPTER XXX

CONCLUSION

WHEN La Touche's senses returned he found himself lying in the open air, with Farol, his other assistant, bending over him. His first thought was for his companion in misfortune.

"Mallet?" he whispered feebly.

"Safe," answered Farol. "We got him out just in time."

"And Boirac?"

"The police are after him."

La Touche lay still. He was badly shaken. But the fresh air rapidly revived him, and he was soon able to sit up.

"Where am I?" he asked presently.

"Just around the corner from Boirac's. The firemen are at work."

"Tell me about it."

Farol's story was short. It seemed that Boirac had returned home that afternoon about three. Shortly after, the detective had been surprised to observe a regular exodus of servants from the

house. Cabs and taxis took away two men and four women, all
with luggage. Lastly, about four o'clock, came François, also with
luggage, and with him Boirac. François closed and locked the
door, handing the key to his master. The two then shook hands
and, stepping into separate vehicles, were driven away. It was
evident the house was being closed for a considerable period.

Farol, entering the taxi he kept in waiting, followed. They
drove to the Gare St. Lazare, where the manufacturer dismissed
his vehicle and entered the station. But instead of taking a ticket,
he simply walked about the concourse and in a few minutes left
by another door. Travelling by the Metro, he reached Alma Station,
walked down the Avenue, and, with a hurried look round, re-entered
his house. To Farol it was obvious that something was in the wind.
He withdrew to some distance and watched.

His surprise at these strange proceedings was not lessened when
he saw La Touche and Mallet drive up to the door and ring. He
hurried forward to warn them, but before he could do so the door
opened and they disappeared within. Growing more and more
anxious, Farol waited till, after a considerable time, he saw Boirac
leave the house alone. Now certain that something was wrong,
he decided he must let the manufacturer go, while he telephoned
his suspicions to the Sûreté. A car with some men was sent
immediately, and they drove up to the door just as Farol returned
to it on foot. Smoke was beginning to issue from the upper
windows, and one man was sent for the fire brigade, while the
others attempted to break into the house. In this they succeeded
only after considerable trouble. Through the smoke they saw La
Touche's body lying half in the hall and half in François's room.
Only just in time they got the men out, the back of the hall being a
sheet of flame before they reached the open air.

"We better go to the Sûreté," said La Touche, who, by this
time, had practically recovered.

Twenty minutes later M. Chauvet was in possession of the facts,
and operations for the tracing of Boirac had begun.

La Touche then confidentially told the Chief all that he had
learnt about the mystery. M. Chauvet was utterly astounded, and
chagrined beyond measure at the blunder he and his men had
fallen into.

"Clever devil!" he exclaimed. "He knew that nothing but the
absolute truth would put you off your guard. But we'll get him,
M. La Touche. He can't get out of the city. By now, every route
will be barred."

The Chief's prophecy was fulfilled earlier than even he expected.

Only an hour later they had news. Evidently believing himself
secure in the destruction of the only two men who, so far as he was
aware, knew enough to convict him, Boirac, after setting the house
on fire, had gone openly to his club. A detective who went there
to make inquiries, found him calmly sitting smoking in the lounge.
He had, it appeared, made a desperate effort to escape arrest, and
attempted to shoot the officer. Then, seeing it was all up with him,
he turned the revolver upon himself, and, before he could be stopped,
shot himself through the head.

So perished one of the most callous and cold-blooded criminals
of the century.

In a curious manner Felix received his reparation. Heppenstall,
who had learnt to respect and appreciate his client, engaged him
to paint a portrait of his wife. While thus occupied the artist made
the acquaintance of the K.C.'s daughter. The two young people
promptly fell in love. Six months later they were quietly married,
and, his bride bringing a not inconsiderable dot, Felix threw up his
appointment and moved to a new St. Malo on the sunny shores of
the Mediterranean. Here he divided his attention between his
young wife and the painting of that masterpiece which had so
long remained an unattainable dream.

THE TERROR
By
EDGAR WALLACE

THE TERROR

CHAPTER I

O'SHEA was in his maddest mood, had been like it all night. Stalking up and down the grassy slope, muttering to himself, waving his hands at some invisible audience, cackling with laughter at his own mysterious jokes; and at dawn he had fallen upon little Lipski, who had dared light a cigarette in defiance of instructions, and had beaten him with savage brutality, and the other two men had not dared interfere.

Joe Connor sprawled on the ground, chewing a blade of grass, and watching with sombre eyes the restless figure. Marks, who sat cross-legged by his side, watched too, but there was a twisted and sneering smile on his thin lips.

"Mad as a coot," said Joe Connor in a low voice. "If he pulls this job off without getting us in jail for the rest of our lives we'll be lucky."

Soapy Marks licked his dry lips.

"He's cleverest when he's mad." He spoke like a man of culture. Some said that Soapy was intended for the Church before a desire for an easier and more illicit method of living made him one of the most skilful, and nearly the most dangerous, gangster, in England.

"Lunacy, my dear fellow, does not mean stupidity. Can't you stop that fellow blubbering?"

Joe Connor did not rise; he turned his eyes in the direction of the prostrate figure of Lipski, who was groaning and swearing sobbingly.

"He'll get over it," he said indifferently. "The bigger beating he gets the more he respects O'Shea."

He wriggled a little closer to his confederate.

"Have you ever seen O'Shea—his face, I mean?" he asked, dropping his voice a note lower. "I never have, and I've done two"—he thought—"three," he corrected, "jobs with him. He's always had that coat on he's got now, with the collar right up to his nose, the same old hat over his eyes. I never used to believe there was that kind of crook—thought they were only seen on the stage. First time I ever heard of him was when he sent for me— met him on the St. Albans Road about twelve o'clock, but never saw his face. He knew all about me; told me how many convictions I'd had, and the kind of work he wanted me for——"

"And paid you well," said Marks lazily, when the other paused. "He always pays well; he always picks up his 'staff' in the same way."

He pursed his lips as though he were going to whistle, examined the restless figure of the master thoughtfully.

"He's mad—and he pays well. He will pay better this time."

Connor looked up sharply.

"Two hundred and fifty quid and fifty getaway money—that's fair, ain't it?"

"He will pay better," said Marks suavely. "This little job deserves it. Am I to drive a motor lorry containing three tons of Australian sovereigns through the streets of London, possibly risk hanging, for two hundred and fifty pounds—and getaway money? I think not."

He rose to his feet and dusted his knees daintily. O'Shea had disappeared over the crest of the hill, was possibly behind the hedge line which swept round in a semi-circle till it came within half a dozen feet of where the men were talking of him.

"Three tons of gold; nearly half a million pounds. At least I think we're entitled to ten per cent."

Connor grinned and jerked his head towards the whimpering Lipski.

"And him?"

Marks bit his lip.

"I don't think we could include him."

He glanced round again for some sign of O'Shea, and dropped down beside his companion.

"'We've got the whole thing in our hands," he said in a voice that was little more than a whisper. "He'll be sane tomorrow. These fits only come on him at rare intervals; and a sane man will listen to reason. We're holding up this gold convoy—that's one of O'Shea's oldest tricks, to fill a deep cutting full of gas. I wonder he dare repeat it. I am driving the lorry to town and hiding it. Would O'Shea give us our share if he had to decide between an unpleasant interview with us and a more unpleasant interview with Inspector Bradley?"

Connor plucked another blade of grass and chewed on it gloomily.

"He's clever," he began, and again Marks's lips curled.

"Aren't they all?" he demanded. "Isn't Dartmoor full of clever people? That's old Hallick's great joke—he calls all the prisoners collegers. No, my dear Connor, believe me, cleverness is a relative term——"

"What does that mean?" growled Connor with a frown. "Don't try swank on me, Soapy—use words I can understand."

He looked around again a little anxiously for the vanished O'Shea. Behind the hill crest, in a narrow lane, O'Shea's big car was parked that would carry him to safety after the job. His confederates would be left to take all the risks, face the real dangers which would follow, however cleverly the coup was organized.

A little distance away to the left, on the edge of the deep cutting, four big steel gas cylinders lay in line. Even from where he sprawled he could see the long white road leading into the cutting, on which presently would appear the flickering lights of the gold convoy. His gas mask lay under his hand; Marks had his sticking out of his coat pocket.

"He must have a lot of stuff," he said.

"Who—O'Shea?" Marks shrugged his shoulders. "I don't know. He spends money like a lunatic. I should think he was broke. It's nearly twelve months since he had a big haul."

"What does he do with the money?" asked Connor curiously.

"Spends it, as we all do," was the laconic answer. "He talked about buying a big country house last time I saw him; he was going to settle down and live the life of a gentleman. Last night, when I had a chat with him, he said it would take half this loot to pay his debts."

Marks examined his well-manicured nails.

"Amongst other things he's a liar," he said lightly. "What's that?"

He looked towards the line of bushes a few yards distant. He had heard a rustle, the snap of a twig, and was on his feet instantly. Crossing the short intervening space, he peered over the bushes. There was nobody in sight. He came back thoughtfully to Connor.

"I wonder if the devil was listening," he said, "and how long he's been listening!"

"Who—O'Shea?" asked the startled Connor.

Marks did not reply, but drew a deep breath. Obviously he was uncomfortable.

"If he'd heard anything he would have come for me. He's moody—he's been moody all night."

At this point Connor got up and stretched himself.

"I'd like to know how he lives. I'll bet he's got a wife and family tucked away somewhere—that kind of bird always has. There he is!"

The figure of O'Shea had appeared across the rise; he was coming towards them.

"Get your masks ready. You don't want any further instructions, Soapy?"

The voice, muffled by the high collar which reached to the tip of his nose, was rational, almost amiable.

"Pick that fellow up." He pointed to Lipski, and, when the order had been obeyed, he called the cringing man before him. "You'll go to the end of the road, put your red lantern on and stop them. By stop them I mean slow them down. Don't let yourself be seen; there are ten armed men on the lorry."

He examined the cylinders; from the nozzle of each a thick rubber pipe trailed down into the cutting. With a spanner he opened the valve of each, and the silence was broken by the deep hissing of the gas as it escaped.

"It'll lie in the bottom, so you needn't put on your masks till we're ready," he said.

He followed Lipski to the end of the cutting, watched the red lamp lit, and pointed out the place where the man was to hide. Then he came back to Marks. Not by word or sign did he betray the fact that he had overhead the two men talking. If there was to be a quarrel this was not the moment for it. O'Shea was intensely sane at that moment.

They heard the sound of the oncoming lorry before they saw the flicker of its lights emerge from the cover of Felsted Wood.

"Now," said O'Shea sharply.

He made no attempt to draw on a mask, as did his two assistants.

"You won't have to use your guns, but keep them handy in case anything goes wrong—don't forget that if the guard isn't knocked out immediately it will shoot at sight. You know where to meet me tomorrow?"

The shrouded head of Soapy nodded.

Nearer and nearer came the gold convoy. Evidently the driver had seen the red light at the end of the cutting, for his siren sounded. From where O'Shea crouched he commanded a complete view of the road.

The lorry was within fifty yards of the cutting and had slowed perceptibly when he saw a man leap up, not from the place where he had posted him, but a dozen yards farther up the road. It was Lipski, and as he ran towards the moving lorry his hand went up, there was a flash and a report. He was firing to attract attention. O'Shea's eyes glowed like coals. Lipski had betrayed him.

" Stand by to run! " His voice was like a rasp.

And then the miracle happened. From the lorry leapt two pencils of flame, and Lipski crumpled up and fell by the side of the road as the lorry rumbled past. The guard had misunderstood his action; they thought he was attempting to hold them up.

" Glorious," whispered O'Shea huskily, and at that instant the lorry went down into the gas-filled cutting.

It was all over in a second. The driver fell forward in his seat, and, released of his guidance, the front wheels of the lorry jammed into a bank.

O'Shea thought of everything. But for that warning red light, the lorry would have been wrecked and his plans brought to naught. As it was, Marks had only to climb into the driver's seat, and reverse the engine, to extricate it from the temporary block.

A minute later the gold convoy had climbed up to the other side of the depression. The unconscious guard and driver had been bundled out and laid on the side of the road. The final preparations took no more than five minutes. Marks stripped his mask, pulled on a uniform cap, and Connor took his place in the lorry where the gold was stored in small white boxes.

" Go on," said O'Shea, and the lorry moved forward and four minutes later was out of sight.

O'Shea went back to his big, high-powered car and drove off in the opposite direction, leaving only the unconscious figures of the guard to testify to his ruthlessness.

CHAPTER II

IT was a rainy night in London. Connor, who had preferred it so, turned into the side door of a little restaurant in Soho, mounted the narrow stairs and knocked on a door. He heard a chair move and the snap of the lock as the door was opened.

Soapy Marks was there alone.

" Did you see him? " asked Connor eagerly.

" O'Shea? Yes, I met him on the Embankment. Have you seen the newspapers? "

Connor grinned.

" I m glad those birds didn't die," he said.

Mr. Marks sneered.

"Your humanity is very creditable, my dear friend," he said. On the table was a newspaper, and the big headlines stared out, almost shouted their excitement:—

GREATEST GOLD ROBBERY OF OUR TIME.
THREE TONS OF GOLD DISAPPEAR BETWEEN SOUTHAMPTON AND LONDON.
DEAD ROBBER FOUND BY THE ROADSIDE.
THE VANISHED LORRY.

In the early hours of yesterday morning a daring outrage was committed which might have lead to the death of six members of the C.I.D., and resulted in the loss to the Bank of England of gold valued at half a million pounds.

The *Aritania,* which arrived in Southampton last night, brought a heavy consignment of gold from Australia, and in order that this should be removed to London with the least possible ostentation, it was arranged that a lorry carrying the treasure should leave Southampton at three o'clock in the morning, arriving in London before the normal flow of traffic started. At a spot near Felsted Wood the road runs down into a depression and through a deep cutting. Evidently this had been laid with gas, and the car dashed into what was practically a lethal chamber without warning.

That an attack was projected, however, was revealed to the guard before they reached the fatal spot. A man sprang out from a hedge and shot at the lorry. The detectives in charge of the convoy immediately replied, and the man was later found in a dying condition. He made no statement except to mention a name which is believed to be that of the leader of the gang.

Sub-Inspectors Bradley and Hallick of Scotland Yard are in charge of the case. . . .

There followed a more detailed account, together with an official statement issued by the police, containing a brief narrative by one of the guard.

"It seems to have created something of a sensation," smiled Marks, as he folded up the paper.

"What about O'Shea?" asked the other impatiently. "Did he agree to split?"

Marks nodded.

"He was a little annoyed—naturally. But in his sane moments our friend, O'Shea, is a very intelligent man. What really annoyed him was the fact that we had parked the lorry in another place than where he ordered it to be taken. He was most anxious to discover our little secret, and I think his ignorance of the whereabouts of the gold was our biggest pull with him."

"What's going to happen?" asked Connor in a troubled tone.

"We're taking the lorry tonight to Barnes Common. He doesn't realize, though he will, that we've transferred the gold to a small three-ton van. He ought to be very grateful to me for my foresight, for the real van was discovered this evening by Hallick in the place where O'Shea told me to park it. And of course it was empty."

Connor rubbed his hand across his unshaven chin.

"O'Shea won't let us get away with it," he said, with a worried frown. "You know him, Soapy."

"We shall see," said Mr. Marks, with a confident smile.

He poured out a whisky and soda.

"Drink up and we'll go." He glanced at his watch. "We've got plenty of time—thank God there's a war on, and the active and intelligent constabulary are looking for spies, the streets are nicely darkened, and all is favourable to our little arrangement. By the way, I've had a red cross painted on the tilt of our van—it looks almost official!"

That there was a war on, they discovered soon after they turned into the Embankment. Warning maroons were banging from a dozen stations; the darkened tram which carried them to the south had hardly reached Kennington Oval before the anti-aircraft guns were blazing at the unseen marauders of the skies. A bomb dropped all too close for the comfort of the nervous Connor. The car had stopped.

"We had better get out here," whispered Marks. "They won't move till the raid is over."

The two men descended to the deserted street and walked southward. The beams of giant searchlights swept the skies; from somewhere up above came the rattle of a machine-gun.

"This should keep the police thoroughly occupied," said Marks, as they turned into a narrow street in a poor neighbourhood. "I don't think we need miss our date, and our little ambulance should pass unchallenged."

"I wish to God you'd speak English!" growled Connor irritably.

Marks had stopped before the gates of a stable yard, pushing them. One yielded to his touch and they walked down the uneven drive to the small building where the car was housed. Soapy put his key into the gate of the lock-up and turned it.

"Here we are," he said, as he stepped inside.

And then a hand gripped him, and he reached for his gun.

"Don't make any fuss," said the hated voice of Inspecto Hallick. "I want you, Soapy. Perhaps you'll tell me what' happened to this ambulance of yours?"

Soapy Marks stared towards the man he could not see, and for moment was thrown off his guard.

"The lorry?" he gasped. "Isn't it here?"

"Been gone an hour," said a second voice. "Come across Soapy; what have you done with it?"

Soapy said nothing; he heard the steel handcuffs click on th wrist of Joe Connor, heard that man's babble of incoherent rag and blasphemy as he was hustled towards the car which had draw up silently at the gate, and knew that Mr. O'Shea was indeed ver sane on that particular day.

CHAPTER III

To Mary Redmayne life had been a series of inequalities. Sh could remember the alternate prosperity and depression of he father; had lived in beautiful hotel suites and cheap lodgings, on following the other with extraordinary rapidity; and had grow so accustomed to the violent changes of his fortune that she woul never have been surprised to have been taken from the pretentiou school where she was educated, and planted amongst county schoo scholars at any moment.

People who knew him called him Colonel, but he himsel preferred his civilian title, and volunteered no information to he as to his military career. It was after he had taken Monkshall tha he permitted "Colonel" to appear on his cards. It was a grand sounding name, but even as a child Mary Redmayne had accepted such appellations with the greatest caution. She had once been brought back from her preparatory school to a "Mortimer Lodge," to discover it was a tiny semi-detached villa in a Wimbledon by-street

But Monkshall had fulfilled all her dreams of magnificence; veritable relic of Tudor times, and possibly of an earlier period, i stood in forty acres of timbered ground, a dignified and venerable pile, which had such association with antiquity that, until Colone Redmayne forbade the practice, charabancs full of American visitor used to come up the broad drive and gaze upon the ruins of what had been a veritable abbey.

Fortune had come to Colonel Redmayne when she was about eleven. It came unexpectedly, almost violently. Whence it came, she could not even guess; she only knew that one week he was poor, harassed by debt collectors, moving through side streets in order to avoid the creditors; the next week—or was it month?—he was the master of Monkshall, ordering furniture worth thousands of pounds.

When she went to live at Monkshall she had reached that gracious period of interregnum between child and woman. A slim girl above middle height, straight of back, free of limb, she held the eye of men to whom more mature charms would have had no appeal.

Ferdie Fane, the young man who came to the " Red Lion " so often, summer and winter, and who drank so much more than was good for him, watched her passing along the road with her father. She was hatless; the golden-brown hair had a glory of its own; the faultless face, the proud little lift of her chin.

" Spring is here, Adolphus," he addressed the landlord gravely. " I have seen it pass."

He was a man of thirty-five, long-faced, rather good-looking in spite of his huge horn-rimmed spectacles. He had a large tankard of beer in his hand now, which was unusual, for he did most of his drinking secretly in his room. He used to come down to the ' Red Lion " at all sorts of odd and sometimes inconvenient moments. He was, in a way, rather a bore, and the apparition of Mary Redmayne and her grim-looking father offered the landlord an opportunity for which he had been seeking.

" I wonder you don't go and stay at Monkshall, Mr. Fane," he suggested.

Mr. Fane stared at him reproachfully.

" Are you tired of me, mine host," he asked gently, " that you should shuffle me into other hands?" He shook his head. " I am no paying guest—besides which, I am not respectable. Why does Redmayne take paying guests at all?"

The landlord could offer no satisfactory solution to this mystery.

" I'm blest if I know. The colonel's got plenty of money. I think it is because he's lonely, but he's had paying guests at Monkshall this past ten years. Of course, it's very select."

" Exactly," said Ferdie Fane with great gravity. " And that is why I should not be selected! No, I fear you will have to endure my erratic visits."

"I don't mind your being here, sir," said the landlord, anxious to assure him. "You never give me any trouble, only——"

"Only you'd like somebody more regular in his habits—good luck!"

He lifted the foaming pewter to his lips, took a long drink, and then he began to laugh softly, as though at some joke. In another minute he was serious again, frowning down into the tankard.

"Pretty girl, that. Mary Redmayne, eh?"

"She's only been back from school a month—or college, rather," said the landlord. "She's the nicest young lady that ever drew the breath of life."

"They all are," said the other vaguely.

He went away the next day with his fishing rod that he hadn't used, and his golf bag which had remained unstrapped throughout his stay.

Life at Monkshall promised so well that Mary Redmayne was prepared to love the place. She liked Mr. Goodman, the grey-haired, slow-spoken gentleman who was the first of her father's boarders; she loved the grounds, the quaint old house; could even contemplate, without any great uneasiness, the growing taciturnity of her father. He was older, much older than he had been; his face had a new pallor; he seldom smiled. He was a nervous man, too; she had found him walking about in the middle of the night, and once had surprised him in his room, suspiciously thick of speech, with an empty whisky bottle a silent witness to his peculiar weakness.

It was the house that began to get on her nerves. Sometimes she would wake up in the middle of the night suddenly and sit up in bed, trying to recall the horror that had snatched her from sleep and brought her through a dread cloud of fear to wakefulness. Once she had heard peculiar sounds that had sent cold shivers down her spine. Not once, but many times, she thought she heard the faint sound of a distant organ.

She asked Cotton, the dour butler, but he had heard nothing. Other servants had been more sensitive, however; there came a constant procession of cooks and housemaids giving notice. She interviewed one or two of these, but afterwards her father forbade her seeing them, and himself accepted their hasty resignations.

"This place gives me the creeps, miss," a weeping housemaid had told her. "Do you hear them screams at night? I do; I sleep in the east wing. The place is haunted——"

"Nonsense, Anna!" scoffed the girl, concealing a shudder. "How can you believe such things!"

"It is, miss," persisted the girl. "I've seen a ghost on the lawn, walking about in the moonlight."

Later, Mary herself began to see things; and a guest who came and stayed two nights had departed a nervous wreck.

"Imagination," said the colonel testily. "My dear Mary, you're getting the mentality of a housemaid!"

He was very apologetic afterwards for his rudeness, but Mary continued to hear, and presently to listen; and finally she saw. . . . Sights that made her doubt her own wisdom, her own intelligence, her own sanity.

One day, when she was walking alone through the village, she saw a man in a golf suit; he was very tall and wore horn-rimmed spectacles, and greeted her with a friendly smile. It was the first time she had seen Ferdie Fane. She was to see very much of him in the strenuous months that followed.

CHAPTER IV

SUPERINTENDENT HALLICK went down to Princetown in Devonshire to make his final appeal—an appeal which, he knew, was foredoomed to failure. The Deputy-Governor met him as the iron gates closed upon the burly superintendent.

"I don't think you're going to get very much out of these fellows, superintendent," he said. "I think they're too near to the end of their sentence."

"You never know," said Hallick, with a smile. "I once had the best information in the world from a prisoner on the day he was released."

He went down to the low-roofed building which constitutes the Deputy-Governor's office.

"My head warder says they'll never talk, and he has a knack of getting into their confidence," said the deputy. "If you remember, superintendent, you did your best to make them speak ten years ago, when they first came here. There's a lot of people in this prison who'd like to know where the gold is hidden. Personally, I don't think they had it at all, and the story they told at the trial, that O'Shea had got away with it, is probably true."

The superintendent pursed his lips.

"I wonder," he said thoughtfully. "That was the impression I had the night I arrested them, but I've changed my opinion since."

The chief warder came in at that moment and gave a friendly nod to the superintendent.

"I've kept those two men in their cells this morning. You want to see them both, don't you, superintendent?"

"I'd like to see Connor first."

"Now?" asked the warder. "I'll bring him down."

He went out, passed across the asphalt yard to the entrance of the big, ugly building. A steel grille covered the door, and this he unlocked, opening the wooden door behind, and passed into the hall, lined on each side with galleries from which opened narrow cell doors. He went to one of these on the lower tier, snapped back the lock and pulled open the door. The man in convict garb who was sitting on the edge of the bed, his face in his hands, rose and eyed him sullenly.

"Connor, a gentleman from Scotland Yard has come down to see you. If you're sensible you'll give him the information he asks."

Connor glowered at him.

"I've nothing to tell, sir," he said sullenly. "Why don't they leave me alone? If I knew where the stuff was I wouldn't tell 'em."

"Don't be a fool," said the chief good-humouredly. "What have you to gain by hiding up——"

"A fool, sir?" interrupted Connor. "I've had all the fool knocked out of me here!" His hand swept round the cell. "I've been in this same cell for seven years; I know every brick of it—who is it wants to see me?"

"Superintendent Hallick."

Connor made a wry face.

"Is he seeing Marks too? Hallick, eh? I thought he was dead."

"He's alive enough."

The chief beckoned him out into the hall, and, accompanied by a warder, Connor was taken to the deputy's office. He recognized Hallick with a nod. He bore no malice; between these two men, thief-taker and thief, was that curious camaraderie which exists between the police and the criminal classes.

"You're wasting your time with me, Mr. Hallick," said Connor. And then, with a sudden burst of anger: "I've got nothing to give you. Find O'Shea—he'll tell you! And find him before I do, if you want him to talk."

"We want to find him, Connor," said Hallick soothingly.

"You want the money," sneered Connor; "that's what you want. You want to find the money for the bank and pull in the reward."

He laughed harshly. "Try Soapy Marks—maybe he'll sit in your game and take his corner."

The lock turned at that moment and another convict was ushered into the room. Soapy Marks had not changed in his ten years of incarceration. The gaunt, ascetic face had perhaps grown a little harder; the thin lips were firmer, and the deep-set eyes had sunk a little more into his head. But his cultured voice, his exaggerated politeness, and that oiliness which had earned him his nickname, remained constant.

"Why, it's Mr. Hallick!" His voice was a gentle drawl. "Come down to see us at our country house!"

He saw Connor and nodded, almost bowed to him.

"Well, this is most kind of you, Mr. Hallick. You haven't seen the park or the garage? Nor our beautiful billiard room?"

"That'll do, Marks," said the warder sternly.

"I beg your pardon, sir, I'm sure." The bow to the warder was a little deeper, a little more sarcastic. "Just badinage—nothing wrong intended. Fancy meeting you on the moor, Mr. Hallick! I suppose this is only a brief visit? You're not staying with us, are you?"

Hallick accepted the insult with a little smile.

"I'm sorry," said Marks. "Even the police make little errors of judgment sometimes. It's deplorable, but it's true. We once had an ex-inspector in the hall where I am living."

"You know why I've come?" said Hallick.

Marks shook his head, and then a look of simulated surprise and consternation came to his face.

"You haven't come to ask me and my poor friend about that horrible gold robbery? I see you have. Dear me, how very unfortunate! You want to know where the money was hidden? I wish I could tell you. I wish my poor friend could tell you, or even your old friend, Mr. Leonard O'Shea." He smiled blandly. "But I can't!"

Connor was chafing under the strain of the interview.

"You don't want me any more——"

Marks waved his hand.

"Be patient with dear Mr. Hallick."

"Now look here, Soapy," said Connor angrily, and a look of pain came to Marks's face.

"Not Soapy—that's vulgar. Don't you agree, Mr. Hallick?"

"I'm going to answer no questions. You can do as you like," said Connor. "If you haven't found O'Shea, I will, and the day I get my hands on him he'll know all about it! There's another thing you've got to know, Hallick; I'm on my own from the day I get out of this hell. I'm not asking Soapy to help me to find O'Shea. I've seen Marks every day for ten years, and I hate the sight of him. I'm working single-handed to find the man who shopped me."

"You think you'll find him, do you?" said Hallick quickly. "Do you know where he is?"

"I only know one thing," said Connor huskily, "and Soapy knows it too. He let it out that morning we were waiting for the gold lorry. It just slipped out—what O'Shea's idea was of a quiet hiding-place. But I'm not going to tell you. I've got four months to serve, and when that time is up I'll find O'Shea."

"You poor fool!" said Hallick roughly. "The police have been looking for him for ten years."

"Looking for what?" demanded Connor, ignoring Marks's warning look.

"For Len O'Shea," said Hallick.

There came a burst of laughter from the convict.

"You're looking for a sane man, and that's where you went wrong! I didn't tell you before why you'll never find him. It's because he's mad. You didn't know that, but Soapy knows. O'Shea was crazy ten years ago. God knows what he is now! Got the cunning of a madman. Ask Soapy."

It was news to Hallick. His eyes questioned Marks, and the little man smiled.

"I'm afraid our dear friend is right," said Marks suavely. "A cunning madman! Even in Dartmoor we get news, Mr. Hallick, and a rumour has reached me that some years ago three officers of Scotland Yard disappeared in the space of a few minutes—just vanished as though they had evaporated like dew before the morning sun! Forgive me if I am poetical; Dartmoor makes you that way. And would you be betraying an official secret if you told me these men were looking for O'Shea?"

He saw Hallick's face change, and chuckled.

"I see they were. The story was that they had left England and they sent their resignations—from Paris, wasn't it? O'Shea could copy anybody's handwriting—they never left England."

Hallick's face was white.

"By God, if I thought that——" he began.

"They never left England," said Marks remorselessly. "They were looking for O'Shea—and O'Shea found them first."

"You mean they're dead?" asked the other.

Marks nodded slowly.

"For twenty-two hours a day he is a sane, reasonable man. For two hours——" He shrugged his shoulders. "Mr. Hallick, your men must have met him in one of his bad moments."

"When *I* meet him——" interrupted Connor, and Marks turned on him in a flash.

"When you meet him you will die!" he hissed. "When *I* meet him——" That mild face of his became suddenly contorted, and Hallick looked into the eyes of a demon.

"When you meet him?" challenged Hallick. "Where will you meet him?"

Marks's arm shot out stiffly; his long fingers gripped an invisible enemy.

"I know just where I can put my hand on him," he breathed. "That hand!"

Hallick went back to London that afternoon, a baffled man. He had gone to make his last effort to secure information about the missing gold, and had learned nothing—except that O'Shea was sane for twenty-two hours in the day.

CHAPTER V

IT was a beautiful spring morning. There was a tang in the air which melted in the yellow sunlight.

Mr. Goodman had not gone to the city that morning, though it was his day, for he made a practice of attending at his office for two or three days every month. Mrs. Elvery, that garrulous woman, was engaged in putting the final touches to her complexion; and Veronica, her gawkish daughter, was struggling, by the aid of a dictionary, with a recalcitrant poem—for she wooed the gentler muse in her own gentler moments.

Mr. Goodman sat on a sofa, dozing over his newspaper. No sound broke the silence but the scratching of Veronica's pen and the ticking of the big grandfather's clock.

This vaulted chamber, which was the lounge of Monkshall, had changed very little since the days when it was the ante-room to a veritable refectory. The columns that monkish hands had chiselled had crumbled a little, but their chiselled piety, hidden now behind the oak panelling, was almost as legible as on the day the holy men had written them.

Through the open french windows there was a view of the broad, green park, with its clumps of trees and its little heap of ruins that had once been the Mecca of the antiquarian.

Mr. Goodman did not hear the excited chattering of the birds, but Miss Veronica, in that irritable frame of mind which a young poet can so readily reach, turned her head once or twice in mute protest.

" Mr. Goodman," she said softly.

There was no answer, and she repeated his name impatiently. " Mr. Goodman!"

" Eh?" He looked up, startled.

" What rhymes with ' supercilious?' " asked Veronica sweetly.

Mr. Goodman considered, stroking his chin reflectively .

" Bilious?" he suggested.

Miss Elvery gave a despairing cluck.

" That won't do at all. It's such an ugly word."

" And such an ugly feeling," shuddered Mr. Goodman. Then: " What are you writing?" he asked.

She confessed to her task.

" Good heavens!" he said despairingly. "Fancy writing poetry at this time in the morning! It's almost like drinking before lunch. Who is it about?"

She favoured him with an arch smile.

" You'll think I'm an awful cat if I tell you." And, as he reached out to take her manuscript: " Oh, I really couldn't—it's about somebody you know."

Mr. Goodman frowned.

" ' Supercilious' was the word you used. Who on earth is supercilious?"

Veronica sniffed—she always sniffed when she was being unpleasant.

" Don't you think she is—a little bit? After all, her father only keeps a boarding house."

" Oh, you mean Miss Redmayne?" asked Goodman quietly. He put down his paper. " A very nice girl. A boarding house, eh? Well, I was the first boarder her father ever had, and I've never regarded this place as a boarding house."

There was a silence, which the girl broke.

" Mr. Goodman, do you mind if I say something?"

" Well, I haven't objected so far, have I?" he smiled.

" I suppose I'm naturally romantic," she said. " I see mystery in almost everything. Even you are mysterious." And, when he looked alarmed: " Oh, I don't mean sinister!"

He was glad she did not.

"But Colonel Redmayne *is* sinister," she said emphatically.

He considered this.

"He never struck me that way," he said slowly.

"But he is," she persisted. "Why did he buy this place miles from everywhere and turn it into a boarding house?"

"To make money, I suppose."

She smiled triumphantly and shook her head.

"But he doesn't. Mamma says that he must lose an awful lot of money. Monkshall is very beautiful, but it has got an awful reputation. You know that it is haunted, don't you?"

He laughed good-naturedly at this. Mr. Goodman was an old boarder and had heard this story before.

"*I've* heard things and seen things. Mamma says that there must have been a terrible crime committed here. It is!" She was more emphatic.

Mr. Goodman thought that her mother let her mind dwell too much on murders and crimes. For the stout and fussy Mrs. Elvery wallowed in the latest tragedies which filled the columns of the Sunday newspapers.

"She *does* love a good murder," agreed Veronica. "We had to put off our trip to Switzerland last year because of the River Bicycle Mystery. Do you think Colonel Redmayne ever committed a murder?"

"What a perfectly awful thing to say!" said her shocked audience.

"Why is he so nervous?" asked Veronica intensely. "What is he afraid of? He is always refusing boarders. He refused that nice young man who came yesterday."

"Well, we've got a new boarder coming tomorrow," said Goodman, finding his newspaper again.

"A parson!" said Veronica contemptuously. "Everybody knows that parsons have no money."

He could chuckle at this innocent revelation of Veronica's mind.

"The colonel could make this place pay, but he won't." She grew confidential. "And I'll tell you something more. Mamma knew Colonel Redmayne before he bought this place. He got into terrible trouble over some money—Mamma doesn't exactly know what it was. But he had no money at all. How did he buy this house?"

Mr. Goodman beamed.

"Now that I happen to know all about! He came into a legacy."

Veronica was disappointed and made no effort to hide the fact.

What comment she might have offered was silenced by the arrival of her mother.

Not that Mrs. Elvery ever " arrived." She bustled or exploded into a room, according to the measure of her exuberance. She came straight across to the settee where Mr. Goodman was unfolding his paper again.

" Did you hear anything last night?" she asked dramatically. He nodded.

" Somebody in the next room to me was snoring like the devil," he began.

" I occupy the next room to you, Mr. Goodman," said the lady icily. " Did you hear a shriek?"

" Shriek?" He was startled.

" And I heard the organ again last night!"

Goodman sighed.

" Fortunately I am a little deaf. I never hear any organs or shrieks. The only thing I can hear distinctly is the dinner gong."

" There is a mystery here." Mrs. Elvery was even more intense than her daughter. " I saw that the day I came. Originally I intended staying a week; now I remain here until the mystery is solved."

He smiled good-humouredly.

" You're a permanent fixture, Mrs. Elvery."

" It rather reminds me," Mrs. Elvery recited rapidly, but with evident relish, " of Pangleton Abbey, where John Roehampton cut the throats of his three nieces, aged respectively, nineteeen, twenty-two and twenty-four, afterwards burying them in cement, for which crime he was executed at Exeter Jail. He had to be supported to the scaffold, and left a full confession admitting his guilt!"

Mr. Goodman rose hastily to fly from the gruesome recital. Happily, rescue came in the shape of the tall, soldierly person of Colonel Redmayne. He was a man of fifty-five, rather nervous and absent of manner and address. His attire was careless and somewhat slovenly. Goodman had seen this carelessness of appearance grow from day to day.

The colonel looked from one to the other.

" Good morning. Is everything all right?"

" Comparatively, I think," said Goodman with a smile. He hoped that Mrs. Elvery would find another topic of conversation, but she was not to be denied.

" Colonel, did you hear anything in the night?"

" Hear anything?" he frowned. " What was there to hear?"

She ticked off the events of the night on her podgy fingers.

"First of all the organ, and then a most awful, blood-curdling shriek. It came from the grounds—from the direction of the Monk's Tomb."

She waited, but he shook his head.

"No, I heard nothing. I was asleep," he said in a low voice.

Veronica, an interested listener, broke in.

"Oh, what a fib! I saw your light burning long after mamma and I heard the noise. I can see your room by looking out of my window."

He scowled at her.

"Can you? I went to sleep with the light on. Has anyone seen Mary?"

Goodman pointed across the park.

"I saw her half an hour ago," he said.

Colonel Redmayne stood hesitating, then, without a word, strode from the room, and they watched him crossing the park with long strides.

"There's a mystery here!" Mrs. Elvery drew a long breath. "He's mad. Mr. Goodman, do you know that awfully nice-looking man who came yesterday morning? He wanted a room, and when I asked the colonel why he didn't let him stay he turned on me like a fiend! Said he was not the kind of man he wanted to have in the house; said he dared—'dared' was the word he used—to try to scrape acquaintance with his daughter, and that he didn't want any good-for-nothing drunkards under the same roof."

"In fact," said Mr. Goodman, "he was annoyed! You mustn't take the colonel too seriously—he's a little upset this morning."

He took up the letters that had come to him by the morning post and began to open them.

"The airs he gives himself!" she went on. "And his daughter is no better. I must say it, Mr. Goodman. It may sound awfully uncharitable, but she's got just as much——" She hesitated.

"Swank?" suggested Veronica, and her mother was shocked. "It's a common expression," said Veronica.

"But we aren't common people," protested Mrs. Elvery. "You may say that she gives herself airs. She certainly does. And her manners are deplorable. I was telling her the other day about the Grange Road murder. You remember, the man who poisoned his mother-in-law to get the insurance money—a most interesting case—when she simply turned her back on me and said she wasn't interested in horrors."

Cotton, the butler, came in at that moment with the mail. He was a gloomy man who seldom spoke. He was leaving the room when Mrs. Elvery called him back.

"Did you hear any noise last night, Cotton?"

He turned sourly.

"No, ma'am. I don't get a long time to sleep—you couldn't wake me with a gun."

"Didn't you hear the organ?" she insisted.

"I never hear anything."

"I think the man's a fool," said the exasperated lady.

"I think so too, ma'am," agreed Cotton, and went out.

CHAPTER VI

MARY went to the village that morning to buy a week's supply of stamps. She barely noticed the young man in plus fours who sat on a bench outside the "Red Lion," though she was conscious of his presence; conscious, too, of the stories she had heard about him.

She had ceased being sorry for him. He was the type of man, she decided, who had gone over the margin of redemption; and, besides, she was annoyed with him because he had irritated her father, for Mr. Ferdie Fane had had the temerity to apply for lodging at Monkshall.

Until that morning she had never spoken to him, nor had she any idea that such a misfortune would overtake her, until she came back through the village and turned into the little lane whence ran a footpath across Monkshall Park.

He was sitting on a stile, his long hands tightly clasped between his knees, a drooping cigarette in his mouth, gazing mournfully through his horn-rimmed spectacles into vacancy. She stood for a moment, thinking he had not seen her, and hesitating whether she should take a more roundabout route in order to avoid him. At that moment he got down lazily, took off his cap with a flourish.

"Pass, friend; all's well," he said.

He had rather a delightful smile, she noticed, but at the moment she was far from being delighted.

"If I accompany you to your ancestral home, does your revered father take a gun or loose a dog?"

She faced him squarely.

"You're Mr. Fane, aren't you?"

He bowed; the gesture was a little extravagant, and she went hot at his impertinence.

"I think in the circumstances, Mr. Fane, it is hardly the act of a gentleman to attempt to get into conversation with me."

"It may not be the act of a gentleman, but it is the act of an intelligent human being who loves all that is lovely," he smiled. "Have you ever noticed how few really pleasant-looking people there are in the world? I once stood at the corner of a street——"

"At present you're standing in my way," she interrupted him.

She was not feeling at her best that morning; her nerves were tense and on edge. She had spent a night of terror, listening to strange whispers, to sounds that made her go cold, to that booming note of a distant organ which made her head tingle. Otherwise, she might have handled the situation more commandingly. And she had seen something, too—something she had never seen before; a wild, mouthing shape that had darted across the lawn under her window and had vanished.

He was looking at her keenly, this man who swayed slightly on his feet.

"Does your father love you?" he asked, in a gentle, caressing tone.

She was too startled to answer.

"If he does he can refuse you nothing, my dear Miss Redmayne. If you said to him, 'Here is a young man who requires board and lodging——'"

"Will you let me pass, please?" She was trembling with suppressed anger.

Again he stepped aside with elaborate courtesy, and without a word she stepped over the stile, feeling singularly undignified. She was half-way across the park before she looked back. To her indignation, he was following, at a respectful distance, it was true, but undoubtedly following.

Neither saw the other unwanted visitor. He had arrived soon after Mrs. Elvery and Goodman had gone out with their golf clubs to practice putting on the smooth lawn to the south of the house. He was a rough-looking man, with a leather apron, and carried under his arm a number of broken umbrellas. He did not go to the kitchen, but after making a stealthy reconnaissance, had passed round to the lawn and was standing in the open doorway, watching Cotton as he gathered up the debris which the poetess had left behind.

Cotton was suddenly aware of the new-comer and jerked his head round.

"Hallo, what do you want?" he asked roughly.

"Got any umbrellas or chairs to mend—any old kettles or pans?" asked the man mechanically.

Cotton pointed in his lordliest manner.

"Outside! Who let you in?"

"The lodge-keeper said you wanted something mended," growled the tinker.

"Couldn't you come to the service door? Hop it."

But the man did not move.

"Who lives here?" he asked.

"Colonel Redmayne, if you want to know—and the kitchen door is round the corner. Don't argue!"

The tinker looked over the room with approval.

"Pretty snug place this, eh?"

Mr. Cotton's sallow face grew red.

"Can't you understand plain English? The kitchen door's round the corner. If you don't want to go there, push off!"

Instead, the man came farther into the room.

"How long has he been living here—this feller you call Redmayne?"

"Ten years," said the exasperated butler. "Is that all you want to know? You don't know how near to trouble you are."

"Ten years, eh?" The man nodded. "I want to see this colonel."

"I'll give you an introduction to him," said Cotton sarcastically. "He loves tinkers!"

It was then that Mary came in breathlessly.

"Will you send that young man away?" She pointed to the oncoming Ferdie; for the moment she did not see the tinker.

"Young man, miss?" Cotton went to the window. "Why, it's the gent who came yesterday—a very nice young gentleman he is, too."

"I don't care who he is or what he is," she said angrily. "He is to be sent away."

"Can I be of any help, miss?"

She was startled to see the tinker, and looked from him to the butler.

"No, you can't," snapped Cotton.

"Who are you?" asked Mary.

"Just a tinker, miss." He was eyeing her thoughtfully, and something in his gaze frightened her.

"He—he came in here, and I told him to go to the kitchen," Cotton said. "If you hadn't come he'd have been chucked out!"

"I don't care who he is—he must help you to get rid of this wretched young man," said Mary desperately. "He——"

She became suddenly dumb. Mr. Ferdinand Fane was surveying her from the open window.

"How d'ye do, everybody? *Comment ça va?*"

"How dare you follow me?" She stamped her foot in her fury, but he was unperturbed.

"You told me to keep out of your sight, so I walked behind. It's all perfectly clear."

It would have been dignified to have left the room in silence—he had the curious faculty of compelling her to be undignified.

"Don't you understand that your presence is objectionable to me and to my father? We don't want you here. We don't wish to know you."

"You *don't* know me." He was hurt. "I'll bet you don't even know that my Christian name is Ferdie."

"You've tried to force your acquaintance on me, and I've told you plainly that I have no desire to know you——"

"I wan' to stay here," he interrupted. "Why shouldn't I?"

"You don't need a room here—you have a room at the 'Red Lion,' and it seems a very appropriate lodging."

It was then that the watchful tinker took a hand.

"Look here, governor, this lady doesn't want you here—get out."

But he was ignored.

"I'm not going back to the 'Red Lion,'" said Mr. Fane gravely. "I don't like the beer—I can see through it——"

A hand dropped on his shoulder.

"Are you going quietly?"

Mr. Fane looked round into the tinker's face.

"Don't do that, old boy—that's rude. Never be rude, old boy. The presence of a lady——"

"Come on," began the tinker.

And then a hand like a steel vice gripped his wrist; he was swung from his feet and fell to the floor with a crash.

"Ju-juishoo," said Mr. Fane very gently.

He heard an angry exclamation and turned to Colonel Redmayne.

"What is the meaning of this?"

He heard his daughter's incoherent explanation.

"Take that man to the kitchen," he said. When they were gone: "Now, sir, what do you want?"

Her father's tone was milder than Mary had expected.

" Food an' comfort for man an' beast," said the younger man coolly, and with an effort the colonel restrained his temper.

" You can't stay here—I told you that yesterday. I've no room for you, and I don't want you."

He nodded to the door, and Mary left. His voice changed.

" Do you think I'd let you contaminate this house? A drunken beast without a sense of chivalry or decency—with nothing to do with his money but spend it in drink?"

" I thought you might," said Ferdie.

A touch of the bell brought Cotton.

" Show this—gentleman out of the house—and well off the estate," he said.

It looked as though his visitor would prove truculent, but to his relief Mr. Fane obeyed, waving aside the butler's escort.

He had left the house when a man stepped from the cover of a clump of bushes and barred his way. It was the tinker. For a few seconds they looked at one another in silence.

" There's only one man who could ever put that grip on me, and I want to have a look at you," said the tinker.

He peered at the face of Ferdie Fane, and then stepped back.

" God! It is you! I haven't seen you for ten years, and I wouldn't have known you but for that grip!" he breathed.

" I wear very well." There was no slur in the voice of Fane now. Every sentence rang like steel. " You've seen a great deal more than you ought to have seen, Mr. Connor!"

" I'm not afraid of you!" growled the man. " Don't try to scare me. The old trick, eh? Made up like a boozy mug!"

" Connor, I'm going to give you a chance for your life." Fane spoke slowly and deliberately. " Get away from this place as quickly as you can. If you're here tonight, you're a dead man!"

Neither saw the girl who, from a window above, had watched—and heard.

CHAPTER VII

Mrs. elvery described herself as an observant woman. Less charitable people complained bitterly of her spying. Cotton disliked her most intensely for that reason, and had a special

grievance by reason of the fact that she had surprised him that afternoon when he was deeply engaged in conversation with a certain
tinker who had called that morning, and who now held him
fascinated by stories of immense wealth that might be stored within
the cellars and vaults of Monkshall.

She came with her news to Colonel Redmayne, and found that
gentleman a little dazed and certainly apathetic. He had got into
the habit of retiring to his small study and locking the door. There
was a cupboard there, just big enough for a bottle and two glasses,
handy enough to hide them away when somebody knocked.

He was not favourably disposed towards Mrs. Elvery, and this
may have been the reason why he gave such scant attention to her
story.

"He's like a bear, my dear," said that good lady to her daughter.

She pulled aside the blind nervously and peered out into the
dark grounds.

"I am sure we're going to have a visitation tonight," she said.
"I told Mr. Goodman so. He said 'Stuff and nonsense!'"

"I wish to heaven you wouldn't do that, mother," snapped the
girl. "You give me the jumps."

Mrs. Elvery looked in the glass and patted her hair.

"I've seen it twice," she said, with a certain uneasy complacency.

Veronica shivered.

For a little while Mrs. Elvery said nothing, then turning
dramatically, she lifted her fat forefinger.

"Cotton!" she said mysteriously. "If that butler's a butler,
I've never seen a butler."

Veronica stared at her aghast.

"Good Lord, ma, what do you mean?"

"He's been snooping around all day. I caught him coming up
those stairs from the cellars, and when he saw me he was so taken
aback he didn't know whether he was on his head or his heels."

"How do you know he didn't know?" asked the practical
Veronica, and Mrs. Elvery's testy reply was perhaps justifiable.

Veronica looked at her mother thoughtfully.

"What *did* you see, mother—when you squealed the other
night?"

"I wish to goodness you wouldn't say 'squeal,'" snapped Mrs.
Elvery. "It's not a word you should use to your mother. I
screamed—so would you have. There it was, running about the
lawn, waving its hands—ugh!"

"What was it?" asked Veronica faintly.

Mrs. Elvery turned round in her chair.

"A monk," she said; "all black; his face hidden behind a cowl or something. Hark at that!"

It was a night of wind and rain, and the rattle of the lattice had made Mrs. Elvery jump.

"Let's go downstairs, for heaven's sake," she said.

The cheerful Mr. Goodman was alone when they reached the lounge, and he gave a little groan at the sight of her and hoped that she had not heard him.

"Mr. Goodman"—he was not prepared for Veronica's attack—"did mother tell you what she saw?"

Goodman looked over his glasses with a pained expression.

"If you're going to talk about ghosts——"

"Monks!" said Veronica, in a hollow voice.

"One monk," corrected Mrs. Elvery. "I never said I saw more than one."

Goodman's eyebrows rose.

"A monk?" He began to laugh softly, and, rising from the settee which formed his invariable resting place, he walked across the room and tapped at the panelled wall. "If it was a monk, this is the way he should come."

Mrs. Elvery stared at him open-mouthed.

"Which way?" she asked.

"This is the monk's door," explained Mr. Goodman with some relish. "It is part of the original panelling."

Mrs. Elvery fixed her glasses and looked. She saw now what she had thought was part of the panelling was indeed a door. The oak was warped and in places worm-eaten.

"This is the way the old monks came in," said Mr. Goodman. "The legend is that it communicated with an underground chapel which was used in the days of the Reformation. This lounge was the lobby that opened on to the refectory. Of course, it's all been altered—probably the old passage to the monks' chapel has been bricked up. The monks used to pass through the chapel every day, two by two—part of their ritual, I suppose, to remind them that life was a very short business."

Veronica drew a deep breath.

"On the whole I prefer to talk about mother's murders," she said.

"A chapel," repeated Mrs. Elvery intensely. "That would explain the organ, wouldn't it?"

Goodman shook his head.

"Nothing explains the organ," he said. "Rich foods, poor digestion."

And then, to change the subject :—

"You told me that that young man, Fane, was coming here."

"He isn't," said Mrs. Elvery emphatically. "He's too interesting. They don't want anybody here but old fogies," and, as he smiled, she added hastily : "I don't mean you, Mr. Goodman."

She heard the door open and looked round. It was Mary Redmayne.

"We were talking about Mr. Fane," she said.

"Were you?" said Mary, a little coldly. "It must have been a very dismal conversation."

All kind of conversation languished after that. The evening seemed an interminable time before the three guests of the house said good night and went to bed. Her father had not put in an appearance all the evening. He had been sitting behind the locked door of his study. She waited till the last guest had gone and then went and knocked at the door. She heard the cupboard close before the door unlocked.

"Good night, my dear," he said thickly.

"I want to talk to you, father."

He threw out his arms with a weary gesture.

"I wish you wouldn't, I'm all nerves tonight."

She closed the door behind her and came to where he was sitting, resting her hand upon his shoulder.

"Daddy, can't we get away from this place? Can't you sell it?"

He did not look up, but mumbled something about it being dull for her.

"It isn't more dull than it was at school," she said; "but "—she shivered—"it's awful! There's something vile about this place."

He did not meet her eyes.

"I don't understand——"

"Father, you know that there's something horrible. No, no, it isn't my nerves. I heard it last night—first the organ and then that scream!" She covered her face with her hands. "I can't bear it! I saw him running across the lawn—a terrifying thing in black. Mrs. Elvery heard it too—what's that?"

He saw her start and her face go white. She was listening.

"Can you hear?" she whispered.

"It's the wind," he said hoarsely, "nothing but the wind."

"Listen!"

Even he must have heard the faint, low tones of an organ as they rose and fell.

"Can you hear?"

"I hear nothing," he said stolidly.

She bent towards the floor and listened.

"Do you hear?" she asked again. "The sound of feet shuffling on stones, and—my God, what's that!"

It was the sound of knocking, heavy and persistent.

"Somebody is at the door," she whispered, white to the lips.

Redmayne opened a drawer and took out something which he slipped into the pocket of his dressing-gown.

"Go up to your room," he said.

He passed through the darkened lounge, stopped to switch on a light, and, as he did so, Cotton appeared from the servants' quarters. He was fully dressed.

"What is that?" asked Redmayne.

"Someone at the door, I think. Shall I open it?"

For a second the colonel hesitated.

"Yes," he said at last.

Cotton took off the chain, and, turning the key, jerked the door open. A lank figure stood on the doorstep; a figure that swayed uneasily.

"Sorry to disturb you." Ferdie Fane, his coat drenched and soaking, lurched into the room. He stared from one to the other. "I'm the second visitor you've had tonight."

"What do you want?" asked Redmayne.

In a queer, indefinable way the sight of this contemptible man gave him a certain amount of relief.

"They've turned me out of the ' Red Lion,' " Ferdie's glassy eyes were fixed on him. "I want to stay here."

"Let him stay, daddy."

Redmayne turned; it was the girl.

"Please let him stay. He can sleep in number seven."

A slow smile dawned on Mr. Fane's good-looking face.

"Thanks for invitation," he said, "which is accepted."

She looked at him in wonder. The rain had soaked his coat, and, as he stood, the drops were dripping from it, forming pools on the floor. He must have been out in the storm for hours—where had he been? And he was strangely untalkative; allowed himself to be led away by Cotton to room No. 7, which was in the farther wing. Mary's own pretty little bedroom was above the lounge. After taking leave of her father, she locked and bolted the door of her room, slowly undressed and went to bed. Her mind was too much alive to make sleep possible, and she turned from side to side restlessly.

She was dozing off when she heard a sound and sat up in bed. The wind was shrieking round the corners of the house, the patter of the rain came fitfully against her window, but that had not wakened her up. It was the sound of low voices in the room below. She thought she heard Cotton—or was it her father? They both had the same deep tone.

Then she heard a sound which made her blood freeze—a maniacal burst of laughter from the room below. For a second she sat paralysed, and then, springing out of bed, she seized her dressing-gown and went pattering down the stairs, and she saw over the banisters a figure moving in the hall below.

" Who is that?"

" It's all right, my dear."

It was her father. His room adjoined his study on the ground floor.

" Did you hear anything, daddy?"

" Nothing—nothing," he said harshly. " Go to bed."

But Mary Redmayne was not deficient in courage.

" I will not go to bed," she said, and came down the stairs. " There was somebody in the lounge—I heard them."

Her hand was on the lounge door when he gripped her arm.

" For God's sake, Mary, don't go in!"

She shook him off impatiently, and threw open the door.

No light burned; she reached out for the switch and turned it. For a second she saw nothing, and then——

Sprawling in the middle of the room lay the body of a man, a terrifying grin on his dead face.

It was the tinker, the man who had quarrelled with Ferdie Fane that morning, the man whom Fane had threatened.

CHAPTER VIII

SUPERINTENDENT HALLICK came down by car with his photographer and assistants, saw the body with the local chief of police, and instantly recognized the dead man.

Connor! Connor, the convict, who said he would follow O'Shea to the end of the world—dead, with his neck broken, in that neat way which was O'Shea's speciality.

One by one Hallick interviewed the guests and the servants. Cotton was voluble; he remembered the man, but had no idea how

he came into the room. The doors were locked and barred, none
of the windows had been forced. Goodman apparently was a
heavy sleeper and lived in the distant wing. Mrs. Elvery was full
of theories and clues, but singularly deficient in information.

" Fane—who is Fane?" asked Hallick.

Cotton explained Mr. Fane's peculiar position and the hour of
his arrival.

" I'll see him later. You have another guest on the books?"
He turned the pages of the visitors' ledger.

" He doesn't come till today. He's a parson, sir," said Cotton.

Hallick scrutinized the ill-favoured face.

" Have I seen you before?"

" Not me, sir." Cotton was pardonably agitated.

" Humph!" said Hallick. " That will do. I'll see Miss
Redmayne."

Goodman was in the room and now came forward.

" I hope you are not going to bother Miss Redmayne, superintendent. She is an extremely nice girl—I may say I am—fond
of her. If I were a younger man——" He smiled. " You see, even
tea merchants have their romances."

" And detectives," said Hallick dryly.

He looked at Mr. Goodman with a new interest. He had
betrayed from this middle-aged man a romance which none
suspected. Goodman was in love with the girl and had probably
concealed the fact from everybody in the house.

" I suppose you think I am a sentimental jackass——"

Hallick shook his head.

" Being in love isn't a crime, Mr. Goodman," he said quietly.

Goodman pursed his lips thoughtfully.

" I suppose it isn't—imbecility isn't a crime, anyway," he said

He was going in the direction whence Mary would come, when
Hallick stopped him, and obediently the favoured guest shuffled
out of another door.

Mary had been waiting for the summons, and her heart was cold
within her as she followed the detective to Hallick's presence. She
had not seen him before and was agreeably surprised. She had
expected a hectoring, bullying police officer and found a very stout
and genial man with a kindly face. He was talking to Cotton when
she came in, and for a moment he took no notice of her.

" You're sure you've no idea how this man got in last night?"

" No, sir," said Cotton.

" No window was forced, the door was locked and bolted, wasn'
it?"

Cotton nodded.

" I never let him in," he said.

Hallick's eyelids narrowed.

" Twice you've said that. When I arrived this morning you volunteered the same statement. You also said you passed Mr. Fane's room on your way in, that the door was open and the room was empty."

Cotton nodded.

" You also said that the man who rung up the police and gave the name of Cotton was not you."

" That's true, sir."

It was then that the detective became aware of the girl's presence and signalled Cotton to leave the room.

" Now, Miss Redmayne; you didn't see this man, I suppose?"

" Only for a moment."

" Did you recognize him?"

She nodded. Hallick looked down at the floor, considering.

" Where do you sleep?" he asked.

" In the room above this hall."

She was aware that the second detective was writing down all that she said.

" You must have heard something—the sound of a struggle—a cry?" suggested Hallick, and, when she shook her head: " Do you know what time the murder occurred?"

" My father said it was about one o'clock."

" You were in bed? Where was your father—anywhere near this room?"

" No." Her tone was emphatic.

" Why are you so sure?" he asked keenly.

" Because when I heard the door close——"

" Which door?" quickly.

He confused her for a moment.

" This door." She pointed to the entrance of the lounge. " Then I looked over the landing and saw my father in the passage."

" Yes. He was coming from or going to this room. How was he dressed?"

" I didn't see him," she answered desperately. " There was no light in the passage. I'm not even certain that it was his door."

Hallick smiled.

" Don't get rattled, Miss Redmayne. This man, Connor, was a well-known burglar; it is quite possible that your father might have tackled him and accidentally killed him. I mean, such a thing might occur."

Mary shook her head.

"You don't think that happened? You don't think that he got frightened when he found the man was dead, and said he knew nothing about it?"

"No," she said.

"You heard nothing last night of a terrifying or startling nature?" She did not answer.

"Have you ever seen anything at Monkshall?"

"It was all imagination," she said in a low voice; "but once I thought I saw a figure on the lawn—a figure in the robes of a monk."

"A ghost, in fact?" he smiled, and she nodded.

"You see, I'm rather nervous," she went on. "I imagine things. Sometimes when I've been in my room I've heard the sound of feet moving here—and the sound of an organ."

"Does the noise seem distinct?"

"Yes. You see, the floor isn't very thick."

"I see," he said dryly. "And yet you heard no struggle last night? Come, come, Miss Redmayne, try to remember."

She was in a panic.

"I don't remember anything—I heard nothing."

"Nothing at all?" He was gently insistent. "I mean, the man must have fallen with a terrific thud. It would have wakened you if you had been asleep—and you weren't asleep. Come now, Miss Redmayne. I think you're making a mystery of nothing. You were terribly frightened by this monk you saw, or thought you saw, and your nerves were all jagged. You heard a sound and opened your door, and your father's voice said, 'It's all right,' or something like that. Isn't that what occurred?"

He was so kindly that she was deceived.

"Yes."

"He was in his dressing-gown, I suppose—ready for bed?"

"Yes," she said again.

"Just now you told me you didn't see him—that there was no light in the passage!"

She sprang up and confronted him.

"You're trying to catch me out. I won't answer you. I heard nothing, I saw nothing. My father was never in this room—it wasn't his voice——"

"My voice, old son!"

Hallick turned quickly. A smiling man was standing in the doorway.

"How d'ye do? My name's Fane—Ferdie Fane. How's the late departed?"

" Fane, eh?" Hallick was interested in this lank man.

" My voice, old son," said Fane again.

" Indeed!"

Then the detective did an unaccountable thing. He broke off the cross-examination, and, beckoning his assistant, the two men went out of the room together.

Mary stared at the new boarder wonderingly.

" It was not your voice," she said. " Why did you say it was? Can't you see that they are suspecting everybody? Are you mad? They will think you and I are in collusion."

He beamed at her.

" C'lusion's a good word. I can say that quite distinctly, but It's a good word."

She went to the door and looked out. Hallick and his assistant were in earnest consultation on the lawn, and her heart sank.

He was helping himself to a whisky when she returned to him.

" They'll come back soon, and then what questions will they ask me? Oh, I wish you were somebody I could talk to, somebody I could ask to help! It's so horrible to see a man like you—a drunken weakling."

" Don't call me names," he said severely. " You ought to be ashamed of yourself. Tell me anything you like."

If only she could!

It was Cotton who interrupted her confidence. He came in that sly, furtive way of his.

" The new boarder's arrived, miss—the parson gentleman," he said, and stood aside to allow the new-comer to enter the lounge.

It was a slim and aged clergyman, white-haired, bespectacled. His tone was gentle, a little unctuous perhaps, his manner that of a man who lavished friendliness.

" Have I the pleasure of speaking to dear Miss Redmayne? I am the Reverend Ernest Partridge. I've had to walk up. I thought I was to be met at the station."

He gave her a limp hand to shake.

The last thing in the world she craved at that moment was the distraction of a new boarder.

" I'm very sorry, Mr. Partridge—we are all rather upset this morning. Cotton, take the bag to number three."

Mr. Partridge was mildly shocked.

" Upset? I hope that no untoward incident has marred the perfect beauty of this wonderful spot?"

" My father will tell you all about it. This is Mr. Fane."

She had to force herself to this act of common politeness.

At this moment Hallick came in hurriedly.

"Have you any actors in the grounds, Miss Redmayne?" he asked quickly.

"Actors?" She stared at him.

"Anybody dressed up." He was impatient. "Film actors—they come to these old places. My man tells me he's just seen a man in a black habit come out of the monk's tomb—he had a rifle in his hand. By God, there he is!"

He pointed through the lawn window, and at that moment Mary felt a pair of strong arms clasped about her, and she was swung round. It was Fane who held her, and she struggled, speechless with indignation. And then——

"*Ping!*"

The staccato crack of a rifle, and a bullet zipped past her and smashed the mirror above the fireplace. So close it came that she thought at first it had struck her, and in that fractional space of time realized that only Ferdinand Fane's embrace had saved her life.

CHAPTER IX

HALLICK, after an extensive search of the grounds which produced no other clue than an expended cartridge case, went up to town, leaving Sergeant Dobie in charge.

Mary never distinctly remembered how that dreadful day dragged to its end. The presence of the Scotland Yard man in the house gave her a little confidence, though it seemed to irritate her father. Happily, the detective kept himself unobtrusively in the background.

The two people who seemed unaffected by the drama of the morning were Mr. Fane and the new clerical boarder. He was a loquacious man, primed with all kinds of uninteresting anecdotes; but Mrs. Elvery found him a fascinating relief.

Ferdie Fane puzzled Mary. There was so much about him that she liked, and but for this horrid tippling practice of his she might have liked him more—how much more she did not dare admit to herself. He alone remained completely unperturbed by that shot which had nearly ended her life and his.

In the afternoon she had a little talk with him and found him singularly coherent.

"Shooting at me? Good Lord, no!" He scoffed. "It must have been a Nonconformist—we high church parsons have all sorts of enemies."

"Have you?" she asked quietly, and there was an odd look in his eyes when he answered:—

"Maybe. There are quite a number of people who want to get even with me for my past misdeeds."

"Mrs. Elvery said they were going to send Bradley down."

"Bradley!" contemptuously. "That back number at Scotland Yard!" And then, as though he could read her thoughts, he asked quickly: "Did that interesting old lady say anything else?"

They were walking through the long avenue of elms that stretched down to the main gates of the park. Two days ago she would have fled from him, but now she found a strange comfort in his society. She could not understand herself; found it equally difficult to recover a sense of her old aversion.

"Mrs. Elvery's a criminologist." She smiled whimsically, though she never felt less like smiling in her life. "She keeps press cuttings of all the horrors of the past years, and she says she's sure that that poor man Connor was connected with a big gold robbery during the war. She said there was a man named O'Shea in it——"

"O'Shea?" said Fane quickly, and she saw his face change. "What the devil is she talking about O'Shea for? She had better be careful—I beg your pardon." He was all smiles again.

"Have you heard of him?"

"The merest rumour," he said almost gaily. "Tell me what Mrs. Elvery said."

"She said that a lot of gold disappeared and was buried somewhere, and she's got a theory that it was buried in Monkshall or in the grounds; that Connor was looking for it, and that he got Cotton, the butler, to let him in—that's how he came to be in the house. I heard her telling Mr. Partridge the story. She doesn't like me well enough to tell me."

They paced in silence for awhile.

"Do you like him—Partridge, I mean?" asked Ferdie.

She thought he was very nice.

"That means he bores you." He chuckled softly to himself. And then: "Why don't you go up to town?"

She stopped dead and stared at him.

"Leave Monkshall? Why?"

He looked at her steadily.

"I don't think Monkshall is very healthy; in fact, it's a little dangerous."

"To me?" she said incredulously, and he nodded.

"To you, in spite of the fact that there are people living at Monkshall who adore you, who would probably give their own lives to save you from hurt."

"You mean my father?" She tried to pass off what might easily develop into an embarrassing conversation.

"I mean two people—for example, Mr. Goodman."

At first she was inclined to be angry and then she laughed.

"How absurd! Mr. Goodman is old enough to be my father."

"And young enough to love you," said Fane quietly. "That middle-aged gentleman is genuinely fond of you, Miss Redmayne. There is one who is not so middle-aged who is equally fond of you——"

"In sober moments?" she challenged.

And then Mary thought it expedient to remember an engagement she had in the house. He did not attempt to stop her. They walked back towards Monkshall a little more quickly.

Inspector Hallick went back to London a very puzzled man, though he was not as hopelessly baffled as his immediate subordinates thought. He was satisfied in his mind that behind the mystery of Monkshall was the more definite mystery of O'Shea.

When he reached his office he rang for his clerk, and when the officer appeared :

"Get me the record of the O'Shea gold robbery, will you?" he said. "And data of any kind we have about O'Shea."

It was not the first time he had made the last request and the response had been more or less valueless, but the Record Department of Scotland Yard had a trick of securing new evidence from day to day from unexpected sources. The sordid life histories that were compiled in that business-like room touched life at many points; the political branch that dealt with foreign anarchists had once exposed the biggest plot of modern times through a chance remark made by an old woman arrested for begging.

When the clerk had gone Hallick opened his note-book and jotted down the meagre facts he had compiled. Undoubtedly the shot had been fired from the ruins which, he discovered, were those of an old chapel in the grounds, now covered with ivy and almost hidden by sturdy chestnut trees. How the assassin had made his escape was a mystery. He did not preclude the possibility that some of these wizened slabs of stone hidden under thickets of alderberry and hawthorn trees might conceal the entrance to an underground passage.

He offered that solution to one of the inspectors who strolled in to gossip. It was the famous Inspector Elk, saturnine and sceptical.

"Underground passages!" scoffed Elk. "Why, that's the last resource, or resort—I am not certain which—of the novel writer. Underground passages and secret panels! I never pick up a book which isn't full of 'em!"

"I don't rule out either possibility," said Hallick quietly. "Monkshall was one of the oldest inhabited buildings in England. I looked it up in the library. It flourished even in the days of Elizabeth——"

Elk groaned.

"That woman! There's nothing we didn't have in her days!"

Inspector Elk had a genuine grievance against Queen Elizabeth; for years he had sought to pass an education test which would have secured him promotion, but always it was the reign of the virgin queen and the many unrememberable incidents which, from his point of view, disfigured that reign, that had brought about his undoing.

"She would have secret panels, *and* underground passages!"

And then a thought struck Hallick.

"Sit down, Elk," he said. "I want to ask you something."

"If it's history save yourself the trouble. I know no more about that woman except that she was not in any way a virgin. Whoever started this silly idea about the virgin queen?"

"Have you ever met O'Shea?" asked Hallick.

Elk stared at him.

"O'Shea—the bank smasher? No, I never met him. He is in America, isn't he?"

"I think he is very much in England," said Hallick, and the other man shook his head.

"I doubt it." Then after a moment's thought: "There's no reason why he should be in England. I am only going on the fact that he has been very quiet these years, but then a man who made the money he did can afford to sit quiet. As a rule, a crook who gets money takes it to the nearest spieling club and does it in, and as he is a natural lunatic——"

"How do you know that?" asked Hallick sharply.

Before he answered, Elk took a ragged cigar from his pocket and lit it.

"O'Shea is a madman," he said deliberately. "It is one of the facts that is not disputed."

"One of the facts that I knew nothing about till I interviewed old Connor in prison, and I don't remember that I put it on record," said Hallick. "How did you know?"

Elk had an explanation which was new to his superior.

" I went into the case years ago. We could never get O'Shea or any particulars about him except a scrap of his writing. I am talking about the days before the gold robbery and before you came into the case. I was just a plain detective officer at the time and if I couldn't get his picture and his finger-prints I got on to his family. His father died in a lunatic asylum, his sister committed suicide, his grandfather was a homicide who died whilst he was awaiting his trial for murder. I've often wondered why one of these clever fellows didn't write a history of the family."

This was indeed news to John Hallick, but it tallied with the information that Connor had given to him.

The clerk came back at this moment with a formidable dossier and one thin folder. The contents of the latter showed the inspector that nothing further had been added to the sketchy details he had read before concerning O'Shea. Elk watched him curiously.

" Refreshing your mind about the gold robbery? Doesn't it make your mouth water to think that all these golden sovereigns are hidden somewhere. Pity Bradley isn't on this job. He knows the case like I know the back of my hand, and if you think this murder has got anything to do with O'Shea, I'd cable him to come back if I were you."

Hallick was turning the pages of the typewritten sheets slowly.

" As far as Connor is concerned, he only got what was coming to him. He squealed a lot at the time of his conviction about being double-crossed, but Connor double-crossed more crooks than any man on the records, and Soapy Marks. I happen to know both of them. They were quite prepared to squeak about O'Shea just before the gold robbery. Where is Soapy?"

Hallick shook his head and closed the folder.

" I don't know. I wish you would put the word round to the divisions that I'd like to see Soapy Marks," he said. " He usually hangs out in Hammersmith, and I should like to give him a word of warning."

Elk grinned.

" You couldn't warn Soapy," he said. " He knows too much. Soapy is so clever that one of these days we'll find him at Oxford or Cambridge. Personally," he ruminated reflectively, " I prefer clever crooks. They don't take much catching; they catch themselves."

" I am not worrying about his catching himself," said Hallick. " But I am a little anxious as to whether O'Shea will catch him first. That is by no means outside the bounds of possibility."

And here he spoke prophetically.

He got through by phone to Monkshall, but Sergeant Dobie, who had been left in charge, had no information.

"Has that woman, Elvery, left?" asked Hallick.

"Not she!" came the reply. "She will hang on to the last minute. That woman is a regular crime hound. And, Mr. Hallick, that fellow Fane is tight again."

"Is he ever sober?" asked Hallick.

He did not trouble about Fane's insobriety, but he was interested to learn that life in Monkshall, despite the tragedy and the startling event of the morning, was going on as though nothing had happened. Reporters had called and had tried to interview the colonel.

"But I shunted them off. The general theory here is that Connor had somebody with him, that they got hold of the money and quarrelled about it. The other fellow killed Connor and got away with the stuff. When I said 'The general idea,'" said Dobie carefully, "I meant it is my idea. What do you think of that, sir?"

"Rotten," said Hallick, and hung up the receiver.

CHAPTER X

ALL the machinery of Scotland Yard was at work. Inquiries had gone out in every direction and not even Mrs. Elvery and her daughter had been spared. By midnight Hallick learned the private history, as far as it could be ascertained, of every inmate of Monkshall.

Mrs. Elvery was a woman in fairly comfortable circumstances, and, since her husband's death had released her from a gloomy house in Devonshire, she had no permanent home. She was more than comfortably off, by certain standards she was a wealthy woman, one of that mysterious band of middle-aged women who move from one hotel to another, and live frugally in fashionable resorts in the season. You find them on the Lido in August, in Deauville in July, on the Riviera or in Egypt in the winter.

Mr. Goodman held a sleeping partnership in an old-established and not too prosperous firm of tea importers. Probably, thought Hallick, the days of its prosperity expired before Goodman retired from business.

Cotton, the butler, had the least savoury record. He was a man who had been discharged from three jobs under suspicion of pilfering, but no conviction could be traced against him. (Hallick wrote in his note-book: "Find some way of getting Cotton's fingerprints.") In every case Cotton had been employed at boarding houses and always small articles of jewellery had disappeared in circumstances which suggested that he was not entirely ignorant of the reason for such disappearance.

Colonel Redmayne's record occupied a sheet of foolscap. He had been an impecunious officer in the Auxiliary Medical Staff, had been court-martialled in the last week of the war for drunkenness and severely reprimanded. He had, by some miracle, been appointed to a responsible position in a military charity. The disappearance of funds had led to an investigation, there had been some talk of prosecution, and Scotland Yard had actually been consulted, but had been advised against such a prosecution in the absence of direct proof that the colonel was guilty of anything but culpable negligence. The missing money had been refunded and the matter was dropped. He was next heard of when he bought Monkshall.

The information concerning Redmayne's military career was news to Hallick.

"A doctor, eh?"

Elk nodded. He had been charged with collecting the information.

"He joined up in the beginning of the war and got his rank towards the finish," he said. "Funny how these birds hang on to their military rank—'doctor' would be good enough for me."

"Was he ever in the regular army?" Elk shook his head.

"So far as I could find out, no. Owing to the trouble he got into at the end of the war he was not offered a permanent commission."

Hallick spent the evening studying a large plan of Monkshall and its grounds, and even a larger one of the room in which Connor had been found. There was one thing certain: Connor had not "broken and entered." It was, in a sense, an inside job, he must have been admitted by—whom? Not by Redmayne, certainly not by his daughter. By a servant, and that servant was Cotton. The house was almost impossible to burgle from outside without inside assistance; there were alarms in all the windows and he had seen electric controls on the doors. Monkshall was almost prepared for a siege. Indeed, it seemed as though Colonel Redmayne expected sooner or later the visitation of a burglar.

Hallick went to bed a very tired man that night, fully expecting to be called by telephone, but nothing happened. He phoned Monkshall before he left his house and Dobie reported "All is well." He had not been to bed that night, and nothing untoward had occurred. There was neither sound nor sight of the ghostly visitor.

"Ghosts!" scoffed Hallick. "Did you expect to see one?"

"Well," said Dobie's half-apologetic voice, "I am really beginning to believe there is something here that isn't quite natural."

"There is nothing anywhere that is not natural, sergeant," said Hallick sharply.

There was another case in which he was engaged, and he spent two unprofitable hours interviewing a particularly stupid servant girl concerning the mysterious disappearance of a large quantity of jewellery. It was nearly noon when he got back to his office and his clerk greeted him with a piece of unexpected information.

"Mr. Goodman is waiting to see you, sir. I put him in the reception room."

"Goodman?" Hallick frowned. At the moment he could not recall the name. "Oh, yes, from Monkshall? What does he want?"

"He said he wished to see you. He was quite willing to wait."

"Bring him in," said Hallick.

Mr. Goodman came into the tidy office a rather timid and diffident man.

"I quite expected you to throw me out for I realize how busy you are, inspector," he said, putting down his hat and umbrella very carefully; "but as I had some business in town I thought I'd come along and see you."

"I am very glad to see you, Mr. Goodman," Hallick placed a chair for him. "Are you coming to enlarge on your theories?"

Goodman smiled.

"I think I told you before I had no theories. I am terribly worried about Miss Redmayne, though." He hesitated. "You cross-examined her. She was distressed about it." He paused a little helplessly, but Hallick did not help him. "I think I told you that I am—fond of Mary Redmayne. I would do anything to clear up this matter so that you would see, what I am sure is a fact, that her father had nothing whatever to do with this terrible affair."

"I never said he had," interrupted Hallick.

Mr. Goodman nodded.

"That I realize. But I am not as foolish as, perhaps, I appear to be; I know that he is under suspicion, in fact, I imagine that everybody in the house, including myself, must of necessity be suspected."

Again he waited and again Hallick was wilfully silent. He was wondering what was coming next.

" I am a fairly wealthy man," Goodman went on at last. He gave the impression that it required a desperate effort on his part to put his proposition into words. " And I would be quite willing to spend a very considerable sum, not necessarily to help the police, but to clear Redmayne from all suspicion. I don't understand the methods of Scotland Yard and I feel I needn't tell you this "—he smiled—" and probably I am exposing my ignorance with every word I utter. But what I came to see you about is this—is it possible for me to engage a Scotland Yard detective ? "

Hallick shook his head.

" If you mean in the same way as you engage a private detective— no," he said.

Goodman's face fell.

" That's a pity. I had heard so much from Mrs. Elvery—a very loquacious and trying lady, but with an extraordinary knowledge of —er—criminality, that there is a gentleman at Scotland Yard who would have been of the greatest assistance to me—Inspector Bradley."

Hallick laughed.

" Inspector Bradley is at the moment abroad," he said.

" Oh," replied Mr. Goodman, getting glum. " That is a great pity. Mrs. Elvery says—— "

" I am afraid she says a great deal that is not very helpful," said Hallick good-humouredly. " No, Mr. Goodman, it is impossible to oblige you and I am afraid you will have to leave the matter in our hands. I don't think you will be a loser by that. We have no other desire than to get the truth. We are just as anxious to clear any person who is wrongfully suspected, as we are to convict any person who comes under suspicion and who justifies that suspicion."

That should have finished the matter, but Mr. Goodman sat on looking very embarrassed.

" It is a thousand pities," he said at last. " Mr. Bradley is abroad? So I shan't be able even to satisfy my curiosity. You see, Mr. Hallick, the lady in question was talking so much about this superman—I suppose he is clever ? "

" Very," said Hallick. " One of the ablest men we have had at the Yard."

" Ah." Goodman nodded. " That makes my disappointment a little more keen. I would have liked to have seen what he looked like. When one hears so much about a person—— "

Hallick looked at him for a second, then turning his back upon the visitor, he scanned the wall where were hanging three framed portrait groups. One of these he lifted down from the hook and laid on the table. It was a conventional group of about thirty men sitting or standing in three rows and beneath were the words " H.Q. Staff."

" I can satisfy your curiosity," he said. " The fourth man on the left from the commissioner who is seated in the centre is Inspector Bradley."

Mr. Goodman adjusted his glasses and looked. He saw a large, florid-looking man of fifty, heavy-featured, heavily built. The last person in the group he would have picked out.

" That's Bradley; he isn't much to look at, is he?" smiled Hallick. " He is the livest wire in this department."

Goodman stared at the photograph rather nervously, and then he smiled.

" That's very good of you, Mr. Hallick," he said. " He doesn't look like a detective, but then no detective ever does. That is the peculiar thing about them. They look rather—er——"

" A commonplace lot, eh?" said Hallick, his eyes twinkling. " So they are."

He hung up the portrait on the wall.

" Don't bother about Miss Redmayne," he said, " and for heaven's sake don't think that the employment of a detective, private or public, on her behalf will be of the slightest use to her or her father. Innocent people have nothing to fear. Guilty people have a great deal. You have known Colonel Redmayne for a long time, I think?"

" All my life."

" You know about his past?"

The old tea merchant hesitated.

" Yes, I think I know," he said quietly. " There were one or two incidents which were a little discreditable, were there not? He told me himself. He drinks a great deal too much, which is unfortunate. I think he was drinking more heavily at the time these unfortunate incidents occurred."

He picked up his hat and umbrella, took out his pipe with a mechanical gesture, looked at it, rubbed the bowl, and replaced it hastily.

" You can smoke, Mr. Goodman, we shan't hang you for it," chuckled Hallick.

He himself walked through the long corridor and down the stairs to the entrance hall with his visitor, and saw him off the premises. He hoped and believed that he had sent Goodman away feeling a great deal happier, and his hope was not without reason.

CHAPTER XI

IT was four o'clock when Goodman reached the little station which is some four miles distant from Monkshall, and, declining the offer of the solitary fly, started to walk across to the village. He had gone a mile when he heard the whir of a motor behind him. He did not attempt to turn his head, and was surprised when he heard the car slacken speed and a voice hailing him. It was Ferdie Fane who sat at the wheel.

"Hop in, brother. Why waste your own shoe leather when somebody else's rubber tyres are available?"

The face was flushed and the eyes behind the horn-rimmed spectacles glistened. Mr. Goodman feared the worst.

"No, no, thank you. I'd rather walk," he said.

"Stuff! Get in," scoffed Ferdie. "I am a better driver when I am tight than when I am sober, but I am not tight."

Very reluctantly the tea merchant took the seat beside the driver.

"I'll go very slowly," the new inmate of Monkshall went on. "There's nothing to be afraid of."

"You think I am afraid?" said Mr. Goodman with a certain asperity.

"I'm certain," said the other cheerfully. "Where have you been this fine day?"

"I went up to London," said Mr. Goodman.

"An interesting place to go to," said Fane; "but a deuced uncomfortable place to live in."

He was keeping his word and driving with remarkable care, Mr. Goodman discovered to his relief.

He was puzzled as to where Ferdie had obtained the car and ventured upon an inquiry.

"I hired it from a brigand in the village," said Ferdie. "Do you drive a car?"

Mr. Goodman shook his head.

"It is an easy road for a car, but a pretty poisonous one for a lorry, especially a lorry with a lot of weight in it. You know Lark Hill?"

Mr. Goodman nodded.

"A lorry was stuck there. I guess it will be there still, even though the road is as dry as a bone. What it must be like to run up that hill with a heavy load on a wet and slippery night heaven knows. I bet that hill has broken more hearts than any other in the county."

He rambled on aimlessly about nothing until they reached the foot of the redoubtable hill where the heavy lorry was still standing disconsolate by the side of the road.

"There she is," said Ferdie with the satisfaction of one who is responsible. "And it will take a bit of haulage to get her to the top, eh? Only a super-driver could have got her there. Only a man with a brain and imagination could have nursed her."

Goodman smiled.

"I didn't know there were such things as super-brains amongst lorry drivers," he said. "But I suppose every trade, however humble, has its Napoleon."

"You bet," said Ferdie.

He brought the car up the long drive to Monkshall, paid the garage hand who was waiting to take it from him, and disappeared into the house.

Goodman looked round. In spite of his age his eyesight was remarkably good, and he noticed the slim figure walking on the far side of the ruins. Handing his umbrella to Cotton he walked across to Mary. She recognized and turned to meet him. Her father was in his study and she was going back for tea. He thought that she looked a little peaked and paler than usual.

"Nothing has happened today?" he asked quickly.

She shook her head.

"Nothing. Mr. Goodman, I am dreading the night."

He patted her gently on the shoulder.

"My dear, you ought to get away out of this. I will speak to the colonel."

"Please don't," she said quickly. "Father does not want me to go. My nerves are a little on edge."

"Has that young man been——" he began.

"No, no. You mean Mr. Fane? He has been quite nice. I have only seen him for a few minutes today. He is out driving a motor car. He asked me——" She stopped.

"To go with him? That young man is certainly not troubled with nerves!"

"He was quite nice," she said quickly; "only I didn't feel like motoring. I thought it was he who had just come back, but I suppose it was you who came in the car."

He explained the circumstances of his meeting with Ferdie Fane. She smiled for the first time that day.

"He is—rather queer," she said. "Sometimes he is quite

sensible and nice. Cotton hates him for some reason or other. He told me today that unless Mr. Fane left he would."

Mr. Goodman smiled.

"You seem to have a very troublesome household," he said; "except myself—oh, I beg his pardon, the new guest. What is his name? Mr. Partridge? I hope he is behaving himself."

She smiled faintly.

"Yes, he's quite charming. I don't think I have seen him today," she added inconsequently.

"You can see him now." Mr. Goodman nodded towards the lawn.

The slim, black figure of Mr. Partridge was not easily discernible against the dark background of the foliage. He was strolling slowly up and down, reading a book as he walked; but evidently his eyes and attention were not entirely for the literature which he studied, for he closed his book and walked towards them.

"A de-lightful place, my dear Miss Redmayne," he said. "A most charming place! A little heaven upon earth, if I may use a sacred expression to describe terrestrial beauties."

In the light of day, and without the softening effect of curtains, his face was not too pleasant, she thought. It was a hard face, angular, wasted. The dark eyes which surveyed her were not his least unpleasant feature. His voice was gentle enough—gentle to the point of unctuousness. Instinctively she had disliked him the first time they had met; her second impression of him did not help her to overcome her prejudice.

"I saw you come up. Mr. Fane was driving you." There was a gentle reproach in his tone. "A curious young man, Mr. Fane—given, I fear, to the inordinate consumption of alcoholic beverage. 'Oh,' as the prophet said, 'that a man should put an enemy into his mouth to steal away his brains!'"

"I can testify," interrupted Mr. Goodman staunchly, "that Mr. Fane is perfectly sober. He drove me with the greatest care and skill. I think he is a very excitable young man, and one may often do him an injustice because of his peculiar mannerisms."

The reverend gentleman sniffed. He was obviously no lover of Fane, and sceptical of his virtues. Yet he might find no fault with Ferdie, who came into the lounge soon after tea was served, and would have sat alone if Goodman had not invited him to the little circle which included himself, Mrs. Elvery and Mary. He was unusually quiet, and though many opportunities presented themselves he was neither flippant nor aggressive.

Mary watched him furtively, more than interested in the normal man. He was older than she had thought; her father had made the same discovery. There was a touch of grey in his hair, and though the face was unlined it had the set-ness of a man who was well past his thirties, and possibly his forties.

His voice was deep, rather brusque. She thought she detected signs of nervousness, for once or twice, when he was addressed, he started so violently as to spill from the cup of tea which he held in his hand.

She saw him after the party had dispersed. " You're very subdued today, Mr. Fane."

" Am I?" He made an attempt at gaiety and failed. " It's funny, parsons always depress me. I suppose my conscience gets to work, and there's nothing more depressing than a conscience."

" What have you been doing all day?" she asked.

She told herself she was not really interested. The question was one of the commonplaces of speech that she had employed a dozen times with guests.

" Ghost hunting," he said, and when he saw her pale he was instantly penitent. " Sorry—terribly sorry! I was being funny."

But he had been very much in earnest; she realized that when she was in the privacy of her own room, where she could think without distraction. Ferdie Fane had spent that day looking for the Terror. Was he himself the Terror? That she could not believe.

CHAPTER XII

NIGHT came—the dreary night with its black mysteries and its suggestive horrors.

The telephone in the deserted lounge rang shrilly. Cotton came from some mysterious recess in a hurry to answer it. He heard Hallick's voice and winced painfully. He did not like Hallick, and wondered how soon this officer of Scotland Yard, with the resources at his disposal, would discover his own unsavoury antecedents.

" I want to speak to Dobie," said Hallick's voice.

" Yes, sir; I'll call him."

There was no need to call Sergeant Dobie; he was at Cotton's elbow.

" Is that for me?"

Cotton passed him across the instrument.

"Yes, sir . . .?" He glanced out of the corner of his eye and saw the interested Cotton. "Hop it," he said under his breath, and Cotton withdrew reluctantly.

"Have you found anything further?" asked Hallick.

"Nothing, sir. Another spent cartridge—you saw one of them before you left."

There was a long pause at the other end of the wire, and then Hallick spoke again.

"I've got an idea something may happen tonight. You have my private telephone number? . . . Good! Call me if anything happens that has an unusual appearance. Don't be afraid of bringing me down on a fool's errand. I shall have a car waiting, and I can be with you in an hour."

Dobie hung up the receiver as Mr. Goodman came ambling into the lounge. He wore his black velvet smoking jacket; his old pipe was gripped between his teeth. Dobie was on his way to the door when the tea merchant called him back.

"You're staying with us tonight, aren't you, Mr. Dobie? . . . Thank goodness for that!"

"You're nervous, are you, sir?" smiled Dobie, and Goodman's good-natured face reflected the smile.

"Why, yes, I am a little—raw. If anybody had told me I should get jumpy I should have laughed."

He took out his cigar case and offered it to the detective, who chose one with considerable care.

"There's no new clue, I suppose?" said Goodman, making himself comfortable at the end of the settee.

"No, sir," said Dobie.

Goodman chuckled.

"If you had any you wouldn't tell me, eh? That isn't one of the peculiar weaknesses of Scotland Yard officers, that they wear their—I won't say hearts, but their brains, upon their sleeves. You didn't find the gentleman who did the shooting yesterday? I ask you because I have been in town all day, and was a little disappointed when I came back to find that apparently nothing had happened."

"No, we haven't found the shooter," said Dobie.

Neither of them saw the door open, nor the pale face of Mr. Partridge peeping through.

"I was at Scotland Yard today," said Goodman; "and I had a chat with Mr. Hallick. A nice man."

"Very," agreed Dobie heartily.

John Hallick was one of the few men at the Yard who had no

enemies amongst his subordinate staff. He was the type who placed the service first, and individual kudos second, so that it was a tradition that any officer who deserved praise invariably received his full meed of recognition.

"The whole thing is really extraordinary," said Goodman thoughtfully; "in fact, the most extraordinary thing that has ever happened. Do you know, I am developing a theory?"

Dobie paused in the act of lighting his cigar.

"You're like Mrs. Elvery," he said, and Goodman groaned.

"That's the rudest thing that's been said to me today! No, it is about this unfortunate man, Connor, who was found dead in this room yesterday morning. The moment I heard the name I remembered the case—the gold robbery during the war. There were three men in it—O'Shea, the gang leader; a man named Marks—Soapy Marks; and Connor. I wouldn't like to confess as much to Mrs. Elvery for fear she never left me to myself, but I was tremendously interested in war crimes, and I am pretty sure that this dead man was Connor."

"Do you think so, sir?"

Mr. Goodman smiled.

"No, I am perfectly sure now, from your badly simulated innocence! That was the Connor, wasn't it?"

"Did you ask Mr. Hallick;" asked Dobie, and, when the other shook his head : " Well, Scotland Yard is issuing a statement tonight, so you might as well know that it was Connor."

"H'm!" Goodman frowned. "I am trying to reckon up how long he was in prison. He must have been released very recently?"

"A month ago," said Dobie. "He and Marks came out within a few hours of each other."

Mr. Goodman was beaming.

"I knew that I was right! I've got rather a good memory for names."

Dobie lingered. There was nothing for him to do, but he had a human weakness for human society.

"I suppose you're not staying on after tonight?" he suggested. "All these boarding house murders clear out the tenants and generally ruin the man or woman who's running the show."

Goodman shook his head.

"I don't know. I'm an old bachelor and I hate change. I suppose I must be a little callous, but I am not as affected as some of the other people are."

And then he went back to his original thesis.

"Now, suppose this crime is in connection with the gold robbery——"

But here he came across the official policeman. It was not a matter which Dobie could discuss, and he said so.

"Certainly—perfectly correct," said Goodman hurriedly. "I am sorry I was so indiscreet."

"Not at all," replied Dobie, and Goodman saw that he was aching to tell him all he knew. "Perhaps you're nearer the truth than you imagine."

Whatever revelation he might have made after that was interrupted by the arrival of Mrs. Elvery and her daughter. The Rev. Mr. Partridge followed, carrying in his hand a skein of wool.

Mrs. Elvery at any rate was not so reticent. She was trembling with excitement, had information to give to the bored tea merchant.

"I'm going to give you a surprise, Mr. Goodman," she said, and Goodman closed his book with an expression of resignation. "Do you know that Mr. Partridge is an authority on spiritualism?"

"And I am an authority on good coffee," said Mr. Goodman. Cotton had come in with a tray full of little cups, and Goodman selected one. "And if this coffee is good you can thank me, for I have taught the cook, after many years, how to prepare coffee that doesn't taste like dish-water. Spiritualism, eh? B-r-r! I don't want to know anything about spirits!"

Mr. Partridge was all apologies.

"You rather exaggerate, I fear, my dear friend. Do you mind my saying that? I certainly have studied the science from an outsider's point of view, but I am no authority."

"Then you won't object to a few spooks?" said Goodman, smiling.

"Spooks?" The reverend gentleman was puzzled. "Ah, you mean—thank you, Cotton." He took his coffee. "I know what you mean."

Mary came in at this uncomfortable moment, when Mr. Partridge chose to discuss the tragedy of the previous day.

"How terrible it must have been for all you poor souls! How staggering! How——"

Mary was looking at the girl, saw her suddenly stare towards the window and turn pale. Veronica leapt to her feet and screamed.

"I saw a face at the window!" she gasped.

"Draw the curtains," said Mr. Goodman testily.

A few minutes later Fane strolled into the room, and Mary saw there were raindrops on his shoulders.

"Have you been out?"

" Yes, I've been strolling around," he said.

Mary thought he had been drinking; his speech was slurred and he walked none too steadily.

" Did you see the monk?" asked Veronica spitefully.

Ferdie smiled broadly.

" If I had I'd have called his reverence to lay the ghost."

Mr. Partridge looked up, reproach in his eyes.

" It is all very dreadful. I only heard by accident of the tragedy that occurred here last night."

" Don't talk about it, please!" wailed Veronica.

" A fellow creature cut off in his prime," said the Reverend Partridge sonorously. " I confess that I had a cold shiver run through me when I heard of this awful happening. The man's name is not known, I understand?"

He was reaching for a cup of coffee.

" Oh, yes, it is." It was Fane who spoke. " I wonder somebody didn't tell you."

Their eyes met.

" The name of the murdered man," said Fane deliberately, " was Connor—Joe Connor."

The coffee cup slipped from the parson's hand and was shattered on the parquet floor. The yellow face turned a dirty white.

" Connor!" he faltered. " Joe Connor!"

Ferdie, watching him, nodded.

" You know the name?"

" I—I have heard it."

Mr. Partridge was talking with difficulty; he was a little breathless.

" Joe Connor!" he muttered again, and soon after went out of the room.

Mary noticed this and was puzzled. She wondered if Goodman had seen, but apparently he was unobservant, and he was more interested in another inmate of Monkshall. The first moment they were together he opened his heart on the subject.

" You may not believe me, my dear, but Mrs. Elvery has been very interesting tonight. She showed me her press-cutting book—about this man Connor. There is no doubt it was he—I saw a picture in one of the cuttings. And I saw another photograph which rather interested me—had you ever met Mr. Fane before he came here?"

" Was it his?" she asked.

He hesitated.

" Yes, I think it was."

And then she remembered. She had been in the village that afternoon and had seen Goodman at the post office, in the little private telephone booth, and the postmistress had volunteered the information, rather proudly, that he was speaking to Scotland Yard. She had thought no more of this than that Goodman was getting further details about the crime of last night, and she realized that his call had a deeper significance when he went on :—

"I have been making a few inquiries, and I think there is no doubt that Mr. Fane is—um—well, Mr. Fane is not all that he appears to be." And then, earnestly : "I beg of you not to mention this to him in any circumstances."

She was amazed by his vehemence, and laughed.

"Why, of course I won't."

"Mary"—he glanced over his shoulder—the rest of the company were engaged in their own affairs, and he dropped his hand timidly upon hers—"Mary, my dear, why don't you leave this place—go to London?"

"How curious!" she laughed. "That is exactly what Mr. Fane suggested."

"Mr. Fane made the suggestion for another reason," he said, with a touch of grimness in his usually mild voice. "I suggest it because—well, because I am very fond of you. Don't think I'm stupid or sentimental. In spite of the disparity in our ages, I love you as I have never loved any woman in my life."

She was unprepared for the declaration, could only look at him wonderingly.

"Think it over, my dear; and if you say 'No'—well, I shall understand."

She was glad when Cotton came in at that moment and told her her father wished to see her about some domestic trifle. She did not go back to the room until Cotton came to the study with the request that he should be allowed to lock up.

"They're all in bed except Mr. Fane," he said. "I've got an idea he's waiting for you, miss."

"Why should he be?" demanded Redmayne wrathfully.

Cotton did not know.

It was a shrewd guess on his part. Ferdie Fane sat on the sofa, hoping against hope that the girl would return. There was something he wanted to tell her, an urgent message of warning he wished to give to her. He heard the door click and turned quickly. It was the Reverend Mr. Partridge.

"Pardon me," said the clergyman, who seemed to have recovered something of his equilibrium; "I left a book here."

Fane did not speak until the white-haired man was turning to leave the room. Then:—

"You were awfully rattled, Mr. Partridge."

"Rattled?" The parson frowned. "That is a strange term to employ. I was naturally distressed to hear of this poor man's death."

Fane grinned.

"Cotton was more distressed—he had to pick up the pieces of your coffee cup," he said. "Will you sit down for a second?"

The clergyman hesitated, and then sat down on the settee by Ferdie's side.

"What a terrible fate—poor soul!" he muttered.

"Silly—that was what was the matter with Connor," said Fane coolly. "You see, he wasn't as clever as his pal—the other fellow wouldn't have been so crude."

"The other fellow?" Mr. Partridge appeared to be puzzled.

"Soapy Marks—you've never heard of him? O'Shea's right-hand man. You've never heard of O'Shea? I'll bet you've not only heard of him, but if you haven't recognized him you'll know him pretty soon."

The other man shook his head.

"This is Greek to me. Whom am I to recognize?"

"Soapy's got brains," Fane went on. "I'm going to give them a chance."

Suddenly he reached out, gripped the white hair of the clergyman and pulled. The wig came away in his hand.

"Soapy!"

Soapy Marks leapt up.

"What the hell——" he began, but the face of Fane thrust forward into his.

"Go whilst the going's good," he said deliberately. "Go whilst there's life in you. I'm telling you, as I told Connor. You're asking for death—and you'll get it!"

"Well, I'll take it," said Marks savagely. "That's what! I'll take anything that's going."

Ferdie Fane nodded.

"You never could take a warning, could you? Clever Mr. Soapy—all brain and confidence!"

"You can't frighten me." Marks was breathing heavily. "You know what I've come for? My share of the swag—and I'm not going away till I get it!"

"You're going out feet first," said Fane sombrely.

"I am, am I? You think you're damned clever, but I'll tell you something. I knew you the moment you told me about Connor. And there's somebody else in this house who knows you—that guy Goodman. He's no fool—he's knocked about the world. I saw him looking at you."

Fane was startled.

"Goodman? You're crazy mad!"

"Mad, am I? I was down in the village this afternoon, and he was putting calls through to London—making inquiries about you. That girl, Redmayne, was in the post office too. That's made you sit up. What'll you do now, my dear friend? Get Goodman out of the way. I know your methods—I know that old drunk trick of yours too."

Fane had recovered from his consternation.

"Whether he knows or whether he doesn't, I'm warning you," he said sternly. "You'll go the way of Connor."

Marks moved to the door.

"That's fair warning. The man that gets me has got to be quick."

In another second he passed through the curtains which hid the long french windows. Fane heard the click of them as the man opened them and stepped into the night.

Fane waited some time; he heard a step outside in the hall and slipped out through a door which would bring him to the lawn by another route.

He saw the door open slowly. It was Mr. Goodman. He came in, grumbling to himself, looking from table to table for his pipe. Presently he found it. He put it in his pocket and was walking slowly back to the door when he saw something on the ground, and, stopping, picked it up. It was the wig that Marks had dropped in his flight. He looked at this for a long time, and then, conscious of the draught which came through the open french windows, moved towards the closed curtains.

His hand was on the point of drawing them back when two hands shot out, gripped him by the throat and drew him into the alcove.

Mary was half undressed when she heard the struggle below; heard the cry of a man in pain, and, pulling on her gown, fled down the stairs. She pushed open the door of the hall; it was in darkness, as it had been the night before.

"All right," cried out a voice from the darkness, and the lights came on suddenly.

Ferdie Fane was standing by the window, his coat and hair dishevelled.

"Mr. Goodman!" she gasped. "I heard his voice—where is he?"

"I haven't the slightest idea," he said.

And then she saw the smear of blood across the white expanse of his shirt front. . . . As she fell fainting to the ground he caught her in his arms and the blood of a murdered man stained her kimono.

CHAPTER XIII

IT was half-past two in the morning, and Monkshall was awake. The mud-stained car of Hallick's stood at the door; the carpets were rolled up, in the search for hidden traps; and Mrs. Elvery, in a pink dressing-gown, dozed and snored in the most comfortable arm-chair. There Hallick found her when he came in from a search of the grounds.

"Take my advice and go to bed," he said, shaking her to wakefulness. "It's nearly three o'clock."

Mrs. Elvery blinked herself awake and began to cry softly.

"Poor Mr. Goodman! He was such a nice man, and there are so few bachelors left!" she wailed.

"We don't even know that he's dead yet," snapped Hallick.

"There was blood all over the floor," she whimpered. "And that nice Mr. Partridge—have you found him?"

"That nice Mr. Partridge," said Mr. Hallick irritably, "is on his way to London. You needn't worry about him; he's an old lag, and his name is Soapy Marks."

Suddenly Mrs. Elvery became galvanized to life.

"Have you questioned Cotton? He's been behaving very strangely this evening. Twice he's been down to the cellar, and when he came up the last time his knees were covered with dust—and do you know why?"

"I don't want to know why," said the weary Hallick.

"He's searching for the gold that's hidden in this house. Ah, that makes you jump, Mr. Inspector."

"Superintendent," said Hallick coldly. "The gold in this house, eh? So you've got that O'Shea story, have you? Where did you get it?"

"Out of my press cuttings," said Mrs. Elvery triumphantly.

"Will you kindly go to bed?" snapped Hallick, and succeeded in hustling her from the room.

His assistant, Sergeant Dobie, had a theory that needed a little investigation, and now that they were alone for a minute Dobie stated his views.

"Redmayne? Nonsense! Why should he——"

"That's what I was going to tell you, sir. Redmayne is broke; he borrowed all his money from Goodman. The first thing he did after the disappearance of Goodman was to go up into the old man's room, open a box there and take out a promissory note. Here it is."

Hallick examined the slip of paper thoughtfully.

"Get Redmayne here."

The colonel almost staggered into the room. His nerve was gone, he was the wreck of the man he had been.

"I want to ask you a few questions," said Hallick brusquely, and Redmayne scowled at him.

"I'm tired of answering questions," he snapped.

"I'm sure you are," said the other sarcastically. "There's a ghost in Monkshall." He produced the promissory note and held it out for the colonel to see. "Is that the secret of all the queer happenings in this house? Is that the real explanation of the Terror?"

"It was money I borrowed," said Redmayne in a low voice.

Hallick nodded.

"Ten years ago you were the secretary of a military fund. There was an audit and a large sum was missing. You were almost on the point of being arrested when you found the money—you borrowed it from Goodman?"

"Yes."

"An hour or two ago you were searching Goodman's papers. Was it to find this?" asked the detective sternly.

"I refuse to be cross-examined by you," said Redmayne, with something of his old spirit. "You have no right to question me as to my private affairs."

Hallick shook his head.

"Colonel Redmayne," he said quietly, "last night a man was murdered in your house; tonight a gentleman has disappeared in circumstances which suggest murder. I have every right to question you. I have even the right of arresting you, if I wish."

"Then arrest me." The colonel's voice quavered.

"I want you to realize the position you are in. There is

somebody in this house whom no man has seen—somebody you are sheltering!"

"What do you mean?" The shaft had struck home.

"I am suggesting," Hallick went on, "that this loan of yours from Goodman was a blind; that at the time you borrowed it you had command of immense sums of money; that you bought this house to protect a desperate criminal wanted by the police— Leonard O'Shea!"

"It's a lie," said the other hoarsely.

"Then I'll tell you another," retorted Hallick. "Somewhere in this house there is hidden hundreds of thousands of pounds in gold, the proceeds of the *Aritania* robbery; somewhere in these underground rooms of yours is a man half-sane, half-mad."

The colonel cringed back.

"I did my best to keep him away. Do you think I wanted him here—where my daughter is . . ." he whined.

"We'll get the truth about this," said Hallick.

He signalled to Dobie, who led the unresisting man to his study. Hallick followed, and, as the door closed behind them, Mr. Ferdinand Fane came through the closed curtains. He had changed his clothes and was wearing a golfing suit.

Going back to the window, he called softly and Mary came out of the darkness.

"The coast is clear," he said extravagantly, "and nobody need ever know that you have committed the indiscretion of walking in the dark with me."

She pulled off her raincoat and dropped wearily into a chair.

"It is part of the night's madness," she said; "and yet I felt safer there than in the house."

"I never feel safe anywhere," said Ferdic. "I'm going to sleep in this room tonight—where's Cotton?"

"What do you want?"

"A drink," he said, and rang the bell.

Cotton came in so quickly that he might have been standing outside the door. His coat was wet, his boots muddy.

"Hallo!" Fane eyed him keenly. "Why have you been sneaking about the grounds, my young friend?"

"Just looking round, sir. There's no harm in that, is there?" The man's voice was hollow and tremulous.

Then Mary remembered.

"Cotton, you have been with the detectives. What do they say?" Fane laughed softly, and she interpreted his scorn.

"I want to know," she said impatiently.

"I'll tell you what they say." He stared at her. "They think Mr. Goodman's dead—somewhere in this room." He leered at her. "That's a queer idea, ain't it?"

She shuddered.

"And they think that old parson's dead too," he went on with relish. "I heard Dobie telling the superintendent that the parson must have come into the room when the fight was goin' on and that the Terror killed 'em both!"

"The Terror?" she repeated.

"That's what they call him. They say he goes mad two hours every day. That's a queer thing to happen, ain't it, miss? Fancy having a lunatic around, and nobody knows who he is. It might be you, sir—it might be me—it might be me."

"Most likely you, I should think," said Fane sharply. "Cotton, bring me a pint of champagne."

"Haven't you had enough tonight?" pleaded Mary.

He shook his head.

"There's no such thing."

She waited till Cotton was out of the room, then:—

"Mr. Fane, what happened to Mr. Goodman?"

He made no attempt to answer her until Cotton had brought the wine and gone away again.

"This really *is* champagne," he said as he poured out the foaming liquor. "Gosh, I've got a headache."

"I wish you'd have such a headache that you'd never drink again," she said passionately.

"In other words, you wish I were dead?" he suggested.

He was disappointing her terribly; she had thought that in time like this he would have been a help.

And then a thought struck her.

"What do you mean by 'this really *is* champagne'?" she asked.

"I mean that this is the first drink of wine I've had for a week," he said. "Don't ask me any more about my habits—I'm a modest man."

Was he serious? Was this drunkenness of his affected?

"What happened tonight when I found you in this room?" she asked. "When that terrible fight was going on?"

He shook his head.

"I don't know. Some feller hit me in the jaw. I began to feel that I wasn't amongst friends."

Then suddenly he became unexpectedly embarrassed.

"I say, would you really like me to—sort of—well, you know— look after you?"

"I don't know what you mean," she said. And yet she knew well enough.

"I mean, to be around when you want somebody to protect you."
He had come closer to her, but he did not touch her.

"Do you think you're in a fit state to protect anybody?" she asked, and knew that she was begging the question.

"Do you know, Mary, that I'd do a tremendous lot for you? You see, Mary——"

"Must you call me Mary?" she asked.

"Unless your name's Jemima. You can call me Ferdie if you like."

"I don't like—not at the moment," she said, a little out of breath.

"Did Goodman tell you he was awfully keen on you?"
She nodded.

"Poor Mr. Goodman! Yes, he was very fond of me, and I liked him too."

She looked round suddenly and he saw her face.

"What is the matter?" he asked quickly.

She shook her head.

"I don't know, but I've got a horrible feeling that somebody is listening. I wish that man would come," she added inconsequently.

"Expecting somebody?" He was surprised.

"Yes, another detective—Mrs. Elvery calls him the great Bradley. He is coming tomorrow morning."

"Poor old blighter!" he chuckled. "What's the use of bringing in a feller like that? I'm as good as a thousand detectives. I'm as good as O'Shea." He laughed. "O'Shea! There's a lad!"

She stepped back from him.

"I've heard of O'Shea," she said slowly. "What does he look like?"

He laughed again.

"Something like me—only not so good looking."

She nodded and her voice sank to a whisper.

"You know too well who O'Shea is."

The accusation took him aback.

"Yesterday, when you spoke to that man Connor, I was at the window and I heard you threaten him."

He was silent.

"I warned him," he said at last.

As though to put an end to the conversation, he wheeled an easy-chair until it faced the panelled wall, and dragged forward a screen which he placed at its back.

"What are you going to do?" she asked.

"Sleep," was the laconic answer.

"But why do you put the chair there?" she asked in amazement.

"Old monks' door!" he smiled. "Any ghost of a monk is bound to come through the monks' door! If it was a ghost of a cook-general, she'd come through the kitchen door. You can't tell me anything about ghosts."

She was compelled to laugh at the absurdity.

Hallick came back at that moment with the colonel.

"What the dickens are you doing?" he asked.

Ferdie had found a rug, left behind by Mrs. Elvery, and this he was wrapping about himself.

"I'm going to sleep."

"Sleep in your room," said Redmayne harshly.

"Let him alone." Hallick was rather indulgent to this eccentric man.

He felt a draught and pulled back the curtains. The windows were open.

"Bolt this after we go out, Miss Redmayne, and don't let anybody in unless you hear your father's voice. We're going into the grounds."

"You'd better go to your room, my darling," said the colonel, but she shook her head.

"I'll wait here."

"But, my dear——"

"Leave her, leave her," said Hallick impatiently. "He'll do her no harm."

Ferdie, wrapped in the rug, had ensconced himself in the chair. He thought he heard her go out, but she was still there, and presently she peeped round the corner, and, seeing that his eyes were closed, switched out all the lights save one. She thought that she would speak to him, but changed her mind, tiptoed softly to the door and pulled it open. Her head was turned towards where Ferdie sat behind the screen. She did not see the man who suddenly appeared in the doorway, within inches of her. A tall shape, draped from head to foot in black, two eyes gleaming through the slits of the cowl.

She had no warning, no premonition of her danger, till an arm like steel slipped round her waist and a great hand covered her mouth.

She looked round, frozen with horror; saw the gleam of those gloomy eyes and went limp in the arms of the black monk.

Without a sound he lifted her into the passage, closed the door softly behind him, and carried her, as though she had no weight, past the door of her father's study to a little room that was used as a store. Had she been conscious, she would have remembered the big trap-door in the middle of the room which was always fastened. Stooping, he pulled the trap open, and, hoisting her to his shoulder, descended a flight of stone stairs. He left her for a moment, came back and fastened the trap from the inside.

CHAPTER XIV

HALLICK and the colonel visited the men they had stationed in the grounds round about, but nothing at all had been seen of the mysterious apparition, nor had any trace been found of Goodman or Marks.

"Marks is in London by now," said Hallick as they squelched across the sodden grass to the house. "He won't take much finding."

"Why did he come here?"

"To get the stuff that's hidden here—the gold your friend, O'Shea, has cached somewhere in this house," said Hallick. "I am taking O'Shea tonight, and I advise you to keep out of the way, because I have an idea somebody is going to be badly hurt. My suggestion to you is that you take your daughter to London tonight; use one of my cars."

"She will not go. How can I explain to her——" began the colonel.

"There's no need for explanations," said the other shortly. "You can tell her the truth, or you can wait till the case comes up for trial. O'Shea, I presume, gave you the money to buy this house."

"He had already bought it, before the robbery," said the colonel. "I was in a terrible state of mind, expecting arrest at any moment. I can't tell you how he got to know of my situation. I'd never heard of the man before. But when he offered me a loan, a fixed income, and a decent house over my head, I jumped at it. You see, I'm not a fighting soldier—I'm an army doctor; and when he explained that he had these little troubles I very naturally thought he'd be easy to deal with. I didn't even know he really was O'Shea till a year or so ago."

They trudged on in silence, and then Hallick said :—

" Have other men been here—other boarders?" He mentioned two names, and the colonel nodded.

" Yes, they came for a day or two, and then disappeared without paying their bills."

" They died here," said Hallick grimly; " and died at O'Shea's hands—if they'd had the sense to tell me that they'd located O'Shea I could have saved them. But they wanted all the credit for themselves, I suppose, poor chaps!"

" Killed them—here!" gasped the colonel.

By this time they had come to the house, and Hallick tapped gently on the french windows. There was no response. He tapped again, but there was no answer.

" We'd better come to the door and wake Cotton,"' he said.

It was a long time before Cotton heard the knocking, and a longer time before he opened the door.

" Where's Miss Redmayne?" asked Hallick.

The man shook his head.

" Haven't seen her, sir. There's somebody sleeping here—he's covered up with a blanket—gave me quite a start when I peeped round the screen."

" That's Fane; leave him alone."

He turned on all the lights.

And then suddenly a cold feeling came to this hardened detective, a sense of impending disaster.

" Go and find your daughter," he said.

Redmayne went out, and the detective heard his feet on the floor above. He came back in five minutes, white and shaking.

" She's not in her room and I don't think she's in the house. I've looked everywhere."

" Have you seen her, Cotton?"

" No, sir, I haven't seen the young lady at all."

" What's that?" said Hallick.

He picked up something from the floor; it was a girdle. The two men looked at one another.

" He's been here—the monk!" said Redmayne in horror.

Hallick had turned back the screen and dragged the chair, with its slumbering form, into the middle of the room.

" Wake up, Fane—Miss Redmayne has disappeared."

With a quick movement he jerked away the corner of the rug that covered the sleeper's face, and started back with a cry. For the man who lay in that chair was not Fane. He looked down at the dead face of Soapy Marks!

CHAPTER XV

MARY came to consciousness with a curious sensation of discomfort. She was lying on something hard and cold. She looked up and her eyes were attracted by a pale blue lantern which hung from a vaulted roof; and to her ears came the sound of music; the deep, bass notes of an organ.

She struggled to a sitting position, and looked round. She was in a tiny chapel. In a recess stood a white-draped altar. Great wooden pillars supported the roof, and between these she saw a small organ, at which there was seated a black-robed monk.

He heard her move and, looking round, came stealthily towards her. She was paralysed with fear and could not move.

" Don't be afraid," he whispered. " There is nothing to be afraid of, my little lamb."

The voice was muffled by the thick cowl that hid the face.

" Who are you? " she whispered.

" Your friend—your lover—your worshipper! "

Was she dreaming? Was this some hideous nightmare? No, it was real enough.

She saw now that there were two entrances to the vault, one on either side. Two recesses whence stone steps wound upward.

" Who are you? " she asked again, and slowly he pulled back the hood.

She could not believe her eyes. It was Goodman. The grey hair was ruffled, the keen face less serene than she had known it. His eyes were like burning fires.

" Mr. Goodman! " she whispered.

" Leonard, you shall call me," he said in the same tone.

He reached his trembling hands down and caught her by the shoulders.

" Mary, my love, I have waited—oh, so long—for this glorious moment. For you are to me as a divinity."

She came to her feet and shrank back from him.

" You're not afraid of me, Mary? "

She drew to herself all her reserves of courage and strength, and shook her head.

" No, Mr. Goodman. Why should I be afraid of you? I'm glad that you're alive. I was afraid—something had happened to you."

" Nothing could happen to me, my lamb." His smile was full

of confidence. "Nothing could happen to your lover. The very gods protected him and reserved him for this glorious reward."

Her knees were trembling under her. She was sick, and would have fainted again, but by sheer force of will maintained her consciousness.

"Your lover," he was saying. "I've loved you all this time. Sometimes I've wanted you so that there was a fire in my heart and in my brain that was beyond my control."

He took her cold hand in his and brought it to his lips. She tried to pull it away, but he held it firmly, and his eyes smiled into hers. They were bigger than she had ever seen them—wide, glowing eyes that transfigured his face.

"You're not afraid of me?" he breathed. "Not afraid of the lover who can give you all your heart's desire?"

Suddenly he caught her arm, and waved his hand about the room.

"There's money here; gold—thousands and thousands of golden pieces. Beautiful golden pieces, all hidden away. I hid them with my own hands."

And then he waxed confidential, and was more like his normal self.

"This chapel is full of hollow places. I found deep cavities where the bodies of the dead monks lay. I took them out and purified their charnel houses with beautiful gold." He pointed. "That wall behind that old seat there, these wooden pillars, are packed tight with it."

She tried to keep him in that saner mood.

"What is this place, Mr. Goodman? I have never seen it before."

He looked at her strangely, and a slow smile spread over his face.

"This is a sanctuary for my bride." His arms went round her, and she steeled herself to offer no resistance. "Men and women have been married here," he said. "Can't you smell the fragrance of the bride's hair? We will be married here," he nodded. "And men have died here—hundreds of years ago. We may die here too."

He laughed. She had heard that laugh in the night, and the horror of it turned her blood to ice.

"I've buried men here—there!" He pointed. "And there!" He pointed again. "They came in search of me—clever men from Scotland Yard!"

He knelt down on the floor and put his face to the joints of a stone slab.

"There's one there. Do you hear me, you dead man—you who came, so full of life, to catch O'Shea? Do you hear me? I am alive. And you—what are you?"

"Please, please don't!" she gasped. "You are terrifying me!"
He chuckled at this.

"The Terror—ah! That is what they call me—the Terror that walks by night. Biblical—a strange thing to call poor old Goodman. I used to sit, smoking my pipe, in that room of ours "—he pointed up —" and hear that stupid old woman talk of the Terror. And inside me my heart was laughing. She never knew how near she was."
He reached out his long hand, and it clenched horribly.

"Mr. Goodman!" She strove to bring him back to a rational level. "You'll let me go now, won't you? My father will give you anything you want, will do anything for you—he has been a doctor, you know."

Not once did his hand release the grip on her arm.

"Your father?" He was amused, and chuckled for a long time. "He'll do as I tell him, because he's afraid of me. You never thought he was afraid of me, but he is. He thinks I'm mad. That's why he's looking after me. I know he's a doctor—of course he's a doctor. Sometimes he used to lock me up in a cell. I used to scream and tear at the walls, but he kept me there. He's mad—they're all mad!"

She was swooning with fright, and with a superhuman effort tore her arm from his grip and fled to the stairs. Before one foot was on the lowest step he had caught her and dragged her back again.

"Not yet—not yet."

"Let me go." She did not struggle. "I swear I won't attempt to run away again. You can believe me, can't you?"

He nodded and released her. She crouched down on the stone seat before the altar.

"I'll play to you," he said, with sudden inspiration. "Lovely music——"

As his fingers wandered over the keys he was talking disjointedly to himself. Presently he began to play, so softly that his voice sounded harsh and grating against that wonderful background of melody.

"You've heard this old organ?" He looked round over his shoulder at her. "I play to the dead and make them live! Old monks walk here—long lines of them, marching two and two. And people bring young brides to wed and old men to die. And sometimes I see men here that I know—dead men——"

He dropped again into a conversational tone. Suddenly the music stopped, and he pointed to an invisible shape.

"Look—Joe Connor!"

She tried to pierce the gloom but saw nothing. Goodman was talking now, beckoning to the invisible shape.

"Come here, Connor; I want to talk to you. Been to prison, have you? Poor fellow! And all because of that wicked man O'Shea. Come for your share of the swag? You shall have it, my boy."

The organ ceased. He went across and put his arm around something that was invisible to Mary, but was plain to his crazy eyes. And then he led the thing he saw over to the stone seat she had vacated.

"You shall have it, my boy. It's all here, Connor—the good red gold that I got away with. Sit down, Connor—I want to tell you all about it. I'd bought this old house months before—you see, Connor? And I brought the gold here in the lorry by night, and I hid it in the hollow places. Weeks and months I worked, filling hollow pillars and the graves of old monks. Clever, eh, Connor? No wonder you smile."

He rose and stood behind the ghostly shape he saw.

"I tell you this because you're dead—and dead men never tell. And then I got Redmayne as a blind, put him in charge of the house. He had to do it, Connor"—he lowered his voice to a confidential note—"because I had a hold on him. I used to go a little queer and he looked after me—that's what I paid him for. I was nothing—he was the master of Monkshall. He, he—that's how I fooled the police. Nobody dreamed that I was O'Shea. You want your share —damn you! You dog! I'll choke the life out of you first, you hound!"

His voice rose to a yell as he gripped the spirit throat and, in his imagination, hurled it to the ground. He was kneeling on the floor now, his face demoniacal in its fury.

And then he remembered the girl and looked round.

"I'm frightening you." His voice was soft. He came nearer to her and suddenly clasped her in his arms.

She screamed, but he hushed her.

"I don't want to frighten you. Don't scream. I love you too much to frighten you." His lips sought hers, but she managed to avoid them.

"No, not yet—give me a little time."

He loosed his hold on her.

"But you will love me? Did you see those little doors in the passage walls? The old monks lived there. You and I will find a bridal suite there."

She was fighting desperately for time. At any moment this madness might pass. She knew now he was O'Shea—sane for twenty-two hours a day.

"Wait. I want to talk to you, Mr. Goodman. You said you loved me."

"You are God to me," he said reverently.

"You would not want me to love you if I loved someone else, would you?"

"Loved someone else? No, no. I would not ask it. But do you love someone else?"

"Yes—I—I'm awfully fond of—of Mr. Fane."

For a second he neither spoke nor moved, then his hand shot out to her throat. She thought she was doomed, but at that moment she was gripped by the arm and swung aside, and O'Shea looked into the levelled muzzle of an automatic.

"I want you, O'Shea!"

It was Fane's voice, Fane's arm that encircled her.

"Come away from that switch. That's right. I don't want to be in the dark. Farther. Now stand still."

"Who are you?" O'Shea's voice was surprisingly gentle.

"My name's Bradley!" said Fane quietly. "Inspector Bradley of Scotland Yard. I want you, O'Shea. For three years I have been waiting for this opportunity, and now I know all that I want to know."

O'Shea nodded.

"You know what I have done to Marks?"

"You killed him—yes."

"He tried to strangle me—I think he must have recognized me. His body——"

"I found it behind the monks' door and left it in my place. If he and Connor had taken my advice they would have been alive today."

O'Shea gave a deep sigh and smiled.

"I'm afraid I've given everybody a lot of trouble," he said blandly. "So you're Bradley, the man who arrested Connor and the man who arrested our old friend, Soapy Marks, and now you have done the hat trick! Really, I deserve everything for not recognizing you. Miss Redmayne, will you accept my apologies? I am afraid at times I get a little out of hand—a mere passing folly—um. May I take off this ridiculous robe?" He stripped the black robe from him, slowly.

" Be careful. He is not quite sane yet," said Mary in a low whisper.

He heard her.

" Oh, my dear Miss Redmayne "—he smiled—" you must be a very poor judge of sanity. And now, I suppose, inspector—or is it superintendent?—you will marry this charming young lady who has so touchingly declared her love for you? I wish I could find you a little wedding present."

So quickly did he move that Bradley could not have escaped death had not the foot of the assassin slipped. The knife struck one of the pillars, and in the impact the rotting wood broke and a stream of gold flowed from its hollow depth.

O'Shea glared at the gold that had cost him so much, and then he began to laugh.

" A wedding present," he chuckled.

He was still laughing when Hallick and three detectives took him by car to London.

THE W PLAN

By

GRAHAM SETON

THE W PLAN

CHAPTER I

OBSESSION

THE Commander-in-chief, as was his habit when a decision of importance had to be taken, was alone. The walls of the large salon in the Norman château overlooking the English Channel were hung with maps and messages, the table piled with documents and reports. The general paced up and down the wooden floor, from time to time pausing before a great map dotted with coloured flags. It was now after three in the afternoon. In the morning the general had conferred with his army commanders, the chiefs of artillery and of the air, engineers and other technical experts. Later, over lunch, he had discussed the question of man power, reinforcement, transport, the various theatres of war and supply of munitions with officials from London.

Now he was left to make momentous decisions, the result of which might affect the whole course of the war, certainly its higher strategy, for many months to come. The general was satisfied that unless the improbable occurred, his dispositions and supplies were adequate, and when the large reserves from home were fully trained he would be able to take that initiative in offensive action for which he had so long waited.

But in war, it is the improbable, even the preposterous, which so often has reduced plans to pulp and armies to annihilation, rout and defeat.

The enemy had been singularly quiet of late, yet there was no evidence of exhaustion. Prisoners taken in raids were well conditioned and equipped: enemy air-reconnaissance and night raids were consistent, irritating, sometimes almost dominating. The artillery up and down the line was effective with ample ammunition; yet was the enemy inactive. The Foreign Office, through its network of espionage, gave no hint as to the moves the enemy would or could make, what strategy the Commander-in-chief should adopt to force his hand.

Information tested in the light of reality had proved misleading. Officers taken prisoner in those raids, which were becoming increasingly costly, were arrogant, and very silent; the soldiers, mostly unreliable and influenced chiefly to provide witness calculated to give them the quickest comfort in an enemy's hands, gave no clue as to what might be the designs of the enemy one month, possibly

three or four months ahead. There was no sure indication whether
the enemy commander was nervous as to the loyalty and fighting
spirit of an army, now nearly three years in the field.

No one knew, or would tell where and when the enemy would
strike, with what force and with what new instrument of warfare
as the first shock with which to spread dismay and to break the morale
of the British army. These were the problems which confronted the
general staff.

But there was a vague uneasiness in the mind of the Commander-
in-chief. The quietness of the front disturbed him. It was now over
five months since there had been any trial of strength. Many weeks
had elapsed since the great offensive in Italy through which Germany
had sought to break the blockade and open a way out through the
Mediterranean.

The general felt that something momentous was about to happen,
but when? where? His uneasiness had been increased within the
last two days by a note in a report from the Intelligence Branch. It
is one of those odd things, so far inexplicable in psychic research or
in the realm of psychology, that the mind pre-occupied with major
problems will become obsessed with a trivial detail. No one had
paid any special attention to this paragraph, nor had the staff made
reference to it.

It was inserted among a collection of miscellaneous information,
mostly of the character of rumour or hearsay.

A major of engineers, unattached to any particular enemy
division, had been captured in one of our periodical raids, severely
wounded. In delirium he had raved incessantly, and the medical
officer in charge of the casualty clearing station had thought fit
to send for the divisional intelligence officer, a young man
apparently thoroughly conversant with the language, but probably
unskilled in military affairs.

The report stated that the major had referred repeatedly to " the
inverted M breach." He had died of wounds the following day.
The bare statement of fact was there, but no comment. The general
sat down at his desk and glanced quickly through the latest reports.
Pencil in hand he marked those paragraphs the significance of which
he did not understand, or which appeared important. Whilst he
was reading, his hand, led to action by some unconscious thought,
traced upon the wide blotting-pad a series of inverted M's—the letter
W. He pushed his chair back and rose, thrusting his papers back
upon the desk. Dismissing the thought with irritation from his
mind, he again strode up and down the wooden floor.

The conferences had declared nothing new. The Intelligence

Service, espionage, aerial reconnaissance, raids, had provided nothing definite, no facts which correlated.

The general opened his door, and walked down the white-washed corridor to the room of Colonel Jervois, his military secretary.

" Jervois, do you remember a hot-headed young fellow commanding a battalion of the Inverness Highlanders at a dugout we visited near Arras in May last year? He was feeding a brace of Boches on port, and lecturing like a university professor. He pushed out his guests with his foot, and then said if I had nothing specially important to do he could give me some first-hand information, there and then, saving the necessity of writing a long report and delaying the information."

Jervois paused a moment. " Yes, sir, I recall the incident well. You remember, sir, how having passed over his information he outlined a plan whereby we could obtain definite information about the enemy's plans."

" It was just that plan," said the general, " which made me ask you if you recollected the lad. Is he still alive?" Jervois walked across to his disposition chart. " The 2nd Inverness Regiment is now with the 7th Division, 3rd Corps, 1st Army. I will get the operator to put me right through to the battalion.

" Hullo, orderly, have my line cleared—urgent—through to the 2nd Inverness Regiment, 1st Army."

The general was thinking aloud. . . . " Yes, a lad typical of his breed. . . . A shock of fair hair, bright blue eyes, strong; independent, too : spoke German like a native . . . told us he had been discussing Marx and Nietzsche with his night club . . . had a great idea of being flown behind the lines, left to his own devices, and then being picked up again, and bringing information, seen through the eyes of a soldier trained to appreciate a situation on the model of Hamley, Henderson and Clausewitz in place of what he described as the clumsy, indefinite methods pursued, forsooth, by General Headquarters."

" 2nd Inverness Regiment coming through, sir."

" Hullo, Inverness. . . . General Staff speaking here. Is your commanding officer there?"

" Yes, sir, I'll get him to come on the line."

" I've turned up the Order of Battle. I see Duncan Grant is commanding, appointed November, 1916. Should be the same officer," intervened Jervois.

" Commanding officer, 2nd Battalion Inverness Regiment, speaking."

" I am Colonel Jervois, the Military Secretary. You are to report to me personally forthwith. I am informing your brigadier and division, who will send a car with instructions as to destination to meet you at Brigade Headquarters. I shall expect you here within two hours."

Duncan Grant arrived at G.H.Q. shortly after 6.30 p.m. An orderly showed him straight into the office of Colonel Jervois.

"Good evening, Grant, the Commander-in-chief expects you to dinner with him. The orderly will show you where to get a wash. Look sharp and then ask for the Commander-in-chief. I will join you with him."

Grant's mixed feelings were adjusted to those of pleasure and excitement. Dinner with the Commander-in-chief was one thing: a reprimand from an irate staff officer, for any one of a regimental officer's sins of commission or omission, was quite another. He quickly washed away the dust of the journey, followed by a vigorous brush from the orderly, and presented himself in the room of the Commander-in-chief.

The general was standing before the great fireplace, a fine figure of a man, broad-shouldered, tall, dark hair tinged with grey, ruddy complexion, a close-clipped moustache, dark piercing eyes, now a little heavy. His tunic was unbuttoned, and his hands thrust deep into the thigh pockets of his riding breeches—an active, strong man.

The general came forward, his hand outstretched.

"I remember meeting you, Grant, up at Hargicourt. You were entertaining two German professors and . . . then told me how to conduct my Intelligence Service."

"I beg your pardon, sir, nothing was ever . . ."

"No need to apologize. Quite enlightening. I wish I could get a few more hints from young men of your type. Too many commanders agree with me. An army commander needs ideas and we have no monopoly of brains or imagination at headquarters," he looked up, "have we, Jervois? In fact your lecture has brought about this little dinner party. So, after dinner—and that will be short—we will resume." The general rang a bell.

"Sergeant Case, have dinner served at once."

"Very good, sir."

Both the general and Colonel Jervois were very genial during dinner, the general searching in his inquiry—the stamina of young recruits, training of specialists, effectiveness and co-operation of the newly-formed machine-gun battalions, quality of the rations . . . and here Duncan told him that it was a little difficult to induce Jock's belief that pork and beans, with very little discernible pork, were more nutritious than beef steak, despite the medicinal legend imprinted on each tin as to protein and vitamin values. Duncan felt at ease and happy. Dinner, soup, and a meat dish followed by fruit, was pleasantly spiced with easy conversation.

Dinner lasted less than half an hour. The orderly placed the port decanter on the table, but it was a formality : it was not proffered.

" Close the door, orderly. See I am disturbed by nobody." The general rose, and, calling Jervois and Grant, passed through a side door which communicated with his office. He turned on the lights and crossed to the telephone.

" Orderly, put all calls for me through to the General Staff. Colonel Jervois is with me : any calls for him will also be put through to the Staff. We are not to be disturbed." Then turning to Grant he waved him to a chair.

" You will remember outlining to me a plan—it was when I visited your headquarters at Hargicourt—whereby information could be quickly and readily obtained. You stated that you yourself were prepared to give effect to this scheme : and that you were convinced of its success."

" Yes, sir."

" There is information which I require, possibly of supreme importance. It is essential that it be obtained in the minimum of time and its accuracy must be unqualified. You will put your plan into operation, and anything which you may require for the purpose is completely at your disposal. I shall inform you exactly as to the situation, and what is the information in particular which I require. Thereafter you will inform me, please, as to your requirements and proposals. You are prepared, I am assuming, to undertake the task of which you told me some months ago."

" Yes, sir."

" Very well, then, I will outline the position in general. Any further details will be explained and amplified to you by Colonel Jervois, who will also give you such information which we have as to the disposition of the enemy, his plans and the reports which we have secured through the Secret and Intelligence Services.

" You can appreciate the fact that our front has been unusually quiet. We have no information which indicates for certain how, when or where the enemy will move. In some respects, as you will probably have noted, namely in the air and in heavy artillery, we are dominated, at least equalled. Our Foreign Office informs us that there is a grave shortage of foodstuffs causing disaffection among the civil population in the larger towns—but that, of course, in measure we, too, are experiencing at home.

"To me it is clear that an enemy, acting on interior lines, cannot indefinitely remain quiescent. Moreover, the enemy will be well informed as to our own position, and will know that within the space of a few weeks—it was confirmed to me this morning— we shall have available considerable reinforcements both of men and ammunition. We can assume that the enemy is as familiar with this fact as is our own government. The simple deduction is, therefore, that he will strike. Where? How? His quiescence also leads me to suppose that there is a new element of surprise which is now being prepared. I will tell you quite frankly that our Intelligence Service has so far been unable to answer the questions—where will he strike, how will he strike, what is the element of surprise which is being prepared? As, frankly, also I will tell you that the situation, calm as it is reported in our home press, and in fact, as it is, causes me grave anxiety.

"I shall require you to answer those three questions. You will have opportunity to read through our Intelligence reports, both in *précis* and in full, and to examine any prisoners or officers of my own staff; but so far as I can judge there is no information yet available which serves even as a clue to the answer of any of these three questions."

The general had been pacing up and down the salon, and now sat down at his desk. The reports which he had been examining prior to dinner were still lying on the table; he shook these together and passed them to his Chief of Staff. The removal of the papers disclosed what he had earlier pencilled on the blotting-pad—the inverted M. A look of irritation crossed the general's face, and this did not escape the eyes of Duncan Grant. The general, old in diplomacy, quickly realized that the change in the even tenor of his recitation had been detected and he looked up, smiling, he would have confessed to himself, a little guiltily.

"I expect, Colonel Grant, you smoke," and he offered him a cigar.

"Thank you, sir; and how soon should I start to obtain your information? At dawn, I presume, or just before? Perhaps you never noticed, sir, how the smell of Havana smoke clings to the hair. There are few Havanas in Germany, nor do active soldiers often keep their company."

The general was about to light his own cigar and Grant swiftly plucked the lighted match from his hand.

"Pardon me, sir, I want to start on my journey without any incriminating evidence."

The general looked intently at Grant. The glance was not one of severity, but partly of surprise and partly interest. Colonel Grant, possessed, also, a fine sense of discipline, and realizing the unintentional insult of his action to his Commander-in-chief let his eyes fall before those of his general. They rested on the blotting-pad. They saw the repetitions of W, . . . W, . . . W pencilled thereon. Quickly the eye, communicating with the brain, informed Grant that since the blotting-pad was otherwise blank, the cause of the chief's change of countenance and of subject, was connected with these hieroglyphics. He raised his eyes and met those of the general, who was smiling. Jervois was standing at his side a little perplexed.

Colonel Grant picked up a pencil from the table and without removing his eyes from those of the general, wrote on the blotting-pad a single capital letter W. He then laid the pencil down, lowering his gaze at the same time. Looking up quickly he saw that the general too was staring at the pad.

There is a curious bond of sympathy which can often be awakened between persons in any walk of life, when one discovers the other's guilty secret. No man or woman can endure keeping a secret exclusively with himself. If it is one which augurs happiness, its retention is a rising crescendo of pleasure, until, emotion overriding reason, the pleasure must be shared with another. Secrets of guilt gnaw steadily into the very vitals of sanity. Murder will out.

Every policeman knows that, sooner or later, there will be a confessor of an accomplice in crime; and often the master-detective to whom the secret of crime is revealed has saved his prisoner from insanity, though he may bring him to the gallows : so with the Commander-in-chief. He had a guilty secret, something which although apparently absurd, perpetually deranged every logical thought. He had found a friend, someone confident, self-assured, and so much his junior that he could afford to be absurd, in order to rid himself of his obsession.

" Jervois, just hand me back those reports. There is a note in one of them, I do not remember which, but it is of quite recent date, concerning the interrogation of a prisoner, a major of engineers at a casualty clearing station. The Intelligence Branch did not appear to consider it of any significance, and I suppose you will not have it in mind."

" No, General, I can't say that I have."

" Just so. I happened to be reading through these reports, and there was something about this note which struck me as odd. Here it is. You will see that this poor devil in a delirium repeatedly referred to the ' inverted M breach.' Well, people in delirium talk abominable nonsense, but there is something curious about an inverted M, I don't say of any military significance, but of course an inverted M is a double U, and I tried it out on my blotting-pad. Some ribald jest probably accounts for the inversion of the M; and, when you think of it, the officer, although in delirium, held high rank, and was not of the infantry occupying that sector, but of the engineers. It is true, of course, that he was raving and there is probably nothing in it; but as you know, Jervois . . . I am looking for a clue. Perhaps you will say the agitation of an over-wrought, over-anxious man, but I discovered myself pencilling this wretched inverted M, unwittingly, I suppose subconsciously, on my blotting-pad. I am going to ask Colonel Grant, who says that he is ready to start at dawn—how and whither as yet I do not know—whether, now that I have made what amounts to a confession of which I might be a little ashamed, he wants to know anything more about the major of engineers. Now Grant——"

"Yes, sir, the report says he's dead. If any papers were taken off him I want them sent here to me at once. I presume he has been buried. I want the body, complete as it is, and I want also the whole of the effects. The report is dated two days ago. I want everything that belonged to the major, including the body, sent to me."

The general unhooked his telephone receiver.

"Hallo, put me through to Major Gaynor . . . is that you, Gaynor? This is the Commander-in-chief speaking. Come straight to my room immediately."

After a few minutes there was a knock at the door and Major Gaynor came in.

"Gaynor, since I telephoned to you, we have seen, from the Order of Battle, that the 27th Division is in the Bailleul area. The casualty clearing station is at Neuve Eglise. We assume that there is a cemetery beside the C.C.S. Two days ago a German officer, Major Ulrich Muller, died at the C.C.S. Neuve Eglise is about an hour and a half by car from here. I want you to go straight to Neuve Eglise and bring back to this office the body of Major Muller and any articles of clothing, equipment, or uniform, books, papers, or other effects. Jervois will telephone to the division to expedite matters. It is now twenty past seven, and I shall expect you back here at the latest by ten-thirty p.m. Jervois has a written instruction here for your authority. That's all, and be quick."

Colonel Jervois communicated with the division; and having instructed the Intelligence Officer to report at the casualty clearing station with all the effects and papers of Major Muller, he asked to speak with its officer in charge.

"I want to speak with the senior officer in charge."

"He is doing an operation, sir; told me he wasn't to be bothered on the telephone."

"Tell him the General Staff requests his presence on the telephone immediately," he said irritably.

After a few minutes a voice exclaimed: "This is impossible, preposterous . . . one of the most interesting operations I have ever performed . . . trepanning . . . and, apart from that, the fellow will die."

"Listen to me, doctor. Colonel Jervois, G.H.Q. speaking. . . . Major Gaynor of my staff is on his way now to your C.C.S. Whatever else may occupy you, these orders are to be carried out implicitly and quickly. A German, Major Ulrich Muller, is reported to have died of wounds at your C.C.S."

"That's true, he did."

"Very well, where is he buried?"

"In the cemetery beside the C.C.S."

"Was the body clothed when it was buried or not?"

"I really don't know . . . yes, I expect so. I was very busy here with cases from the last raid. No time to do anything . . . but, yes, I remember he died of shock . . . I saw him after he was dead. Sure to be buried in his uniform."

"Had he any papers or matter in his pocket?"

"I really don't know—not my business. I sent for the Intelligence Officer as he was raving. . . . I don't understand the lingo, anyway. They will know all about it at divisional headquarters. I'm busy. There's a man dying. . . ."

"One of my staff officers will be with you shortly. You are to have the body disinterred at once . . . at once, you understand. Gaynor can bring it back in the car. See that Major Muller's effects are complete so far as you are concerned."

"But we cannot put the body in a car. There wouldn't be room for a stretcher, sir. Shall I have it sent in an ambulance tomorrow?"

"No, do what I say. There will be Gaynor, the chauffeur and the Intelligence Officer in the car, and there is room for one more. Sit Major Muller upright in the car. Gaynor must bring the body back. You understand me? This is to be done forthwith, and see to it yourself. You can get on with your operation afterwards; or, if it isn't necessary, Major Muller's hole will be vacant. Good-bye, and look sharp."

The general rose and sat on the edge of his desk, regarding Colonel Grant.

"Grant, your wishes, you see, are being executed. Jervois, you were a little hard on the doctor, weren't you? Now, Grant, you must consider what you are going to do, and what is the plan. You may be able to make something of Major Muller. I have my own theory as to his possible importance at the present situation.

"We have first of all to determine whether Muller was an officer of the German division occupying the sector, or whether he had been sent there on some special duty.

"As he was not attached to this German division, it is clear that Muller was there upon some special mission. We shall see from his badges if he belonged to any special unit. Jervois, you can tell me if the division was about to be relieved. That, of course, might account for Muller's presence . . . just having a look round."

"No, this division had only been in the line for five days prior to the raid, which was carried out for identification purposes. Muller might have been taking up a new appointment in the division."

"That is quite possible," said the general, "we must not allow ourselves to imagine improbables, though you are right to expect it. Have you got the Order of Battle, Jervois?"

"Yes, general."

"Well, is Muller's name on it?"

"Not mentioned: he held no staff appointment, nor was he in command of any of the engineer formations."

"Well, we must have a look at him when he arrives," said Grant, "and, until then, general, with your permission, I would be glad to be given all the information available as to the strategic position, and as to any evidence from the Intelligence reports which you consider important, and which require investigation or verification. I will trust to my memory to retain the essentials. And, sir, before you explain the situation to me will you send for a highly competent air pilot, and place at my disposal an aeroplane, capable of a long flight."

"Of course, that was the essence of your plan. Hullo, orderly, give General Lister my compliments, and ask him to come to my room at once."

In a moment General Lister, who had been in the staff mess-room across the passage, entered—"Lister, this is Colonel Grant of the Inverness Regiment. He is an expert German linguist. I am sending him tonight to a point to be chosen by himself, a considerable distance behind the German lines. I want your best available machine and pilot for the task."

"Mayne's the lad for this job, general."

"Where is he now?"

" XY bombing squadron. He led the Tourcoing raid last week."

" All right, phone for him to come here at once. Grant wants a word with him. And, give orders for his machine to be put ready, maximum load petrol, no bombs."

" General," interposed Grant, " I want one of your draughtsmen from the map section. He must be a man whom we can trust. I believe you've still got a friend of mine down here—John Collett— camouflage officer or something of that kind."

" That's true," said the general.

" Well, sir," said Grant with a broad smile, " I've been waiting for an opportunity to give him orders and see how he likes it. He's under the impression, or was, that he's a great artist. I've got a job after his own heart," he said, now laughing. " He must make at once two crosses painted on strong canvas. These will be pasted over our own aircraft signs on the under wing of the machine. Sorry, sir, we must fly under German colours. For the return trip, I will detach the crosses. It's just to cover my landing."

General Lister looked questioningly at the general.

" That's all right, Lister. I have given Grant *carte blanche*."

" I'll stick 'em on, myself," said Grant, " just before we start. Mayne and we three will be in the know. No one else. You will let me have the dimension of the wing, general, please, and I'll get the artist busy right away."

" That's all, Lister," said the general. " As soon as Mayne has fixed up his machine and is ready, send him here."

The Commander-in-chief then outlined the strategic position.

" Frankly, I'm mystified by the present apparent inactivity," he concluded. " So far as we can judge, the enemy has ample men for an offensive, munitions, everything. He must strike. But where? We have a front one hundred and eighty miles long. He must know that I shall not be ready for three months. He must anticipate me, but where and with what?" The general had been speaking for some forty minutes, explaining with the aid of maps the position and disposition of his own forces, and what he believed were those of the enemy. He showed the strategic points of our lines, their strength and weakness; he detailed the probable moves of the enemy, the advantages of one against another. Grant followed him with close attention and understanding.

A knock came at the door. It was now ten-twenty. Without pausing for a reply, Gaynor came in.

" I've brought the Intelligence Officer, 27th Division, and—er— Major Muller."

" Bring them in."

"Muller's in the car, sir."

"Well, go and fetch him. Tell your chauffeur to hold his tongue. Grant, give Gaynor a hand with Major Muller."

The dead German was tightly wrapped in a blanket, still damp and muddy from the grave. The three officers carried in their burden and laid him on the floor.

"This is your business," said the Commander-in-chief as he turned his back and walked over to the fireplace. Grant and Gaynor had already commenced unwrapping the blanket from the body. It was soon completely exposed to view. A man not yet of middle age, with fair hair and complexion, dressed in green-grey uniform. Its badges revealed nothing other than that he belonged to the Corps of Engineers. Grant folded back one of his eyes to ascertain its colour and opened the mouth and examined the teeth. The eyes were of a very dark brown colour, in sharp contrast to the general Nordic colouring. The second and third fingers of the right hand were missing. Grant examined them closely. It was clear that this feature was no new occurrence, no recent wound. The body was completely clothed with the exception of field boots and socks, which had been removed from the shattered legs, from which the right foot was wholly missing. Duncan then turned to the Intelligence Officer and said : "Help me strip the body. I shall require all these clothes."

In silence the gruesome task of removing the clothes, tunic and riding-breeches, linen shirt and undervest, was accomplished. Grant carefully examined the body to see if there were any marks upon it other than those of wounds. The figure was that of a well-developed and muscular man; and in size, colouring and general structure that of any average soldier of the Teuton type. After a careful scrutiny, the body was wrapped up again in the blanket; and speaking to the general, Grant said that it could be returned to the cemetery or otherwise disposed of; while requesting that the clothing be placed in an oven to be dried and cleansed of the grave. The general rang for his orderly and instructed him to take the uniform and clothing and have it thoroughly dried in the kitchen within the next hour. Grant then asked the Intelligence Officer for any effects taken from the body. The young officer produced a military chronometer of first-class workmanship, a compass, barometer, both of them in leather cases. A cigar case, which on examination proved to contain four cigars, two of which Grant removed and laid on the general's desk. There was also a small map of the whole front, one in common use among senior officers, some dividers and a notebook. The Intelligence Officer stated that he had been right through the notebook, but that it contained nothing other than a miscellaneous number of addresses, many of them of women in a variety of towns in the Essen district, and, underneath, Ulrich Muller's own name and address in the village of Hatzberg, which the map showed to be some six miles north-west of Barmen.

"It would appear that Major Muller is a native of Hatzberg; and it is clear from his appointments that he was not a regular officer but of the reserve. The instruments in his possession are of the finest procurable, and I do not recollect," said he, "having seen any quite as good hitherto."

"Was there anything else?" asked Duncan Grant.

"Yes, there was a small piece of paper which I found in the barometer case. Here it is."

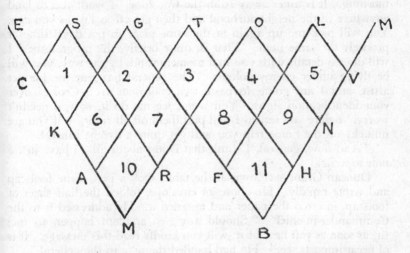

"I didn't attach any importance to the paper, but connected it, of course, with my interrogation of Muller because it is marked with a W, 'the inverted M,' to which he referred. It crossed my mind that probably Muller was proud of his instruments, and in delirium was worried about something technically wrong, or by some alteration in the barometer which he was planning, and that is why this paper was in the case."

"Well, Grant," said the general, "time's getting on, you know. It is already ten minutes to eleven, and I don't think that Major Muller takes us anywhere, so perhaps we can dismiss the question of the inverted M once and for all. I take it you have got your plan pretty well cut and dried now, in fact, you have had it so for many months and the sooner you make your arrangements with Mayne to get away the better. Jervois has just told me that Mayne is all ready and waiting for you outside."

"Yes, general, but I am not going to dismiss Muller. I am adopting him. Just so soon as those clothes are dried, I shall put them on; and by the way, general, I should like to offer you a smoke. I have put two very excellent cigars on your desk. I am sorry my supply is limited; I will be glad if you will honour me by taking one. I would like now to have a talk with Mayne."

In a minute or two Colonel Jervois returned with Flight Commander Mayne. Grant took him over to the large scale map on the wall, and pointed to the town of Barmen. "I want to reach the neighbourhood of that town between four and five tomorrow morning. It is miles away from the war zone. I want you to land anywhere in the neighbourhood and then get off as fast as you can. You will pick me up again at the same place in ten days' time at precisely the same hour. That is, quite briefly, the programme. I will discuss details with you in a moment; and, by the way, you will be flying under enemy colours. The general has lent me his pet artist, and I am going to paste two enormous Iron Crosses over your identification signs. You won't see me do it, so you needn't worry. Before you return I will pull them off all right, so if you are unlucky on the home trip you will get quite a decent funeral.

"And now, general, I think that is just about all. I have just a note to write."

Duncan Grant sat down at the table, took a pen, some foolscap and wrote rapidly. He chose an envelope, folded the half sheet of foolscap, inserted the paper and fastened it. He addressed it to the Commander-in-chief. "Should any . . . accident happen to me, sir, as soon as you hear of it, will you kindly read this message. It is of great importance." He had handed the note to the general.

"Of course, Grant," said the latter genially—probably a note to his nearest relative, but the general would not inquire. Grant repeated: "The note is of great importance." The general placed it in his breast pocket.

"I will report back to your headquarters in this room about dinner time on June 16, today being June 5. I would rather, sir, you didn't see me in the guise of Major Muller, so unless you have any further orders to give me,"—and he pulled himself up to attention— "I should like to say good-bye, sir. I will do my best."

The Commander-in-chief came across from the fireplace. He was visibly touched. It was obvious at least to his chief of staff that a load had been taken from his mind, even though, as Colonel Jervois reflected, the Commander-in-chief appeared to be clutching at a straw. The general laid both hands on Grant's shoulders and said: "Even should you fail, Colonel Grant, your country and I are grateful. Good luck! I will send my orderly to you."

The general left the room. Grant instructed Gaynor and the Intelligence Officer to remove the blanketed body, and, with murmured expressions of good luck, Jervois and the two staff officers passed out into the whitewashed passage. Mayne and Grant were left alone, but only for a moment, for the general's orderly came in.

"Have you dried that uniform yet?"

"Yes, sir."

"Well, bring it right in to me, and find me a safety razor, tooth brush, soap, the latter French, by the way. And, orderly, clear off and go to bed. We don't want anything else. I am leaving a parcel here. Keep it in the general's room until I return. I will call for it in ten days' time."

The orderly returned with the uniform and articles of toilet, laid them on the chair and withdrew. Colonel Grant quickly undressed and then arrayed himself in the uniform of a German major of engineers, tunic, breeches, underclothing, everything complete except the socks and boots. His own black field boots satisfactorily completed the figure, with the field service cap in which the Intelligence Officer had gathered the major's papers and effects.

"And now, Mayne, if you are ready, we'll be off. It's now eleven-fifteen." Grant parcelled up his own uniform in some paper from a shelf in the office, marked it with his name, put on his overcoat and, following Mayne, left the farmhouse unobserved. They walked down the road about a mile to the aerodrome; and there found Flight Commander Mayne's machine in readiness. One of the mechanics came forward and said: "There is an officer from the topographical section here who wants to speak with a Colonel Grant." Grant stepped forward and took two large sheets of canvas and a glue-pot from John Collett.

"Well done, John," he said. "You're a better painter than I thought." He laughed.

"Oh, by the way, Mayne, send your mechanics over to that hangar. I want a private word with you," and while the six mechanics were moving across the grass to the hangar Grant swiftly knelt down under first one wing, then the other, and firmly pasted the two newly-painted crosses over the British identification marks.

"That's all right, Mayne. You can tell your lads to come back again." Mayne blew his whistle and within a few minutes pilot and passenger were seated in the aeroplane ready to move off. The

mechanics swung the propeller; and in a flood of light from the
flares in the aerodrome, the aeroplane swept into the skies.

"Crikey! Did you see that, Sid? That machine was marked
with Iron Crosses. Saw it with me own eyes, I did."

"Och, awa'," jeered a Scotch mechanic as they moved off back
to bed, "ye've been up in t' canteen."

"They was Iron Crosses. I see'd 'em with me own eyes," and
the aircraftman stood gazing after the machine, now fast disappearing into the night.

CHAPTER II

AT THE WIDOW'S HOUSE

THE aeroplane rose swiftly from the ground, and soon was
climbing far into the starlit night. Altitude was the first
essential. Neither Mayne nor Grant had any desire to come within
the range of either friendly or enemy searchlights, or to become
the object of scrutiny or suspicion from " night hawks."

The machine climbed steadily until an altitude of fifteen
thousand feet had been reached. Then, setting a course due east,
Mayne headed his machine to span the two hundred and forty miles
from G.H.Q. to Barmen, crossing Belgium, during the remaining
hours of darkness.

Time was the essence of the contract. The flight had begun
shortly before midnight. Barmen must be reached by four at the
latest. By that time the stars would be paling before the coming
dawn, the dark skies melting into the neutral grey-blue tints which
herald the first approach of the sun below the horizon. All would
be still, very still. A few twinkling lights from the larger towns,
the belching smoke of a hard pressed factory, its night furnaces being
stoked for the coming working day, making a black smear across
the landscape; forest silhouetted black against the undefined pasture
lands, and rivers pale and iridescent would be distinguished.

Then before the light strode through the gloom, Mayne must
select a landing spot, far removed from any town, village or
dwelling, so that no one too curious should observe the slipping
of the passenger. That was the first essential. But the problem of
landing was in itself hazardous. The fields stood high in corn,
maize and barley. It was mid-June. Neither the crops, nor the

hay would yet have been cut. A forest clearing would have been attractive but the probable stumps of the felled trees would render this impracticable. Mayne and Grant had discussed this problem.

A parachute landing was suggested. There were, however, two outstanding objections which finally ruled out such a mode of landing. It was essential to find a landing ground because the aeroplane must return to the same spot for Grant after ten days. Moreover, landings by parachute were not always entirely successful; even a sprained ankle would destroy the possibility of subsequent success. It might, too, be difficult, quickly at any rate, to dispose of the envelope itself, at least, without arousing suspicion.

Mayne considered the problem anew. The season had been exceptionally dry. A study of the maps had revealed a narrow area shown as swamp some two miles long and half a mile wide, flanked on the one side by the River Wupper, and on the other by the forest. This region was some ten miles south-east of Barmen. No buildings were shown within two or three miles of this place, and then the forest intervened. On the farther side the contours showed that the land rose almost abruptly some eighty feet to form a plateau of pasture or arable lands, with farm buildings dotted here and there.

As he piloted his machine, Mayne reflected carefully upon the problem of landing. Much seemed to depend upon the height of the river. Although there had been little rain to render life more unpleasant for those in the Western trenches, or alternatively to please an avaricious peasantry in swelling the ears of corn, Mayne felt a momentary annoyance that he had not inquired at G.H.Q. what had been the extent of recent rains in the Ebbe Gebirge where the Wupper rises.

A pilot engaged in a long flight has much time for self-recrimination. . . . The machine gave a lurch. . . . That is always the pilot's reminder that introspection is a dangerous habit, physically as well as psychologically. " Wait and see," mused the pilot. . . . Surely, the most English thing ever said by an Englishman about English policy and English habit, albeit to an audience of Scots. Mayne wondered what Grant would see, if he waited, if only for ten days, and incidentally, if Flight Commander Mayne waited, whether he would ever see Colonel Grant, the Scot, again.

So time passed : the machine sped on, aided by a light following wind. The sky remained clear. No word was interchanged between the two passengers, except the almost automatic checking of the half-hours and compass bearings, by Grant, who acted as observer. So far no lights had been observed : the towns were plunged in fearful darkness. War-time curfew and the dread of the unknown

horror from the skies extinguished every light. After the passing of
the fifth half-hour, however, the blurred lights of a city were visible.

"Passed the scare zone—the River Maas——" shouted Grant.
"One hundred and ninety-five miles. That's seventy-one miles an
hour. We should reach Barmen about ten minutes to four."

Duncan Grant, too, had been facing his own problems. His
original plan had been a simple one, in conception, if not in execution. . . . It was this . . . that he should be flown to some spot in a
remote part of Germany, assuming for the purpose the uniform,
papers, field book and other effects taken from the dead body of a
soldier in No Man's Land. Such a soldier would be reported missing.
It would not be known for certain, at least for several months,
perhaps never, whether he had been taken prisoner or had been
killed.

So long as Grant did not visit the immediate district in which the
man lived his domestic and working life, he would be able to move
about fairly freely, mingling with other soldiers in the taverns,
visiting the towns and villages, and, using his intelligence and
military knowledge, acquire information of a very varied character
which, after analysis, would prove of high value. Grant possessed
a keen appreciation of the dangers involved, of the possibility of
detection, but he felt quite confident that an imaginative mind, a
capacity for improvisation and some inventive genius, would be his
defence in any untoward situation, or should a too awkward curiosity
arouse suspicion. His surest weapon of defence was a perfect mastery
of the German language.

The plan had not been materially altered by the general's Muller
obsession. Grant chuckled to himself—he was Major Muller of the
Corps of Engineers, but not quite a perfect replica, blue eyes against
brown, five fingers in place of two. Perhaps he might be obliged to
wear coloured glasses and remain gloved as an additional camouflage.

He wondered what the Inverness Regiment was doing, who had
taken command: "Probably that stiff MacNair" . . . "Two-
thirty, fifteen thousand, four hundred feet, compass bearing
correct" . . . and his mind reverted to the problem in hand.

"After all, even if there was nothing in the Muller complex, at
least he was a peg upon which to hang the plan. There were certain
advantages in making his first bow as a field officer of engineers. He
would not be required to produce a field service book to inquisitive
military policemen: he was independent of money and . . . oh . . .
Hell!" Grant realized that he had no money, not a mark to bless
himself with. That was a tragic error. An ordinary soldier, if he
happened in peace time to be a burglar, and why not? could steal

with impunity. A major of engineers, a thief? . . . Easier, perhaps.
The mind travelled this line of thought for a while.

Grant was discovering it difficult to appreciate the reality of the
position now that definitely he had assumed the role of Major Ulrich
Muller, whose clothes had been disinterred from the cemetery of
Neuve Eglise. Would a colonel of the historic Inverness Regiment
masquerading as a major of the almost equally historic corps of
German engineers stoop to steal? Damn funny!

Anyway, he would soon be walking the countryside near, but
not too near, to Muller's home. He must find out all about Muller :
that was certain : and quickly. What was his job prior to the war?
What was his job now? To what section of engineers was he
attached? When last at home? Whither had he gone? After all,
too, one officer's uniform was much like another. Perhaps Muller's
tailor—he probably owed him a bit—or his girl, or his wife or both,
could recognize Muller's uniform; but for the rest, well, if Muller
was unattached, Grant could be unattached too—just a major of
engineers, on leave. Such a role would perhaps bring him nearer to
Muller's history and home—and to his special duties—than a Muller
masquerade presented conveniently some distance from the Muller
home. Wilhelm, that was patriotic enough, and, Schaeffer, not too
common and not too distinguished—Wilhelm Schaeffer, Major, of
the Corps of Engineers. " Good old Muller . . . old pal, met him
up the line . . . must visit the family." He might be reported
missing by now. Schaeffer could hand out the sympathy to the
family. That might be troublesome; details as to how poor Muller
died or went missing . . . too trying . . . and the tailor might
come round—probably some whiskered Polish Jew—a vulture
coming for the pickings. No, Grant had no time to waste. The
Muller mare's-nest must first be exploded—inverted M's, fiddle-
sticks! The mother or sister would put the M back in its right
place—the alphabet—for appropriate selection when needed.
Delirium, yes, inverted brain-box. Anyhow, the uniform was useful,
a safe passport. He could begin that way. Events after that could
look after themselves.

He was taking his life in his hands, but, after all, this adventure
was no more dangerous than going over the top, or dodging " flying
pigs " and other missiles which relieved the stagnation of life in the
trenches. But he would be alone, no cheerful, selfless batman beside
him, no one to see him fall or to share his fate. If he died he would
die alone.

Well, that wouldn't matter much to anyone else. His mother
would care, but she had been warned so often both by intuition and

by the scraps of news which Duncan imparted, while there was the ever growing casualty list with names of family and of friends to steel her against the shock of loss. And there was no one else; no one who would refuse comfort in her loss. . . . He had cut all that out years ago; after she had written *finis* to his dream. . . . He wondered what had become of Rosa. . . . Memory refashioned the picture . . . there was his uncle's house at Ardersier. It stood upon a little promontory with a background of firs overlooking the Moray Firth, and was built of grey stone. Long windows opened upon close-cut grass, broken by rosebeds and fringed with herbaceous borders and shrubs which sloped away to the water's edge. Beyond lay the narrow sea, backed by yellowing fields and the low hills of the Black Isle. What days he had spent with Rosa there! Rosa von Gleiwitz, the daughter of a German squire, and now he was at war with Germany. Well, thank God, she had terminated that affair. . . .

But how exquisite she had been, a mass of deep golden hair woven in trim plaits, clear violet blue eyes from under heavy lashes sparkled brightly from a face of perfect loveliness. . . . How cool her brow, her lips like rose petals. How quickly the weeks had passed, fishing, tramping . . . laughter like a peal of bells, music divine. And then she had disappeared, quietly, firmly, irrevocably from his life. His pulse quickened with the thought, the old desire was stirred. And when Rosa had faded, he had thrown himself fiercely into the study of his profession. And now, superbly equipped, technically proficient, he was being winged to Rosa's country . . . the country of his enemies. . . . Enemies? Grant reflected . . . why were the British, Nordic and Teutons, allied with Latins and Slavs? How well could Britons and Germans pull together. The Germans brave and ingenious, the British stolid, liberal-minded, an innate sense of justice . . . playing the game . . . some indefinable quality . . . the British the colonizers, Germans the colonials . . . and Rosa . . . typical of her race . . . what an ally . . . a wife.

"Hullo, old man, are you asleep?" Mayne shouted through the speaking-tube. "It's gone three and I can spot lights, front, right."

Grant's reflections and planning had carried him away from the automatic duty of the observer. His mind returned in a flash to his maps, compass and bearings.

"We're just crossing the River Maas—town of Limburg on our left. There is no raid scare here. Look ahead a bit and you can just see a red glow. Those will be the blast furnaces of Crefeld and Dusseldorf. We shall be well over Dusseldorf in the next half-hour, and in a further ten minutes should reach Elberfeld and Barmen. I hope I shall be able to spot the town. At Barmen I want to turn south-east on a bearing of 125 degrees, and we shall then have to come down and choose our landing ground."

Within a short while a mosaic of lights could be discerned below. The machine was travelling over the vast arsenals, steel and iron works, mines and closely settled area of the Rhineland industrial belt. Huge blast furnaces, flickering like candles below, belched forth their black smoke into the night, making its atmosphere even darker. As the aeroplane passed immediately above the towns of Elberfeld and Barmen, a thick pall of smoke hanging over the towns completely hid them from view.

The smoke had the appearance of a great black sea, the light wind gently rocking its sullen surface into a swell, and occasionally tossing its edges into billows and waves flecked with fleeting spray. This cloud of smoke, by its very density, would dull the sound of the aeroplane to the ears of the inquisitive in the town below, but it rendered Grant's maps momentarily useless. He was able to judge, however, from the speed record and chronometer the moment at which the direction should be changed for landing. A few minutes after the course had been altered the lights of the landscape could again be distinguished. Looking back and across to his right, Grant could pick out the towns in series . . . of Dusseldorf, Elberfeld and Barmen, the latter being almost directly behind the course of the machine.

It was now nearly four o'clock, and as yet too dark to effect a landing. In the east, however, from this altitude the faintest suggestion of the coming dawn could be discerned. The stars were paling and the deep blue-black of night changing to that almost green tint which heralds the coming variations of a new day. It takes but little time from this phase for light to break upon the world. Mayne decided that he would utilize the time in hand by reducing his elevation gradually and continuing the flight in the direction of the Ebbe Gebirge mountains flanking the Sauerland, a territory thinly populated and well wooded.

When the light permitted a landing—the least possible light for the purpose—he decided to turn the machine, flying from west to east. A flight in this direction would certainly occasion no alarm or suspicion, and probably at this stage of air development and war activity would arouse scarcely any curiosity, even from those few peasants and workers who, sleepily enough no doubt, would be going forth to the fields and other daily tasks. In ten minutes the altitude had been decreased to some eight thousand feet, and the landscape was becoming distinguishable. Dark patches indicated the forests, interwoven with little silver threads, the rivers and streams of the Ebbe Oberland. Mayne made a wide turn and began to dip the machine more steeply to earth. He called to Grant through the speaking-tube : "Look out for a landing place. If we can spot something better than the map reference, all the conditions are ideal for a landing here."

He shut off his engine and glided swiftly to within a few hundred feet of the ground. Light had rapidly established its domination over the passing night. It was now nearly half-past four, and the sun was stretching its yellow fingers over the hills while, with the exception of a few fairy lamps still hanging high in the skies, the stars had been wiped away by the gleam of a new day.

Mayne did not dare to traverse the ground more than once for fear of arousing suspicion. The area appeared too rugged in formation and densely covered with forests, while wherever a clearing indicated a village, every yard seemed to be covered with yellowing crops. The rivers, however, shown as being of some size on the map, were very low, as could be observed from the bridges which now stood high over the water, their piles, for many feet above water level, green with lichen moss; while the stream itself flowed now only through one or two spans, where the bridges were designed to cover a far wider flow of water. Grant passed this comment across the speaking-tube, remarking also that the indication was to try first the previous plan of landing on the swamp by Viersberg. Time was now the essence of procedure. Decisions must be made and carried out. The hazard had now to be taken. Closely following the map with the landscape below, Grant directed Mayne, who had again opened up his engine, to the Wupper River line, on which was situated the chosen place.

" Here we are !" shouted Grant.

Mayne dipped the nose of the machine, shut off his engine and sped the approach to the swamp. The landscape was noted in a flash. The right bank of the river, a sluggish deep stream some fifty yards across, rose steeply for thirty feet. There was a gradual bend in the river, almost at right angles, about a mile and a half long. That would account for the steep bank against the hillside which above it rolled in a broad down, tufted with tangled scrub, bracken, and broom, to a high plateau of waving corn. The left bank of the river stretched back to the edge of a thick pine forest. The bed of the stream showed boulder and shingle, then mud flat; then tree stumps and logs piled in confusion by the river in winter torrent; then a belt of reeds and finally a stretch of ground, light brown in colour, flat in texture, some sixty yards in depth beyond the reeds leading up to the forest edge and a bare mile in length.

The landing looked good. Mayne skimmed over the surface of the approach. The wind from the west, caught in the bend between the forest and the high bank as the river bent to the south, caused the machine to lilt from side to side. Two dangers only presented themselves: bog-land which would grip the landing-wheels, or a hidden tuft which might overturn the machine as it sped in a taxi to rest.

Grant called through the tube: " Make over the river. I'll take the water; don't land."

" Damn it all! " shouted Mayne, " we're both in this," and the machine grounded.

The light brown mass proved to be long, dried grass. The ground was hard underneath. The machine bumped heavily with a tendency to pitch forward, as the forward wheels sank into the grass, but the rear skid dragged more heavily and the machine came to rest.

Grant climbed out, and threw his overcoat and flying cap back into the cockpit. There was no time to lose. He dipped under the wings and ripped off the sticky black enemy crosses.

" You're flying under our colours now. Go like blazes, kid." He reached his hand up to Mayne in the pilot's seat. " So long, old man, give my love to the Commander-in-chief, don't forget that—my love. Tell Jervois I'll send him a postcard; and, by the way, especially, ask Jervois to wire my regiment as soon as you get back . . . say I've gone on ten days' special leave. Bring breakfast for two with you on the fifteenth, and make the landing a bit farther upstream. You haven't much room on this heavy stuff to clear the trees and bank in front.

" *Auf wiedersehen!* " shouted Grant. They gripped hands.

" Good luck, Scottie . . . my God, you've got some guts," and Mayne, guilty of unsoldierly emotion, pulled his hand away quickly. " Give the prop a spin."

The machine bumped like a camel rising, then began to plough heavily forward. It gained speed, then seemed to hang, another spurt forward and the wheels lifted, but the tail still dragged reluctantly in the stubby grass. Then as the machine moved towards the river bend the wind, coming strongly off the cliff face, lifted it, as if by the tug of a string on a kite. It flopped heavily again, and then rose high over the steep bank, Mayne skilfully taking the turn of the river and meeting the breeze full in the face. A perfect start . . . Mayne glanced over his left shoulder. There was Grant waving . . . then the tree tops blotted him from view. The machine climbed steeply up, up, up, higher and higher, five, eight, fifteen thousand feet towards Barmen. Then due west. Keep the compass west and nothing else mattered. Mayne could pick up his bearings later on. Four, possibly four and a half hours' flying in a head-wind and he would be safe from the danger of " dog-fights " or scouts dropping out of the blue. Anyhow, he had the altitude. Grant moved into the trees, and watched the aeroplane until it was a tiny speck . . . now only a dot . . . going . . . gone. No one had observed the landing. That was the probability.

Just on five o'clock on a fine morning. Majors of engineers do not prowl about lone pine forests in back war areas at five in the morning; so Grant decided to wait, and for the reason, too, that if his individual landing had been observed curiosity would bring the observer to the spot within a short space of time. He looked through Muller's kit again . . . and there was a parcel of shaving gear . . . a bit bulky, surely. He unwrapped it. . . . God bless the orderly! . . . two ham sandwiches and a hard-boiled egg—a wonderful fellow the British batman, probably a waiter from a club in St. James's, and all the restaurants packed with greasy, grasping dagoes! No one came. The sun rose and topped the river bank. Suppose the landing, as such, had been observed from a farmhouse or village. Perhaps some curious person would visit the river bank. Grant must examine the ground. Perhaps there were wheel tracks, and their measurement, not coinciding with the measurement of a German machine, aroused suspicion. Grant walked the distance of the rolled out grass. The ground showed no indentations : the grass had been laid out flat, and the marks might have been those of any machine. Good! And now for plans. He would walk upstream to where the forest and scrub touched the water's edge. There, under cover, he would walk slowly, following the river in the direction of Barmen. He had twelve miles to go, but would strike the road about four miles outside the town.

A major of engineers on ten days' leave. . . . Wilhelm Schaeffer, pal of poor old Muller, giving up a day of his leave to visit the relatives, and tell them what a fine fellow Muller was—that would pass as a tale in a credulous world. In wartime those not engaged in the battle area will believe anything.

Grant reflected upon the yarns being spun in drawing-rooms and hotel lounges by elderly officers with dim memories of a South African picnic, and by young staff officers whose chief military qualification was kinship to a bold politician or to a manufacturer selling mock marmalade at immense prices to an over-worked and too often not very scrupulous government department. None of these gentlemen had ever heard a shell in flight, far less a bullet. But, ye gods! the tales! and what a mental intoxication for those at home. Duncan had some tales too . . . but he would keep them.

So, having shaved and washed himself, Grant strolled leisurely along the river bank. He passed two lads operating a saw mill beside the river. First blood! and simple. He would test his disguise. He must play the actor to perfection. Here was a not too critical provincial audience. As he entered the shed the lads looked up and stopped work.

" *Guten morgen, Herr Major!*"

Grant glowed with pleasure—a slight swagger, a condescension, and seated himself upon a pile of logs. " Pit props?" he queried.

" *Ja, Herr Major,*" answered the boys in unison. He asked the lads about their brothers and fathers. They had nothing to tell, a brother killed, an uncle prisoner, nothing known about the course of the war : and the miners were weary of long hours of work. Some strike agitators had been shot in the square at Elberfeld. But Germany was winning the war . . . the master stroke was being prepared. . . . Everyone said so. Food, a little short in the towns; but not for the peasants, however, said one of the boys shyly, as the major became more expansive and appreciative. Grant decided to move on.

He was really enjoying himself, experiencing the emotions of the actor. He bade the boys a friendly good-bye and tramped on towards Barmen. The lack of money worried him and he was growing hungry. He came to a bridge at Beyenburg carrying the high road, and leaving the course of the stream he swung down the road to the town, whose chimneys, church tower and buildings were now clearly visible four miles distant. He passed some peasants' carts, a few heavy lorries, but the way was mainly deserted. A road mender saluted him as he approached the outskirts of the town.

A line of new villas led up to the railway crossing at Langerfeld. Children were playing in the road. They saw him coming, and drawing themselves into line gravely saluted. He patted the diminutive sergeant-major on the head : " Now charge the dirty English," he cried, and with fierce yells the children scrambled in mock attack down the street.

There's war spirit right enough, he mused. The kids may be a bit anæmic as the result of the blockade, but the rot hasn't yet set in. Strikes at Elberfeld, Dusseldorf and Essen? Perhaps? That was natural enough. There was plenty of money . . . behind the lines. The patriotic middle class were pouring their savings into the national coffers, and being taxed out of existence. They had sacrificed a generation of their children to the fatherland. Money? Why, God bless my soul! the *schiebers* are raking it in. . . . Profiteers having a wonderful time and the workers mean to have their bit while the going's good . . . a strike's not against the immorality of war, but to secure a bit more of the boodle . . . the profiteers couldn't have it all . . . and, what the hell did it matter anyway? . . . higher wages, higher prices. . . . The *schiebers* could pass the buck to the taxpayer . . . no, there was nothing in these strikes other than human selfishness . . . no moral issue involved, no weakening of national spirit. Look at the kiddies!

He entered into the spirit of the game.

"*Ich bin Englander,*" he cried. "Fix bayonets! charge!"

The children, who had now come to a standstill at the end of the row of cottages, bore down upon him with renewed fury. He picked up the leader, a thick-set little boy blue-bottle, lightly spanked him and set him on his feet. . . .

Major Schaeffer passed over the level crossing and had entered the town of Barmen. He had decided to seek the best hotel. That would provide both shelter and food with certainly a week's credit. As he had not the remotest intention to remain long so far removed from the battle area, the plan suited admirably. He inquired for the main square of the town, which, from its shop fronts, appeared to be prosperous, with its streets now just before the luncheon hour filled with comfortable citizens; and after a few minutes' walk stood at one corner of the Neumarkt. It was surrounded by pretentious stone buildings, the Rathaus with its fine pillared façade, municipal library and usual local government offices. In the centre was an equestrian statue of the Emperor Frederick the Great; electric trams rattled over the cross points; flower and newspaper sellers occupied kiosks, upon which were posted patriotic posters urging the populace to contribute to the victory loan and to work for the fatherland; motor cars, some few bearing official signs pasted upon the wind screen, but mostly private cars, were closely packed one side of the square.

The restaurants were busy, tables set in the open, some men lunching, others drinking lager from deep glass mugs, gossiping and smoking. Grant looked at the signs and advertisements, searching for an hotel. . . . Hotel Imperial. He strolled across the square, a soldier saluted; a lieutenant of infantry sprang to attention.

He crossed the threshold of the hotel, went to the reception office, and asked for a room, one of the best bedrooms. "A double room?" inquired the clerk, familiar with the habits of officers on leave.

Grant, fulfilling the rôle of Schaeffer, decided that he must conform to plan. It might, too, be useful. *"Naturlich,"* he replied.

"And your baggage?"

"It has been mislaid," said Grant.

"Will the *Herr Major* give instructions to the valet to procure anything he requires? . . . They will be entered on his account. . . . Will the major sign the register?"

Grant took up the pen. Good God! . . . He must replay that part of Muller. . . . Schaeffer was not in the Army list. . . . He would be under suspicion within an hour. . . . He must take that risk and make a short stay. . . . Jekyll and Hyde, not in one person but as two . . . he signed the register—Ulrich Muller. Grant then followed the page to the lift and was shown to a large double-bedded room. He rang for the valet, ordered fresh underclothes—those from the grave would not look so inviting upon a new morning—pyjamas and some miscellaneous toilet requisites.

He washed, and descended again to the great lounge, now filled with an animated group of men and women. There were several uniforms among the crowd; a slim, fair boy on crutches dragged himself painfully to the restaurant; several women, obviously those butterflies who flit through every prosperous town, were sipping wine. Major Schaeffer strolled into lunch. He was shown to a table laid for two. He sat down alone and carefully selected a substantial and attractive lunch, a bottle of Rudesheimer and called for a newspaper. Several women passed slowly beside his table, obviously inviting themselves to be the guest. He continued to read his paper, without looking up, but he took stock of them.

He might require a *confidante* . . . one of these women, probably a harpy, hard-bitten, callous, her attractions brightly-painted to hide the imperfections of age and the ravages of a vicious life, rather than a younger woman with a readier market and too many lovers . . . yes, she might be useful.

But he was hungry : he would first do ample justice to the menu and fortify the inner man. After that there was work to do. He studied the newspaper carefully; then, having finished his lunch, he called for a cigar and ordered a box to be sent to his room and signed the bill, Muller, room 23. He went straight up to his apartment. He must now be quick. He would walk to Hatzberg, just five miles distance. Even as Muller he would doubtless be known in Barmen, though as a major of the reserve he might be far less prominent in a war involving comet promotions than his rank would signify in a regular officer. That was comforting.

As Wilhelm Schaeffer, therefore, he left the hotel and inquired the road to Hatzberg. He walked rapidly. The road left the town and ran through an ugly, blackened countryside decorated with slag heaps, winding apparatus and the tall, smoking chimneys of textile factories. Every yard between the factories was cultivated. After walking for over an hour, after which the countryside became more picturesque, undulating and wooded, Schaeffer overtook an elderly priest. He passed him good day and inquired his destination.

The priest was glad of someone with whom to converse. He had taken over duty in Hatzberg only recently to replace a younger zealot who had gone to the front . . . yes, he knew the Mullers . . . he had been summoned the evening previously, and had heard the terrible news, another son of the village gone—killed, a prisoner, who knew? . . . Ah! Schaeffer had known him . . . he was dead . . . Gentle God have pity! . . . his poor mother. Muller was so clever . . . a mining engineer. Schaeffer agreed, and added: " Selected for special duty, a great loss."

" Yes, ability turned to such waste and destruction. It was he who planned and sunk the new shafts in the Bismarkhütte, by Kattowitz in Silesia." He had not been much with his mother, a widow, during recent years . . . he had only returned home shortly before his summons to the front . . . he was to have taken an appointment as chief engineeer in Elberfeld . . . dead, ah, dear God! . . . That will kill his mother, so proud, so good a servant of the Church. . . . Devoted to each other . . . her only son . . . dear God! . . .

Grant was inclined to feel sympathetic. Then he almost chuckled aloud; a fleeting smile crossed his face. Muller would not be known in Barmen except perhaps by reputation. Grant would, therefore, be safe from recognition for a short while. Meanwhile, the devoted, proud mother with whom, doubtless, the equally devoted son shared his secrets, would have much to tell. He would discover what was Muller's mission. The general was right . . . there was something worth while discovering in the Muller affair. He enjoined the priest to silence. No one must know that Muller was dead. He, the comrade in arms, would break the news gently, then summon the priest, for his ministrations.

They were approaching the village, its little white church centring the cluster of buildings. The priest pointed to a low, double-fronted house standing back from the road. Behind a holly hedge a neat grass lawn stretched up to its walls. Between the trimmed edges of the grass and banked by standard roses and a profusion of old-fashioned flowers, a red brick path led up to the creeper-clad porch. The lawn was intersected by gnarled apple trees, and through the squat windows Grant could observe the sheen of brass and clear glaze of china ornaments.

He lifted the latch of the gate. He must risk the discerning mother-eye upon his uniform. His footsteps rung alarmingly on the path, his heart beat in his throat. The tragic reality of the situation was contributing that stage fright which unawares will assail even the most skilful and experienced actor. His powers of deception would be highly tried. He was to act alone before the most gifted critic, the mother who had borne and known her son from the cradle up. Her questions would be searching. He would bide his time. He must obtain his facts first. Then he would break the dread news and leave the lone widow to her grief, her priest, and, he could not help hoping, her death. . . .

Women . . . mothers . . . had intuitions. . . . If his story should in one single respect raise suspicion, a mother's faith and hope would discredit the whole tale. She would cling to hope. She would disbelieve his story of Muller's death. Hope eternal . . . Grant would be discredited. Schaeffer would not save him from discovery. These thoughts flitted through his brain. He knocked upon the low green door. A servant girl, bare-footed, opened it to him: " *Ja wohl!* Frau Muller will be in the garden behind the house."

Grant declared that he would announce himself, and the maid showed the way across the house and out through the casement windows. He saw a little lady, some sixty to seventy years of age, frail like some porcelain figure from the Dresden potteries, silvered hair, delicate features, fine hands albeit strong with toil, clad in dark blue satin, her delicate throat graced with old lace. She was bending to the pea-sticks, but at the sound of voices she turned and started.

" Ah, good afternoon, little mother. Your son prayed me if ever I were in this neighbourhood to be sure to call upon you. We are close friends, comrades in battle. I know him well. He speaks so often of you. I have some days' leave in Dusseldorf. . . . I felt I already knew you. I have come, you see. . . ."

" Ah! *mein Herr,* you have news." The little woman came across, both hands outstretched in welcome. " My son's friend is my friend. But you have news. . . ." A sob caught her throat, it shook her frail body, " Good news."

" Oh, yes, yes," rejoined Grant. " It is a long story. I will tell it to you. Your son is safe."

" I have received a telegram last night," said the widow. " He is reported missing, but that cannot be true; he is so strong, so clever, so brave and . . . God is good . . . I did not credit it," Frau Muller was regaining courage. Hope buoyed her. She was satisfied. Yes, she would hear the story . . . but yes, later would do . . . she was happy now. . . . "Major. . . ." "Wilhelm Schaeffer," repeated Grant, ". . . will take wine, fruit and cakes. We will go to the salon, and I will tell the *madchen* to serve refreshments. You are thrice welcome, Wilhelm, my son's friend."

They entered the low salon. Frau Muller seated herself in a deep upright chair : Grant selected an armchair removed from the light, in shadow. He wanted to avoid the watery, blue eyes. Muller's mother disturbed him. Curse these blasted clothes; even Muller's vest, the initials probably worked by those deft, delicate fingers. But he must give Frau Muller her head. Now that anxiety was removed she would be willing to sing her pæan of praises. Ulrich would be whitewashed in a verbal shroud. . . . What a horrible idea! He must pull himself together. This was a bad start. The actor would break down and forget his lines. Then what would the master critic say?

Well, he had some war stories—truth . . . stranger than the fiction of West End drawing-rooms. He would whet her appetite, arouse her pride and then hear some of Muller's experiences. That was the line. Grant had a storehouse of tales, some of which had never been told, secrets in the recesses of his mind. He must tear the widow's heart, capture her pride, enslave her spirituality. No matter if his story were told of the other side. She would not know the difference. In this warfare the experience of British or Germans, Italians, Russians, were all much alike—shells, fear, mud, corpses, lice, blood, panic, drunkenness, sweat, dust, harlots, marching—a kaleidoscope of bestiality, broken by acts of matchless self-sacrifice. Grant would create the atmosphere in which the old lady would unburden her secrets—Muller's secrets.

" I will try to give you a picture of life . . . up at the front. In it you will be able to visualize better the life of your son. . . . I remember being appointed to my command. It was a new formation. The officers too fond of alcohol, the older soldiers good material but gone to seed, because they could not get the stimulant which the officers imbibed, and . . . the officers themselves provided no other . . . for the rest . . . a host of untried youngsters, kids of eighteen and nineteen. I am always very grateful for these kids and curse myself eternally for what I had to teach them. My job was, and is, to win the war. I remember that I had to deny myself the stimulant of appearing to be heroic before my men—and I can imagine this must be a glorious intoxication—and go about my job organizing little groups into a sense of sanity, infusing courage by appealing to the manhood in men turned curs, threatening, cajoling, even shooting as a salutary lesson. And I had also to refuse myself the fun of shooting back at the enemy—and it is fun under war conditions— because the brains of my life were wanted to organize a front which was rapidly decomposing. We were hard pressed. . . ."

The widow was leaning forward in her chair, her eyes wide with eagerness, following every word of the story with fixed attention. She was like one hypnotized. Grant had forgotten the widow, all else but his story—untold. He was living again the mental agony of years of war. His acting before the most critical audience in the world was supreme.

"I had formed a little body of scouts. Not one of them was over twenty years of age. They were fresh, clean, bright-eyed, just little adventurers. They had no vices, no fears. They lived with me, where I went, they went. It was like a school treat with this difference, that it was my job to harden their hearts to shocks, and to spoil their minds to the sight and sound of death and bestiality—a face half shot off, turned up to the sky isn't pleasant; a man with his bowels torn out by high explosive can make a strong man physically sick; an old corpse, bloated and black, is terrifying."

Frau Muller covered her face with her hands. "Go on," she said.

"I had to make them coarse to stand the racket of things which I loathed personally, and which I feared too, lest they should weaken when I needed most their confidence, the power and inexperience of their youth and their manhood. I have lived pretty hard, and had seen by that time more than three years of war; but sometimes alone, in danger, I reflect upon how I have deliberately coarsened the minds of these lads by profanity and jibe—anything beastly so long as it neither hurt the brain like drink, nor the body, like women, I utilized to steel these lads for the task which must be theirs.

"I trained them diligently as scouts, and demanded their confidence and love with every artifice of which a commander can make use, in order that on any part of the battlefield, they should be my eyes, telling me accurately what I must know without embroidery, but telling me also without an eye to the main chance— safety or glory—and I knew each one individually for what he was worth. I tested them—a walk here, ten minutes and a cigarette there, sometimes sharing a blanket, a lad by himself as himself, not in the artificiality of the presence of a corporal, or their comrades—I needed them to do my will: I required their confidence, my external and internal spies, my intelligence corps, my scouts. I have degraded these lads, debauched my soul to win a battle; my personal honour has been seduced by the habit of war, my brains prostituted by its necessities."

G.M.N.—N*

Grant checked himself. He had confessed to this stranger, this little waxen figure, the mother of his enemy, now dead and naked in a damp blanket, the innermost secrets of his soul, the hellish agony of his mind. He stopped and sipped his wine, reflecting that now again would war's grave necessity make a supreme call upon his finer instincts. He must excuse himself. The situation was horrible.

He continued: "History will provide evidence of the practical effect of such training, but it will tell nothing of what it cost me personally, in giving it. I am ashamed of war's necessity—that it has compelled me deliberately so to debase the souls of men. It is not as though I lack culture or like so many others am submerged in an orgy of drink. I love beauty in nature, in art, literature, in little children, in the minds of philosophers and . . ," he hesitated, "in women such as you, little mother."

Frau Muller bowed her head. Grant's story, his final thrust, had struck home. His very sincerity loosened the widow's tongue. He had won her sympathy, her mother love . . . he sensed the reality of the situation, he had won her confidence and all her secrets. Frau Muller must be used. He would pile her ruin upon that of the minds of fresh lads from the hills and vales of his highland home. . . . The massacre of the innocents!—their minds, not their bodies. He ceased.

"My Ulrich has felt like that, too. His brain and inventive genius degraded to the service of futility. You know him well: his fine character. From what you say I can see that you were comrades, close and intimate. How he dreaded the summons to war! It was not his courage that ever failed. His work in the mines had proved that. He feared only the enslaving of his skill to the machine of war. But when the summons came, he faced it bravely."

"I know, I know," interposed Grant, "we were together."

The widow continued: "I remember when he was summoned to army headquarters by the chief engineer some eight months ago. He was glad, but afraid. They needed his brains, a great engineer. He left me for three days. Then he returned—so proud. He remained for just a week. Daily he went to a disused mine near Hattingen. He experimented in secret. They placed several hundred prisoners, French, English, Russian miners at his disposal from the big camp at Elberfeld. I have seen them, poor devils. They worked in long shifts. The escorts kept the inquisitive far from the pit head. They came and went in silence. And Ulrich would sit late at night working on his plans. I would not leave him. While he worked I sat with him. He begged me to go to my bed, but I should see so little of him. I sat and watched him working: and I, too, worked. He must wear the uniform of a major of

Imperial Engineers. The tailor came. I worked its appointments. The week was all too short. Then one day he had completed his tests. He told me he must go to the army headquarters. His workings were placed in my little bureau. When the war was over he told me he would use them for the industry which was his pride, his life.

"And then he went away. He has not been back since. He has written often. I have his letters, too, in my bureau. I do not understand the war : I cannot even guess. Then he remains in one place, so it seems, for his letters come more regularly. He is working hard. He is confident. He tells me his great work for the fatherland is nearing completion. The plans are perfected, but I cannot know what is his work." The widow sighed. "I am lonely. I have my flowers, my housework, the church. I feel alone. Ah, Wilhelm, it is good of you to have come. You will describe him to me, his work, his pride. I need to feel him. He is all I have. I have his last letter. It is in my bureau in my bedroom. You can tell me what it means, fill in between the lines. I am old and lonely. I want to feel him again."

"So," reflected Grant, no longer under the spell of his own reflections, "the bureau is in her bedroom. Muller's papers are there."

Frau Muller rose. She glided quietly from the room, Grant holding the door to let her pass. There was colour in her cheeks, her eyes bright. She smiled at Grant as she passed, grasping his arm lightly and pressing it affectionately.

Grant was alone. He had time to think, to formulate some scheme. He must obtain the plans from the bureau upstairs in Frau Muller's bedroom. He listened acutely for her steps above; one . . . two . . . three . . . eleven steps along the corridor upstairs, the latch of a door clicked; he could hear her moving overhead, not directly above, but towards the front of the house. He could find that room . . . up the stairs, along the corridor, eleven short paces, a room to the right. He heard the jingle of a bunch of keys. Then a drawer was opened.

He must secure those plans . . . at any price. He would take his time. He heard the *madchen* humming a doubtful marching ditty. He looked carefully round the little salon. Portraits of Ulrich, an illuminated address to Professor Muller of Bonn University. That would, doubtless, be the husband of the *Witwe* Muller—a fine head. He examined the bookcase; it was lined with scientific works—mathematics, geometry, chemistry. Professor Muller was a scientist. His mantle, then, had fallen upon Ulrich.

Grant opened the case; and, haphazard, he chose a work upon statics, the author, Heinrich Muller. It was well thumb-marked. He hurried over its pages. There were pencil notes upon stresses and strains, perhaps in the handwriting of Ulrich. That might be important. He would hold the book in his hand when Frau Muller returned. She would probably volunteer information. Footsteps came along the passage, twelve this time, the rustle of satin as the back of her dress swept the stairway.

Frau Muller entered. Grant was standing before the open bookcase, Heinrich Muller's text work in his hand. To his unspoken question she nodded and smiled : " My husband's," she said.

" Of course. To me, also, that is a very interesting little library," he remarked. " No wonder Ulrich gained distinction : his genius inborn. I see Ulrich has been a keen student too. His handwriting?" he hazarded.

" Oh, yes, he used my husband's work for his plans. He frequently referred to this book. It is a great treasure. I know little of these things. My life was for my husband—entertaining his little family of students, many of whom, his favourite, the most able, visited our house in Bonn. Then he was taken from me. I moved to this quiet village. It was sufficiently close to the mines for Ulrich's studies and apprenticeship. Before he finally went away he used my husband's book as I sat with him. His handwriting, you ask? Oh, yes; Ulrich produced his master scheme from my husband's theory. He called it the W plan, and then, you know, of course, it was his jest—inverted M."

" I know, I know," interposed Grant. " We have worked upon it together."

" Ah, I guessed that would be so. All his heart, his whole mind was in that scheme. He left me and went to the front in order to put it into operation. That was seven weeks ago. He reckoned that it would require ten weeks to give effect to the whole plan. He complained that the prisoners would not work : they were too slow. He experimented at Elberfeld, and arranged his time schedule by their performance. The engineeer-in-chief would give him no more than ten weeks. He complained that even so many entailed risks were too long. The English must be trapped. They would soon be reinforced.

" Ulrich worked furiously, long hours, to perfect his plan, and now it will not be long before all is ready. You have been with him, working with him. How you must have needed respite before the final stage of the plan is completed! That will end the war : Ulrich was so confident. The English will be taken unawares, thrown into disorder, their lines penetrated in a dozen places.

"But," she said wistfully, "I am sorry for the English. I have had an affection for them. We have received their professors from Cambridge at our home in Bonn, and students too. We have a lady in this village—Fraulein Maurer—she frequently visits me, who has spent several years in England. She taught our language and our music—Bach, Schubert, Beethoven—Germany has the world's music —in the home of a Scottish nobleman. They are different, the Scotch—so she always insists. But there is so much hate in Germany for the English today."

The old lady rambled on. "She insists that the Scotch are different. They have fought against the English. I have suspected that perhaps she may have loved a Scot. She returned to Germany four years ago. She is ill. She would not go to her home in Koln. She preferred, she has told me, to bury herself among the people. She nurses voluntarily in the prisoners' camp at Elberfeld. No matter her illness, there are few willing—they need those who can speak English. In the evenings she comes often to my house. She lives in a flat by herself near the Stadt Baurat. And she is much alone, perhaps her health is worse than I know. We two are alone, so she comes and plays to me and we talk together. She had her secrets, perhaps as I have said she had a lover. I know not. I do not care to ask. She plays to me, and I feel less lonely."

The widow sighed, then continued :—

"Ah! but I have Ulrich's letters. Read his last for yourself, you can tell me. He hopes to visit me within a month. Would that mean the end of his work? He has scarcely slept. He is confident. The work goes forward. Everything is quiet. Our airmen—are they not gallant?—they keep the enemy away. The English cannot observe; dare not attack. He meets friends everywhere : but he may not talk. Few know of his work. The English make raids. They are repulsed, so many English taken prisoners, others lying dead.

"He says the prisoners are often fine specimens, but young and badly led. The officers untrained. They throw themselves away. They do not understand technique. He is a technician. He observes that always. War is a technique like mining engineering. Ulrich is an engineer : he does not pretend to understand warfare. But we have our experts, have we not? He likes to listen to them. His plans must harmonize with those of other experts. And the English, they are brave, but everything haphazard. They kill their men with their own artillery, their machine-guns are without organization, they play at soldiers—see, he says it—as they play at their football."

Grant nodded an assent. How bitterly he understood. "But it

is horrible, this war. Everyone is infected with its fever : morality has died. God is forgotten. The workmen clamour always for more money. Prices go up; there is extravagance, no control. I live alone : my *madchen* comes every day for a few hours. Then, at six, she goes home. She was a good girl; but now, well, I have my fears." Grant recalled the dirty ditty. So the *madchen* would soon be gone. That was good. He could still wait.

"Ulrich has written regularly. Every four or five days I receive his letters but there has been no letter now for nine days. See the date. Today it is the sixth of June. His last letter is dated the twenty-fourth of May. I was afraid.

"Then last night I have received the telegram. He is missing." Frau Muller leant forward and clasped Grant's hands. The colour had departed from her cheeks, her hands were cold. Her eyes searched his own. Involuntarily he shivered. "But you have brought me news," and her fingers tightened upon his wrists.

"Yes, yes. I must tell you his story," he stammered. "He is safe. He has brought honour to your house." Her grip relaxed, the faded colour crept back to her cheeks.

Grant's capacity for improvisation must produce a story—"We were working together in the battle zone, just behind the firing line. My engineers were weary. The English had been shelling the front line and support trenches. It was heavy shelling. I lost many men, some killed, others wounded. We were expecting a surprise attack. The infantry and machine-gunners were ready. We had orders to withdraw.

"A heavy shell burst in the trench just beside us. Its walls collapsed. It was dark. We extricated ourselves. I thought that Ulrich was with us, as we withdrew. When we reached the reserve line, we sought shelter in the galleries. Ulrich was not with us.

"I asked my lieutenant. He said that Major Muller was safe at the headquarters of the battalion holding the line, in a deep dugout. When dawn came there was a roll-call of our men. There were some known to be killed, others had been reported wounded through the aid posts, a few unaccounted.

"I telephoned to the battalion headquarters for Major Muller. He was not there, had not been there, he was missing. The lists were drawn up. The clerk reported the names as was his duty—killed, wounded, missing. Of course that of Major Muller was among them.

"But, have no fear now, Frau Muller. I went out at once to find the truth. I was distracted. I searched the lines where we had been. I found Ulrich. He had been crushed by the falling parapet. He had lain there the night through at the bottom of the trench—no safer place—his leg pinned by the weight of earth, but he was safe."

" *Gott sei dank,*" murmured the widow, crossing herself devoutly.

Grant continued : " These messages take time to pass through headquarters. Your telegram is three days since the event. In a week maybe, or soon, you will receive another communication . . . perhaps sooner than you think. I will tell you more. You must know of his life and of his work."

CHAPTER III

ACROSS FOUR YEARS

A LIGHT step was heard on the red brick path leading from the road to the house. The sun had sunk low behind the little village, and the room was deepening in gloom. Grant looked up.

" It is Fraulein Maurer," said the widow. " She will be glad to meet you." The latch of the green front door was lifted. A light step passed across the little hall and the door of the salon opened.

In the dim light, almost behind her, too, as she entered, Grant could see little of the woman's face. She was of tall stature, elegant in her carriage, but thin, almost emaciated. The shaft of light from the setting sun caught a wisp of her hair which had escaped from the careful plaits arranged on either side of her head. The hair was like spun gold.

" Ah, my dear, I must present to you Major Schaeffer, Ulrich's friend. He is visiting me and has brought good news. Ulrich is safe."

The girl stepped forward, her hand outstretched. Grant, following the usual courtesy of the country, drew his heels together, bent his head, meeting her outstretched hand with his lips, while he touched it with his fingers. Her hand was thin—he felt the bone, so cold, even upon this warm summer evening. Frau Muller took the girl's cold hands in her own.

" Play for me—a prelude of praise : then you shall hear Major Schaeffer's story. I, too, will hear it again."

Fraulein Maurer choked a little, then sat before the keys . . . her fingers dwelt upon the keyboard. " It shall be Liszt," she said. " He played and prayed, perhaps the greatest of all pianists, pathfinder in music, big-souled philosopher, triumphing out of sorrow—Liszt—It shall be the 'The Mountain Symphony.'" She was now facing the window, the last light of day playing upon her tired face, her glorious hair deep gold but softened here and there with a streak of silver.

Grant, deep in his chair, was wrapt in thought. Plans were taking shape in his mind. The general's odd obsession was the master-key.

The music swept through his soul—warbling birds, rippling streams; the hills mounting higher and higher, crag upon crag, boulder upon boulder, even as a ladder to Heaven; the sweep of eagles' wings, a soft breeze singing through the pines, laughter and echo. . . . The girl appeared buried deep in her music, her head sometimes pressed affectionately over the instrument, listening, inquiring for those deep, true melodious notes with all their variation of light and shade, which were interwoven by a master in the mosaic of the symphony. The music of Liszt was enthroned.

The widow sat forward in her chair, her face transfigured with joy. "Never have you played like this, my dear," she said softly, then relapsed again into silence. The weariness had passed from the face of the player.

Grant raised himself to see her better. The eyes were closed as if in sleep, her fingers finding the notes with certainty. A rare beauty enriched her pale face. The mouth was upturned in a wistful smile.

Rosa . . . the piano which sang. A rush of memory over four intervening years. . . . Rosa, the same glorious hair, the bewitching smile, figure, form, atmosphere. Rosa, his flower bud, the same, yet how different. The little *fraulein* in a widow's house, a faded flower, so pale, playing music which charmed the ear and lacerated the heart. She stifled a cough; it shook her emaciated bosom. She played on, a glorious soft melody which she filled with the shy sweetness of a wild rose—Rosa.

He moved from his chair to see her more closely. It could not be . . . not the same Rosa. He leant his arms gently upon the piano, his head between his hands. His eyes searched her. He could see now how thin, how drawn, almost haggard she was; the bones in her neck stood out.

His eyes dropped to those skilful hands, fingers of velvet, yet when they conjured a rising crescendo, a torrent of sound, as if forged of bronze. Fingers, on one a ring—diamonds clustering a single ruby. Rosa, his ring. Her eyelids lifted. Her eyes, deep blue, met those of Grant. . . . Her fingers trailed from the piano . . . the notes ceased. Frau Muller rose. She crossed to the piano, her hands outstretched. She touched the girl delicately upon the shoulder, kissed her lightly on the brow.

"Thank you, Rosa. Thank you. How happy I am tonight with you and Wilhelm. I will fetch the lamb and prepare a little supper. You will both tonight sup with me. Wilhelm can tell you the story of Ulrich's escape. Then, perhaps, after supper, unless Major Schaeffer must depart—and I have not even asked him where he is staying—we may have a little more music. I am so happy. God is good to me."

Frau Muller moved from the room, a smile of sweet ecstasy upon her face. Grant's mind was in a torment—the plans and . . . Rosa. What to do? He must go, wait in hiding; watch for the departure of Rosa, return upon some pretext, take the papers from the bureau— by diplomacy, by force if necessary. And here was Rosa, his Rosa . . . impossible, yet. . . .

"I cannot trespass further," he stammered, "and my time is so short. . . ." He hurried after Frau Muller into the hall.

Rosa still sat as if in a trance at the piano.

"But you must remain for supper; is that not right, Rosa?"

"Major Schaeffer—will remain," a voice so low as to be almost inaudible was heard from the salon.

"Very well," he said. He stood for a moment in hesitation in the hall. Then slowly he returned to the salon, closing the door behind him.

"Duncan, I felt, I knew it was you. I do not understand. Why are you here? It is for me you have come? I do not understand." A sob shook her frame, ending in a cough which racked her whole body.

Grant moved forward swiftly. He pressed the shaking body to him, buried his face in her hair.

"Rosa, poor Rosa," he murmured.

A hollow cough rent her body. Duncan held her. Her body was limp in his arms, she gasped for breath. Then he looked into her eyes, taking her thin hands in his own. Their eyes met. Years were swept away. . . .

It was an evening just such as this, a summer evening, the sun dipping into the sea, painting it a vivid gold. His uncle's home, overlooking the beauty of the loch. The casement windows of the music-room were thrown wide open, revealing a stretch of cool green lawn leading down to the inlet from the Moray Firth in which some boats lay lazily, the idle water rippling gently against their sides. Away across the water lay the purple hills of the Black Isle. They had rambled across the moor and through the pine forests all the

afternoon, tea with great scones and cookies with dear old Miss
Aitken in Ardesier, then slowly walking back to the home. Three
weeks they had been together. Her sweet voice trilled German
songs on a Scottish hillside. How she had rejoiced in his knowledge
of her country's literature and art . . . the daughter of Graf von
Gleiwitz—the name Maurer with which the widow introduced her
to him he could not understand.

Then that day he had discovered his love; the serene beauty of
her character, the magic of her art, the glory of her beauty enslaved
him. So they had wandered back to the great, grey stone house at
the water's edge.

His uncle and the children had driven into Inverness. The house
was empty. Rosa and Duncan had passed into the music-room. She
played with her polished technique—Schubert, Beethoven, Schu-
mann—light and shade with all the emotions, her passion volcanic
in Rachmaninoff's Prelude, thunder and lightning; the tenderness of
her touch melting the heart in a passage from Beethoven's Sonata
Pathetique.

Duncan was leaning over the end of the grand piano, as he had
today, feasting his eyes upon her, the rise and fall of her breast, her
hair, her sweet almost childish face, the eyes lowered upon the
keyboard. Then as she looked up their eyes met—as today. Her
face was transfigured in rapture. He could see her now as she was
then—Rosa—they had kept their secret for a little while. They had
journeyed one day together to Inverness, to hunt for books, and there
together, they had chosen a ring, a ruby . . . red, red rose; set in
diamonds . . . the dew-drops of purity.

He knelt now beside her, his arms entwined round the poor, thin
body. Her fingers played with his hair. "Duncan," she murmured,
and bent her head. So they remained for many minutes as the light
faded, and a quiet gloom stole softly over the room.

A footstep sounded in the hall, a light flickered under the door
which opened. Frau Muller carried an oil lamp in her frail hands.
Duncan had moved towards the door.

"Twenty minutes to half an hour, my dears," said the widow, "I
am preparing the feast and you can well entertain each other." The
spell was broken. Facts must be faced. There was much to tell.
Grant must tell the truth. He could trust Rosa. He would not ask
her aid. He must tell her . . . everything.

"Rosa, I will tell you my story quickly. You will believe me, I
know. I am here in disguise. No one knows. I am seeking
information. It is my duty. War is horrible. This war . . . my
God! I have a duty. It brought me here. No matter how. In a

day or two I shall have gone away again. Then I shall return to our own lines. . . . That is all."

There was a pause.

"I can understand," said Rosa slowly . . . "all." There was silence in the little room for a while, then Rosa spoke again.

"You are in danger, every minute, every day. I must aid you, if I can. I know nothing, want to know nothing, of your plans. Perhaps I can help you, not in them," Rosa covered her face with her hands, "but to keep you safe. I have known you were at the front. Every day I pray for you—even now the bell rings for vespers—I pray for you, Duncan. Let me help you. Tell me what I must do."

"Rosa, Rosa, I cannot ask you to help me. You may, perhaps, be of service to this poor widow in her grief."

"Her grief?" she questioned.

"Oh, yes, Ulrich Muller is dead."

"But you have told her . . ."

"I know, I know. That is part of my plan . . . a ruse . . . diplomacy, call it what you will; and . . . it has served her well. Better for her to have this news broken gently than for her to nurse the fears of the unknown, or the shock and anguish of a sudden discovery. He was taken prisoner. He died of wounds on the second of June. I have seen him. He is buried at Neuve Eglise. One day, after I have gone away, you will tell her gently, and tell her also that I am sorrowful. When this war is over I will come to see her, if she will, and will tell her the whole truth. Today, not yet, she must not know. You will do this for me, Rosa."

"I will. Poor little lady . . . she is to me as a mother."

"Rosa, dear, I have waited for this day all these years. I have a little time. Can we not talk? Why did you leave me, my sweet rose? You loved me, ah . . . how I knew it, but you left me to my sorrow. Four years I have waited and now . . . I want you as before. You remember our hills at Black Isle . . . Rosa," and he knelt again beside her, tenderly stroking her wasted arms and hands.

"But you are ill, Rosa, you have been ill for long. I know. And you toil in the camp. It is not fit; you must leave this work for others. There are plenty of women with nothing to do. Rosa, I implore you, make yourself well. This war will not last for ever. We shall meet afterwards . . . I will take you home. My rose."

"Duncan, I cannot do this. You ask me why I left you. I will tell you. I could not marry you. I was ill. I fought it. There was no cure. . . . I cannot live long. That is true, Duncan. I can still serve, so I work where none others will, and where at least I can aid those who need it most.

" So I left you . . . I hoped that you would forget me. I had your memory and your ring. I took the name of Maurer. No one knows, but my sister. She is mother superior in the convent at Santa Maria near Geneva. She sends me the money my father left me in trust. He is dead, and my mother too. So what does it matter? I am Rosa Maurer, the nurse who speaks English and visits the prisoners' camp. I can help there. I have had news of you once, Duncan dear. I was glad. Do not ask me to promise anything. I was content; and . . . now that I have seen you again and felt you near me, I am happy. Dear, dear Duncan. But, Duncan, I must help you. We will leave the house together soon after supper. We may talk a little together then. You will . . ."

" Now come along, my dears, the feast is served. Bring the lamp, Wilhelm. We shall require more light."

Frau Muller seated herself at the head of the table in the high-backed arm-chair, Rosa to her right, Wilhelm at the left. A bowl of freshly-cut roses stood mirrored upon the polished board, old point lace mats supported the dishes. There was a decanter of Rhine wine and tall-stemmed glasses whose iridescence caught the light of the lamp, claiming, too, the delicate tints of the roses. A vegetable soup with mint and flaked cheese opened the feast.

" Pray serve the wine, Wilhelm—Echloss Johanisberg, a rare vintage. . . . I seldom take it." She raised her glass, inclining her head first to Rosa and then towards Wilhelm. " Your very good health, my dears."

" God keep you, little mother," Grant smiled at her.

Then he studied Rosa's face. Her lips moved. She sipped her wine, looking deeply at him across the brim of the glass, the colour of whose golden contents fought for mastery with the reflection of her hair.

The widow was in high spirits. She prattled on, of Ulrich, of her home in Bonn. Both Duncan and Rosa were relieved, sunk in their own thoughts—the love that had been and still was, and Duncan with his plans. The dinner was a high success. The soup was followed by a dish of beaten eggs with asparagus tips. The widow would hurry to the kitchen, while Grant reset the table for another course. Then tiny fillets of veal—" the meat was hard to secure "—and then a sponge trifle, spiced and warm with Kirsch. Some strawberries completed the repast.

" You will like to smoke?" asked Frau Muller. His hand went instinctively to his breast pocket—Muller's cigar case! He remembered only just in time.

" I seldom smoke. No, I think not, thank you."

Now to his task; he must cast the die. "Ulrich requested me to bring his plans—his workings from the experiments. I had almost forgotten . . . your kind hospitality makes me forget." He avoided Rosa's eyes. She was looking at him : he felt it, reading his motive. She had detected the purpose of his visit to the little home of Frau Muller.

"Why, of course, but the papers are so many. I have placed them in my bureau. Have you to depart tonight? Perhaps tomorrow; you will come tomorrow as you wish. You may then go through the papers. You will know which relate to his work. Tomorrow." It was, of course, a widow's plea to preserve her joy. She wanted Wilhelm to return. The balm was working wonders. She could not lose Wilhelm so soon.

"Tomorrow morning, Wilhelm?" she asked.

"Oh, yes, tomorrow will do." He laughed with gaiety, a little forced. Rosa was watching him. "And now, little mother, it is late. I must return to Barmen. I shall like the walk in the cool of the night; and you must rest, little mother. Perhaps I may accompany Fraulein—Maurer to her home."

"We will go now," said Rosa. "It is past nine. It is late for me, and I have my work tomorrow." They rose from the table. "Play to me once more, Rosa," requested the widow, "before you go. I shall like to go to rest with your music in my ears. I am happy, so happy."

They moved to the little salon. Rosa seated herself at the piano. She sighed, closed her eyes, then her fingers sought the keyboard—a refrain from Beethoven's Pastoral Symphony—the sun painting the waters of Moray, red and gold . . . Rosa and Duncan alone in the music-room of the grey stone house . . . distant purple hills.

"Good night, little mother, until tomorrow. Sleep well, and thank you. Good night."

Grant held the door as Rosa passed out beneath the little porch. Then he closed it.

"Rosa," Grant was agitated. "Is it possible for you to see the priest tonight? Tell him to say nothing to Frau Muller. Yes, he knows that Ulrich is dead. He must not see her."

"I know what you have come to seek, Duncan. I will help you. The priest will not see Frau Muller. Take me to his house. I shall not go to the prisoners' camp tomorrow. I do not always go. sometimes . . . I am not well enough. Tomorrow, they will think I am not well. I shall come to Frau Muller's. Then we will talk.

"Duncan," Rosa grasped him tightly by the arm. "I must help

you . . . my Duncan . . . I can help you . . . we will meet tomorrow. Now take me to the priest."

They walked in the darkness of the silent village street, his right arm round her, Rosa's two hands clasping his arm. They reached the priest's house. A light burned in the window.

Grant raised her face to his own. "Good night, my love, my sweet rose." He kissed her lips, a long kiss. . . .

"Now go, Duncan." Their hands fell apart. She knocked at the door while Colonel Grant strode on into the night.

The door opened. "Father, I have just left the *Witwe* Muller. The major, Ulrich's friend, was there. I know the truth. He could not tell her then. He will come back tomorrow. He tells me you know of Ulrich's death. Do not see the widow. I pray you. There is time yet for her sorrow. I see her often. I am a woman, and, how well you know it—with my sorrow, too. I can aid her as only a woman can. Then later I will send for you. You may help her with the comforts of Mother Church."

"I understand," said the priest. "You are wise. It is good of his friend. There is always time for bad news. In these days I have carried so many sorrows and there are many sick. You will tell me, *fraulein,* when the poor widow needs my ministration."

"And now, good night, Father. . . . I am not so well tonight. I need rest."

"Good night, *fraulein,* do not work too hard. We have need of such sweetness as yours today."

The door closed. Rosa walked slowly to her little apartment at the Stadt Baurat.

Grant paced quickly down the road to Barmen. He lit a cigar . . . and in a moment had cast it away. He must think. His mind was in a whirl . . . his plans . . . his safety . . . his Rosa. A vague uneasiness had settled upon him . . . his thoughts danced and distorted themselves within his mind.

He entered the hotel. The large hall was filled with people, a babel of sound . . . shrieks of forced gaiety coming out of the restaurant. He sat at a little table . . . weary and preoccupied. But he desired conversation. . . . He must talk . . . sing . . . shout . . . do anything. He nodded to a heated, over-fed man mopping his brow at a table opposite: then called for a bottle of sparkling hock.

Several women passed him with questioning eyes. Then he observed that older woman whom he had noted at luncheon. An old man, coarse, and a little tipsy, pressed his blandishments upon her boredom. She caught Grant's eye. With a bare apology she left the gross one to his mutterings and his wine and threaded a passage through the crowd to Grant's table. He waved her a seat, called for another glass while he lazily toyed with the scintillating stem of his own. The wine, brilliant in the glare of the lamps, poppled into her glass with beaded bubbles floating and winking at the brim.

"*Prosit! Herr Major.* . . . You are on leave?" she queried.

Grant would be cautious. These creatures were everywhere, international, in every capital, in every town, without home or fatherland. They gathered like vultures; money, excitement, and drink to drown their sorrows, to banish the haunting shadow of mother love, a childhood and other happier days. Spies, too, many of them . . . in the pay of both sides . . . the older, the more experienced, the underworld of the diplomatic corps, secret agents. Perhaps this creature was a spy . . . setting a thief to catch a thief. . . . What a jest! Perhaps even she intrigued for his own Foreign Office.

"Do not let us talk of the war," parried Grant. "Amuse me; I am bored."

"Poor boy," lisped the harlot, quickly scenting money, the supreme incentive, relapsing to the tawdry of the *maison meublée.* She stretched a smile at him. An effort, Grant noted.

"Staying in the hotel?" she asked.

"A bird of passage," he said. "Tell me about these people, that old devil who was chucking kisses at you." He refilled her glass.

"Oh, that's Herr Messer, president of the Messer Werke. He's made a pile of money and lost two sons in the early days, killed by the English. Christ!" she chuckled, "you should hear him revile the English. The shock killed his wife . . . that's where I come in. He's hard, though; he won't part with a mark. That's his youngest son, the pale-faced kid with crutches—had his leg shot off in the air —no use for me, a sanctimonious little devil, but tolerates me for dad's sake. He's trying to reform him." She giggled.

"I'd like to have a yarn with the lad," Grant said.

The woman rose and went across to the young officer. Grant beckoned him to come over; then realizing his disability walked over to join the pair. The lieutenant attempted to rise. Grant acknowledged the courtesy, and waving him back drew up a chair. The woman had already seated herself and called for wine. Conversation fell to the war, aerial domination, the spirit of the army, developments. The young man had a keen intelligence. Grant did not particularize. The woman was either bored, or pretending to be so. Finally the possibility of easier money lured her away from a conversation growing too technical to a Herr Messer with the simpler vocabulary of Bacchus.

" My father," indicated Lieutenant Messer, waving his hand towards the woman's companion.

" Poor devil! there are many such. Don't worry too much. You can put that right when this dirty business is over."

" I live with him—I'm the ewe lamb," and he laughed a little. " Poor dad. I'm the only one left. He's got his work. That was fine . . . before war made it too easy for him. Then he lost his sheet anchor—my mother. But you don't want to hear our family troubles?" and he broke off for a moment.

Resuming, he said: " Funny thing, this morning. I get up early . . . force of habit . . . and my leg won't let me sleep much anyhow. I fancied I heard an aeroplane overhead. They come sometimes, and I always have my field glasses handy. I like to see the types of machines . . . improvements and so on. The sound died away going east.

" It was a gorgeous morning, and I sat in my chair marvelling at the changes in the sky and watching the stars go out one by one. My window faces east. I had been there just over half an hour when I heard an aero engine again. It was coming nearer. I got my glasses and hopped to the end of the veranda, and I could see the machine distinctly." He glanced round him, lowered his voice and bent forward. " It was about two miles south, and going in a westerly direction rising all the time. I raised my glasses to obtain a better view. I judged the height then to be about eight thousand feet." His voice sank to a whisper. " It was an English aeroplane, English markings on the under wings, going like the devil. I told dad. He laughed at me. ' Dreams, sonny,' he said, ' just dreams.' But I can swear to it. I know an English machine when I see one. . . . My God, I've been in a few dog fights! What do you think, *Herr Major*?"

Grant considered for a moment. So Mayne had been observed! " Very probably you are right, my lieutenant. Strange things happen in war. An English aeroplane perhaps, probably: but have you considered? . . . an English pilot? It was very early in the morning, you say. You should tell no one of what you have seen. Probably a new ruse for observation. An early start keeps the inquisitive in bed . . . like our friend sitting with your father. I never trust that type, but their line is the gossip of beer halls. I suppose it has its value and its price. Take my advice and keep what you have seen to yourself."

" Very good, *Herr Major*. You will excuse me now. I will ask the porter to call dad's chauffeur. I must take him home."

" I, too, will retire." Grant rose and yawned, a little more

obviously than good manners would have permitted him, in order
to impress the lady.

"Good night, sonny. Don't fret yourself. Look after your
father. He will need you. Get well soon." They shook hands.
Grant held the lad's hand in his own firm grip, and tightened it as
he whispered confidentially: "Remember to keep what you have
seen to yourself. . . . Good night."

Grant moved towards the lift, and, passing the waiter, said:
"Waiter—the wine to my account." He must get some ready
money. It was awkward. Twenty marks to the woman would
make her less inquisitive; a tip to the waiter would keep his tongue
from gossip. Rosa—she had offered help. No, he could not take
money from her. . . . Yes. Rosa. How necessity drives! He
went to the lift and straight to his room. He threw off his clothes—
Muller's clothes. Thank God . . . clean, new pyjamas: the
ecstasy, the purifying of a bath. He jumped into bed, switched off
the light—Rosa, sweet music, evening sunlight upon a loch, purple
hills, a kiss, Rosa. . . .

*　　　*　　　*　　　*　　　*

Grant awoke, refreshed. It was after eight o'clock. He jumped
out of bed, bathed and shaved, and dressed rapidly. He rang for
coffee, and drank it, munching rusks as he dressed. He put on the
clean underclothes, the others he threw into a drawer. He went
straight out, taking the high road again to Hatzberg. He was in
high spirits, his step buoyant. Soon he would see Rosa. By half-past
ten he had reached the little village. He went straight to the little
gate. He knew that from some window Rosa was watching for his
approach.

As he walked down the red brick path he called cheerily—" Frau
Muller! Good day to you, little mother!"

"Is that yourself, Wilhelm? Come into the salon."

Grant hung up his cap: then crossed the hall to the salon. Frau
Muller rose from the table which she had cleared and set in the
window. It was covered with documents, some tied with tape,
others piled with brass ornaments set as weights to prevent the
breeze from the window disturbing them. The widow came across
to him, raising her hands which she placed on his shoulders. She
raised her face to him affectionately. He kissed her brow lightly.
She clung to him and buried her head on his bosom. She wept a
little. Grant felt a sharp pang of embarrassment. He had made
up his mind to keep sentiment at arm's length. His duty

summoned him to a different task . . . a little diplomacy, all that was necessary . . . and he had much to do. He felt an impatience, but he must be tolerant of the widow.

" There . . . there . . . little mother. Now let us look at the papers."

" I have them all here. I used to collect them into bundles for Ulrich, and after he had gone, I carefully put them altogether. See, I have set them out upon this table, just as I did for Ulrich. I can explain when you wish. In this bundle are the markings upon the W Plan." She laughed a little : " Inverted M, I should say. You will find the plans complete. Ulrich went through them : these he wished to use in his work after the war. In this pile are the results of his week's experiments with the prisoners at Elberfeld : you will find these also complete. Here tied in the green ribbon are the results of his tests with various explosives.

" I do not understand these things, but they concern, I think, the different charges, angle of laying and density of soil to be blown. In this pile you will find a number of maps of the front with some notes; and here in this roll tied with the red ribbon is the model of the W. Plan. There are two maps.

" Among these papers are the notes which he made towards the end . . . they are not complete. Ulrich took his notes with him," she smiled. " And now I will leave you for a while. You are familiar with the subject and will be able to go through the papers and select what you and Ulrich will require from them. You will stay to lunch. I will see to this and go about my household duties."

Grant seated himself before the papers. He was no engineer. This was a large task even for one with high technical qualifications. First he would rapidly examine each bundle. He selected the maps, the easiest task. With topographical plans he was familiar. He unrolled them. One was a large scale map of the whole front upon which was pasted a transparent plan. The transparency bore fine black lines in the form of almost regular trellis work, broad at one end, narrowing down to two points. At the points of the trellis on the wider end were red spots. Grant pressed the transparency down upon the map and read.

The network covered a front of some fifteen miles—Poperinghe, Abeele, Flêtre, Strazeele, the River Lys. A number of lines crossed and recrossed the tracery to which there was a key at the foot of the map. Muller, reflected Grant, was captured at Scottish Wood, just east of Dickebusch. This was important. He turned to the other map. It was a large scale repetition of the former, masses of figures, a time table, many more lines drawn direct upon the map, but all conforming in general plan to the trellis tracery. He rolled them up, but as he did so the triangles of the tracery remained in his mind's eye—a series of W's.

He rapidly unrolled again the second plan. Quite plain, the letter W, intersected, one after the other, conforming to a definite plan. Inverted M. . . . Grant chuckled with joy. He tied up the maps and put them on one side. He took up the bundle tied with green tape. He slipped off the ribbon and rapidly turned over the papers. Charge 1, Charge 2, and so on, many of them detailed workings: lower down, instructions to engineer in charge of Section 1, 2, 3. He counted seven of these. At the bottom some plans in pencil referring to charges showing the angles, charges required, time schedule of detonations. The plans were in Section, each one conforming to the shibboleth . . . W. He would examine these later.

So it was, of course it was, a mining plan on a large scale. Ypres to the Lys. But what the hell for? That didn't get the Germans very far. After all, we blew a few mines at Fricourt to open the Somme break-through. What a fiasco! . . . held up at High Wood after fifteen days, and bogged at Les Boeufs up to the present day! Anyhow it was interesting, but nothing yet to cause G.H.Q. to become unduly agitated.

He selected another dossier—experiments with prisoners at Elberfeld. This was quite straightforward. The papers were pinned together, first day, second, third, fourth, and fifth. He looked over the first day: two hundred and fifty men, task of digging and clearing a shaft and laying narrow gauge rail track; cleared X tons of soil from shaft. Another calculation showed a time schedule using the Messer excavator and single track running gear. Only forty men used in the shaft, the balance utilized for emptying track wagons, except for trained miners employed in propping the shafts.

He rapidly glanced at the fifth day's workings—Messer excavator used almost entirely. Large numbers of men employed on emptying wagons and removing soil from endless winding gear . . . miners engaged on expert work. "Scottish the best workmen and well disciplined" was a note which met his eye. Hell! the native genius of his race and the discipline which he himself had helped to inculcate being utilized in some foul scheme against his own country. Grant's pulse quickened with excitement and indignation.

He was collecting and putting aside the papers when his eye fell on a single sheet of foolscap not attached to the rest—the names and addresses of a number of women. Dear Ulrich had been careless, reflected Grant. Mother wouldn't like this little list—but where had he seen a list like this before? . . . Ulrich's pocket book! He whipped it out of his breast pocket, ran through the pages. Emilie Gartner, Malapaner Strasse 15, Breslau. The same upon the foolscap. The names and addresses in the notebook tallied exactly with those on the foolscap. Well, he wouldn't require evidence twice, and the mother wouldn't like it. He folded the foolscap, and placed it in his breast pocket, replacing Muller's book.

He then took up the first pile of papers which Frau Muller had indicated as the completed plans. They revealed an analysis of the experiments with prisoners and with the Messer excavator.

Messer! how stupid not to think of it before . . . the bloated old man at the hotel! That is how he made his pile. Grant wondered how much his mistress knew. At any rate, she hadn't made much use of her knowledge. The Foreign Office hadn't an idea. Perhaps she was only in the stage of finding out. She complained the old man was hard . . . perhaps even tighter and shrewder with his secrets—business instinct, even ex alcohol—than with his profits. However, he wouldn't need the papers, a bulky lot, relating to the experiments with prisoners. " Scottish the best workers, well disciplined." That stuck in his throat! However, here was a summary. The plan, the Messer excavator with prisoners to be employed . . . the W Plan—vertical and horizontal—time schedules, storm troop concentration in short galleries, mine charges, excavations by Mont Kemmel and Steenwerk.

Grant pondered the situation as he had left it . . . no wonder the Boche fought like cats at Kemmel and pushed the French out at the end of April! " The first among all causes of victory," says Clausewitz, " is to pursue a great object with energy and perseverance." Germany needed, must have, Mont Kemmel at any price—the backbone of the W Plan. He turned to re-examine the papers. The plan was taking shape in his mind. He must take away these papers and study them. He reached again for the maps of the W Plan.

Deep in reflection, he had not heard the step of Rosa. She entered quietly. Grant glanced up from his work. Rosa . . . God, how ill she looked, but how beautiful! He caught a sob, and hurried to her. A feeling of great pity swept over him. He clasped her to him. Then he coloured with shame. She had seen his work, his treachery to the widow. Rosa knew what was passing through Duncan's mind.

" My dear," she said. " I knew what your work would be. I have come to help, if I can. I have told them at my apartment that I am going away for a little rest. I am free to do your bidding.

If you have nothing for me to do, if you cannot, will not, use me, I will sit here. Shall I play to you? . . . but I want to help you. Duncan, say I may. Tell me how I can help you."

Duncan placed her in an arm-chair and seated himself upon its arm.

"Rosa, I do not want you to help me. Perhaps your aid might soil our love. I have my duty. It is not a woman's work . . . not women of your type. I want as clear a conscience as I can have. The war has already sufficiently degraded my instincts, my sense of honour. That is a duty—right or wrong, it is not my part to question —but our love is apart."

"My dear, if I cannot aid you now when you may need my help most, of what use is our love? Remember I abandoned it once." A cough racked her. "Duncan," tears welled to her eyes, "let me help you."

"Rosa, this is a sordid business. It will defile the purity of your nature . . . I have nearly completed my plans; but . . . there is still much to do . . . and so little time. . . ." He paused and regarded her searchingly. "If you wish it, Rosa . . . yes . . . you can help me."

"I do wish it, Duncan," she replied earnestly, the colour flooding her face and neck, and then very quietly she sighed : "For better or worse, Duncan. Can't I give myself to you, dear . . . feel you close to me . . . replenish these barren years of your life . . . and of mine . . . Duncan. I am yours . . . do with me what you will. . . ." She looked up into his face. . . . "I need you, dearest. Give to me your love. . . . As your wife I may help you, as Rosa von Gleiwitz, I cannot."

Duncan relinquished his hold of her, stepped back, and regarded her. After many moments he spoke : "Rosa . . . you have my love . . . as my wife you shall help me. . . . We can go to Barmen this afternoon. We will go to the hotel. You can veil yourself. I will explain later. And, Rosa," he laughed, "what a confession! . . . I have no money, not a blessed mark. Bring all the money you can."

Rosa smiled. They kissed. "Now get on with your work, Duncan. I will play to you for ten minutes—Mendelssohn, the Wedding March." She seated herself at the piano and struck the first chords.

Frau Muller entered. "Why, Rosa, I did not hear you come in. I am preparing luncheon. You play . . . how delightful . . . but why the Wedding March?"

Rosa continued to play, and smiled at the widow wistfully.

" You can keep a secret, little mother. Wilhelm and I are old, very old friends."

" Wilhelm?" A look of astonishment crossed the widow's face.

The march swept on to a triumphal end. The last chords seemed to quiver and vibrate for a moment about those in the room . . . then faded away.

" You will bless us, little mother," said Rosa. " We shall need your blessing." Frau Muller sank upon her knees, her head buried in the cushions of the settee. Her frail body shook. Intense emotion swept her. . . .

" Dear little lady," said Grant, as he bent over her, " it is true : but Rosa will return to you. You two will comfort each other."

When the echo of the last notes had died away, Frau Muller joined the hands of the two lovers, kissed them, and then bustled away again to the kitchen. " Another feast, Rosa and Wilhelm."

" It is a secret, little mother," Grant called after her. " Now, Rosa, go quickly, and prepare."

With heightened colour, the light of happiness in her eyes, and buoyancy in her step, she waved him farewell.

Duncan gazed from the window until she had passed out of sight, then turned again to his task. It was nearly completed. He gathered together the files, discarding one pile and some odd papers; parcelled and tied them up in a large piece of paper which Frau Muller had thoughtfully provided for the purpose. Then he wandered into the little back garden, and lit a cigar.

It was just past noon. He must reflect. It would take him time to go through the papers, to study the technique of the operations planned. He must take them to some quiet spot, master them, and then go to the front area and discover what was being done. There might not be much time : he must allow, too, for accidents. Eight days in hand : then he must return to Barmen and slip away at dawn with Mayne. He had the plans, he would take no unnecessary risks, but he must assure himself that they were being operated. The facts were of vital importance. The wits of one general were being pitted against those of another. Colonel Grant's task would utilize all his skill, his resources, reserves, mental and physical. He was a spy—more often than not a title to which stigma and dishonour are attached.

But the profession of espionage probably demands more varied attainments, harder work and greater courage than any other. The physician not only has the whole-hearted co-operation of his patient, but suffers no penalty for error : the barrister, however unskilfully he may conduct his case, enjoys the protection of the law and cheerfully collects his fee : the soldier has the support of the nation; the clergy the privilege of their cloth; the business man the backing of the bank : while even the journalist is entrenched and camouflaged in an anonymity.

But the spy has no protection, no privileges, no entrenchments, no cover. He spends every hour of his existence in launching the attack, and from the moment he shows his head he is liable to attack. He is bombarded from front and rear, he is enfiladed and walks between fires. He is eternally committed to the offensive. For him there is no retreat, he must advance or perish. He must be a linguist of the first order. He must be forceful yet persuasive, both simple and subtle. He must be an advocate, a logician and a diplomat. He must be as versatile as a politician and as consistent as tempered steel. He must be a judge of form, of colour, and have a ripe knowledge of human nature. He must possess a fighting instinct, and he must have invincible courage. He must be opportunist, tactician, strategist. He must be confident and he must be cheerful, and he must have the saving grace of humour, but he must be neither a braggart nor a buffoon. He must be dogged, yet never dogmatic. He must be an optimist, but he must not inhabit a fool's paradise. To sum up he must be a metaphysician, psychologist and philosopher, in a word both Man and Superman.

The province of an Intelligence Service is sufficiently wide to embrace the whole earth, and engage the whole life, experience and knowledge of the spy. It demands the complete surrender of every social and diplomatic quality he may possess. It demands every moment of his conscious hours, for the born spy is he who from dawn to dark—and long after—each hour and each day, whether of work or leisure, keeps his mind receptive to every impression, every thought, every chance human contact which may add conviction to his argument, supply the missing link in a chain of evidence. If he does this successfully he has found the Philosopher's Stone. But always he must be alone. Every man's hand is against him. He is fearful of substance and of shadow. He has no friends, but everywhere enemies, alone, always alone.

Grant passed slowly up and down the little garden path. He smiled to himself; he laughed aloud; he inhaled the air deeply; his heart was pulsating; he dug his hands deeper and deeper into his pockets and slapped his thighs with delight; he was almost in a seventh heaven, if there be such a thing : he felt almost overcome with exhilaration; he wanted to shout aloud like the Greek philosopher in his bath—Eureka! . . . he had found the Philosopher's Stone.

Rosa and the plans, the plans and Rosa.

He discovered himself humming the words to the first odd ragtime ditty which escaped from the maelstrom of his mind. Life was good, extraordinarily good; he possessed everything he wanted in the world. He thrilled with excitement when he thought of leaving with Rosa that very afternoon. Here, indeed, was romance!

He perceived Rosa through the casement windows. She had returned, a smile of triumph on her lips. Grant called to her softly and she came into the garden. Then came Frau Muller—luncheon was ready. Rose petals had been strewn upon the table. The little party was silent, each preoccupied with thought. Frau Muller would weep a little, then gaily apologize. Little justice was done to the dexterity and industry of Frau Muller's feast. They went into the salon. Rosa played again, happily and lightly.

Then the widow kissed them both affectionately; and secretly to live as husband and wife they left the little village of Hatzberg on the road to Barmen.

CHAPTER IV

MEN LIKE MOLES

"DUNCAN, dear, we must send the announcement to *The Times*. All the best people do that," exclaimed Rosa with that old gaiety which Grant remembered so well.

"And, Rosa, we're going to talk home language for just one little hour. My grandfather always used to tell his London friends that the Inverness cabmen speak better English than Mr. Balfour or Lord Rosebery. We'll talk the best English—from Scotland. And now for your announcement. What is it to be?"

"Here we are," cried Rosa, "listen! The betrothal is announced between Lieutenant-Colonel Duncan Grant, Inverness Highlanders, only son of General Ian Grant of Culbokie, and Rosa, daughter of the late Graf von Gleiwitz."

They laughed together, and then leaving the high road crossed to a pine copse upon a little knoll overlooking Barmen.

"And now, Duncan, the help you need. That must come first. Let us discuss your plans and tell me what I can do."

Grant told the bare story of Ulrich Muller, of his flight and of the landing at Viersberg. And then he told her of the hotel clerk.

"Suppose," he said, "I had told him I shall be joined by my wife, would he have believed me? I doubt it. But all will be ready for us. And you have married a penniless—markless—man. I shall need money. It silences the curious, and gives freedom from anxiety."

"I have brought six hundred marks."

Grant was silent for a moment. "Rosa," he said, "Rosa . . . how good of you." Then he laughed. "I was anxious about the hotel bill. Suspicion would be aroused if I left without paying it. A young lieutenant, Messer, son of Messer, the steel magnate, knows that a British aeroplane was over Barmen on the fifth. I advised him to tell no one. But there might be a hue and cry. Things would move quickly. Muller—who was Muller? . . . from Hatzberg. But no, surely he was reported missing. And Major Schaeffer, who was he? Answering to the description of Muller of the Hotel Imperial. Whence did he come? Who was he? Rosa, how I have needed your help! But you, too, are in danger, great danger. Rosa, dear, I hadn't thought of it. Rosa Maurer and Wilhelm Schaeffer. Who is this Schaeffer? Suppose questions are asked? We must think this out together. I have asked too much of you, Rosa, dear."

"Silly one, do you think I had not thought of this? I wanted to share your danger, your life. Why not? And there are many ways. But you will leave Barmen without suspicion. And," she added wistfully, "we will go—together, you and I, for a little while. We cannot remain in the hotel."

"We will go tomorrow. I must read through these papers carefully as soon as we reach Barmen. Then I will plan for the future. There is much to do. This will not be too much strain for you, dear? Take my arm now. We will take the tramway at the Quellen Strasse to the Neumarkt. You have your veil; you can cover yourself before we enter the hotel, and we will go straight to my room. Then we will plan. Now we will talk of ourselves."

"I remember reading somewhere," said Rosa:

" ' Greater than my need of thee
Greater than my misery
Greater than Eternity
My love of thee!' "

he sighed. He pressed her closely to him. "My beloved, I have almost learned to bless the hour you left me. If I have lived alone for this hour, I am happy—Rosa." He kissed her lips.

Then with her arm pressed lightly upon his, they walked slowly through the wooded way to the outskirts of the town.

A short rest upon a seat; and then came the rattling tramcar, filled with workmen and girls. They made way respectfully for the officer and his lady. They had no bitterness towards the man from the front and the lady, so delicate, pale and beautiful. With good humour they exchanged jests. At the Neumarkt, Duncan and Rosa alighted. Rosa drew the veil, one of thick buff lace, over her face, then took Duncan's arm and they walked across the square to the hotel. It was after five o'clock. A few were drinking beer and wine, but the lounge was almost deserted. He drew up a chair for Rosa.

" I will tell the clerk that my wife has arrived. She is tired after her journey; we will dine in our room, perhaps, later. That will give us several hours, undisturbed for work." He strolled across to the reception desk. The clerk received his message with an ill-concealed smirk. Grant felt a strong desire to strike the man; but he forced a smile. He must comply with war's convention and licentiousness . . . nay, more, and he passed ten marks across the desk. . . . After all, the clerk had anticipated it and Major Muller had readily accepted the suggestion. Rosa and Duncan went to room No. 23. He turned the key.

" Now we will make ourselves comfortable." He took her hat and coat and threw off his tunic. Then he drew out the table, placed two chairs, and unwrapped his parcel.

" Here are all the plans. I must completely master these tonight. Will you take notes—in German—in this pocket book? It was Muller's."

For two . . . three hours . . . more . . . with scarcely a word exchanged between them . . . Grant re-examined the plans, charts, schedules and maps. Rosa helped him by making an occasional note and by rearranging the papers.

And this is a summary of the plan as Grant discovered it and realized it. Every German effort to break through the cordon of steel around the frontiers had suffered defeat. The Germans had struck through Russia and Italy. They were thwarted. The effort to strangle Belgium and Roumania both by invasion and with every diplomatic artifice, with the object of disrupting the allies, of weakening the blockade, and of creating difficulties in the eastern theatre of war, had failed. Money, men, experts had been poured into Asia Minor in order to create a diversion, without success. It is true that a treaty of little value to Germany had been signed with revolutionary Russia. Doom had overtaken the depravity of a sunken nation, and Russia was in very consequence no ally for a Germany fighting for its very national existence. Rather was the treaty of Brest Litovsk a dangerous, insidious drug, though it might temporarily relieve German pain.

The two main theatres of war were in the East—Russia . . . that was disposed of; and, in the West—England, the French and Belgians on a front of over two hundred miles. The French were weakened: men spoke of mutiny, of wholesale desertion. Belgium was invested, her army infinitesimal. America had declared upon the side of the Allies; the first troops, raw, untried, led by inexperience were already coming into the line. England stood firm, though weakened, with a growing political faction clamouring for peace.

The offensive at Verdun, fought with matchless gallantry on both sides, had been broken by the stubborn, heroic defence of the French —"They shall not pass!" cried Marshal Foch, with courage unquenchable, great in leadership. . . . The massed assaults against the British in bitter fighting had been checked before the Belgian hills—the jagged tower of the Ypres Cloth Hall still kept its eastern watch. The British, stubborn as their mules in defence, vigorous and fierce in attack, were yet unconquered and as unconquerable as had been the "Contemptible Little Army."

The Allies were girding their loins. Germany must act. To break the English lines and gain sight of the Channel ports . . . that was the supreme task, the final, the only objective. Unless England were broken, the Allies on the Western front divided, the doom of Germany was sealed.

Germany must make a discovery. The Imperial State and its commanders must summon to its council any who could help solve the insoluble riddle—statesmen and diplomats; military, naval and air chiefs. The plans of the strategist are determined by diplomacy and where strategy ends, tactics begin. The silver threads of continuity of strategic and diplomatic purpose runs throughout a campaign, drawing in its train not only commanders-in-chief but all subordinate leaders.

Therefore had the English front received the deepest consideration. The line from north to south ran through from the ghastly Passchendaele salient, thence east of Mont Kemmel, through Méteren and Merris, crossing the River Lys by Merville, then Givenchy and Cambrin, west of Béthune to the battlefields beside Arras, and farther south through the wastes of the Somme fighting, with Bapaume and Peronne as names to mark the debris. No special tactical advantage lay with either side except at Mont Kemmel. Here the Germans by a supreme effort, with extraordinary tenacity of purpose and heroic courage, had wrested this dominating hill from the French.

The tactical advantages lay with Germany. The British defences and communications were overlooked for miles. Mont Kemmel was a vantage point of immense value, and the king-pin of the tactical and strategic position. The breaking of the English line on a sufficiently wide front at this point, would imperil the Channel ports, would gravely interrupt the main line of communication and supplies, and followed resolutely would throw the English back upon the Channel and drive a wedge between them and their French Allies. This was the task.

A plan had, therefore, been formulated by the chief engineer to undermine the English lines by a series of galleries on a wide front and to force a passage for the storm troops. That was the genesis of the idea. To accomplish this practically was a different matter. This task appeared a superhuman feat, involving the construction of a vast number of galleries several miles long, the concentration of great numbers of troops below ground probably for many days, the draining of a wide area, the surface of which in great part was permanently a swamp.

The foremost engineers of Germany had been summoned in conference. Ulrich Muller, engineer from the Bismarkhütte, and recently appointed as a chief engineer at Dusseldorf, had been included. Alone he had said that the project was possible. The time factor was his difficulty. He was prepared to stake—the older engineers had laughed—his young reputation upon it. More, for that was of little importance, his plans were fully prepared.

Ulrich Muller had recently thrown out some experimental shafts at the Bismarkhütte with the object of penetrating the rich and so far unmined coal seams of Kreis Pless. His object had been to utilize the existing organization, elevators, railway power, sorting screens, administration, welfare establishments at the pit head, and bring coal by mechanical process, five, possibly even thirty miles underground by a new process and method of shaft sinking, drainage, ventilation and haulage. He had tested all the necessary apparatus over two or three years of arduous work and the whole of the working plans and experiments had been reduced to a series of formulæ to which he had for lack of any other comprehensive term, given the name of the V Plan. The project of the chief engineer could be accomplished. It would take some three months to prepare; but, granted the necessary skilled labour, unlimited resources in machinery and a free hand, Muller declared definitely that the project could be carried out in its entirety. These facts were briefly stated in the notes. The scheme was accepted. Muller was provided with a week in which to finalize his plans. Thus the project took shape.

Two shafts were to be sunk just east of the Mont Kemmel group of hills. Galleries were then to be thrown forward undermining the

British lines on a front of fifteen miles and penetrating westwards
for eight miles. The galleries were to be so constructed that large
numbers of men, artillery, ammunition, supplies, could be concentrated in them. Drainage was carefully provided. The galleries
ended with long arms reaching obliquely across the lines, and finally
quitting their depth terminating near the surface, while throughout
they were connected with each other by a series of shorter galleries
thrown also obliquely and almost at right angles to the main gallery,
meeting each other at a right angle bend, part of which thrust
towards the enemy lines westwards.

Thus did the general concept in plan conform to a series of the
letter W, linked together by and at the extremities of the outer arms.

Underneath the main galleries, which ran horizontally east and
west, were constructed another series of galleries conforming exactly
in dimension to those above, and connected with the upper tunnels
by yet another series of similar shafts thrown vertically downwards,
but conforming always to the W Plan. This was the trellis work plan
which Grant had noted.

Troops, ammunition, guns were to be concentrated in those
galleries which formed the angle connecting the two long arms of
the letter, the latter being kept clear as roadways to permit the
different arms and services to be hurried forward as required, in
conformation with the battle plan.

Where the long arms terminated to the west, penetrating far
behind the British lines of organized defence, namely the last line
of entrenchment, and concrete strong points, a series of mines was
sown each of which was connected by electric cable with a point
central in the trellis work. The mines would be blown, and in their
craters machine-gun strongholds would immediately be established
to cover with enfilade crossing fire the deployment of the hidden
troops from the points formed by the angles between the two connecting arms. The main arms of the upper system, which in series
formed continuous roads converging to a central point of communication and control, would then be utilized for the rapid transit of
artillery, wagons and stores, while the intersecting angle arms would
be used for the passage of infantry and cavalry.

The main arms of the lower system would be similarly used, but
with reserve troops consisting for the most part of armoured cars
brought from the Russian front and light troops, whose objective
would be to sever the lines of communications running south from the
Channel ports through Bailleul, Arras, Amiens, and to capture the
Channel ports.

The vertical section was to provide a system of rapid and easy lateral communication, while the angle of slope was so arranged that troops, mounted and dismounted, could pass from one section of galleries to another, utilizing the short angle roadways without interrupting the progress of the westward traffic along the main arms.

The scheme was one of astonishing ingenuity. Nothing had been overlooked. Every detail had been carefully worked out with mathematical precision. From the minute that the mines were blown a steady passage of men would begin to defile from behind the main British lines—horse, foot and guns—an army complete, a whole expeditionary force coming like moles from underground. The plan was made possible by the utilization of the Messer excavator and single-track, endless winding gear, capable of mining and clearing thousands of tons of soil every hour. An additional contrivance was arranged for the automatic erection of props to secure the roof and sides of the galleries, but here the plan required the eye of an expert. The angles of the W system—and as a harmony much depended upon angle—provided for the blowing of the craters as the means of exit, while a further series of much smaller W galleries constructed at the extremities of the long arms would prevent blow back and provide safety for the hosts secreted in the galleries.

The necessity to success, as in every other military operation, was secrecy—a secrecy which must be preserved for two, possibly three months. Elaborate precautions had, therefore, been taken to ensure that the work should be carried out so that a leakage of information was impossible. The troops in the line, at that time the 31st Division from the Rhineland Province, were relieved by a whole corps of Jägers, troops tried, dependable, with the highest fighting reputation. The number of rifles in the front and support lines was trebled in order to defend them against enemy operations which might be designed on a minor scale to improve his tactical position. The most urgent orders were conveyed to local commanders to suppress all raids with the utmost energy, and in any case to prevent their penetrating through the support lines.

The Jäger Corps consisted of three divisions. Two of these were placed in the front lines. All leave, even of the most urgent nature, was stopped. Generals of brigade, even the divisional commander and his staff, were placed in the forward area, and west of the head of the shafts. The division in reserve was placed in a wire enclosure at Courtrai; while thick wire entanglements were thrown out from west to east on both sides of the sector and enclosed in the rear, so that the divisions in the line were equally shut off from outside communication.

An order was published declaring that the Jäger Corps had been specially selected for intensive training and as an iron example to the nation, the object being to promote the will-to-win spirit through the armies. The overthrow of the Russians on the eastern front was, with a purpose, stressed. This order was cleverly conceived and cunningly phrased with the object of diverting suspicion, and it was allowed to fall into enemy hands and into those of any persons suspected of Allied sympathies. It had the further object of discouraging British raids upon the sector, since the name of the corps and the intention was stated, while a raid upon a sector so strongly held would hardly invite an enemy anxiously conserving its man power. The corps responsible for holding the front would, therefore, have no knowledge of the mining operation proceeding in its rear, while the internal relief of the divisions could be carried out without fear of secrets being revealed to an inquisitive population with no sympathy with its invaders.

Instructions had been issued to the officers commanding prisoners' camps to select all miners from the ranks of ordinary soldiers of whatever nationality and dispatch them without delay to Mors, the centre of the Lower Rhenish coalfield. It would be assumed that the miners were to be utilized in coal production. The Guard Grenadier Regiment was dispatched to Mors and a cordon placed round the railway station.

The prisoners in large batches with interpreters were herded into covered wagons as soon as they reached Mors, strong guards placed in charge of each wagon and train loads dispatched to Menin. After each train load reached a point in the open country some twenty miles from Mors, it was halted, and the prisoners were served out with fresh clothing and the uniform of the Reichswehr. Any who showed truculence or refused were instantly shot by the guards. A staff formed from the Intelligence Service was placed in command of the camp, and dummy orders were formulated and promulgated daily to allay suspicion. The formation, consisting of nearly ten thousand men—British, French, Italians, Belgians, Poles, Russians— was designated the 15th Composite Reichswehr Division.

In addition, any German soldiers under sentence of death for desertion or mutiny were dispatched to this camp for work to remove them wholly from their comrades, but to conserve a depleted man power. Indents for rations, supplies, clothing and all the varied requirements of a large body of men under active service conditions bore this nomenclature.

A double barbed wire entanglement, electrified, was thrown up round the camp, and the Guard Grenadier Regiment gradually transferred with each train load to prevent the individual escape or mutiny of any of the prisoners. Upon arrival they were formed into battalions and companies by their nationality and an interpreter placed in charge of each group.

Thus was quietly and with the utmost secrecy formed a division of miners from prisoners of war for the purpose of constructing the W breach. Rigid orders were issued that any attempt to communicate, or any speech with any person outside the confines of the camp would be met with instant death without the formality of court martial.

The camp itself was well furnished and equipped—a large canteen, tobacco, a daily ration of wine, musical instruments, gramophones, reading matter in various languages, good food. The General Staff exercised every ingenuity to promote bodily well-being and mental satisfaction. With the exception of the orders as to communication and the strictest obedience the men were accorded the utmost licence. *Pro formae* of the orders were included in the notes.

Grant marvelled at the comprehensiveness of the scheme, its thoroughness, its ingenuity. As a military operation, albeit, without doubt, a flagrant breach of International Law, it was a masterpiece. And as to Hague Conventions . . . an eye for an eye, a tooth for a tooth!

The experiments at Elberfeld demonstrated that this vast work could be accomplished in sixty-eight days. Muller had allowed a further week in case of accidents or any hitch in the provision of the necessary machinery. But the date must be reckoned from the capture of Mont Kemmel and its surrounding hills. Grant was able, therefore, to determine how far the work had proceeded, it being assumed that it had already commenced.

He remembered the fierce fighting for Mont Kemmel. The French Chasseurs d'Alpin, picked troops, were thrown back, and the Germans established themselves well to the west, their posts being thrust out into the half water-logged country, a feature of which is the Dickebusch Lake. That was on the twenty-eighth of April. He might assume that it would require a week at least before operations could commence, though in the quiet lull on both sides which followed the fury of the battles of the Lys in March and April, an enemy ready to commit itself to an operation behind the battle area could quickly and without fear of interruption put it into operation. He might assume, therefore, that mining had commenced about the fourth of May. He rapidly figured . . . all would, therefore, be ready by the first week in August, possibly as late as the sixth.

The plan provided, also, that drainage of the galleries would be accomplished by the sinking of further vertical W-shaped shafts below the second tier of galleries ending in deep sumps. The water level would be retained below the apex of the letter, preventing a flow back, and a subsidiary system by utilizing the Speyer method of rapid absorption with tranium. Vast quantities of earth, hundreds of thousands of tons, were to be excavated. It was arranged that this would be automatically unloaded and spread on the slopes of the main hills. The fact of the hills and their irregular topography would prevent detection of the increasing elevation, while by a careful spread of the excavations they would not be observed obliquely by aerial observation. The air defence by day over the whole of the British front was strengthened so that it would predominate in order to prevent low flying observation.

The whole of the Seventh Army from the Russian front was to be dispatched to Mons for special training, refitting, equipment. The general plan of the staff provided then that orders were to be issued to these corps to concentrate ten days prior to X day in the Forêt de Mormal, east of Maubeuge. Dummy arrangements were to be made for their reception, billeting, and the skeleton move. Advanced troops, a few men from every formation, would be dispatched and the Intelligence Staff arrange that the civilian inhabitants and the troops occupying the Peronne sector be well informed, so that with all necessary speed the enemy would obtain knowledge of the concentration.

It was plain that the purpose was to draw suspicion from the Ypres-Lys sector farther south to the Somme, and to encourage the concentration of British reserves in that area. The operation of the W Plan would, furthermore, separate these reserves from their main bases at Dieppe, Boulogne, Calais, Dunkirk. The forest of Mormal itself and its scattered valleys would prevent observation. Similarly, orders were to be issued to the Third Army occupying the front between the Rivers Scarpe and the Somme to strike towards Amiens as the objective, as a feint to weaken the British front and reserves in the Ypres area. The British would conceive that an attack on a very large scale by two armies was intended to drive a wedge between them and their French allies as had been previously attempted and had so nearly succeeded. The French would be drawn to meet this threat, acting upon British information, and then the dramatic discovery of its falseness would, without doubt, give reality to the whispered dissensions between the Allies.

Muller's function was simple—to provide the necessary galleries and shafts—the technique of the engineering plan. The notes were the strategic and tactical elaboration of the General Staff, utilizing the W Plan as the fulcrum of a general campaign. But the plan was perfectly clear : nor was Grant concerned with the more intricate details of the installations of Messer equipment and of Speyer absorption.

The plan was almost diabolical in its conception and thoroughness. That it would succeed, Grant had not the least shadow of doubt. That if it were carried through, it would certainly overthrow the British and destroy for ever the Allied cause he could at once understand.

He selected the essential plans and notes—now reduced to very few. He re-examined the maps. He noticed what he had not previously noted, namely, that each rectangle formed by the trellis was numbered. These numbers were keyed at the foot of the map and against each number was the name of a town. The red points at the tips of the long arms—now known to be the main galleries and exits and the positions of the mines—were lettered, not in sequence, but, as it appeared, haphazard. He ran his eye over the list of towns then quickly took from his vest pocket the list of names which he had placed there to keep them from Frau Muller's eyes. The names tallied—Berlin, Dusseldorf, Coblenz, Worms, Stuttgart and so on.

He read the names over carefully, checking them with any lettering which might appear on the map. The letters at the red points were similar to those of the initial letters of the ladies' names. The initial letter of the name of the street conformed to a letter denoting a main arm gallery running south-west—M.R.B.H.N.V.—and the final letter denoting one running north-west—B.F.M.A.K.C. It was a simple code.

Muller had copied it into his notebook obviously to refresh his memory as he supervised the progress of the plan, and had coded it in this simple fashion for security. The code had been safe enough . . . up to this moment, it had expressed nothing more to Grant than a list conveniently to be forgotten, and, in any case, to be hidden from its author's mother.

Each complete rectangle in the trellis was numbered in sequence, but there were other numbers, namely, those in the list of addresses . . . what of them? For example, Malapaner Strasse, 14 . . . Fraulein Emilie Gartner, Malapaner Strasse, 14. That was the rectangle on the extreme left. . . . Emilie . . . E.—that indicated the culmination of the first mine at the end of the main gallery. . . Malapaner—M showed the main gallery from the shaft to the end and R, another gallery for troops and communication culminating a

O, the apex to be utilized for the first exit of storm troops. The street numbers would indicate complete sections.

Grant re-examined the plan carefully, and it was clear to him that three or four of the galleries, together with the connecting angles, by now were complete.

It was already past nine o'clock. Grant's immediate work was finished.

The element of surprise is the keystone of success. Thus, the scheme in its entirety was a masterpiece, a supreme combination of all the forces contributing to striking power—infantry, artillery, cavalry, engineers, transport, the air, the mine, mechanics, chemistry. It was a plan proceeding from great generalship similar in its essential character of surprise to Napoleon's passage of the Alps before Marengo; Lee's flank and rear attack at Chancellorsville, Marlborough's march to the Danube before Blenheim. War, Grant recalled, is " first and foremost a matter of movement." Great God! The Germans were about to give a practical demonstration of that principle. Afterwards " War is a matter of supply, destruction and well-organized co-operation against a definite objective." The stagnation of the western front was to be ended. Germany intended war, and one which fully complied with every canon and precept of its science.

Grant rose and stretched himself.

" Rosa, dearest, I had forgotten you. We have had nothing to eat since lunch time, and then neither of us ate anything at all. You must be famished. I will place all the papers inside my tunic and we will go to a little restaurant away from this hotel and have dinner."

They went out, Rosa veiled as before. Grant observed that their exit was followed by the jealous eyes of the harpy. He waved a sign of recognition to Lieutenant Messer, who was seated with his father and a group of friends.

" Tomorrow, I must leave for the front. I will take the train to Brussels. I must see what I can see. On the night of the fourteenth I will return. You will keep all the papers and we will meet at this restaurant at nine o'clock. If I do not return, take the papers. You must write what report you can—you know almost as much as I do now—then when the aeroplane comes down at Viersberg . . . remember—I have given you a little map showing the landing place . . . hand the papers to the pilot. I want you to keep Muller's instruments and chronometer, and when you judge right, give them to his mother. I shall not need them. We cannot go together, but we will meet again on the fourteenth, my dear."

They returned to the hotel. Muller settled his account, remarking: " We leave early in the morning. . . ."

*　　*　　*　　*　　*

" Duncan . . . I love you." He entwined his fingers in her glorious hair now spread like cloth of gold over the white linen. " Dearest heart, we have found each other. Let me feel you near me, Duncan . . . your life and mine. I can live now."

" Rosa . . ."

CHAPTER V

SEEN FROM A BARLEY FIELD

A T six o'clock in the morning Grant awoke. Rosa was still sleeping, a smile on her lips, her pale beauty encompassed by the golden halo of her hair. Duncan kissed her. She stirred and was awakened by the passion of his embrace. She clung to him. " I am happy now . . . content," she sighed.

" Paradise—lost and regained," murmured Duncan.

They rose. Grant rang for coffee and dressed rapidly. By seven o'clock he was clothed. They left the hotel together. The railway station was crowded—workmen and girls coming in from the suburbs to the textile and engineering workshops, others departing for the short daily journey to the loom, the pit, the bench and the office; business men carrying dispatch cases and a number of soldiers in uniform returning to the front.

The people, Grant noted, were much like those of any other provincial town in western Europe, good, honest, plain folk, preoccupied with the small affairs of life, laughing in little groups; a maid and her man; a tearful peasant woman, the mother of a stripling weighed down with pack, accoutrements and rifle. Transpose the scene to Edinburgh, Leicester, Bristol—it would scarcely occasion comment.

He booked his ticket for Brussels, and entered the train. A change would be necessary at Dusseldorf. In his carriage were already seated two or three civilians, professional or business men. They bade him good morning. The train would leave in a quarter of an hour. He stood with Rosa. Few words were exchanged.

She placed her hand through his arm, he held her fingers lightly in his hand.

"And now, Rosa, you will return to Hatzberg. The image of your beauty remains with me . . . our little hour."

Grant entered the train already panting with impatience. He held her hands and kissed her lips, a stray wisp of her hair caressing his cheek. "*Auf wiedersehen.*" He leaned far from the window, his hand reaching towards her until a bend in the track hid her from view. He then seated himself in the corner deep in his own reflections. The short journey had no event—his companions solicitous and friendly. The change at Dusseldorf brought him back to his task.

After a short wait he embarked on the journey to Brussels. The train was full: his compartment crowded, officers and civilians. Grant was glad indeed that his companions were his junior in rank. This contributed a natural defence against embarrassing questions. The conversation was of small experiences. He had been wounded in the fighting on the Somme in April. Now he was returning. He lent a ready ear to criticism of the English gunnery, the effect of tanks—how the English had bungled that!—to the detailed history of the great German offensive in the battles of the Lys and the various impressions it had made by its victories . . . and disappointments upon the populations of those areas in which the officers had their homes; and of the impression made in battle contact with English, Scottish, Australian and American troops. He heard lewd tales of brothels in Brussels, Lille and elsewhere—flotsam and jetsam of war. It was all valuable. The younger officers found a ready listener, a mirthful companion, a senior officer with sympathy, and their tongues wagged eagerly.

The terminus was at Brussels. Grant with his light haversack sought the first hotel and commanded a room. He must now quickly reach the forward area. He must make certain that the plans now clearly focused in his brain were in fact being pursued. He could not approach the front in the uniform of a field officer. He would excite attention. A change of rôle was a necessity. As a civilian he would be immediately suspect. He must appear now as a common soldier, one of those hundreds of thousands all so much alike passing hither and thither upon a thousand different missions and engaged in a thousand diverse capacities. He would pass unnoticed, he would mingle freely in the towns and billeting areas, tramp the roads, seek shelter in a base camp, any way-side farm house. He could take his chance almost anywhere. The back areas of the battle zone were honeycombed with every kind of formation, men passing to and from leave or the hospitals, transport, laundries, bakeries, road menders, railway guards. He would pass unnoticed.

One condition only was necessary. He must possess himself of the uniform and of the papers, field service book and equipment of an ordinary soldier, and he must obliterate for ever the physical facts of Major Muller and of Major Schaeffer. He wandered out into the streets. There were many soldiers. The taverns and pavements were crowded—a hostile civil population mingling freely and easily with a crowd of soldiery.

A project quickly sketched itself in his mind. . . . He would procure a motor car: then upon some pretext or another he would induce—and the offer of money to the ordinary soldier would, he considered, prove a sufficient inducement—or command, a likely looking lad, to accompany him. He would drive out into the country and then . . . Grant considered. He could not commit the horrible act which forced itself upon his mind. Murder . . . murder in cold blood. He could not do it.

He reconsidered the whole plan. Perhaps he could successfully make the man hopelessly drunk. But that would take time. A drunken man's company is a heavy liability, nor could a major of engineers be observed in company with a bibulous soldier.

His conscience battled with the problem. Duty as an advocate came to its aid with keen cross-examination. In how far did the killing of a German soldier by a British officer differ from the cold-blooded assassination of a thoughtless sentry by a concealed sniper? Was not war, after all, a matter of killing? Did it matter where or how the killing took place so long as it was achieved successfully? Would there not be one soldier less to fight the British? Was not shelling the killing of the unseen by the unknown, and did not the heavy gunners glory in their work? Did not our airmen only last week drop bombs upon Tourcoing? Was this not cold-blooded murder? The risk involved to his whole scheme would be immense if he did not silence for ever the man whom he proposed to rob. He would kill him. Then he would dispose of the body . . . and the motor car, too, and the uniform of Major Muller.

Having once overtaken the qualm of his conscience, he faced the problem with keen interest. He would strip the soldier's body and would array it in the uniform of Major Muller, place it at the wheel of the car, start up the engine, put it in top gear, leap clear of the car as it gained speed, and permit it to wreck itself. He could choose a place where an incline on the road would encourage a triumphant smash. His own underlinen was new: he would remove any marks of the place of purchase . . . and he would himself set fire to the car after the smash, so that the authorities might spend anxious days with inquests, and, he chuckled, would not be able possibly to affix a name to the headstone of the grave of the charred remains. Safe-guarded by the soldier's papers, he could entrain for the forward area, and make his inquiry and observation. But he must first discover a soldier drawn from the area north or south of the sector occupied by the Jäger Corps. He could then approach sufficiently close . . . but not too close.

He went first to his hotel and interrogated the clerk—he must have a motor car . . . but that would be difficult . . . they were requisitioned . . . but for the major, possibly . . . he would inquire. He passed ten marks to the clerk . . . an automobile could be found. . . yes . . . a Benz . . . he would telephone to make the appointment. Grant went out to the garage in the Rue Dolfus, where its proprietor was ready. He drove the car away, leaving fifty marks as good faith with the proprietor; and stationed it in a quiet square near the hotel.

Grant then left the main boulevards and walked into the narrower streets in which the soldiers were accustomed to congregate. Feigning a little inebriation, he entered a tavern. A group of soldiers rose from a table. He waved them back to their seats and com-manded a bottle of wine. He called for more glasses and wine. They were good fellows. He would drink with them. They were going on short leave. The trains ran irregularly—no accommodation until the following morning.

Two men were from the 139th Saxon Regiment occupying the Passchendaele front. One of them, a lad of some twenty years of age, was about his own build. He measured him with his eye. He was a soft-eyed lad, wavy hair, smooth-skinned, too red, wet, full lips, the lower of which sagged sensuously.

Grant turned the talk to home, always an open sesame with soldiers proceeding on or returning from leave. Letter-cases and books came from the recesses of tunic pockets. Photographs, leave papers, tickets were produced—all the trivial trinkets of a soldier's prized possessions. But they would be short of money? The major was well paid. How much had they drawn? Field Service pocket books containing the pay entries were shown. He passed each of the seven men several marks apiece, and then turning to the lad whom he had selected, said: "My servant is not with me. Come and help me with my kit. You can rejoin your companions later." An elder soldier laughed loudly. Flattered by Major Muller's notice and selection, the youth accepted the suggestion with eagerness.

"Good night, comrades, enjoy yourselves."

Major Muller, followed by the soldier, smiling sheepishly, left the tavern. He walked quickly to the waiting motor car.

"I am billeted outside the town," he said, licking his dried lips. The horror of what he was contemplating obsessed him. As the car passed through the pleasant suburbs he chattered hysterically to defeat the ravages of conscience upon his peace of mind. The air was warm, but the rush of the speeding car brought a fresh breeze to his throbbing temples.

They left the long rows of little red-roofed villas set down in square gardens, then the more pretentious mansions with their broad acres in the suburbs, and passed into the open country, travelling at a high speed. Beyond Assche, Grant observed a side road, a rough track from which the ground dropped abruptly to the left side. He slowed down, and, remarking that he had nearly missed the turning, backed the car to the crossing, and thrust his way up the track.

Two hundred yards farther on he stopped the car. "It seems as if there is a puncture in the tyre—offside hind wheel. Jump out and have a look."

As the young soldier turned and scrambled out of his seat, Grant bent down and seized a heavy spanner which he had placed in readiness by his feet.

"My God, I can't do it," said his conscience. "An eye for an eye," said the advocate.

The soldier bent a moment to examine the tyre. He fingered and punched it, dusted his hand . . . then looked up. Grant was kneeling on the driving seat, his trunk twisted, muscles gathered and arm raised to deliver the blow. The insipid smile faded from the face . . . the sluggish intelligence slowly grasped the pending tragedy arrested for a moment in mid air . . . the jaw dropped, the eyes wide with horror gazed into the face of the merry man suddenly turned murderer. The arm descended.

The unholy fire in Grant's brain had died. He looked down. Something lay sprawling grotesquely—almost ludicrously—beside the wheel. No sound, no movement . . . silence.

Swiftly he unclothed the body. The light, thank God, was failing. Poor devil! He exchanged his clothes with those of the soldier—the name was Otto Gedern, 139th Saxon Regiment. It was an unpleasant business, but at least the clothes were warm. He hesitated a little and then clung to his new underclothes : they would comfort him against the obscenity of this new masquerade. He was now fully and properly dressed, and realized that it is a considerable physical effort to clothe an inanimate man.

The task was complete. He raised the body and with difficulty

placed it in the driving seat, the right foot on the accelerator, the leg
slightly bent from the knee—the pressure of the limp, unrestrained leg
would effectively depress the pedal. He swung the engine, and,
standing on the dash-board, bent over and placed the car in gear,
first, second, top. The car was moving nicely. Pulling the wheel
hard over with his left hand, he jumped clear to the right, rolling
on to the grass. Grant jumped up. The car had plunged over the
embankment, and had overturned on to its side where it was held
by two young birches which bent to its weight. The grotesque
figure had slipped from the driver's seat, and was lolling limply over
the side. Grant pushed it back into the seat, locking the right arm
in the steering wheel. He dug the man's bayonet into the petrol
tank and from its squirting filled a tin with spirit. He threw this
over the figure, and drenched the fore part of the car. Then he
struck a match, lit a wad of paper and threw it into the car. Grant
ran, then climbed the bank. The flames greedily licked the spirit.
Grant could see the horrible figure as it were at the stake. The tank
burst with a loud explosion : flames mounted with renewed violence.
The figure was encompassed, then lost in a sheet of flame, dimmed
by columns of smoke.

Grant ran—Muller and Schaeffer had disappeared. Soldier Otto
Gedern remained, with nine days' leave of absence, blessed freedom.

He rejoined the high road and turned west, hurrying from the
glare of the burning car. He could not be far from Alost. He was
in high spirits—Otto Gedern would have a good time in Belgium.
He had no desire to expend his leave in his Saxon home, enough
sorrow and unhappiness there. He possessed the larger portion of
four hundred marks. He had wished to visit the gaiety of Brussels,
and having satiated his desires, he was now seeking the quiet of
Belgian villages where his money would prove the best passport
to hospitality. That was the plan. In an upside-down world, the
idiosyncrasies of one soldier wouldn't worry anyone. He was as free
as the air—his papers were in order. He could spend his leave as he
liked, provided he reported back to the 3rd Echelon of his regiment
upon the prescribed date. He was free.

He walked the road happily. He must now reach the forward
area quickly. He only wanted confirmation of all he had learned.
He would return by train to the forward area, using Otto Gedern's
pass. It was June 8—how he had lived ! He had seven clear days
left to complete his task. On the fifteenth at dawn he would meet
Mayne again, and . . . on the fourteenth—Rosa. Seven clear days
—if everything went well more than time enough; at any rate, ample.
He would make for Tourcoing. It would probably take him a whole

day, the lines would be sure to be congested. Tourcoing would be a good jumping-off place; the 139th Regiment was quite sufficiently far away, but he was near enough, as a soldier proceeding on leave, to pass without comment. He struck a match and examined the leave pass. Ten days granted from the sixth. That was two days ago, and the poor devil had already wasted one day. His leave expired on the sixteenth at 3rd Echelon . . . so did that of Grant, but at Viersberg. From Alost he would board the first possible train for Tourcoing. On the fifteenth he would be able to tell little Mayne from personal observation what kind of mess he had made with the " eggs " he dropped last week.

Grant wandered into a dismal looking inn near the station. A sour-faced Belgian told him he had no accommodation. Grant produced five marks. Acquisitiveness overcame prejudice . . . the innkeeper would see what he could do. Grant accepted the offer in stuttering French and German—the lingua franca of the invading army. He ordered a simple meal and turned in. He was tired, an exhausting, nerve-racking day. He awoke at six, dressed and quickly walked across to the railway station.

He was accosting a blue-smocked railway man when a corporal of military police touched him on the shoulder. For one brief second Grant experienced all the horrors of a criminal apprehended in crime by the majesty of the law. " Show your pass," said the corporal. Grant produced it. It was examined. The photograph of a girl slipped from between its pages and fluttered to the ground. Grant stooped and picked it up. He fingered it in half guilt, his eyes cast down. Damn it all! he hadn't noticed it before—taken in Dresden. He looked up : the corporal was grinning at him.

" You're a long way . . . from her," commented the soldier, jerking his head towards the photograph, " and you're wasting your leave. Better get on the next train through Brussels," he said, not unkindly.

Grant hesitated. " No, corporal, I'm going back. . . . They don't want me at home . . . she doesn't. I'm going back—have a good time Tourcoing way—I know a girl there—have a good sleep and crawl back on the sixteenth . . . I'm fed up with leave."

" You're an odd one. All right, there's a train at nine-twenty-five, over an hour to wait. Come and have a yarn."

They sat in the little waiting-room, now the military headquarters and post. A corporal and three men, greybeards, formed the garrison—two asleep—the other Grant could see dismally guarding the points by the signal box, a carbine slung over his shoulder. A dull place, Alost, except when the leave, hospital, and reinforcement trains passed through. They had been busy last month with wounded from the great offensive, and later division after division from the Russian front had passed through. The corporal was glad of a change of companionship. He had been severely wounded in the lungs at Verdun . . . a bloody business that! . . . now he was cursed with the companionship of men old enough to be his father. Soldiers . . . it made him sick!

"Your train is signalled . . . Good luck," cried the little garrison.

Grant climbed into a train crowded with soldiery. He thrust himself into a seat, yawned and closed his eyes. He feigned sleep for two hours, listening to the conversation. They took him for granted. The men were returning from leave. They had travelled together from Hanover, men of the same division, except one gunner who was too drunk to participate in the desultory conversation. Grant stretched himself and nodded. He lit a cigar and joined in the fragmentary talk, which, as the heat grew, faded away. The train with many delays wandered through the peaceful countryside.

It was after three when it dragged into Tourcoing. Grant got out. He showed his pass at the barrier and walked out into the streets, mingling with their crowded soldiery. He went to the Catholic rest house established in a temporarily disused factory. Then, greatly daring, he wrote a little letter—just love—to Rosa. It would cause no suspicion. Then, regret tugging at his heart strings, he destroyed it. The act might be taking a chance with Fate. He was getting irregular in his meals. He dropped into the canteen, gorged himself, and then joined a group in the billiard-room. He moved about from one group to another: then out into the streets again; drinks in a tavern . . . he was popular, for he had money to spend.

From this group and from that the evidence which he had gleaned from the plan was partly confirmed—the Jäger Corps, disciplinary troops, were occupying the Kemmel sector. There was a rumour that a new Army Corps from the Russian front was going down to the Somme area—so the bluff was being noised abroad.

There was other news too . . . the British bombing raid of the past week had made a devil of a mess of the remount depot, hundreds of horses blown sky-high, and very many others had to be destroyed. Another bomb had narrowly missed the area commander's quarters, and had killed several women employed at the laundry. Several of the bombs, fortunately those which had been best placed, had proved to be duds . . . curse these profiteering manufacturers, was Grant's mental comment. One was embedded in the Rue de Lille. All traffic was diverted and the houses in the near vicinity had been cleared. The town engineers, Belgian civilians, had orders to unearth the bomb and remove it. "They fairly had the wind up," sniggered a staff sergeant who had never heard a shot fired.

Grant knew enough . . . he would strike the road for Wervicq and hope to obtain a lift in a lorry. He must see more. This information was hearsay, good confirmatory circumstantial evidence, but not sufficient. He set out to walk. It was hot and dusty. No lorries came along. Otto Gedern's boots pinched his toes, the heels mocked him at every step, chafing the flesh. The mental strain had been enough : he was beginning now to feel its effects physically.

He reached a wayside inn, now half-past seven. He called for a *bock* of beer, and took off his boots and socks. Both heels were blistered. He stretched his toes. He could not proceed much farther in this condition. . . . Blast the fellow's boots! He sat in a shabby chair beside the road, drinking beer.

Grant was admirably fulfilling the rôle of common soldier. Otto Gedern—fed up . . . and far from home—the silly expression appeared as a rainbow on his mental horizon. He grinned. Well, life wasn't so bad—even as Otto Gedern . . . though his heels were sore. He heard the sound of heavy wheels and a motor engine. He put on his socks and boots quickly and stood in the road, boot laces trailing, tunic unbuttoned, typical soldier returning from leave.

He hailed the lorry driver, who pulled up. Grant offered him a drink of beer : then requested a lift anywhere a bit farther on. The driver in his shirt sleeves, face smothered in dust and streaked with sweat, got down from his seat. He mopped his face with an oily rag. They drank beer. Then both men got up on to the driver's seat. The lorry was going to the Guard Grenadier store depot—load of electric cable.

"Very particular, the Guards," commented the driver, "this bloody stuff has to be unloaded and then reloaded into the Guards' own wagons."

He would be at the job half the night, and had orders as soon as unloading had been completed to return straight to his depot in Lille. He had been for a damn joy ride half round Europe already. He would drop Grant at Garde Dieu—that would be about two miles short of the Guards' store, reflected Grant. He would dearly like to see the store depot and get confirmation of the Guard Grenadier Regiment. It might be a risk.

He inquired : "Don't you usually carry a relief driver?" . . . That was true. . . . The relief had gone sick : there was no one else available and they were in a hurry. Grant volunteered that he

was accustomed to motors and spoke of technique. The driver
allowed him to take the wheel . . . he was satisfied and drove on.

"My leave's nearly up," said Grant. "I ought to reach
Armentières first thing tomorrow morning. Can't you take me on
with you to the depot? I can help you as second driver, and you
could drop me on your road to Lille." The driver agreed.

"Take off that tunic and put it under the cushion." He took over
the wheel again.

"You must look the part," said the driver with a gruff laugh,
passing him the grease rag, with which Grant smeared his arms and
hands, and then reaching the dash-board added dust to his make-up.
They drove on. Night had fallen. A half curl of moon climbed up
over the horizon : a swift car overtook them. They came to a cross-
road : the driver pulled up and inquired the road of the military
policeman who checked his pass. He was given directions—about
half an hour from the cross-road. He drove on.

The shaded beam of a lantern showed down the road. He
reduced speed to a crawl. A voice rang out. "Halt!" The lorry
was pulled up. A sentry came forward. "Your pass and direction
order." The driver produced his oily pass and order. "Spare driver
with you," said the sentry, nodding his head at Grant. The driver
acquiesced. "All right, go ahead slowly—two hundred yards.
There's another sentry there." The lorry moved on and was halted
again. "What is your load?" asked the sentry. "Electric cables."
"Turn in to the right." A sergeant jumped on the dash-board and
blew a whistle. A party of about a dozen men ran out handling a
run-way. They placed it against the tail of the lorry, then swarmed
into it and slowly lowered the great wheels carrying the cables.
Grant had had ample time to examine the men. Guard Grenadier
Regiment all of them. He slammed up the tail board. The sergeant
wrote out a pass. "Hand this to the second sentry. Turn the lorry
here and get out quick."

Grant climbed back into his seat. He could see a number of
lorries and loading parties but could discern no encampment. This
then was only a ration and store dump. The dummy division took
wise precautions. The lorry turned out into the road. The sentry
repeated : "Hand your pass to Post No. 1." Grant delivered the
pass to the sentry, adding "Good night." The courtesy was not
returned : Grant remembered . . . no communication outside . . .
penalty death. These Guards adhered to that order to the letter.
The lorry returned to the cross-roads where the driver inquired the
road to Lille. Directions were given, and they drove on into the
night. The driver indicated a tumble-down village on the

Armentières road. Grant pulled out his tunic and equipment and slipped from the footboard, thanking his friend.

The lorry rattled on, its noise reverberating through the silent village. Grant stood for a moment in meditation. He must turn in somewhere for the night. He walked down the village. A light showed from under the doorway of a large barn. He listened— voices speaking German. He knocked at a small door inset in the great gate. It yielded to the pressure.

" *Wer ist da?*" cried a voice. The light blinded him.

" Returning from leave. I've lost my way. Can I sleep here?"

" Come in," shouted several men.

The focus of his eyes were adjusting themselves to the lamp light. A jeer greeted his appearance, and Grant suddenly realizing that he was in a motley of grease and dust stood grinning broadly. He saw some fifteen or twenty men in various postures of ease, clothed and stripped, reading, smoking, playing cards and engaged in that perennial entertainment of rounding up the ubiquitous louse. He was told that he could find a corner in the straw, the corporal adding that there was a pump in the yard outside.

Grant threw down his equipment, divested himself of his tunic, shirt, boots and socks and went out. The French soap from G.H.Q. was balm but he had no towel. He came back dripping : someone tossed him a towel. Then he drew up to the light of the lamp to examine his blistered feet. His right heel was angry red and raw. A kind soul offered him lint and iodine.

It is a universal habit that when man engages in the self-application of that universal antiseptic, his fellows always watch with intense interest and excitement. Men revel in the iodine comedy. Every head looked up. Grant dabbed the iodine on the wound, winced . . . whew! He had played the comedy well. Everyone laughed.

He was in good company, soldiers in reserve, resting from their tour in the line. He shared a blanket in the straw and slept happily —physically tired. The men were early astir and woke him. He redressed, carefully packing the offending boots with lint. The soldiers passed him part of their breakfast with strong coffee. He was a very smart soldier indeed when he left the billet, and moved off in a northerly direction. The day, the tenth of June, was overcast, a strong north-westerly breeze had arisen and drove the scudding clouds before it. He was only some ten miles from Kemmel. He must see for himself the prisoner division somewhere on the road, and if possible obtain some nearer view of the activity behind the hills. He had a mental picture of what he was seeking.

He took the road for Houplines passing through L'Epinette and skirting Armentières. Grant felt quite at home. . . . Back in Armentières of all places . . . and he laughed . . . billeted inside the lunatic asylum during November in the first months of the war : and then, in the Rue de Nieppe—literally blown from his bath by a crump! . . . living like a water-rat, leg-bound by mud as thick as treacle, while continuous rain poured from Heaven as from a bucket . . . rain fell upon June the tenth . . . Grant, a veritable Jonah, was back in the boat!

The line was very quiet. No one took any notice of him. He walked on, going due north. He came to a canteen and filled his belly. Continuing north, he struck out towards Ploegsteert— " Plugstreet " of bitter memory. He must not go north of a line lying roughly between Kemmel and Courtrai, and he must give the appearance of leaving or rejoining his regiment, which lay in the sector some miles north-west of this line.

He sought shelter with an engineer group engaged in road upkeep . . . yes, he was a bit off his beat . . . he would have to make a detour . . . The Jäger disciplinary division. They laughed uproariously. They had been engaged keeping a section of road in good repair for three years. Life was pretty good, food, warmth, comfort, entertainment, and buxom Belgian girls in the village. . . . Roll on the war! . . .

But the Jägers, and, of course, the silent division quartered with the Guard Grenadier. No one knew anything about them . . . from the Russian front, new allies; possibly released convicts—God knew! Each day a large party went up the line for training with the Jägers . . . the ideas of the staff were crazy, the ways of authority to be marvelled at . . . no, they did not work that section of the road but he would cross the Menin road at Wulverghem . . . The camp would not be far from there.

Grant went out again into the rain. Heavy dark clouds had gathered and the rain was descending heavily. He was soaked to the skin. He came to a rest camp—fragments of every regiment and corps. He would shelter for a while. He saw some men of the 19th Saxon Corps, but not the regiment of Otto Gedern, deceased. He avoided them, and mingling with the crowd, laid aside his equipment, and took off his tunic to let it dry. He purchased a flask of cognac and ample food at the canteen and again set out. He reached Gapaard cross-roads where he learnt that the main Courtrai road was " *Verboten*." That probably would be the way to the camp of the 15th Composite Division.

He must secrete himself and watch the road. He walked about

two miles north, then leaving the road, passed through fields of corn, now bowed and dripping with the rain. He could see the telegraph poles along the forbidden road leading diagonally across his path to Courtrai. He followed a trench which divided the fields, corn from barley. The high, yellow barley stretched to the edge of the road to which it yielded with reluctance. Grant plunged in among the wet stalks, and moving carefully forward so as not to disturb their appearance from above, crept to within about ten yards of the roadside, from which position through the stalks he could see clearly, being shielded from above by the thickening ears of the barley and veiled by the criss-cross of whiskers.

He lay down to wait. The rain had slackened to a steady drizzle. The barley ears dripped steadily upon him . . . seven . . . eight o'clock. The road remained deserted. He was cold and chilled to the bone. The rain had ceased. The flying clouds opened fitfully to admit a shaft from the setting sun. Dusk crept about him and the road remained silent. He took another nip of brandy and chewed bread and cheese. His limbs were stiff, he was cramped and began to shiver with cold. Night fell. It was very dark. Grant stood up, flinging his arms cabman-fashion to revitalize and warm his cramped, cold limbs. He slapped his thighs with his hands, beat his chest and had another nip of brandy. He was prepared to stay all night, if necessary all next day. He was at the end of his task. Identification of the 15th Division was vitally necessary. Alternately he sat in the midst of the wet barley and stood up for exercise.

Then he heard the heavy thunder of a column of motor lorries approaching along the road from the east. That would be from the encampment. He stretched out among the barley stalks, dragged himself a little nearer to the roadside, and bent the stalks above his head.

The column was quite near. The lorries carried no lights. The first drew level. He dimly saw the outline of the covered wagon, the driver and the silhouette of a soldier seated beside him. A second, a third, four, five . . . twenty-five lorries passed at a few yards' distance from each other, moving steadily. He could see nothing but the dim shadows of the two men on the driving seat, and the outline of the wagons. Twenty-five lorries. That would mean five or six hundred men, if they contained men. Grant cowered down again in the barley, stretching farther forward. More lorries began to pass . . . two and then . . . an open wagon. Four . . . five . . . more and more . . . Grant could see the silhouetted heads of men, bodies packed tightly on the floors of the jolting wagons.

Twenty-seven wagons passed, mostly uncovered—a host of men.

Then all was silence. Cold banished fatigue. The hours, with intermittent rain storm dragged by, Grant punctuating his boredom with brandy, cheese, chocolate, and humid bread. The wind had relaxed and Grant's clothes hung heavily from him, those next to the skin clinging with a clammy embrace. A cock crew in the village, then another. Light, shadowy and unreal, stole upon the deserted countryside. Grant, to warm himself, ran along the grass flanking the road. Then he heard the muffled sound of motor engines, the trundle of wheels to the west.

He fled back, re-entered the field by the trench dividing corn from barley, and crept back to his hiding-place. The roar increased. He covered his hands, sank his body to the earth, scarcely dared raise his eyes, his green cap pressed down over the forehead. He noted the driver : close to him on the near side sat an armed soldier of the Guard Grenadier Regiment. The wagon, a covered one, had passed. Followed another, a similar soldier; then . . . another. The back of the wagon was open. Grant could see heads, bearded men mostly. Another wagon . . . Grant's eyes were for its tail end. It was closed. Another; it was an open wagon, twenty, possibly thirty heads, some bearded, the shoulders were dirty, earthy. The back of a man rested on the tail board. It was streaked with clay. Grant knew that clay . . . its yellow, mawkish colour. Lorry after lorry passed. Grant failed to count. These were no ordinary soldiers, bearded and dishevelled, the spruce Guard Grenadier in charge so different. The column passed on.

Rain fell again. Grant had had sufficient confirmation. It was the twelfth of June. He was shaking with ague. He took out his flask of cognac . . . the smell of spirits always made him shudder in the early hours . . . he drained the flask. Its stream warmed the course of his throat. He was seized with sickness, retched and sank limp with perspiration, fatigue and chill against the side of the ditch. He must get away from this place. Precaution fired him to action. He broke into a jog-trot across the sodden fields. He would rejoin the Tourcoing road, anywhere. He stumbled on, avoiding the index of telephone posts indicating roads proceeding north. So he went on for an hour, or more. It was after six o'clock. The weather looked more hopeful, but it was still overcast. A strong flight of aeroplanes passed overhead going back to their hangars. Others, high up, droned their warning patrol.

He came to a farmhouse. It was astir. A thin wisp of smoke curled lazily from the crumbling chimney, to float awhile in the still air before fading into the dim haze above. Grant walked in through the tiled porchway. The inviting smell of coffee smote his nostrils.

Madame *la bonne femme* was busy with her pots; bowls were upon the table. A yellow-haired youth sat blinking at the table, two little girls were seated upon a bench, the elder weaving her younger sister's tousled hair into plaits. He bade them good morning, and asked for coffee. He threw down some marks upon the table as the first move in the game of diplomacy.

He told them he was going home on leave. . . . Poor boy, he was tired, hungry, yes? . . . and from the *sales tranchées* . . . his mother, wife, sisters, sweetheart, would be glad to see him? She prattled on. The sight of the marks had worked wonders with her day-to-day heart. He was wet through, yes? . . . he must draw up to the fire. She poked it vigorously. Grant took off his tunic. A cloud of evaporation was drawn off. He must dry everything . . . he would catch his death of cold.

So, with gladness, he divested himself of all his clothes, and naked yet quite unashamed, for the first time since he set out, Duncan Grant, lieutenant-colonel, without camouflage, uniform or decoration, as God made him, mothered and fussed over by this Belgian housewife . . . he sat before the fire sipping hot coffee, the clothes of Otto Gedern, soldier deceased, steaming before a cracking fire.

The farmer came in from the cow byres. His wife nodded to the marks still lying upon the table. They were a passport. He extended a welcome, drank his coffee, ate cheese and bread and went about his daily task. The woman brought him a blanket and she wrapped it around him. He slipped forward in his chair; his eyelids were heavy. He blinked at the glowing embers, then pulled the blanket closely round him. His head sank upon his chest. He slept. His work was done. Back to Barmen . . . and Rosa.

* * * * *

In the snug warmth of the blanket before the blazing fire, the exhausting nervous tension of the past few days relaxed, the physical hardship banished, Duncan Grant had slept deeply.

A light hand shook him. He was roused to that half-consciousness which, in the warmth of blankets, is so infinitely pleasant. Thoughts chase each other by selection through the quietness of the mind. He drowsed with visions of green fields, and waving corn, soft lapping seas and shingled coves, the cottage and the stook, rolling hills, glen and moorland stream. His mind refashioned the days when all the world was young, the smell of the loam, the music of the stream, the tang of the myrtle berry, the caress of the upland breeze, and the sight of the rolling purple hills. He recalled schooldays in the pleasant vales and cottages of Berkshire, shrouded in a blue film of smoke and haze; the minarets, waving palms, and placid waters of the Nile, the red-roofed villages of Surrey; the snow-capped peaks, forests and temples of the Indian foothills; the whole kaleidoscope of a regimental soldier's joy days, hunting, fishing, shooting, in good company; but always he bent his wayward mind to that picture of shady glens, purple hillsides, and triumphant peaks of the Highlands which formed the background to a face set in a golden halo . . . Rosa.

The housewife shook him again; the sleeper awoke. It was high noon. A savoury smell greeted him. He blinked at the hot embers, stood up, yawned, and stretched his limbs, the blanket falling from his well-knit frame. A loud laugh greeted him. Little heads turned, and, remarking his nakedness, sniggered and buried themselves in plates of steaming vegetables and bread. The man, returned from his farm work, was engaged upon his midday meal, the children, too, at the table, the good wife busy with the cooking and service, snatching a bite, or a sip of coffee, in the intervals of her work. The man, munching a husk of bread, spluttered in his deep guttural : " *Ne dérangez vous, c'est tout égal.*"

Grant was at home. The woman tossed him the dried garments and trousers, into which he slipped, and then set before him soup, bread, cheese, and coffee. Grant was amply rested, his spirits high. He permitted his command of the French language to excel the dictates of caution and conversed merrily. They were fed up with the war, its restrictions, impositions, requisitions . . . otherwise things went on much as usual . . . the messes were good customers with good money, and . . . there was always the washing done for officers.

Grant nodded with delight. Here was a nation divided in twain by two invading armies of different races, with no common language. The peasantry were suffering untold hardships and inconveniences; they knew little of the causes of the war, nothing of its strategy and wide-flung campaign; but it had its compensations—vegetables and eggs at famine prices to the invaders, and . . . there was always washing to be done for officers. He rocked with laughter. The midday meal over, he placed ten marks on the table. Ah! he was a *bon garçon* . . . God would protect him. That, too, was amusing ever—the conception of God as some kind of unseen, remote, charity organization society handing out His Divine protection to those who paid in good cash for small earthly services and often grudging hospitality. The peasants were like the gypsies on a Derby Day . . . " Gawd bless yer pretty faice, dearie," as the shillings passed from the smooth, small hand of the lady to the horned, dirt-engrained paw of the woman of the caravan.

Grant put on his tunic; then sat to gird again his feet in Otto's boots. In the soggy dampness of the leather, they had passed unnoticed. Now, dried before the hot fire, they resisted his feet as would a small size in steel armour. Madame bent her muscular frame, and seized the obstinate footwear. Her strong thumbs kneaded the hard leather with tallow. Her sinewy arm basted toes and heels. They resisted a little less; and, Grant hoped, the shrinkage would try his heels the less. He slung his pack and equipment, and went out into the day. The sun shone again, but not too hotly. He had all the appearance of a soldier from the trenches, unshaven, unwashed, his hair tousled, uniform coated in the mud from the barley field in which he had lain. Specks of rust tinted the steel of his rifle and equipment. He was going on leave. It was the eleventh of June. He still possessed three days of freedom and . . . he had been delayed . . . *une affaire* . . . a little too much to drink . . . a little sickness. But much could be done with three days' leave.

He struck the road to Tourcoing. A light railway, used for carrying stores, engineering apparatus and artillery ammunition ran beside it. An empty train with odd details of men, sick, lightly wounded, the miscellaneous from the battle front sat on the empty trucks. It puffed busily along. Grant ran : willing hands took his rifle and pulled him into a moving truck. Now he would have a little peace from Otto's boots. The train rolled into Tourcoing. He went down to the station and presented his leave warrant. The transport officer jeered at him for a fool, then more kindly bundled him into a waiting train filled with soldiers. They were in merry mood. Grant now familiar with the front could without restraint take an easy part in the conversation. He was enjoying himself.

The train was bumped into sidings, where it remained for hours, while convoy after convoy of wagons, propelled by panting engines, pushed past—material of war, guns, limbers, men, always more men of every formation and from every kingdom, principality and district in Germany. The stage was being set, reflected Grant. The merry spirits flagged. The night was spent in jolting and shunting with little eastward progress. It was the morning of the twelfth and the train rumbled into Brussels. Six hours' delay. Grant sat in the canteen, listening to chance gossip. He dared not go out into the streets for relaxation.

Evil thoughts preyed upon his mind which the activity and

interest of the past forty-eight hours had banished . . . the murderer revisiting the scene of his crime . . . he must occupy his mind. He would buy a new pair of boots. So he went out and fitted his feet with the extravagance which every gentleman loves—good, well-fitting boots, not quite adaptable to the grouse moor, a little too . . . well, they lacked the square toe, homely, intimate, leathery appearance of the brogue or shooting boot from a bespoke maker in one of those shy turnings off Regent Street or the Strand. A little too flashy, made to look the part, to proclaim a shooting boot—he thought of Tartarin—but they were well-formed, soft, clinging, and comfortable—good, comfortable boots. No longer would he be dogged by the footsteps of Otto, nor would his feet at every step chant a *Danse Macabre*, in requiem to a battered figure at the stake.

The qualms and fear which afflicted the conscience of Duncan Grant were becoming doped by the advocacy of reason, of logic and of duty. No one ever truly lives who carries a load of self-denial ordinances and penances. They are the dugouts of cowards, the funkholes of the afraid. All progress depends upon untrammelled mental ability and activity. The smaller things of life, lived thus, fall into their proper perspective—a killing at a cross-road to frustrate a devilish design, to enable a victory with consequences which would reverberate throughout civilization and amid remote savagery. Poof! . . . Grant had no rabbit-hole for his conscience . . . and the haunting boots had gone.

He returned to the canteen. There was a further delay. Two o'clock on the twelfth. How he longed to tell Rosa that he was coming probably a little earlier. He dare not. The train would leave for Dusseldorf at seven o'clock in the evening. He busied himself with chance gossip—a tale here and there. Each yarn brought confirmation to all he had read and seen.

He boarded the train, empty goods-wagons returning to the great arsenals at Dusseldorf, Crefeld and Elberfeld. There was a two days' congestion of leave: men were herded into the wagons. They sought rest anywhere on the wooden floors, packs stacked as pillows against the creaking sides, rifles and equipment, sufficiently hap-hazard to irritate a neighbour and to devastate his chances of peaceful sleep. The train drew out from the station, fitfully, making loud protest and raining showers of coal dust upon the wagon roofs. There was little ventilation. All the confused smells of unwashed, well-fed humanity rose to choke the heat of the night—sweat, tobacco smoke, damp, unwashed clothes, food, spirits, wet leather. Some were drugged and slept fitfully in their corners, or against the wagon walls. Those less fortunate who occupied the centre of the floor kicked by restless sleepers, discomforted with equipment, cursed freely and perspired . . . the stench appalled.

Daylight, after the long night was welcome. The exhilaration of anticipation again gripped the men. The train rumbled over the points, then came to a standstill. The wagon doors were thrown open—Dusseldorf. The soldiers, thirsty, hungry, unwashed, mud-soiled, and their eyes blood-shot with fatigue and the suffocation of the night, hair tousled, partly dressed, swarmed out upon the platform where coffee, soda water, ginger bread cakes were prepared and waiting. Kindly, quiet women, from some voluntary organization, ministered to the wants of these elemental, rough and roughly-used men, but whose blasphemies were strangely stifled in their presence. As hunger and thirst were appeased, each collected his equipment, and the grey-green mass disintegrated into small groups bound for their several destinations.

Grant examined the direction board on the main platforms. There was barely an hour before the first train to Barmen, a workmen's train, similar to that which had carried him to the front. He washed, shaved off a two days' growth of beard, and then seated on the platform cleaned his rifle and equipment. The train drew into the platform. He climbed in with a score of mechanics and artisans. In less than an hour he was in Elberfeld. He alighted and was lost in the hurrying crowd, waving his leave warrant to the blear-eyed official as he passed through the ticket barrier. He entered a restaurant and partook of a very good breakfast. And now for his final plans . . . and Rosa.

Mayne would meet him in two days' time. Supposing he did not come, or there was an accident in landing . . . two possibilities. What then? . . . supposing the aeroplane was wrecked, or shot down on the return to the British lines . . . what then? The information which he possessed was of supreme importance. At all costs it must reach the Commander-in-chief within two or three weeks at the latest. At any rate Grant must improvise two lines of communication with G.H.Q. A memorandum outlining the plan must be prepared in duplicate. He himself must take one, the other . . . ? There was no one but Rosa. But how? What could she do? And the effort and strain were far, far more than she could possibly undertake. He pondered. He paid for his breakfast, then entered a shop and purchased writing materials and carbons for copying. He would find a quiet place to prepare his memorandum and draw the sketch maps. Perhaps an idea would occur to him as to how Rosa could help. But she would know best; she would have ideas, but he dared not enter the village of Hatzberg. Perhaps he could send her a note by a messenger or telephone to the Stadt Baurat asking that a message be given her.

But Heaven knew . . . Rosa might already be under suspicion, even in difficulty. Grant struggled with the desire to see her, prompting always his designs and plans. Then he discovered himself unreasonably creating barriers against such a meeting, when more than probably their brains—and hearts—in co-operation could find a solution of the problem. Grant decided upon communication. He went to the public telephone . . . could he speak with the Stadt Baurat? . . . Why, certainly . . . was it possible to speak with Fraulein Maurer? . . . Oh, yes, it was important—a friend with news from her sister. But Fraulein Maurer was not well, she was in her apartment . . . Grant insisted that the matter was important . . . they would bring her to the telepone. . . . He must tell her somehow in the first breath of conversation that it was himself.

" *Fraulein Maurer?*" he inquired, eagerly awaiting the sound of her voice.

" *Ja, hier Fraulein Maurer.*"

" Is all well with the widow?" That sentence would surely indicate himself.

" Yes, yes." Grant intervened rapidly. . . . She must say nothing. " I must meet you quickly, important news of your sister. At the tramway terminus by the Quellen Strasse, twelve noon. You can do this?"

" Yes."

" And no one knows?"

" No one."

" *Auf wiedersehen,*" and he hung up the receiver. Rosa again, blessed news. He went out, took the tram car to the Quellen Strasse, and with two hours to wait, crossed into a shady clump of trees and shrubs, took off his equipment, unpacked the writing materials and settled himself on his stomach, elbows resting on the ground. The memorandum must be concise, definite. It must briefly set out the simple facts. He commenced writing.

Grant considered his notes. He could say no more. It was impossible to convey in words the magnitude of the operation, the seriousness of the situation, the threat to the safety of the British lines.

Then he re-wrote his memorandum carefully stressing the main points of the message in capitals, and underlining the passages commanding action.

URGENT. IMMEDIATE ACTION.
VERY URGENT.—To G.H.Q. W PLAN.

1. Major Muller, buried Neuve Eglise, June 2, was engineer in charge gigantic offensive operation.

2. Germans have extensively UNDERMINED sector from YPRES to LYS using new engineering (Messer) process.

3. UTMOST SECRECY has been kept. Jäger Corps know nothing of this operation.

4. MINESHAFTS are sunk East of MONT KEMMEL and STEENWERK. Exact location undetermined. (See plan.)

5. Underground GALLERIES extend from KEMMEL and STEENWERK westwards for about six miles.

6. Plan provides for SEVEN EXITS approximately at LOVIE CHATEAU, The POPERINGHE-STEENWOORDE Road, ABEELE Railway Station, KRUYSTRAETE, FLETRE, STRAZEELE Station, LA MOTTE.

7. Three EXITS are probably now complete, at LOVIE CHATEAU, FLETRE, KRUYSTRAETE.

8. Galleries are in two strata, upper and lower, intercommunicating.

9. GENERAL OFFENSIVE IS PLANNED TO COMMENCE FIRST WEEK AUGUST (possibly a little later). SIXTH AUGUST the date by present order.

10. ATTACKING TROOPS WILL EMERGE from UNDERGROUND at Seven Exits preceded by explosion of MINES.

11. Two ARMY CORPS with armoured cars and cavalry in advance will be utilized.

12. Concentration of two army corps in the SOMME area is a skeleton blind. A feint attack will be made against AMIENS.

13. Objective of Main Offensive—CUT COMMUNICATIONS from CHANNEL PORTS and Capture the latter.

14. Whole resources of German Armies to be thrown into this offensive.

15. 15th Composite Reichswehr Division is conducting whole mining operation. This consists of PRISONERS of WAR— British, French, Russian, Italian. IN GERMAN UNIFORM. Guard Grenadier Regiment are with them as guards and German soldiers as interpreters. Encampment is west of TOURCOING. Exact location undetermined. Large parties proceed to and from Shafts by night in motor convoys. Route passes GAPAARD X Roads.

16. Sketch plan attached.

WHOEVER RECEIVES THIS MESSAGE DISPATCH SECRET UTMOST URGENCY TO G.H.Q. TO G.O.C. IN C. AT ALL COSTS.

Transmitted through two sources at 5.0 a.m. June 15 by the man who went to find the W Plan on June 6 last.

URGENT   URGENT   URGENT

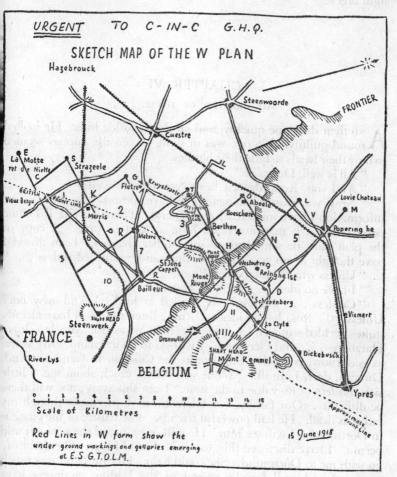

The memorandum was completed. Then he prepared the map in outline. The details he could not supply without the aid of the plans and papers in Rosa's possession. Would she bring them with her? He had plenty of time. He folded the papers, placed them in two envelopes, and secreted them in his tunic pocket. Then he repacked his equipment, and wandered down to the seat at the tramway halt. Twenty minutes still remained. He lit a cigar, thrust his hands into his pockets, thrust out his legs, and with his head thrown back idly watched the smoke curl into the air and drift away in the light breeze.

CHAPTER VI

THE GREATEST OF THESE. . . .

A ND then she came quickly, and sat down beside him. He looked round guiltily. No one was in sight. Even the poplars seemed to bow their heads to hide their blushes.

" All is well, Duncan?"

" And you, Rosa, dearest heart, you too are well?"

" Now we must plan again. I have almost two days. The information I have must reach the general. There is a risk if I alone possess it that it may not reach him, at least in time. A copy of the plan must be sent through some other channel. I am afraid I have thought of no way in which this can be achieved unless . . ."

" Unless what?" intervened Rosa.

" I have no idea . . . no . . . none."

" Confess . . . confess," she smiled at him. " And why not? Unless . . . Rosa has an idea . . . now listen to me. I have already quite decided—indeed it was my first news for you—to leave Hatzberg . . . and Germany. I will go to Switzerland. My sister, as you know, is Mother Superior at the Convent in Geneva. And, Duncan, dear, I am ill. No one will bother much about me, a little sick *fraulein* of no value to the state. I can slip away; nor will there be difficulty. Our family, von Gleiwitz, have privileges though my father is dead. He had powerful friends. The trustee of the estate is in Dortmund. I will see him. He will recommend the passport and permit. I have discussed this, too, with Frau Muller. She desires to go with me to Dortmund. She could help. Her husband was much respected and well loved: several of the leading engineers have studied under him. She will help me if necessary. That has been my little surprise. Then quickly I will go. I will be near my sister and live quietly in the mountains. My sister has asked me many

times to go, but I have not cared. I have had strength for a little
work—which I have loved—service which no one else would do.
From Switzerland," her eyes brightened, " I could write to you,
dearest, and you to me. We should be near to each other."

Rosa spoke slowly, wistfully; she choked a little. " Perhaps . . .
I could . . . live for you, Duncan, and I could carry the plans to
Geneva—is that what you wish? . . . Duncan, can I do that . . .
for you? It would not be difficult . . . for Rosa von Gleiwitz. Then
I can . . . yes, I can pass them through to the English Legation."

" Rosa . . . dear, what a wonderful idea . . . one of perfection
. . . but I fear it will not be so easy to obtain the necessary pass.
It will take time, of course. But do not . . . promise me . . .
harm yourself in this endeavour . . . you will promise, Rosa?"

" I promise, Duncan, to do my best . . . for you."

" Then you shall . . . we must discover a quiet retreat. I am on
leave. You are my wife . . . Rosa? We will go to the Barmen
Wald. You will perhaps know of a little inn where we can stay.
The tramway will take us. We can sit in the wood, you and I, Rosa,
we may plan . . . and love. And you have brought the plans with
you, Rosa?"

" I have everything."

Hand in hand they sat under the shady poplars, the leaves
beating a merry tattoo in the light wind, two lovers, almost
unnoticeable, the soldier and his maid sitting beneath the trees, at
the head of the Quellen Strasse. The tram came. Rosa and Duncan
seated themselves shyly amid approving and smiling faces. Alighting at the Neumarkt they crossed to the south of the town and
boarded the light railway to the Toelleturn. The woods greeted
them and soft hills rose in salute. They found a little inn, the
Schutzen Haus, an unpretentious wooden structure with a large
restaurant, a popular centre upon Sundays and holidays. They were
most welcome . . . for one or two nights . . . why certainly. The
good *haus frau* was delighted . . . nay, honoured. . . . The soldier
had come from the trenches . . . and now with his bride . . . they
should feast and be given the best guest-room. The patriot rose in
her buxom bosom . . . more, it should be the room of honour. So
they lunched; and then taking the plans wandered into the wood.

Duncan made a little nest of pine needles, a cushion of moss for
Rosa, and there seated, on a summer afternoon, the light of a high
sun dancing a fairy ballet through the close leaves, they examined
the plans afresh. The memorandum in its two envelopes was
rediscussed. Rosa would take one copy . . . she would fold it and
secrete it in her clothes . . . she would think out a method . . . she

would sew Duncan's copy into his tunic. He took it off for her examination. It would, she considered, be safest in the stiff lapel of the collar. This could be unstitched and the memorandum and map inserted on either side. She would finish that in the evening. Duncan opened up the haversack and brought out the writing materials. Together they drew the W Plan upon a sketch map showing the threatened sector. The drawing of the plan occupied some two hours. Each had a copy. They were folded and placed in envelopes.

Grant considered. " Rosa, what will you do with Muller's papers? You cannot take those with you."

" No, that would be unwise."

" I think I will take them," said Grant, after reflection. He placed them together, and slipping them into his tunic buttoned them securely in.

" Now, Rosa, as to your plans . . . not one day . . . even for ourselves, should be lost."

Rosa sighed. " Tomorrow . . . not today, Duncan . . . I need you for a little hour . . . then I will go back to Hatzberg. I will tell Frau Muller that I am ready. We will go to Dortmund the next day; and, then . . . Duncan . . . I will do my best . . . I cannot say. . . . But I will reach Switzerland."

The evening hour closed in. The long shadows stretched themselves upon the grass, the warm glow of the setting sun gently caressing two lovers who had forgotten all but the serenity of devotion which now filled four barren years.

At twilight . . . the little inn : and night . . . so quiet, so peaceful.

*   *   *   *   *

Duncan walked with Rosa to the little station. A lover's farewell . . . and he was left to his own thoughts and plans.

Less than twenty-four hours remained. He would wander slowly to Viersberg through the woods. And he would hide among the trees and shrubs, first disposing of his rifle and equipment which made him now perhaps an object of curiosity and remark. He plunged into a lonely pine copse. With his bayonet he dug a trench, and laid in it his rifle, covering it with earth. He walked on to another clump of trees and similarly disposed of his bayonet, pack and equipment. Then he strolled on.

He partook of a meal at an inn, purchasing bread, cheese, dried meat and a bottle of Kirsch. He plunged again into the woods, moving south-east. As night fell he walked rapidly to the course of the upper stream. He could not tell precisely at what point he had met it, but judged his position to be north of the rendezvous, and the moon was not yet up. He waited for some hours in darkness. By the light of the moon he followed the pathway, which followed the course of the stream, walking in a southerly direction. Everything was well. He passed the saw-mill at the water's edge, finally reaching the marsh. There he paced up and down to test its surface after the recent rains. The level of the river was considerably higher and the marsh a little spongy to the tread. He paced its surface carefully. He must find the place of most severe resistance for Mayne's landing, as far up river as possible. Even if the aeroplane landed well it might have difficulty in gaining sufficient speed to rise off the heavy ground. This reconnaissance of the ground took considerable time.

Grant was glad to be able thus to pass the anxious hours. He found his nerves in a state of high tension. The creak of a branch made him start, the sound of a snapping twig chilled him. He placed his cap to mark the best position for alighting. Very early in the morning he would flag this point with his shirt and Mayne would see the signal. The night dragged on. Grant munched a little bread and cheese, and swallowed a mouthful of Kirsch. His nerves were on edge . . . anti-climax was setting in.

He watched for dawn. He felt it slowly coming, though the stars persisted in their brilliance. Alternately he watched them, and the east, for a paling of the dark pall of darkness. Almost suddenly it seemed to grow lighter. He listened, straining his hearing. He re-examined the ground, then taking off his shirt laid it out upon the tufted grass.

Light was wading in upon the darkness. He listened. He strained his eyes to pierce the bluer blackness. The stars went out one by one . . . an orange streak painted the horizon . . . he could now discern the trees, the curve of the river.

He gazed up into the vanishing night. . . . Dawn . . . the sun rose triumphantly. He searched the heavens anew. Light painted them orange, yellow, deep blue, paling to cerulean and cobalt.

He began to fear. But Mayne would come . . . must come.

The sun as if by great bounds mounted before his straining eyes . . . the skies were clear . . . the trees threw long, fantastic shadows on the ground. The sun mocked him. He began to tremble, prayed incoherently . . . Mayne must come, he almost screamed. My God! He stifled a sob. The hour of safety had passed . . . yet hope remained. He gazed up into the limitless roof of Heaven, hand to ear—no speck in the sky . . . no drone of an engine. He grew cold, the perspiration of fear drenched him;

hoping without hope. The sun climbed always up, now painting the landscape in all its summer clothing. He stumbled back to the trees . . . hope had vanished. Colonel Duncan Grant wept.

Then hope came again to his rescue. Perhaps the date had been mistaken; or something had gone wrong. He would wait. Tomorrow Mayne would come : the sixteenth. The marsh would be drier still under the heat of another day's sunshine. He pulled out his flask and drank deeply of the Kirsch. The warming spirit buoyed him. He put on his shirt, marking the landing spot with a large stone. He would wander in the woods, or watch a fisherman higher up. There were peasants and woodcutters. He could obtain food. He sauntered up the river bank. It was deserted. Four miles up he met an old man accompanied by two lads. They were rolling logs towards the swollen stream. He was on leave . . . nothing much to do . . . he would help them for a while. The physical energy required would soften his nervous tension.

He worked hard, furiously, the thoughts playing mad hide-and-seek in the recesses of his mind . . . Rosa was leaving for Dortmund, and Mayne would come tomorrow . . . a log splashed to the river's edge. That was a heavy one. . . . But why hadn't Mayne come today? Hell! . . . he laid his shoulder under the end of another log, raised it with all his strength, every muscle taut . . . it tipped on end . . . almost like tossing the caber at the Inverness games . . Rosa . . . purple hills . . . the sun, curse it!. . . painting the loch, orange and red . . . and, as he threw the log forward . . Mayne is coming tomorrow.

It was midday . . . the men drew out their meal. He would share it? The physical work had been as a tonic. Hope now ran high. He toiled all day happily, then returning in the evening with the peasants to their wood-built home. Plenty of food was hidden within the house. He told them stories of the trenches : the old man nodded . . . he remembered 1870 . . . the boys sat agape.

Before dusk he bade them farewell, and wandered back along the river's edge to keep his silent vigil. Clouds had drifted over curtaining the stars. A light drizzle fell and the night was muffled in black. Grant made a covering of pine needles, and propped his back against a tree trunk. His eyes were heavy with sleep, his heart with disappointment and bitterness. His courage was ebbing . . he wanted Rosa. His head dropped forward. . . . This was surrender . . . he forced his eyes wide open, staring into the darkness. He must not sleep. He must think clearly. Suppose the aeroplane did not come tomorrow or . . . was it yet today? He must discover some new way out . . . he was wide awake now.

He must make an appreciation of the situation . . . what a bright idea? . . . Just like being a kid again. Appreciate the situation . . . dear old Sandhurst, cavalry sketching board, a bicycle, canvas case fitted with many coloured chalks, his whole body hung round like a Christmas tree with field glasses, clinometer, map case, and . . . a pub with good beer at Frensham . . . appreciate the situation. . . . " The Blue force holds the line from—" Bunkum. . . . Why! they hadn't even visualized a war of three dimensions, in the air, upon land and sea . . . and . . . underground . . . the W Plan.

He dared not wait indefinitely for an aeroplane, not even after tomorrow. But, of course, Mayne would come. But . . . suppose he did not. One line was secure. . . . Rosa would be able to get through to Geneva, but . . . Heaven knew when! If the wheels of the German bureaucracy turned as slowly as those of Whitehall, the pass might be granted in two, three or six months' time. Slow, yes, but sure . . . if in time. And if Rosa could go through Switzerland so could Colonel Grant, or Otto Gedern—but . . . in a different manner.

Did it matter if he were interned? He would declare himself a British officer. The Legation would substantiate that. Then he could hand over his information. Interned . . . Grant began to wish for that—on parole with Rosa beneath the shadow of the great white peaks in which he had climbed, and loved so well. His mind fashioned a new life of love and perfect tranquillity. He must reach the Swiss frontier.

But Colonel Grant had been transformed . . . the spectre of wretched Otto Gedern loomed before him . . . Otto, soldier of the 139th Saxon Regiment whose leave expired on the sixteenth of June . . . tomorrow.

What a jest! . . . Mayne was coming and Otto would take French leave . . . to France.

Always it came back to him—appreciate the situation. Mayne . . . Mayne might not arrive. Grant must reach the Swiss frontier. At Bâle would be the nearest point. Trains would be running but he could not enter a railway station. He no longer had a valid pass. He must board a train going south, always south, following the course of the Rhine . . . it must be at least two hundred and fifty miles—so many miles full of danger, of the risk of detection. He could board a goods train in a siding; that would be safer than a passenger train.

Perhaps he could change his rôle . . . as a plate layer this time, and hop from train to train. He yet possessed an ample supply of money—a little palm oil would accomplish wonders. At least he could cover a large part of the journey by rail, probably by goods train . . . that would be the way of least resistance . . . no curious officials or inquisitive police scrutinized the passage of a goods train. The engine driver and the stoker were fully occupied with steam pressure, coal and signals; the guards were concerned with brakes. He could discreetly make the necessary inquiry as to the destination of the wagons, secrete himself amid the miscellany of a goods siding near Elberfeld and board the train as it slowly moved out. The stations were well marked. He could note these and jump off as the train slowed down before signals, or, in shunting operations, if it turned at a junction in a false direction. The process could be repeated, or perhaps later he could steal a bicycle. There were many ways, but he must avoid the towns and the inquisitive. . . . But, of course, Mayne would come. . . .

The dark night passed slowly, the trees dripping a tattoo upon the hard ground. Grant stood up, yawned widely and stretched his limbs, drank Kirsch from his flask. He discovered a day's growth of beard on his chin . . . he was dirty and disreputable, hardly a credit to the Inverness Regiment . . . not even to the 139th Saxon Regiment. A distant cock called a strident note, the first herald of a new day. An hour and a half, perhaps two hours more, he judged. He gazed up through the dripping branches: the rain had ceased, though the pines still wept great tear drops. He left the belt of sheltering trees and re-examined the landing ground. The rain had soaked the tufted dry grass, but, underneath, the earth surface remained firm.

Through the mist of the passing cloud the stars peeped down upon him shyly. Cock crew again, answered by a jealous neighbour. Mayne was coming . . . he would soon pass overhead flying down towards the Ebbe Gebirge . . . he would wheel round and land . . . then breakfast, blessed breakfast, for two, and later . . . a bath, blessed bath. The auto-intoxication of high hope touched him. He paced to and fro upon the landing ground. He sought the stone: the darkness was breaking . . . he found it readily. Mayne is coming! Clouds and rain might have held him up a little.

The east paled, then light began to steal upon the western world. Mayne is coming! . . . in a few minutes now. He strained his eyes to pierce the cloud.

He heard a drone, surely an aeroplane . . . but, no . . . he had always heard that sound . . . damned monotony . . . only the rush of the stream. Mayne must come! He clenched his hands until the bones stood out white. They were raised in supplication.

"God! . . . speed Mayne," he muttered in anguish.

It was light.

He spread his shirt again, and paced the landing track, angrily kicking the tufts of grass as they rose and defied his footstep. Grant prayed, then cursed. Mayne must come! He walked almost in a delirium of fatigue and mental anguish. Half an hour passed.

He stood still. . . . Blast them! He was forgotten! . . . but . . . little Mayne . . . he would come! No aeroplane appeared. Hope . . . courage . . . deserted him. Tears welled into his eyes, a great sob choked his throat; something unexplainable, unknown, undiscovered . . . snapped; and Grant abandoned himself to his grief, stumbling back to his little nest among the pines . . . he was forgotten.

Sleep, that kind, unseen nurse of the broken, whose soft ministrations bring new hope, new life to the mourner and the afflicted, gently took him, pillowing the weary head upon the pine needles, closing the hot, anguished eyes. Duncan, the child who had lost his plaything, cradled in his nest beneath the trees, slept the sleep of utter exhaustion.

* * * * *

He sat up and rubbed his eyes. He was refreshed, infinitely so. He looked out through the trees. There was his shirt, laid out to dry. He jumped up and shook the clinging pine needles from his clothes. Of course, Mayne hadn't arrived. There was no time to lose. He must begin the adventure over again. Everything seemed so very long ago. . . . Frau Muller . . . and Rosa. All like a dream. He had been asleep. Otto Gedern . . . dirty dog who had overstayed his leave.

He went down to the river, and splashed the cool water over his head and breast; and scooping it in his hands, drank. He put on his shirt. There were the plans, the bulky parcel of papers thrust into the inside pocket of his tunic. He could not carry these any longer. They would have been useful. But he had all he wanted . . . the essentials. He would burn the W Plan. He re-entered the wood. The thin curl of smoke would not be observed above the tree tops. He struck a match. The papers, plans and maps burnt slowly. He watched them . . . then as they warmed, a sheet of flame gripped the mass—how like his last conflagration on a small scale—it twisted the blackened papers . . . smoke enveloped the flames. Grant fanned it with his hands to dissipate the incriminating signal above the tree tops.

G.M.N.—P*

The fire flickered, then went out. The W Plan had disappeared.
He threw earth over the dead embers, stamped upon it, then,
turning on his heel abruptly, strode westwards. He would not be
worried in Elberfeld; everyone was too busy. He picked up the
light railway and followed the track to Barmen, left it outside the
town, threaded his way through the pleasant gardens of the southern
suburbs of the town, and strolled across to the Bahnhof Steinbeck.
He peered over the fencing at the sidings, busy with shunting and
loading. He joined a group of workmen loafing beside a gateway
giving entrance to the goods yard . . . casual labourers . . . there
was always a job in the goods yard . . . short of men. Then having
crossed to the station and filled his pockets and haversack with
refreshments and another flask of spirit he rejoined the group.

A call came for loaders. He pushed his way among the workmen,
taking his check-in pass from a railway official at the pay-box beside
the gate. With two others his task was to load drums containing
chemicals. He examined the chalk marks, indicating destination,
drawn upon the wagons. They were consigned to Crefeld. He
edged away from his task and sought another working party : they
were loading pit-props—destination Courtrai. He returned to the
task, working hard and methodically, chaffing his fellows for their
tardiness. He sidled away from them, the task more than half
completed, and strolled round the yard. Four men were loading
large barrels into an open wagon. The destination was Mainz.
The barrels were heavy. Grant lent his aid. He peered again at
the chalk marks. . . . " Despatch 16th June " . . . today. Mainz
. . . that would be well on the way. The barrels were empty—
tallow vats—a musty smell pervaded the atmosphere—nauseating,
rancid. He struck, as if accidentally, the top of a barrel as he thrust
it up towards a man standing in the wagon : the top tilted a little
under the force of his blow. Grant had decided he would travel to
Mainz in a tub . . . the cynical wisdom of Diogenes . . . the
cunning of Forty Thieves.

The task was completed. He noted the exact location of the
wagon in the sidings. He must give up his pass, then he could
scale the railings later, and under cover of darkness board the wagon
and clamber into the tub. He accompanied the men to the gate. He
must conserve his rations, so entered a small restaurant beside the
station, filling his stomach. He lounged about the station until dusk,
then hastily looking around to see if he was observed, pulled himself
to the ridge of the fencing and jumped lightly to the ground the
other side. He waited in the shadow of the fence, holding his
breath. He had not been observed. He ran quickly, threading his

way through the wagons. He broke into a walk as he passed some
railway men engaged upon a routine task. Scrambling under some
covered wagons he reached the siding. He spied the truck which he
had been loading in the morning. He clambered up quickly. The
tops of the tubs did not show above the level of the wagon line. How
the place stank ! . . . tallow.

As an engine noisily shunted he beat open one of the tubs and
climbed in. The stench nauseated him, but . . . he would get used
to it. Another long wait—agonizing, uncomfortable, beastly. Then
the wagons were shunted together. He was jolted horribly in the
tub. Men came and hitched the couplings. After hours, as it seemed,
the long line drew out. The journey had started. During the night
he could sit at ease and in comfort on top of the tubs, or lie at full
length. By daytime he must be careful . . . no looking for men,
honest or dishonest, at midday . . . wise Diogenes would merge his
personality into that of one of the Forty Thieves . . . he would
forsake Greece for Baghdad . . . and, if only he could, escape at
last from the appalling stench of tallow!

The long convoy struggled fitfully, yet it continued with little
delay. Night passed. Grant wriggled into the tub. By pressing his
knees against one side and his back against another he could rest in
comparative comfort. He pulled the top lightly over his head.
Playing at Diogenes was really rather fun . . . if only the barrels
had been clean. From time to time he would cautiously tilt the
top of the tub and look over its edge, straightening his body. He
stood upright and could peer over the edge of the wagon and note
the names of the stations. They were following the course of the
Rhine, had passed through Koln and Coblenz, and were nearing
Mainz. Grant peeped out and noted Bingen. He would be alert
now. When the train slowed down, or preferably halted, as
undoubtedly it would before Mainz, he would emerge from his tub,
clamber along to the brake van and jump off from its lower step.

The train was passing through the market gardens, and beyond
he could see the domes, spires and chimneys of the fine capital city
of Rhenish Hesse. He pushed up the lid of the tub, sliding it upon
its neighbour. He looked round and saw that he was unobserved.
He jumped, pressing up with his arms, and scrambled along the
tops of the tubs, upon which, for a moment, he lay at full length.
The train was slowing down with brakes applied. He ran quickly
to the brake van, swinging himself into it and jumped down upon the
metal step. He glanced out and forward, to the left and to the right.
He chose a place to alight which afforded the almost immediate
cover of a clump of poplars and low shrubs. The train was slowing

down, the couplings of the wagons, as they were jerked and compressed, making a deafening sound. Grant jumped. He stumbled against a sleeper, recovered his balance and, running for cover, threw himself among the shrubs. The long convoy of wagons was passing. No guard looked his way as the train vanished towards Mainz. So far so good . . . now he must move on.

He leapt up and began walking towards the city, striking the road at Amöneburg. The hour was now after six in the evening. He was about to enter a small restaurant when suddenly he met his appearance in a mirror advertising a popular wine. His face was grossly unshaved, his clothing creased and marked with stains. The restaurant was filled with people taking the pleasure of a summer evening away from the busy city. Grant turned and hurried away, but . . . he was hungry.

He entered an inn, unkempt and poor in appearance, its ragged façade and windows covered in dust. Three bicycles were leaning against the wall. He pushed into the dimly-lighted, rudely furnished *wein stube,* and called for wine. The workman lounging against the counter nodded to him. Grant requested supper, throwing upon the counter a twenty-mark note. The slattern cut bread and dried meat, piled the plate with fresh green vegetables and potatoes and passed it over to him. He ate greedily, reflecting, and feeling sorely tempted by the bicycles . . . but there would be an immediate cry, and he was in such thin company as to be too noticeable. He took up his change, and sauntered out, proceeding towards Mainz.

He entered the suburbs and replenished his pocket rations at a shop and having inquired the way to the railway station, he walked in the fading light down the Mombacher Strasse to the Haupt Bahnhof. He hoped there to discover another train proceeding south through Baden. Grant considered that it would be an advantage to be shaven. He would still pass as a soldier on leave as long as he avoided the possibility of scrutiny and examination by police or other officials. But he must not permit the time taken over such a luxury to militate against the immediate journey.

He sauntered up to the busy railway station and passing it walked upon a bridge from which he could view the metals and rolling stock, and probably discover the way of entry to the goods yard. He perceived long lines of wagons being loaded, and crossed over to the goods yard, walking beside the high fencing until he came to a gateway. It was closed. Through the crack, Grant could see a small box lighted by an unshaded electric bulb. A railway official was seated reading a newspaper, obviously on guard over the gate in order to prevent intruders.

Keeping his eye to the crack, Grant pushed the gate very gently. It began to yield to his pressure. He pushed it a little farther. The man looked up over his paper. Grant felt his eye meet that of the guard, who leaned forward a little. Grant held his breath. The man resumed his reading. Grant waited, then pushed the gate again. Damn! It creaked on its hinges. The eyes looked up. Then the man rose from his chair, newspaper still in hand and looked out of his box. Grant stood very still. The guard laid aside his newspaper and crossed over to the gate. He observed that it was opened. Then he looked round the gap, observed the unkempt dirty soldier, told him to go to the devil and slammed the gate. Grant heard the key turn on the inside.

Curse it! He must find another way. He could, of course, pass through the main entrance of the station, then slip down upon the track and make his way to the goods yard. That would entail risks, but he would adopt the habit of a wounded man from hospital and cultivate a generous limp. He approached the main entrance walking slowly, his right leg trailing with assumed difficulty. The main hall was thronged with people, men and women and soldiers, of all classes and grades. He limped through the crowds to the turnstiles leading to the platforms and track ways. He noted that at those barriers conducting to local train services the officials were perfunctory in their duties, while at others leading to the main lines, the tickets and passes were carefully scrutinized.

It was of no importance to Grant from which platform he dropped down upon the track. If he were held up at the barrier he could readily excuse himself that he had no ticket, and, of course, he could purchase one for a short journey. He joined a crowd of workmen and artisans at a barrier. As he limped a man offered his arm. Grant took it, while those in front allowed them precedence of entry. The official allowed them easy passage.

Grant was now on the platform, and thanking the man for his courtesy, sought a seat. He would jump on to the track at the end of the platform when the train had passed out. It came in, waited for a few minutes, its carriages filled, then a whistle blew and the train steamed out. Grant rose, and forgetting his limp, walked to the edge of the platform.

He felt that he was being watched from the barrier. He slowly turned his head. A soldier was looking at him . . . one of the military police. Grant feigned an unconcern which certainly he did not feel. He lit a cigar and strolled up the platform out of sight of the barrier. He would wait a minute, then run like the wind and disappear.

A step echoed from under the archway. Grant's heart beat in his throat. He dared not turn his head in the direction of the footstep. It approached slowly. Grant turned and confronted a military policeman, a domineering, big man. His thumbs were thrust into his belt, his legs wide apart. A cynical smile smeared his red, meaty face.

"So, you're a wounded soldier, are you? . . . And which leg hurts the most?" he guffawed . . . "Show your pass," he ordered abruptly.

Grant measured him under his eyelids . . . the man was big, certainly, but the spread legs made him a fair target. Grant unbuttoned his tunic pocket saying: "It's all right, corporal," and withdrawing his pass with his left hand, swung his weight behind the right with closed fist, and struck the unbalanced man full under the jaw. His great legs sank and he dropped.

Grant turned and ran. He jumped from the platform down upon the track. He heard a savage voice shouting after him. Grant fled towards the goods yard. The voice followed him. A man jumped out as if from nowhere to impede his progress. Grant swept by him. He could hear the voice in his wake . . . he was being followed . . . a cry had been raised . . . the warning whistle of a train blew behind him . . . he looked over his shoulder and saw the bright red lights of an engine with steam up bearing down upon him . . . he jumped to one side . . . a passenger train was passing, gaining speed, a yard from where he paused . . . a crowd yelled behind him . . . Grant leapt to the train . . . his fingers found a handrail . . . he pulled himself up on to the footboard . . . his face was against the glass of a carriage window, through which he could discern the travellers. They looked up in astonishment at the sudden apparition. Grant pulled himself to the forward side of the door, and opened it . . . hands helped him in.

"Nearly missed the train," he gasped, for lack of a better introduction with which to excuse himself.

"Karlsruhe train," said someone.

"Thank God," breathlessly gasped Grant.

An official came for the tickets. Grant still possessed ample money and to spare to cover the journey—Rosa had ensured that. The collector eyed him suspiciously. After leaving Worms the official entered the compartment, and scrutinized him closely. Grant began to feel very discomfited . . . the train was moving too swiftly for him to jump off again . . . and perhaps, he was unduly anxious . . . the train was proceeding fast. . . . At Karlsruhe he would be well on his journey . . . from there it would not be so difficult . . . the train drew up outside Karlsruhe station by a signal. Grant considered quickly . . . he would jump off . . . he had had enough of railways . . . he would bicycle, or become a civilian, unsuspected and respectable.

As he was thus sunk in reflection the collector reappeared. Close behind him was a sergeant of the military police with an escort. Grant looked up. It took him a second to reach for the door handle. He bounded for safety. Hands like a vice gripped his right ankle. He pitched forward, striking his face against the foot-board. He was dragged back into the compartment from which the other passengers had fled and now stood in the corridor excited and anxious. Grant's face was bleeding freely from a severe cut. His wrists were handcuffed behind his back. The sergeant thrust him into a corner of the compartment nearest to the corridor. Grant smiled at him through the blood which dripped from his cheek.

The sergeant spoke. "We've had a message about you from Mainz. Let's have a look at your papers." He reached forward unbuttoning Grant's tunic and took from his pocket his leave pass and other papers. "Leave to Dresden," he commented, "Soldier Otto Gedern, 139th Saxon Regiment; leave expired morning of the sixteenth. So that's it, is it? Posing as a wounded soldier at Mainz, struck the military policeman on duty at the station, and now we've got you at Karlsruhe.

"You're a deserter. You'll be charged with desertion, and with striking your superior officer in the execution of his duty." He smiled broadly. "You haven't got much time to live, Otto Gedern. We don't waste much time over these matters nowadays."

Grant said nothing. He was at the end of his resources, a captive. Sickened by the blow which he had received, he continued to smile stupidly through the clotting blood on his face.

The train drew into Karlsruhe. The sergeant hustled Grant out of the compartment, and handcuffed him to the escort. A crowd gathered—one or two soldiers who looked on sympathetically, curious boys pressing close about the escort . . . in Karlsruhe this was all they saw of war and they liked to register its rare impressions—some unlucky devil handcuffed to a policeman, hustled and hurried through the streets . . . a sleek, comfortable man shook his fist in Grant's face; a fragile woman caught in the crowd turned her head not to see his bloody face; a workman laughed. The sergeant strode ahead, pushing aside the gaping, curious crowd which closed up again behind the escort and its victim as they passed from the station to the military barracks on the outskirts of the city.

The sergeant dropped back and walked beside his prisoner and escort. Now that his duty was accomplished he was beginning to feel a common humanity with his victim. He spoke to him. "What's the game anyway? . . . Trying to desert?"

"No," said Grant.

That, in fact, was the truth, and he very fully realized not only the ignominy of his position, but the impossibility of extricating himself from it. The sergeant would have to make a report, the more complete the better for his reputation. . . . "Did you strike the corporal of military police on duty at Mainz Station?"

"I did," said Grant.

"What for?" queried the sergeant.

"Oh, I don't know," said Grant wearily, "perhaps I didn't like the look of him." The sergeant laughed.

"Even if you aren't a deserter, as you say, you'll receive sentence for striking your superior officer . . . in the execution of his duty. You know that, don't you?"

"Yes, sergeant," replied Grant, yawning. "When I've had a sleep I can tell you all about it. . . . Let's leave it till the morning."

They entered the barracks. A group of young soldiers were lounging by the gateway. "Make way there," shouted the sergeant. They withdrew on either side, gaping at the unshaven, dirty, blood-stained figure as it passed. Grant was taken into the guard-room, his wrist unfettered from that of the escort. The sergeant of police went through the formality of handing over the prisoner to the sergeant of the guard. Grant was pushed into a narrow cell, its only light proceeding from the barred grille above the door. The handcuffs were taken from his wrists. He asked for water. He drank, and then sponged his face, drying it with a soiled handkerchief. Then taking off the stained tunic and folding it under his head, he stretched himself on the plank bed, and slept.

CHAPTER VII

SUNSET AND SUNRISE

THE morning sun of the sixteenth of June painted the façade of the creeper-clad mansion and its gardens with all the vivid tints and quiet shadows of an early summer's day, bright emerald melting into deep olive greens, scarlet and crimson offset by opaque purples, yellow and orange piled upon russet and browns.

An elderly butler, clad in a green apron, watering-can in hand, moved with spongy tread among the flowers and ferns, which banked both sides of the porchway leading to a massive, double-fronted door. A host of additional, though small, duties had fallen upon him, since the general mobilization of men for service; but, with the help of the head gardener, whose age and years of devotion to the Blesch household vied with his own, he filled in the mosaic of a day's duties with serene composure and exactitude.

Hearing the sound of footsteps, he pushed the watering-can upon one side among the flower pots and hurried busily into the house, closing the door quietly behind him. He bustled to the pantry, stripping off the green apron, and quickly slipped into the black coat of his higher and appropriate office.

A bell rang. The doors of the Blesch house never opened quickly to the unexpected caller. Having allowed a few dignified minutes to elapse, the butler, who had tiptoed across the marble floor of the great hall, ceremoniously opened the doors. Two women stood nervously between the flower banks. The younger, advancing, asked if Herr Blesch was at home. The butler, in reply, with dignity said: "The Herr Kommercienrat Blesch receives no callers except by appointment."

"But you will tell him," said the woman, "that it is Fraulein von Gleiwitz who desires to speak with him."

The old retainer stood back shading pale eyes with his hand, and gazed at her. "Pardon me, *fraulein,* surely not the daughter of Graf von Gleiwitz?" he inquired.

"The same," replied Rosa, smiling, "and this is my friend, Frau Muller. We desire to speak with Herr Blesch."

Restraint and dignity fell from the old servant. He stretched out trembling hands in welcome.

"Your father was one of our oldest friends, Fraulein Rosa. Ah! and I remember you so many years ago, our little golden Rosa, but" —he paused, holding her thin hand in his own—"you seem cold, you are not well, Fraulein Rosa. . . . You will come in. . . . Ah, pardon, I had forgotten myself; pray come into the inner hall and be seated. The master himself is not at home. . . . He has great affairs. . . . This terrible war. . . . He is always busy with immense responsibilities."

He conducted the women across the pillared hall to a wide lounge, from which stairways led to the upper apartments, and offered chairs.

"Herr Blesch is not at home," he explained, "but the countess, his wife . . . perhaps you may know her . . . is, I think, in the library, and I will acquaint her of your visit."

Then he moved away with clasped fingers, a new buoyancy in his gait, muttering cheerfully, in search of the countess.

The Countess von Arenfels, the second and young wife of Herr Blesch, industrialist, sat before a wide escritoire engaged upon a correspondence which increased always with her husband's ramifications in the control of manufactures and of men, and with her consequent duties as hostess. The line of her nostril and the curve of her lip connoted a superiority which the blending of aristocratic inheritance with new-found wealth had amplified, while the restlessness of head and hands implied an impatience and irritability, which gave place to a certain cold charm only when she was the focal point of social activity arising from her husband's affairs.

To Herr Blesch, the social status, youth, classic beauty and ability of the countess were valuable assets. His first wife he had loved; the countess he regarded as capital on the credit side of his estate, so far not depreciating in value : nor had the countess herself any illusions upon the point. Herr Blesch denied her nothing, but his own time and intimacy, and she responded faithfully, if cynically, to the bargain.

The butler quietly opened the door, paused and discreetly awaited the countess's pleasure.

" Well, what is it, Joseph?" she inquired irritably, without looking up from her desk. " I am very busy. I observed two women pass the window. What do they want? You know I never see people of that class. If it's some claim, tell them to submit it by letter through the appropriate organization."

" No, madam. These ladies are not ordinary callers. They desire to see the Kommercienrat."

" What nonsense, Joseph!" interrupted the countess. " I expect you to have more sense."

" I beg your pardon, madam. It is the Fraulein von Gleiwitz, a daughter of the Graf von Gleiwitz, a very old friend of the Kommercienrat . . . in the old days, madam. I remember the *fraulein* as a quite little girl. I felt sure madam, the countess, would see her."

" I'm very busy, Joseph. . . . I have told you. What does she want?" exclaimed the countess tapping a toe with impatience upon the parquet floor.

" That I do not know, madam, but if it is your pleasure, I will show the ladies in. The Graf von Gleiwitz was very closely associated with Herr Blesch, and the *fraulein* seems ill. If I may say so, I feel sure that the master would desire that you should see this lady."

" As usual, Joseph," said the countess dryly, " you are indeed presumptuous. You may be right : at least, I can save my husband the inconvenience of an interview. Show the ladies in, please."

" I thank you, madam." The butler retired, while the countess seated herself again before her desk, ensuring, however that her back was turned a little farther towards the door, from which, by experience, she realized that her profile could be seen with advantage mirrored in the gilded overmantel.

The door re-opened. In quiet tones the butler announced : " Fraulein von Gleiwitz and Frau Muller to see the Countess von Arenfels," and then closed the door behind them. The countess did not raise her eyes from the desk for some moments, and then glanced at the mirror, meeting the timid inquiry of Rosa and the widow. She rose slowly and turned.

" Ah," she said, " the *fraulein* . . . I did not properly catch the name . . . but no matter."

" Von Gleiwitz and Frau Muller," interposed the widow.

" Why, of course," said the countess, " friends, so Joseph tells me, of the Kommercienrat . . ." she paused, " from the old days. . . . We are living in different times now. . . . He is, as you may know, very occupied, his days, hours, minutes, engaged in the service of the state. . . . Perhaps I can, what shall I say ? . . . assist you. Ah, please be seated. . . . Forgive me. . . . I forget others, as his wife I have little time for such relaxation.

" I do not recall the name, von Gleiwitz. It is some years since you have seen my husband. Yours, of course, will not be an ordinary social visit. You will have, I presume," said the countess with a slight sneer, " some favour to prefer, an interest, perhaps, relating to my husband's more obscure past. I endeavour, where possible, to relieve him of such small irritations." And, smiling unpleasantly, she added : " You may confide in me."

Rosa was distressed by the chilliness of the reception, and her tongue tied by the querulous austerity of the countess.

Frau Muller spoke. " It is very good of you, countess, to receive us. We had hoped rather to make an appointment convenient to Herr Blesch. It is a small matter that has brought us to see him, but one in which his good offices can greatly assist the daughter of his old friend, the Graf von Gleiwitz. Perhaps you have observed, countess," she continued, " that Rosa is very far from well. She has been ill now for many months, and has been advised to go to a sanatorium for treatment in Switzerland. There are difficulties about passport formalities. We felt sure that the Kommercienrat, by virtue of his high position in the state, could facilitate such matters."

The countess, flattered by this reference to the power of the Blesch household, smiled with genuine pleasure. "I am quite certain," she said, "that my husband can assist you. It is, as you say, a small matter, and you may leave it with me."

Rosa leaned forward in her chair, a new animation lighting and flushing her face. "That is most kind of you, countess. My father and Herr Blesch were colleagues, and I came often to this house. When old Joseph opened the door, I felt just as if I had come home again."

The pleasant smile on the face of the countess withered. "Joseph," she said, "is a veritable encyclopædia as to the past ages, but a little inconvenient and embarrassing to me with his reminiscences."

Rosa, realizing that she had touched a delicate spot, continued quickly: "I have been urged by my sister, who is the Mother Superior of the Convent of Santa Maria, at Geneva, to come to Switzerland. My health, as my friend, Frau Muller has told you, has been failing. Your very kind offer of help relieves my anxiety. It is most good of you."

The countess relaxed a little. If she had little in common with her husband, at least she studied his interests with meticulous care. This was a small matter. It would please Herr Blesch to assist this pale and sickly child of his old friend. She would unbend and be gracious. "My husband will not return until dinner time. You will be our guests for a few days, perhaps. We are understaffed and a little primitive," she said. "Have you luggage with you?"

"Oh, dear no," replied Rosa, laughing. "Our small requirements are at the station."

"Very well. I shall send for them, and will have rooms prepared for you. It will be a happy surprise for my husband when he returns," added the countess.

Later, while the widow sat upon the veranda dreaming before gay borders and cool lawns, Rosa and the countess walked quietly in the Dutch garden. The two women were of an age, socially of equal distinction. The countess was drawn towards this frail and lonely girl. She surveyed her, and saw that she possessed both beauty and rare charm. She became friendly, took Rosa's arm in her own, and invited confidence. Rosa had desired that Frau Muller should make no mention of her hurried betrothal to the Major Schaeffer, and her secret would certainly remain inviolate in the Blesch household.

The countess, with her own sterile love, breathed sympathy for the beautiful girl, whose illness had removed her from the grand emotions. She expressed, too, her own disappointments and found Rosa a sympathetic listener.

"Ah," she said, "your music must bring you consolations. For myself, I direct my desires into business channels. For my husband I am a kind of female dragoman, labelled wife for convenience. He has no interests outside his affairs. I am his prisoner, but I can never get close to him. . . . I am, I think, on the whole, satisfied. You are free, Rosa : when you are well, perhaps your music will not suffice."

Rosa remained silent, her eyes upon the ground, thinking of Duncan.

"We have much in common, Rosa. It will be a real pleasure to me, as I know also it will be to my husband, to have you with us for a few days, until this matter is arranged. You will, too, be able to entertain a young officer, who will be with us in a short while. His father—you probably know the name—is Herr Messer, my husband's closest business colleague. I do not see him," she added acidly. "You perhaps know of his reputation in Elberfeld; but the boy is a soulful lad." She paused. "He has lost a leg. He has a great future, I believe. Do you know him?"

Rosa shook her head. "No," she replied, "we have not met. I live very quietly."

"I sometimes think," continued the countess, "his experiences have made him a little light-headed; and, of course, his life at home . . . his mother died from shock some months ago, when she lost two sons . . . his life is impossible. Your music, I am sure, will comfort him. What I have seen of the boy is attractive; he has dangerous views, but he is discreet. . . . Now you will like to rest before dinner," the countess concluded, "you will make yourself entirely at home. I have matters which need attention, but I shall look forward to further little talks with you." She took her hands in her own and kissed her with affection.

Dinner was not served until nearly nine in the evening. The ladies awaited the arrival of Herr Blesch in the drawing-room. He entered swiftly, a man of fine presence, over six feet in height, of firm figure and muscular gait despite his fifty-seven years. He kissed his wife lightly, passing with hands outstretched to Rosa.

"Our little sunbeam, little Rosa. How like your mother!" he exclaimed. "The same expression, the same hair. It must be nearly ten years since we met. . . . This is indeed a pleasure. . . . And Frau Muller, of course . . . your husband was a genius, a great man. We owe much to him in these days." He paused, then in lowered and serious voice continued : "And your son, my dear lady.

I trust that all will be well. . . . You have my deepest sympathy in what I know must be your present anxiety."

"Oh, dear, oh, dear," exclaimed the widow brightly, " I assure you I have no longer any anxiety. I am . . ." Rosa regarded her searchingly and anxiously . . . " I am quite sure," said the widow firmly, " that he is safe."

"Then you have received news?" asked Herr Blesch.

Rosa intercepted, covering her own anxiety. " Frau Muller," she said quietly, " has her faith, and in that she trusts."

"Naturally," replied Herr Blesch, " faith is a wonderful comfort in these dark days. We few who are familiar with the work of your son must, too, have faith. You have courage, madam, which I am proud to say is an example to myself." He dismissed the subject with a sweep of the hand. " Now let us dine."

The intimacy of the dinner table was a happy one. Herr Blesch, who, as Rosa had perceived, was disturbed by the disappearance of Major Muller, of the circumstances of which he obviously possessed a fuller knowledge than did the widow, was grateful to Rosa for her interception. An embarrassing moment had passed, and he was glad to talk of the little affairs of Rosa's childhood, and of the distinguished days of Professor Muller's occupation of a Chair of Science at Bonn University. But he carefully avoided any further reference to Major Ulrich Muller. As to the passport and necessary visas for Switzerland, there would be no difficulty. He hoped within a few days to be able to conclude the formalities, and would press the matter forward personally through the Foreign Office without delay. He was delighted to have two old friends as his guests again, especially since, as he could observe, Rosa and his wife had already established the intimacy of friendship.

Five days passed in comfort, rest and quietness. Before dinner on the twentieth of June, a motor car brought Lieutenant Messer to the house. Rosa and Frau Muller were in the garden reading. Herr Blesch would return for dinner. The lad had important letters from his father to deliver, and these would require, perhaps, some verbal explanation. The three women went into the dining-room and were joined by Herr Blesch and the lieutenant some ten minutes later.

"Permit me to present the Lieutenant Messer, a very gallant officer of our air forces, and the son of another old friend, Herr Adolf Messer. Perhaps you may have met him in Barmen, Rosa?" said Herr Blesch.

"I am proud, indeed, to meet you, *Herr* Lieutenant. But we have not met before, I think," said Rosa.

"Fraulein von Gleiwitz lives in Hatzberg," interposed the countess.

"Oh, yes, but I go out very seldom," replied Rosa. "I live near my friend, Frau Muller."

Heinrich Messer bowed to the widow.

"Ah, how interesting!" exclaimed Frau Muller. "You will know my son, Ulrich, perhaps? He has spent much time at the works with your father. He is an engineer."

Herr Blesch grunted assent.

"Surely he cannot be Major Ulrich Muller of the Corps of Engineers?" questioned Heinrich.

"Why certainly! And you know him?" asked the widow eagerly.

"I could not say that," replied Heinrich. "He is a very great engineer. My father says he is a genius; one of Germany's master brains. No, I cannot say that I know him."

"Then perhaps you know his friend, Major Schaeffer?" put in the widow quickly. Rosa looked across at her and frowned, catching her breath, but Frau Muller did not observe the glance. "Major Schaeffer has just been with us for a day or two." The widow turned to Herr Blesch. "It was he who gave me the first assurances as to Ulrich's safety. But, of course, Herr Blesch, as you know, I never doubted."

"I know, I know, of course. . . . But who is this Major Schaeffer? I have not heard his name in connection with . . . ah . . . Major Muller's activity."

"Probably not," laughed Rosa, determined to turn the conversation, "there are so many majors of engineers. Just a friend, I think."

"Oh, no," said Frau Muller warmly, "a very close friend. His most intimate. You do not do him justice, Rosa. Major Schaeffer was with him everywhere in his work."

"I think I should tell you, Frau Muller," interposed Heinrich Messer, "that I was not right in giving you to understand that I have not met Major Muller. Certainly, I do not know him. But just a few days ago, an officer spoke with me, very kindly, in the lounge of the Imperial Hotel in Barmen . . . only for a few moments. . . . I did not know his name, but he was a major of the Corps of Engineers. . . . He was very courteous and friendly to me. . . . I observed that he was a resident in the hotel, and I asked the clerk his name. . . . I then realized that I had been honoured indeed. . . . I saw the signature at the reception desk. . . . It was Major Ulrich Muller."

The widow leaned across the table towards Lieutenant Messer, her face animated with excitement. She caught the look of fear in Rosa's eyes. There was a still silence for some seconds, then a fork dropped with a tinkle upon the widow's plate, and she fell back limply in her chair. The countess hurried to the widow's aid, and sought to compose her. Herr Blesch was speaking; Rosa, pale as parchment.

"You spoke with Ulrich Muller in Barmen, Heinrich?" he questioned. "Are you sure? Major Muller has been missing since the fifth of June. You observe the shock which you have given to his mother. Are you sure? For me and for your father, the fate of Major Muller is of the utmost importance."

Heinrich appeared bewildered at the consternation which his remarks had caused. "Of course it was Ulrich Muller. I saw his signature in the register."

Rosa had been thinking rapidly. She must protect the identity of Duncan at all costs. This inquiry was leading along a difficult path. "There are probably a score of Ulrich Mullers in the army." she said with forced gaiety.

"Describe the appearance of your acquaintance. That will quickly clear the matter up," demanded Herr Blesch.

"He was tall," said Heinrich quietly. "I should say six feet; sandy hair, blue eyes, big boned; hands, large and practical, just as I thought he might be."

"That might be a description of our Major Ulrich Muller," said Herr Blesch grimly. "But you are positive the eyes were blue, Heinrich?" he questioned. "And you noticed his hands? Had he any fingers missing?"

"No, certainly not. As to his eyes, I am quite sure. I marked him particularly. I saw him again the following day with a woman, heavily veiled, and he waved recognition to me as he was passing through the lounge."

"You are sure," pursued Herr Blesch, "that you would have noticed had fingers been missing from his right hand?"

"Positively certain," replied Heinrich, without hesitation.

"You may compose yourself, Frau Muller," said Herr Blesch kindly. "There is certainly some mistake. I am sure your son was not in Barmen; nor could he have been."

"I heard what the *Herr* Lieutenant said," replied the widow faintly. "It is odd. His was a description of Ulrich's friend, Major Schaeffer . . . very odd."

"Or a description of anyone else," added Rosa gaily. "This must have been a practical joke, or perhaps someone wished to hide

his own identity from the curious. One can never tell in wartime "
—she laughed—" can one, *Herr* Lieutenant?"

" It seems queer to take the name of one's friend, who is, as I
understand, reported missing."

" Very queer indeed in the circumstances," added Herr Blesch.
" You will excuse me, ladies. I have important matters to which to
attend. You will not be anxious, Frau Muller. Heinrich, when you
have finished, please join me in my study."

Conversation languished. Both Frau Muller and Rosa were
obviously greatly disturbed. Heinrich after a few awkward minutes
made his excuses and joined Herr Blesch in the study.

The Kommercienrat was seated at his desk. " Sit down,
Heinrich, I want to talk to you. I have already telephoned to the
chief-of-staff. There is as yet no trace of Ulrich Muller. The name
of Major Schaeffer is not known. I must tell you, in confidence,
the facts. Muller was reported missing after an English raid. He
was, as you have said, a genius, and responsible for certain engineering plans of high importance to me and to your father, and to the
state. His loss has greatly disturbed us. You are positive both as
to the name and as to the correctness of your description of the
man?"

" Quite positive," replied Heinrich. " I remember, too, my
conversation with him very well." Heinrich related his experience
of having seen the aeroplane, and of his talk with the major of
engineers. Herr Blesch listened with grave attention.

" However painful this may be to Frau Muller and to Rosa, too,
I must question these ladies closely. There is something very curious
about this matter. It may be, as Rosa suggests, just a practical
joke, though I can scarcely believe it. I shall require you to be
present. We must discover the identity of this Major Schaeffer.
Now let us go to the ladies."

When Herr Blesch and Heinrich entered the drawing-room,
Rosa was seated at the piano. Frau Muller sat in a small, straight-
backed arm-chair, her eyes closed in quiet ecstasy; the countess
reclined upon a sofa turning over the pages of an illustrated paper.

" Rosa plays exquisitely," she remarked to her husband as he
entered. " You are fond of music, are you not, Heinrich? We have
just had Beethoven's *Pastoral*; now what shall it be?"

" Just one moment, Sophie," intervened Herr Blesch. " I want
to ask one or two questions as to Major Schaeffer."

The widow reopened her eyes, and sat up abruptly, clasping the
carved arms of the chair in her thin fingers.

" My dear Karl," sighed the countess, " please let us have a little post-prandial peace. This subject is distressing to Frau Muller. Why, Rosa told you it was just a practical joke, and Heinrich has been mistaken. You really are becoming absurdly apprehensive, and very fussy. Take a rest, Karl. Now, Rosa, let us have more music."

Rosa allowed her fingers again to stray bewitchingly over the keyboard.

Herr Blesch had coloured darkly with annoyance. He smoked in silence for a moment and then said harshly, with impatience: " You may play in a minute or two. . . . I am sorry if I pain you, Frau Muller . . . you will forgive me . . . but, no doubt, I can help you further. Tell me," he said, addressing himself to her, " who is this Major Schaeffer?"

" Karl, do sit down, or go to your study and leave us in peace."

" Who is Major Schaeffer?" barked Herr Blesch angrily to the widow.

" I really do not know," stammered the widow nervously.

" You do not know, what do you mean?" inquired Herr Blesch, his voice rising.

" He is a friend of my son Ulrich. . . . He told me so," replied Frau Muller quietly.

" There you are," said the countess. " A friend of Ulrich's."

" Yes, indeed," continued the widow, " and an old and intimate friend of yours, Rosa, is he not?"

Rosa fingered the notes, played a stanza of chords, with lowered eyes, while she fought for self-composure, and reasoned quickly as to her reply. " Oh, yes, of course. There is no mystery about Major Schaeffer. Both Frau Muller and I know him well. He was on leave and came in to see us."

" And," put in Frau Muller, " he told me of Ulrich. Major Schaeffer had only recently been with him. Why," she said with assurance, " I gave him some of Ulrich's papers to take back to him in the trenches."

" Papers," roared Herr Blesch, " what papers?"

" Don't you think we have had enough of this, Karl? You make me quite ashamed. Rosa, play to us a little more."

Herr Blesch crossed to the bay window, puffing his cigar in anger. He passed out on to the veranda. Rosa played, she scarcely knew what; excuses, explanations chasing each other through her mind. Herr Blesch was more than agitated; that was plain, nor would he be baulked in his inquiry. There was danger. This Rosa realized . . . but for herself alone. Duncan was safe. It was now five days since he had returned to the British lines. But could she be sure? He had told her that she would hear the aeroplane and perhaps see it on the morning of the fifteenth. How she had strained her hearing and eyes. She had heard and seen nothing; but Duncan was safe. An intuition told her so; the secret telepathic message of love. She would take the offensive in question, and remain no longer the passive witness beneath cross-examination.

After several minutes Herr Blesch, whose footsteps had been heard pacing the veranda, re-entered. He was calm and smiled as he entered. "It is," he said, "most interesting to me to hear details of Ulrich Muller and his colleague from his mother and friends. Your son's work is known to me and to this boy's father intimately. We are honoured to be his servants."

Frau Muller's face glowed with pleasure.

"I should so much have enjoyed meeting his colleague, Major Schaeffer. That is why, Sophie," he said with a curve of the lip, "I have appeared a little importunate. Perhaps, Frau Muller, you may be able to suggest where I could get in touch with Major Schaeffer?"

"I really do not know," replied Frau Muller. "He returned immediately, or almost at once, to the front, I believe to rejoin Ulrich in his work . . . but Rosa will tell you. She was with him after he left my house."

Rosa had hidden her face behind some manuscripts of music which she had raised upon the rest above the grand piano.

"I have not the slightest idea where he is now. How should I? There is such secrecy in these matters; is there not, *Herr* Lieutenant?" said Rosa, gaily addressing herself to Heinrich. "What do you say? . . . 'somewhere in France' . . . and that may mean Belgium, Luxemburg, Poland or even Turkey."

"Then he has gone back to the line, Rosa?" questioned Herr Blesch. "What a pity! When did you first meet him, Frau Muller?"

"Oh, only a day or two ago," replied the widow.

"What date?" said Herr Blesch sharply.

"Let me see now . . . it would be about the sixth, no, surely, the fifth of June. I remember well now; yes, it was the fifth of June."

"That was the date, Herr Blesch, upon which I saw the aeroplane," intercepted Heinrich.

"An aeroplane," exclaimed Rosa, "how exciting! He never told us, did he, little mother? Did he come in an aeroplane?"

"It is quite possible that he did," replied Herr Blesch dryly. "So you never met Major Schaeffer before the fifth of June. . . . You were speaking of some papers a little while ago, Frau Muller. What papers were these?"

" Oh, dear me, just the papers Ulrich left behind, after he had finished his experimental work in the mines, before he went to the front—maps and plans. Ulrich wanted some of them, so his friend had come for them."

" And you gave them to him, Frau Muller?" asked Herr Blesch sternly.

" Why, certainly."

Herr Blesch smoked in silence for a moment, then he said : " Will you play a little, Rosa? Frau Muller is tired." When she paused in her playing, Herr Blesch continued : —

" Rosa, dear, how long have you known Major Schaeffer?"

" Quite a long time. Not very well, until recently, but surely you must remember him. It must have been at your house that I first met him, years ago."

" Ah, ha," laughed the countess. " Oh, fickle memory ! At last you stand convicted, Karl : it was you who introduced the mystery man to Rosa."

" I am quite certain that this was not so," replied Herr Blesch with some heat. " Perhaps Rosa will describe this major."

For a moment Rosa sat in reflection, then she answered : " He is tall . . . very dark, both in hair and complexion. . . . A striking figure, thin, æsthetic. But surely you will remember him now I have produced this little picture."

" Rosa," exclaimed the widow, " you must be mistaken. Wilhelm is fair, a fine figure of a man, in build much like Ulrich."

" But such a one was the Major Muller who spoke with me at the Imperial Hotel on the fifth," interposed Heinrich, " and I saw him with a lady thickly veiled on the following morning."

" Your happiness must have dimmed your eyes, Mother Muller," laughed Rosa gaily. " Oh, no, Major Schaeffer was dark." Rosa must mystify and mislead now, whatever the cost. The effort of control was taxing her strength. She choked suddenly, then, for a moment, was overcome with a paroxysm of coughing.

Frau Muller leant forward quickly in her chair, then half rose. " Poor, poor Rosa; she is not strong," she said in explanation. " I . . . I do not understand," she faltered, " all this curiosity concerning my son and Wilhelm. I was happy and satisfied until tonight. . . . I do not understand . . . let us leave it . . . Rosa is not well." She appealed to Herr Blesch, whose expression hardened perceptibly.

" Countess," she continued, " this is all very painful. What does it matter if Wilhelm was fair or dark? I am old, my eyes are dimmed. . . . I am sure Rosa must be right. . . ." The widow paused, shook her head as she mused, then smiled softly, " Rosa knows . . . she and Wilhelm are very dear friends . . . they are betrothed."

" Is that true?" cried the countess shrilly.

" I have said so," replied Frau Muller quietly, and she rose and crossed the room to where Rosa sat before the piano, exhausted, breathing heavily and gazing before her with wide, staring eyes. The widow gathered Rosa to her. Rosa whispered : " Wilhelm was dark, little mother." The widow spoke. " Rosa will tell you that she and Wilhelm love one another. It is true! Are you not glad? . . . She has waited for her happiness. . . . It has come."

" I had understood," said the countess with a sneer, " that Rosa's affections were confined to her music. I am sure we must all congratulate her upon this discovery of her attachment to the . . . ah! . . . dark man of mystery." Silence followed.

" Rosa," said Herr Blesch stiffly after a while, " as your trustee, I am glad indeed to be one of the first to congratulate you. Can you now tell us something about this Major Schaeffer?"

Rosa coughed to defer her reply. Then she said faintly : " There is very little to tell . . . I have been much alone . . . he was kind, very kind, to me. Are you not glad?"

" I think," replied Herr Blesch, " that I must give you some information which perhaps will shock you. . . . I ask you to be calm. . . . For me . . . this matter may be of . . . great importance."

" As they would say in Germany's new territory," laughed the countess, mocking him : " ' L'Etat, c'est moi.' But continue, Karl. I love to hear you in the grand manner."

" Don't be a fool, Sophie . . ." he replied testily.

" Fool?" she sneered, " I've been fooled enough during the past few days by this friend . . . from the old days, Karl."

Herr Blesch lit another cigar, and puffed the smoke in silence, then continued. " The information which I have to give is as follows. After leaving the dinner table, I telephoned to my friend, the chief-of-staff. I asked if there was any further news of Major Ulrich Muller. I am sorry to have to tell you, Frau Muller, that at nine-fifteen this evening, he is still missing : there is no news. Major Schaeffer's encouragement to your hopes was, I fear, unfounded."

" Oh, dear God!" cried Frau Muller.

" But do not alarm yourself. No news is good news, you know, and . . . you have your faith. Take courage, madam . . . Major Schaeffer's story to you was not true . . . the name of Major Schaeffer is not known at Army Headquarters : no man with such a name was at any time associated with Ulrich Muller. . . ." He paused while the burden of this information penetrated the minds of the little audience, now entirely under his control, awaiting the next words with breathless expectation.

"Rosa, tell us, please, is Wilhelm Schaeffer the name of your lover?"

"Yes," breathed Rosa.

"Then Wilhelm Schaeffer is a liar," he said dryly.

"Go on," said the countess quickly, her eyes bright with excitement.

"I am going to ask Lieutenant Messer to tell you of what he saw on the morning of the fifth of June."

Heinrich told of what he had observed, of hearing and seeing an aeroplane. When he had completed the story Rosa leant forward upon her arms across the piano. She had gathered all her courage and strength. Her mind had quickly sought an avenue of escape and of excuse, by question and answer, by self-examination and cross-examination. She must fight for Duncan with every artifice and power at her command, the strength of her mind, the weakness of her body. She must utilize all her resources. The urge to action roused her. The pale cheeks were flushed.

"How thrilling, *Herr Lieutenant*," she exclaimed. "I do wish I had seen it, too. Tell me, if I had been awake, should I have heard the aeroplane, and seen it, too?"

"Of course you would," answered Heinrich, speaking with the enthusiasm of a master of technique. "You couldn't miss it. You could hear the drone of its engine miles away."

The light died from Rosa's eyes—"You could hear the drone miles away," said the airman. Duncan had said so too. She had heard nothing . . . seen nothing. Had the aeroplane come back? Where was Duncan now? Perhaps still in Germany. . . . She must save the discovery of Duncan's identity.

"Now," said Herr Blesch, addressing himself to Rosa. "It will be interesting to go over what we have learnt. The evidence will help you, I feel sure. . . . As your trustee I have, too, a duty in your protection. . . . Perhaps you may not have chosen as wisely as you had hoped. Let us see. Heinrich tells us that on the evening of the fifth of June, a major of the Corps of Engineers spoke with him. . . . The name in the hotel register was that of Ulrich Muller. It is quite plain that this visitor was not the Ulrich Muller whom we all know. . . . In conversation he warned Heinrich not to disclose the evidence as to an aeroplane. . . . This man coincided exactly with Frau Muller's visitor."

"No," cried Rosa.

"Let me conclude," said Herr Blesch swiftly. "Frau Muller insisted before you corrected her."

"I am not sure," sighed the widow, interrupting.

"I . . . am quite sure," replied Herr Blesch. "Wilhelm Schaeffer and the visitor at the Hotel Imperial were one and the same person—the description and dates are agreed. Rosa alone disagrees. This man is to marry Rosa. We do not know when they first met, certainly not at this house; of that I am sure. Wilhelm Schaeffer is unknown to Army Headquarters. He posed as a colleague of Ulrich Muller. . . . He lied. . . . He examined Major Muller's papers. And then we have the story of an aeroplane . . . with English markings. . . . Can you not put two and two together? Am I so apprehensive, Sophie?" he asked, turning towards the countess.

"Rosa," he said sharply, the rasp in his voice rudely breaking the silence, "when did you first meet Wilhelm Schaeffer?"

Rosa gasped for breath. Her bosom heaved; she paled with emotion. The evidence was overwhelming, she felt herself being pressed back and back; the space for manœuvre narrowing, always narrowing . . . evidence, like walls, was closing in upon her; there was no avenue of escape. She had reached the last line of defence; yet not hers . . . that she must surrender . . . Duncan's identity alone could be shielded.

"I suppose," she replied slowly, feeling the eyes of all fixed upon her, "that my first meeting with Wilhelm Schaeffer was . . . yes . . . at the house of Frau Muller . . . no . . . I cannot tell you." She coughed and fought breathlessly for self-mastery, her fingers fumbling the silent keyboard. Frau Muller, whose eyes were closed, had swooned. She lay back in her chair unnoticed.

"You had not then met him before?" pursued Herr Blesch sternly.

"Of course not," cried Rosa, uttering a sound in part chuckle, part sob.

"And your description of this Wilhelm Schaeffer? Was he this fair man or another?"

"I do not quite understand," replied Rosa. "Fair or . . Wilhelm . . . my . . ."

"Lover," supplied the countess acidly.

"My lover, if you like. He is tall . . . dark. I have described him."

"But we are not certain," said Herr Blesch gravely. "Are you quite sure?"

Rosa's moment had come—she must play her part now. Rosa

rose from her seat, triumph writ upon her face. She threw her trump card.

"Quite sure," she said firmly. "Heinrich observed a veiled woman at the Hotel Imperial. . . . That woman was Rosa von Gleiwitz. . . . I am quite sure of my lover's description. . . . It was I who spent the night with Major Schaeffer!"

Rosa's words swept on. "You are apprehensive, Herr Blesch . . . you have your secrets, jealously guarded, fenced round with barbed wire and with bayonets. . . . I, too, have my secrets . . . trivial things, little hopes, emotions, fears, desires. . . . I have nothing but my honour to defend. . . . You have torn down my defences . . . you are apprehensive? As my trustee, perhaps you have acted within your rights." Her voice rose in staccato tones. "Yes, I slept with Wilhelm. . . . He gave me what no one else has ever even offered. . . . You have his description. Do you need more?"

Rosa covered her face with her hands and stumbled from the room, her body shaken with great sobs. Duncan's identity was secure. Rosa had carried conviction by the very baldness of her confession. She had stripped herself of modesty, to ride naked through the highways of their cynosure, while the countess played at Peeping Tom. Now, in her shame, Rosa fled.

"How disgusting," murmured the countess, yawning as Rosa passed. "From the old days, Karl . . . a common prostitute . . . yet . . . I could almost be sympathetic with her." She laughed harshly. "Send the little *poupée* away and forget it. . . . Stick to business, Karl; it's more profitable. . . . Ring for my maid : we will take Frau Muller to her apartment."

Herr Blesch and Heinrich were alone. Both were silent for many minutes wrapt in thought. Herr Blesch spoke at last. "Well, Heinrich, you are a soldier. What would you do?"

"I do not know. Nothing is plain to me," replied Heinrich.

"Not plain? You don't know?" shouted Herr Blesch. "It's as plain as a pikestaff. Someone came. I don't know who . . . a spy, probably. He sought to rob Frau Muller of evidence vital to the state. Frau Muller has told us she had nothing of importance. Thank God, our secrets are inviolate. No one can steal them from us. Who is this fellow? No one knows. He seduced this girl in order to make her a party to his plots. Probably he had accomplices, your fair friend for one. . . . The dark man ravished Rosa. She must pay! . . . You don't know what to do . . . send for the police . . . arrest her! She gave herself to a spy, and you don't know what to do? Does a German woman's honour mean nothing to you, Heinrich? Send for the military police. I'll have the woman shot as an example to the others."

The lad had grown very white. He stood up, gripping the edge of the writing table to support his weight.

"Do you suppose," Heinrich stammered through his tears, "I gave my mother and brothers in order to have to listen to venom of this kind. . . . When I looked down at the bloody pulp which had been a leg, I thought that was the dirtiest sight I should be asked to see . . . I've seen something more beastly now!"

Herr von Blesch, who had regained his composure, remained quite unruffled. "Be quiet, Heinrich," he said sternly.

"Be quiet be damned!" shouted the lad. "We're not all cogs in this infernal machine of war, going round and round and round, while you and dad, and a few others sit back and rake in the profits . . . you have no right to accuse this woman," he continued breathlessly. "You know nothing of her life, which has brought her little love or joy, except . . . in a work which no others would do. You are dug in here in smug complacency, while the lads, and women, like Fraulein von Gleiwitz, dance in Hell. You call the tune, and, just because you think, only think, mark you, that she's been a party, willing or unwilling, to something which will stand between you and your profits, you vilify her in your own house."

The countess had returned and stood within the half-opened door.

"Heinrich," her bosom heaved as she fought for words. She strode toward the lad, and thrust him roughly into the chair.

"Sit down. I will not have such words in my house. Sit down or get out at once. My husband has his clear duty to the state of which, as you have rightly, though intemperately, observed, he is a major part," she said acidly, with greater calm. "How dare you defend a harlot who gave herself, and the secrets of the empire, for what you call love? You boys don't know what love is." She passed across to her husband and took his arm, standing beside him.

"Love?" inquired Heinrich, his voice rising and falling as the words in ebb and flow came from him. "My God! I know what love is and what it means. I've seen it in Barmen. Did you use the word harlot? Very well, then, I have my answer. If one word is said against this woman, I will use the influence of an airman who gave a limb, the remaining son of a family well known in Elberfeld, with the workmen. You have strikes and unrest here. We have them in Elberfeld. The fires of revolution are laid among our workers. I can kindle those fires.

"How does my father expend his leisure hours? . . . poor devil!

. . . in the arms of every woman in Barmen. He is your friend, Herr Blesch, your closest business associate, the founder of your fortune. I know his profits. If you inform against this woman, I will declare my father's profits . . . your profits . . . to the workmen. I will tell them, too, in what manner he disposes of them. That evidence will recoil on your head. The workmen are waiting for a torch with which to light the fire of revolution. I hold it. You will no longer ride roughshod over us all. If you touch this woman, who has suffered, perhaps more than I, I will light that fire." He laughed hysterically. "Now think of that in terms of profit and loss, Herr Blesch."

"You are mad, Heinrich," exclaimed the countess.

Heinrich remained motionless for some seconds. Quite calmly he continued : "In a sense we are all mad, but I am not blind. . . . Every ambition, every desire you have is satisfied. Power immense, complete domination over thousands of men, and wealth untold. You are supported by the whole resources of the state, by law, police, military force."

"What do we get out of the war?" . . . The face of Herr Blesch set itself in an ugly smile. "Yes, I know I'm only a kid," retorted Heinrich, "but I've only got one life, and I have as much title to a viewpoint as you have, Herr Blesch. Every ideal I had has been shattered. My brothers are gone, my mother is dead, my father so debauched that I am ashamed to be his son. Do you really imagine the soldiers or the workmen care a snap any longer for your war, your plans, your victories, your rule? . . . They don't. They are goaded on by threat of court martial and imprisonment, while you sit back and have all the fun."

Herr Blesch shook his head in negation.

"Oh, yes," cried Heinrich, "it is fun organizing this, that, and the other; creating grandiose schemes, holding the destinies of thousands of human lives in your hands, ordering, disposing . . . the greatest game in the world. You are so preoccupied with schemes that you have no moments for friendship or life . . . everything, everybody is utilized to serve only your ambitions . . . until they are saturated, like those of dad . . . then when the brain no longer makes its demands of all the physical resources, you and your kind give themselves to the body, pouring out wealth and expending power in the seduction of anyone whom the whim of the moment commends to the eye and to the senses.

"I'm not blind. I've seen it. I have been brought up among your kind. There may be rare exceptions. You, perhaps, are one . . . but you're having your fun, the greatest game in the world. . . .

Rosa von Gleiwitz, and I . . . where do we come in? . . Just pawns in the game . . . Rosa and a spy . . . nonsense . . . Rosa and . . . a lover . . . that's her secret. . . ."

"So," interrupted the countess, "you class yourself with her, Heinrich?"

"What is the worst you can say of her?" stammered the lad. "You imagine she may have been the tool of some plot which might thwart or hinder your own ambitions and schemes. So you set up yourself upon a high pedestal and preach nonsense about morality and the state. What is the truth? As I believe, Rosa has loved, perhaps does love, this man in a way you have never known . . . or have forgotten. She found what life never gave to her before."

"I think we have heard quite enough, Heinrich," said Herr Blesch in heated tones. "Your views might be interesting later. We . . . do not expect a woman of this class to behave . . . ah . . . as a prostitute."

"Let me continue," interrupted the countess, realizing that perhaps Heinrich unwittingly was fighting her own battle.

"Thank you, countess, but I refuse to be silenced. . . ." Heinrich continued breathlessly. "At the lowest estimate, supposing your interpretation can be admitted to be right, Rosa's had her little fun . . . just as you are having yours . . . and, as every girl and every lad, marshalled and dragooned by your kind, snatches it whenever a chance offers, whether in Berlin or Brussels, Elberfeld or Lille. Do you grudge her just that?

"You have yet to disassociate yourself from my father upon the grounds that he has wearied of profits and prefers seduction, Herr Blesch. I warn you . . . you may be a paladin in organization, a master of mechanical technique, the supreme industrial force, but you have lost touch with the people; you fail to understand their emotions, ambitions, fears, anxieties. You may be able to control them with the aid of martial law . . . though personally I doubt it. But the people are the key to the situation, military, social, political, industrial. Keep faith with the people, Herr Blesch . . . or, I warn you, they will break you."

"Young man," said the Kommercienrat, rising, "I have listened to you with patience. Were it not for your wounds, and for my friendship with your father, I should persuade myself to send for the police. I have listened to vituperation of this kind before. For you, I have pity, an overwrought, hysterical lad. Your utterances are treason. Men who have dared to speak in this vein to my workmen have been shot, or are now in jail. You had better go to bed and cool your head. . . . I have my duty."

" Herr Blesch, I, too, have my duty. You must help this young woman in her trouble; she, too, is the child of a friend whose life was devoted to the foundation of your fortune. You must help her."

" You dare say ' must ' to me?"

" I do. My alternative is clear. I go to the workmen in Elberfeld. I know the secrets, I hold the torch. I will fire the revolt. Then, what of your ambitions, your plans and schemes, Herr Blesch?"

" You threaten me, Heinrich? You are a public danger, a madman!" He placed his hand swiftly within the centre drawer of the desk and drew out a revolver.

" Shoot me like a dog, if you will," jeered Heinrich. " Then telephone to dad, and tell him what you have done! You forget I'm all he's got. He still possesses one absorbing hobby—myself. . . . You have not realized that his other ambitions are satiated." Heinrich sank back exhausted by his effort, then said very quietly: " Consider; what I ask is simple. Give Rosa her passport to the frontier . . . and forget."

" Heinrich," said the countess, " leave us for a little while. . . . I wish to consult with my husband." With uncommon grace and sympathy she assisted the lieutenant to the door. " You will find wine set in the library. We . . . I will join you later." The Countess von Arenfels closed the door and turned to her husband.

" The boy is mad," said Herr Blesch bluntly.

" Oh, yes, perhaps . . . but there is wisdom in his madness, Karl."

" Wisdom? . . . Where? . . . What?" demanded the Kommercienrat.

Tears dimmed the countess's eyes as she placed her hands upon her husband's broad shoulders. Rosa in all her weakness had fought and won, where the countess, with all her natural gifts, for three years had feared to do battle.

" Karl, what does it matter? . . . Rosa has had her fun . . . you have had yours . . . within a few weeks, it will be finished . . . the W Plan," she whispered. . . . " Where do I come in, Karl?"

The countess ran her delicate fingers lightly over the rugged set face, then pressing her body against the massive frame she kissed him. She clung to her husband, weeping quietly. The countess must not lose this fight; as it was her first, so it must be her last. The man held her back from him with strong arms, looking down upon this woman shorn of pride, who was his wife. She felt his finger quiver, and then looked up, an appeal smiling through the tears in her eyes.

" Sophie," he whispered, " you are so true, so good, so perfect, that I had forgotten . . . you are also beautiful." He gathered the woman to him.

The countess and her husband entered the library. Lieutenant Messer rose awkwardly and stiffly as they entered. Herr Blesch poured three glasses of wine, and raised his glass. "Heinrich," he said simply, "I salute you"; then smiling to his wife he touched her glass.

"Within a day or two, Heinrich, I shall ask you to take Rosa to the frontier. . . . My wife and I go to her now. . . . Good night."

Herr Blesch held the door open for his wife. In the hall stood the butler.

"Shall I put out the lights and lock up now, sir?" he inquired.

"In a minute or two, Joseph, but see Lieutenant Messer to his room."

"Certainly, sir," he added wistfully, "just like the old days with Fraulein von Gleiwitz in the house again."

"Just like old days, Joseph," replied the countess, placing her arm upon that of her husband. "We need the old days over again."

"They say," said the butler, "that history always repeats itself. God be with you both."

The countess softly entered Rosa's apartment. The girl, weary to exhaustion, sat before the empty fireplace, still fully dressed. The thin ashes of what had once been the W Plan lay scattered at her feet. Rosa had, too, offered up as a burnt sacrifice the selfless devotion of her life, the sanctity of her love. . . .

They might think that she had some secret lover who had masqueraded in Barmen, and lied glibly to the stricken widow, while she herself silently applauded, then had satisfied his lust; but the willing sacrifice of her honour had saved the discovery of Duncan's identity. She could do no more. What did it matter now? She might remain in Barmen . . . her work lay there so long as she had strength for the task: possibly she would one day go to her sister. . . .

The vision of the Cross was before her eyes . . . sacrifice was still the science of power. . . . Her life was ended. . . . Duncan would remain a memory in her dreams—rippling waters; purple hills and love sublime; little hours in the forest . . . sunset.

The countess sank upon her knees beside the still, wan figure. "Rosa, dear, you will be glad. . . . You will go to Switzerland. . . . My husband has arranged this for you. . . . I want to ask your forgiveness . . . and to thank you. Through you, I have found Karl. My debt to you is a heavy one. . . . Will you forgive me?"

Rosa sighed. "I have nothing to forgive. . . . You cannot

know all," replied Rosa through her tears. "You have given me hospitality and help; your friendship and affection. . . . Is that not enough? For me, everything is in the past . . . and I am happy. I will go to my sister . . . you, too, are happy, Sophie . . . your sunrise over the hills. . . . I am glad." And so they remained quietly talking for many minutes, until the door gently opened.

"Sophie," whispered Herr Blesch, "I want you."

"Come and join us for a little moment, Karl."

He entered and leant over the chair. "Good night, Rosa." He kissed her tired face. . . . "Come, Sophie." . . . The door closed again.

CHAPTER VIII

IN THE DEPTHS

A SHAFT of light stole through the iron grille into the cell. Colonel Duncan Grant slept on peacefully, the light playing on his face.

A soldier, his heavy boots ringing upon the stone passage-way, came to the door. He fumbled with a bunch of keys which he held in his right hand, finally inserting one in the lock. The noise stirred the sleeper. He opened his eyes but did not move. The soldier set down some bread and a metal cup of water upon the end of the plank bed, glancing furtively at the sleeper. Seeing he was awake, he smiled sheepishly and said: "Your breakfast." Grant needed friends. Even a shy lout of a peasant temporarily imprisoned in a military uniform, with a woeful smile, might colour the misery of the hours ahead.

"Thank you," said Grant, stretching and sitting up. "What happens next?"

"I don't know," said the sentry, "I'll try and find out."

Rye bread, dry and hard—the water helped it upon its course . . . and Grant was hungry. The atmosphere was close. He could hear the sound of voices. He walked across to the grille, and pressed his head hard against the iron bars. He could distinguish nothing of the conversation from the blurred voices: he could see only the walls and floor of the passage, upon which the shadow of the passing sentry from time to time fell. He sat down upon the bed. He would like to wash and shave. The sentry re-appeared. The key turned and he came into the cell.

"Any chance of a wash?" Grant questioned, adding, "and a shave?"

"I'll fetch some soap and water," said the sentry.

"And a towel," added Grant.

The sentry went out, taking the cup with him, returning with a bowl of water, soap and a towel.

"The barber will come later," he said, "if the officer of the guard permits." He turned the key on the inside and stood watching the prisoner wash himself. Grant took off his shirt, throwing the water over his chest and head.

"What's the next move?" said the captive.

The sentry glanced cautiously over his shoulder through the grille. "You'll go before the officer at ten o'clock."

"What's the charge?" said Grant.

"Desertion and striking superior officer. The evidence isn't all here yet. Court martial case, the sergeant says."

Grant dried himself briskly, then handed the bowl, soap and towel back to the sentry, who left the cell, locking it behind him. Grant sat down again. His watch, papers, money had been taken from him. But he possessed his precious tunic and his mind was alert.

He walked round the cell examining it. There was no means of exit. He had better wait and think. He would for the present play the part of the docile captive . . . events would shape themselves . . . he must first discover the nature of the charge, the attitude of the officer . . . perhaps a cunningly devised excuse would save him from a severe penalty . . . after all, many men had appeared before him as commanding officer charged with desertion, often merely technical offences and with striking a superior officer, perhaps the result of a drunken brawl . . . the men were contrite. England, still less Germany, could not afford to lose good officers and able men, who expressed willingness . . . he himself had tempered justice with mercy . . . he would plead not guilty to the charge of desertion and the extenuating circumstances of drink . . . no, that would not do . . . of a drug as the excuse for striking . . . but not self-administered . . . he had had a large sum of money in his possession . . . that he could prove . . . he had gone to a brothel . . . they had drugged him in order to secure his money. He had been sufficiently sane to realize that, and had staggered to the railway station . . . after that he could remember nothing until his arrest in the train. It was a slender hope, but he could tell the story with conviction, and plead for mercy.

And if he were not sentenced to death, then he would be sent back to his regiment—the 139th Saxon Regiment, under escort. He was Otto Gedern. But . . . he would then be in a worse plight than he was now . . . he bore no resemblance whatever to Otto . . . where was Otto? . . . Well, no one would ever discover that. He must avoid being sent back to that regiment at all costs. Why did he desert? . . . Perhaps that was the key to the riddle . . . but he had pleaded not guilty to desertion. . . .

Grant considered. Here was a new line of thought . . . he wasn't a Saxon. . . . They had made life Hell for him . . . for he was a Bavarian. That was why he had had the idea of going south to Bavaria. He wanted to fight, but in the ranks of his own mother blood. . . . It had become an obsession with him. The excuse was very thin. Why! he himself could riddle it with objections. But it would do for want of any other at the moment. He would wait until he had been charged, and would demonstrate a soldier's best behaviour.

The sound of footsteps came along the corridor. They halted before the door of his cell. He stood up. A voice called him to attention. He sprang to the alert facing the door, his body rigid, head thrown back. The key turned and the door opened. An officer, one sleeve empty and pinned across his breast, closely followed by a sergeant, an elderly man of the reserve, and the friendly sentry entered the cell.

" What's the man charged with?" said the officer.

" Desertion and striking his superior officer in the execution of his duty."

" These are very grave charges," said the officer. " You have, of course, your defence?"

" Yes, sir," said Grant.

" The commandant will see you at ten o'clock. Meanwhile, anything you want?"

" I would like to clean myself up a bit, sir," said Grant with humility. " A shave, sir, and clean my boots."

" A very serious charge, sir," said the sergeant. " Most irregular to allow privileges in such cases. The sergeant of the police told me he is a most violent man."

" I'm sorry, sir," Grant sighed.

" I'm afraid you'll have to go without the shave, but you can clean your boots," said the officer, not unkindly. " Please see to that, sergeant."

The door clanged to, and Grant was left in silence. Later the sergeant returned with an escort of two men, to one of whom Grant was again handcuffed. They left the cell, and marched across the wide barrack square, upon which youths, almost children, in small squads were being drilled. They glanced in his direction, their eyes frightened at the dishevelled figure. Grant held his head high, a gaiety in his pace. The file was halted, and he fell in at the tail of a line with other defaulters. Duty sergeants and corporals strolled along to look at the curiosity. Some laughed, others whispered anxiously among themselves.

The defaulters went within the charge-room one by one. Most came out unescorted; two with escort were marched to the guard-room from whence Grant had come. He was the last of the line. A call to the alert . . . and he was pushed through the door of the charge-room . . . confronting the commandant. For a moment the light coming full from the window dazed his vision, then a figure, regarding him intently, loomed before his eyes.

A man with a blotched face, and puffy eyes, brushed grey mustachios and bald head sat behind a table, supported by two officers who stood beside him. He bent his head to examine the charge sheet, then again looked Grant over carefully.

His lips sneered sarcastically: "Sergeant, who is this dirty creature disgracing my barracks?" Grant felt the rage of bitterness overtake him. He set his teeth.

"Otto Gedern of the 139th Saxon Regiment," replied the sergeant quickly.

The commandant evidently had had a disagreeable morning. His complex was to be cruel; he was soured with disappointment by the loss of a higher command; and, fretting in this senile backwater, when a chance chivvied the malice of his mind, savage passion possessed him.

"You dirty *schweinhund!*" he jeered. "You are charged with desertion and with striking your superior officer. What is the evidence, sergeant?"

"The leave pass of this man was granted from the sixth to the sixteenth of June, from his regiment in the line. The leave was granted to Dresden. The ticket had been used as far as Dusseldorf. He was found in possession of two hundred and fifty-one marks, whereas his pay book shows recent withdrawals of only forty marks . . . that was on the fifth. He was seen at Mainz Station by a corporal of the military police . . . you have, sir, his telegraphed statement before you . . . posing as a wounded soldier. He struck the corporal of police. He boarded a train and was arrested by Sergeant Ulms of the military police at Karlsruhe. His papers and effects are on the table, sir."

"Send in Sergeant Ulms. . . ."

"What do you know about this case, sergeant?"

"Received a message from the military police post at Mainz that a man answering to the description of the prisoner was travelling in the main line train due at Karlsruhe at twelve-thirty after midnight. I went to the station, caused the train to be stopped at the signal halt and boarded it. The conductor who had this man already under suspicion took me to the compartment. As I was about to interrogate him he attempted to jump through the doorway. I arrested him and handed him over to the sergeant of the main guard. He was charged with desertion and with striking. I questioned him. He stated that he was not a deserter and that he struck the corporal of police," he paused and glanced towards the prisoner, "because he didn't like the look of him."

The commandant half rose, fixing a monocle; a look of wonder, followed by one of intense satisfaction, entered his gleaming eyes. He sat back again deep in his chair, rubbing his hands together.

"*Mein Gott!*" he swore quietly. "You . . . you dirty lout . . . Otto Gedern . . . you dare to say that you struck one of the military police . . . because . . . you did not like his face?" He uttered a foul blasphemy.

"Not at that moment, sir," interjected Grant briskly. A subaltern tittered. The commandant glared at him.

"What do you mean, 'not at that moment '?"

"I was not quite myself," said Grant. The comic truth of his statement suddenly struck him. He smiled broadly. The sergeant, sensing the situation, and hoping for approval, struck him on the back, saying: "Take that grin off your face."

"Any further evidence?" demanded the commandant.

"None, sir," replied the adjutant beside him. "The corporal of police from Mainz is on his way. I would ask for a remand, unless you wish to proceed with the case."

"Are you guilty, Otto Gedern?"

"Not guilty of the first charge, technically guilty, I regret, sir, to the second. I was ill, sir."

"You are remanded. . . . Get out," the commandant screamed. The file marched.

Grant returned to the cell. The key turned and he was left alone. He dreaded another appearance before the commandant. He was familiar with the type. Here was a popinjay turned vulture . . . a failure in war he had been deprived of his command, and his services relegated to the trivial duties of a barrack commandant . . . here, his wings clipped of authority, performing the routine of a clerk, the repression from which he suffered had discovered an outlet in tyranny.

He was a bully, the last resort of incompetent authority. . . . His disappointed, degraded spirit wreaked a daily revenge upon his distracted lieutenants, most of whom had been severely wounded in the early days of the campaign . . . he delighted to torture young recruits with the whip lash of sarcastic blasphemy and obscenities, while enjoying the protection of his rank and uniform. He was hated and despised, and he knew it. The debased mind gloried in victimization, revelled at the sight of men squirming under his tyranny. Grant had observed such types at home, fortunately very few. But he could not hope for help or mercy from the commandant, nor was it probable from the subordinate officers whose reputations were in his hands.

Grant lay upon his bed in reflection. The sun had moved round to another side of the building and no longer lighted the cell. The air was heavy. The exhaustion and anxiety of the past days were playing havoc with mind and body. He felt physically sick. Food was brought : he ignored it.

Fantastic thoughts crowded in upon his mind. He was a beaten man . . . he could not escape . . . he would be shot as a deserter . . . and his soul in just retribution, sent to join that of Otto Gedern . . . no, never that! He would defy this commandant . . . declare himself a British officer, a colonel of the Inverness Regiment . . . they would shoot him like a dog . . . and . . . one day his regiment would know. That would be a better way out. But probably at home they would sneer at him . . . no one would know that he had secured the W Plan. . . . It would die with him . . . and . . . Britain would be overwhelmed.

The works were going steadily forward, men tunnelling day after day, completing the galleries . . . and Scots, too . . . they were willing workers! God curse it. He would rather be with his regiment, enemy in front and rear. The idea fired his imagination. . . . How they would have fought, his regiment, his men! Surrounded, no surrender, to the last round of ammunition, a battalion eclipsed in imperishable glory . . . years hence his name would be writ large in the annals of his regiment : a glorious tragedy like those at Darghai, Magersfontein, Le Cateau. . . . What an end!

But this . . . the vile uniform of a besotted enemy . . . and . . . God damn it! why had he bragged to the Commander-in-chief? He was dishonoured, had achieved nothing . . . nothing . . . nothing! . . . Yes, yes, he had . . . he possessed the W Plan . . . the general had been right . . . Duncan Grant had done his best. "Oh, God, help me," the spirit cried. But reason quickly undermined the hope of the spirit . . . God wasn't on his side . . .

there wasn't a God at all, and . . . even if God did exist, He didn't care a damn about the British. The Germans were just as good . . . no God had stepped in at Loos, why should He now?

The W Plan was inspired, it was a *coup d'état,* a master plan . . . God had made it . . . Curse God! The W Plan. . . . Yes, of course . . . Rosa had it . . . Rosa hadn't seen him for years . . . she had run away and left him . . . of course she had an excuse, a good one . . . then they had again met by chance . . . Rosa recognized him . . . he was a spy . . . she had pierced his armour . . . then she had made love to him. . . . Christ! what a fool he had been. Rosa was no different from any other woman . . . she was a German . . . she had wrung his secrets from him . . . she possessed the W Plan . . . Rosa was just like the harlot in Barmen!

Grant sprang up, kicked the planks savagely, and smote his head with clenched fists. Rosa like . . . my God! . . . No. . . . His brain was reeling . . . Rosa! He had doubted her . . . he was only fit to die. Rosa . . . my God! The tears welled into his eyes, great sobs shook him. Rosa was going to Switzerland. . . . She would reach the British Legation. . . . No matter about him . . . his work was finished.

He would be tried and condemned to death . . . as they led him out he would declare himself—Colonel Duncan Grant of the Inverness Regiment . . . a spy. He had failed . . . but Rosa would succeed—God speed her! . . . Rosa would succeed . . . through her his work would be completed . . . in death he would triumph . . . again doubt, bitter doubt gnawed into his reason . . . if she failed?

He strode up and down the cell. He beat the walls with his hands and wept, then collapsed in exhaustion upon the bed, where he lay for many minutes. He looked up, with scared eyes. Someone was watching him through the grille . . . a helmeted head . . . it was the commandant. A chuckle escaped from the officer's lips, as he called with an oath for the key. He would like to interrogate the prisoner. The sergeant of the guard, a new-comer, with a file of men came to the cell door. It was opened.

Grant stood up. His frame was quivering with rage and terror. The commandant leaned against the wall folding his arms, and delicately fingered his moustache.

" So you do not care for our hospitality, Otto Gedern," he said with a sneer. " The commandant comes to comfort you. Your wife. . . . I presume the photograph in the pay-book is your wife . . . will be anxious. We shall, of course, acquaint her with your burial . . . the dung heap of our barracks is well kept, is it not, sergeant?" He roared with laughter. "Your body in due course will grace our Bavarian fields. Thus will you give back to the Fatherland what you sought to steal away."

His voice was rising in a thin crescendo. "You damn swine! dirty rat! You sit and snivel in my barracks." His glance fell upon the untasted food. "You despise our food. You're a cur, a coward, a traitor." The commandant was squealing in uncontrolled passion . . . . "I'll teach you to strike a superior officer. You bastard! . . . you don't like the look of our police. . . . I'll beautify your own bloody face!" and snatching a riding switch which dangled at his side, he struck Grant savagely across the face. A deep red line ran from the chin across the forehead as the switch had bent itself round his head. Blood began to ooze from the cut.

The immobility of the man enraged the commandant . . . the sight of the blood had only whetted his appetite . . . he was living in a mental El Dorado; such a rare opportunity seldom presented itself. Grant reeled under the blow, but braced himself to meet the storm.

The commandant panted heavily, the physical exertion of his passion extracting heavy toll from his overwrought nerves. He advanced a pace. "You deserve to bleed "—the soldiers of the escort blanched with terror, anticipating a further outrage—" You damned pig, posing as a wounded soldier."

"Sergeant," he bellowed, "have the swine stripped and see if there is a wound on his body and report to me tomorrow morning."

He advanced near to the prisoner, "I know your regiment, you dirty renegade—Saxons," he jeered, "you slunk away even from that white-livered mob of skunks!"

Grant's tottering reason gripped one fact . . . the very accusation of the infuriated commandant was a part of his plea against the charge of desertion . . . he would use it.

The commandant gibbered with excitement. He had ceased to control the rush of words. Such sanity as he possessed deserted him. He was a devil. He advanced a step nearer, and struck at Grant with his fist . . . he longed to feel the hot blood of his victim wetting the palms of his hand . . . he lusted for blood. Grant warded off the blow with his arm. His reason was going . . . he would strike this foul creature to the ground. Seeing the light in his eye, the commandant, like every bully, a coward at heart, recoiled, and struck fiercely with his riding whip in self-protection at the white-angered, blood-smeared face. The sergeant intervened as the prisoner fell as if lifeless upon the bed. Grant's mind was stunned, his consciousness deserted him.

The commandant chuckled with sensuous joy as if leaving the bull ring after a private rehearsal. What a day! . . . He would dine with relish upon pork . . . pouring red wine down his throat.

The sergeant watched the dreaded figure swagger across to the commandant's house . . . then he turned swiftly. His soldier's honour had been besmirched by the commandant's cruel, cowardly attack. . . . This wretched man had done nothing to deserve this . . . nothing . . . he had stood immovable before the storm, inflexible under the first savage blow. The prisoner was no coward —deserter perhaps . . . but not prompted by any craven spirit.

The soldier returned to the guard-room in which the men were whispering together in fright. "Bring water and towels. Give me the key, quick."

He ran to the cell and entered. The prisoner was lying huddled upon the bed, his arms drooping limply to the floor upon which blood was dripping from a gash in his head and two hideous wounds upon his face. The sergeant raised the senseless body. The guards bathed the blood from the head and face and cleansed the wounds, removing the stained shirt.

"Fetch blankets and a palliasse," said the sergeant. They laid him in comfort, spread a blanket and raised the head upon a pillow. The prisoner opened his eyes. He looked round with terror, breaking to rage.

"It's all right, my lad," said the sergeant. "He's . . . gone." Grant sank back. The sergeant left the cell, returning with lint, bandages, rum and water and a portion of his own rations. He bound the head, reviving the prisoner with the spirit.

Grant sat up. . . . "That's better," he said.

"Now eat; you need it." Grant ate slowly. Life was coming back at the hands of kindness.

"Thank you . . . comrades."

"That's all right, lad," said the sergeant gruffly, and withdrew, leaving one man in the cell with the prisoner. Grant lay back and closed his eyes. His head throbbed: he drew the blanket closer round him. On a summer evening he was shivering. The sentry passed him more rum. Then the weary, stricken man slept. The sentries were relieved every two hours in the cell.

As the night passed, the sleeper grew restless. He called aloud from the profound unconsciousness of sleep. Words came in torrents, bitter and sweet, rage and infinite pity, in the German and in the English tongue. The young sentry called for the sergeant. He came bustling into the cell.

"He speaks English," said the sergeant. Grant awoke and sat

up. They changed the bandages. The bleeding had been checked. "Now take some more rum and have another sleep." Grant lay down again and slept. It was almost nine before he opened his eyes. The shock had passed. His head was clear. They brought him an ample breakfast with hot coffee.

The sergeant looked in. "The commandant will want to see you at ten o'clock. We'll take off the bandages and make you look as spruce as possible." The guard helped him . . . clean boots . . . a comb and brush. He was handcuffed again to the sentry and marched across the square.

The story of the commandant's foul assault had echoed round the barrack rooms. Now came his victim. Curious glances were thrown in his direction, heads craned from barrack windows. He walked resolutely. The duty non-commissioned officers outside the charge-room regarded him with sympathy. He was marched in before the commandant, and avoiding the man's eyes looked straight before him above the man's head.

The commandant surveyed him with curiosity. He spoke to the sergeant.

"You have carried out my orders, sergeant?"

"Which, sir?"

"Fool . . . you had him stripped?"

"Yes, sir!"

"Well?"

The sergeant spoke deliberately and slowly. "He . . . had . . . no wounds, sir."

"He has something to go on with now," said the commandant with a sneer, turning to his adjutant beside him. "When I visited the cell, the man tried to strike me, and I taught him a lesson."

Grant caught the adjutant's eye and saw it flicker.

The commandant pursued his theme. "You were a witness of the assault, sergeant." The clock ticked off the passing seconds of silence.

"You heard me, you damned idiot, didn't you? You saw the assault?" he screamed.

Again, deliberately, the sergeant replied: "I did, sir."

"Is there any further evidence, *Herr* Adjutant?"

"Yes, sir, the corporal of military police from Mainz."

"Send him in then."

The corporal, with some heat, told the story of the assault, and of the subsequent chase at Mainz Station.

"Have you any questions to ask the witness?" snapped the commandant.

"Yes, sir," said Grant speaking for the first time; and, turning his head towards the big man, his mouth quivered in a smile. "I'm sorry, corporal. I hope I didn't hurt you."

The policeman's face wreathed itself in smiles. Otto Gedern was evidently a sportsman, and he had heard how he had stood under the commandant's whip.

"That's all right, my man," said the corporal, addressing the prisoner.

"Hold your blasted tongue," screamed the commandant. "Get out, all of you! Remanded for court martial."

Grant was back in his cell. The sergeant came to him after a short while. "The court is convened for tomorrow morning. You are entitled to the advice of an officer as your counsel. Is it your wish to see an officer before the court assembles?"

Grant considered . . . hope was creeping back . . . sympathy was with him . . . the flimsy defence which he had concocted in his despair had gained immeasurably from the commandant's assault . . . but what was it that the commandant had said which had impressed his reeling mind? He pressed his head with his hands. . . . "Cowardly Saxons, dirty pigs." That statement linked itself with his line of defence. He was not a Saxon, but a Bavarian, and he wanted to fight beside his own kinsmen . . . so he had run south . . . he had overstayed his leave, but only by two days, but he had surely shown an endeavour . . . the drug story weakened that part of the case: perhaps he had better plead that he struck the corporal in temper—the man was a good fellow, he would not overstate his evidence after the incident of that morning in the charge-room.—Otto's plan, almost complete, was being foiled by the policeman at Mainz. He had shown that he had pluck . . . the court, even if the fact did not come out in evidence, as it would not, would have heard of the outrage committed. Grant was calm now, and resigned . . . almost happy.

He knelt by his bed and prayed: his prayers gave him confidence and contributed strength. Then he called to the guard and requested a pencil and paper, and noted down the points of the case which he proposed to present. Later a voice in the corridor asked: "Where is soldier Otto Gedern?" The sergeant of the guard brought an officer and escort to the cell.

"I have seen you before, Otto Gedern," said the officer, whom Grant recognized as the lieutenant with the armless sleeve who had visited him previously in the cell. "I have orders to act as your counsel. The court assembles tomorrow. Since this little affair occurred," and he smiled, looking down upon his empty sleeve, "I have resumed my study as a barrister. I may be able to help you, but you must first tell me frankly the whole story, and I will see what I can make of it. You are no coward, Otto; you may be a fool . . . and I have heard also that you can speak English. Is that true?" Grant nodded. "That is a qualification which is valuable and our army cannot afford readily to lose." He turned to the sergeant. "You may withdraw with the escort. If I want you, I will call."

"You are advised not to plead guilty," the barrister continued. "Now tell me your story."

Grant placed the notes before the officer. His paybook would reveal three years' faithful and regular service in the field. He had committed no previous offence of any seriousness. He was unpopular with the Saxons and could not achieve promotion, his ambition . . . he was a Bavarian. He had taken advantage of his leave to try and join his Bavarian comrades . . . the journey south proved that. He had overstayed his leave by two days. And . . . had not the commandant cursed him for a Saxon?

"What was that?" interjected the officer. . . . "That is important. . . . I must use that." His zeal as a barrister was being fired. Soldiering days would be over one day, perhaps soon. He was a lawyer today. "Who are the witnesses? Who heard him say that?"

"The sergeant of the guard and the escort of two men."

"Perhaps I shall be obliged to call the commandant," he smiled. "Now as to striking your superior officer. Were you drunk?" Grant wavered for a moment. The officer eyed him keenly. "I want the truth."

"No, sir," said Grant.

"Well, why did you do it?"

Grant considered a moment. "The truth," reminded the officer "He was going to interfere with my plans," replied Grant.

"Perfect," commented the barrister, rubbing his one hand upon his cheek, a little mannerism. "Quite enough . . . quite reasonable. Now I want a little more in support of my case. Tell me about yesterday evening . . . this mess," and he indicated the cuts upon Grant's head and face. "Tell me the story."

Grant narrated the events simply. "What a devil!" whispered the officer below his breath. "And what did you do?"

"I stood quite still, sir," said Grant.

"Have you evidence of that?"

"The sergeant and the escort saw it."

"Very well, Otto Gedern, don't worry over much: and, by the way, I want you to look your best. As orderly officer I refused

you the barber : as your counsel, I will now order him. My client,"
he smiled, " is going to win the sympathy of the court. Those cuts
will show themselves when you have had a shave. The commandant
is your best friend . . . and don't forget it. Now remember, tell
your story before the court, as you have told it to me . . . exactly
as you have just told it. . . . The truth. . . . I do not wish you to
refer to the commandant or to any events which have taken place
since your arrest. Leave all that to me. I can best judge the temper
of the court. I must take my cue from the prosecutor."

" Thank you, indeed, sir," said Grant, standing up.

" I will see you before the court sits, and the barber will come
tomorrow morning."

" Thank you again, sir."

Grant was left in the cell with his own reflections. He was happy.
His mind wandered back to happy days upon the heathered moors
of his own home, fishing in the swift water . . . a sand grouse shoot
upon the sand flats of the Blue Nile . . . stalking gooral in the
Indian foothills . . . and his thoughts were much with Rosa. . . .
He wished some at home could peep and observe the gruff kindness
of the sergeant, the tenderness of rough-handed peasants turned
soldiers. Even the commandant had his prototype in British base
camps. His mind was elevated. . . . Englishmen in their tens of
thousands, Germans, too, had gone forth in their millions, aided by
their women, each one with a vision—intangible, ethereal, divine,
love of family and pride of race . . . their thoughts were of boyhood
days, when youth stepped forth from his cities to find his god in
all the wonders of nature.

Civilization had culminated in the most furious output of man's
created works that ever disgraced the history of human progress—
guns, munitions, tanks, machine-guns, bombs, poisonous gases,
mines, and every conceivable device for the wholesale slaughter of
mankind, the destruction of his works and of the beauty of God. . .
what a monument indeed to civilization !

The poet and philosopher in the man swept him . . . even as a
burbling brook tumbles headlong from the snow-capped peaks of
the mountains, stretching white fingers to Heaven, and rolls onwards
in a great stream, carrying upon its troubled waters the obstacles
which would impede its progress; and, ever swelling into a mighty
river, belches forth into the ocean . . . so is the stream of human
progress . . . it sprang from Heaven on high : it has tumbled and
cascaded through the dim ages; it has swelled in the stream of
mediævalism, and has driven on, dashing its sure course through
barriers of repression; it has passed through the maelstrom of

conflicting civilizations and now is surely rolling on into the open sea of the boundless brotherhood of man. Nothing shall stay its torrent . . . its destiny is sure . . . for the destiny of man is in God.

And Rosa, his sweet love, she was with him. . . . He pulled the blanket over him. He was tired and happy. He slept. A sentry peered through the grille and returned to the guard-room. " He's asleep, sergeant."

" Leave the poor devil, then. I see the commandant has added a further charge of striking. . . . He's got enough trouble now. Let him sleep."

CHAPTER IX

JUSTICE

GRANT awoke early and lay meditating on his presentation of the case until the barrack barber came. The inflammation and swelling of his face and head had gone, but there remained two accusing red weals across his face which the removal of a four days' beard made only the more apparent. Grant carefully dressed and brushed himself. Breakfast was brought, and shortly before nine the officer acting as counsel looked in through the grille.

" Ah, that's better," he said. " Keep your courage up; you'll need all of it. I should tell you that the commandant has preferred an additional charge against you, that of striking, or alternatively of attempting to strike, him in the execution of his duty when he visited you in the guard-room."

Grant stood back, aghast. Observing his consternation, the officer added : " Don't you worry about that. You can leave it to me."

An hour later he was conducted across the barrack square under escort of a sergeant and three men. The court was to sit in the library and its members with the witnesses were already assembling. Grant noted them carefully in turn. The two military policemen were standing together in conversation with their backs turned towards him. Two officers of artillery in field-service dress carrying sheathed swords, obviously members of the court, were smoking. They glanced in his direction. The sergeant of the guard and two soldiers who had witnessed the commandant's assault were drawn up in line with other formal witnesses of arrest, among them the conductor of the train, who appeared ill at ease. The party was called to attention as the adjutant crossed from the charge-room, and entered the library. A moment later an officer of field rank, limping slightly, and who aided his progress with a stick, approached in company with two other officers, one of whom Grant noted as having been present in the charge-room upon his last appearance there.

He studied the face of the field officer, certainly the president of the court. He was a man of slight build and small in stature, dark hair and moustache edged with grey, his face lined and pale, æsthetic rather than that of the typical soldier. The two officers with him, one of whom carried a folio of papers, looked hurriedly in the direction of the prisoner. Grant placed the latter as the prosecutor.

After a few minutes' delay, all those attending the proceedings were summoned to the court room where its members, Major von Oppeln, the president, Captain Reichman, Lieutenants Meichner and Deusel, were duly sworn. The prosecutor, Captain Brauen, and the defender, Lieutenant Mettelinck, were formally introduced and sworn. The court took their seats, the prosecutor his place at the end of the table, the officer acting in defence beside the prisoner.

The proceedings were formally opened by the president.

" Soldier Otto Gedern of the 139th Saxon Regiment is charged—Firstly—with desertion upon active service. . . . Secondly—with striking his superior officer in the execution of his duty. . . . Thirdly—with striking his superior officer in the execution of his duty." He looked up for a moment. " You are Otto Gedern?"

Grant replied : " Yes, sir."

" There are three charges. Do you desire the charges to be proceeded with separately or together?" he said, addressing Captain Brauen.

The prosecutor rose. " Separately, sir."

" And you?" he said, looking towards the defending officer.

" All together," said the latter.

" We seem to have some conflict of opinion in regard to procedure. What reasons have you, Captain Brauen?" said the president.

" Each of the charges against the prisoner is very grave. The court must weigh each one separately," replied the prosecutor.

" And you, Lieutenant Mettelinck?"

" It is clear, as the president must know from the précis of the case, that the first two charges are closely identified the one with the other. The second arises from the first. That is the defence. The prisoner was only acquainted as to the third charge this morning. I have, of course, read the summary of evidence. I would also prefer this charge to be related to the first."

"I must require the court to be cleared," said the president, "while we consider the question of procedure."

With the exception of the officers composing the court, all present withdrew from the library. A sergeant, acting as usher, after a few minutes recalled the prosecutor, defender and the prisoner with escort.

Major von Oppeln then addressed the court. "We have decided," he said quietly, "to hear the three charges concurrently. The summary of evidence suggests that they are closely correlated and it will suit our convenience in determining the guilt, or otherwise, of the accused, to hear the whole matter." Then, turning to the prosecutor, he said: "Will you open your case, please?"

The prosecution first produced the field service books of Otto Gedern and his other effects in proof of the fact of determined desertion.

The evidence then of the police corporal from Mainz was heard.

"Do you wish to cross-examine this witness?" said the president.

Lieutenant Mettelinck rose. "Had you ever seen the prisoner or spoken to him before you demanded his pass?"

"No, sir."

"What precisely was he doing when you spoke to him?"

"He was standing on the platform smoking a cigar."

"Did any words of anger pass between you before he struck you?"

"No, sir."

"Will you show the court exactly what he did?"

"He raised both hands unbuttoning his tunic pocket . . . so," the corporal demonstrated. "Then he made as if to remove his warrant and . . . well . . . he struck me."

"From the prisoner's demeanour at the time would you say that he was angered or intoxicated?"

"Certainly not, sir. . . . He answered me civilly. I was never so surprised in my life as when he struck me."

"Thank you. That is all."

There followed the other witnesses with formal evidence as to arrest.

The president, looking towards the prosecutor, said: "That disposes of your case in respect of the first two charges. Do you now desire to proceed with the further charge? In determining our verdict we shall, of course, as I have indicated, have regard to this last, but I think it may be confusing to the issue to introduce it at the present time."

"That was my wish, sir," said the prosecutor, adding: "Since the court has ruled that the three charges be taken concurrently, a course with which I respectfully disagree, I do not think it will be necessary for me to proceed with the further charge. The facts as to the first two will doubtless be sufficient."

"That," said the president, "I must remind you is a matter for the court. The case for the prosecution is so far closed, is it not?"

"So far, yes, sir," said Captain Brauen.

"The court will now hear the defence."

Lieutenant Mettelinck rose again. "The defence of the accused is a simple one," he said. "This man, Otto Gedern, as the court will observe from his field service books, has served with his regiment in the field for two years and seven months. He has not been subject to stoppages of pay, his character has been good."

Captain Brauen rose quickly from his seat, thumping the table. "I object to evidence as to character at the present stage."

"Please sit down, Captain Brauen. I have assumed from the depositions that the case of the defence is that the charge of desertion bears only a technical interpretation. Is that so, *Herr* Lieutenant?"

"Thank you, sir, that is part of my case. Have I your permission to proceed?" The president nodded. "The accused has served without promotion, nor has he been wounded. He has the appearance and demeanour, as the court will note, of a good soldier. He is a Bavarian and in consequence he found himself out of sympathy with his comrades. Desiring to serve with his own kith and kin he took the opportunity of leave to try to come south. The evidence for the prosecution substantiates this. He was well on his way, when he found his plan being foiled by the well-meaning interrogation of a corporal of military police at the Mainz railway station. The court has heard that no angry words passed: the prisoner was standing on the platform smoking. He did not realize that he was striking a superior officer: his case is that there was someone obstructing a well-intentioned and, I suggest, honourable project, and he struck to remove the obstruction. He has expressed his sorrow. . . ."

"I object," interjected the prosecutor, raising his arm.

"I think," said the president to the defender, "that every accused person on trial for his life, where the facts are not disputed, expresses sorrow. We can leave that till later." The prosecutor sat down, a sardonic smile of satisfaction on his face.

"Very well, sir. That concludes the case for the defence. The papers of the accused and the evidence before you amply substantiate his case."

Major von Oppeln fixed his regard upon the prisoner. "We have now heard both sides of this case, Otto Gedern—that is, so far as the first two charges are concerned. Do you desire to give evidence on oath?"

Grant winced as if he had been struck. A still silence fell upon the library. Captain Brauen leaned forward across the table keenly watching the prisoner, whose eyes were closed, his lips slightly moving. Grant must perjure his soul . . . for England.

Lieutenant Mettelinck was beside him. "You heard the president's question, did you not?"

Grant re-opened his eyes. "I ask your pardon, sir. I should like to give evidence on oath." He was sworn. Categorically, clearly, and in detail he reiterated upon oath the case as outlined by his defender.

"Have you any questions to ask the accused?" asked the president of the prosecutor, who immediately rose to cross-examine.

"Your leave commenced on the sixth of June, did it not?"

"Yes, sir."

"Upon what date did this brilliant idea of deserting from the 139th Saxon Regiment and joining some Bavarian formation first strike you?"

"I had been thinking about it for a long time."

"Why, then, didn't you proceed at once on the sixth or seventh of June?"

"I was trying to make up my mind."

"Where did you spend the days between the sixth of June and the sixteenth?"

"In Brussels."

"What were you doing in Brussels?"

"Nothing in particular, sir."

"Is this court to believe that you were eight or ten days in Brussels doing . . . nothing in particular. You know, as well as I do, how soldiers who expend their leave in Brussels spin out the days and hours . . . creeping from one wine house to another, from the brothel to every low haunt of vice. . . ."

"I," interjected the prisoner quietly, "I . . . have no experience."

"Then this was a last-minute idea, was it?"

"Yes, sir."

"How came you in possession of so large a sum of money?"

"I have saved it."

"With what object?"

"Getting down to Bavaria."

"And yet when the opportunity legitimately came for you to proceed on leave and make the proper inquiry in Bavaria, you remained as a coward in Brussels, as you state, trying to make up your mind?"

"Not as a coward, sir."

The prosecutor shrugged his shoulders with a sneer upon his face, and threw his papers down upon the table.

"My cross-examination," he paused for dramatic effect, "is finished."

"Please clear the court for a few minutes," said the president, and when its members were alone he turned to his colleagues. "The case so far is quite clear, I think. It will be for you, gentlemen, to consider your verdict. But we are agreed to hear the third charge before we proceed to such consideration. Are there any further questions which any of you would like to ask of the witnesses, including the accused?"

The president turned to each officer in turn. None desired further evidence. "Then we will proceed," he said. The sergeant-usher reassembled the court.

"Now, Captain Brauen," said the president, "there is a further charge preferred against the accused, arising as the court has determined from the first two which we have heard."

"I do not propose to call any evidence. The facts as to the first two charges, and what the court has heard are sufficient."

Captain Brauen had heard the facts concerning the commandant's assault. His case was a good one. He had considered that the mere fact of preferring a third charge, and then of dismissing it after hearing the earlier evidence would be sufficiently damning and would definitely establish the superiority of the prosecution over the minds of the court.

"You will call no evidence, then? Is the court to dismiss the third charge?"

"Yes, sir. You have ruled that the charge shall not be taken separately. It is only additional evidence as to the base character of the accused. . . ."

"Captain Brauen," said the president sharply. "The court has not asked the prosecution for evidence as to character. You have determined not to proceed with this charge. You have no right, therefore, to refer to evidence which has not been contributed. Sit down. I shall now call upon Lieutenant Mettelinck to make his pleading upon behalf of the accused."

The defender rose briskly.

"If I may speak personally, I regard myself as being happy in being able to advise and defend the accused, Otto Gedern. The facts before the court clearly establish that this man is a good soldier. The prosecution has been anxious to demonstrate that the fact of Gedern's tarrying in Brussels is proof of his cowardice, and intention to desert.

"I submit that here was a man with a fixed idea, but an imbued sense of discipline prevented him from giving effect to his project, until the moment came—near the end of his leave. He was at the parting of the ways.

"He chose a hazardous course of which his present position is sufficient proof; but may I be permitted to remind this court of the writing of the great authority, von Clausewitz, who in a treatise upon the virtues of leadership and courage said: 'Even foolhardiness . . . that is not to be despised.'

"He carried through his project with enterprise and resource. The fact of his striking the corporal, and the instant decision for which the act called, are in a sense—a strictly military one—not discreditable. The procedure of the accused admittedly was foolish. I suggest, however, very seriously that the intention was noble, even praiseworthy.

"I propose now to prove to the court that this man is worthy of its sympathy and respect. I am not pleading in mitigation of any severe sentence but that he may be permitted to go forward with a project, which I have already suggested may be praiseworthy. The prosecution has elected not to proceed with the third charge, nor to call evidence. The defence has a right to refer to this charge, which I feel sure the court will admit."

The president bowed his head.

"This man, Otto Gedern, has shown exemplary behaviour since his arrest. He is no coward." Lieutenant Mettelinck was speaking not with the voice of the perfunctory advocate but with conviction, a sense of fervent duty, and from the heart.

He waved his hand towards the accused. "The wounds upon this man's head were inflicted with a riding-whip. He stood unflinching under the first blow. A field officer," he paused, " struck him, piling contempt upon abuse. Part of the accusation made against him was that his regiment is a mob of white-livered skunks!

"It is no part of the defence of the accused that his regiment consists of men unworthy. The defence is that due to misunderstanding upon a territorial, I might even be permitted to say, upon a racial basis, he desired rather to serve, not with this fine regiment, but with a Bavarian unit.

"But it is, on the contrary, a part of the case for the prosecution, arising from the third charge with which process has not been taken, that because this man is Saxon, as the prosecution supposed, he, a prisoner and an innocent man, is therefore an object of contempt and fitted to be vilified, struck and wounded, while he suffered such insult and assault in silence and without defence.

" This man is no coward! My whole case is that he is a Bavarian, and a man of singular bravery. The court elected to consider the three charges concurrently. The prosecution has repudiated its right to call evidence in support of the third charge. I ask for my right to call such evidence in defence of this brave man. The wounds which he bears alone fully substantiate what I have said. If this man has erred technically, his bearing and the evidence clearly demonstrate that he is not guilty of the grave charges preferred." The defender ceased, and quietly folded together his notes.

The president looked up and addressing the prisoner and escort said: " You may sit down." The sergeant drew up a bench. " I will now hear the prosecution."

" The court has just heard the speech for the defence," said Captain Brauen with a sneer. " Not a single plea in substantiation of the prisoner's case has been adumbrated. The defence has introduced matter quite irrelevant."

" I gave my sanction," interjected the president quickly.

" The facts which I would clarify are that this man deserted his regiment in the line. Presumably, then, he sought various ways of escape. Hiding first in the purlieus and alleys of Brussels, he finally, with an artful cunning, stowed himself away in a goods train, reaching Mainz. Here he posed as a wounded soldier; and as such stole sympathy, and, but for the vigilance of the military police, would perhaps have escaped. As it was, he violently assaulted the police, but due to the excellence of our system of detection was arrested.

" His whole story I submit is a tissue of lies. The court will have observed how this man, realizing the sentence which will shortly be passed upon him, hesitated in taking the oath."

" Captain Brauen," said the president dryly, " you must not attempt to anticipate the verdict of this court."

" I apologize, sir. But the facts. . . ." His voice trailed. The president was watching him keenly. He hesitated : then recommenced. " I shall not refer to matters raised by the defence in regard to the third charge."

" You may not," the voice of the president rose in staccato tones.

The prosecutor continued : " The charges I submit are amply proven. Even supposing, which I cannot, that there is any truth whatever in the ridiculous plea of the accused, I suggest that rather than such serving in mitigation of the offence, this plea is in itself an aggravation. The cohesion of the army depends upon loyalty. Chaos would result if every soldier with a grievance elected to impose his will upon that of the state. But, I suggest, it is sufficiently obvious that the prisoner's plea has no validity whatever. I submit that this man is guilty of cowardice, of desertion; and when he found himself in a corner, he struck his superior officer, as a fox driven to earth would snap at a terrier."

Grant's hopes sank. The prosecutor in his final words had seized upon the weakness of his case.

The president spoke. "We do not desire to hear any further evidence. The court is closed while we consider our verdict." The prisoner and escort were ushered outside. Captain Brauen and Lieutenant Mettelinck withdrew, saluting the president.

Major von Oppeln addressed the court. "In determining our verdict it is no part of our duty to be guided by consideration as to whether this man is brave or a craven. The law is quite clear. We are here, in the first instance, to decide whether the charges are proven. With any other matter we may deal when we consider what sentence shall be imposed."

He turned to each member of the court and asked for a verdict. Each member without hesitation in respect of both charges quickly gave his reply—" Guilty."

"My own judgment confirms your opinions."

The president called out : " Sergeant, open the court."

All those who had attended the trial crowded into the library.

"The court," said the president, speaking deliberately, "finds the prisoner ' Guilty ' upon both charges."

A pause followed. . . . "Lieutenant Mettelinck, on behalf of the accused, do you desire to submit any evidence, or to make a statement in mitigation of sentence?"

" Sir, I have already stated—and I suggest it is also proven—that this man is no coward. He is willing and anxious to serve. He is a man of good education also. He speaks English fluently. This is an asset with which the army cannot lightly afford to dispense. I appeal to the clemency of the court."

" The court will now be closed while the sentence is considered."

Men rose . . . feet shuffled . . . a general sigh of relief from the tense atmosphere . . . the court was cleared.

The president again addressed himself to his colleagues. "It is now our duty to consider the sentence which will be imposed. The law, as you know, gentlemen, prescribes the death penalty in respect of both the two charges which have been submitted and proven. It is within our competence, however, to mete out a less sentence if in our opinion, after careful consideration, there is anything which can properly be urged in extenuation on behalf of this man.

"I am inclined myself to think that there is something behind this case which has not appeared in the evidence either for the prosecution or the defence. Human nature is a curious complex, subject, especially under war conditions, to strange hallucinations, obsessions, and passions. In my judgment Otto Gedern is obviously a man of courage, resource and initiative. His plea upon oath was made with conviction, which was not shaken after cross-examination. The fact that the third charge was not proceeded with is entirely in the prisoner's favour. We must pay due regard to this.

"Nevertheless, a point of first importance was urged by the prosecution, namely, that if any man with a grievance takes the law into his own hands and seeks to impose his will upon that of the state, the result would be chaos. For disciplinary reasons, therefore, you may consider, gentlemen, that the extreme penalty should be imposed. First, I would like to have your views, Lieutenant Deusel?"

"Well, sir, I think it certainly is a point in favour of the accused that no evidence was produced to disprove his own story. Everything that he has stated was supported by the facts as produced by the prosecutor, and, sir, I think he's a brave man. I would not impose the death penalty."

"And you, Lieutenant Meichner."

"I agree with Lieutenant Deusel, sir. He's a fine type of man, and his offence is largely technical."

"Captain Reichman, what is your view?"

"This man has been proved guilty. The facts as to the case are generally known in the barracks; the sentence which the court imposes will have its influence upon the recruits in training. Since many are drawn from the ranks of industrial workers, now being rigorously combed, we are experiencing difficulty. A severe disciplinary example will be of value at the present time, not alone in respect of recruits, but upon the civil population, who will doubtless learn quickly about this case. This man has been proved guilty. In my view the death penalty should be exacted."

The president spoke. "I am obliged to you, Captain Reichman. The points to which you have drawn the court's notice are important. Before this court assembled I was handed an envelope containing an army order. It is marked 'Secret and confidential.' It is unnecessary to remind you that you are upon oath not to disclose matters arising from process in this court. The order which I have here is an instruction to presidents of courts martial. It gives powers to such courts to exercise clemency in cases where, in the court's judgment, the accused may have acted upon impulse, and especially where, if other factors stand to his credit, he possesses any expert military qualifications.

"In such cases, the order instructs the court to impose the death penalty, but, without awaiting any further directions from higher authority, to inform the accused of the extenuating circumstances which its members have in mind, and to commute the sentence to one of service with the 15th Reichswehr Composite Division, in disciplinary charge of whom is the 3rd Guard Grenadier Regiment. Such men will be sent under escort to the base depot of the Guard Grenadier Regiment in the Lille command."

The president continued : " I concur with the view advanced by Captain Reichman. The order of the court will be that sentence of death has been duly imposed. This I think will have the effect which you desire, Captain Reichman. But, in my view, there are circumstances in this case, some of which we can only surmise, since evidence has not been offered, which declare it to be our plain duty to commute the irrevocable sentence of death. I understand, Lieutenants Deusel and Meichner, that this, too, broadly is your view. Now that I have read this army order, I should like, also, to carry you with me, Captain Reichman."

" I agree, sir. And, in fact, were it not for the reasons which I advanced, I should greatly regret the exaction of the extreme penalty."

"Very well, then, we are agreed," said the president. "I will cause the court to be reassembled."

This was the end of the drama. Grant was pale, but he stepped briskly into the court-room beside his escort. Prosecutor, defender and witnesses ranged themselves behind the accused. When the court was duly assembled, and after a short space of silence, the president rose.

Addressing himself to the prisoner, he spoke quietly. " We have, with meticulous care, considered this case. Having due regard also to your character and service, our verdict was unanimous. The sentence, also, which the court will impose is our unanimous decision.

" Soldier Otto Gedern, you have been found guilty upon the charge of desertion upon active service, and upon that also of striking your superior officer in the execution of his duty. The sentence of this court is death."

Tense silence prevailed. So it was all over, reflected Grant. Days of futility . . . everything lost . . . a failure. Rosa . . . lost to him for ever . . . his Rosa, alone, now and for ever. . . . And the plan . . . the W Plan.

A wry, mirthless smile fleeted across his lined face . . . **God!**
What a failure! His mind was numbed.

The president was speaking again : to the condemned man the
voice seemed to come from very far away. " The court has, however,
as I have indicated, had in mind your previous service and qualifications, and acting with the powers conferred upon us, the sentence of
death, which we have imposed, is commuted, again unanimously,
to that of service under rigorous discipline with the 15th Reichswehr
Composite Division." A sigh of relief escaped the lips of the police
corporal from Mainz. " You will proceed under escort as soon as
arrangements are made." In compliance with the army order to
the court, the president ordered the sergeant-usher to remove Grant's
shoulder straps upon which were woven the regimental numerals.

" Have you anything to say, Otto Gedern?"

Grant did not answer at once. Indeed, the full meaning of the
president's words had not yet filtered through the blanket of black,
hopeless fog which shrouded the nerve centres of his brain. What
was it that the president was saying? God! Couldn't they leave
him alone? ". . . the sentence of death, which we have imposed, is
commuted "? What was this? And then suddenly light filtered
through the gloom . . . his mind struggled from its hell.

" May I say, sir, that . . ." He hesitated, " I thank you."

The president bowed while the faintest smile passed across his
face as he said : " Germany will look to you to repay the clemency
of this court."

He then handed the documents to the adjutant, and the court
closed. The prisoner returned to the cell. The handcuffs were
removed, and his property, with the exception of his pay book and
official papers, was restored.

A few minutes later Lieutenant Mettelinck entered the cell.
Grant sprang up. " Thank you, sir, from the bottom of my heart."
Then slowly he added : " Perhaps one day, sir, I may be able to be of
some service to you. . . . I shall hope so."

" There's something curious about you, Gedern. I believe there
to be more behind this case than I know, or than you have told the
court. But never mind that, you have my very sincere good
wish. . . . Farewell."

" Thank you again, sir," said Grant, with emotion.

Late in the afternoon the corporal of police from Mainz, accompanied by an escort of two men, visited him. " You are to come
with me now to the railway station. And . . . no more tricks, Otto
Gedern."

Grant, remembering the sigh in court, put out his hand. It was generously gripped by the big corporal, who then, with that curious paternal affection which often characterizes men whose duty calls them to disciplinary service, took kindly charge of the prisoner. After his deficiencies in kit had been made good, Grant was marched to the railway station. The prisoner and escort were provided with accommodation in the guard's van; and Grant, sleeping soundly, was awakened to find the train slowly entering Koln Railway Station.

The party changed at Koln and after some hours' delay joined a leave train proceeding to Lille.

Recovered from the shock of the past few days, although his face bore the wounds of the commandant's whip, and a pallor had replaced the warmer glow of his skin, the mind of the prisoner began again to engage itself with that part of his life which had been so dramatically interrupted. A decade of time seemed to have elapsed since he parted from Rosa.

Some queer, psychological change appeared to have wrought itself in him : his ego seemed to be altered. It was almost impossible to realize that he and Colonel Duncan Grant were the same personality . . . his feelings more readily adjusted themselves to a conception of an emancipated Otto . . . for his gratitude to the court and to the defender were genuine and sincere, but such an expression came from himself as Otto Gedern, reprieved deserter, not from Colonel Duncan Grant, the spy.

This introspection was extraordinarily confusing. He could scarcely realize his position nor had he yet capacity to analyse his attitude towards the two conflicting duties which displayed themselves before his mind—the W Plan, the Commander-in-chief, England; and the new lease of life generously granted to Otto Gedern, soldier. It was all overwhelmingly difficult. Of course there was Rosa.

Telegrams began to flash through his mind. . . . Where was Rosa? . . . Going to Switzerland. Why? The W Plan. . . . Were they not united? . . . More so than ever through the W Plan. . . . His duty must be clear. . . . The W Plan. What was the date? . . . Of course it must be the twenty-first of June . . . where was he going? . . . he had scarcely heard what the president had said. At any rate to his stunned mind it had meant nothing, but life instead of the grave.

" Corporal," he said, " where are we going?"

" To Lille."

" What regiment . . . didn't the president of the court say something about a disciplinary corps . . . I didn't hear."

" Yes, you're to be posted to the 15th Reichswehr Division with the Guard Grenadier Regiment."

The mind's wireless operator began again to send out messages. Guard Grenadiers . . . seen from a barley field . . . convoys of lorries . . . prisoners of war . . . Scots, willing workers . . . condemned German prisoners working with them . . . interpreters . . . men like moles . . . the destruction of the British Army . . . the W Plan.

He began again to reflect—so this was then his fate. Colonel Grant's life had been spared in order that, as Soldier Otto Gedern, he might participate actively in the work of destruction . . . a Scot . . . a willing worker . . . the just retribution of fate. But he would see what he had not seen—the W Plan in being . . . how amazingly interesting!

He was neither Duncan Grant nor Otto Gedern. He was living in a new dimension . . . almost a resurrection from the dead . . . he had been so near to the commandant's dung heap . . . he was a new man, reborn. But where was Rosa . . . she had a claim, nay more she was of him, Duncan of her—inseparable—" Till death us do part. . . ." Death had been foiled . . . he must be Duncan Grant!

The train dragged into Lille. The party marched to the military police headquarters and reported for instructions. They washed, shaved, and ate a hearty meal. A little later orders were received to march to the 2nd Motor Convoy column. A lorry would be proceeding during the night to the Guards' depot, where the prisoner would be handed over and the escort relieved of further duty. As night fell the escort was placed in a ration and supply lorry forming part of a column. They arrived at the sentry post. How well Grant recollected its stern discipline. The lorries drew into the park behind the barbed wire enclosure. The escort and their prisoner climbed down.

" Report at the guard-room over there," said a sergeant, pointing to gleams of light coming from a muffled window. The sergeant of the guard took over the papers with quick decision. " Name?" he queried, addressing Grant.

" Otto Gedern."

" Spell it." He was entering information upon a foolscap form. " Your number is 60719. 15th Reichswehr Composite Division. Read this order." He passed a typewritten order pasted upon a board. " Prisoners are forbidden to converse under penalty of instant death. You understand?"

" Yes, sergeant."

"Corporal, march your escort back to the lorry. Here is the receipt for Otto Gedern. Look sharp now."

*　　　*　　　*　　　*　　　*

Grant found himself in a large encampment of wooden huts. Immediately upon arrival he was conducted before an officer, who examined the papers relating to the court martial, handed to him by the sergeant in charge of the escort. The officer studied the papers and then addressed himself to the prisoner.

"You are under sentence of death, Otto Gedern. You will find in this command that you will enjoy complete liberty within the confines of the camp. You will have every opportunity to be happy. The work upon which you will be employed is of a special character. It is hard and demands the best of which you are capable. We allow no shirkers here : no second chances. The penalty imposed for non-compliance with any order of whatsoever nature is instant death at the sole discretion of the officer responsible for the issue of that order. You have been fortunate so far that the court martial has dealt leniently with your offence. In this command there is no appeal to the clemency of a court, no extenuating circumstance for offence which can be permissible. Orders must be immediately, energetically executed. That is the spirit of this command. The penalty for failure, I repeat, is instant death. Do you understand?"

"I do, sir," said Grant.

"I observe," said the officer, "that a qualification noted is that you can speak English. Is that so?"

The officer rang a bell and upon the entry of an orderly, said : "Send the interpreter from C. Battalion to me at once," and then addressed himself again to Grant. "The interpreter of C. Battalion, consisting of Englishmen, will examine your proficiency. If the test is satisfactory you will be posted for duty to that battalion."

Every doubt was swept from Grant's mind. The events and revelations of the twelve days, prior to his arrest, sketched themselves vividly in his mind . . . he was back again in the barley field . . . a convoy of men whose black silhouettes stood out against the night. Englishmen, French, Italian, Russian, Poles and Scots, were passing . . . men going to and from the underground galleries which formed the W Plan. Now he was to be a cog in the wheel of this vast machine designed literally to undermine the whole strength of Britain—a mechanical Samson, willing Scots, figuratively shorn of their hair, to bring down the temple of an empire in ruins. He was a free man now, a new man, living in a new world hedged in by iron discipline and barbed-wire entanglements.

G.M.N.—R

But he was different from any of the inhabitants of that new world for he alone knew the W Plan, at least in its entirety. Even if the Commander-in-chief had failed him, within the confined limits of his new world he could still serve his general and England. He would wait for events to develop. Perhaps his chances of success today were greater than ever previously.

A knock was heard upon the door, which immediately opened to admit a short, brusque little figure, somewhat grotesque in military uniform. He saluted clumsily.

"Good evening, Herr Hauptmann. You sent for me?" he queried.

"I want you to test this man as an interpreter in English. He claims facility in the language."

Some five minutes of conversation between the two men, the one a gentleman of culture, who carefully feigned a little hesitancy, the other a German whose business habits prior to the war had brought him daily in touch with those of wealth and culture in London, made it plain to the examiner that Grant possessed a rare fluency in the English tongue.

"I am satisfied," he said, turning to the officer. "This man possesses a satisfactory knowledge of English."

"Then he will be posted for duty to C. Battalion." He wrote out an order. "Take this to the adjutant, and you, soldier Gedern, accompany the battalion interpreter."

CHAPTER X

A GAME OF CARDS

GRANT was posted to the 3rd Company of the battalion, and found himself in a narrow, dimly lighted hut, on either side of which were two tiers of bunks in which were men sleeping. At regular intervals equipment, but no arms, were hung at the foot of the bunks. An armed sentry stood at the door. Grant passed in.

"You will be for duty at three o'clock tomorrow morning," said the grenadier, and he pointed to a vacant place in the row of bunks. Grant hung up his equipment, and climbed up to a straw palliasse, suspended upon tightly-stretched fencing wire. Lulled by the warm atmosphere and the rhythmic sound of the deep breathing of many men, sleep took him to herself.

He was rudely awakened. Voices, familiar as from some other age, urged him to show a leg. He was one of a company of some sixty men, speaking what passes for English in a dozen different dialects, cursing, tumbling against each other in the dim light, pulling on short field boots, adjusting equipment. He was unnoticed. A sharp order was called out and the men filed outside, Grant among them. Their names were called, familiar English names, with a few of German origin as it were to give leaven to the list. His own was the last to be called by the company interpreter.

"Otto Gedern, take your place with the second squad." A gap was made in the ranks for the new recruit, and the party marched to the canteen at which coffee and bread were served and every man issued with a haversack ration. They were then packed, squad by squad, into a convoy of waiting motor wagons. Through the gloom Grant could observe other groups of men filing from out of the huts and canteen towards the waiting convoy. Not one single word had been spoken by anyone with the exception of the short, sharp orders of the guards. The men sat huddled together upon the floors of the wagons which rumbled steadily towards the forward zone. It was still dark when the column came to a halt.

The men clambered out, and were formed into parties of fifties, each accompanied by two grenadiers and an interpreter, a German soldier, with the rank of corporal. They marched in file towards the mount of Kemmel which loomed in the near distance. An occasional star shell illuminated the ragged outline of the hill, the sharp sound of musketry, the heavier report of shrapnel told of that timidity and nervousness which heralds dawn in the battle area. As they reached the hillside, the way led through huge mounds of tumbled earth banked upon either side of the narrow path. The figures of men, dimly defined, could be observed high upon the slopes of the deepening channel, throwing aside the tons of new earth and debris which poured upon the hillside from the wide mouths of enormous tubes which thrust themselves from the hillside. "The Messer excavator," was Grant's mental comment.

The party entered a large tunnel, opening out to a great subterranean hall, the roof of which was supported by concrete pillars and which was brilliantly illuminated. Grant could discern the sound of smooth-running machinery, as of a great power station : at regular intervals heavier vibrations as of some distant explosion could be heard, followed immediately by the tumult of huge chains locking swiftly in the cogs of giant wheels, and then the muffled noise of loose earth falling.

This sepulchral orchestra was accompanied by yet another sound, entirely distinctive, as if of a torrent of water swiftly intaken to the mouth of some phantom mammoth of the depths. Here was the Messer excavator and endless winding gear in motion, accompanied by the Speyer drainage system by absorption. A continuous stream of men swathed in clay came from the mouths of two tunnels leading from the main galleries to the great hall, upon either side of which were stationed begrimed engineers in charge of the intricate controls governing the complex machinery.

Above each of the tunnel entrances was fixed a large letter of the alphabet. Grant noted them carefully. These entrances indicated the commencement of the long galleries leading to the heads of the mined shafts. A large party of men was now drawn up upon one side of the great hall, while an officer, megaphone in hand, standing before a chart, detailed the parties and numbers of men required for each section of the work. As the instructions were given, the parties left the hall and disappeared through the mouths of the tunnels, while the noise of machinery continued without interruption.

Orders came to the squad to which Grant was attached. They were marched away in file, passing into B gallery. In its wide mouth an electrically driven light-railway train was waiting. First the train was loaded to capacity with heavy shells: the working party was then crowded into empty trucks, and the train proceeded along the wide, lighted gallery. The sound of machinery within the enclosed space became almost deafening; it was difficult to separate from each other the variations of sound which Grant had noted while in the main hall, but insistent always was that of the mammoth suction of water.

At regular intervals the gallery opened to right and left of the track and gave way to galleries sloping downwards running at right angles to the main track. These were the shafts connecting the upper series, upon which Grant's party was travelling, with the lower trellis of the W system.

Where these communication galleries met the main shaft, the track opened out to admit sidings upon which were trucks heavily laden with all the munitions of war, rations and fodder. Large parties of men were at work unloading the wagons, and reloading them into hand-operated trucks to be taken for store to the more remote parts of the shafts, or for immediate service to the farther ends of the lower system galleries. Everything was organized and the work proceeding as with mathematical precision.

As the train passed these points Grant noted above the clamour of machinery a sharp order in French and again in some unfamiliar language which he thought to be Polish or Russian. The train drew on, moving rapidly for about half an hour, at the end of which it drew into one of many sidings at the foot of a gradual slope upwards, about one hundred yards long. The letter G was posted at the foot of this gangway, and Grant realized that in the course of his journey he had penetrated some five miles beneath the British entrenched positions and that now he was standing almost directly beneath the village of Flètre.

It was almost impossible to give credence to such an extravagant conception . . . of the W Plan in being, being driven forward with increasing energy and faultless organization . . . and, of the ignorance of the armies of the Allies, with all their elaborate systems of espionage and intelligence, aided by every device known to the usages of modern warfare . . . and of the fact that outside those closely-guarded ranks of workers, over whose head the penalty of death hung always, he alone knew the details of the plan, he alone, a workman unloading the heavy shells which would complete the downfall of Britain, and change a world's history and geography . . . he alone appreciated the significance of the gigantic scheme which his hands were helping to complete.

The party worked steadily for some hours, and was then moved back along the railway track, as Grant judged it, by some four miles. The wagons were placed upon a siding and the party disembarked. A truck was waiting to be unloaded, piled high with cases of explosives. The interpreter in charge of the group called the men around him.

" Be careful of that stuff. It's dynamite. Load it in these trucks."

The explosives were carefully handled and disposed in hand-operated trolleys. The interpreter leading the party carried a plan of this section of the galleries in his hand, while the two Guard Grenadiers posted themselves respectively at the head and tail of the column. They marched forward diagonally from the direction of the shaft which they had left, but on the same level. This gallery, Grant realized, would be one of the short arms connecting the main galleries. At the apex of the two short arms the party was halted. The dynamite was carefully stored against the wall of the shaft, obviously preparatory to being moved forward to the end of a main shaft, when the works were completed ready for the blowing of the mines.

The party returned to the trucks when a rest of half an hour was ordered and the men brought out their rations, and were permitted to converse. Grant found himself in conversation with a corporal of Royal Engineers. The men talked listlessly of the last game of cards, or of the simple matters of home life. Grant noted that all reference to the work in hand or to the life of war was studiously avoided. He made an effort to engage the interest of the corporal, who prior to the war had lived in a Berkshire village. Grant had hunted around Newbury and knew the Thames reaches by Pangbourne intimately : as a boy he had swum a lake to find swans' eggs, and had tickled trout in the Pang.

The corporal was friendly. They would have a yarn when they were back again in camp. Grant had penetrated the stoic reserve of the southern county estate carpenter, which had previously been the man's familiar occupation.

A plan, desperate though it might be, was beginning to sketch itself in Grant's mind . . . even if he could not deliver the W Plan . . . could never reach headquarters . . . even if Rosa, now so far away, heaven knew where, separated from his life, might not reach Geneva . . . would it not, perhaps, be possible prematurely to blow up one section of the galleries and at least give some warning of the approaching danger?

He reflected upon such a project . . . a small explosion would be useless for his purpose . . . the detonation would perhaps do little more than suggest that probably one of the larger dumps of shells or other explosives had gone off behind the lines . . . but surely it would indicate something most unusual. He dared not examine again the map still secreted in the collar of his jacket. An explosion of the tons of dynamite which they had just handled would, so far as he could judge it, erupt somewhere in the forward zone if indeed it succeeded in accomplishing anything beyond temporarily wrecking some of the subterranean galleries . . . if it were possible correctly to tamp the charges and lay a mine, without doubt a surface explosion could be caused . . . then again if the dynamite could be moved to the far end of one of the long arms of the galleries and fired from such a point, a vast explosion could be occasioned behind the British lines, for example at Flètre or Poperinghe . . . supposing such a thing did happen, there would, of course, be an inquiry . . . engineers would be summoned who would investigate the cause and this labyrinth of devilment would then be exposed.

But what could he do in order to achieve such a project? . . . he knew nothing of mine laying, of the technique of charges, or tamping explosives. Moreover, it would be impossible to move the loads of dynamite from their present position, and, in any case, to explode them meant certain death for himself and for any others whom he might persuade to assist him.

Death held no terrors for him : but, for those deadened, hopeless souls with whom he toiled amid the din and in the fetid atmosphere of this living tomb, death might still hold out the fear of the unknown, a sting so far untried. The very silence of these men, their mute obedience to orders, a minute breach of which would cause the certain fall of the sword hanging always over their heads, was a token of their fearfulness . . . and they still possessed their compensations within the camp—drink, tobacco, good food, hectic music and the deep sleep of exhaustion and forgetfulness . . . The sun still shone in the sky; perhaps one day even the prison gates would open.

Grant might take one man into his confidence, two or three, but of more he doubted. The company was filtered with informers, English-speaking Germans, and he must first convince one or two men of his true identity in order to break down the barriers of reserve and fear with which each individual was hedged.

The long hours passed in toil, disposing of munitions, penetrating in and out of the long galleries, with which in this section of the works the party seemed to be familiar. This part of the stage was being set finally for the great drama. In the lower galleries Grant had a glimpse of long lines of armoured cars and guns of heavy calibre; in the upper a whole treasury of all the most modern appliances relating to mobile warfare. At one time the party crossed a new gallery in the course of construction—the Messer machine was at work, blasting, breaking, hauling, swallowing tons of new soil, carried by the endless winding gear to great tubes which took them in and threw them miles away upon the slopes of Mont Kemmel.

Twenty-four hours of continuous work, with short intervals for rest, had passed. A relieving squad mechanically took over the task. The men composing the working party were pallid with physical exhaustion, stifled with the damp heat of the atmosphere, numbed by the roar of machinery. They now tumbled into the waiting wagons which took them back through the long gallery to the main hall, filled with lines of fresh men from the encampment, relieving groups in other parts of the workings.

As they left the shaft head and passed into the cool night a great sigh involuntarily escaped from each man as he greeted the fresh air, and drank it deeply into his lungs. The sound of machinery receded and was blanketed by the growing walls of the long avenue through which the files of men shuffled to the waiting motor convoy. The men sprawled in the bottoms of the wagons, some in deep slumber, others sleeping fitfully as they were jolted against each other by the swinging wagons. Within the encampment the men, after being provided with hot coffee and rum, went back to the long low hut to sleep. . . .

*   *   *   *   *

Grant woke, refreshed. Some men were cleaning uniforms and equipment, others sitting about conversing, while others still slept heavily. Grant joined a little group who were stripping the mud from their equipment and laughing over some ancient jest, the corporal of engineers, Waller by name, among them. They strolled together towards the canteen already filled with men, some leaning against the counter, others playing a variety of games—cards, billiards, darts.

The men were separated by instinct into their varied national groups, though, against each little coterie, inquisitive spectators stood idly watching the varied recreations of a new and strange race. Through an aperture Grant could see the bound and rebound of a football, and heard the cries of Englishmen, though many of various races were participating in the rough and tumble, ruleless game.

Grant and Waller seated themselves at a little table, smoking, with cups of steaming coffee before them, and resumed the discourse upon trout. Waller confessed to having been an accomplished poacher; and, when the spirit moved him, still had given a Sunday to this pastime. He found that the excitement of lawlessness stimulated the blood of his veins, and by its adventure provided spice to an otherwise monotonous existence.

Grant encouraged him with enthusiasm, commenting: " It would be grand to have a little adventure again. This life must get on your nerves a bit."

Waller regarded him suspiciously, and added in an unfriendly tone : " It is forbidden to criticize . . . here."

" Of course," said Grant. . . . " Let's go out and sit in the sun."

Grant led the way and deliberately chose a clear space of ground, removed from the sound of English voices and beside a group of Russians noisily playing together. They lay down. Grant must win this man's confidence. He sketched the configuration of the English countryside by heaping the dust with his fingers until the three ridges between Reading and Newbury, and flanking the course of the Thames to Wallingford, with the intervening Hog's Back running high through Bradfield and Bucklebury, lay planned upon the ground, the contours roughly conforming to the letter W. Then he filled in the villages by placing pebbles and stuck pieces of dried grass into the ground to denote the woods.

"You know this ground very well . . . for a German soldier," commented the corporal.

"I remember as a boy, my father was staying at Englefield for the shooting."

"Your father . . . shooting?" questioned the corporal slowly.

"Yes; he was with friends. I remember that I stole away from the house down to a stream haunted by trout which runs through Bradfield. I lay so still beside a tiny foot-bridge, bare arm dangling in the water. The trout came snuffling to my finger-tips like a favourite hunter for lumps of sugar. There was a big sleek fellow I had spied under the bridge. My finger felt his fat belly as he snuggled to the invitation of my gentle tickling. Then my fingers closed and I hurled him over my shoulder into the green meadow. . . . Great fun that! . . . Better than sniping at some poor devil's head, corporal?"

"You talk like an English gent, but you aren't an interpreter with this lot"—he jerked his thumb over his shoulder—"are you? That seems a waste to me. You know our interpreter—well, you've heard him, anyway—some bloated waiter. If it wasn't for . . ." He checked himself deliberately and smiled wryly.

"Can you keep a secret?" said Grant in a lowered voice, looking the man straight in the eyes.

"We have to, here," said the corporal quietly. "Why, I daren't even think for fear of talking in my sleep."

"Well, don't worry about your sleep," laughed Grant, and added very seriously: "You must believe me. . . ." He paused without taking his eyes from those of the corporal. "I am a British officer . . . my name is Colonel Duncan Grant, Inverness Highlanders."

Corporal Waller gasped, frowned and then shook his head, saying: "You're kidding me."

Grant thrust his face nearer to that of the corporal. "You've got to believe me," he said, and then pointing to the map which they had drawn in the dust, whispered: "We worked in galleries shaped like that"—he traced his finger along the course of the hills—"last night . . . think it out."

The corporal pondered. "What are you doing here? What are you getting at, anyway?" he said with hesitation.

Grant parried him. "Do you want to break this damned monotony? . . . If I'm a German I'm pretty well off as things go in wartime . . . well fed and safe . . . that's true, isn't it?" The corporal nodded. . . . "But I am British . . . this plan," he clapped his hand emphatically upon the little heaps before him, so that tiny springs of dust squirted up through his fingers, "will destroy England . . . you must have thought about it . . . it undermines the whole of the British lines. . . . The dynamite we shifted yesterday, one day soon will be exploded . . . just like those little puffs of dust. . . . Thousands of men . . . Englishmen . . . will be destroyed. Do you believe me?"

"Yes," said Waller reluctantly, "I believe that . . . I've figured it out . . . we all know that . . . but we dare not discuss it. . . . Even if you are a British officer, what can you do? We go on with the work, driven to it. It's no business of ours, anyway."

"Corporal Waller," said Grant, "you have my life in your hands . . . I have delivered it to you. . . . I, too, have yours . . . so far as any man knows here, I am soldier Otto Gedern, qualified as an interpreter . . . but I need you . . . I'm here to defeat this plan . . . think, man, of those Berkshire hills and vales . . . compare that sweet countryside with this foul business . . . you, an Englishman, will help me, Waller? . . . and keep my secret."

The man glanced up at Grant suddenly. Then his eyes lighted; the heavy bearded jaw thrust itself forward. "By Christ, I will," he said between his teeth. Grant placed his hand in that of the big, characteristic yeoman and gripped it tightly.

"But it's you must give the orders," Waller added; "I'll do what you tell me."

"How many of the others in our group understand what we're working upon?" asked Grant.

"I can't rightly say," said Waller, pausing. "Generally speaking, I suppose most of the lads have some idea, but they daren't talk about it. It's only occasionally that a chance word in the course of the work, or when we're alone together, gives me the impression that most of them have figured it the same as me."

"Do you understand mining, corporal?"

"No, I'm a carpenter by trade, but I've had some experience in the 'Brickstacks' 'way back in nineteen-fifteen . . . I've got a pal here, McTavish, of the Borderers . . . he's been a miner all his life and was taken prisoner with me on the La Bassée Canal . . . he was a sergeant in the mining company."

"Do you trust him, Waller?"

"Yes; he thinks much the same as me . . . he'd had a bit too much to drink one day . . . I had a hell of a job with him . . . he turned savage . . . said he'd like to blow up the whole bloody business and go west in the mess.

"Thank God! no one heard him, but I got the wind up properly. Every other man is a spy, at least, one begins to think so with everyone dressed the same, and these interpreters hanging round every odd corner . . . the guards don't matter to us : they just stand around like statues unless there's any shooting to be done . . . and even that doesn't happen now."

He paused, and then said with weariness in his voice : "We just go backwards and forwards."

"Now, Waller, listen to me. I am determined to blow up these galleries. It's our job . . . mine . . . yours. We're British . . . we're going to have one gigantic adventure together . . . better than poaching, Waller . . . blow the whole business sky high. There's enough dynamite down there to bust up Europe. . . . Are you game, corporal?"

"I'll do what you tell me," the man said slowly.

"Well, go and find friend McTavish and bring a pack of cards with you. We'll find some more volunteers for this job before we're through with it; and then they can join our card party as a bit of camouflage."

Corporal Waller slouched away, hands thrust deep in his pockets, shoulders hunched, his shaggy head gazing gloomily upon the ground. Grant rolled over on to his back and lit a cigarette. The plan, a final throw of the dice, was taking shape in his brain as he watched the thin smoke eddying up to be lost in the deeper blue of the sky. He was lying thus when Waller returned with McTavish, a bow-legged, rugged little man, with a shock of red hair. They squatted beside him.

"Waller and I," said Grant, "have been talking over old days together. He pleads guilty to being a poacher . . . so do I."

"He's a gent," interjected Waller . . . "one of the landed gentry." The three men laughed. "He was a poacher just for a kid's bit of devilment . . . I'm a craftsman at the game."

Grant laughed merrily and said : "As a matter of fact . . . I'm a Scot."

McTavish had opened his wizened eyes a little wider. "So you're a gentleman, are ye?" and he was gazing at Grant with increasing astonishment. . . . "Then, what the hell are ye doing here?"

"I was just going to tell you, McTavish, when . . . you've dealt the cards." Grant continued : "Waller trusts me; he's under my orders. Is that right, corporal?"

The man expressed an affirmative by a poise of the head and a deep-throated "Aye."

"Don't get excited, McTavish . . . you're coming in with us . . . my name's Grant, Colonel. . . ." The man sat back on his heels in bewilderment. "Yes . . . Colonel of the Inverness Regiment." Then speaking deliberately and pausing between each sentence he said: "I know . . . Waller knows . . . you, too, McTavish, know, the nature of the work upon which we are engaged. You're a miner. . . . Could you blow up the dynamite we were shifting yesterday?"

"I certainly could, sir."

"Could you wreck the galleries, McTavish?"

The man considered. "With some preparation I could do that, sir," he said slowly. "At least, in part."

"Not entirely, then."

"No, sir, that would mean . . . well, I don't know; but what's the idea, anyway?"

"Waller and I have agreed to blow that dynamite sky high . . . you understand how to do it . . . we need your help . . . we're going to have it, aren't we, McTavish?"

The man's eyes narrowed until their bright blue irises were lost in wrinkles of reddened skin, the mouth spread with a broad grin exposing an interrupted row of teeth, yellowed with tobacco chewing.

"Help you?" he queried. "If it hadn't been for Waller, I'd have blown the lot up long ago. Help you?" his voice was rising. Grant hit him playfully, saying: "Your deal, McTavish."

Grant then outlined the plan in his mind. It was to allow eight or ten trusted men into the secret of the project. The party would be sent to work upon this portion of the gallery on the morrow. As the forepart of the column turned the apex connecting the two communicating galleries, the men at the head and tail of the column would turn upon the guards and interpreter and overpower them; quickly the fuses would be laid and the dynamite exploded. That might be the end, but what matter? . . . one glorious adventure. The plan they considered was feasible if sufficient men could be pledged to the scheme. They agreed to meet again together for a game of cards during the afternoon. Meanwhile, each of the three would try quietly to win recruits for their enterprise among his friends.

*　*　*　*　*

The interpreter to the group had long nursed the desire to obtain employment in the canteen in which his experience and proficiency in European languages would render him valuable; and moreover, the prospect of such ease and plenty cried loudly day by day from the temple of his being—a fat stomach, the symmetry of whose curves was in danger by reason of the arduous nature of the toil to which the body was exposed. He discovered Grant in the canteen, and bringing two tankards of lager seated himself beside him.

The interpreter purred his flattery. Otto Gedern was obviously a fine soldier; he had noted the zeal with which he applied himself to his work, while he himself—he waved his hand in deprecation—was scarcely fitted for such tasks. Herr Gedern, too, spoke the English language with perfection. The interpreter would recommend him for control of the group, while he himself would ask to be relieved and relegated to a more humble office, that was, of course, if Otto Gedern desired the post which self-effacement could create. His beady eyes twinkled with eagerness as he gazed over the brim of the tankard into which he had plunged to hide his excitement.

Grant, the player of many parts, took his cue. He was flattered at the suggestion and would desire such an opportunity better to serve the Fatherland, but requested the interpreter to tell him how such an appointment could be arranged.

The plump little man would see the adjutant: he would go at once and, so saying, he rose from the table, hurrying busily from the canteen, in whose atmosphere, as he threaded his way quickly by long practice through the tables, he already felt the reincarnation of his former cosmopolitan life.

Grant sat in meditation . . . in sole charge of a group working in a comparatively isolated part of the workings, issuing orders in a language not understood by the armed guards, he would be master of the situation. The guards could be overpowered, and then in the secrecy of the workings the explosives could be disposed by experts, the fuses laid, and a great mine blown which would vomit forth somewhere near the British front and support lines, and would, whatever other result was achieved, certainly wreck a part of the galleries, delay the progress of the plan, and probably provoke suspicion within the British lines. He had already won over two good men to the project, and before the party set out to the workings on the morrow he felt sure that the adherence of three or four other men would be secured. He would be able to deal with the rest of the party within the workings when the time came.

The interpreter came hurrying through the crowded canteen, making his way swiftly, his face wreathed in smiles. Obviously, his project had succeeded.

"The adjutant would like to see you at once," he said. "I am promoted," he gushed, "to the office of second corporal in the canteen; you will be elevated to that of interpreter."

"I am very much obliged to you," Grant said. "Come along; we will return to the canteen in celebration." They left the canteen, the fat little figure pirouetting across the floor with the air of the *maître d'hôtel* disposing an honoured guest.

"The interpreter tells me that you are a zealous soldier and very fluent in the English language. He recommends you for promotion to the office of interpreter, not I think," he said dryly, "without some less obvious motive that his own services might better be employed in the canteen. With this latter view I happen to concur," and he smiled as he viewed the fat figure now bent in humility. "I have looked through your papers, Otto Gedern, and am satisfied that you possess the qualities necessary. I am glad to have this confirmed," he laughed a little, "by our ambitious friend here. You will take over his duties at once." And turning to the orders of the day, he added, "And will be in charge of your group tomorrow. You understand?"

In the afternoon Grant met Waller and McTavish in the hut. His appointment as interpreter had already been posted in the daily orders. Five other men were seated at a table conversing, and looked up quickly as Grant entered the room.

"What about a game of cards?" said Grant.

"Come on, boys," Waller called out over his shoulder.

The eight men formed one of many little groups resting and playing in the sun. With legs stretched out in a circle and heads together they began playing. Waller introduced the five men, Clarkson, Davis, Hughes, Partington, Maulkin—adding: "We're all in the game . . . the other one . . . with you."

Between the throw of the cards, as they fell almost automatically, Grant outlined his plan. McTavish, Clarkson, Davis, and himself would lead the column; Waller, Partington, Maulkin and Hughes would bring up the rear. As the first part of the column turned the bend and the apex of the two connecting galleries where the explosives were stored, upon an order from Grant, they would turn on the guards, disarm and destroy them. Clarkson and Hughes at the end of the column would take over the arms of the guards, and prevent entry or exit from the gallery, while McTavish with other skilled miners laid the charges. Events would then shape themselves. Grant informed the men that he possessed plans of the whole system secreted in his collar. It had been his project to deliver them to the British lines. They were to understand that this was the W Plan.

McTavish suggested the possibility, after the mine had been blown of being able to force an exit through the crater, if the miners were not destroyed by the force of the explosion itself. That would depend upon what could be arranged to prevent a blow-back down both the galleries intersecting at this point.

The party broke up and strolled across to the canteen where, in twos and threes, they joined the main body of the men of their own group, who were making merry in one corner. Grant set himself out to cultivate friendship with the men, to which advances, in place of those of the alternately ingratiating and hectoring little fellow whom he had replaced, they readily responded. At eight o'clock they had orders to be within the hut, and the roll was called; the sentries took post while the men climbed into their bunks. Grant was in a state of high excitement and slept but fitfully.

At three o'clock on the following morning the hut was astir, and throwing on their equipment, the men stumbled through the darkness to the waiting lorries. After a jolting journey to the shaft head, they reached the great hall. An officer came across to Grant, and handed him a plan of a part of the workings with a detail of instructions for the working day . . . the dynamite was first to be shifted clear of the gangway, and a recess cut and strutted in the wall, to be constructed to contain it . . . thereafter, the group was to report at the head of G shaft for digging operations. They were given picks and shovels, and entrained for the cross gallery halt.

Having detrained, Grant assembled his party within the gallery and addressed them.

" We have important and dangerous work to do today. My orders will be obeyed . . . immediately and absolutely. I want you to understand that."

He then marshalled the column with his chosen men at its front and rear, himself leading the way, walking beside the armed sentry. He judged the gallery to be about two miles in length, along which the party was moving briskly in step. Thirty to forty minutes had passed before he saw in the distance the wall facing the end of the gallery, which denoted its abrupt change in direction. He glanced backwards to McTavish and his confederates, and, in a moment, had turned the corner.

He cried to the party to halt, at the same time wresting the rifle from the hands of the sentry beside him. The three men behind sprang upon the astonished man, stifling his cries and throwing him upon the ground, while Clarkson, rifle in hand, took post closing the gallery. Grant ran round the bend and discovered that Waller with his comrades had as effectively dispatched the rear guard. The

working party stood huddled in amazement and fear against the
wall of the gallery.

Grant called them to attention and spoke.

"I am a British officer : there are men here who know the fact."

"That's right, sir," cried voices from the end of the gallery.

"Men skilled in mine laying will report to Sergeant McTavish
in front; the others will remain with Corporal Waller here under
my orders. Anyone who attempts to leave the gallery will be shot.
Get to your posts."

A dozen men joined McTavish, the other thirty odd remaining
with Waller. A conference then took place between the miners and
Grant as to the best means of blowing up the gallery. After a quick
discussion it was decided to move the dynamite some twenty yards
from the apex down one arm of the gallery, which at the turn would
be blocked with soil dug from the sides of the shaft, so as to afford
some protection for the mining party from the force of the explosion.
The men set to work with fury to dig out a cave in the wall, piling
the soil as they did so. Within a short space of time a wall with a
small aperture to be filled later had been made. The miners, with
the assistance of a carrying party, then stacked the charges of
dynamite in the recess, while the main body of the party withdrew
through the aperture to within the other gallery, where they
used every effort to strengthen the wall to give them all the protection
possible.

McTavish carefully laid the fuse, which Grant then lit.
Enthusiasm and excitement had given added strength to the working party, who toiled without respite. Grant and the miners
returned to the main body of men in the adjoining gallery and the
aperture was hastily filled. There lay now between the working
party and the mine not only the thick triangular wall, but another
built around the end of the gallery some ten feet thick, and every
moment growing stronger in its resistance.

CHAPTER XI

NO MAN'S LAND

GRANT stood, watch in hand . . . two minutes to go. . . . He
called upon the men to cease work. "Thank you lads," he
cried. "Splendid. This . . . is for England." Then glancing at

his watch he said : "We have just over one minute to go," adding with a laugh : "Better sport than tickling trout, Corporal Waller."

The second ticked loudly from his watch; his heart thumped in his throat . . . in a moment a tremendous roar engulfed his ears and senses. The men, who had withdrawn some thirty yards down the gallery, were thrown from their feet and hurled against the walls. The soil rocked beneath their feet; the roof, balks of timber, pit props and tons of earth descended upon prostrate bodies. Mountains of soil from the barrier were thrown violently down the gallery and were carried by a tempest of wind. The lights had gone out; the air was heavy with dust.

Grant recovered consciousness to discover one leg pinned beneath a considerable weight, otherwise he was a free man in the blackness of the devastated pit. He struggled with the loose soil and timbers, freeing the imprisoned leg; then thrust out his hand which met the soft warm body of a man. He moved his fingers over it and shook it. The faculty of hearing was creeping back. He heard sounds—a man shouting hysterically, low moans as of someone in pain; the man beside him stirred.

Grant shouted through the darkness : "Call out your names, one by one." He counted sixteen, among them McTavish, Hughes and Partington. He could detect their muffled groans from the depths of the gallery. He then cried : "Are you free to move?" Three men answered that they were imprisoned by the fallen roof. To the remainder Grant called to come over to him if they could. He waited, and could hear them laboriously working their way over and through the debris towards him. He still possessed the matches with which the fuse had been lit. He must carefully conserve these, though their light could be spun out considerably by lighting torches of splintered timber. But he feared also to illuminate the devastation, for fear that the urgent call of humanity might delay the party from extricating themselves from the shaft, while seeking for buried comrades. The possibility, sketched by McTavish, of emerging from the galleries somewhere within the British lines, possessed him. The men were now gathered round him.

McTavish stretched out his hand : it met Grant's shoulder. He shifted it clumsily upwards, patting Grant on the cheek. "Good for you, sir," he half sobbed.

Grant had made a rapid mental appreciation of the situation. They must make their way past the barricade and try to find an exit upwards. They crept forward slowly over mountains of debris which seemed at times as if it would entirely block further progress. At one time Grant felt his back touch the roof, but the gallery had been constructed securely. Later, as they groped forward the surface of the wreckage inclined downwards. The air was fresher, distinctly so.

"Where do you reckon we are now, McTavish?"

The man considered. "Weel," he said in his high-pitched voice, "I should say aboot th' bend." Grant struck his first match and they gazed around. Someone laughed: then for a moment all were convulsed with mirth.

They were in a part of the gallery not very severely damaged. Behind them were vast piles of earth and timber in grotesque disorder. The undamaged gallery wall curved slightly. McTavish suggested a line of progress to the left. He and some of the men still gripped their shovels. The match flickered out. Grant lit another and sought for pieces of timber from which strips were taken of which to make a continuous torch. The men with shovels, under the direction of McTavish, commenced digging, propping the roof of the new gallery with loose timbering from amid the wreckage. The earth was piled loosely, and, as they worked, heavy falls from above continually choked the mouth of the tunnel.

McTavish inspected with his keen understanding. "We're no so far frae fresh air," he said, sniffing deeply. The workers in short reliefs continued cutting and then, having cleared a wide area at the foot of the incline, began to proceed at a steeper angle. Avalanches of soil necessitated extreme caution, but they were skilled in such a task, which hour after hour, almost in silence, went forward. At last a cry came from the new tunnel. A shaft of light filtered through the loosened earth some twelve feet above the foremost workers.

"It goes against me leaving th' other lads behind," said McTavish wistfully, resting for a moment on his shovel.

Grant pondered the unspoken question. "We may be able to bring relief later. Our first duty is to go forward."

The Scot sighed and continued his work, until the intervening earth suddenly collapsed, rolling pell-mell down the shaft, revealing the clear blue of the sky above.

A new sound met their ears, that of the continuous burst of shells and of rifle fire. A black curl of smoke for a moment blotted out the sky. The mine had burst in one or other of the opposing lines, perhaps even in no man's land between them. Grant moved cautiously towards the lip of the crater and listened. He could detect the sharp crack of machine-gun and rifle fire upon either side—the crater then was somewhere in between the lines. The hour he judged from the sun, was between one and two in the afternoon, eight or nine hours since the mine had exploded. Clearly, whatever result had been achieved in the underground galleries, and that could only be a matter for conjecture, the springing of the mine had made a considerable impression upon the battle area. The intensity of defensive firing clearly indicated that both sides were in a state of high nervous tension.

He ordered the men to go a little way back into the tunnel, where a conference was held. It was agreed that after nightfall each should make an attempt to reach the British lines. He divided the paper which he had been given into thirteen pieces, and with charcoal traced upon the back of each piece the words: "W Plan." These were placed in the breast pockets of the men, to whom also Grant clearly outlined the main features and intentions of the Plan itself. They were instructed that anyone successful in reaching the British lines, should ask immediately for a message to be sent to General Headquarters, referring definitely to the W Plan.

If Grant himself failed to reach the lines, the full detailed W Plan was sewn into the collar of his tunic, and the ground could be searched by patrols for his body. This could be readily identified by the two white armlets which he tied round them by tearing off the arms from his shirt.

As the afternoon drew on the noise of firing diminished. Grant sent a man forward to the crater lip to observe. Twenty minutes later the man returned to report that so far as could be judged, they were encircled. The sound of fitful firing came from three sides at a distance of not more than one hundred yards, while from the back, similar sounds appeared to be some distance farther away.

Grant judged that the explosion must have undermined, at least, the front British line, and that the latter had been redisposed to meet a threatened attack. As dusk fell the rattle of machine-guns and rifle fire increased from the British lines, while a barrage of shrapnel fell across no man's land and upon the crater itself. Grant withdrew his men into the safety of the tunnel . . . they would wait until the night life outside became calmer. As the moon rose fully, casting a beam into the crater mouth, the firing gradually ceased.

The night became silent—broken only by an occasional burst of fire and a stray shell: while light rockets soared into the air. Then Grant, with McTavish, leading the party, crept up the tunnel to the top of the crater. Grant found himself in a turmoil of broken trenches, barbed-wire entanglements, deep shell craters and shattered trees. The force of the explosion had thrown aloft limbs, clothing and fragments of flesh. Battered bodies, piled themselves beside abandoned stretchers. The stench of blood and of gas pervaded the hot night air: it sickened the palate and caught the throat tightly.

Now, as Grant crept forward, wriggling upon his stomach, he felt the touch of broken bodies, portions of which protruded hideously from the debris of a wrecked trench: ammunition boxes, splintered rifles, coils of wire, trench stores of all kinds, impeded him at every move and turn. Rats, the four-footed vultures of the Western battle-fields, scurried across his path. The mine had devastated the front and support lines—Heaven alone knew at what a cost of British lives. Death had cut swiftly with his scythe, and now, his foul breath fanned the nostrils with the nauseating smell of blood: he winked his eye from aloft with each burst of shrapnel; and his dry laugh chattered from the mouths of a score of machine-guns.

The W Plan was coming home very . . . very . . . slowly.

Grant was near the line now, not more than seventy yards, McTavish beside him, their bodies cleaving to the ground. A sudden burst of rifle fire commencing at one point and spreading itself up the line caused Grant to sink low into the depths of a shell-hole. Star-shells illumined the sky and lighted the ragged landscape.

McTavish thrust his head cautiously above the edge of the hole. He whispered to Grant. "I can see some men moving. They may be our boys trying to get in." A loud cry was heard above the musketry. "Some poor devil's hit," commented the observer. The rifle fire and illuminations ceased abruptly.

After a few minutes Grant crept on from shell-hole to shell-hole. When within fifty yards of the line he could dimly discern the moving silhouette of heads above the trench parapet. A little to their left a small patrol was leaving the front line. It passed through the wire carefully, crouched low as a star-shell from the German line faintly lit the panorama, then bore away to the left, either searching for wounded or investigating the cause of the latest alarm. It was agreed then between Grant and McTavish that one alone should first attempt to penetrate the line, while the other waited in a shell-hole. If one was detected, the other would raise cries to attract attention and allay alarm. In this project McTavish insisted upon leading.

Grant watched the wizened active body writhe its way across the ruins of a trench system, nearer, always nearer, to the head which bobbed above the trench. Then he heard McTavish shout: "Hey, Jock!" and rise to his feet. The startled sentry fired. McTavish, still crying aloud, ran towards the trench. Panic had seized the men who now thickly manned the line.

A flash momentarily blinded Grant, bullets whistled past his ears, and then he saw the body of McTavish hanging limp, jerking upon a strand of wire. From his position in the shell-hole Grant cried desperately in English . . . "Cease fire!" The troops, their nerves tried to exhaustion with the events of the past twenty-four hours, every moment expecting a fresh catastrophe or attack, renewed their furious indiscriminate fire in his direction. Bombs falling short of his position, added to the chaos and din, while trench mortars searching the ground, shrieked spitefully beside his retreat.

Placing his hands before his mouth in fury he shouted: "Cease fire, you bloody fools. . . . Cease fire! . . . Cease fire!" A whistle was blown from the line: the firing, now desultory, ceased. Men climbed out over the parapet towards the body of McTavish.

Grant started to run, staggering through twisted barbed wire which clutched at the cloth of his trousers and lacerated his flesh . . . he shouted continuously . . . "Don't shoot" . . . Someone threw a bomb in his direction which burst beside him, cutting his forehead and face . . . he heard the patrol upon the parapet cursing . . . he plunged forward, eyes blinded by blood and perspiration, deafened with the panic of rifle fire and a babel of sound, his limbs weary almost to exhaustion . . . there was a blinding flash . . . a roar! Grant collapsed in a heap just short of the riddled body of his friend and compatriot.

The panic-stricken patrol gathered the two bodies roughly into the trench. A young officer commanding the company in the line came forward and inquired if the men were dead. He flashed an electric torch upon their faces and uniforms.

"Bloody Huns," he commented . . . "this devil's still breathing . . . take them down to the aid post . . . I'll report at battalion headquarters."

He passed through the communication trench, which the troops were feverishly reconstructing, to a concrete, dome-shaped, stronghold and passed through the blanket shielding the door, revealing the officer-commanding seated before a rough table.

"We've got two Huns, sir. One dead, the other is still breathing. I've sent them down to the aid post."

"Have you got their papers, or any identifications?"

"No, sir," he stammered, "I forgot."

"Go and get them quick." Then turning to the adjutant, the colonel said: "Go with him, Mason."

When they reached the post they found one body, that of McTavish, laid outside the dug-out upon a stretcher. "Dead," commented the adjutant as he entered. Grant was seated limply upon the skeleton of a chair. The blood had been washed from his head and the skin wounds bandaged. He was unconscious. The orderlies had cut away the rags of trousers, exposing legs hideously torn by wire, and one, the right, broken below the knee.

The tunic had been thrown upon one side. Mason took it up and searched the pockets. He extracted a small piece of paper bearing the words in English : " W Plan." There was nothing else. He examined the pockets of the dead man, and discovered a similar slip. The orderlies sponged Grant's leg, while the medical officer pressed rum and water to his lips.

" What's the matter with this man?" questioned the adjutant sharply. " Anything serious?"

" Nothing much . . . to you," acidly replied the doctor, a civilian drawn from a comfortable country practice, weary of military imperiousness.

" Can't you make him talk?" snapped Mason.

" I'm trying first to bring him to life," said the doctor dryly.

Dismissing the company commander with the two slips of paper and the tunics of the men to report to the colonel, Mason stood impatiently beside the wounded man.

Grant opened his eyes, stared vacantly before him, and mumbled a few words in German. Several minutes passed : he shivered as a deep draught of rum coursed down his throat.

Then he sat erect, suddenly, crying : " Don't shoot, don't shoot, you bloody fools!" The effort caused him to sink back with a groan.

" Take it easy," said the doctor, sponging his head.

" What's your name?" interjected the adjutant.

Grant blinked and paused, then said mechanically : " Otto Gedern." . . . Where was he? back in the cell . . . his face was bandaged . . . what had become of the commandant? . . . his mind was drifting . . . the sentence of the court . . . death . . . commuted . . . the pot-bellied interpreter—he chuckled—the galleries . . . the mine . . . Waller, little McTavish . . . where was McTavish . . . hanging on the wire. . . .

Duncan Grant, propped by two stretcher-bearers in his chair, his tortured mind assailed by rage and despair, alternately shouted hoarsely and wept.

Convulsions shook the battered body . . . the soul in its no man's land struggled to reach the mocking light of sanity. Suddenly he raised his hands to his neck. The fingers felt for his collar. " Where's my tunic?" he shrieked, " . . . the W Plan."

"That's better," said the adjutant. "What's this W Plan?"

Grant gazed at him for a full minute, then lurched forward in his chair. "Are you a British officer?" he groaned. Mason nodded.

"Good God! then why the Hell . . ." The voice trailed away.

"Are you English?" snarled Mason. "What's this blasted uniform?"

Grant attempted to rise, his eyes blazing. "I . . . must . . . telephone . . . to the Commander . . . in . . . chief," he jerked, the words coming in staccato.

Mason laughed. "That's rich—Otto talks to the Commander-in-chief—wouldn't the correspondents love it?"

"If you don't want to drive this poor devil off his head—he's pretty near it, Captain Mason—" said the doctor, "you'd better leave him alone for a bit. I'll patch him up and when he's got over the shock I'll send him to battalion headquarters."

The elder man sternly faced the younger, who turned and left the dug-out.

The doctor loved all humanity . . . his profession, for himself, was the highest calling to service for mankind. He knew village life unknown to the vicar . . . he had carried an ever-growing family from birth, through childish complaints, the maids through their first birth pangs, the men through secret foolishnesses—some he had buried. He hated war . . . the shattered bodies . . . the futility of it all . . . this weary, broken figure, except for some uncontrollable chance might be some lad from his own Dorset Downs. Carefully he smoothed the brow and waited. A sigh escaped from the drowsing figure. The doctor bent over him, holding his two hands firmly between his own. Grant looked up into the doctor's eyes. The master of healing had drawn the patient under the spell of his skill.

Quite calmly and very slowly Grant spoke. "They shouldn't have shot McTavish . . . I called out, ' Don't shoot ' . . . but they went on. I . . . I'm Duncan Grant, no . . . not Otto Gedern . . . I've got the W Plan . . . my tunic. . . . Tell . . . tell. . . ." the voice was fading away, "the Commander . . . in . . . chief."

Fatigue, wounds, rum and morphia had had their effect. Grant was asleep, his reason saved by that constant, wonderful, unerring skill, love and knowledge of a country doctor.

The medical officer not only disdained the restriction and regulations of military life, but himself possessed initiative and a will of his own. Placing the wounded in charge of stretcher-bearers, he left the aid post, and avoiding the battalion headquarters, walked through the communication trench to the signallers' dug-out.

"Hullo, sergeant! good evening," he said cheerily. "No trouble here I hope. I want to talk to someone of the staff. Against regulations, maybe, but I'll stand the wigging for this."

With some reluctance the sergeant cleared the line, and when communication was established the doctor asked to speak with the chief of staff. There was some delay; then he was informed that he could speak, but only for a moment, with the military secretary.

He opened the conversation at once. "I'm a doctor. I've got a man in my aid post, wounded. German uniform . . . says he's Duncan Grant . . . W Plan . . . he has something to report to the Commander-in-chief."

"What's that?" shouted Colonel Jervois. "Grant . . . W Plan . . . with you . . . he must be brought here to me at once."

"He's asleep," said the doctor, "but I'll pack him into an ambulance as soon as I can. . . . Be careful of him . . . he's wounded and it may be touch and go with his brain-box. . . . I'll send him to No. 7 General Hospital."

The doctor hung up the receiver, and standing in the trench he stroked his greying moustache thoughtfully. "I'll get his tunic from the colonel . . . it seems to be important . . . Duncan Grant . . . poor devil . . . W Plan . . . wonder what it's all about . . ." He slipped through the blanket into battalion headquarters.

"Well, how's your pet patient?" sneered the adjutant.

"He's a little chilly," parried the doctor, "and I've come for his tunic."

"Dear old nurse," laughed the colonel. "Well, we don't need that any more. By the way, has he said anything? I can't make head or tail of this W Plan business . . . seems odd written in English . . . and he speaks English, too, doesn't he, Mason?"

"Yes, fluently; probably a deserter."

"I must report the matter to the brigadier," said the colonel.

"I," said the doctor, "must take the responsibility for having already informed the chief-of-staff direct . . . the patient is asleep . . . he will wake up in No. 7 General Hospital. . . . I must get him off in the ambulance. . . . Good night, colonel."

*　　*　　*　　*　　*

A fresh breeze was blowing off the sea through the wide-flung windows and gently fanned a face upon the white pillow. A man was sunk in deep slumber; and so, for many hours, motionless, except for the rise and fall of the white linen to his regular breathing, he had rested in the quiet peacefulness of this room overlooking the sea.

A nurse, keeping her patient vigil, sat beside the bed reading, sometimes glancing through the window across the white-flecked, blue waters as some great ship, following the curve of the coast-line, slowly entered the harbour, or steamed out, accompanied by a busy escort, to that homeland whose white cliffs lay just beyond the horizon.

After long hours the patient stirred a little; his lips moved murmuring—"Rosa." His eyes opened for a moment. Then he slept again, the mouth parted in a faint smile.

The door opened quietly to admit Colonel Jervois, who quietly beckoned the nurse to him.

"Has he yet waked?" he whispered.

"Not yet, but he has moved. I do not think he will sleep much longer."

"I will remain, then."

For a full hour he sat upon the window ledge in the bright sun, wrapt in thought . . . eleven men, eight of them wounded, had been brought in during the night . . . patrols had brought in two dead bodies . . . they were in German uniform . . . the men were English, and, one, Hughes, unwounded, a former Welsh miner, had been sent to headquarters . . . the man was dazed and had told a wild, incoherent, incredible story interlaced always with the name of a Colonel Grant, with the white armlets, who had the W Plan . . . and here was Grant back again, haggard, torn and dishevelled beyond belief, twenty-two days after he had flown away upon his mission.

The patient stirred again, opened his eyes, then tried to move while the nurse gently held him, and smilingly inquired if he was ready for breakfast. As she moved to raise the pillows, Grant recognized Jervois, seated behind her, framed in the window.

The staff officer rose, and, crossing to the bed, took one hand in his, pressing it.

"You're home again, Grant . . . home . . . thank God."

"Home. . . ." Grant's brow puckered. . . . "Yes. . . . I suppose so . . . where's McTavish . . . and the others?"

"Eleven came in during the night," answered Jervois, who had been warned against agitating the patient in a too eager quest for information. There was silence for many minutes.

Grant considered, his fingers nervously plucking at the sheets, then spoke slowly. "There are still many, about thirty men, down the shaft. . . . McTavish wanted to dig them out before we left . . . and there were thirteen men with me. . . . I tried to stop the shooting. . . ."

"We'll find these men," said Jervois, pressing his hand. "Don't worry about that. . . . I've already had a talk with one of your men—Hughes by name."

"What did he say?"

A nurse entered carrying a steaming tray which was placed upon a table astride the bed, while pillows were packed behind the patient's back. Jervois poured out the coffee and Grant smiled happily. This was comfort indeed. He sipped it.

"What did Hughes say?" asked Grant after a while.

Slowly and deliberately Jervois spoke. "That you had the W Plan."

"Yes, yes, of course, in my tunic . . . where's my tunic?"

The nurse, rising swiftly, glided to the door. She reappeared after a few moments. Grant was talking rapidly, Jervois seated at the foot of the bed wrapt in attention.

"Get on with your breakfast," mocked the nurse. "Here's your tunic." Grant took the mudstained, grey-green garment in his hands, and asked for scissors—Rosa's stitches—he reflected and paused.

"Have you any . . . other news, colonel?"

Jervois shook his head.

"Not from Switzerland . . . our Legation . . . a lady?"

"None whatever," said Jervois.

Grant quickly slit the collar. Two envelopes, one from either side, soiled and damp, were exposed. "These are the W Plans . . . Everything you want is here."

Grant's brow puckered. "Colonel," he asked, "what happened to little Mayne. . . . I waited for him."

"Ah, a brave lad, Mayne . . . he did not return. We have heard since that he was detected and shot down over Tourcoing. He brought down two enemy machines with him."

"Poor little Mayne," said Grant quietly. "I knew he would come . . . if he could."

Jervois rose from the bed. "I must go at once to the Commander-in-chief. Grant. . . ." he said, the voice broken with emotion, "you've saved the army."

A wan smile crossed the wounded man's face.

Jervois was leaving the room but turned again to meet Grant's voice. "Don't forget my men . . . Hughes will tell you."

The wounds and fracture had been dressed and set, and Grant

was lying back upon his pillow, his gaze turned towards the sea. He watched the afternoon leave-boat steaming out from the harbour, the whirling seagulls in its wake. He was deep in meditation . . . purple hills . . . a sea melting into the crimson of an evening sky . . . a face framed in gold . . . Rosa.

The door opened softly. The Commander-in-chief, the man who could win a battle in the morning and in the evening help Belgian farmers to stack their corn, stood watching, his eyes filled with that devotion which three years of cruel war and its fierce necessities had failed to dim.

Grant turned his head—" General!" he exclaimed.

The general swiftly sank upon one knee beside the bed: and, as he had done on parting, so now his strong hands affectionately gathered the young man to him, as he studied the face beneath the bandages. Tears dimmed his eyes.

"I cannot thank you," he stammered, and remained, his head bowed, dumb with emotion: then rising he stood before the open window, his broad back to the patient.

The general drew a chair beside the bed. "Grant," he said, "will you tell me the story . . . not about the plans. I have already issued my orders," adding firmly: "The W Plan will never be put into operation. It is dead . . . You, thank God, have killed it . . . for ever."

"There is nothing to add, general. I left a letter with you, sir; it is a request that no one will ever know that I have been concerned with this, that no . . . I don't know how to put it . . . reward shall be given if I am successful."

"My dear boy," exclaimed the general, "that is absurd. Of course. . . ."

"I have your word, sir. Can't we leave it at that?"

"If that is your wish, Grant," said the general quietly, "I can say nothing else. . . . I'm sorry; but is there nothing I can do?"

"Yes, sir, yes," the wounded man's voice was rising with emotion. "I hate this war. . . . It's Hell! . . . I'm degraded, foul, I can't escape; I am haunted. . . . Let me go, sir. . . . Let me go." The general gripped his hands.

"Steady, lad, steady. . . . I know what you feel. Do not I feel it, too? But, I am sure now . . . quite sure, that we are near the end. I am going to send you to England among your friends."

"No, sir, I beg of you, let me stay here until I can walk . . . then . . . let me go away. I wish to hide in some quiet place in Switzerland. . . . Is that possible?"

"That I will arrange," said the general. "I will come to see

you again, Grant . . . now I must go to the conference which waits
for me. God bless you . . . Duncan Grant . . . and from the
bottom of my heart, I thank you." The door closed gently behind
him.

CHAPTER XII

THE GARDENER

IT was now late in the afternoon. The garden so brilliant with
colour in the sunlight, its fountains and miniature streams twinkling like a myriad gems, was now bathed in soft reflected light
from the mountain tops, while the firs, pines and larches which at
midday provided pleasant shade were stretching long shadows over
the green lawns.

High up on either side grand forest-covered hills arose, culminating in majestic peaks, some formed in fantastic shapes, great rocky
pinnacles, others festooned with glaciers, tipped with snow.

The gardener still toiled, his work at once his leisure, and his
whole life. Duncan Grant had seen him in the early morning
when the dew sparkled on the ground. Again, at midday, he was
standing in a fairy pond stripped to the waist removing every stray
leaf which might mar the mirror of its loveliness, or break the
perfect reflection of the surrounding flowers and shrubs.

A fountain sprayed his bronzed body glistening in the sunlight:
it was sculptured to perfection, the torso beautiful to see as he
twisted and bent, the body straight as a larch, the arms like the
roots of some giant conifer, the fingers, despite the nature of their
work, long and delicate as its fibres.

Duncan, leaning upon a stick, stood beside Rosa, the pale
delicacy of whose features contrasted vividly with the transcendent
loveliness of her golden hair. He spoke to the gardener, making
some comment of approval. The gardener's face, swarthy in colour
rugged of feature, broke into a happy smile. He showed some of
the rarest jewels, miniature alpines, gentians, primulas, violas
soldanella, collected from the high passes and last green patches
which cling to the snowline.

As they moved about this part of the garden he found one gem,
perhaps the choicest, snapped and sapped of its vitality. Hard by
a slug, swollen and obscene, spread its grossness upon a stone. A

new light came into the eyes of the gardener; swiftly he squeezed out its life between his strong thumb and forefinger. He shrugged his shoulders, looked at Rosa as if with a question; then added simply that it was because of the slugs that he must work to protect his defenceless flowers.

The garden, with its long borders of bright antirrhinums backed by tall dahlias and delphiniums, its cool lawns, pools and fountains, winding paths which at every turn presented a new vista of beauty or of grandeur, lay high over the tempestuous waters of the Inn in the Lower Engadine.

Many people, from many lands, had come thither to find rest, leisure, recreation and new health in this wonderful fairy valley. Some were older men from the cities, weary with the irritations and pressure of industrial life and finding freedom again after more than three years of blockade and uninterrupted industry: some, women, exhausted with the pleasures and dissipations of European capitals: others, just tourists retreading long forbidden paths, passing through, yet often remaining in a scene so wholly captivating; while here and there were men broken, maimed and shattered, who in the stillness of the mountains sought to gather the fleeting fragments of a youth snatched by the rude hands of war.

Thus through his work was the gardener himself the healer and evangelist. Often he would pluck some fragrant, perfect bloom and lay it beside a dreamer as he slept. Many weeks after the last sound of battle had been stilled in silence, Duncan Grant and Rosa had been reunited in Geneva, where they had been quietly married. Now in the peace of Vulpera, amid the rugged grandeur and sublime beauty of jagged peaks and soft valleys, they stood hand-in-hand in contemplation of the ever-changing landscape in its evening kaleidoscope of colour.

Duncan pointed to the majestic mediæval castle of Tarasp, perched high upon a rocky eminence dominating the valley, and idly told Rosa of the tyrannies which in the name of God, religion, and civilization had in past ages spread misery, rapine, and death throughout the villages, which, some high on the mountain side, some beside the rushing river, give life to the valley.

Their reflections were broken by the sound of a heavy footstep. Half turning, Grant observed a gross person approaching. He was heavy eyed with dissipation, a vast belly protruded itself in front of the body, rolls of flesh piled themselves above his collar, fat fingers decked with diamonds thrust themselves from the starched linen of his sleeve ends: a great cigar lay between the bulging lips.

It was Herr Adolf Messer.

The creature shuffled up the pathway, pausing before the fairy pond; and, flicking cigar ash upon its placid waters, broke the mirror, making an ugly stain upon the picture.

The gardener was watching.

The man, who had so richly profited from his country's ruin, and whose very presence constituted a living memorial to his shame, leaned heavily against a young spruce, which bent itself as if recoiling from his touch. He raised one foot heavily among the graceful flowers. As earlier, so now, the stem of a choice flower snapped, and was ground under foot.

The gardener was watching. The light in his eyes changed to fierce hatred. He moved forward swiftly, the muscles in his arms tightening so that the bone of his fingers showed white under the bronzed skin, until he faced the human slug.

Duncan held Rosa's frail hand tight in his own. He whispered to her—" Tyranny . . . in the twentieth century."

The human slug, its bloodshot, glittering eyes beneath languid lids, observed the gardener. He discerned the hatred in the eyes, the threat in demeanour. Savagely he pushed his foot among the alpine gems; then, again flicking his ash into the pool, he sneered . . . as long ago a Pharisee regarded a publican. He spat and shuffled back along the path, while the gardener cleansed his garden.

The gardener looked up from his toil at the lovers and smiled. . . . " Another slug," he said. . . .

The evening passed into sublime afterglow. Duncan drew Rosa to him. Their voices were soft, so that the sigh of a gentle wind in the pine tops formed an accompaniment to the matchless refrain of love.

" You remember the boy, Heinrich, old Messer's son. He had lost everything, but his ideal . . . a love for all humanity . . . for that, and unknown to him, for us, he fought . . . and won."

" Our love, too, is symbolic," murmured Grant, " something greater, more profound than we know. We are the embodiment of a great human principle . . . some new force growing out of all the misery of mankind, against a world whose motive has been sheer force. . . . The gardener is the living symbol of our new world; that other . . . of the old."

THE SECRET OF TANGLES

By

LEONARD R. GRIBBLE

THE SECRET OF TANGLES

CHAPTER I

THE MAROON SALOON

"HEADQUARTERS calling all cars in western area! Headquarters calling all cars in western area!"

In the wireless-control room at Scotland Yard the operator paused to glance expectantly at the frowning man standing beside his chair. The paper in Detective-Inspector Anthony Slade's hand crinkled. His face was grave, his grey eyes were thoughtful.

"All right, Jones," he said. "Send it out."

The wireless operator took the paper from Slade, cast an eye over the first typewritten lines, and leaned towards the microphone.

"Headquarters calling all cars in western area! Stand by for important call from Department X2!"

The operator stopped, cleared his throat, and began to read aloud the message Slade had given him.

* * * * *

A grey touring-car cruised along a quiet street in Ealing. On its radiator were the silver winged hands of the Flying Squad. It was dark, and the heavy clouds above threatened rain. There was no moon, and each time the wind swept down the street in a fierce gust the street-lamps flickered.

Suddenly one of the two men in the rear seat leaned forward.

"A call from the Yard, sir," he announced to the heavy figure seated next to the driver.

The car drew to a halt, and the man addressed twisted about, inclining his head to one side.

"What is it, Drew?"

There was a pause before the man replied. In the gloom presiding inside the car the nickel band of his headphones shone with eerie whiteness.

"A message coming through from Department X2, sir," were his next words.

The man next to the driver rasped his chin. Abe Brawley, the redoubtable leader of the Flying Squad, was a close friend of Slade's. The two men had worked together on a number of cases, and on many raids had ducked to avoid the same bullet. They had been

together in that strange affair of Sir Giles Gillespie's " suicide," and
they had gone hunting the Marsden rubies on one of the wildest and
most hazardous adventures either of them had experienced.   Each
figured in the other's record at the Yard, and each held high admiration for his friend's quality as a detective.   On the one hand, the
senior officer of Department X2 frankly admired Brawley's characteristic forthrightness, his ability to concentrate on one particular
angle of a case, and his fine sense of organization; on the other hand,
the Flying Squad leader was never silent or slow in offering his
opinion of Slade's merit as a C.I.D. officer.   On more than one
occasion he had expressed good-hearted envy of Slade's logical
methods in tackling a case, of that dogged obstinacy which was a
marked characteristic of the man, and which had brought him to
triumph many times when the chances of the police seemed to be
hopeless.

Brawley waited now, wondering what Slade's message would be
about. He knew that Department X2 rarely phoned the Squad cars.
It must mean that this was a fresh case; probably a bank robbery
or . . . a number of possibilities passed through his mind. The band
of ghostly light over the wireless man's head wavered.

" Message coming through now," he reported.

The other three men in the car shifted their positions slightly.
Each man felt a thrill of excitement pass through him. Then the
wireless man was repeating the message as he received it.

"Information wanted about a maroon-coloured saloon car,
believed to have been concerned in a burglary in Cheviot Crescent,
Mayfair. Number of people in car not known. Possibly four.
Number of car PV 73—last figures of number not known. Car last
observed travelling west in Kensington. All stations will be warned.
This is headquarters calling all cars in western area."

The wireless man's voice stopped.

" Turn south, Hopkins, then take a run out towards Southall.
We'll turn south again then."

The man at the wheel set the car in motion, turned it, and a few
minutes later the Flying Squad patrol was making speed along
Ealing Broadway. The wireless man still sat with the headphones
clamped to his ears. Next to him a plain-clothes man peered through
a pair of night-glasses. Brawley was scanning the road ahead through
a similar pair of glasses. There was a fair amount of traffic on the
road. Small cars swung in and out among the buses and lumbering
trams, and every now and then an intrepid cyclist would graze his
way between two motors. The man at the wheel, however, was one
of the coolest drivers in the metropolis. Nothing on four wheels

daunted him, and the Flying Squad car seemed to skim in and out among the other traffic with the ease of a hovering bird. More than one traffic policeman shot a suspicious glance at the low-bodied, powerful grey car hurtling towards him, only to swing back on his heels as he glimpsed the magic symbol of those winged hands. Yet by the time the Flying Squad car reached Southall only two red motors had been seen, one an M.G. " Midget " and the other a mail-van.

" We'll make a wide detour, heading south, and bearing west at the same time," said Brawley.

But the car had not proceeded more than another quarter of a mile when Drew, the wireless man, announced another message. The patrol car was quickly drawn to a halt. Each man waited impatiently as the man with the headphones repeated the message sent out from Scotland Yard.

" Telephone message from call-box in Chiswick reports wanted car to be travelling westward parallel with river. When noticed was making about forty-five miles an hour. This is headquarters calling all cars in western area."

Brawley turned to the driver.

" Let her have her head, Hopkins. We've a chance to head that car off, though Number Fourteen might make it before us."

The patrol car leapt forward with an eager purr, and the dark ribbon of road began slipping fast away. Drew waited patiently for any further message, while Brawley and the man seated behind the driver scanned the road ahead. Hopkins sat crouched over the wheel, which was pressed against his chest. One arm hung at his side. The fingers of his other hand toyed with the knob of the electric horn. Hopkins knew his area well; he could have driven round it and through it on a night of thick fog.

As the car passed through wider thoroughfares, along roads lined with the stripped shapes of plane-trees, its speed increased. The wind blew more keenly in the faces of the Flying Squad searchers. Brawley and the man behind the driver tucked their collars up. Drew was too intent on listening for a morse code sign to think of the wind. As for Hopkins, a gleam of almost wild glee lit his narrowed eyes. His jaw was set grimly. This was what the man lived for, speeding through the night like a phantom, a thing of power and motion controlled by the slightest pressure of his gloved hand.

A quarter of an hour later Brawley's patrol met No. 14 of the Flying Squad, but the latter had not sighted the maroon saloon. The two cars continued westward until they reached a crossroads, and then they separated, Brawley's car taking the southern road, which ran nearer to the river.

For half an hour the grey car continued along that road, stopping each car it met to make enquiries, but no news of the maroon saloon was received. Rain came on. It swept down in a sheet, and in the glare of the patrol car's powerful headlights the great drops broke and spread themselves into a glistening ribbon of light. Puddles formed, and the car ploughed through them like a speed-boat.

Suddenly the waiting Drew hissed a warning, and Hopkins jammed down his brakes. The wireless man repeated the Yard message in his customary inflexionless voice.

"Flying Squad cars in western area covering all main east-west roads. No further news of wanted car to hand. Last sighted in Chiswick travelling westward at forty-five miles an hour."

Drew's voice stopped, and the car sprang forward again. Brawley took out a handkerchief and wiped raindrops from his night-glasses. The grey car was speeding along a straight stretch of black, gleaming road. Trees rose on both sides, and beyond them dark spaces that were fields. Hopkins pressed his foot down harder, and the note of the racing engine rose to a shrill whine. Ten minutes later trees and fields gave place to hedgerows.

Brawley wiped his glasses again.

"Looks as though that car made a getaway all right, unless it's turned north," he remarked.

No one answered. The car raced on.

At the next A.A. box Hopkins halted, and Brawley barked questions at the man inside, but received no satisfactory answers. Several cars had passed within the last twenty minutes, but he had not noticed them specially. The patrol car went on, and five minutes later drew to another halt at a crossroads. Brawley made up his mind instantly.

"Left!" he snapped.

The car swung south again, and after about a mile the road narrowed considerably. The car bounced over ruts, and Hopkins slackened to just over thirty. The road began to wind towards the right. A couple of miles farther on the surface was again smoothly metalled, and Hopkins was keeping the speedometer at fifty-five when Brawley sighted another A.A. box. Here they met with news that revived their hopes. A general telephone call had been sent out to the A.A. and R.A.C. scouts in that district, and thanks to the timely warning this man had been on the look-out some seven minutes before when a dark red saloon car flashed by. He had not been able to read its number. But he was certain that the letters on the number-plate were PV. However, the message had said that probably four persons were in the car. There had been only one person in this car, the driver; on that point the man was definite. He told Brawley that there was another branch road about three miles farther on.

Luck was with the Flying Squad patrol. Just before reaching the branch road they met a heavily laden lorry, which Brawley stopped. The driver was positive that he had not passed another car for the last quarter of an hour. Hearing that, Brawley took a chance. The grey car turned down the branch road, which at first ran almost due south.

"Now, Hopkins, let her out," ordered Brawley.

A thin grin curved the driver's lips. His eyes puckered until they were almost shut. He nodded.

The next instant the car was hurtling forward at a speed eclipsing anything she had done before on that night. How the mad rush continued was a miracle. Trees loomed up and vanished all in the same movement. From side to side the racing car swerved, taking bends on the straight. The strong headlights sent two powerful beams ahead through the darkness. Not another word was spoken until the road bore west again. Brawley took a map from his pocket and flashed his electric torch on it, but he was unable to make out their position. He cursed under his breath, and put the map away. Three more miles were traversed, and then the headlights picked out the white shape of a signpost. At that point the road bifurcated. Brawley climbed out, glanced at the names on the post's fingers, and examined the muddy surface of the road. He came back.

"Left again, Hopkins," he directed. "The road to Ploverton, know it?"

The driver nodded.

"It's as bad as a ploughed field."

"Well, do what you can."

Half a mile down the road they met a motor-cyclist, whom Brawley hailed. Yes, the man had seen a dark red saloon car, only a few minutes before. No, it was not travelling very fast. Not much more than from about twenty-five to thirty he should imagine.

Hopkins made thirty-five, and five minutes after leaving the cyclist Brawley's night-glasses picked out a dim red speck ahead. Hopkins, every nerve strung high, kept up the pace, though the grey car pumped and pitched perilously. The red speck grew brighter, larger. Brawley pressed the driver's arm, and obediently the pace slackened. The Flying Squad patrol was now tailing the other. Brawley knew how to play follow-my-leader. If the car ahead was the one Tony Slade wanted, it would lead them to the thieves' hide-away. He began wondering what sort of a haul they would make.

Suddenly the red speck ahead grew quickly larger. The other car had stopped.

"Catch up, Hopkins!" muttered Brawley. "We've got 'em now."

The Flying Squad car spurted forward, and slowed up behind a red car drawn into the hedge-side. The Yard car's headlights revealed the slim figure of a girl struggling with the rusty latch of an iron gate.

Brawley gaped. Leaving his night-glasses on the seat, he climbed out. He stared from the girl to the number-plate of her car—PV 73542.

"Where are the others?" he snapped brusquely.

The girl's figure straightened, and under the close-fitting green felt hat she wore a pair of large brown eyes surveyed the Flying Squad leader calmly.

"I'm afraid I don't understand. Who are you? What do you want?"

Her voice was slightly husky.

"So that's the line you're going to take—eh?"

"I repeat, I don't understand."

"Look here, miss," said Brawley severely, "I'm from Scotland Yard. Where have you come from?"

She paused a moment before replying, as though weighing her words. She was dressed in a dark green mackintosh with a grey fur collar. Crocodile-skin walking-shoes encased her small feet, and her hands were concealed in a pair of green leather gauntlets. Brawley studied her closely, and wondered much.

"I've come from London."

"Not Cheviot Crescent by any chance?"

"I've never heard of the place."

Brawley grinned, but it was not a pleasant grin.

"No, I thought not. Where, then?"

"My flat, if you must know."

"I see. Did you pass through Chiswick?"

"Yes. Now, if that is all will you kindly——"

Brawley held up a hand.

"Not so fast, young lady. You would call your car maroon coloured, wouldn't you?"

A little frown crossed her face. It might have been of perplexity or anxiety. Brawley couldn't be sure.

"Why, yes, that's right." This time she sounded a trifle less sure of herself.

"Well, now, let me tell you something. A maroon saloon number PV 73 something or other is believed to have been used by a party who broke into a house in Cheviot Crescent, Mayfair, this evening. What about it?"

Her lips parted.

"You mean you think my car was the one that was used?"

Brawley nodded.

"Something like that. I'm afraid you'll have to come back to London, miss."

"Oh, but I can't!" she cried, for the first time showing any sign of excitement. "I've come here to see my uncle. He rang me up. Said he had to see me urgently."

Brawley's grin became almost tolerant.

"I believe I've heard that one before."

"But it's the truth!" she expostulated, and the huskiness left her voice. "I don't know what's the matter, but it must be something very important or he would never have sent for me."

The Yard man glanced at the iron gate.

"This where he lives?"

"Yes."

"What's the name of the place?"

"Tangles."

"Queer name, isn't it?"

"I don't see that that matters to you."

Brawley shrugged. He had had long experience of raiding West End night-clubs, and knew that there were some women who could not help snubbing policemen.

"You wouldn't, of course." He took the snub lightly. "But you will have to come back with me after you have seen your uncle."

"You don't believe me, then?" A note of hauteur had crept into her voice.

"What I believe is neither here nor there. It depends upon what you can prove."

She bit her lip, and her eyes flashed.

"You think my car was the one used in the burglary in Cheviot Crescent, don't you? And you think I'm mixed up with a gang of thieves?"

"I think that car"—Brawley pointed to maroon saloon—"was

the one used. I don't know whether it's yours or not. And I think that quite probably, somewhere between here and Cheviot Crescent, you dropped three passengers."

She drew herself up stiffly, and under the brim of her green hat Brawley caught a glimpse of brown curls.

"In that case I suppose there's nothing else for it but to go back with you after I've seen my uncle, Mr——?"

"Brawley."

"Mr. Brawley. I trust you won't find it necessary to mention this fantastic charge to him——"

"I'm making no charge, miss. Don't misunderstand the situation. Anyway, I won't say anything to your uncle—yet."

"What do you mean?"

"If your story's true he'll be able to verify that he phoned you, won't he?"

She nodded shortly.

"But before we go inside I should like your name."

"Claire Merrell. And my address is 27A Stanthorpe Mansions, South Kensington."

"Kensington—eh?"

"Yes. What of it?"

"Oh, nothing." But Brawley had remembered that the wanted car had been seen in Kensington that evening. He took out a notebook, and in the glare of the headlights noted her name and address. "Your uncle's name?" he asked.

"Morton Haunchwood. This place is Tangles, Lower Ploverton."

"Thank you, Miss Merrill," said Brawley when he had replaced his notebook in his pocket. "Now we'll go along to the house. Payne!" he called to the fourth member of the Flying Squad patrol.

The man got out of the car.

"Yes, sir?"

"I want you to come with me up to the house."

Brawley stepped forward, opened the rusty gate, on which, in fancy scroll-work, was the name "Tangles," and stood back for the girl to enter. The two Yard men followed her.

She led them along a soaking wet gravel path overgrown with weeds. The laurel hedges on either side of the path, revealed in the ray from Brawley's torch, were straggly and untrimmed. Large puddles had formed on the path where the gravel had sunk and had not been repaired and rolled out. A general air of neglect enveloped the place. The dark shape of a large house rose before them, fronted with a high porch upheld by four chipped stone columns. Small weeds had even been allowed to invade the crazy-paving under the porch.

Brawley turned his torch on the door, and the girl gave a short cry.

"Why, it's open!"

The large, massive door was ajar. Brawley played his torch round the door-frame. There was no bell, he noted; only the rusty knocker above a weather-eaten iron letter-box.

"Looks as though you were expected all right," he remarked dryly.

The girl turned serious eyes on him.

"There's something wrong. Uncle would never have had that door left open."

"We'll soon see."

Brawley pushed the door wide open and stepped inside, flashing his torch round the hall. The air inside was cold and damp.

"Can't say it's a very cheery place," he admitted, walking to the foot of a large staircase.

"It isn't," said the girl unexpectedly, and crossed to a door at the side of the staircase. "This is my uncle's study," she explained.

Brawley said nothing. He was frowning. He did not like this place Tangles. It gave him the creeps. He watched the girl open the door of the study, step quickly inside, and fumble for the light switch.

The next moment she gave a piercing cry and stumbled forward into the room. Brawley sprang after her, Payne close at his heels. Claire Merrell was stooping over the form of a man which lay sprawled across a worn carpet.

The girl turned round, her deep brown eyes wide with fright and fear.

"He's dead!" she gasped.

Brawley was scanning the crumpled figure with narrowed eyes. The man's breast was soaked with blood, and there was blood beside him on the carpet. Brawley drew the girl to her feet, and passed her to Payne, who led her to a chair. Then he stooped over the body and slipped a hand under the man's waistcoat, raising the sticky shirt-front. He rose to his feet slowly after kneeling down and peering close at the wound.

"Is that your uncle, Miss Merrell?" he asked.

The girl nodded mutely.

"He's been murdered," he told her gravely.

CHAPTER II

THE MAN WITH THE TWISTED SMILE

"Hello, Tony! Made it in good time, old man."

Brawley met Slade at the rusty gate. It was now drizzling, and the wind was colder. Slade shivered as he stepped out of the car in which he had arrived.

"Only two false turns, Abe," he grinned, striding up to the Flying Squad leader. "Well, what's the complication this end?"

"Murder."

"So I understand. But how does it connect with that message I had sent out?"

Brawley shook his head.

"Don't ask me, Tony. But it does. The maroon saloon's here."

"Here!" exclaimed Slade, staring at the other.

"Oh, you'd be surprised what we fellows can produce once we're on the search," said Brawley loftily, and added seriously: "There's more than meets the eye to this affair, Tony."

"What do you mean?"

"When we caught up with that car the only person in it was a girl. She gave her name as Claire Merrell. Said she hadn't been anywhere near Mayfair, hadn't ever heard of Cheviot Crescent, and had certainly not dropped any passengers between there and here. Well, that for a start, after the description of her car and its number fit the broadcast particulars. Oh, yes, and she has a flat in Kensington. She's received an urgent phone call from her uncle, a Morton Haunchwood, if that means anything to you——"

"Not yet."

"——and had driven here direct. Must have been mighty urgent for her to have put out so quickly on such a filthy night——"

"Some people might think murder rather urgent," murmured Slade.

"When she got here we were on her tail. She tried to put me off, but I partnered her up to the house door, which we found open. We stepped into the hall, and she crossed to the door of her uncle's study, went inside and switched on the light, and there he was."

As Brawley paused Slade's chief assistant, Sergeant Clinton, walked up. He had backed the car into the hedge. Slade turned to him.

"Oh, Clinton, take Dr. Herrick up to the house, and Polton can get his snaps. I'll be along in a few minutes."

Clinton, followed by the doctor with his attaché case, and Polton with a camera, proceeded up the dark path towards the house. Slade fell in step with Brawley, and the two continued after the others more slowly.

"You're wrong about the maroon car, Abe," said Slade suddenly. "It's been found."

Brawley stared at his friend.

"Where?" he asked.

"In a back street behind the Edgware Road."

"Remember its number?"

"Yes. PV 73542——"

"What!" exclaimed the Flying Squad leader, wheeling round. "Why, that's the number on this girl Merrell's car!"

Slade stopped.

"Let's have a look at that car, Abe. It seems as though someone's been playing a practical joke in bad taste."

"I've got it parked at the side of the house. There's no garage to the place."

Slade examined the girl's car by the light of his own flash-lamp and Brawley's.

"Abe," he said, "this car's of the same model as the one used on that burglary job. The only difference is the number-plate. This one has stamped metal figures; the other's figures are painted on. Someone's been pretty smart."

"If we're lucky someone's going to swing for Haunchwood's murder. Think there's a connection between the two jobs?"

"Not a doubt," replied Slade, putting his electric torch back in his pocket. "The girl was a decoy. The point is—was she framed or is she working with a gang?"

"She strikes me as genuine," Brawley admitted.

"But you've no proof the man was her uncle?"

"No. I'm going by the way she acted. I'd swear she was genuinely upset when she came upon him, though I confess it struck me as funny that she went straight to the study."

The two detectives turned towards the house. Brawley pointed to a lighted window on the ground floor.

"That's the study where he was shot. The gun's not here. There's an old flower-bed under the window—it's nothing but a mess of mud and weeds now—but it shows how the murderer left?"

"Left?" echoed Slade.

"Yes, the prints all point outwards."

"If the murderer left that way, what about the open front door?"

"I take it that's the way the manservant left?"

"Oh, so there was one? Any maids?"

"No. Haunchwood, from the girl's account, was a bit of an eccentric cove. Couldn't bear women around the place. He lived here alone with one man, a chap named Ferriss. But Ferriss is missing."

"Well, let's go in, Abe. Herrick and Polton should be through their jobs by now."

The two detectives walked round to the front door and entered the hall. For a moment Slade stood staring round, and then moved after Brawley to the study. It was a large, high room, with merely a desk, an arm-chair, a wastepaper basket, smoking companion, and a smaller chair. Three of the four walls were lined with well-filled bookcases. Slade glanced at the backs of the volumes. All sorts were crammed between the shelves : paper-backed cheap editions, lurid fiction with bright yellow paper covers, massive, calf-bound tomes with tiny gilt lettering on the backs, small pocket editions, quarto volumes, thin in bulk, with mottled edges to the leaves. It was the library of a man with wide and varied tastes. There wasn't an ornament in the room. The curtains were of some heavy brown material, with velvet fringes, severe in tone, severe in appearance.

Dr. Herrick was fumbling with his cuffs, and Polton was tying the strap of his camera case. Slade turned to the former.

"Got the bullet, doctor?" he asked.

The other shook his head.

"Afraid not, inspector. It smashed a couple of ribs, went through the right ventricle of the heart, and brought up inside him somewhere. A nasty wound, and, as you can see, he bled freely. Death was instantaneous, however, and I should say he had been dead about two hours or two hours and a half before I examined him. There are slight powder-burns on the flesh of the chest, and the hole in his shirt-front is singed a little. I should say that he was shot from a distance of two or three feet."

"Do you think he had been moved after being shot, or was he lying where he fell, doctor?"

Dr. Herrick pondered the question for a few moments, but finally shook his head.

"I'm afraid I can't be sure on that point, inspector. I don't think the body had been moved. But from the nature of the wound you may be sure that if it had been carried any distance—say, from another room, for example—there would be blood-stains to show from where."

"Thank you, doctor." Slade turned to Polton, one of the plain-clothes men of Department X2. "Finished?" he asked.

"Yes, sir. I took three shots."

"Well, don't tie your camera up, Polton. I want some shots of those footprints out there. Inspector Brawley will show you the place." Slade walked across to Brawley. "Where's the girl, Abe? I've a few things to ask her. Is she all right?"

"She won't throw hysterics, if that's what you mean," said Brawley. "She's in what she calls the drawing-room. I'll show you in. Payne, one of my men, is in there with her."

It was the most masculine drawing-room Slade had ever stepped into; like the study, there was not a single ornament in it, no pictures hung from the walls, which were damp, and from which the paper hung in strips at places, nor was there much furniture, and what few pieces there were looked uninviting. A straight-backed settee that was "modern" in the early years of the century was set between the two tall windows, hung with curtains similar to those in the study, except that these were more faded and stained. There was an arm-chair, the hide of which was torn over one arm. An old-fashioned cottage piano stood coyly upon green glass domes, lost in that large room, its silk-pleated front faded. At the opposite end of the room was the only imposing piece of furniture, a large sideboard, upon which reposed an old briar pipe and a couple of books. There was no table in the room. In the centre was a single straight-backed chair. Upon this sat a girl in a green woollen jumper-suit.

Claire Merrell looked up as Slade moved towards her. For several seconds she and the detective regarded each other in silence. Slade noted that she was dressed with care and taste. Her clothes suited her, and they fitted her well. Her brown eyes appeared frank, and her chin had a firm yet delicate line. She was not beautiful; but she was very good-looking. There was something about her that suggested the word "capable."

Slade was the first to speak.

"Miss Merrell? I am Inspector Slade, of Scotland Yard. There are some questions I must ask you."

For an instant a tired expression crossed her face, but it was gone almost as it appeared.

"Yes, of course. I'll tell you what I can."

"First," continued Slade, "I understand your uncle was of a retiring nature. How often did you come to visit him?"

"Oh, very seldom. In fact, only when he specially invited me."

"Is your mother still alive?"

Her eyes widened.

"My mother?" she queried.

"Yes. She was his sister, wasn't she?"

A slight colour stole into the girl's cheeks. She looked hurriedly away.

"Why, yes, that's right. But no, my mother isn't alive, Mr. Slade."

The detective regarded the girl gravely. What was the cause of her confusion just then? He advanced a few steps nearer.

"Tell me, Miss Merrell, have you any idea who murdered your uncle?"

His voice was cold, impassive, and to the girl sitting before him it sounded strangely enigmatic.

"Of course not, inspector!" She raised her face, and in her brown eyes was a hunted look. "It is all a complete mystery to me—too terrible!"

"What do you mean by 'all,' Miss Merrell?"

Her hands fumbled together. She was growing more uneasy each minute. She gazed round the room more frequently, as though seeking some way out of the place.

"I mean the telephone call, coming here and being stopped by that other detective, finding my uncle in here, dead, the front door open, and Ferriss not here——"

"Ah, yes—Ferriss. Was he quite reliable?"

"Really, I know little about him. He—he has been with my uncle for a number of years."

"And you were surprised to find him not here?"

"Naturally."

"Tell me, Miss Merrell, did your uncle keep anything of value here at Tangles?"

She shook her head.

"No. To be perfectly truthful, inspector, I don't think he had much of value. I've never understood that he was rich. Surely if he had been he wouldn't have let this place go to rack and ruin."

Slade took a turn up the room.

"Do you think this man Ferriss shot your uncle, Miss Merrell?" he asked bluntly.

Her shoulders slumped; the line of her chin became a little less resolute. To Slade, watching the girl closely, it seemed as if she were suddenly in doubt how to reply. Her glance round the room was almost desperate.

"I don't know what to think!" she cried, more shrilly, jumping to her feet. She crossed to one of the windows, and stood there with the light playing upon her brown hair, her features, her locked hands and drooping shoulders. In a moment she had changed. She now looked frail, forlorn. Slade felt a slight pity for her, but he told himself that she was a poor liar. Sooner or later she would make a slip.

"You mean you think he *might* have done it?" he questioned coldly.

"Might have done it!" she exclaimed. "Of course he might have done it! Anyone might have done it——"

"True," nodded the detective. "Even you, Miss Merrell."

She stared at him, fascinated by the possibility he had suggested.

"Me?" It was but a whisper.

"Your uncle has been dead from two to two and a half hours. You *could* have killed him, driven fast to London, and driven back again. . . . You were playing the part of a decoy. You know that, don't you?"

There was something almost brutal about the way Slade said that; but he realized that he had to pin the girl down somewhere, and she was not proving easy.

She laughed brokenly.

"So that's what you think, is it?"

The detective shrugged.

"A house in Cheviot Crescent was broken into, and the two men who left the house were driven off in a maroon-coloured saloon car with a number known to be PV 73 and three other figures. That car was later noted racing through Kensington and still later through Chiswick."

"Well?" she demanded, her face very white.

"An hour and a half later that car was found deserted in a back street behind the Edgware Road. Meanwhile you were hurrying here, drawing a Flying Squad car after you. Now can you honestly tell me, Miss Merrell, you think this is all pure coincidence?"

She regarded him intently.

"Not pure coincidence, inspector." She emphasized the second word.

"I see. You mean someone arranged things, procured a car similar to yours, and then dropped out of the race while the police car followed you. In other words, you allowed the crooks to make a nice getaway. Is that what you mean?"

She walked back to the chair, and sat down heavily. She looked suddenly tired. This time she made no effort to straighten her slack shoulders.

"Something like that, I suppose——"

Slade's voice cut in, cynical, mocking.

"Oh, you merely suppose so! And you arrive here and find your uncle dead. You suppose so!" Slade advanced on the girl, his eyes scanning every feature of her face, which was drawn and haggard-looking. "Miss Merrell, I suggest that you are not telling the truth, or that you are purposely holding something back."

She winced at the words, and Slade could see that she had to exercise a great self-control to remain from crying. The girl knew something that she did not want to tell. That was obvious. She stared at the detective with wide eyes that did not see him. Her lips were pressed together.

Slade took another turn up the room. Standing with back against the door, Payne remained motionless, regarding the scene without interest. Clinton sat on the edge of the arm-chair, notebook opened on his knee.

Slade spoke again, and the words were uttered incisively.

"I further suggest, Miss Merrell, that you told a deliberate lie when you said that Morton Haunchwood was your uncle. If that is the man's name, he is certainly not your uncle. Tell me the truth, now! And, remember, this is a murder case!"

There was something about the detective as he stood there before her that filled the girl with a nameless dread, so terrifying that it almost superseded that other dread which had been with her for the past weeks. A lump rose in her throat, and desperately she tried to swallow. There was a pulse beating feverishly somewhere in her head; she did not know where, except that it seemed to make her eyes smart under the strain.

She jumped to her feet, swayed a moment, but steadied herself immediately. Slade realized that she was deadly calm.

"It's true. He's not my uncle. I never saw him before in my life." The words fell from her lips mechanically.

The detective took a deep breath.

"That's better, Miss Merrell," he said encouragingly, and more gently. "Now we can begin to understand each other."

"There you're wrong!" she flashed, colour returning to her cheeks. "That's the truth that I've just told you, but I can't tell you anything else. You must understand that. . . . I have nothing more to tell you."

"Indeed! This is a sudden change of front, Miss Merrell. By the way, *is* your name Claire Merrell?"

She threw him a bitter glance.

"It is. But you might as well know that I don't know whether Morton Haunchwood was his real name. That was the name I was told."

She walked over to the settee and dropped on to it. Her hands hung limp at her sides. Slade strode to the left-hand window, pulled aside the curtain, peered into the darkness, and then came back to the centre of the room, his hands rove deep in his trousers pockets.

"It's still raining," he remarked.

The girl made no reply, but she began tapping with her toe. Slade waited; the tapping became quicker.

"Well, what are you going to do—arrest me?"

Slade smiled.

"Not yet, Miss Merrell. There are some more questions I want answered first, and before I arrest you I shall give you the usual warning. You've probably read it in mystery stories."

"I loathe mystery stories," she retorted. "And I'll answer no more questions."

"You're not being blackmailed, are you?"

"Don't be absurd! I work for my living."

"As I thought, it's someone else. Most likely a man."

The flush in her cheeks deepened, and she bit her lip.

"Do you mind if I smoke?"

She shrugged, signifying that it made no difference to her. Slade filled his pipe and lit it.

"It's either a brother or a lover," he ruminated, as though to himself, but she made no reply. "Whoever it is," he continued, "you're both in a mess. Who was Ferriss?" he fired at her suddenly.

"I was told he was Morton Haunchwood's servant."

"Know what he looks like?"

She opened her handbag, which she had brought into the room with her, and extracted a photograph. She passed it to the Yard man.

"That's Ferriss."

Slade glanced at the photograph, and started. It was the likeness of a man's head and shoulders. The man was almost bald, but his eyes were very deep-set, and the brows jutting over them were dark and bushy, lending his face a peculiar expression, almost Mongolian. He was clean-shaven, and his necktie was badly knotted. But the most striking feature about the man's face was the mouth. It was lifted at one corner in a strange smile, a sort of twisted smile, that gave the entire face a sneering expression. It was not a pleasant face, but it was a face one would remember for a long time after seeing it.

" So this is Ferriss."

The girl glanced at the detective quickly.

" You know him?"

Slade did not look up; he remained looking at the photograph in his hand.

" I've only seen him once," he said. " That was a short while ago at Cheviot Crescent."

The girl sprang forward excitedly and clutched his arm.

" What is it?" she demanded. " What do you mean?"

" Miss Merrell, we found the body of this man "—he tapped the photograph—" when we arrived at the house in Cheviot Crescent that had been broken into. He had been shot through the heart."

She stared at him unbelievingly.

" Then there are—there have been two murders!" she faltered.

The Yard man nodded, his face grave.

" You realize now why you must tell me——" He broke off suddenly. He had caught a faint sound outside the window. He pushed the girl from him and at the same moment called out : " Payne—turn out the light!"

The man at the door sprang to the switch, and the room was plunged in darkness. At the same instant that the light went out there was the sound of falling glass and the report of a shot.

In the darkness Slade heard the girl give a short sigh, and then she crumpled up and slid to the floor.

CHAPTER III

SLADE MAKES A DISCOVERY

SLADE sprang to the window, ripped aside the curtain, fumbled with the latch for a moment, and stepped out on to a low terrace. Drops of rain fell on his face. As he turned to run down the terrace he heard a pounding on the door of the drawing-room and Brawley's gruff voice raised in loud inquiry.

" Right, sir—you go that way, I'll go this."

The words were spoken by Clinton, who was close behind his chief.

Without answering, Slade leapt the few steps at the end of the terrace and raced off into the darkness. Clinton turned in the opposite direction. The grounds stretching behind the house were fairly extensive. From the little Slade could judge in the scramble in the darkness the wide stretch behind the house must at one time have comprised a fair-sized park. The ground sloped slightly, and he found himself blundering into root-stumps and bumping into indiscernible tree-shapes. But though he stopped several times to listen he heard no sound of any movement in front of him. Save for the thin patter of the raindrops on the leaves and the *drip-drip* from the leaves all was still. Not even the sound of a passing car on the road beyond the grounds, and the wind seemed to have dropped. It was a dismal search, and, as Slade felt, hopeless from the start. Whoever had fired that shot had had a couple of minutes' start, and the chances were that he knew every inch of these grounds. But while there remained a remote possibility of coming up with the person who had fired at the girl Slade kept on; and as he progressed he experienced a keener desire to learn where this stretch of parkland that had been let run wild and apparently remained untended for years led. He noted that he was traversing slightly downhill, and, looking back from time to time, he watched the position of the lights in the house. He kept as near as he could in a straight line.

He had been wandering about in the darkness under the trees for about twenty minutes when a familiar sound caught his ear, the lapping of water. He hurried forward, and a couple of minutes later stood beyond the fringe of trees on a shelving, grassy slope, staring at a stretch of dark water that he knew must be the Thames. The grass was tall and rank, sedgy, and the ground underneath was soft and muddy. Cautiously he picked his way to the bank, and stood there listening. Then his ear heard what he had expected to hear, the fading *chug-chug* of a speeding motor boat. There was little doubt now in Slade's mind that the person who had shot the man at Tangles and who had fired at the girl were one and the same, or that that person had arrived by the way he had left—across the water.

The rain blew out of the night from across the invisible face of the river—invisible, that is, save from where runnels of light from a house on the opposite bank streaked its darkness. Tucking his coat collar about his ears, the Yard man took out his flash-lamp, and, turning on its bright ray, picked his way more slowly along the bank. Some twenty yards along from the point where he had emerged from the wooded parkland he came upon an old, broken-down pier, a frail structure that looked as though it might have been erected for the convenience of punting parties. The ray from his torch revealed gaps in the rotten flooring. The iron bolts were rusty and in places almost eaten away by the action of the water and the weather. Treading gingerly, he stepped on to the pier and moved along, flashing his light ahead. This was evidently where the person in the motor boat had landed and moored the craft. The pier was not long, being built on piles, and extended into the river some twelve feet or so. Slade reached its end and knelt down.

Several rust-red ring-bolts were fastened to each side, and from the one on the farther side dangled a piece of knotted rope which had been hacked through with a sharp knife. The sever had been recently made, for it was a fresh cut, and the strands of hemp had not commenced to unravel. He glanced at the knot. It was an ordinary reef knot, secured with a couple of half-hitches. Placing his torch on the planking beside him, Slade unfastened the knot and drew the piece of rope out of the ring-bolt. He coiled it up and stuffed it in his pocket. Then he took a look round the other side of the pier. He was about to take a step forward when his foot trod on something hard wedged between the rotted boards. He stooped.

He had trodden upon the handle of a clasp-knife, the open blade of which hung down between the boards. Only by great good luck had the knife remained suspended in that position. It had plainly slipped from someone's hand, and had it fallen a couple of feet farther down the pier it would certainly have disappeared into the river.

The handle was wet, so there was no need to treat it carefully; what fingerprints it might have held were destroyed. It was an ordinary knife, with a single heavy blade, that folded into the handle. But cut into the handle of one side were three letters: T. G. B. As a clue it might be worth much or nothing. Slade placed it in his pocket with the pieces of rope.

At that moment Clinton, who had gone rambling among the trees along a circuitous route, stepped into the clearing above the bank. He saw the ray from Slade's torch and hailed him.

" Careful, Clinton," warned Slade. " This pier's nearly falling to bits."

The bulky form of Slade's chief assistant stepped on to the pier and moved cautiously to the side of the other.

" Did you spot him, sir?"

Clinton had been hurrying, and had not yet recovered his breath.

" No. He made a hurried getaway in a motor boat if I'm not mistaken, Clinton. But there's one thing I do know—he went up-river."

" How does that help, sir?"

Clinton took out a handkerchief that was already wet through and wiped the rain from his face.

" It means that most likely he's headed for Ploverton. It's only about a mile and a half up-river from here, I believe," explained Slade. " I also found these. They show something of the hurry he was in."

He took the rope and clasp-knife from his pocket and held them out.

" Well, the knife should prove useful, at any rate," said the sergeant. " But——" He broke off and stood peering out across the water. " Hello!" he exclaimed, " that light's gone out."

" Eh?"

Slade turned round and followed Clinton's gaze. The streaks of light had vanished from the surface of the water, for the light in the house on the opposite bank had vanished.

" Probably somebody's bedtime."

" Still, it's funny that it should go out like that, just after the fellow made his getaway."

" We don't know that it was a fellow, Clinton."

The sergeant sounded surprised.

" You don't think it was a girl, do you?"

" After what we've stumbled on tonight I'm not thinking anything until I've found out more. Clinton, this is one of the most puzzling cases I've come across, and, as you know, that's saying something. There's something almost uncanny in these two murders after hearing Claire Merrell's tale. Let's be moving back to the house. I want to know what's happened to her."

They arrived back at the house to find that Dr. Herrick had placed the girl in a bed in a room on the first floor. A bullet had pierced her shoulder, inflicting a nasty flesh wound. It had narrowly missed smashing the bone. The girl had fainted, he explained. That final shock had been too much for her system. She had been highly strung, and the wound had administered a mental as well as physical knock-out. He had got through on the phone to Ploverton Cottage Hospital, and a nurse was being sent out immediately to attend the girl.

Slade went down to the drawing-room, where Brawley was walking up and down looking like a caged lion who had no great idea of captivity. As soon as Slade entered the room he pounced on him.

" What do you make of it all, Tony?"

Slade dropped on to the settee.

" To be frank, Abe—nothing. I don't know enough. . . . Oh, here's her bag ! "

He picked up the girl's handbag, which had been placed on the settee, and unfastened the clasp. He took out a small purse containing three pound notes and some small change, a small bunch of keys, a silver case containing powder compact and lipstick, and a slip of paper on which was typed :—

MORTON HAUNCHWOOD
HAROLD FERRISS
JOHN RIDLEY
STANLEY MERTON

That was all the bag contained. Slade replaced the other articles, retaining the slip of paper. He read the names typed on it a second time, then held it out to Brawley.

" Does this tell you anything, Abe?" he asked.

The Flying Squad leader looked glum.

" Just about as much as you get out of it, Tony—no more."

Slade grinned.

" Which isn't much, is it? Well, Haunchwood and Ferriss are out of the running. Looks as though we've got to find Ridley and Merton pretty soon. They might be booked to go the same way."

" Did she say much."

" No. But you were wrong, Abe. She was lying. Haunchwood —if that was his name—wasn't her uncle——"

" Wasn't?" queried Brawley, a pained look spreading across his face. " Why, I'd have bet——"

" Just be glad you didn't. You'd have lost. But she was about to open up, Abe, when she was shot."

Brawley's face drew longer, and his expression became glummer.

" She won't talk now."

" She's got to talk soon," said Slade evenly, but from his tone he meant the words. " I've left Farrar to look after that business in Cheviot Crescent, but he won't be able to straighten out much. The real mystery's here."

Brawley looked interested at that.

" How do you arrive there?" he asked.

" Well, Ferriss was supposed to be a servant here. He's murdered, and on the same night that Haunchwood, the man who is supposed to employ him, is murdered here. Then of all places that girl has to come here with a cock-and-bull tale about an urgent phone call from her uncle. Well, she comes here, and it's not long before someone takes a pot-shot at *her*. You see, this place Tangles is the centre of the mystery—whatever the mystery is. One thing we know, Abe. There is someone pretty desperate going about, a killer who will stop at nothing. The odds are that the stake is large, worth securing. Before we can become very effective we've got to know what the stake is. Only the girl and two other people, I should say, can tell us."

"Ridley and Merton?"

Slade nodded.

"Yes, they're the other two. Listen, Abe. In the house in Cheviot Crescent the safe had been broken open. Money, securities, anything one would have expected to find in it, were gone. But in a drawer of a desk I found a letter, a very formal letter ostensibly upon a matter of business, addressed to Harold Ferriss and signed John Ridley. The sheet of paper bore the heading of the Summerdale Brickmaking Company, Ploverton. That's getting near home, isn't it?"

Brawley was silent for a moment.

"You didn't come across any reference to the other chappie, did you? Merton?"

"No." Slade glanced down at the slip of paper. "This is the first time I've come across Merton's name. But I shouldn't be surprised if I learned that he lived in Ploverton. I've an idea these people—the four whose names are here and the girl—were watching each other mighty carefully. Probably one of them thought he had waited long enough——"

"That means either Ridley or Merton."

"Looks like it, Abe. But we're going to have a job getting enough evidence to make an arrest. From the way the girl's kept the secret I shouldn't say the other two will prove talkative. And, of course, there's always the possibility that our search won't be limited to these two. There may be others."

"What're you going to do now, Tony? I'll have to get my patrol back."

"When that nurse arrives I'll get in touch with the local station, and tomorrow morning I'll have to take another look at the house in Cheviot Crescent. I think we shall be able to seal that up and concentrate down here. A visit to Mr. Ridley at the Summerdale Brickmaking Works is clearly indicated."

"Well, don't forget to ask him if he ever owned a clasp-knife, Tony."

"I'll remember that," grinned Slade. "That'll be the nurse," he added, as the sound of a car drawing to a halt came from the direction of the road.

A few minutes later Nurse Bunton, small, competent-looking, quick-eyed, was shown into the hall. She slipped off her cape and turned to Dr. Herrick.

"Well, doctor, where's my patient?" she asked.

Slade breathed a sigh of relief. The woman knew her job, and a single glance at her face revealed that she could keep her mouth closed. As Dr. Herrick stepped aside with the nurse Slade interrupted.

"Oh, excuse me, doctor, but there's one thing I should like to ask Nurse Bunton to do for me."

"Certainly." Herrick moved off, and Slade was left with the nurse.

"What is it, inspector?" she asked quietly, her dark eyes quizzing him.

"I want you to pay special attention to this patient, nurse—watch her closely. If she tries to do anything unusual say nothing here, but get in touch with me as quickly as you can. Do you understand?"

She nodded gravely.

"I think I do, inspector. And where shall I phone you—at the Yard?"

"Yes. If I am not there leave a message, saying you'll ring again within, say, half an hour. I'll get back to my office as soon as I learn you've got through. Is that quite clear, nurse? Anything unusual, mind——"

Nurse Bunton smiled.

"Isn't 'suspicious' a better word, inspector?"

Slade smiled in turn.

"A much better word."

They understood each other.

When Dr. Herrick had at last taken the nurse upstairs Slade turned to the telephone and the directory on the small table in the hall. Three minutes later he was speaking to the desk-sergeant at Ploverton Police Station. The man sounded amazed at the short recital Slade treated him to, but promised that he would get in touch with his superior, Inspector Rayner, immediately. Leaving the hall, Slade went in search of Clinton, whom he found inspecting the drawing-room.

"Clinton, I'm going to leave you down here. I've got through to the local people, and there'll be an Inspector Rayner down shortly. Do what you can." Clinton nodded; he understood very well what Slade meant. "I've told the nurse," went on Slade, "to keep a close eye on her patient, and if she sees anything suspicious to get through to me at the Yard, and say nothing here. That was merely a precaution."

The dour-faced Clinton almost smiled.

" I get you, sir."

" Very good, then, Clinton. I'll be getting back to report, and see if Farrar has anything further. Everything clear?"

" Yes, sir."

Slade found Brawley talking to a couple of his men in the study. The corpse had been placed on the floor at the foot of one of the large bookcases, and had been draped with a blanket taken from a bedroom upstairs. The Flying Squad leader swung round when he saw his colleague.

" Well, all set, Tony? I shan't be sorry to get out of this dismal place. I thank my stars I haven't got your job and the prospect of coming back here—even in daylight."

" Don't be too sure of your not coming back, Abe. After all, you found the place."

Brawley snorted.

" And a pretty peck of trouble too. Come on—let's be going."

CHAPTER IV

FORESTALLED

Pale autumn sunlight lit one side of Cheviot Crescent as Slade's car drew to a halt. It was not a long thoroughfare. Running parallel to and behind several large blocks of hotels, it was one of those crescent-shaped streets, with house fronts on one side and backs on the other, that are peculiar to London. A plain-clothes man saluted as Slade and Sergeant Farrar climbed out of the car.

" Anything to report, Irvin?" asked Slade.

" No, sir. I came downstairs three minutes ago."

" Let's go up, then."

The three Yard men passed through the front door of the house outside which Slade had stopped his car. In the square and rather lofty hall sat the uniformed figure of one of the divisional constables. The man scrambled to his feet when he saw Slade.

" 'Morning, inspector."

" 'Morning."

Slade strode forward and continued up the wide staircase. On the first landing he turned aside into a room on the left, cast a sharp eye round the apartment, and turned to Farrar, who had followed him into the room.

" Just as I left it."

Farrar nodded.

" As I said, sir, I've been through everything here—but without coming across a thing that'll help."

Slade nodded, his face puckered in thought. Suddenly he bent over the open and empty safe. Straightening his back, he returned to the centre of the room and pulled open the drawers of the table. He closed them with a bang, frowning more intently.

" Well, whoever opened the safe, Farrar, knew where to get the key—and though he left the safe open he took the key with him. I can't think up an answer to why just now. Can you?"

Farrar shook his head.

" No, I don't get that, sir. The other rooms are all locked, too. No sign of their having been searched."

" All right, Farrar, we're not going to waste time here. There are two things I want. One, the agent for this place. He'll be at his office this morning, and I want to know who was renting this place. Two, I want a man set to check up the address of the man who told the constable he saw two men run out of the house and pile into a maroon saloon car which he thought already held a couple of men. I'm going to leave you in charge at this end then, Farrar, and if you want me you will have to phone that place Tangles."

" Very good, sir." Farrar produced a notebook. " The agent's name is Cyril Flutterbee; he has an office in Piccadilly. I'll get the witness's address checked up right away. Do you want to see the man, sir?"

" No. Mr. Flutterbee will be enough for me."

Mr. Flutterbee was stout, slightly bald, and a single glance was sufficient to show the detective that he suffered from an inflated sense of his own importance. His paunch was ample, and his black vicuna waistcoat was ornamented with the taut line of a thin platinum watchchain. When his pretty ash-blonde secretary ushered Slade into the estate agent's inner sanctum Mr. Flutterbee had jammed a monocle into his left eye and was regarding the blank expanse of the door expectantly. With a curt wave of the hand he banished the girl, and, continuing the motion, indicated a chair on the other side of a magnificent mahogany desk.

" Well, now, inspector," he began, with a smirking grimace, " what can I do for you?"

The finger-tips of one pudgy hand tapped the finger-tips of

another pudgy hand. Slade regarded the man closely, and was aware that Mr. Flutterbee's small eyes were very much alive.

"You've seen this morning's paper, Mr. Flutterbee?" Slade opened crisply.

"Er—yes." Mr. Flutterbee was very cautious. He blinked, and the effect of the monocle was to make his face seem like that of an owl with a squint.

"And you are the agent for number seventeen Cheviot Crescent, I understand?"

Mr. Flutterbee rose and affected great agitation. He walked to the window, bathed himself in the thin sunlight for a moment, while contemplating the traffic in Piccadilly, then turned about and nodded vigorously.

"I am, inspector. It *is* my misfortune to be the agent for that very desirable—ahem!" Just in time had he recalled himself; he blinked more owlishly than before. "I was hoping you had come to see me about something else," he finished lamely.

Slade gave the man a straight, hard look, and came to the conclusion that he was in a funk; he was afraid for his reputation. For a moment the detective had considered the possibility of the estate agent's being mixed in something crooked; but a closer glance reassured him on this point. Mr. Flutterbee was thinking only of himself—and his reputation. His next words confirmed the detective's impression.

"Inspector," he went on, a more genial and confidential tone in his voice as he sat down again, "can't you handle this case without so much publicity? What I mean is I fail to see what advantage to yourself—as a detective, of course—can accrue from spreading this unpleasantness in the columns of the Press——"

Slade cut in; he had sized up Mr. Flutterbee fairly accurately, and had no wish for his time to be wasted while the other listened to himself spouting.

"I've nothing to do with the reports published in the newspapers, Mr. Flutterbee. If you've any complaint you should write to the editor of the paper concerned. And I consider murder something more disturbing than a mere unpleasantness."

Mr. Flutterbee hastened to correct his mistake.

"Oh, no, no, don't misunderstand me, inspector. Don't think I don't regret this sad occurrence——"

"I've no doubt on that score," remarked the Yard man dryly, and received a baleful stare from the other, who, after a moment's pause, rubbed his hands together again.

"Very well, then, what is it that I can do for you?"

Slade smiled grimly. This was capitulation.

"First, Mr. Flutterbee, I want the name of the person who took the house."

The estate agent made no move. "Anything else, inspector?"

"Yes, the time that person occupied the house, any personal details in the contract, previous address, references if any, and date of expiration of contract."

"Very good," said Mr. Flutterbee, but his expression was sour as he reached forward and pressed a desk-button. The monocle slipped from his eye, and evidently he was too disgruntled to notice the omission.

The ash-blonde secretary brought in a file and a ledger, and by referring from one to the other Mr. Flutterbee eventually found what he was seeking. He sat back and puffed, and Slade noticed that the line of his watchchain was slightly less taut.

"The occupier's name, inspector, is Morton Haunchwood, if that conveys anything to you."

He glanced at the Yard man swiftly. Slade nodded, his face impassive.

"Just a little."

"I see. Well, now, we need not go into the matter of the rental—I hardly think that matters—but I see from my book that the house was taken for eighteen months. Let me see, now—why, yes, the lease will be up at the end of this month."

Slade leaned forward more eagerly. This was news. Haunchwood had taken the house in Mayfair for eighteen months, and shortly before the expiration of that time he and another man who had been associated with him are both shot—murdered. The case became more interesting at every stage.

"What about Haunchwood's previous address?"

Mr. Flutterbee puckered his lips, and held them between finger and thumb.

"Well, it's hardly a previous address that is given, inspector. Mr. Haunchwood gave his country address."

"I can guess it," said Slade. "Tangles, Lower Ploverton."

Mr. Flutterbee raised surprised brows.

"You surprise me," he remarked, aloofly polite. "However, it appears that the only reference Mr. Haunchwood gave was his bank, and in the circumstances I considered that sufficient."

"Tell me, Mr. Flutterbee, did Haunchwood live in town much or only occasionally?"

The estate agent visibly appeared to freeze.

"I'm afraid I cannot enlighten you on that point, inspector. My clients' respective lives do not concern me, and you must understand that my interest is purely professional."

Slade could cheerfully have kicked the pompous fool. He said nothing, however, waiting for a question he knew the other was saving. Mr. Flutterbee suddenly found that he could wait no longer.

"Doubtless you consider all this very much to the point, inspector, but it wasn't Mr. Haunchwood that was found dead in the house, was it?"

"No," admitted Slade, not to be drawn.

"The account in the paper this morning stated that the dead man's identity was not known to the police. Well—er—don't you think you had better apply to Mr. Haunchwood direct?"

Mr. Flutterbee's eyes were ogling with suppressed excitement. He felt he had made a worthy suggestion, had shown remarkable perspicacity.

"I'm afraid that's impossible, Mr. Flutterbee."

"Oh?"

"Yes, quite impossible."

Mr. Flutterbee wriggled—or, rather, squirmed—in his chair. He did not like this man who had been sent from Scotland Yard. He had an annoying habit of causing one to feel inquisitive—consciously inquisitive.

"And might I inquire why?"

Mr. Flutterbee was groping for his monocle with his left hand; his brows were very arched; but their archness vanished at Slade's next words.

"Haunchwood has been murdered."

Mr. Flutterbee quivered.

"Murdered!" he gasped protestingly, and threw up an arm as though to ward off something that was about to assail him. "But you said that man was *not* Mr. Haunchwood."

"I know. Haunchwood was murdered at Tangles. Just a minute, Mr. Flutterbee." Slade drew a photograph from his pocket. "Have you ever seen that man before?"

He held out the photograph of Ferriss.

The estate agent gave it one glance, and then looked up at the detective as though he suspected him of some trick.

"*Seen* him? Why, that's Mr. Haunchwood himself!"

It was Slade's turn to appear surprised; but the next moment he had recovered himself.

"Of course," he said nonchalantly. "But can you be certain, Mr. Flutterbee—absolutely positive?"

The estate agent chose to look supercilious. He patted the sides of his mouth.

"Do you think I could forget a man with a grin like that, inspector?"

Slade stared at the face of the man with the twisted smile.

"No, I don't suppose you could," he said at length, and rose. "Mr. Flutterbee," he cautioned, "you realize of course that this inquiry concerns murder. I need hardly add that it would be exceedingly unwise of you to repeat anything I may have mentioned to you just now."

Mr. Flutterbee quivered again. For the first time since the Yard man had entered he really felt himself in the presence of an emissary of the law.

"You can depend upon me to be most discreet, inspector," he hastened to assure the other. "In fact, I can give you my word that not a syllable shall be breathed outside this office."

"Better make it inside too," said Slade ungraciously, and with a nod went out. He had had about all he could stand of Mr. Cyril Flutterbee.

At the house in Cheviot Crescent Slade found Farrar awaiting him with news. There had been a couple of phone calls from the Yard. It appeared that a Nurse Bunton was inquiring for Slade from Tangles, a place near Ploverton. The last call had come through from the Yard barely three minutes before Slade had arrived from the estate office in Piccadilly.

Slade went back to his car and drove to the Yard. He had been in his office ten minutes when Nurse Bunton's next call came through.

"Is that Inspector Slade?"

The Yard man recognized the nurse's sharp tones.

"Yes, speaking, Nurse Bunton. You have something to tell me?"

"Yes, sir. I've been trying to get on to you for about an hour. This is my third call——"

"So I understand, nurse. I got back as soon as I heard you had phoned. I'm sorry for the delay."

He heard something that might have been a sniff at the other end of the wire; then Nurse Bunton was speaking again, and Slade listened with close attention.

"Dr. Herrick, as you know, sir, gave the patient a sleeping-draught last night. He told me she would not be awake until about half-past nine this morning. Well, it was just after that time that I happened to cross into the hall from the dining-room. Just as I turned down the corridor I heard a click. I stopped for a moment, wondering what it could be; then it occurred to me that it might be the telephone receiver replaced on its hook. I hurried into the hall, and as I went past the foot of the staircase I chanced to look up, and there was my patient hurrying across the landing at the top of the first flight, sir. She didn't see me; she was too intent upon getting back to her room. But it was pretty obvious what she had been doing—phoning someone. It looked strange to me, so I thought I had better phone to you as you told me to, sir."

Slade's face was grave.

"You did quite right, nurse, and I'm very grateful for this timely notice. Tell me, please, is Inspector Rayner at the house?"

"Yes, sir. He came last night, and left after speaking to Sergeant Clinton for some time; and he came back about nine o'clock this morning. He's with Sergeant Clinton now, sir. Did you want him?"

"No—no, thanks, nurse."

Slade was about to ring off when she spoke again.

"I'm being relieved at eleven o'clock, sir. Dr. Herrick said someone should remain with the patient today, and he has arranged for a staff nurse from Ploverton Cottage Hospital to come out here."

"Very good, nurse. I'll remember that—and thanks very much. Good-bye."

Slade replaced the receiver and got to his feet. He paced up and down the office several times, pondering this last item of news. Whom had the girl phoned? And why had she been so anxious to get in touch with someone? She had been fired at. Only by a miracle had the bullet missed killing her.

Slade sat down again, heavily. There was a deep mystery surrounding the girl, surrounding that old, neglected house with the peculiar name of Tangles. Two murders on his hands already —almost three—and he had no clear idea of where to start his investigation. The girl would have to talk—true. But meantime! What wheels had that phone call from Tangles set in motion. Had the message been a warning?

The more he thought about it the more disconcertingly sure he became that it had. But what sort of warning— Why——

The house-phone on his desk shrilled, and he picked up the receiver. One of the divisional plain-clothes men was below with a report for Department X2. He had been sent out by Sergeant Farrar.

A few minutes later the man knocked and entered. He had further bewildering news to offer Slade. He had been sent to check the address given by the witness in Cheviot Crescent and to tell the man that he would be required to attend the inquest—and he had discovered that the man had given the constable a faked address. There was no such street as the one he had named in all London.

"Looks as though our friend's covered his tracks, then—doesn't it?" said Slade.

"It certainly does, sir. And if you don't mind my adding, sir, it looks to me as though his being there on the spot was something more than a coincidence."

Slade gave the man a sharp look, then nodded.

"You're right. It *is* something more than a coincidence."

And when the man had gone he told himself that there wasn't a single coincidence in the whole affair. It was all a carefully planned and connected scheme. But what puzzled him was where the girl fitted in. Had there not been those two cars of the same colour and make and with the same number on their number-plates he would have had graver doubts about her—but there *were* the two cars. No doubt about that. And someone *had* tried to kill her too.

It was all a maze, with not a thread of sense to lead him.

He stuffed tobacco in his pipe, lit it, and began pacing again, his hands deep in his trousers pockets. Time and again he told himself that the girl was his best lead. The very fact that someone wanted to get her out of the way—permanently—showed that she knew something dangerous to that person's interest.

Suddenly he picked up the receiver and asked to be put through to the office of the Yard's firearms expert. When Slade next replaced the receiver a keener gleam was in his eye. The Yard expert had established that the bullets which had killed both men might have been fired from the same gun. That pointed to a single murderer—and another problem. Herrick had said the man at Tangles had been dead from two to two and a half hours before he arrived. Then it was possible that the murderer of the man at Tangles had driven fast to London—say, in half an hour or forty minutes—killed the man with the twisted smile in the Mayfair house—and driven back to Ploverton and been waiting for the girl when she arrived.

It sounded melodramatic, the conception of someone mentally unstable; but Slade had had long years of experience of murderers and their ways. He knew that no one on earth works faster or more untiringly than the man who has planned a murder or series of murders and is intent upon carrying out his design.

But there was a fresh point. Which man had been killed at which place? Haunchwood at Tangles—or Ferriss? Ferriss at the house in Mayfair—or Haunchwood? The girl had said that the man at Tangles was Haunchwood, while the estate agent had purported to recognize the photograph of the man found dead in Mayfair as Haunchwood.

Slade realized bitterly that the more he probed the less sure he found himself of what he had already learned. He took out his notebook and flicked over some leaves.

CLAIRE MERRELL, 27A Stanthorpe Mansions, South Kensington.

For a minute or two he studied the address, speculating. Suddenly he slipped the notebook into his pocket, donned his coat and hat, and went down into Derby Street, where he had left his car. A couple of minutes later he was tailing a Green Liner along Victoria Street, *en route* to South Kensington.

It was almost noon when he found Stanthorpe Mansions, a modest-looking block of flats in a road called Burling Grove. As he cruised along the kerbside, looking for No. 27A, he saw someone cross the pavement hurriedly, step into a dark blue *coupé,* and drive off. When he found No. 27A at last it was to realize with a start that the man who had driven off in the *coupé* had come from that particular building. Of course, he might have left any of the other flats comprising No. 27A, but——

A white-moustached porter in a peaked cap was fixing a light switch in the hall.

" Miss Merrell's flat? " inquired Slade of the old man.

The latter paused in his task and squinted.

" 'Oo did you say, mister? "

" Miss Merrell," repeated Slade.

The old man scratched his head.

" Ain't no Miss Merrell lives 'ere, sir."

He screwed his scraggy red neck round in its too-large collar and glared at Slade through gold-rimmed spectacles, for all the world like a human turkey.

" Don't 'appen to know the lidy's Christian name, do you, mister? " he inquired, grinning as roguishly as his toothless gums would allow.

" I'm looking for the apartment of a Miss Claire Merrell, and the address I was given is 27A Stanthorpe Mansions."

The old man chuckled.

"That's right, sir, that's right. On'y it's *Mrs.* Claire Merrell you're wantin'. Number Twelve on the third floor—you'll see her plate outside the door."

And he continued persevering with the recalcitrant light switch, chuckling long and deeply to himself.

Slade, cursing under his breath at the delay, ran up the stairs three at a time, thereby bringing down upon his head the vitriolic wrath of a very large lady in a very loud purple dress, who chanced to step out of a second-floor doorway as he ran by.

He found No. 12 on the third floor. In the centre of the door was a small brass frame with a cardboard slip inserted, bearing the caption:

CLAIRE MERRELL

He took from his pocket a bunch of skeleton keys, and after trying several found one that opened the latch. He stepped inside the door and closed it quietly. A single glance round the room in which he found himself revealed the truth. He had been forestalled!

He passed from one room to another. In each were signs of someone having searched hurriedly. Drawers were pulled open, cupboard doors swung back, and in the grate of what was apparently the sitting-room was a fresh pile of black ash. Someone had been burning papers.

Slade thought again of the man who had driven off in the dark blue *coupé,* and swore under his breath.

It had been a matter of seconds.

CHAPTER V

LORETTE'S

A QUARTER of an hour later Slade returned to the sitting-room and contemplated the black ashes in the grate with a frown. He had found nothing in the flat that gave any clue to the girl's personality. In the wardrobe were her dresses; personal articles were to be found in each room, in fact, but nothing of the nature Slade sought: no letters, accounts, diary, or notes. As he stared at the ashes he wondered.

He bent down and ran his fingers through them. They were brittle and crumpled at his touch. There were a few ends that were not entirely burned: several of these were obviously corners of bills; and there were one or two scorched tips of letters. But not one of them was likely to offer him any aid. He was about to get up when his exploring fingers felt a piece of something thicker and stiffer among the charred remnants. He picked it up and softly blew the powdered ash from its surface.

It was a piece of the bottom of a photograph. The likeness had been completely destroyed, and what he held in his hand was a portion of the mount. The piece of cardboard was scorched a deep brown by the flames, and it was only by running his finger over the surface that Slade discovered several small raised markings. He held the piece of cardboard up to the light, but the scorch was too deep for him to see what those markings were. Then suddenly it occurred to him—the photographer's name and address in small raised letters!

This was heartening. Although the find might not prove in the least helpful, he took it as a sign that his luck was not altogether out. Carefully he sorted over all the other ashes in the grate, and he found three pieces more of the photo-mount, but none of these bore any distinguishing mark, and in each case the portion of the photograph itself had been wholly destroyed.

Slade left the flat and went down the stairs again, slowly this time; he was thoughtful. The white-moustached porter was still tinkering with the light switch in the hall. He looked up when Slade approached.

" Have you an office here?" asked the detective.

He spoke abruptly, in a tone that caused the other to peer at him closely.

" No, sir," said the old man. " But if it's something you want to ask me we can go down into the kitchen."

" That'll do."

It took Slade some minutes to convince his fresh host that he was a Scotland Yard detective, and not a practical joker. It appeared that the old man had had more experience of the latter.

" Well, yer want ter know wot *I* know about this 'ere Mrs. Merrell, inspector," he ruminated. " I can tell yer this fer a start— it ain't much."

" Never mind—let's have it."

" Now," continued the old man cautiously, " don't go thinkin' I'm a nosey parker——"

" I won't," promised Slade, with a grin.

" Or that I meddle with things as don't concern me——"

" No, of course not."

" But, if you arsk me, inspector, *I* thinks as it's funny when a

married woman—as she calls 'erself—comes to a block o' flats like
this an' sets up on 'er own an' 'er 'usband on'y comes to see 'er
now and agen. A course, I know there's 'er business to——"

"Do you know her husband by sight?"

"Well, sir, it's as much as I do, if you understand. I 'aven't
spoken to 'im more than about twice—or three times at most, say—
and we've a lot o' people in and out o' these flats."

"How long has Mrs. Merrell been here?"

The old man racked his brains for a few seconds.

"Well, not more than eighteen months, sir."

Slade nodded thoughtfully. Haunchwood had occupied the
house in Mayfair about that time.

"I see. When did you last see Mr. Merrell?"

"To tell the truth, sir, I thought at first that I saw 'im go out
just afore you came in. But I can't be sure. You see, I on'y caught
a glimpse of 'is back as 'e went out and down the steps."

The man who had driven off in the dark blue *coupé*. That
meant that the girl had phoned her husband from Tangles, and
he had driven here to the Kensington flat and destroyed some
evidence—of what? And as the old porter had remarked, if the
two were not separated why did they live apart in this way?

"You mentioned a business. What sort of business has Mrs.
Merrell?" Slade inquired.

"Dress-shop, sir. One o' these 'ere places where you puts a
couple o' gowns in the winder an' rig the shop up with mirrers.
It's called Lorette's."

"And where is the shop?"

"In Shaftesbury Avenue, sir."

"Is Mrs. Merrell employed there?"

"Lummy, no, sir! She owns the business. She is that there
Lorette—though w'y she's got ter pick a name like that to run a
shop with beats me."

"It does me too," the detective confessed as he got up. "Do
you happen to know if Mrs. Merrell has many callers—gentlemen
friends?"

The old man winked knowingly.

"She ain't that sort, sir. Bit too serious-minded fer 'er age,
if you arsks me. I s'pose it's that business; must be an awful
worry. And blowed if 'er 'usband's about much ter 'elp 'er, as
you might say."

"You'd say, then, that she leads a fairly quiet life?"

"Yers, there's plenty as 'ud call it quiet, an' there's them I
know as 'ud say it wasn't livin' at all."

"I see. Right." Slade slipped a half-crown into the old man's brown paw. "Now, don't forget. Not a word to anyone—understand——"

"Yers, sir," said the porter, pocketing the coin readily, "but if yer don't mind me arskin' one question——"

"Well, what is it?"

The old man gulped.

"Wot's she bin up to? I mean, sir, wot's she done as you should be 'ere makin' these inquiries?"

Slade smiled disarmingly.

"I hope she's done nothing. In that case the inquiries can't hurt her, can they?"

The old man shook his head, mumbling to himself, and led the way out of the kitchen. As he went back to the light switch in the hall Slade passed down the front steps and climbed into his car. He turned eastwards and drove to Piccadilly Circus, where he turned into Lower Regent Street and parked the car, and then set out along Shaftesbury Avenue on foot. He found Lorette's on the left-hand side progressing towards Charing Cross Road, almost opposite the Shaftesbury Theatre. The old porter's description was correct. Two model gowns were shown in the window, and beyond the white-and-gold partition the detective caught the reflection of large mirrors.

He passed inside, and his first glance assured him that the establishment catered for a high class of custom. No Whitechapel-made garments found their way into Lorette's. The piled carpet and tasteful furnishings were proof of that.

A tall woman with dark auburn hair, dressed fashionably in black and oyster satin, approached him with a doubtful expression on her face.

"Is there something I can do for you, sir?" she began, but Slade cut her short.

"I'm from the Yard. Are you in charge?"

The woman's eyes hardened.

"At the moment. Madame is away."

"I know about that—and why she's away. Where can I speak to you without being interrupted?"

For a moment the woman hesitated, as though in doubt; but Slade's face wore a determined look.

"There's an office behind this curtain. If you will follow me——?"

She paused on a note of interrogation. Slade supplied his name.

"Inspector Slade." He handed her one of his official cards.

She gave it a cursory glance and led the way across the shop to the office, which was a small, compact little apartment, with wooden partitions, glass-panelled at the tops, and room only for a desk and two chairs. On a four-shelf bookcase were ranged the account books of the business.

"Now, if you'll excuse me, Miss——"

"Clissold."

"——Miss Clissold, I'll speak bluntly. I want to know what you can tell me about Mrs. Merrell. Furthermore, I want you to regard what passes between us as strictly confidential. Remember, this is a murder case!"

It was rather dramatic, but Slade realized that he would have to make an early impression upon the competent-looking woman. His method was justified. At mention of the word "murder" the woman flinched.

"Oh, inspector, but you can't think that Mrs. Merrell——"

"I'm thinking nothing about Mrs. Merrell at the moment," Slade reminded her frigidly. "I've come for information. But let me tell you this, Miss Clissold. You'll be helping Mrs. Merrell best by being frank——"

"But there's really nothing I can tell you about madame," the woman hastened to assure him. "There's practically nothing I know. Of course, I have her address here, and the details of the business, if those facts are of any use to you——"

"They might be later, but I am not interested in them now." Slade considered. After a moment he leaned forward. "Perhaps it would be better if you answered my questions, Miss Clissold. We might get on faster that way."

"Well, very good, then."

"How long has Lorette's been established?"

"I should say nearly three years."

"And have you been in the firm all that time, Miss Clissold?"

"No. I joined madame about two years ago, shortly before her marriage. As a matter of fact, it was on account of her marriage that I came here."

"Do you know Mr. Merrell?"

She shrugged.

"I've seen him several times of course. But he does not come here very frequently. Indeed, madame herself has not been here so much as usual during the past few months."

"Now I have a more personal question to ask, Miss Clissold. Do you think Mrs. Merrell is happily married?"

The woman looked her surprise.

"Why certainly! What makes you think——"

But Slade held up a hand.

"I'm afraid I cannot admit to thinking much at this stage, Miss Clissold. Now, tell me candidly, do you think Mrs. Merrell has a lover?"

Miss Clissold's rather lean and intellectual face lengthened in an expression of distaste.

"Really, inspector, if all this is for a divorce case——"

"I didn't say divorce—I said murder," rasped Slade, evidently annoyed.

The woman's glance fell. Her white fingers fumbled with a paper-knife on the desk. Plainly there was something in her mind that was troubling her. Slade waited patiently.

"No, Mrs. Merrell isn't the sort who would have a lover—I mean of her own choosing." The woman lifted her eyes, and gazed straight at the detective. Slade admired her loyalty. "But since you've asked me, I must admit that I have seen a man hanging about outside the shop several times, and each time I saw him it certainly occurred to me that he was waiting for madame to come out."

"What makes you sure?"

"Well"—the woman hesitated—"I've only noticed him waiting outside when madame has been in, and he always disappeared after she had gone out."

"Was he a young man?"

"I can't say. I never saw him close. . . . I should say about forty. He had a reddish moustache, and each time I've seen him he was wearing either a mackintosh or overcoat."

Slade took out his notebook and jotted down several points for future reference.

"Mrs. Merrell was not very confiding, was she?" he asked, looking up suddenly.

"Do you mean about the business or about her private affairs?"

"Both."

"Well, in that case I must explain. She made it a rule that each person here knew exactly how to carry on no matter whoever was away. It was part of her principle: the place was to run itself. And I must say, from my own experience, it has been a wise policy. On the other hand, madame has never mentioned her private affairs much to the people here. She treats every member of the staff friendlily, but she is not really intimate with any of us."

"Thank you, Miss Clissold, that makes things plain for me. So I can take it Mrs. Merrell did not mention this man with the reddish moustache to you."

The woman shook her head.

"Do you know if she has any address other than the one in South Kensington?"

"No, inspector, that's the only address we have in the books here."

"Who handles the firm's correspondence?"

"Well, I open anything addressed to the firm. Any private correspondence, or even any letters relating to the firm's business addressed to any special member of the staff, is passed on to the person addressed to."

"I see. Then you have never acted in a secretarial capacity to Mrs. Merrell?"

Miss Clissold's intelligent looks did her no more than justice.

"If you mean, inspector, do I know what was contained in her private correspondence—no, I don't."

Slade smiled grimly.

"I see you understand, Miss Clissold."

"I could hardly fail to!" she asseverated tartly.

Slade moved off on to a different tack.

"You know of no trouble Mrs. Merrell has experienced recently?"

"No. I believe I mentioned that lately she has not been attending the shop quite so regularly. But that's the only difference I am aware of."

"And the firm's finances are in sound order?"

"Perfectly."

"Mrs. Merrell's?"

"Again, I am afraid I cannot help you, inspector. Madame's private account is in a different bank from the firm's account."

"You know then of no one who bore her a grudge——"

"Bore?" The woman had quickly settled on that use of the past tense.

Slade made haste to retrieve his slip.

"I should have said 'bears.'"

But he saw that the woman was not satisfied. A doubt had been sown in her mind. She half rose.

"Inspector," she said, clutching the table, and there was more emotion in her voice now than at any moment since Slade had entered, "you said this case you are on is a murder case. . . . You don't mean that—that——"

The detective regarded her calmly.

"Of course not, Miss Clissold! Mrs. Merrell is quite well. As a matter of fact, she sustained a slight accident, and in a few days she'll——"

"Someone tried to kill her?"

The woman's face had drained white. She stood there, half leaning over the desk, her eyes fixed on Slade's face, the knuckles of her fingers gleaming whitely through the skin. Slade saw a tiny pulse beating frantically in her throat.

"What is it you know, Miss Clissold?"

His voice was stern, uncompromising. For a moment the woman continued to stare at him with a blank expression on her face, as though her thought had come to a sudden standstill. Slowly the expression changed; intelligence brightened her eyes and the tenseness of her arms relaxed. She sank down into her chair.

"I didn't want to tell you, as it doesn't seem right to repeat what one overheard by accident——"

"Scruples are very good things to have at the right time; but, like a great many things, they can be misused," Slade pointed out.

The woman nodded.

"You're probably right." She frowned at the desk-top. "I remember coming in here one day shortly after noticing that the man with the reddish moustache was hanging about outside. I didn't know that madame was in here, and when I entered she was standing against the bookcase, with her back towards me, and she was talking to herself, as though trying to convince herself about something. I heard her mutter something about, 'It'll be dangerous if he finds out, but it's a chance—at least it's a chance.' That was all I heard. I didn't want her to know that I had overheard anything, so I crept out again. A little while afterwards she came out, dressed for the street, and I noticed that after she had passed the man waiting outside he turned and walked off in the direction she had taken. That's all I know. It's nothing much really, and probably there's nothing to it, but I must confess it has set me thinking several times."

Both became silent for a spell. They were interrupted by a rap at the door, and another darkly clad assistant squeezed her way into the small office.

"Excuse me, Miss Clissold, but there's a gentleman outside inquiring for madame."

"Very well, Marie. Tell him I'll be along in a minute or two. Don't say madame's not here."

The assistant threw a sharp glance from Miss Clissold to the detective.

" Very good, Miss Clissold."

The door closed after her, and the woman at the desk rose.

" Is this another detective?"

Slade too had risen. He shook his head.

" No, you won't have any other Yard men calling here, Miss Clissold, you may be assured of that."

The woman looked at the detective with a new expression.

" I'll go and see who it is, inspector. If you care to stand on that chair you'll be able to see him through the glass panel."

Slade nodded and smiled.

" Thanks for the tip."

" Well, I'll go and see what he wants."

Miss Clissold went out, and as soon as the door had closed Slade drew the chair he had occupied up against the wooden partition next to the shop. He waited for a moment or two, and then carefully stepped on the chair and raised his head level with the glass panel. He saw Miss Clissold speaking to a man of about her own height, but whose back was turned to the detective. In his hand the man held a bowler hat; and he wore a dark grey overcoat, while from his crooked arm hung suspended a tightly rolled umbrella. Miss Clissold, Slade saw, was speaking rapidly, and gesturing with her arms in the Continental fashion. At last she walked quickly to the telephone, but the man stepped across to intercept her. Slade heard his voice, raised louder.

" No, do not trouble. Really it is not important. . . ."

It was a deep, guttural voice, without any special characteristic.

Miss Clissold came back, crossing to the other side of the man, so that he had to face round. Slade started. The man's upper lip was shaded by a bushy red moustache. As he continued to stare he was aware that Miss Clissold was surreptitiously glancing upward towards the glass panel of the office. He raised his head a trifle higher and caught her eye.

She nodded.

CHAPTER VI

IN PLOVERTON

As soon as the man had gone out of the shop Slade hurried from the tiny office, and, stopping only to ask Miss Clissold to phone the Yard and ask Inspector Brawley to look after his car, he passed

out into Shaftesbury Avenue and took up the chase. His quarry
had set off at a smart pace in the direction of Charing Cross Road.
At Cambridge Circus he turned south towards Trafalgar Square,
and, crossing to the Strand, entered the ever-open portals of the
Corner House. Slade now realized that he had missed his lunch,
and was grateful for the man's turning into the restaurant. He
followed him to the second floor, and chose a table in a corner
near the band dais, screened by the spreading shape of a palm
with long, spiky fronds.

There he sat for three-quarters of an hour, slowly consuming
food and still more slowly sipping coffee. He had time and
opportunity for studying the man he had followed, as the other
had chosen to sit half facing the orchestra. The man's head was
crowned by a mass of reddish hair, long above the ears; unruly
hair, for it was not slicked back, and there was no parting at the
side. His brows were bushy, and as he sat smoking a cigar the
expression on his face was hard to define. The eyes were deepset
and unfathomable. He was dressed in a well-fitting navy-blue suit,
and his tie was of navy-blue silk, dotted with small white spots. For
the most part the man sat there after the plates had been cleared
away, his elbows on the table, the fingers of one hand twined round
the cigar, listening to the strains of the orchestra. Yet appeared not
to be listening with appreciation. Several times Slade detected a
far-away expression in the man's eyes, and he guessed that his
thoughts were miles away from that orchestra. Once or twice he saw
the man twist about and cast a rapid glance round the assembled
company. At length, when his cigar was half smoked, he rose and
signed for his bill. As he strode towards the desk Slade rose in
his turn. When the Yard man stepped out into the Strand his
quarry was giving instructions to a taxi-driver. The man climbed
into the taxi, the driver plunged down his meter-flag, and the cab
moved off. Glancing round desperately, Slade saw a taxi with its
flag up coming out of Charing Cross Station. He held up his hand.

"Follow that cab—and don't lose sight of it—this is a Yard
job," he reeled off.

The cab was in motion as he clambered inside and dropped into
the seat. After a quarter of an hour he knew whither the chase
led—Paddington Station. He was not mistaken. At the Great
Western terminus he paid off his driver and hurried after the man
into the booking-hall. He saw him cross to the first-class booking-
office. Tearing an excursion leaflet from the notice-board, he drew
close enough to overhear the man's request to the clerk. A first-
class single to Ploverton!

Luckily the excursion leaflet screened his face, for as the man moved away from the grille he threw the detective a sharp glance, but passed on without hesitating towards the indicator. Slade took his opportunity to slip along to the third-class booking-office, where he took a single to Ploverton also. He was still studying the excursion pamphlet when he approached the indicator.

A train was leaving for Ploverton within ten minutes. Slade ambled along towards the platform, and on a seat by the gate picked out his man, who was leaning on his umbrella and finishing his cigar.

They were ten minutes full of strain. At any moment Slade was prepared to see his quarry rise and stroll out of the station, or go to meet someone, but when at length the train steamed in and the gate was opened he watched the man he had followed from Shaftesbury Avenue move down the platform with a feeling of sharp relief. The Yard man chose a third-class compartment three or four behind the first-class compartment into which the other disappeared, and, settling himself in a corner seat, filled his pipe, and took the opportunity of thinking things over. There had been a sharp development since he had set out that morning for Cheviot Crescent, and he was pleased to find that he was completing a circle, travelling back to Ploverton. Miss Clissold had not known who this man with the reddish hair and moustache was, but if she had been telling the truth Claire Merrell was something more than interested in him.

The man had entered Lorette's and inquired for the girl; the first time he had entered the shop to Miss Clissold's knowledge— and Mrs. Merrell was lying wounded miles away. Had the man known the girl was not there, or had he some other reason for calling at which Slade could not guess? Even so, was the man connected with the mystery centred round Tangles?

Those were the questions that chiefly occupied the C.I.D. man's mind during the run to Ploverton. He found no answer to them, and realized that he would have to travel a much greater distance before he could hope to offer himself an explanation. The more he considered the several and apparently unconnected facts in the case the more perplexed he became. At every turn he was stumbling upon a fresh individual who was in some way or other concerned with one or other of the principals. By the time the train steamed into Ploverton Station he still maintained that his best bet was the girl herself. It somehow seemed strange to consider her a married woman owning a fairly prosperous business; but then, he reflected philosophically, looks tell one nothing these days—except untruths.

However, it was strange that he had not been able to learn more about Mr. Merrell—if there was such a person. There remained still two people linked to the mystery whom he had yet to find: Stanley Merton and John Ridley, the latter in some way or other connected with the Summerdale Brickmaking Company, whose works were in Ploverton.

The red-haired man, smoking a fresh cigar, strode quickly across the platform and through a door into a waiting-hall. Only three other passengers besides the detective alighted at that station, and Slade was the last to surrender his ticket. When he emerged in the street the man he was following was nowhere in sight. Casually he scanned the faces of the passengers inside a single-deck bus waiting outside the station, and saw his man seated near the front. Slade got aboard, and sat down next to a rather stout lady with a large shopping-basket perched on her lap.

The man with the red hair got out at a stopping-place about a quarter of a mile beyond the main street of shops. The houses in this part of Ploverton were large, and screened from the road by the trees of their own grounds. The bus started up, turned a corner, and then Slade rose and pressed the bell-knob. He walked back to the stopping-place, hastened to the corner of a road with hedgerows on one side and front gardens on the other, and saw his man hurrying along some fifty yards away. The chase continued past the front gardens to a stretch of the road bounded by hedges on both sides, and all at once the man in front turned, as it seemed, into the hedge.

Slade crossed to the other side of the road and approached cautiously. He had seen enough of what befell unwary persons in Ploverton not to take every care to avoid being sniped. Nearly a quarter of an hour passed before he drew level with the place where the man had disappeared, and then he chuckled.

In the hedge was a small wooden gate, on the other side of which a grey gravel path led to a small cottage, almost hidden by a row of beeches. Slade crossed the road to the gate, and stood for a moment pondering his next move. At last he unfastened the latch and stepped on to the gravel path. He saw that the cottage was situated at one end of a large plot of ground, which sloped gradually. Beyond the cottage, seen through the nude branches of the trees, was a large house of red brick.

As he approached the cottage he thought he saw one of the curtains in the front window quiver, but could not be sure. He knocked upon the old-fashioned iron knocker, and waited. No one came in answer to the summons, so he knocked again, more loudly. This time he heard a shuffling sound, and the door was opened a little way. In the opening appeared the wrinkled face of a little old lady with a pile of grey hair knotted in a peculiar manner on the top of her head.

"Yes, and who are you?" she squeaked.

"I'm sorry to disturb you, madam," said Slade, with a smile, feeling at a complete loss, "but have you a visitor?"

"A visitor?" She laughed on a crackling note. "Why, no one comes to visit Old Mother Hubbard, not these days—not even the vicar."

And she laughed that queer, crackling laugh again, and shook her head so that the thread of black velvet running through the grey strands became loosened.

"You are Mrs. Hubbard, then?" said the detective quickly.

"Yes, I am Mrs. Hubbard, sir. As I haven't a visitor, what is it I can do for you? But come in; come in."

She held the door open, and Slade entered.

The tiny hallway was gloomy and smelled faintly damp. The little old lady, who apparently was known locally as Old Mother Hubbard, led the way into a small sitting-room, furnished with a few old and cheap sticks, and beckoned her visitor into an ancient rocking-chair. Slade sat himself down gingerly, and was a trifle alarmed when the chair gave under his weight, and began rocking to and fro. He tried his best to appear as though sitting in such a chair was an everyday occurrence with him, and smiled self-consciously at Mrs. Hubbard, who sat her bent form on a broken-down couch of antique design, through rents in the leather of which the horsehair stuffing showed.

Mutely Slade wondered into what strange parlour his inquisitiveness had drawn him.

"Now, then, sir." She perked up her face, which was not clearly discernible, as the small window was shielded by dark stuff curtains, and patted the dress across her knees. She was dressed entirely in black and Slade could see that in her youth the old lady must have been a buxom girl.

"Well, I'm really sorry for troubling you, Mrs. Hubbard," he explained, "but I am almost sure I saw a gentleman pass up your path——"

"What sort of a gentleman?"

"Oh, of average size. He had reddish hair and a moustache——"
She shook her head.

"He hasn't called here, sir. Would you be wanting him?"
As her interest grew her voice became even huskier. "Of course,

he might have gone up through the grounds to the house," she added.

"The house?"

"Yes, Mr. Ridley's place. You see, this cottage belongs to Mr. Ridley—it used to be the caretaker's home, I believe—and he lets me live here. It's very kind of him. I never did like what are known as charity homes, sir. Why, I once heard of an alms-house in Birmingham—Birmingham's my home, you know, sir——"

"Yes, yes," interrupted Slade, who had no wish for her to become garrulous. "But Mr. Ridley—is he the Mr. John Ridley of the Summerdale Brickmaking Company?"

"That's him, sir. A nice gentleman. He's been very good to me, though I knows there are some who don't give nobody a good word——"

"And do you do anything for Mr. Ridley, Mrs. Hubbard? I mean, look after things at——"

"No, sir," she interposed quickly. "Mr. Ridley wouldn't hear of me doin' a thing, though I told him as I didn't like takin'——"

"No—quite. Then you don't know much about Mr. Ridley's affairs?"

She cackled.

"Not more than what gossip knows. Mr. Ridley's one who keeps himself to himself. Doesn't mix with Ploverton folk much, sir. He's a lot in London, I understand."

"Then he doesn't entertain much, have many visitors here?"

"Never known him what you call entertain, sir, since I've bin here."

Slade rose. He felt that to stay longer would merely be a waste of time. It was obvious that the woman knew little about the man whose name had been included on the list he had found in Claire Merrell's handbag.

"I suppose callers on Mr. Ridley frequently use your path, Mrs. Hubbard?"

"Not frequently, sir. Sometimes a body has walked up to the house through the grounds, but no, not frequent, sir."

She glanced up, and squinted at the detective.

"What, ready to go already, sir? A bit o' company's welcome to me these days. Not many come nigh Old Mother Hubbard."

It took Slade another quarter of an hour before he found himself outside the cottage, and with the door closed he turned and walked round to the other side of Mrs. Hubbard's creeper-covered abode and came upon a winding path which apparently led to "the house" and which ran between high clipped hedges of evergreen shrubs. There was a fresh tang in the air, which smelled all the sweeter after the almost airless atmosphere of the cottage. Six minutes' walking brought Slade to the rear of the red-brick house, enclosed by a brick wall covered with creeper similar to that which twined over the cottage. Picking his way carefully, so as to avoid being seen by any servants, he made his way round to the front of the house, the name of which he now saw was Orton Lodge.

He rang the bell and waited. Presently the door was opened by a manservant, a nondescript-looking individual garbed in rusty black.

"Yes, sir?" inquired the man gruffly, and craned his neck forward, his head twisted to one side, in the manner of a deaf person.

"Is Mr. Ridley at home?" asked Slade.

The man shook his head.

"No, sir. Hasn't been home since this morning. Can I take a message?"

Slade thought fast. He was wondering about the man with the red hair. If *he* was Ridley——

"Oh, I made sure I should find him in. In fact, I thought I saw him precede me along the road."

The man's smile of denial was almost a sneer.

"No, sir. Couldn't have been Mr. Ridley. If it's urgent you'll probably find him at the works, though. He mentioned about calling in there this afternoon some time."

"Very well, I'll try the works. Er—do you know what time he will be back here?"

"Can't say, sir. Mr. Ridley doesn't keep what you'd call regular hours."

"All right—thanks."

The door closed, and the detective turned away, feeling that since he had left the station things had not progressed altogether satisfactorily. Twice he had been baulked, and he was feeling distinctly annoyed. He had been as curious as he dared appear before Mrs. Hubbard without rousing the old woman's suspicions, and had learned little; and now he had drawn a complete blank. Yet he had not been mistaken. The man with the red hair and red moustache *had* turned in at the cottage gate. But where had he vanished?

Slade glanced back at the house, and told himself he did not like the looks of that manservant. Then he moved off down the road at a sharp pace. The next place of call was the Summerdale Brickmaking Works.

It took him some little while to learn from passers-by the direction in which the works lay, and it was not until he had twice taken a wrong turning and been walking the best part of half an hour that he saw before him, at the end of a broad lane opening from a road that was being freshly made up, the squat shapes of brick-kilns. A lorry laden with tiles was leaving the muddy and littered yard at the end of the lane as Slade approached, and he saw painted in large white letters on its green sides: Summerdale Brickmaking Company—Ploverton. The man who was closing the gates stopped and straightened his back as Slade walked up. He jerked his head interrogatively.

"Can you show me to Mr. Ridley's office?" asked the Yard man.

At the request the man's demeanour became more respectful.

"Certainly, sir. Go straight across the yard and through that wooden door at the end—that one, sir "—he pointed to the door he meant—" and you'll come to the offices. The doorman there'll take you through, sir."

The doorman was a squat, consumptive man with a brilliant orange tie.

"Yers?" he inquired, jerking his head like the other man.

"I want to see Mr. Ridley."

"Name?"

"Slade."

"Ain't a traveller, are yer? The boss ain't got no time to waste on 'em."

"No, I'm not a traveller."

"Got a card?"

Slade took a deep breath and selected a card from his pocket-book. The doorman took it in a grubby hand, gave it one swift, arched glance, and then jerked his head back.

"Gawd!" he muttered, scrambling off his stool, and scuttled down a corridor.

Slade smiled to himself and waited. It might have taught the man a lesson in manners, but he doubted it.

"Mr. Ridley'll see you at once, sir."

When Slade first set eyes on John Ridley he cursed silently. Here was not his red-haired man with hirsute upper lip, but a blond-headed, clean-shaven business man, with deepset piercing blue eyes and thin lips pressed in a straight line. The squat doorman closed the door after announcing the visitor's full name, and Slade moved towards the desk by the side of which the other stood, hands in the pockets of a double-breasted jacket, a look of interest on his lean face.

"What is it I can do for you, inspector? Anybody here been giving trouble?"

Ridley motioned the detective to a comfortable-looking chair, and sat himself in his swivel-chair.

"I'm not certain yet, Mr. Ridley."

Slade was thinking fast and studying the other. Ridley raised his brows, nodded slowly, and displayed some excellent teeth.

"It's not myself that's worrying you, is it, inspector? I'm generally considered a good boy."

He smiled, but his eyes remained keen; and suddenly Slade decided to say nothing about the man with red hair.

"Do you know a Mrs. Merrell at all, Mr. Ridley?"

The other appeared to ponder.

"Not that I can recall off-hand. How old is she?"

Slade smiled thinly.

"A difficult question to answer in these days, Mr. Ridley. However, if you don't know the lady that's that. But you know a Mr. Harold Ferriss, don't you?"

The interested smile remained on Ridley's face, but Slade could feel the burning glare of the man's eyes after he had asked the question.

"Yes, I know Mr. Ferriss—or, rather, a Mr. Ferriss—and, yes, I believe his name is Harold, now you mention it. But I don't think I've ever met him personally. I've had dealings with him on behalf of the firm, you understand?"

"Then you can't tell me anything about him apart from your business relations?"

"I'm afraid not, inspector. You see, Ferriss is an agent for another firm, a Continental firm, as a matter of fact. Our products are good articles, rather higher-priced than most, but we've our market. There are certain Continental firms that import our bricks despite duty because they want an article somewhat better than the average. Mr. Ferriss is an agent for one of those companies."

It sounded plausible.

"May I have the name of the foreign company Mr. Ferriss represents?"

Mr. Ridley nodded, and stretched out a hand to one of the drawers of his desk. He paused suddenly and looked up.

"Excuse me, inspector, but before I give you this information, will you tell me one thing—are you after Ferriss? Is he a wrong 'un?"

Slade's smile was sphinx-like.

"It doesn't matter much now if he was—he's dead."

"Dead! Oh, I'm sorry to hear that! Of course, you're looking into the matter of his effects——"

"I'm looking into the matter of his murder!"

There was a short silence, during which each man eyed his *vis-à-vis*. Ridley was the first to break it. He shook his head from side to side, in a dazed fashion.

"But are you sure, inspector? Surely it is not as bad as that. I mean——"

"It's worse!"

Ridley stared, and Slade felt that the man was acting cleverly.

"Worse?" he muttered, and abstractedly passed a hand over his sleek blond hair.

"Ferriss is corpse number one. There's a number two."

"But I don't understand!" protested Ridley.

"Ever heard of Morton Haunchwood?"

The other started.

"Haunchwood? The old hermit who's tucked himself away at that lonely place called Tangles? Yes, I know him slightly. But you don't mean——"

"I do. Haunchwood is corpse number two. But listen, Mr. Ridley, I'm not certain which of the two is Haunchwood and which Ferriss."

"What do you mean, inspector? You don't——"

Slade drew his chair close to the desk.

"Never mind that now." He waved a hand. "Who's that?" He pushed the photograph of the man with the twisted smile into Ridley's hands.

He gave it barely a glance.

"Why, this is Haunchwood's valet!" he exclaimed, and looked up. "You think he did it—killed Haunchwood, I mean?"

"No he didn't kill Haunchwood. He was killed himself——"

"Killed?"

"He's corpse number one."

"But you said——"

"I know. He's Ferriss all right. You've settled that point."

"I?"

Ridley's expression was one of amazement; he looked at the detective like a man who has suddenly walked out of a dark room into brilliant sunlight. But Slade did not intend to offer an explanation. He held his hand out for the photograph, which the other passed to him after another quick glance at it.

"That's Ferriss all right," the Yard man repeated. "He was murdered in a house in Mayfair."

"Wait a minute," said Ridley, pulling open a drawer. He searched through a blue folder and took out a sheet covered with red typing. Starting half-way down the column, he ran his finger to the bottom and continued searching the next column. Slade took out his pipe and lit it. Ridley looked up.

"Here's the address we have for Ferriss—Cheviot Crescent, Mayfair."

"That's where his body was found—in a room where the safe had been robbed."

Ridley's amazement grew with each minute that passed. He gaped at the Yard man. His deep blue eyes were opened wide in a vacuous stare.

"But there must be some mistake, inspector——"

He stopped short. Slade had risen; he towered over the desk, a threatening figure.

"You're damned right, Ridley—there is!" Finesse was gone; the detective was wielding a naked blade. "You're stalling and keeping something under cover." He drew from his pocket the letter he had found in the house in Mayfair. "Read that—it may refresh your memory. And note the signature—your own; and the address—Tangles!"

Ridley's eyes were narrowed; his lips were pressed tightly together in a thin pink strip of colour.

The letter bore the heading of the Summerdale Brickmaking Company, Ploverton, and ran:

H. FERRISS, ESQ.,
Tangles,
Lower Ploverton.

DEAR SIR,

We are sorry to have to inform you that our representative will not be free to see you at time and place agreed upon. We trust this will save you any delay or inconvenience.

We are,
Yours faithfully,
THE SUMMERDALE BRICKMAKING COMPANY.

Ridley's hand clenched, crumpling the sheet of notepaper.

"That signature's a damned forgery!" he shouted. "I never sent that letter."

He seemed strangely excited. A tinge of colour stole into his pale cheeks, and his eyes again glittered. Slade took the precaution of picking up the letter as it dropped from the other's fingers.

"A forgery, eh?" He sounded sceptical. "Isn't that the firm's notepaper?"

"Of course it is!" snapped Ridley. "But can't you see someone's pulled a trick there? I didn't know the man, I tell you. It's all Greek to me. If you want samples of my signature there are plenty here. Look."

He drew several papers from a folder on his desk and passed them to Slade. The detective compared the signatures on them with that on the letter; there could be no doubt that the latter was a clumsy forgery of the former. Unreasonably he felt that in some indefinable way Ridley had scored over him, and it was a feeling he did not relish. He passed the papers back to the other.

"Any idea who sent that letter—who *could* have sent it?"

"Anyone here who can handle a typewriter *could* have sent it!"

"How many typists have you?"

"Three."

"Who do they work for?"

Ridley took a deep breath and dropped back into his chair. Slade was pressing the pace.

"Myself—Miss Vines; Mr. Merton—Miss Moffett; and Miss Gale is attached to the counting-house."

Slade sat down.

"And Mr. Merton——"

"He is our sales manager."

"Is he Mr. *Stanley* Merton?"

A fresh look of surprise crossed Ridley's face.

"Why, yes! Do you know him, inspector?"

"No—but I'd very much like to see him. Now!"

CHAPTER VII

A DISAPPEARANCE

JOHN RIDLEY sat back in his chair, and spread the palms of his carefully manicured hands upon the top of his desk.

"I'm afraid that's not possible, inspector. Mr. Merton called in first thing this morning, and left shortly afterwards. He will not be back again today."

Slade's pipe had some time before grown cold. He now took it from his mouth and placed it in his pocket.

"A cigarette, inspector?" invited Ridley, proffering a silver box.

Slade shook his head. "No, thanks." His eyes had narrowed, for he had much at which to wonder. In the first place, Ridley had shown the letter not to have been sent by himself; in the second, Stanley Merton, the one remaining person whose name was on the list found in Claire Merrell's handbag, was also engaged at the Summerdale Brickmaking Works; and, thirdly, Merton had left the works early that day and had not returned.

Slade watched Ridley light a cigarette.

"What colour is Merton's hair?" he asked.

The lighted match remained poised in mid-air for a second or two. Then, with a quick turn of the wrist, the tiny flame was quenched.

"Dark brown. A shade or two darker than your own, inspector." The C.I.D. man nodded slowly, but his eyes did not widen.

"Clean-shaven, I suppose?"

Ridley nodded.

"And build?"

"Slightly less stocky than yourself, inspector, if I may say so, but about your height. However, what have these details to do with——"

"Murder?"

Ridley smiled thinly. "I did not say so."

"Or were you thinking of forgery?"

"Well, that would not be so far from your own idea, would it, inspector?"

"No. That's why I want to see Miss Moffett's machine."

Ridley rose. "Very good. Come with me, and I'll show you Merton's office. His typist has a table in there."

Miss Moffett was a prim-looking spinster of uncertain age, the type of female Brawley had once classed as all bone—human and whale. Her faded grey eyes blinked waterily at Ridley through a pair of thick-lensed spectacles.

"What can I do for you, Mr. Ridley?" she intoned.

"Clear out," said Ridley brusquely.

"Er—yes, sir."

Miss Moffett fled precipitately. Before the door had closed on her Ridley had snatched a letter from her typewriter and drawn a fresh sheet of notepaper from the rack on the table. He offered it to the detective, who set it in the machine and typed several lines from memory. Drawing the sheet from the typewriter, Slade compared what he had typed with the letter.

"This is the machine all right," he proclaimed.

Ridley nodded.

"I'm sorry for that," he said.

Slade rose and folded the sheet he had typed upon inside the letter.

"Why?"

"I hate to think of him being a wrong 'un."

"Well, take my tip, Mr. Ridley, and don't talk to him about it when he shows up. I don't want him scared off; and you might caution Miss Moffett. Ever had a quarrel with him?" he asked.

"No. A few business wrangles, that's all; nothing that you might call personal."

"Is he married?"

"Not that I know of."

"Well, if you'll give me his address I think I shan't have to trouble you any more at present."

"Oh, that's all right, inspector. Anything I can do, you know." They went back to Ridley's office.

"Here's Merton's address. It's a lonely spot near the river."

Slade read what Ridley had written upon the slip of paper he had handed him : "The Cedars, Riverside Road, Lower Ploverton."

"Far out?" he asked.

"About a mile along the south side of the river, and——" He broke off with an exclamation that caused Slade to glance at him sharply. "Why, of course! I remember the place now. It's almost opposite that place of Haunchwood's—Tangles—on the opposite bank."

"I see," said Slade evenly. "Well, good day, Mr. Ridley, and thank you."

The detective hardly realized that he was passing out of the building. He was thinking of when he had stood upon the old landing-stage at Tangles the previous evening, watching the runnels of light across the dark river. Clinton had remarked that it was strange the lights had gone out immediately all sound of the motor boat had died away. Was there anything to it? Slade was asking himself. Stanley Merton had been the last person on the list he had learned anything about, and from first appearances it seemed that he might become the most interesting. And then he thought of Ridley. He was uncertain how to make up his mind about the man. He had given Slade the impression of advancing and retreating at the same time; a conflicting impression, and Slade was normally suspicious of such. But superficially there seemed nothing specially to intrigue him about the man, though he admitted he disliked the looks of the manservant who had answered his ring at Orton Lodge.

Dusk was falling, and Slade became aware that several cars that sped past had their lights on. He quickened his pace, and after twenty minutes' walk found himself once more in the main thoroughfare of Ploverton. He turned into a tea-shop and ordered hot buttered toast, poached eggs, and a pot of tea, and while engaged with this simple repast he busied himself with entering notes in his notebook. Leaving the tea-shop, he made his way to a public call-box and put through a call to Tangles, where he asked for Sergeant Clinton. He was kept waiting a couple of minutes while a search was made; then the speaker returned to say that Sergeant Clinton had left half an hour before. Slade asked where to, and gave his name. Another couple of minutes ticked by, and then a fresh voice sounded over the wire, that of Sergeant Wiggins of the local police. He said that Sergeant Clinton had left with Inspector Rayner for Baltch's Yard. Slade asked where the yard was, and after being directed how to get there from the place where he was phoning hung up. Ten minutes later found him outside a premises which a sign announced belonged to Thomas G. Baltch, boat-builder. Another smaller sign proclaimed that Mr. Baltch hired out by the hour or for a longer period rowing-boats, punts, and motor boats. Beside the premises was a concreted yard which opened on to the road.

Slade walked through the iron gate and moved across the yard, and, passing through a wooden door which was half open, came upon a pebbly beach, with the river gently lapping at its rim. Three figures stood silhouetted against the glare of a single electric light, raised on a wooden pier, and moored to the pier were rows of small craft.

The Yard man walked across the shingle, and it was not until he was within a few yards of the three figures that they heard his approach. They all looked round at the same instant, and one started forward.

" Oh, here you are, sir ! "

It was Clinton; and the expression on his face showed that he had news.

" I've taken a roundabout way of getting here, Clinton, but I hope I'm not too late."

Clinton gave his chief a penetrating glance. He knew from the tone of his voice that Slade had uncovered something likely to prove both interesting and important.

" Inspector Rayner and I have traced the owner of the clasp-knife."

The other two approached, and Slade was introduced in turn

to Inspector Rayner and Mr. Thomas G. Baltch himself. The local inspector was a florid-faced man whose attitude towards the case revealed that he had worked his way up from the ranks. He was perfectly willing to let someone else do the worrying and head-work, knowing full well that when the case was settled he would get his full meed of credit. The boat-builder was a different type. Stout, with a pair of twinkling eyes, he spoke in a deep voice that was almost a bellow. His teeth were obviously false, but his good spirits and good nature seemed genuine enough.

The four men repaired to a room Mr. Baltch was pleased to allude to as his office. Old-fashioned oleographs in violent tints hung on the walls. An odour of stale tobacco-smoke pervaded everything, from the blotter on his desk to the faded green curtain hung on a brass rail behind the door. The only light in the compartment was the single bulkhead lamp set in the centre of the ceiling.

"That's my knife right enough," continued Baltch, in a mild roar, after they were seated. "I missed it a couple of days ago."

"Do you know *where* you missed it?" asked Slade.

"Oh, somewhere about the yard, I suppose. I'm always laying it about, but generally it stays there. This time it didn't."

"You've got no idea who took it?"

"No more than the dead," boomed Mr. Baltch, striking a match and lighting a particularly strong-smelling briar.

Slade glanced at Clinton.

"The boat?"

"Yes, taken from the pier. It was brought back, but tied up in a different place, and of course the painter had been cut. That was plain."

Slade turned to the boat-builder.

"Get many undesirables in your yard, Mr. Baltch?"

"No, the inspector here sees to that."

Rayner cackled. "Vagrants don't like Ploverton," he opined. "It's a place they can't get away from very easily."

Slade accepted this information for what it was worth.

"Are there many people hereabouts who can handle a motor boat?" he asked Baltch.

"Plenty," replied the other. "This summer we had an extra run on 'em, and I'm thinkin' of startin' speed-boats next season. Quite a number of visitors spend the week-end in Ploverton during the summer, and most of 'em are what you might call river-minded. And I s'pose it's only natural to take to a motor boat after being used to a car; you want something with speed."

The discussion became general and desultory, and after another quarter of an hour Slade rose.

"I'd like to take a look at the craft that was borrowed last night," he said.

Baltch got up, his pipe blowing like a miniature furnace.

"Sure!" he bellowed.

The four men trooped back to the beach, and Baltch led the way to the pier, flashing an electric torch with a wide, revealing ray.

"Here she is," he said, kneeling down with some difficulty.

Slade knelt beside him on the wet boards. A few inches under his knees the dark water rippled and slipped past with a sleek, sliding motion. The painter had clearly been cut. Slade took the piece of rope from his overcoat pocket and compared the cut end with that of the boat's painter. They fitted.

The detective rose and jumped into the boat, which was not a large craft. Taking out his own flash-lamp, he turned its bright ray over the thwarts and engine; but though he searched carefully he found nothing. He was disappointed, for he had been hoping to come across an empty cartridge-case. He stepped on to the pier and moved back to the beach.

"Well, Clinton, it doesn't look as though we can help ourselves much more here." He glanced at the large boat-builder. "If Mr. Baltch has no objection we should like to retain his knife for a little while longer. It might prove a useful exhibit."

Baltch waved a pair of arms like windmill sails.

"Not at all! Not at all! Keep it as long as you wish, inspector."

In the garage at the side of the premises was Rayner's car. The two Yard men and the local inspector climbed into it, and the latter took the wheel.

"Where to now, Slade?" he asked.

"Tangles," said the Yard man, and turned to Clinton. "Well, you've got something to tell me, Clinton. You were restless all the time Baltch was about. What is it?"

Clinton regarded his chief glumly.

"The girl's disappeared!" he exclaimed.

Slade stared at him, while Rayner opened the throttle.

"Disappeared? But she was in bed with a nasty flesh wound, Herrick said——"

"Well, then, she's got a constitution like a horse—that's all," grunted Clinton disconsolately. "And that damned nurse that was sent to relieve the first one went to sleep reading a book. When she woke the girl had gone—so had her clothes."

"Anybody see her go?"

"No."

"Well?"

"The trouble is we don't know how long she's been gone, although we know one way she couldn't have escaped—along the drive to the road. Inspector Rayner had a man patrolling the drive."

"Which way did she take, then?" asked Slade, giving his assistant a close glance in the darkness of the car.

Clinton shifted in his seat.

"As far as I can make out she must have got away across the river. But I'm certain there wasn't a boat. I know it sounds impossible——"

"Perhaps not so impossible as you think, Clinton," murmured Slade, low enough for the man at the wheel not to hear.

He was thinking of the Cedars, on the opposite bank from Tangles, and of Mr. Stanley Merton.

CHAPTER VIII

A COUNCIL OF WAR

INSPECTOR RAYNER took a large blue silk handkerchief from his pocket and blew his nose vigorously. He was perplexed, and the glance he threw Slade showed it. Slade was staring thoughtfully at the silver buttons on Sergeant Wiggins's tunic; the local sergeant seemed scarcely any brighter than his superior. Next to Slade sat Clinton, his bulky notebook spread open before him, the stump of a pencil in his hand.

A council of war was being held in the drawing-room at Tangles, and Slade had opened the discussion with a brief account of what he had learned. He was careful to prune the narrative. There were several features about his discoveries that he did not allude to; he considered that course wisest in the circumstances. Rayner and Wiggins might be admirable watchdogs, but they would not shine as thinking machines.

Rayner blew his nose a second time, and his red face became even redder.

"Well, that's about where the case stands at the moment," added Slade, pushing his chair back. "Now, Rayner, perhaps you can give me a few ideas about some local people."

The other nodded, waiting, while Wiggins strove to look intelligently occupied with his thoughts.

"Now, first, Haunchwood himself. What do you know about him?"

"Little—precious little. In fact, I'd never seen the man until I saw his corpse here. It was known, of course, that he'd taken this old place, but I don't think he entertained at all or moved among his neighbours. He lived a sort of hermit's life——"

"Yet he was not above middle age," Slade pointed out.

"I know. Looks queer on the face of it; but some people are queer."

"Which bank did he use?"

"I've found that out—the Ploverton branch of Lloyds. But he had only a small current account, few hundreds."

"All right. Tradesmen?"

"Baker, greengrocer, and milkman called regularly, but never saw Haunchwood himself. Either left what was telephoned for at the tradesmen's entrance or saw Ferriss."

"Yes, that brings us to Ferriss. Much known about him?"

"About as much as was known about Haunchwood. They lived out here alone. A woman came two or three times a week to clean the rooms. She's a Mrs. Farmer, lives in a cottage on the other side of the station, but she can't offer us much. She was let in each time she rang at the tradesmen's entrance, and that's all. Never saw a soul from the time she got here till she left; and the last time she came each week her money was always in an envelope in the hall."

Slade struck a match and lit his pipe.

"Got any idea as to who Haunchwood really was, Rayner?" The local man shook his head in vigorous denial.

"Not the remotest. He's always been a crank to my mind—that's all. We've never had cause to worry about him till now; never had reason to think he was something he didn't pretend to be."

"Well, there it is, Rayner. Several people seem to be confused regarding which was Ferriss and which was Haunchwood. There was obviously some jiggery-pokery going on. The Piccadilly estate agent, for instance, was quite definite about Haunchwood——"

"I can only suggest that Haunchwood let Ferriss sort of deputize for him at times," offered Rayner doubtfully.

"Not unlikely," admitted Slade. "But what isn't quite so likely is that Ferriss would be signing Haunchwood's signature. The puzzle's deeper, however. Remember that Ridley recognized

Ferriss's photo—anyhow, we'll still continue to call that one Ferriss—as that of Haunchwood's valet, or whatever the man was; yet he said he had never seen Ferriss."

Rayner frowned.

"Still, Ridley wasn't very thick with Haunchwood. I suppose saw him once or twice in a more or less casual way over something or other, and didn't even learn the name of the valet."

"The girl knew it."

Rayner had a bright idea suddenly.

"She might have been bluffing."

It was an idea that had occurred to Slade in Ridley's office. He looked at Clinton.

"What do you think, Clinton?"

The sergeant's opinions were valuable to Slade. Clinton was one of those practical men who rarely create a theory until they have uncovered all the necessary facts and the truth begins to take definite shape. Slade regarded his sergeant as a kind of mental brake for himself.

Clinton fingered his bluish-brown chin.

"She'll tell us when we find her," he said bluntly, and bent over his notebook again.

Slade smiled to himself as he watched the looks of wonder that appeared on the faces of Rayner and Wiggins.

"Clinton's right," he said. "No use speculating on that topic—the girl's our answer. From appearances she knows as much about this affair as anyone—and more than most. She's got to be found quick."

Rayner tapped his clenched fist several times quickly on the arm of his chair.

"But how're we going to find her? We don't know where to look."

Slade's eyes narrowed, and a far-away look came into them.

"Well, I've one shot to my bow. A long one, it's true, but it might hit the target. However, I'm hoping the girl will show up before long."

"You think she will?"

"If she's as deep in this as she seemed last night she will—she can't keep out. There's something big behind all this, big stakes, or I miss my guess completely." Slade paused for a few moments. "Rayner," he said, in a changed voice, "got many red-haired men in Ploverton?"

"Eh?"

The local inspector looked startled at the question.

"Just that, red-haired men—oh, yes, with reddish moustaches."

Rayner took a deep breath.

"Well, a few, I suppose. They're pretty common," he added caustically.

"I know. Anyway, there's one I specially want to trace, and I've an idea he's living here somewhere. Tell you what I'd like you to do : get your men to check up on as many as you can. Find out where they were this morning and afternoon. If they were in this neighbourhood don't worry; if any of them went to the station and took a first-class to London I want to know immediately."

Rayner continued to stare at the Yard man. To the local inspector the request was a piece of sheer fantasy. Slade had omitted to mention the red-haired man he had followed from London.

"Very well, if you think that's going to get you anywhere, but I frankly don't see——"

"Nor do I yet. There may be no such person."

"What!" Rayner had a suspicion that the other was baiting him.

"You see, it's just an idea of mine. There may be nothing in it because the person I'm thinking of may be someone else entirely, a man disguised."

"Oh!" The exclamation might have been intended to convey anything.

"Know anything about Merton, a fellow at the brickworks?" was Slade's next question.

"Not much. He lives out this way, I believe. Do you know, Wiggins?"

The uniformed sergeant nodded.

"That's right, sir. He lives at the Cedars; other side the river from here."

"What sort of a fellow is he?"

"Well, there's little to tell you really, sir," continued Wiggins after receiving a nod from his superior. "He's in one or two local clubs—tennis, golf, and so on—but I don't think he mixes much, if you understand me. Has a housekeeper. Don't remember who she is, but she lives in the place, I know that, because a relative of hers died and I had a man go down and see her about some formalities."

Slade pondered.

"What do you know about Ridley?" he asked at length.

Rayner shrugged.

"What is there to know? The man's a director of the Summerdale firm—got a big interest in it, too, I believe. Apart from that, well, he keeps himself to himself. Some while ago he let an old woman, a Mrs. Hubbard, come and live in the old cottage at the end of the grounds. I believe she's some poor body without a friend or relative in the world. Rather decent of Ridley to let the old girl have the place, though he couldn't use it himself. Like Haunchwood, he has a man who looks after his things and more or less keeps the place going, for Ridley's a bachelor, though he's certainly not the monkish-looking type. Again, like Merton, he belongs to several local sports clubs—that's right, isn't it, Wiggins?"

"Yes, sir, that's right," agreed the sergeant. "Keen waterman, too, Mr. Ridley is, from accounts. I have heard it said as he's got a yacht somewhere along the coast, but that's only local rumour. Might be nothing to it."

Another short silence fell on the group. Clinton broke it.

"There's another man we mustn't forget at this stage," he said. "The man who gave the false address in Cheviot Crescent."

Slade nodded glumly.

"It looks as though he certainly made a good getaway. We've lost track of him—but I won't forget him, Clinton. He fits in, never fear."

Rayner grunted.

"I wish I could see how any bits of this case fit in. It's all a complete muddle to me. Everybody tangled up with every one else, fighting each other."

"That sort of case always remains tangled till the right moment," explained Slade, with a smile. "I've noticed it several times. It continues a maze so far; then someone tries to move quicker than the others, and that does the trick. There's a break in the pattern; one loose thread is sufficient to unravel the whole design."

"Well, what's the design of this case, if you can tell me?" asked Rayner, with a snort. He was losing his confidence.

Slade struck another match and lit his pipe.

"We have a group of people after something. What that something is I don't know—in fact, none of us has the slightest idea yet. But it's safe to assume that it isn't money——"

"Why?" snapped Rayner.

"Because money can be placed in a bank to one's credit in any country."

"You mean whoever had the money, then, would beat it abroad?"

"That's it."

"I'm not so sure," Rayner frowned.

"Of course, there are special circumstances," conceded Slade, "but normally——"

" All right, let's pass that and get on. If it isn't money, then what?"

" Either jewellery or some sort of securities. In the first case the jewellery would be the proceeds of a robbery; in the second the securities would be the proceeds of a swindle."

" Yes, I follow you," nodded Rayner, a shade more interest in his voice. " But where's the design or pattern come in?"

" Well, it's something of a criss-cross pattern, Rayner. Haunchwood and Ferriss were working together; that much is fairly plain. Against them, I should say, are Mrs. Merrell and the person who killed them. There are at least two other random threads—the man who gave the wrong address in Cheviot Crescent and a red-haired man——"

" The one you want us to look up—if he's here?"

" The same. I don't know his name. All I know is that he is interested in Mrs. Merrell——"

" A lover?" asked Rayner quickly, while Sergeant Wiggins's stoat-like eyes suddenly gleamed.

" Shouldn't think so," replied Slade slowly, " but I can't be positive."

" Hmph! That's not much help." Rayner sat back and eased his stiff serge collar with a forefinger.

" It isn't. That's why I'm not worrying too much about him. The owner of that other maroon saloon might be traced if we get the Press to boost the case——"

" What about the licence?"

" Torn out. And if the number's a fake that won't help us much, will it?"

Rayner resorted to his large blue silk handkerchief once more; he was discouraged. No one answered Slade's question, and it was during the pause which ensued that they heard the raindrops beating against the window-panes. The local inspector rose and crossed to the window on the left-hand side of the fireplace. Pulling aside the curtain, he looked out.

" It's pouring," he announced as he came back to his chair. " Chances are it'll be a regular dirty night."

Slade nodded; his thoughts were elsewhere.

" You've got the bullet that hit the girl, Clinton?" he asked suddenly.

" Yes. Dug it out of the skirting. It tore through her shoulder and brought up in the woodwork."

" Let's have it, then."

Clinton took a small object wrapped in cotton-wool from his

waistcoat pocket and handed it to Slade. He looked across at Rayner.

"As I told you, Rayner, the Yard firearms expert says the bullets that killed Haunchwood and Ferriss were almost certainly fired from the same gun—which means the same person fired them. Of course, we'd have a better check if we had the empty cartridge-cases. However, what I'm wondering is if this bullet matches those others."

He patted his waistcoat pocket.

"You think it will?" Rayner's eyes were narrowed.

"I *think* it will," replied Slade cautiously, "and if I'm right in thinking so, then the murderer is to be found in Ploverton—we've proof positive."

Rayner lit a cigarette and puffed quickly.

"How exactly do you figure that out?" he asked, drawing his chair close to the table and leaning his elbows on it.

"A man was killed here first—Haunchwood. Then the murderer went to London (by car, presumably) and killed a second man—Ferriss. It was shortly after Ferriss was shot that Claire Merrell got that phone message—if she did get it. Very well, I'm having her number checked up, and if she *did* receive a call at the time she says she did we shall know from whom. One thing's certain, though—it didn't come from here."

This time Rayner did not interrupt when Slade stopped. He waited for the Yard man to continue.

"Now, if the same person shot Claire Merrell," he went on at last, "who killed Haunchwood and Ferriss, he must have moved fast—got down here almost as soon as the girl; perhaps sooner. Well, there are two ways of doing that—by car or train. When we consider the first we've got to remember that the maroon saloon had been turned adrift. Begin to see the trend, Rayner?"

The local inspector shook his head, and Slade glanced at Clinton. The latter nodded shortly.

"Think I do, sir. The murderer killed Haunchwood and drove to London in the maroon saloon with the faked number. The car was faked—made a replica of the girl's—because if it was seen the inquiry would be directed to her."

"Right, Clinton. The only slip up was in the duplication of the number-plate. After all, it was natural to suppose that a painted black-and-white number-plate would do. But that fact alone tells us something else—that the murderer didn't know the girl's car too well by sight. He knew the make, and could copy that; he knew the number—but didn't recall the type of plate. Yes, go on."

Rayner was having difficulty in following this fine reasoning; Wiggins had several minutes before given up the unequal contest.

Clinton gave a hurried glance at his notebook, and then continued in the same flat voice.

"Someone saw the maroon car, and probably recognized the murderer. That was the man who gave the false address. He may even have followed the murderer to Cheviot Crescent, and he most likely gave the constable the tale about four people climbing into the saloon car because he knew that if he said one it would look bad for the girl later on——"

"You are presupposing also, Clinton, that this person also knew of the faked car, aren't you?" queried Slade.

"Yes, sir."

"That means this person knows an awful lot about the girl, eh?"

Clinton nodded. "We've a choice of two, sir—her husband and this red-haired fellow."

Slade put his pipe down, got up and folded his arms, and began striding the room.

"You're only getting back to the old theory, Clinton, that the girl is the centre of the riddle. However, go on."

"Well, the murderer makes off with whatever he took from the safe in the house in Cheviot Crescent, turned loose the car behind the Edgware Road in a back-street, walked into the Edgware Road and caught a taxi——"

"Right, Clinton—to Paddington. We've arrived at the same result!" There was a faintly ringing note in Slade's voice, and for a moment his eyes shone brightly. He genuinely felt that this was a step forward in their deductions. "We can check that up roughly with a Bradshaw—make a note of that."

Clinton was already scribbling down the note. Slade turned to Rayner.

"Any criticism of that? If there is, let's have it."

Rayner stood up.

"Good Lord, no, man! I should never have got there in a month of Sundays. That's good work, if I may say so, Slade."

The latter grinned.

"Say it all you like. We thrive on flattery at the Yard; it's a luxury."

"But seriously——" began Rayner, to be cut short by the insistent clamour of the telephone bell in the hall.

Clinton rose and went out of the room. A few moments later he returned and glanced at Slade.

"Something's mighty wrong," he announced to his chief.

"Ridley's on the phone. He's ringing up from his home, and he wants to see you about something that's frightfully urgent. He wouldn't whisper a syllable about it to me. He's holding the line."

"Right. I'll see what it is. He's probably remembered something about Merton."

But that was not the reason for the phone call. When Slade returned to where the others waited his face was grave.

"Ridley's just got in. He found his man bound and gagged, and the whole house has been ransacked from top to bottom."

CHAPTER IX

ROBBERY AT ORTON LODGE

IN the red-brick porch glowed an electric lantern. Raindrops glistened on the glass and copper frame, and slowly the lantern was swinging in the wind.

Rayner's car drew to a stop, and he and the Yard men alighted. Wiggins and two local uniformed men had been left at Tangles.

"It's almost as dreary out this side as it is on the other," commented Rayner.

Slade nodded. Over the fields facing the house the wind moaned. Rain swept across the front of the house in gusts, and as they stepped under the porch they heard the faint grinding sound of the lantern as it swung back and forth. Each man was a hard-bitten policeman, who had served many years in the Force, yet each felt uneasy as he stood there awaiting the answer to Slade's ring. None of them could say what gave rise to the feeling. Perhaps it was the wet and miserable night, the loneliness of the place, or, again, perhaps the feeling was due to some sense of presentiment. At length the front door opened.

In the dim orange glow from the hall lamp stood Ridley, his blond hair ruffled, his eyes wide and wondering. Slade looked at the man's mouth. The thin lips had almost disappeared, so compressed were they.

"Ah, here you are! Hallo, Rayner—you! And who——"

He paused as his eyes rested on Clinton's thickset figure.

"Sergeant Clinton of the Yard," explained Slade crisply.

"Well, come along in."

They hung their hats and coats in the hall and followed Ridley into the drawing-room. Reclining on a settee was the form of the man who had answered Slade's ring earlier that day. His eyes were closed, and one eye was turning a beautiful shade of purple. A few clots of congealed blood clung about his nostrils.

" Jenkins went out to a technical knock-out, as I understand it," said Ridley. " He's feeling pretty sick."

The man opened his one sound eye in a horrible wink, and closed it quickly. He moaned, shuddered, and lay still again.

" What happened?" asked Slade.

" About three-quarters of an hour ago Jenkins went to the door to answer a ring. There was a man outside with a hat pulled down well over his eyes. He asked gruffly if I were in. Now, according to Jenkins, a man had called earlier with a similar request. He wasn't sure whether this was the same person. Anyway, he opened the door wider to get a better look at the man when suddenly the other lunged at him. Jenkins faintly remembers the two blows landing quickly in his face—but he doesn't recall experiencing any pain until he came to, gagged and bound in this room. He was trussed up on the floor, and couldn't move. He had to wait till I got in. As soon as I'd untied him and heard what he had to say I got through to Tangles, where you said you were staying, Mr. Slade."

" Did he come to while the man who outed him was still here?"

" Yes, but he didn't see him again. This room had already been turned topsy-turvy, and the search was going on in the others."

" He doesn't know at what time, then, the man left, Mr. Ridley?"

" No, but the funny part is that he seems to recall hearing voices in the other rooms, low voices, as though two people were arguing."

" Men's voices?" asked Slade.

Ridley passed a hand through his disarranged blond hair.

" Jenkins isn't sure upon that point. I've questioned him, but he rather fancies that one of them was a woman."

The three policemen glanced at one another quickly, and Slade was aware that Ridley was cautiously watching their reaction to this piece of news.

" Are you sure on that score?" Slade queried sharply.

Ridley shrugged.

" Ask him?" He indicated Jenkins.

Slade bent over the man on the sofa.

" Jenkins, are you sure that one of those voices you heard was a woman's?"

The man opened his sound eye again and grunted.

" Yes, of course I'm sure," he grunted surlily. " A man's voice and a woman's. Couldn't hear what they said, but I got the idea they were arguin' about somethin'. My head felt too sore for me to worry much what they were sayin', but it sounded as though they were on the landin' on the first floor and——" He broke off with a sharp exclamation, peering more closely at Slade. "Hey! You're the man what came here earlier, askin' for Mr. Ridley. Was it you who bashed me——"

"Now, lay down, Jenkins. Take it easy. This is Inspector Slade, of the Yard."

With Ridley's hand on his shoulder the man subsided, growling and muttering. He closed his eyes again.

"So you called here, inspector?" said Ridley, turning to the Yard man.

"Yes, didn't I tell you this afternoon?"

Slade's tone was bland. Ridley suddenly smiled.

"Maybe you did. I can't recall now. However, I don't think Jenkins need carry a grudge against you, inspector."

It was heavy humour, and did not sound well. Slade continued as though Ridley had said nothing.

"Tell me, Mr. Ridley, have you any idea what the burglar came for?"

The other's brows went up in surprise.

"That's what puzzles me, inspector. I've no idea at all. There was some money in my bedroom—some forty or fifty pounds in notes and silver, as a matter of fact—and that hasn't been touched——"

"In a safe?"

"Well, no, a small cash-box."

"Then you can rest assured that what this burglar was after was something larger than would go into that cash-box, Mr. Ridley," observed Slade.

"What?" Ridley started, and added quickly, "well, I can't for the life of me guess what it is, inspector——"

Slade gave the other a straight look.

"Are you sure, Mr. Ridley?"

The man met the look without flinching. Slade almost told himself there was something mocking in Ridley's pale eyes; he stopped with the thought half formed.

"Positive." The other's tone was slightly less genial. "The whole affair's a complete and bewildering mystery to me."

"Like the forged letter," murmured Slade, but the comment didn't seem to call for an answer.

"Well, you gentlemen had better make what search you want

to," invited Ridley, gesturing round the room. "The entire house is free to you. Go where you like. I sincerely trust you'll find something that'll clear up this matter. It's all very disturbing."

Slade glanced round the upset room, and agreed. Ridley dropped into a chair and lit a cigarette.

The two Yard men set to work in a manner that suggested this was no new task to them; Rayner followed them from one room to another, switching off the lights when they had finished their inspection of a particular room. Whoever had knocked out Jenkins and ransacked the house had done the job thoroughly, though inexpertly, as Slade very soon detected. It had been a quick job, suggesting that the burglar had been pressed for time and had worked hurriedly. There was little sign of method. Things had been flung out of drawers and cupboards into a heap on the floor and then raked over. But on none of the furniture were there any finger-prints. The dining-room and drawing-room and a small study were searched, and then the detectives, followed by Rayner, mounted to the first floor. Here confusion reigned even more obviously than in the downstairs rooms. In the bedrooms the bed-clothes and contents of wardrobes had been piled in the centre of the floor. Shirts, collars, ties, underclothes, and pyjamas had been recklessly tossed anywhere. In Jenkins's room and Ridley's there was not a sign of anything that pointed to the identity of the person responsible for the pillage. Two spare bedrooms had been hastily searched, and in one a dozen moth-balls had been spilled over the floor. On the second floor there were two small rooms, one that was plainly a lumber-room and a small room set under a gable. The former had been searched perfunctorily. Trunks and suitcases had been hastily forced open, and evidently the searcher had been content with plunging his hand inside, for their contents remained in them. The smaller room was bare of any furniture. It looked out over the grounds. For a moment Slade stood by the window, Clinton at his elbow, Rayner in the doorway.

A step sounded on the stairs, and Ridley appeared on the landing.

"Well, any luck?" he inquired.

Slade shook his head.

"All I can tell you, Mr. Ridley, is that the person who made such a mess of the rooms was a novice at the game. The chances are he missed what he was looking for in his haste."

Ridley's brows went up.

"That so?"

Slade pointed to the window.

"There's no light, Mr. Ridley, from Mrs. Hubbard's cottage. Could one be seen from this window?"

"Oh, yes. As a matter of fact, the old girl's one of those early to bed early to rise people. She's probably been in bed some time."

"I see." Slade came away from the window. "You don't think she would be likely to help us—have seen anything?"

Ridley laughed.

"Old Mother Hubbard? Not a thing! She's like a hermit-crab, and doesn't stir far from her shell. You know," he continued, more conversationally, "she's rather a dear old soul, though people think she's funny. Well, I suppose she is really, but there's something likeable about her I always think——"

"Has she been in the cottage long?"

"Ever since I heard she was wanting a home, inspector. You see, she was a nurse to my mother at one time, and so, in a way, might be considered an old retainer. Yes, she's a dear old soul. Do anything for anyone, though of course I don't ask her to do anything for myself. Her ways are a bit old-fashioned, you know, and she's not above speaking up for her opinions."

He laughed again, and they trooped out of the small room and down the stairs. As they passed into the room where Jenkins still reclined upon the settee Ridley turned to Slade once more.

"Then you've really formed no idea at all about this peculiar affair, inspector?"

"Only the one I told you, Mr. Ridley—that it was performed by an amateur at house-breaking."

Ridley glanced at Jenkins's bruised and swollen face.

"I can't say that *that* looks like an amateur's work, inspector."

"Oh, it was all planned well beforehand—you may rest assured upon that point, Mr. Ridley. . . . Like that forged letter."

Ridley's head swung round, and his chin suddenly jutted out aggressively, as though the man were instantly upon the defensive. He frowned.

"Surely you're not suggesting there's a connection——"

"I'm suggesting nothing, Mr. Ridley. Until you can give me some idea as to the motive behind this burglary I'm afraid I shan't be able to suggest anything."

The other's lips grew thin, as they had been when he answered the door.

"It's no good asking me that again, inspector. I'm at a complete loss to account for the affair. I admit it looks as though someone wanted to get in rather badly." He laughed sheepishly, and the tenseness of his shoulders relaxed. "But couldn't there have been a mistake?"

"There's been a mistake all right—somewhere," the detective replied enigmatically.

Ridley produced a cigarette-case and offered it, but none of the others accepted. He extracted a cigarette himself and lit it with a lighter.

"I don't get you, inspector."

"That's probably because I'm not sure myself. But I know—I feel sure, Mr. Ridley—that this burglary was a blunder. Someone was getting desperate when this job was done, the same as someone was getting desperate when Haunchwood was murdered."

A blue light seemed to flare in Ridley's eyes. He took the cigarette from the corner of his mouth and stared at the detective. He pushed his tongue over his dry lips.

"You mean someone wants to—to murder me too, inspector? Is that what you mean when you say someone is desperate?"

An abstracted look came suddenly to his face. He might have been thinking of anything—or nothing. Slade was puzzled.

"Maybe," he said non-committally. "I should advise you to be on your guard, Mr. Ridley."

Ridley frowned. He threw his cigarette into the grate with a short, impatient gesture.

"I don't understand. I don't follow your drift," he complained. "Why should someone want to kill me——"

"Why did they want to kill Haunchwood—and Ferriss? And why was that letter forged and sent from your office?"

The other shook his head as though to clear it from a mental fog. He dropped into a chair and watched Clinton prowling about the room.

"It's all beyond me—I don't see light anywhere."

Slade shrugged, and crossed to the grate. In the hearth the cigarette stump was smouldering. He glanced round, and saw that Ridley's head was between his hands, which were ruffling his blond hair again. Quickly he stooped and picked up the cigarette stump, squeezed it out against the bar of the grate, and slipped the dead butt into his jacket pocket. He had noticed that those cigarettes bore a large gilt monogram, which made them unusual.

When Ridley looked up Slade was closely scrutinizing a bronze knight in armour who was threatening the clock with upraised sword.

Slade stepped away from the fender.

"I don't think we need trouble you any longer, Mr. Ridley——"

The other rose.

" I'm sorry to have dragged you out upon such a hopeless errand——"

" Oh, I shouldn't call it 'hopeless.'" protested Slade mildly. " At least, it's given me an idea."

" Well, I'm glad of that."

Slade wasn't sure whether Ridley's tone as he said that was bantering or sincere.

As Rayner got his car under way he asked Slade what he thought of the business.

" Putrid!" exclaimed the Yard man heartily, and the local inspector was left to draw his own conclusions.

They were driving through Ploverton when Rayner next spoke.

" Well, what's next?" he asked the Yard man.

Slade was silent for a few moments. He was thinking deeply, puzzling over some idea that had come to him. He glanced at Rayner long and earnestly before he replied.

" The Cedars," he said. " But you'd better make sure your tank's full before you leave the town. We might want a lot of petrol."

Rayner returned the Yard man's level gaze in silence.

" Righto," he said, and asked no question. He was beginning to appreciate Anthony Slade's way of doing things.

CHAPTER X

AT THE CEDARS

AFTER filling up with petrol at a pump-station in the town Rayner crossed Ploverton Bridge to the south side, and turned down Riverside Road. For half a mile or so houses flanked the road on each side; then fields appeared, bounded by small groups of trees and straggling hedgerows with a house dotted in between here and there. The road was bad. The car's headlights picked out large ruts and cracks in the surface, and Rayner had to drive carefully. The rain had stopped, and a moon was trying to break through the clouds when they first saw lights reflected in the surface of the river.

" You've certainly got some dreary patches round hereabouts," remarked Slade.

Rayner grunted into the collar of his coat.

"Wait till next month, when the fogs come. That's the time to call it dreary."

Other remarks were passed, but on the whole conversation did not flourish. Each man in the car had plenty to occupy his thoughts, and was grateful for the chance to consider them without disturbance.

"That's the place," said Rayner suddenly, breaking the silence. His gloved hand pointed to a patch of light to the left of the road stretching ahead. Three minutes later the car drew up outside the Cedars.

It was in every way a different place from Orton Lodge or Tangles. In design and compactness it was modern. Roughcasting covered the top portion of the walls, and the windows were small and framed in metal. A small detached garage stood at the side of the house, and a single gravel path led to both garage and front door. A thick hedge of some description of evergreen topped the low wall fronting the road, and beyond lay a lawn, fringed with bare earthen borders.

A few seconds after Slade rang the front-door bell someone within clicked down a light switch and a light under the porch glowed feebly. Then came the sound of fingers fumbling with the door catch, and a moment later the door was partially opened and a croaking feminine voice asked, "Yes? Who is it?"

"I've called to see Mr. Merton," said Slade. "Will you take him my card?"

For a moment it looked as though the woman holding the door was of a mind to close it in their faces, but she hesitated at Slade's commanding tone, and then slowly drew the door back.

"Come in," she invited ungraciously, and took the visiting-card Slade held out.

She left them standing in the small hall, and ambled into a room at the rear, closing the door after her. She was gone some minutes, and while they waited Slade listened intently, with both ears cocked. He thought he heard the sound of someone moving on the floor above, but was not sure. He was still listening when the woman appeared again, and beckoned him.

"Will you please come this way, sir?" she invited, more respectfully.

Slade nodded to the other two men.

"Come on."

The man standing in front of a wood-fire in the grate stared as the three policemen entered. He was of medium height, with dark brown hair brushed straight back off his forehead, and his features were sharp and regular. His pale brown eyes, almost amber-coloured, stared at them through shell-rimmed spectacles.

"Good Lord, a deputation!" he exclaimed, but there was no humour in the remark. A single glance at the man—he appeared to be about twenty-eight or thirty—told Slade that he was on edge, nervy; he knew the type, temperamental, capable of doing anything in a moment of stress.

"I must apologize, Mr. Merton," began Slade when the other waved a hand.

"Don't," he said, "—not yet."

Slade's jaw squared. He didn't like this kind of reception. It more than suggested that he wasn't going to get anywhere, and Slade hated wasting his time more than he hated most things.

Merton pushed himself away from the mantelpiece, and waved a hand towards some chairs.

"Be seated, gentlemen. It's more difficult to be unpleasant when one's seated." His grin was wry. "I take it you haven't called upon me just to say good evening."

Slade sat himself down, and the other two followed his example. Merton dropped into an arm-chair, and, resting his elbows on the arms, bridged his fingers.

"You're right, Mr. Merton," said Slade coldly. "We haven't just dropped in to pay our respects, but to ask where you've been this evening."

Merton raised his brows, and the movement caused his spectacles to slip slightly down his nose. He pushed them back into their proper place with a forefinger.

"Is that any of your business?" he asked bluntly.

"We shouldn't be here if we didn't think so. Are you going to tell us?"

"Certainly not."

Slade took a deep breath. This man was going to prove difficult to handle—if he was going to be handled at all, which he rather doubted.

"I rather thought that would be your attitude, Mr. Merton," he confessed.

Merton's brows raised again.

"Indeed! You seem to take me for granted upon singularly short acquaintance, Inspector Slade. Or have you been talking to friend Ridley?"

"I have—about a burglary at Orton Lodge."

Merton's hands came down from before his face and he sat forward.

"You don't say!" he exclaimed, but there was no genuine surprise in his tone; it was rather mocking than otherwise. "Well, what's it got to do with me?"

"That's not for me to say——"

"Well, I'm glad of that!" snapped Merton. "And in that case I hardly see any reason for prolonging this—er—inquisition."

"I'm sorry to disagree with you, Mr. Merton, and I must caution you that this attitude you are adopting does not help you in——"

"I'm not aware I require help."

"You may if you can't explain your movements this evening."

"Of course I can explain my movements. But I perceive no earthly reason why I should when you offer no explanation."

Slade had to make his mind up quickly. It was plain that Rayner would not expect to take a part in the duel, and Clinton would not interfere until he got his chief's signal. The Yard sergeant would content himself with making a mental summary of all that passed for future reference.

Slade took the forged letter from his pocket and handed it to Merton.

"Know anything about that?" he asked curtly.

Merton stared at it, and his face grew rigid. He remained staring at the letter for longer than was necessary to read it through twice. He looked up at last, and his eyes were narrowed.

"Appears to have been sent out by Ridley, though that's not his signature."

Slade allowed Merton full marks for shrewdness.

"I asked if you knew anything about it."

"Not a thing." Merton handed the letter back and made himself more comfortable in his chair.

"That signature's a forgery."

"Well, what's it got to do with me? What could be the object in forging a business note of that sort?"

"For instance, to prevent a meeting between a member of the firm and Ferriss."

"Which member of the firm—Ridley?"

Slade thought Merton's eyes were sharper now than they had been since he entered the room. Merton was on his guard, and every nerve was athrob.

"Hardly. Ridley says he never saw Ferriss."

"So that's what he says, is it? But why're you so interested in Ferriss?"

"He was murdered last night."

Merton sat up with a jerk.

"Ferriss—murdered! Good God!—where?"

Slade wasn't satisfied that the show of surprise was real. He ignored the question and took from his pocket the photograph.

"Is that Ferriss?" he asked.

Merton nodded, staring at the photograph as though it had some special significance.

"Yes, that's Ferriss. He was Haunchwood's valet-of-sorts. Know Haunchwood? Old boy who lives across the river from here, at a ramshackle place called Tangles."

"He doesn't live there any longer."

"Eh? Oh, you mean he's moved?"

Slade saw that the man's hands were twitching. He was having difficulty—great difficulty—in appearing calm and undisturbed by the other's questions.

"No, he's dead. Murdered, like Ferriss."

Merton got slowly to his feet, his mouth open; but his eyes swivelled from right to left, like those of some hunted animal which is desperately watching escape being cut off. He sat down suddenly.

"Go on," he said hoarsely. "What is it you want to say? What is it you're going to accuse me of?"

His nerve was fast going.

"I'm not accusing you of anything," said Slade, surprised despite himself at this remarkable change in the other. "I'm asking for an explanation if you have one. That letter with the forged signature of John Ridley was typed on Miss Moffett's machine."

There was a sudden, sharp silence, and while it lasted Slade thought he heard the soft footfall of someone in the room above. But it might have been the woman who had let them in.

"Well?" he demanded at length.

Merton roused himself with an effort.

"I've nothing to say."

"You realize——"

"Oh, go to the devil!" broke out the young man, starting up. "I realize nothing except that I'm not going to make any damn-fool commitment, or be tricked into admitting something I don't mean. Get that, and make no mistake."

His flare of anger died down. His face was pale, and his features seemed more keen, sharper, than before; the movements of his neck were quick, spasmodic.

"Very well, Mr. Merton, there's one other thing I must ask you——"

"Well, what is it?" snapped Merton sharply.

" May I see the room over this one?"

Behind the lenses of his spectacles the young man's eyes flickered. He was trying desperately to understand what was in the other's mind.

" Have you a search warrant, Inspector Slade?"

Slade chewed his lower lip.

" No," he had to admit.

Merton's reply flashed out as soon as the word was uttered.

" Then I'm sorry—you can't see the room upstairs—or any other damned room in this house. Blast it, can't a man have privacy in his own home?"

" Haunchwood couldn't," Slade reminded him grimly. " This place is right opposite Tangles," he added, as though by the way.

Merton flinched.

" You'll be saying next you think I pulled that one," he sneered unwisely.

Slade smiled. At last his man was upon the run.

" You're behaving rather mysteriously, Mr. Merton. Don't you think you'd be well advised to do some explaining—now, while you have the chance?"

But the other rushed at the obstacle bull-headed.

" Threats—eh? Well, they won't wash with me. I suppose I've to thank Ridley for this visit. Well, you can damn' well tell him from me that I prefer to pick my own company and fill my house with my own guests—I don't want his."

Slade rose; there was little point in remaining longer.

" I'll think over what you've said, Mr. Merton. I——" He stopped suddenly. He had glanced at the mirror over the mantel-piece, and his eyes had caught sight of some grains of powder on top of the mantel itself. Before Merton realized what he was about to do he pressed his forefinger upon the grains of powder and raised his finger to his nose.

" Remarkable what delicious perfumes some of the latest face-powders have," he remarked, and turned towards the door.

Merton glared at the Yard man's back, but said nothing. The middle-aged woman who had answered the front door came from somewhere in the region of the kitchen and saw them to the gate; then she shut the front door and switched off the porch light.

Rayner whistled.

" Well, that was a sweet-singing bird! He'd take a prize!"

" He'll take a month in bed if he's not careful," grunted Slade. " That young man's on the verge of a nervous breakdown. His nerves are all frayed, and he's got a temperament that'll keep 'em raw. If I'm not greatly mistaken he's been having a thin time of it lately."

"What d'you mean?" demanded Rayner.

"Well, he's got something on his mind, and he won't get it off while he remains thinking that way about it."

Rayner shook his head, and buttoned up his coat-collar. They climbed into his car.

"What was that you said about perfumed face-powder, Slade?" he asked as Clinton slammed the car door shut.

Slade grinned.

"Wait, Rayner. You'll see. We've been moving in a circle. I guessed it when he recognized that photograph of Ferriss—— Oh, I don't mean recognized Ferriss, but the photograph itself."

"I'm afraid I don't catch on."

"Nor do I—all the way. But listen, Rayner. I want you to coast along this road till you strike a gate where we can pull in. Yes, and, by the way, which is the better road to town, this or the one on the north side?"

"The one on the north side."

"I see. All right, then, we'll move back towards Ploverton and find that gate."

They found a gate on the right-hand side, and after Slade had opened it Rayner half backed the car through.

"Now," said Slade, "if we keep the lights off we've a chance of remaining here unseen. I don't think we'll have long to wait."

Nearly twenty minutes passed before they heard the hum of a car's engine coming along the road, and it was travelling towards Ploverton. The rain had passed over, and now a slim crescent of moon rode the night sky above the dark shapes of the trees. From across the river came the low soughing of the wind, and from somewhere on the opposite bank a dog was barking. The drone of the approaching motor became louder, and presently they caught sight of a thin ribbon of light streaking the surface of the road. The light grew into a glare.

"Watch close," whispered Slade.

The spot where they had chosen to hide was on a bend, and the approaching motorist slowed to take it. As the car drew abreast the moon was bright enough to reveal his face. The man was Stanley Merton, and at his side, wrapped in a concealing fur coat, was a woman. In that momentary glimpse the men crouched in the car backed through the gate could not see her face. Her head was turned, and she was speaking earnestly to Merton, gesturing with a gloved hand.

The car passed the gate and gathered speed.

" Righto! Now get on their tail," said Slade.

Rayner turned his car into the road and drove on towards Ploverton. The red rear-light of the car ahead was soon picked up, and the police car followed Merton's to Ploverton Bridge, where the latter crossed. Five minutes later the cars were moving sharply down the main London road.

" Well, this is a gay jaunt," muttered Rayner, settling down to the task of following the other car all the way to London. " Where's it going to end?"

Slade grinned.

" That's what I can't make my mind up about. But I'm glad we filled up with petrol."

CHAPTER XI

SLADE SPEEDS THINGS UP

As Slade had suspected, Merton drove into London. He passed through Chelsea, skirting the river, and continued along Grosvenor Road, turning along the Vauxhall Bridge Road to Victoria. He bore past the station and made for Hyde Park Corner, turned up Park Lane, and after running round the Marble Arch drove ahead up the Edgware Road.

" Well, I'll say he's leading us a pretty dance. Wonder what his game is," grumbled Rayner, who was finding difficulty in keeping up with the car ahead and at the same time obeying the traffic signals.

" Picking a safe spot, that's all," said Slade.

" Well, I hope he's got it in mind, then."

The car ahead continued to Maida Vale, where it suddenly turned down a side-street, to draw up before the garage of a block of houses that had been converted into the Meridian Hotel. The three policemen waited until Merton and the woman had passed into the hotel, then, while Clinton kept an eye on the hotel entrance, Rayner ran the car into the garage, and a few moments later he and Slade joined the C.I.D. sergeant.

" What's the procedure?" Rayner asked Slade.

The Yard man looked at the glass doors of the hotel entrance and frowned.

" We'll give them a minute or two to get to a room, and then we'll see how he's signed the register. It'll depend upon that."

Rayner didn't understand, but he made no further comment, and Clinton, after a quick glance at his chief, fell to watching the passing traffic. At last Slade said, "All right. We'll go in now."

They passed through the swing-doors, and Rayner's serge overcoat and peaked cap at once aroused the interest of the desk-clerk. That lean-faced individual forgot to smirk when he picked up the card Slade dropped on to the counter.

"I want to see the manager," said the Yard man.

The clerk gave him a glance that trembled.

"Yes, sir—certainly. If you'll wait just a moment——"

The manager—into whose office they were ushered—was a Jew, short, very fat, very bald, and very frightened. Slade's first words did much to reassure him, though the doubtful expression did not leave his fleshy face throughout the interview.

"This is a murder case I'm on, Mr. Rosenstein," said Slade after introductions were over. "I want to see the names of the last people who have registered here—they entered a few moments ago, a man and a woman, and they have left their car in the garage round the corner. If necessary, I may want a room, and if I do I shall want to be informed of when they take breakfast and of when they are leaving—and given plenty of time. You understand?"

Mr. Rosenstein gulped and nodded his large head, which was attached to his shoulders by a wide roll of fat. His beady eyes flickered. He was a wise man, and realized that it would not be well to mention the reputation of his hotel.

"I onderstand perfectly, inspector. You shall have all the help ve can afford you."

"Thank you, Mr. Rosenstein. But, remember, I said I was on a murder case. This is not to be chattered about."

Slade's look was grim. The manager held up a couple of hands and gesticulated forcefully.

"You haf my vord, inspector. I shall see zat none of my staff—chatters."

"Good. Then let's see the register now."

The register was brought in, and Slade turned to the last entry. He started, and held his finger on it. Written in a sloping hand was "Mr. and Mrs. S. Merrell, London" and the date. Clinton's eyes widened, and Rayner whistled softly.

Slade looked at Rosenstein, who was eyeing them with obvious speculation.

"What are you going to do now, Rayner?"

A sudden smile lit the Ploverton inspector's face.

"I think I can leave an empty house to Wiggins. So I'll stay and see this through."

"Good. We'll want a couple of rooms, then, Mr. Rosenstein."

They were given the keys to two rooms next to each other, and were shown up to the fourth floor. Slade ushered the other two into one of the rooms and closed the door.

"Clinton," he said, "I want you to stay here with Inspector Rayner. When they leave in the morning follow them, and if they split up—as I think they will—well, it'll be up to you."

The sergeant nodded.

"I've got an urgent job awaiting me at the Yard," Slade went on, "one I've got to tackle tonight. If anything comes of it that you should know I'll get through on the phone. If you don't hear from me, however, go right ahead, and report when you're through."

Again Clinton nodded.

"Will you want any of my notes, sir?" He tapped the pocket in which he kept his notebook.

"Not yet, Clinton. Time for those later. We've plenty on our hands at the moment, and we can compare notes and make a final check afterwards." Slade turned to Rayner. "This is not putting you out at all——"

"Not a bit," the other hastened to assure him. "Take it from me, Slade, this is a slice more exciting than rounding up folk who've forgotten to pay their dog licences," he grinned. "I wouldn't miss it for worlds."

"Right, then. I'll be getting back to the Yard. Oh, yes, Clinton, if you want an extra man phone for Irvin. I think Farrar's finished with him. So long."

Five minutes later Slade was in a taxi bowling down the Edgware Road. When he entered his office at the Yard it was to find a brief report from Sergeant Farrar. The inquest on the man found shot in Cheviot Crescent would be held on the morrow, and what should be given out to the Press? Slade scribbled a few lines in pencil below the report and then picked up the house-phone and was put through to the photography laboratory.

"Hello, Platt. Just wanted to know if you were in. What, you're still working on those crossed finger-prints? Well, I've got a rush job here, and a ticklish one. I'll bring it down myself; but I want it put through in half-time."

Platt was a tall man with gold-rimmed spectacles and a slight squint. His shoulders drooped, and he was always to be seen with the cuffs of his white jacket rolled above his wrists. He sucked his tongue noisily when Slade showed him the pieces of charred cardboard which he had taken from the grate of the flat in Stanthorpe Mansions.

"What do you think I am, Tony," he groused, "a miracle-worker?"

"Pretty near, old man," grinned Slade, who could see immediately that the task had captured Platt's interest. "It's brittle, and liable to flake——"

"You needn't tell me—I can see that. What is it, a bit of a photo?"

"Yes. The photographer's imprint is on this piece: small raised letters. Luckily this piece is not so badly burned."

"Oh, I'm glad to hear that," snorted Platt, holding the piece of burnt cardboard to the light. The bantering suddenly dropped from his manner. "When do you want it by, Tony?"

"As quick as you can do it. I'm waiting in for the result."

"Good God! Some of you plagued detectives think that all you've——"

But the rest of the harangue was lost to Slade, who had retreated with a chuckle. If Platt didn't ring down to tell him the result within an hour he'd be surprised.

He went back to his office and sat down at his desk. He was feeling suddenly tired. It had been a long day, and a strenuous one. He had been on the go all the time, and now he saw little prospect of getting some sleep before the early hours. It was hard to realize that he had been on the case only about twenty-four hours. So much had happened, and so many conflicting pieces of evidence had been discovered, that the case might well have been in hand a full week.

Slade lit his pipe, and settled down to a browse over the facts. Minutes passed, and he took no account of their passing. The problem that he found himself confronted with absorbed all his interest and attention; but he knew he was faced with a difficult task this time. The only glimmering of light in the entire case had burst through when he had read the entry in the register of the Meridian Hotel. If Merton and Claire Merrell were man and wife a lot was explained: the girl's telephone call that morning, and her disappearance. Merton had not appeared at the brickworks; but someone had crossed the river and taken the girl away. Again, the register had been signed " S. Merrell." Stanley Merton was a very good *nom de guerre* in the circumstances. The initials were the same. And Miss Clissold, at Lorette's, had vouched that the girl's name was Mrs. Mer*rell*. Very well, who were husband and wife working against? If Merton had sent that letter to Ferriss, and had written Ridley's signature, one was provided with much food for reflection. There was that strange robbery at Orton Lodge, Ridley's place, and the hunt for something that had not been found.

Slade turned to another aspect of the case. Someone had planted that maroon saloon to involve the girl in a murder case— at least, to use her as a decoy to insure that someone's safety. Was that same someone the person husband and wife were opposed to in the mystery struggle? It seemed reasonable. But what could be the stakes? He recalled what he had said to Rayner earlier that evening. Jewellery or something convertible into money. . . .

Then there was the primary mystery of Haunchwood and Ferriss. What had been the mystery of those two men's existence? They had shared some secret—what? And was that secret shared by Merrell—or Merton, as Slade still considered him—and his wife? The murderer knew of it; they had been killed because of it. Did the same danger threaten the Merrells? Ridley too—where did he come into the tangle?

Slade had filled his briar for the third time when the phone buzzer at his elbow broke the silence of the office. It was Platt. Slade went up to the photography laboratory, to find Platt with his white jacket stained with yellow and purple splotches. His hair hung over his forehead in dank wisps, and his collar was loosened. But there was a triumphant light in the photographic chemist's eyes.

" Well, I've got you a result, Tony," he grinned cheerily. " But what a job! Three times no result save a bleared stipple; and the third time I thought I'd ruined the subject. That made me mad, you can guess. However, the fourth time— Well, here it is; I'll throw it on the screen. Come and see."

He pulled down a white canvas screen, came back to a magic lantern fixed on a stand, then switched off the light. A moment later the lantern threw a bright ray towards the canvas. Black sketchy words appeared : " P. Sunliss, 16B Grafton Street, London." Below " London " was a dark patch that looked like " AY2 " written hurriedly.

Slade wrote down what he read on the screen, and Platt turned on the light.

" What's the AY2?" asked Slade.

Platt shrugged.

"Don't know, except that it was possibly written in indelible pencil. Might be a catalogue or file number."

"Well, let's hope so," said Slade. "I've got to trace that photograph. I believe it'll be important."

"Good luck, Tony—and good hunting."

Slade looked up "Sunliss, P." in the telephone directory, and found that besides the number of the Grafton Street studio the photographer had a number in Norbury. He got through to the number and asked for Mr. Sunliss, to be told that Mr. Sunliss was speaking. Briefly Slade explained what he wanted of the photographer, and, late though the hour was, Mr. Sunliss did not hesitate to assure the detective that he was perfectly willing to do what he could that very night. If Inspector Slade would be outside the studio in Grafton Street within forty minutes he would find Mr. Sunliss there.

The photographer was as good as his word. Slade found him waiting by his car after thirty-five minutes.

"Is it a photograph for the newspapers, inspector?" he inquired as he unlocked the door of the studio.

"I wish it were as simple as that, Mr. Sunliss," said Slade, with a smile. "I'm afraid it—— Just a moment," he broke off.

A patrolling constable was hurrying towards them, ready to tackle a couple of thieves. The man retired with a salute after a few words with Slade, and the latter followed the photographer up a flight of narrow stairs. When they entered the studio Sunliss turned on the light and faced the Yard man.

"Now, Mr. Slade, if you'll please let me know what it is you want I'll see what I can do."

Slade explained that he was anxious to trace a burned photograph, on the bottom edge of which had been deciphered the caption he had written on a piece of paper. He handed Sunliss the note he had made in Platt's laboratory.

"That"—he pointed to the AY2—"was written in indelible pencil below the last line. AY2, isn't it?"

Sunliss shook his head.

"No. It's a file reference—AYZ actually. It's fortunate you were able to decipher it, inspector, or otherwise I shouldn't be able to trace the photograph. However, with the reference, it ought to be fairly easy. Now, if I'm not mistaken, that reference was in use about two years ago. Let me see."

He unlocked a wall-safe and took out several ledgers. Opening one, he traced a number, which provided him with an index reference to a larger book.

"Ah, here we are—AYZ. The last of the AY series of orders. Now, just a minute, and I'll have the name of the sitter. Yes "—he flicked over a few pages and ran his finger down an alphabetical list of names—"here's the name—Sir Raymond Gelder."

The photographer and the Yard man looked at each other for several seconds in silence. It was a name well known to both of them, a name that, nearly two years before, had figured on the front page of most English newspapers. Sir Raymond Gelder had committed suicide after the failure of the celebrated Gelder Trust, and the result had brought catastrophe to a number of businesses throughout the country which were controlled by the trust. No one had known why the trust had failed just when it had. Upon paper its affairs had appeared sound enough. Sir Raymond's personal fortune had been involved. Slade did not remember offhand the many side-issues of the affair, but he knew there had been a deal of talk about mystery speculations.

"Phew! That's raking up the past, Mr. Sunliss."

The photographer smiled.

"I remember his having the sitting now. A white-haired gentleman, very upstanding, with a genial smile. Yes, I remember him distinctly now. Still, I can get you our file copy of the photograph, if you'd like to see it."

"I should—very much."

The photograph Sunliss handed to Slade a short while later was of a striking-looking man. Generosity and business acumen were blended in the character of the features.

"Would you mind if I borrowed this photo for a while, Mr. Sunliss?" asked the detective.

"Not at all, inspector. We have the negative, of course."

"Thank you very much indeed, sir. This is a great help. Enables me to fit another link to a very short chain."

"That's perfectly all right, Mr. Slade. Only too glad to be of assistance. If there is anything else you would like me to do——"

"Well, there is just one thing." Slade took from his pocket the photograph of Ferriss. "Can you tell me if this was taken professionally—or by an amateur?"

Sunliss took the photograph and examined it with a small lens, which he fitted into his eye.

"I should say that it was taken by a small camera, and an enlargement made. From the lighting I should hazard that it was taken in the open air, and I am rather inclined to think that this little smudge at the top is part of a leaf."

"A leaf!" echoed Slade.

Sunliss nodded, his head still bent over the photograph.

"Yes, I'm almost positive it is a leaf. You know, the photograph may have been taken with the camera concealed, hidden in some foliage."

He took the glass out of his eye and smiled at the Yard man.

"Such things are done. I've been asked to develop some very peculiar photos of that kind."

"You mean photographs that would be used for blackmail?" Sunliss shrugged.

"I won't say that I *have* developed any such, and, again, I won't say that this photo was taken with blackmail as the object. Obviously there is nothing taken in this subject other than the man's head and shoulders. But I shouldn't mind offering it as my opinion that this gentleman "—he tapped the photograph with his lens—" was distinctly averse to having his likeness possessed by other people."

Slade thought of the Haunchwood-Ferriss tangle and considered the possibility quite likely.

"You should be with us at the Yard," he smiled.

Sunliss laughed.

"I don't know about that, inspector. But I've always considered that the better the detective the more profound a student he is of human nature—which is a very funny thing."

So Slade thought as he made his way back to the Yard. However, it was not until his taxi was turning into Whitehall that another thought occurred to him. He picked up the speaking-tube and gave the driver another order. The man turned his taxi round and circled Trafalgar Square, joining the eastward stream of traffic in Duncannon Street. Ten minutes later Slade paid off the man outside the towering structure of Monitor House. His watch told him it was half an hour after midnight; but he knew that Timothy Hagan, the Irish editor of the *Daily Monitor,* would be in his office until one o'clock.

Upon presenting his card he was quickly shown up to the editor's room. He entered, to find "Big Tim" Hagan scanning some copy-sheets. The Irishman looked up when Slade entered and scowled.

"You never look me up, Tony, except when you want something," he growled.

Slade dropped into a moderately comfortable chair of green leather and chromium-plated steel.

"Well, Tim, you can't grouse. You had the end of the Farrell story before anyone else."

Hagan's eyes lit.

"That was a whale of a yarn, Tony." He shrugged his broad shoulders, and looked glum again. "But Home Secretaries don't go mixing themselves up in murder cases every time you drop in here. What is it this time?"

"I want all you can dig me up about the Raymond Gelder case, Tim."

Hagan's eyes widened. He sat back and stared.

"So that's it. Well, I'm damned! When the case was on the police did nothing——"

"We weren't asked to do anything," Slade pointed out agreeably. "And when he committed suicide it was past worrying about."

Hagan shook his head, staring hard at the detective.

"You don't mind taking a little warning from a pal, do you, Tony?"

"No, Tim. What is it?"

"Well, there was a lot of crooked work in that Gelder Trust affair that the general public didn't hear about, and we couldn't print the tale because of the awful stink it would have raised."

The laughter died in Slade's eyes.

"What was the mystery, Tim? Get down to bedrock, like a good fellow."

Hagan leaned over his desk and crossed his arms.

"The real mystery as far as I'm concerned was what became of Gelder's private fortune. Of course, had it been found just after the crash it would have been confiscated. But he was a smart lad. It wasn't found—not a penny of it. And it amounted to a tidy sum——"

"Such as?"

"Well, in the neighbourhood of a hundred and fifty thousand. Pretty good pin-money, ain't it?" grinned Hagan broadly.

Slade nodded sombrely. He was thinking fast.

"You're right, Tim. Pretty good pin-money . . . would buy enough pins to prick a great many bubbles."

"Uh, don't go getting poetical, Tony, for God's sake!" Hagan fingered his jaw. "But you're right at that. It *would* prick a great many bubbles. There's a bubble named Haunchwood, for instance——"

Slade leaned forward.

"That one's pricked, Tim," he announced quietly.

Slowly Timothy Hagan got to his feet and came round his desk to where Slade sat.

"You mean that, Tony—murdered?"

"Twenty-four hours ago. The news'll be given out in another hour—too late for any write-up. That'll give us a little while longer to cook you something up."

But there was no fun now in Hagan's broad, good-humoured face.

"I knew! I knew it!" he said softly. "When you came in here and mentioned Gelder's name I told myself that shooting of Ferriss was going to break something wide open. Oh, there'll be an awful stench if you're not careful, Tony!"

"How big have you played Ferriss's murder?"

"Quarter of a column, not more. Here—see."

Hagan picked up a sheet of proof from his desk and passed it to the detective. Slade read it through. A bare announcement, with the usual tag that the police were in possession of an important clue which was expected to lead to early results.

"Is it worth playing it bigger—yet awhile, Tony?"

Slade shook his head.

"No, not yet, Tim. And personally I think you're wrong. . . ."

"What's that?"

The Irishman spun round.

"There's not going to be much of a stench. . . . But tell me, Tim. Any other bubbles to be pricked besides Haunchwood and Ferriss?"

Hagan eyed the detective long.

"Ever hear of a bird named Ridley? A canary-looking cove: light hair, trim, but a nasty customer, and one I wouldn't trust with the widow's mite."

"John of that ilk? Now running the Summerdale Brickmaking Company?"

"Oh, so he's still keeping up that farce! A pretty piece of cover up that, Tony. But how did you get on to him? He's a wily *avis,* the sort that generally knows the answers before he asks the questions, and he's as tight as a tick on a dog's ear."

Slade regarded the other blandly, and Hagan, who had known the Yard man for a number of years, knew that he was going to be put off.

"Oh, his name just came up, Tim. You know how it is——"

"You bet I do!" grinned the Irishman. "Anybody else's? You're making an interesting collection, Tony!"

Slade rose and leaned against the editor's desk. His expression became more earnest, a change Hagan recognized.

"Did Gelder have any family?"

"Can't tell you offhand. But we've got it all in the records down below. I'll have his card brought up."

The *Daily Monitor's* "Personality Index" was one of Hagan's chief contributions to the efficient routine of the great daily newspaper. By means of it he was never at a loss for news. His staff could always find something to say about someone; and, as Hagan was never tired of reiterating, the best news is always about people—preferably the best people.

He picked up the typewritten card handed him by an assistant and glanced over its contents.

"Here we are," he said, holding it out so that Slade could read what it contained. "Gelder was a knight, chairman of the Gelder Trust, and here's a list of the companies the trust controlled, and, as you see, the Summerdale Brickmaking Company is one of them. Not a very large concern, with not a great turn-over, but sufficient to keep Mr. John Ridley in the picture. Again, Haunchwood and Ferriss have their names here. Apparently they ran the Pyramis Trading Corporation—obviously a dud concern, with a name like that. After the crash the Pyramis disappeared, with most of the others. But, you see, the Summerdale firm kept alive. It's down in the Thames Valley somewhere. Place called Ploverton. Know it?"

"I've heard of it," said Slade.

"A dead hole, in my opinion. But, then, I don't like the Thames Valley—nor anywhere flat. Like to climb a bit when I can get away from E.C.4, though this won't let me climb much longer." Hagan laughed loudly, and rapped his paunch. "But to get back to Gelder," he resumed. "His wife died about seven years ago, and he did not marry again. There are no children, but he had a nephew, the son of his sister, who married a consumptive solicitor. Gelder took the boy under his wing, provided his education when the parents died, and generally brought him up in his own——"

"What is the nephew's name?" asked Slade, interrupting.

Hagan's glance dropped an inch, to a name underlined in red.

"Merrell. Sidney Merrell. Mean anything to you?"

Slade nodded.

"It's beginning to."

"Ah, ha! The mystery deepens!"

"No, Tim. The plot thickens—but the *mystery* is becoming slightly less mysterious. I'm beginning to see daylight. You're a useful fellow, Tim."

"Now, don't get smug, Tony. I don't trust that tone of voice."

"What else do you know about Merrell?"

"Nothing, except that he had little in the bank when his uncle shot himself. I don't know what's become of him. Why?"

"You didn't know he was married, then?"

Hagan's bushy brows lifted in two black arcs.

"No. Who was she?"

"Lorette."

"Conveys nothing to me. But she sounds too romantic to be what some people call 'nice.'"

Slade laughed.

"Lorette of Shaftesbury Avenue. The business is doing well, I believe."

"Smart chap to marry a woman with a good business in these days. Might make a story out of it; specially if Lorette's would consider a little advertising now and again."

Slade shook his head.

"All this is hush-hush for the present, Tim. You'll get the story later, and all in good time for——"

"I seem to have heard there's no time like the present," growled Hagan, dropping the card on to his desk.

"Much more important at the moment is have you heard of a place called Tangles?"

"Tangles? Funny name, isn't it?"

"Well, it fits the place it describes all right. It's in Lower Ploverton."

The editor picked up the card once more and glanced over it.

"Tony," he said severely, "I'm strongly suspecting you of keeping too much up your sleeve. All I can tell you about a house called Tangles is that up to three months before his suicide it was the country home of Raymond Gelder."

Slade smiled at his friend with irritating serenity.

"I was beginning to wonder if it might have been."

CHAPTER XII

A TRICK THAT DID NOT WORK

At twenty minutes to nine the next morning Slade sat in his office at New Scotland Yard. On the desk before him were three daily newspapers, each of which included a long write-up about the mystery of the maroon saloon car and the murder of one Harold Ferriss in a house in Cheviot Crescent. Full details of the Yard's "theory" were given, and the public were promised a lengthy account of the proceedings at the inquest to be held that day. On other pages, almost crowded out by other small news events, were notices of the finding of the dead body of a Mr. Morton Haunchwood, once a fairly well-known figure in the City, at his home

Tangles, in Lower Ploverton. No mention was made of a possible connection between the two deaths.

Slade picked up a typed telephone report from an exchange supervisor. The call received at 27A Stanthorpe Mansions on the evening of Ferriss's murder had been traced not to Tangles, as Claire Merrell had stated, but to a public call-box at the corner of Cheviot Crescent. There could be no mistake. That had been the only call received at the number of the Stanthorpe Mansions phone on that evening.

He thought of the man who had been the only "witness" of the affair in Cheviot Crescent, the man who had given the false address. Could it be that he had been the person who had phoned Claire Merrell? . . . And who would have been most likely to phone her? Who—other than her husband—knew of the Stanthorpe Mansions flat? The staff of Lorette's and perhaps the red-haired man. It was the latter who puzzled Slade most. He fitted nowhere into the picture. As far as Slade could see there was no vacant niche in the case where he should and could fit. Yet he was a factor not to be left out of account. How important he was Slade could not gauge; but he was certain—as certain as he could reasonably be, that is—that he was not the man who had observed the maroon car in Cheviot Crescent; or who had phoned Claire Merrell and told her to go to Tangles and what to say should she walk into a trap.

With a distinct feeling of doubt Slade put the matter from his mind. It was something, he told himself, that would have to be cleared in the course of the investigation; and it was not the only angle that remained obscured. He was certain now, since his talk with Timothy Hagan on the previous evening, that the entire mystery and the murders too concerned Sir Raymond Gelder's disposal of his private fortune, which would have been engulfed in the cataclysm of the Gelder Trust's break-up had Gelder himself not been very farsighted. But what had he done with his fortune—a fortune running into a hundred and fifty thousand pounds? A great bait, such a sum. Men would kill and cheat and rob for a fraction of that wealth. . . .

Slade turned to another matter. The Yard's firearms expert reported that the bullet Clinton had dug from the skirting-board in the drawing-room at Tangles was of the same calibre as those other two bullets—which had not missed their marks. Fresh consideration of that bullet brought Slade's mind back to the girl. Someone had tried to kill her because she was about to tell the police—what?

The evidence and the reasoning it gave rise to had resulted in his describing the usual vicious circle of facts and queries. Argue from any angle as he would, he always came back to the same query: What was the secret of Tangles? If it had been Gelder's place, why had Haunchwood and Ferriss taken it? Why had the murderer been so interested in it? And Gelder's nephew and his wife? There, in that old house that had been let fall into disrepair, the grounds of which were now choked with weeds, lay the crux of the whole affair, the hub of this perplexing mystery.

Slade got up, lit his pipe, and began walking about the office. It was now nine o'clock. In an hour's time he would——

The telephone on his desk shrilled, and he hastened to snatch up the receiver.

The caller was Clinton, phoning from a call-box on Victoria Station. He was taking a train to the little Kentish town of Wenford, not far from Tonbridge. Mrs. Merrell had booked a first-class return ticket to that station, and he was following her. Her husband had seen her to the station, and had then gone off in his car. Rayner had followed him.

Slade suddenly made up his mind.

"Keep behind her at Wenford, Clinton, and find out where she goes to. I'll catch the next train. There have been fresh developments, which I'll explain when I see you."

He rang off, donned his hat and coat, and left the Yard for Victoria Station, where he found that the train Clinton and Mrs. Merrell had travelled by had left some seven minutes before. The next train to Wenford would not be for a couple of hours. It was on a small branch-line. But he learned that he could take a train to Tonbridge, and change on to a local bus, which ran to Wenford every twenty minutes. The next train to Tonbridge left in twenty-two minutes' time.

So Slade passed out of Victoria Station half an hour after his assistant. A mellow sun was glinting over the roof-tops of London, and after the train had passed through Croydon the air smelled fresher. Brighter autumn shades spangled the open spaces between the homes of Sanderstead, and by the time the train was passing through Woldingham long, open stretches of field and downland met the eye. Slade sat back and smoked, feeling a sudden content-ment, which he had not experienced at any time during the past thirty-six hours. He had had little sleep on the night before, and the keenness of the air pouring through the train window seemed to revive him.

He was fortunate at Tonbridge to find a Wenford bus about to start. The journey took about twenty-five minutes, and as soon as Slade alighted he set out for the station, where Clinton would be awaiting him. He came upon his assistant seated upon a low wooden bench against the fence on the opposite side of the road from the station. Clinton was keeping his eyes upon all comers. He rose as Slade approached.

"Can't make out why she came down here, sir," he muttered dolefully. "This place is right off the map. It's got me beat."

"Don't worry, Clinton," enjoined Slade, "that young woman doesn't do much without very good reason. You followed her all the way?"

"All the way to number sixteen Canterbury Road."

"Know whose place it is?"

"Not yet. But I know her visit wasn't expected."

"How?"

"I trailed her on the other side of the road, and watched when the front door was opened. The woman who opened it was obviously surprised to see her, and she spent a minute or two looking at her before she fell on her neck."

"Well, it won't take us long to find out who lives at number sixteen, Clinton."

It didn't. A call at No. 12, with a request if Mrs. Higgins was in, began a discussion regarding who it was the caller really wanted, during which Slade elicited that a Mrs. Ackroyd lived at No. 16. He met Clinton at the corner of Canterbury Road, and imparted his new piece of information.

"Now, Clinton, how was Mrs. Merrell dressed?"

"Same as last night, sir. Felt hat and fur coat, brown walking-shoes, and she had a small brown-leather attache-case."

"Right, then we'll pay a call at number sixteen."

The houses in Canterbury Road were terrace houses all of the same monotonous design. Small front gardens were bounded by wooden fences, painted more shades than the hues of the rainbow. Clinton waited on the pavement while Slade opened the front gate of No. 16 and knocked on the front door. He had to knock twice before approaching footsteps in the hall informed him that his summons had been heard.

The door was opened by a pleasant-faced woman with hair just turning grey. A pair of keen grey eyes that held a twinkle of humour regarded the detective with a level stare.

"Yes, sir, what can I do for you?"

"Excuse me, but I should like to speak to Mrs. Merrell for a moment," said Slade.

There was a long moment's pause, during which the pleasant-faced woman's eyes did not flicker once.

"I'm very sorry," she said at last, "but Mrs. Merrell left only a short while ago. She only paid a flying visit, and I don't think she was expecting anyone——"

"She wasn't," smiled Slade grimly. "Of course, you are quite sure that Mrs. Merrell has left——"

"Quite sure, sir," replied the woman, with a cheery smile, and closed the door.

For a moment Slade stood on the porch step listening to her retreating footsteps. He heard a door closed, and then rejoined Clinton.

"Playing for time, Clinton," he explained. "Of course, she *may* have gone, but I doubt it. She hasn't gone back to the station, that's certain. You would have spotted her——"

"Couldn't have missed her," affirmed the sergeant. "I've had the way to the station covered ever since I got here."

"Then either she's left for somewhere else in the village or else she's just waiting until we've disappeared off the scene—and I think the latter's the more likely. We'll keep this road covered. You take the station end, and I'll take the top end. If either sees her coming along, drop out of sight for a moment and pick her up after she's gone by."

They separated, walking along Canterbury Road in opposite directions. Nearly half an hour passed before Slade noticed a woman leave a house that might be No. 16, and walk quickly in his direction. She was dressed in a close-fitting brownish hat and a fur coat, and her shoes, he saw, were brown. She walked with her head lowered, as though she did not wish to be recognized by passers-by.

Slade turned down the road at the end of Canterbury Road and waited until she had passed by. He saw her cross the road and turn along one that branched off half-right. Giving her a few yards' lead, he turned back and followed her. After fifty yards or so the road the woman was walking down emptied into a country lane. The sun shone brightly on the drying pools in the lane, and birds were chirping in the fields and trees beyond the hedges. From a small hillside in the distance ahead the breeze carried the sound of a plough drawn by horses. They passed a small cottage, in the garden of which a little girl was singing a hymn-tune. She stopped in her play to smile at Slade as he walked by. The detective smiled back.

The woman in front was walking more quickly, and the Yard

man increased his own pace. He was wondering what her object was and where she was going. To tell the truth, he was not altogether easy in his mind. The road seemed to stretch ahead in a winding, unbroken line until it climbed the slope of the hill where the farm team was toiling.

Slade began to catch up with her. When he was almost alongside her she stopped and turned round. Just in time the detective stayed a violent exclamation. It was Mrs. Ackroyd, and her merry eyes were twinkling with mirth.

" It was really a shame, wasn't it?" she said, smiling charmingly. " But I've enjoyed the walk."

Slade had the grace to grin, though he was thinking unprintable things.

" I'm afraid I can hardly say the same, Mrs. Ackroyd. But perhaps I shall enjoy the walk back."

Already they had turned about and were retracing their steps. The woman put a hand on his arm.

" You mustn't think badly of my niece," she said, and her voice was more earnest. " She's not doing anything wrong."

" Well, she might have waited to tell me that herself," replied Slade.

" Yes, but then she would have missed the train back," explained Mrs. Ackroyd sweetly.

Suddenly Slade smiled. If the girl had gone to the station Clinton would have followed her. She would not have tricked him merely by changing her clothes. But the woman's next words caused the smile to disappear.

" She left by the back way," she continued. " You see, she wants to get back to her husband."

" Indeed! You surprise me!" Slade's expression was sour.

" I don't really think I do," murmured the woman gently.

But Slade did not reply, and they proceeded the rest of the way back to Canterbury Road without another word. Before the gate of No. 16 Mrs. Ackroyd paused.

" Well, she's gone now," she said. " Won't you and that other gentleman come in and have a cup of tea? The next train does not leave for some time."

All at once Slade's irate feeling vanished. The woman was really charming, and, after all, he had been tricked fairly. He should have been more awake to the chance of her duping him. It was a generous gesture on her part.

" Very well, Mrs. Ackroyd," he said, " I will fetch my assistant——"

"Yes, do! And perhaps you'll both take a snack of lunch. Oh, I'll see that you don't miss the next train!" she laughed.

"This is indeed very kind of you, Mrs. Ackroyd. I'm only sorry that circumstances——"

"Tut! Don't mention 'em. None of us can help doing our job. It's only that sometimes we don't understand the other fellow's—that's all."

"Yes, perhaps that is it——"

"Of course it is! Now, I'll get along indoors and put that kettle on——"

Slade went to find Clinton. He liked Mrs. Ackroyd. She was homely, and she had a way of making others feel at their ease. He was trying to explain this to an amazed and openly sceptical Clinton, who was tired and heartily sick of the view at the station end of Canterbury Road, when the sound of hurrying footsteps caused him to look round.

Hastening towards them, her hair streaming from under her hat, the fur coat flapping open behind her, was Mrs. Ackroyd. Her eyes were no longer smiling and gay, and her genial face had lost its cheerful expression of good-humour. She ran up to Slade and caught his arm.

"What is it?" he asked.

The woman was panting.

"It's Claire! She's lying on the kitchen floor! And it's gone!"

"What has gone? I don't understand——"

"The key!" said the woman, sobbing. "The key and the safe number she brought me!"

CHAPTER XIII

THE MERRELLS FACE THE FACTS

Mrs. Ackroyd brought a bowl of water, a sponge, and a bottle of smelling-salts into the small sitting-room at No. 16 Canterbury Road. Through the lace-net curtains a thin stream of autumnal sunlight mottled the well-brushed rug before the hearth. A stray beam gilded the bowl of dark red, velvety antirrhinums in the centre of the oak table and touched lightly the pale face of Claire Merrell as she opened her eyes and raised herself into a sitting position.

"What happened?" she murmured weakly.

Mrs. Ackroyd passed the bottle of smelling-salts once or twice more under the girl's nose.

"There, there, you'll feel better now, Claire."

The girl smiled feebly.

"But what *happened,* aunt? I—— Oh!" She held her head in both hands. "My head feels as though it will burst."

"How does your shoulder feel after the fall, Mrs. Merrell?"

The girl's hands dropped from her face. She turned her head suddenly, in a movement that caused her to wince, and she started.

"Inspector Slade—you here!"

She appeared to rally herself, and with a feeling of distinct doubt Slade saw the fighting light come back into her eyes. Wisely he attempted to pass off his presence with a smile.

"I always bring you trouble, don't I, Mrs. Merrell?"

For several moments the girl's eyes still remained hostile; then suddenly she smiled.

"Well, this is only the second time, inspector, but—— Oh, I remember now—that awful Jenkins!"

Slade and Clinton exchanged glances.

"What about Jenkins, Mrs. Merrell?" asked the C.I.D. man quietly, signing to the other woman to remain silent.

"Let me think now. Aunt had gone out after she had put the key"—she glanced at Slade quickly, but realized that it was too late to retrieve the slip, and went on—"in a drawer of the dresser in the kitchen, and I had put on her hat and coat, and was just going out the back way when the kitchen door opened and Jenkins came in."

"You're sure it was Jenkins—Ridley's manservant?"

"Yes, in spite of his purple and green eye! His face had an ugly look, and I could see he had come for trouble—though I didn't know he knew of aunt's place here. He told me to give him the key and the number disk——"

"The key and number disk to what?" asked Slade.

"To my—our—safe deposit."

Slade nodded gravely.

"Thank you. Please continue, Mrs. Merrell."

Before continuing the girl took a few sips from the glass of water her aunt had placed on the table. The beam of sunlight had shifted to a patch of the wall behind her, and in the shade her face now seemed more than usually pale. Deep, anxious lines were revealed beneath her eyes, and there was a furtiveness about her glance that informed the detective of her uneasiness in having to explain at all.

"I told him I did not know what he was talking about, and he just leered at me in a horrible way that was perfectly revolting. 'Give me that key and the number,' he said, 'or I'll smash in that pretty face of yours.' I told him again I did not know what he was talking about, and added that if he did not go I should call a policeman. At that he laughed again. '*You* call a policeman!' he sneered, and then he uttered some frightful oath, finishing up with 'Ain't that rich!' I became angry. I was frightened of the brute, although I could not let him think so. I started to the front door. 'Very well, then, I shall summon a policeman,' I said, but the minute I was out of the kitchen he was at the dresser and had pulled open the drawer. 'Well, give 'im my kind regards, an' don't ferget to tell 'im I got what I came for—*if* you calls 'im!' he shouted in a loud voice. I was dumbfounded. My movement towards the front door had only been bluff, as he must have guessed, and of course he must have been watching through the window of the kitchen door when aunt put the key and number disk in the drawer—that's how he knew where to look. He was laughing as he turned to go out again. That stung me. I realized all that the key meant and—and——"she stumbled, looking hesitantly at the detectives—"I simply had to do something. I rushed back into the kitchen. He turned round, and I seized his arm. I don't remember much more except the horrible look on his face as he swung his arm back. His blow caught me in the chest—and the next thing I remember is aunt here holding the smelling-salts under my nose."

"And your shoulder, Mrs. Merrell?" inquired Slade.

"It's throbbing a little, but I don't think I fell on that side."

The girl placed a hand to her wounded shoulder. She looked at the faces of the Yard men in turn.

"I must get back to my husband!" she exclaimed. "I simply must! This—this means everything to us!"

"I gathered that it meant a great deal, Mrs. Merrell," said Slade. "But I won't press you for details now. Your husband himself shall explain, and I rather think that there is much that requires explaining." He glanced at Mrs. Ackroyd, and the look of inquiry on the good woman's face informed him that she did not share the Merrells' secret, nor realized that they were involved in an ugly murder case. The girl was staring at him with troubled eyes, full of silent pleading. "A great deal, in fact," he added, and left it at that.

Instantly there came into the girl's face a look of grateful relief. "I'm ready to go back with you, inspector, when you are."

Slade regarded her doubtfully.

"Are you sure it wouldn't be taxing your strength too much, Mrs. Merrell?"

"Well, I was in a worse state when I got down to the telephone, wasn't I? And I wasn't in exactly good shape when I got away to the old landing-pier."

Her smile was winsome, and suddenly Slade realized that despite the deceit and artifice she had practised he liked her. She was playing a part, a part dictated by loyalty; the young wife with the finely shaped head and the splendid eyes was not a common crook, could not be. Slade knew enough of human nature and of what human nature was capable of to realize that. The girl was putting up a plucky show for her husband's sake. It was purely on his account that she was involved in this affair at all. But Slade was sure now, after this second strange meeting with the girl, that whatever her reason for being in the dangerous game was, it was an honest one. It needed strength of will, courage, and grit to do what this girl was doing, to go through what she had gone through, and still be prepared to go on with the odds against her. It was while she sat there smiling at him with that little pathetic smile that Slade realized the great clash of personality involved in this case. The hard and ruthless were pitted against the determined and purposeful; and there was danger. . . . Two men already had been slain, and this girl seated before him sat there only as the result of a lucky chance. Perhaps the girl was thinking much the same thoughts herself as she watched the serious light soften in Slade's eyes; she might have been remembering how he had been the one who had realized that danger was threatening from the draped window and had flung himself towards her, to protect her. Had Slade not moved when he had, and called sharply to the man by the door—

"But there is something you want to ask me first, isn't there, inspector?"

Only her lips moved; her glance remained fixed on his face, and it was as though she read his thoughts.

Slade straightened his back.

"Yes—one thing, Mrs. Merrell," he said. "Do you know anything about what happened to Haunchwood and Ferriss?"

She was grateful he had omitted the word "murder."

"Your husband, then?"

Her face clouded, and her glance dropped.

"He would not tell me."

No more was said about the affair then. Mrs. Ackroyd, after her niece had told her for the third time that she did not need to see a doctor, busied herself in preparing lunch for the four of them; and while she was engaged in the kitchen Clinton took a cautionary glance round the garden, whence Jenkins had appeared, and Slade listened to the girl's account of what a dear her aunt really was. Mrs. Ackroyd, it appeared, was the widow of her mother's brother. Her uncle had died years before, leaving a small pension to his widow, and Mrs. Ackroyd had taken the house in Canterbury Road because the rent was small and because Wenford was only a small place and she could easily get out into the Kentish country-side, of which she was particularly fond.

It was nearly three o'clock when the two detectives and Mrs. Merrell caught a train at Tonbridge, and it was half-past five when Slade got his car out of the garage and drove back to Victoria Station, where Clinton was waiting with Mrs. Merrell in the buffet. Slade made good speed along the road to Ploverton, and it was just after five and twenty to seven when he drew up outside the police-station and went in for a few words with Rayner. Luckily the inspector was in his office. As soon as he saw Slade he put aside the work he was engaged upon and swung round to give him all his attention. Briefly the Yard man recounted what had happened that day in the Kentish village, and Rayner's face became a strange study of conflicting impressions. The Yard man finished by asking him what developments had happened in Ploverton.

"None," said Rayner bluntly. "I followed Merton back here—or Merrell, rather—and I've got one of our plain-clothes men watching the Cedars right now. He didn't go into the Summerdale works today—in fact, he hasn't stirred outside the house. Evidently waiting for his wife to come home and report. The inquest on Haunchwood is at ten-thirty tomorrow morning, and I've had a chat with the coroner. Everything's all set for a quick adjournment. By the way," he added, "I see the papers have spread themselves about Ferriss and the mystery of the maroon saloon."

"Yes, I'm hoping for some result from the car, at any rate. I've got a man covering the inquest, which will be purely formal. I take it Haunchwood will be buried after the inquest?"

"Arrangements have already been made. The day following he'll be buried in St. Mary's Cemetery. Well, what've you got on the programme now?"

"I'm going to make Merrell talk. His wife is about done up, and silence won't aid either of them any longer. It's my opinion they're up against a tough proposition, one too hard to tackle on their own. Both of 'em have got to be made to see reason."

Rayner smiled.

"Well, if you're expecting to knock sense into a woman's head—and one who's prepared to pull a stunt like that at Tangles——"

He dropped his arms dramatically, and Slade rose.

"She's had some sense knocked into her, but not by me." He regarded the local man with a wry expression. "I may want you later on, Rayner, to come with me on a visit to Orton Lodge."

"Oh! Ridley again?"

"No, Jenkins this time. We may make him talk; and I've an idea his finger-prints will be known at the Yard."

Slade went out then, leaving the local man gaping.

Claire Merrell threw the Yard man a half-doubtful, half-wondering glance when at length he came out of the police station; but Slade did not look at her.

"Shan't be long now, Mrs. Merrell," was all he said as he set the car in motion again.

It was Merrell himself who answered Slade's ring at the front door. He stared when he caught sight of the two detectives with his wife, and a frown replaced the keen expression on his face.

"Why, Claire," he began, "whatever——"

She interrupted him.

"It's no good, Sid. We can't pretend any longer. Inspector Slade knows you're Sidney Merrell, and not Stanley Merton, and we've got to clear up this mess."

There was a tired inflexion in her voice. Her husband's manner instantly became tender, and the two Yard men were shown another side of Sidney Merrell's character from that they had witnessed the previous evening. He stood back to allow the others to enter, and after the housekeeper had taken Mrs. Merrell's coat and hat he led the way into the drawing-room.

"Claire," he said, in a worried voice, "you're very tired, my dear, and something has happened. You don't mean that——"

He stopped, his face paling as his wife nodded slowly.

"Yes, Sid—the key and number disk have been stolen!"

For an instant the young man flashed an angry glance at the detectives, but his wife hastened to correct his mistake.

"It was Jenkins! He must have found out and been there, expecting me——"

"Then Ridley——" He broke off, unable to find further words.

Claire Merrell sighed.

"Yes, Ridley's beaten us, Sid. We've been clever, but, my dear, not clever enough. We can't hold back the truth any longer, and you'll have to tell what you know."

Merrell took off his glasses and polished them slowly with a silk handkerchief. So far neither Slade nor Clinton had spoken a word. He turned to the former.

"I don't know whether you know what it's all about, inspector," he said, "but if you do you know I've played my hand and lost. . . . As Haunchwood and Ferriss played theirs. . . ."

"I know something, but not all, Mr. Merrell," replied Slade. "There is a great deal I do not understand. But you must realize, first, before you say anything further, that I am investigating two cases of murder. Two men were shot, killed, and the murderer remains at large. First of all I must ask you whether you were concerned in the murder of either Harold Ferriss or Morton Haunchwood—or in the murders of both?"

Merrell replaced his spectacles. He blinked at the electric standard lamp, which stood by the fireplace, casting a warm glow over the girl, who had sunk down into the armchair he himself had occupied during the detectives' previous visit. For several seconds he stared at nothing. Suddenly he faced Slade.

"No!"

Slade nodded curtly.

"Very good, Mr. Merrell. I might add now that the time has arrived to face the facts—so far as I know them. There are a number of questions which will have to be answered, and I'm afraid some of them will not sound quite pleasant——"

"Never mind the pleasantries!" interrupted Merrell. "We're quite willing to face the facts now. There's nothing else to do. I'm ready to answer your questions, inspector, but I can tell you beforehand that I have done nothing criminal—nor has my wife, who has done all she has merely to help me regain that which is mine."

"In that case, Mr. Merrell," said Slade, "I'll ask you, first of all: Do you know who murdered Haunchwood and Ferriss?"

Merrell took a deep breath, and behind the lenses of his spectacles his grey eyes appeared to widen until the whites almost extended to the rims.

"Yes, I do!" he muttered thickly.

CHAPTER XIV

A STRANGE STORY

"WHY—Sid!"

Claire Merrell was sitting forward in her chair, her gaze riveted upon the face of her husband. Merrell set his lips and nodded.

" I mean it, Claire! Remember, I said there was something I couldn't tell you? That was it. I can't say I saw Haunchwood murdered, or Ferriss, but I saw the same man in the two places at the times of the murders. That's good enough, isn't it?"

He thrust out his chin as he addressed the question to Slade.

" It's certainly convincing," agreed the Yard man. " Who was it?"

Merrell was about to reply, his lips were framing a name, when suddenly he thought of something else. He checked himself and levelled another question at the detective.

" Just a moment, inspector, suppose you tell me first what *you* know, eh? How much have you found out?"

An angry crease lined Slade's forehead, but the sight of Claire Merrell, her pale face turned towards him, stayed his sharp retort.

" I know, Mr. Merrell, that you are trying desperately to recover the equivalent of your uncle's missing fortune. Until three days ago you were in the field against Ridley on the one hand and Haunchwood and Ferriss on the other. All three were concerned in the Gelder Trust, operated companies it controlled—at least, on paper. I don't know, but I have an idea, that those three worked to break the trust, thinking to share in your uncle's private fortune, which they considered would be used to help out the trust. But your uncle saw through their game—too late to avert public disaster, but not too late to foil them gaining their real object. Am I right?"

Merrell rose. The last trace of hostility had gone from his face. He was smiling sheepishly.

" Inspector, I'd take off my hat to you—if I had one on. I didn't know there was another person outside we—er—principals, if the word suits, who knew the real game. Obviously Ridley and the other two worked under cover. They didn't know until lately that I was in the running. You see, I changed my name—and they didn't know me personally, you must understand—and with my wife's help got the job in the Summerdale works. I watched Ridley and the other two as a cat watches mice, but they've been deucedly clever; never made a false move. I found out little, though from time to time I believe Ridley had suspicions regarding me. But whenever we met he always kept the same front."

He walked across to a smoking-cabinet and produced a box of cigarettes.

" You'll smoke?"

When each was more comfortably settled with a lighted cigarette Merrell resumed.

"And now I'll answer your first question, inspector. It was Ridley who shot Haunchwood and Ferriss."

The pronouncement was received in silence that lasted for several minutes. Each person in the room was occupied with different thoughts.

It was Slade who spoke next.

"Before you tell me how you know that, Mr. Merrell, I should be glad if you would first explain what it is that you principals in the case—to use your own word—are striving to obtain. I shall understand the rest better once I know that."

Merrell nodded, and tapped an inch of ash from his cigarette.

"That takes us back to the time immediately before my uncle's suicide." He paused, considering what he was about to say. "As I told you, inspector," he continued, staring frowningly at the carpet between his feet, "my uncle realized that his great venture, the Gelder Trust, was being exploited by financial crooks, and the realization came too late to avert public disaster. I cannot explain—or hope to—all the many ramifications of the circumstances and facts, but what it all amounts to is that money was written down on paper that wasn't in the bank. There had been some clever jugglery going on of which my uncle had not been aware. You see, one company could not drop out of the trust without the whole bunch cracking up. The security of one meant the security of all. Well, for one there was no security. That was the Pyramis Trading Corporation, controlled by Haunchwood and Ferriss. When the Pyramis went bust the trust burst wide open, and nothing could patch the rent. You know the story. There was a scare. Stocks fell to rock-bottom, and even fell through the bottom. Options, agreements, contracts—everything was brought to a sharp close. Needless to say, the whole thing had been manipulated, cleverly, over a period of many months. My uncle could do nothing. There remained his considerable fortune that was not involved in any of the trust businesses. That fortune was the outcome of some twenty thousand pounds left him by his father. He had built it to a solid hundred and fifty thousand by clever investing. The trust was purely his own creation, the product of his great organizing ability. He had kept it apart, strictly, from all else with which he was concerned financially. In his later years it was not so much his money-making machine as his hobby, if you understand me. It was what he lived for, strove for, and worked to make prosperous."

Merrell paused. His cigarette had gone out. He flicked the charred stump into the grate. No one offered any comment, so he went on.

" One thing could save the trust, my uncle realized—his private fortune. But when he understood how the disaster had been engineered, when he knew that all the Gelder Trust companies' stock which was really worth anything, and which his own money would inflate, was held by Haunchwood and Ferriss and Ridley, he let the trust take care of itself. Of course, in the opinion of the public he was the prime criminal, the man who had commercially exploited his fellows and squandered their money, and he would be the scapegoat. He knew that once he was put into court his fortune would be taken from him, that he would have no say in the matter. His only object became to foil the schemers who had wrecked his life's greatest achievement. He thereupon decided to take his life, but, before doing so, to dispose of his fortune in a way that would ensure its safety. Let him be declared a bankrupt, not a penny of that hundred and fifty thousand would be touched."

" How did he do it?" asked Slade, who was intensely interested.

Merrell looked up and smiled a slight, wintry smile.

" That was the cause of all this trouble, inspector—the way he did it."

He paused again, weighing his words, and when he resumed he was watching his wife, whose eyes were closed. She seemed to be dozing.

" Of course, in a lifetime of business affairs my uncle made many commercial contacts abroad, inspector. But there was one firm with whom he was very friendly, an Italian firm—Antonio Merillo's, a private banking firm with connections in the States. Several times in the past, so I understand, my uncle arranged pieces of business for the firm in this country, and he had become friendly with Merillo himself. Now, when the trust disaster arrived Merillo's were about to float a short-term loan of about a quarter of a million pounds for some mining venture with sound credentials. You understand, it would be a loan with large interest, a sort of temporary affair among friends—nothing public about it. Only wealthy bankers and suchlike were to be in on it, and Merillo's themselves were putting up about a hundred thousand of the quarter million. To cut the story short, my uncle subscribed the other hundred and fifty thousand—but upon certain conditions, to which Merillo, who was taken into his confidence, agreed. A series of fifteen certificates was arranged for the loan, each for the sum of ten thousand pounds. Number one of the series my uncle sent to myself, his only living relative. I might here interrupt the story, inspector, to tell you that he had been as a father to me. He it was who educated me and brought me up with a taste for art and literature, and made life comfortable. I was married about six months before the trust trouble arose, and he had agreed to give me a really responsible post in one of the trust companies. However, that's all by the by. To get back to the peculiar arrangement he made with Merillo's. The other fourteen certificates he hid somewhere in his old country house of Tangles, on the opposite side of the river from here. I might say that he had left it about the time of my marriage, and until Haunchwood and Ferriss managed to get it after the crash it remained unfurnished."

Again Merrell stopped. But he was telling his story so completely that there was no need for Slade to interrupt with a query. The young man leaned forward and glanced closely at his wife.

"Asleep, Claire?" he asked softly.

The girl opened her eyes and smiled.

"No, Sid, just tired. Go on. You're telling it well."

The husband nodded and moistened his lips with his tongue.

"The arrangement about the certificates, as I understand it to have been, was something like this, inspector. The loan was made for eighteen months, at the end of which time it would be repaid to Merillo's by the company concerned. Now, my uncle arranged with Merillo's that cash should not be given for the certificates at the end of the stipulated period unless they were all surrendered together. However, an exception was made—namely, certificate number one—the one he sent me. If that certificate alone was surrendered any time during the month after the period of the loan was up ten thousand pounds would be paid for it. But in that event the remaining capital would automatically be placed at the discretion of Antonio Merillo for distributing as advantageously as he could, the interest to come to myself. In short, if those other fourteen certificates were not surrendered within that one month, together with certificate number one, then they became valueless."

"I think I understand, Mr. Merrell," said Slade, nodding. "An ingenious scheme—which safeguards you, but which allows you to handle and dispose of the complete capital only if you can present the entire series of certificates during that month. Am I right?"

"Perfectly. But, unfortunately, as you may have guessed, I haven't those certificates—and the first week of that month is nearly gone!"

Slade now began to understand something of the urgency that had dictated the recent movements in this desperate game for a fortune.

"But you still hold the key to the situation, don't you?" he reminded the young man. " You still hold certificate number one."

" Not now."

Slade became more interested.

" How's that, Mr. Merrell?"

" That certificate we placed in a safe deposit. The key was left at my bank until a few days ago, when we decided to have it some-where where we could get it at any hour. You see, we thought we might want it suddenly—if we secured those other certificates! But we didn't, and after what has happened we decided that we had better hide the key somewhere else, and my wife thought of her aunt. She took her the key today. You know the rest."

Slade gave Merrell a straight look.

" I know that your wife said Jenkins took it."

" Of course!" exclaimed the other. " Jenkins is working for Ridley. Now Ridley has the complete series. Let him present those certificates at the London agents of Merillo's and he'll have to be given a hundred and fifty thousand pounds—or its equivalent."

" You're sure Ridley has the other fourteen certificates?"

Merrell laughed harshly.

" Not a doubt."

" But didn't your uncle leave some document or other explaining all this procedure? And wouldn't the presenting of this docu-ment be sufficient to cause Merillo's to suspend payment?"

The young man's expression became cynical.

" There was a letter. It was stolen. My wife saw its contents. I never have. It was stolen within a few hours of my uncle's blowing his brains out. . . . But supposing I *had* the letter, and supposing I *did* present it and Ridley contested Merillo's decision—what would be the result?"

" You mean to say that there would be another inquiry opened, and the money would be confiscated to reimburse the people who suffered in the crash of the——"

" The people who were fleeced by a party of crooks for their own ends!" exclaimed Merrell hotly, and Slade accepted the amendment without comment.

" Very well, then, now tell me how you know Ridley has the complete series, Mr. Merrell," said the detective.

Merrell clasped his fingers and unclasped them. He was growing excited, and the more he talked the more he was working himself up into a state of nervous restlessness. At last he folded his arms and stared moodily across the room to where a sea-etching hung on the wall.

" I told you, inspector, that my wife and I decided to regain those certificates. Well, we were too late to secure Tangles, so we took this place, and, as I've already explained to you, I got the post with the Summerdale Brickmaking Company, whose true history and actual worth I knew, so that I could keep an eye upon Ridley. My wife tells me that in his letter my uncle never actually explained whereabouts in Tangles he had hidden the certificates; but he doubtless thought that in eighteen months I should be able to find them. He hadn't bargained for Haunchwood's stepping into the place before I could. However, the affair resolved itself into a game of watching and waiting. I was watching Ridley and the pair across the river, and Ridley and they were watching each other, and, as I now know, Ridley was watching me also—though when he first suspected me I can't say. Meanwhile we were all waiting—and anxiously. Haunchwood must have discovered the certificates recently, because I was fortunate enough at the works to find in one of Ridley's files some letters addressed to Ferriss at the Mayfair address. You see, Haunchwood and Ferriss were still operating one or two shady concerns in the City, but down here they were man and master. Well, when Haunchwood had made his find Ridley discovered the fact in some way or other, and made overtures to Ferriss. A bargain was struck between them, and I knew that if they pooled chances my own were even more remote than they seemed then—which, heaven knows, were remote enough! But I still had number one then, and was hopeful, as I knew they could do nothing without that first certificate. I was prepared to find Ridley making overtures to me, and had my answers ready— but he was too cunning. However, I gummed up his game with Ferriss, and, in a way, I am responsible for Ferriss's death—though it would have come sooner or later. Ridley is a double-crosser born and bred."

"How do you come to be responsible for Ferriss's murder?" asked Slade, with a curt nod in Clinton's direction.

The sergeant had taken out his notebook, and was engaged in jotting down questions and answers and such of Merrell's story as he deemed necessary for future consideration. Merrell had thrown him several uneasy glances, and Slade hastened now to reassure him.

"You need not feel concerned about the notes Sergeant Clinton is taking down, Mr. Merrell," he said. "They are merely for reference."

Merrell nodded.

"I understand," he said, not, however, without a further doubtful glance at the industrious sergeant. "But to answer your question, inspector." His eyes moved to Slade's face, and remained watching the detective. "When you showed me that letter last night I told you a lie. I had seen it before. I typed it and wrote that signature. I, in fact, sent it to Ferriss—and this was my purpose. I had discovered notes on a piece of paper in Ridley's private-letter file, which he kept locked up in a cupboard in his office, and these told me that he had arranged to meet Ferriss in Ploverton. I precipitated things by sending that letter, which stopped Ferriss from turning up—and as a result Ridley thought he was being double-crossed and got mad. The upshot was that he went up to Tangles in a motor-boat one night. I watched him with a pair of night-glasses. He landed and tied his boat to the old landing-stage. Some time later I heard the sound of a shot across the river. Minutes went by, and at last I saw two figures come down to the moored motor-boat. One, I knew, must be Ridley; the other must be either Haunchwood or Ferriss. I couldn't tell, of course. But it was plain that the second man was being compelled to accompany Ridley. I had no idea what had happened, though murder did cross my mind. Still, I couldn't be sure. The motor-boat left the landing-stage, and headed upstream.

"Well, I dashed outside, got out my car, and rushed to Ploverton. I hung about by the London road on the offchance of catching a sight of the two as they made their way to Orton Lodge. I waited nearly twenty minutes, cursing myself for being such a fool. I was about to give up, thinking I had missed them, when I saw a car I recognized rushing towards me. Ridley's car. Luckily I was in the shade, or he'd have seen me. There were two men in the car, and after it had rushed by where I was waiting I turned about and went after it. The chase led to—Twickenham!"

"Twickenham!" echoed Slade, while Clinton glanced up frowningly.

"Yes. And this will show you how well Ridley's plans had been made. At Twickenham he turned off into a place called Oxford Mews, where he had a lock-up garage. I crept to the end of the mews and watched. He had a gun in his hand and the man he was covering was Ferriss. I can see his face now, white— ghastly white; the man was quaking with fear. I don't think——"

"But why did Ridley stop at the garage?" interrupted Clinton, whose wrist was aching.

Merrell was brought up with a jar.

"Why? . . . Because he wanted to change cars. He left his usual car there, and took out the maroon saloon with the same number as my wife's!"

"Ah! That's a point I want to clear up," said Slade. "How

did Ridley come to know about your wife's car, and why was he so keen to implicate her?"

The young man took a handkerchief from his pocket and wiped his face.

" I'll answer your second question first, inspector," he said. " By implicating my wife—or, at least, getting her involved in some police inquiry—he would have me off my guard, and he would be in a better position to get the all-important first certificate. And now the first question. I've already told you that I don't know when he first came to suspect me, but I've already told you that it was through my wife that I managed to get the job with the Summerdale firm. To be a little more explicit, she got some friends to give me a recommendation which wasn't—well, altogether justified, as I'd had no previous experience of such office work. However, that's merely incidental, a simple fraction of the whole compound equation. What is significant is that Ridley could have traced my wife's part in the recommendation when he suspected me, and when he learned who she was—why, then my secret was out. He knew who I was, what I and my wife were after, of course, and he arranged his hand accordingly.

" For instance, there was a red-haired johnny who used to hang about outside my wife's place of business in Shaftesbury Avenue. He would follow her from place to place, so that she daren't meet me as arranged. That thing went on for some time. We never found out definitely who the man was; he was pretty elusive, and he never appeared when I was around. But I've an idea it was Jenkins, snooping about, thinking Claire would lead him to the hiding-place of the first certificate.

" But I don't know even now if it really was Jenkins, or if——"

" I think I may be able to help you there, Mr. Merrell," said Slade.

" You, inspector!" exclaimed Merrell, starting, and looking at the detective sharply.

" Yes. I was at your wife's shop yesterday. I went there after I drew blank at her flat in Stanthorpe Mansions. You just beat me to it——"

He was interrupted by Mrs. Merrell, who was now sitting upright once more.

" You saw that horrid man outside the shop yesterday. Is that what you mean, inspector?" she queried.

" More than that, Mrs. Merrell. He actually went in the shop and asked for you."

Merrell sprang to his feet.

"That's Jenkins for sure—curse him!" he ejaculated. "Ridley shot you, Claire, at Tangles, thought he'd done for you, and, like the cunning swine he is, he sent Jenkins to London to make sure."

"But why should Ridley have shot your wife, Mr. Merrell?"

The young man's nerves were beginning to fray under the strain of the examination.

"Can't you guess?" he snapped more brusquely than hitherto, and something of his previous truculence appeared in his manner. "He was out there, listening. He was a murderer, and he'd got those fourteen certificates. The time was ripe to cash in. All he'd got to do to get a hundred and fifty thousand pounds was secure the first of the series. Well, what chance would he have if Claire was forced to tell the police the whole complicated rigmarole, spill the names of the parties concerned? He wouldn't be able to get out of the country, for you'd have been after him. He was too clever to consider whether Claire *wanted* to tell, for *our* sake."

Merrell slumped down into his chair again, the fire dying out of his eyes.

"But what's the good of chewing the rag now, anyway? Ridley's got us whacked. He's got the whole bunch of certificates, and he'll be off. Tomorrow he'll be gone, and you won't have a chance to tell him no."

He spoke dispiritedly.

"I can promise you I'll do what I can, Mr. Merrell. But I shall want to know the rest of what happened on the night Haunchwood and Ferriss were murdered. You'd got as far as the lock-up garage in Twickenham—remember?"

Merrell sighed, and once more plunged into this very involved and lengthy story. Again Clinton turned over a new leaf of his notebook and settled his cuff so as to leave his hand free to move more readily.

"In the maroon car Ridley drove to the house in Cheviot Crescent, where he and Ferriss got out. Ferriss had a key in his pocket, and let them in. When the door had closed after them I ran my car into a side-street—I forget its name now—and came back into Cheviot Crescent. Some time passed. At last I saw Ridley come out of the house alone, pause to glance quickly up and down the street, and then dive into his car. The next moment he was tearing off. There was nothing I could do. I was at a complete standstill. I'd followed him and Ferriss to London, but had learned nothing except about the change of cars. I certainly wondered what had happened to Ferriss, but I hadn't heard the sound of a revolver-shot——"

"You wouldn't have," explained Slade. "Ferriss was shot in one of the rear rooms."

"I naturally supposed the obvious," resumed Merrell, "namely, that Ferriss had remained there. However, I had guessed why those two had rushed to London. Although Haunchwood and Ferriss were lying low at Tangles, they were keeping up a few old contacts in London, and Ferriss was the one who was attending to that end of the business from the house in Cheviot Crescent. He may even have used Haunchwood's name. That was a trick that was not unusual to them—to change *rôles*. Ask anyone who has lost money in the Pyramis. I bet you they can't tell you which was Haunchwood and which Ferriss for certain. That's why——"

"Just a moment," interrupted Slade. "Something's occurred to me, which you might be able to explain. You said, earlier, that Haunchwood and Ferriss and Ridley all combined to bring about the crash of the Gelder Trust. Yet here the three prime-movers are divided into opposite camps——"

"Of course they were!" cried Merrell, growing excited again. "Originally their idea was to force my uncle to throw his fortune into the melting-pot they'd prepared. They'd have come out with shares at booming prices, and have cleared three fortunes. But when they found that they'd manipulated the market all for nothing save the disintegration of the trust their joint loyalty terminated abruptly. Further, when they became aware of what my uncle had done it was each for himself—except that Haunchwood and Ferriss had been together in shady dealing so long that they naturally pulled the same strings this time too. Is it clear now, inspector?" added Merrell.

"Yes." Slade nodded thoughtfully. "I see the position more clearly now, thanks. Will you please go on?"

"Well," Merrell resumed, "when Ridley had gone I began wondering about what had happened at Tangles. I didn't know at the time—didn't guess—why Ferriss had come to London, to get the certificates he had hidden in the house there. I thought only of the chance of at last being able to get into Tangles. There had never been an opportunity before. So I phoned my wife, and told her briefly what had happened, and what I wanted her to do. She agreed, and said she would drive down at once. She'd got a key, but we didn't know if there had been a fresh lock put on the door. Anyway, she was game to have a shot. The certificates might be there—and, at least, it was a chance. We agreed that if there was any interruption she was to pretend she had received a phone call from Haunchwood, her uncle, and try to bluff the rest. She knew

Ferriss was the butler—at least supposed butler—at Tangles——"

"Ah! That raises another point," interrupted Slade, turning to Claire Merrell. "That photograph you had in your handbag, Mrs. Merrell. How did you come by it?"

The girl smiled slightly.

"Ask Sid," she invited.

Slade glanced at her husband, and stared when he saw that Merrell was blushing self-consciously.

"You see, inspector," said the young man, "I'm a bit of an amateur photographer. As you know, I've a boat at the end of the garden—the one I rowed Claire across in yesterday—and I've made several trips across to the grounds of Tangles, and upon several occasions I took with me a small folding camera with an automatic snapping device at the end of a longish rubber tube. I had the idea some months ago of getting some snaps of Haunchwood and Ferriss that might later come in useful—that might provide me with a means of arguing my case if it came to a pinch——"

Slade's eyes twinkled. "A gentle form of blackmail, eh?"

Merrell's flush mounted.

"I honestly don't know if it was an intention so criminal as that, inspector. Indeed, it was never any more than a vague notion at the back of my mind, and the only results it ever produced was that snap of Ferriss's head and shoulders between the trees. Claire carried a print about with her. I don't know why. A whim—she thought it might come in useful——"

"It did," Slade assured him. "I found it invaluable. And that photograph has saved you a terrific amount of extra explaining, Mr. Merrell."

"Well, I'm glad to learn the snap's done some good. It nearly got me caught out. Ferriss heard the click of the shutter, and for a moment I thought he had tumbled to what had happened, but after a long glance round he went off, and I was free to get back to the boat. I can tell you that experience cooled my ardour to get some snapshots, inspector!"

"I can well believe you," grinned the Yard man, winking at Clinton, who had just looked up after hiding a smile in his hand.

Merrell wiped his face with his handkerchief again, and settled his spectacles more comfortably on his nose.

"Well, I think you've got about the whole story, inspector. That's the finish of the case, so far as I'm concerned. We're licked."

"Oh, don't say that, Sid!" exclaimed his wife. "Ridley hasn't got away yet. Inspector Slade here——"

She stopped. Slade was obviously thinking of something else. Husband and wife both waited for the Yard man's next question. It was not long in forthcoming.

"How did you get back to Ploverton, Mr. Merrell, upon the night of the murders?"

"Drove back."

"Have you any idea how Ridley got back?"

"I saw this morning's papers, and read about his losing the car in the Edgware Road district. Quite likely he took a train from Paddington. It wasn't very late then. He could have walked from the station to where he had moored the motor-boat, and have gone downstream to Tangles again. Anyway, that's apparently what he did do. The swine, to try to murder Claire!"

There was an uncomfortable silence in the room for a few minutes. Suddenly Slade asked:

"Has Ridley consistently been a trickster, as far as you know, Mr. Merrell?"

The young man snorted.

"About the only decent thing I've ever heard him do is allow that poor old girl to live rent free in the cottage below Orton Lodge. I suppose having her there lends him some sort of reputation in the district. You can bet there's a reason for her being there, inspector. Ridley'll make some use of the poor old thing—don't doubt that!"

Merrell's voice rang cynically. Slade turned to the woman. Her gaze was averted.

"There was a burglary at Orton Lodge last night," the detective inserted casually. "I'm not going to ask either of you if you know anything about it—but one of you tell me this. Were the burglars successful in their search? I didn't think, myself, that they were!"

Husband and wife regarded each other doubtfully. It was the woman who spoke.

"I don't think they were successful, Mr. Slade," she said softly.

Slade turned abruptly to Clinton.

"I think that's all meantime, eh, Clinton?"

The sergeant nodded.

"Yes, I think so, sir."

Slade got to his feet.

"If you'll excuse me for a few moments, there's one of Rayner's men outside that I'd like a word with."

Merrell smiled bitterly.

"That's all right. Go ahead. We've no reason for stopping

you doing what you like—now. Just see—— Oh, it doesn't matter!"

The young man picked up another cigarette and lit it. Slade opened the door and moved into the hall. He trod on a thick carpet, which deadened his footfall, and so the woman bent over the telephone did not hear his approach. The instant he realized what she was doing Slade slunk back against the doorway of the drawing-room. From where he stood he caught a glimpse of the light shining on her darkish grey hair and her bowed shoulders. Her voice was lowered, the conspiratorial tones of someone who is saying something she realizes must not be overheard.

She was saying :

" No, no, Jim! I tell you he's spilt the lot. You'd better look lively now, or those Yard men'll catch up. . . . No, you can't do that. No! Better meet me tonight. Where? What time? Oh . . . somewhere where we can be sure we won't be interrupted. Say the corner of the lane leading to the brickworks about quarter past twelve. Suit you? Good!"

As the receiver clicked home Slade slipped into the darkness of the drawing-room and gently pulled the door to after him.

CHAPTER XV

A TRAP

Rayner stared at Slade unbelievingly.

" But it's absurd, man!" he expostulated. " That house-keeper, Mrs. Stourbridge, has been at the Cedars as long as Merton, or Merrell rather, has had the place. I can't imagine her being linked up in this affair. She's known in Ploverton and——"

" That's all right, Rayner—only this woman isn't Mrs. Stourbridge," said Slade.

" Eh?" Rayner sat more upright. " What's this?"

" A couple of days ago Mrs. Stourbridge said she had to go to Ploverton to look after her daughter-in-law, and she recommended this woman to fill her place while her daughter-in-law was sick. But the point is—who's Jim?"

" Search me?" the local inspector invited. The Yard man had spent half an hour recounting in brief all that had transpired at the Cedars, Merrell's story, the truth about the whole mystery, and that last final surprise as Slade was about to leave the house. At first

Rayner had been openly regretful that he had missed attending the interview, but he had now put aside his regret in order to think more clearly about this new angle to the case.

"Do you believe all this about Ridley?" he asked Slade, point-blank.

"What can I say?" countered the Yard man. "I know no more than you——"

"Sure of that?" interposed Rayner slyly.

"Well," laughed Slade, "not enough to make any appreciable difference to my reasoning. In fact, I know less about the people here. This Jim now——"

But Rayner still had no suggestion to offer. He shook his head.

"There's only one thing for it, then," pronounced Slade at last, in a decisive tone.

"What's that?"

"Find Mrs. Stourbridge's daughter-in-law. That woman's been paid to remain off the scene; you can bet on that, Rayner. Do you know the woman's daughter-in-law?"

"No, but I believe I know how to find where she lives."

Rayner went to the door of his office and shouted down the corridor in an echoing voice: "Bartlett, come along here, man!"

A young policeman appeared and saluted smartly.

"You called me, sir?"

"Yes, Bartlett. You've got a brother in the Ploverton Rovers football team, haven't you?"

"That's right, sir. Alf—the next one to me."

"Does he know a fellow named Stourbridge?"

"Do you mean Ray Stourbridge, the Rovers' centre-half, sir? Well, Alf's rather friendly with him; as a matter of fact, sir——"

"Then you know where Stourbridge lives, Bartlett?"

"Yes, sir. Deacon's Row—number eight."

"Thanks, Bartlett. That'll be all."

The young policeman saluted again and retired after throwing a wondering glance at the silent and seated forms of Slade and Clinton. As the door closed behind him Rayner turned to Slade.

"Well, shall we go along?"

"Seems the best chance of finding out about 'Jim,'" nodded Slade.

Rayner knew where Deacon's Row lay, a narrow street at the station end of the little town. A single-fronted public-house stood on one corner, and at the opposite end of the street was a Salvation Army hall. No. 8 was half-way down, on the more prosperous-looking side of the road—that is, the side boasting the public-house.

The sound of Slade's car driving down the little street caused a few curious heads to appear at windows.

"About the only car that comes down here is the doctor's," Rayner leaned across to confide. "I'll wager a good many are already laying odds as to who's got a fresh addition to the family. Hallo! Here's the house we want."

In answer to Rayner's knock a young woman appeared at the door.

"Who is it?" she inquired, peering up at them out of the darkness of the passage-way.

"I'm Inspector Rayner, Mrs. Stourbridge. I understand your mother-in-law is here. I should like to see her—it's very important."

For several moments the young woman hesitated until a door at the end of the passage opened and a man's voice inquired, "What is it, Mary?"

"Nothing, Ray. Only some gentlemen to see your mother——"

"To see me, Mary?" asked a deeper voice, and another form appeared behind the young woman's. "Who is it wants to see me, Mary?"

"I do, Mrs. Stourbridge. I'm Inspector Rayner, and, as I've just told your daughter-in-law, it's very urgent."

"You'd better come along inside, sir," said the younger Mrs. Stourbridge. "Ray!" she called. "Bring a match and light the gas in the front room."

Her husband entered the front room, scraped a match, lit the crazy gas-mantle, that threatened to disintegrate at the slightest disturbance of the air in the room, and pulled down a lop-sided Venetian blind. The streak of gas-flame escaping through the broken mantle purred insistently on an unpleasant note.

"Sit yourselves down, gentlemen," invited the young man. "Now, mother, you come over here—and if she's been a bad girl, inspector, just you call me," he grinned as he ushered his wife out and left the policemen and the elder woman alone.

Slade nodded to Rayner, and the local man undertook to do the talking.

"Mrs. Stourbridge, you told your employer, Mr. Merton, that you would be away for a few days, because your daughter-in-law needed you. Is that right?"

"Yes, sir." The woman nodded, but she was already looking uneasy.

"You said your daughter-in-law was sick."

"I—well, you see, sir, I had to give some sort of *reasonable* explanation for wanting to be away."

"And also for suggesting that another woman take your place! You've been very rash, Mrs. Stourbridge," said Rayner severely.

The woman's rather bony hand flew to her mouth.

"But nothing's happened, has it, sir? He said it was only for a day or two, and then I could go back . . . and—and he offered me three pounds!"

"Ah! So you were—bribed!" Rayner uttered the word in an unpleasant way that made the woman squirm. Tears gathered in her eyes.

"Oh, sir, I haven't done anything wrong, have I? You see, it was like this, sir. He came to me an' he said a friend of his sister had got the offer of a good job down in Gloucestershire somewhere as housekeeper—but she hadn't got a single reference. He said she was almost certain to get the job—a good, comfortable place, sir—if she had only one reference even—just to sort of show she'd held the position before. In fact, it was all fixed up 'cept for her showing the reference. Well, he said it was worth three pounds to his sister's friend if she could get the chance of serving at the Cedars for a few days—a week at most—so that she could ask Mr. Merton for a reference. He'd be sure to give her one, he said. Well, sir, three pounds is three pounds, and I want some new shoes and a mackintosh, and, after all, it was giving someone else a chance I wasn't likely to get myself in a hurry, and, besides, I've always felt that to be a sort of dog in the manger when one has a real opportunity for doing a bit of a good turn to someone as——"

"Yes, yes!" interposed Rayner quickly, as soon as he saw an opening. "But who is 'he'? Who fixed all this up, and gave you the three pounds?"

The woman opened her eyes wide.

"Why, sir—Jenkins! Mr. Ridley's man. You know, sir, Mr. Ridley that lives at Orton Lodge, the manager of the Summerdale works."

"Oh, so it was Jenkins, was it?"

"Yes, sir. That's right, sir. But he didn't give me the three pounds, as you said. He *promised* it, sir."

"And when are you going back to the Cedars, Mrs. Stourbridge?"

"I don't know. Jenkins was to drop me a line. Then I was to go along and see Mr. Merton, sir."

"I see." Rayner gazed at the woman reflectively. "I wonder, now, Mrs. Stourbridge, could you tell me Jenkins's Christian name?"

"Well, as it happens, sir, I can. Though I shouldn't know it only he took me to meet his sister's friend. You see, I was to take her to the Cedars and explain to Mr. Merton, and sort of introduce her. And it was when we met her that I heard her call him by his Christian name."

" And what was it?" snapped the impatient Rayner.

Mrs. Stourbridge blinked at his sudden change of tone. Tears gathered in her eyes again.

" James, I suppose," she said tremulously. " Leastways, she called him Jim."

The three policemen were driving back to the station in Slade's car before either one of them offered any comment upon this recent discovery.

" It certainly looks as if Ridley meant to get either the certificate or the key to the deposit box that holds it," reflected Rayner aloud, " to go to the length of getting someone on the inside. Now we know how Jenkins came to be down in Kent."

" Exactly," said Slade, watching the road ahead. " She heard Merrell and his wife discussing the matter last night before they left for London, heard what they proposed to do—and phoned Orton Lodge. Jenkins took it easy, doubtless; arrived in Wenford in plenty of time and just strolled round the backways to the houses in Canterbury Road. Pretty easy, eh?"

" Childish!" snorted Rayner. " And it all looked so hellishly complicated!"

" It isn't all cleared up yet—by a long way," promised Slade, and promptly became silent again.

Once more in the inspector's office at the police station, Rayner asked his *confrère,* " What next?"

" Better ring Merrell, Rayner, and tell him to be on the alert about midnight, and follow the woman when she leaves, but to take every precaution against being seen by her, or that'll give the entire show away and ruin a splendid chance we've got to get Jenkins where we want him."

Rayner stared at his blotter.

" Think it's wise to bring Merrell into it?"

Slade nodded.

" Absolutely! This is a trap, Rayner. And one of the things I want to find out is—does Jenkins really know who gave him such a lovely black eye? If he does, the presence of Merrell will set him on edge. I want him to be on edge. I want a set of his finger-prints."

Rayner whistled.

" Think he's an old lag, then?"

"Sure of it, though I've never met him before. What's more, now I know how that woman got to the Cedars, I'd stake a tidy pile of chips that she's seen the inside of quod. When a woman's got a long nose *and* deep-set eyes—look out!"

"I take it she's got 'em," grinned Rayner.

"And a jaw far too square to be beautiful."

Rayner leaned forward and picked up the telephone receiver from its cradle on his desk.

"All right. I'll get Merrell. Hallo! Oh, get me the Cedars on the phone—ask for Mr. Merton."

He put down the receiver and waited for his call to be put through. The three men smoked in silence till the phone bell rang. It did not take Rayner long to make Merrell understand what was wanted of him, and when he put down the receiver for the second time he turned to Slade and said, "Now for the details. What are *we* going to do in setting the trap?"

"We're going to bait it," said Slade thoughtfully.

"But the bait?" queried Rayner, puzzled. "Who'll be the bait?"

"Jenkins," replied Slade and smiled slowly.

CHAPTER XVI

JENKINS TAKES IT QUIETLY

SLADE, Clinton, and Rayner were at their stations at the corner of the lane leading up to the Summerdale brickworks by a quarter past midnight. The night was cold, and across the brickfield blew a steady breeze. Fortunately the moon appeared only at lengthy intervals. High banks of cloud were floating across the sky, and rain threatened. Slade's car had been left farther up the lane, under a hedge. The three policemen did not allow themselves the luxury of a smoke during their wait, and, remaining crouched in a small ditch, the bottom of which was covered with two inches of glutinous mud that did not smell too sweetly, the minutes seemed to drag by with intentional slowness.

It was nearly five and twenty to one when they caught the sound of someone approaching along the road towards the lane. There was nothing they could do save listen.

"A man's step," whispered Rayner. "Jenkins!"

It was Jenkins all right. He stepped round the corner of the lane just as the moon sailed majestically out of a dark bank of cloud.

For several seconds the lane and the road stretching beyond were bathed in a white, clear light; and standing by the hedgeside, not four feet away from the concealed men, smoking a cigarette, was Jenkins. There was no mistaking him. The moonlight struck across his face and revealed the large bruise under one eye.

The moon disappeared; darkness descended again; and the wait continued. Jenkins finished his cigarette and lit another from the glowing stump of the first. He began pacing the end of the lane, stamping his feet. Once he yawned, and stretched his neck as he did so.

"It'd fit a noose beautifully!" grunted Rayner in Slade's ear, as he watched through a leafy screen.

Ten minutes more passed. The clock of the parish church in Ploverton chimed the third quarter. The last note was still reverberating softly in the night air when Slade caught the sound of fresh footsteps, hurrying—small steps, a woman's.

"Oh, 'ere you are at last, Maud! You're blasted punctual, ain't you?"

Mr. Jenkins's temper had not worn well during his wait.

"Couldn't 'elp it, Jim. You said if I was to meet you any time to come this end. Well, it's a longish walk, and that Riverside Road ain't safe at this time o' night——"

"It ain't with you about, Maud!" Jenkins chuckled at this heavy witticism, and the woman clicked her tongue. "Well, let's 'ave it. Wot did you learn?"

The woman clicked her tongue again.

"Plenty. That Yard 'tec Slade, as he calls himself, has got the whole tale out of Merton or whatever he calls hisself, and your boss is in for it—take it from me!"

"How much did Merrell—*that's* 'is name, if you wants to know—say? Did 'e mention those two?"

"Yes. He knew all about the murders. Was watching with night-glasses, and he followed the car to London, and was in Cheviot Crescent when Ferriss was done in."

Jenkins drew a long breath.

"Crikey! It's bad, Maud. It's worse—it's ugly! I don't like it. We ain't all shipshape yet. I got the key today, but that ain't the bit o' paper itself, is it?"

"Jim," said the woman, "what do you stand to get out of this?"

"Now, look here, Maud," said Jenkins severely, "you mind your nose and it won't get tweaked—see? That's 'ow it is with you and me, and don't go forgettin' it, my girl. I'm getting all I want—and more than other people want to give me. I'll tell you that much, but that's all. So mark me words. Jim Jenkins is a bit smarter than some folk give 'im credit for."

"But, Jim," pleaded the woman, "I'm frightened! You got me into this. If those two Yard men find out——"

"Shut up!" snarled Jenkins. "I'm looking after this. Leave it to me, can't you? Didn't bring me all the way out 'ere jus' ter whine, did yer?"

A flood of bright moonshine illuminated the dark world at that moment, and the watchers behind the hedge saw the woman flinch at the man's words.

"Jim, you didn't tell me there'd been *murder*! You left me to find it out, and you can't expect——"

"Huh! I can expect a dammed deal, Maud. What's more— I do! You're going to mind what I say. Keep that mouth of yours shut or——"

He never explained the alternative. A heavy hand placed on his shoulder caused him to swing about with a wild and lurid oath, to stare into the coldly hostile eyes of the chief of Department X2.

"Save it till you get to the station, Jenkins. You'll have a chance there to do all the explaining you want to—and more."

Jenkins tried to wrench his shoulder free of that restraining grasp, found the effort futile, and rounded on the woman angrily.

"This is your doing, Maud—you —— nark!" he swore. "If you've——"

"It wasn't, Jim! Honest it wasn't! I don't know nothing about this!"

She stopped abruptly, to stare at the figures of Clinton and Rayner that had appeared beside her. Slade jerked his head up the lane.

"We'll be moving. This place is getting chilly."

He thrust Jenkins before him, and with a few thickly muttered words the man slunk forward. The fight had suddenly gone out of him, and he had turned sullen.

"Rayner," said Slade, "you drive, and Clinton can look to the woman. You three can manage in the front seat at a pinch. I'll take the rear seat with Jenkins."

It was nearly a quarter past one when that strange company passed under the dim blue light burning outside Ploverton Police Station. Rayner sent one of the night constables for more chairs from the other offices, and when they were all seated he signalled to the uniformed man to shut the door and remain outside in the corridor.

"We shall want some notes taken," he said to Slade.

"That's all right," replied the Yard man. "Clinton will take down."

The sergeant drew out his thick notebook and pencil. Leisurely he rose, and, drawing the wastepaper-basket from under Rayner's desk, sharpened the pencil until its point was to his satisfaction. Then he took his seat again. The others had watched the operation in silence.

"Now, Jenkins," began Slade, turning to the man, who was seated in a crouched attitude, alternately throwing savage glances at the woman and at the detective. "You're mixed up in a murder case. You know what that means. You'd better let's have it straight."

Jenkins cleared his throat and leered.

"I've got nothing to say," he grunted. "Just you prove I 'ave that's all. Go ahead and prove it, if you're so damned sure."

Slade's eyes narrowed.

"So that's the attitude you're going to take, is it, Jenkins?" he said quietly.

The other shot him a quick glance. He didn't like that low voice; didn't know what it signified.

"What're you getting at?" he demanded surlily.

"This, Jenkins. You're an accessory after the fact of murder, and you're likely to get it hot unless you're willing to talk."

The man was about to say something sharp in return, but in time bit back the words.

"Then you've got your murderer, 'ave you?"

Slade rose and stood over the man threateningly. It was obvious that finesse was lost on him. There was only one way to deal with him, the one way he knew and understood, like all his tribe.

"Look here, Jenkins, we'll stop beating about the bush. Either you're going to listen to reason or you're going behind bars—tonight!"

At that Jenkins flinched, and scowled again at the woman seated beside him.

"What do you want to know?" he asked after a long pause.

Slade approached a step nearer, and pointed at the man with a finger.

"Did Ridley kill Haunchwood and Ferriss?"

"I don't know—and that's straight."

"Do you think he did?"

"Can't say. He might have—Merrell might have."

Slade began on a fresh tack.

"You and this woman, Jenkins, are not in this game for your

healths. *You* are working with Ridley because you expect to get a good slice out of what he's after; and *she's* in it for her picking. Right?"

Jenkins wetted his tongue, and glanced up at the detective under frowning brows.

"I'm Ridley's servant—ain't I?" he stated doggedly.

"So people have been given to understand. But let me tell you something. You've got a chance now to save your skin from a bad blistering. If you're not a fool you'll take it. If you are a fool you'll keep your mouth shut, let me check up on you at the Yard and get your record—— Ah! That got you, eh?" he nodded, as the other started violently. "You wouldn't like to have to take your stand in court with that record being read out, would you, Jenkins? How long was the last term?"

The man wetted his lips again, but did not reply. The others heard his breath whistle through his teeth, and when he looked up there was a hunted expression in his eyes. His face appeared suddenly grey and lined, heightening by contrast the deep purplish hue of the bruise under his eye.

"Well?" demanded Slade, more sharply.

Jenkins's feet shuffled under his chair.

"I ain't a-goin' to commit myself," he said less assuredly. "What do you want me to do?"

"You'll hear," promised Slade, and turned his attention to the woman.

She glanced at him and dropped her gaze quickly. Her hands were fumbling with each other in her lap.

"You got into the Cedars by a ruse, giving the name of Mrs. Drew. What's your real name?" demanded Slade.

She saw Jenkins looking at her threateningly and flinched.

"If I tell you he'll——"

"Don't worry about Jenkins," the detective told her. "He'll want all his time looking to himself. Now, what's your name?"

"Maud Ankers."

"And you admit you got into the Cedars under false pretences, that you bribed the housekeeper, Mrs. Stourbridge, into giving you an introduction to——"

"Yes, I got into the place to sort of spy out the land, sir, but I never bribed the woman—it was Jenkins."

At that the man jumped to his feet and shook his fist.

"Damn it, I said you were double-crossing me, you——"

"Sit down, Jenkins!" shouted Slade, and the other obeyed, still glaring.

"Now, Mrs. Ankers, have you any previous convictions? I want the truth!"

The woman nodded her head and sniffed.

"All right. Well, we won't go into them just now; they can wait. Tell me, do you know John Ridley—have you ever met him, seen him, know him to talk to, or worked for him before?"

She shook her head vigorously.

"Don't know a thing about him, 'cept what Jim here told me, and don't think he's got me working for him this time. It was Jim who got me down here."

"How much did he promise you if you did this job properly?"

"Fifty quid," said the woman.

Slade smiled thinly and turned back to the man.

"So you're willing to give Mrs. Ankers——"

"She ain't a missis," snarled Jenkins. "No man 'ud ever live with 'er. Pinchin' things off the counter and kid's clothes—that's all she's 'ad the nerve to try 'er 'and at—blast 'er!"

"You were willing to give her fifty pounds for taking the place of Mrs. Stourbridge, weren't you, Jenkins?"

"That's what I *told* 'er, because we 'ad to git someone to do the job quick. She'd a bin lucky to've got ten!"

"And who is the 'we,' Jenkins?" asked Slade softly.

The other started, and cursed himself for letting his temper run away with him. He glared across the room to where Clinton was faithfully recording each thing he said and each statement he made. Too late he realized that he had blundered, irreparably. He had been tricked into the admission, and he felt sore.

"Me and the boss," he muttered, and glowered as Clinton's hand moved across the open page of his notebook.

"You and Ridley?"

Jenkins gulped.

"Yes—who the hell d'you think I meant? Me an' the Archbishop o' Canterbury?"

The sarcasm was wasted on Slade. He adopted a new tone.

"Has it occurred to you, Jenkins, that Ridley has double-crossed almost everyone he knows? Mightn't he do the same to you?"

Jenkins smiled evilly.

"I'd like to see him try it—once! That's all—once!"

"He's promised you a large reward, hasn't he?"

But this time Jenkins was on his guard.

"He's promised me nothing!" he maintained stoutly.

"Not out of a hundred and fifty thousand?" murmured Slade, in a tone of mock surprise.

He saw Jenkins's small eyes almost close. The man had heard the sum involved for the first time. Slade bent over him.

"Came as a surprise, didn't it Jenkins—that amount? Big money, isn't it? Worth doing two murders for, d'you think?"

Jenkins shrank back, his eyes glittering as the movement brought them directly under the light.

"I don't know nothing about it—not a thing!" he persisted, and suddenly his manner changed completely.

"Look here, guv'nor," he resumed, on a more suppliant note, "honest I didn't know what all this 'ere fuss was about. I thought you were trying to fix me so's I'd split on Ridley—an' I wouldn't, see? No, I wouldn't have squealed on 'im if 'e'd committed forty ruddy murders—not me! I ain't that sort. But I thought all that chow about murders was applesauce, see? To sort of get me started. Get me? Well, that's straight, an' you're welcome to believe me or not, as you bloomin' well like. But understand this: Ridley never let on as 'e was on the game for that much dough! 'E told me ten thou.—that's what 'e told me. An' you say a 'undred an' fifty!"

"I also said, Jenkins, that it was big money! That a man might think it worth committing two murders for such a prize. Remember?"

Jenkins made a short movement with his hand.

"That sort o' talk don't mean nothing to me, guv'nor. *You* know I ain't mixed up in any murders. Do I look that sort?"

Slade gave him a straight look and decided it would be policy if he refrained from admitting what sort he thought Jenkins looked.

"An' didn't you yourself say that Ridley was a double-crosser?" continued Jenkins succinctly. "Well 'e is—if 'e's bin 'avin' me on a bit o' toast about what 'is game was——"

"And just what was his game—according to what he told you, Jenkins?"

"Why, to smash a company Mr. Merton had got a lot o' shares in. For some reason or other 'e's dead set on Mr. Merton."

Jenkins tried to appear lacking in guile at that moment, but Slade was not altogether reassured. He knew Jenkins's type, and his depth; realized that the man was capable of any depth of deception, and of resorting to any trick in order to gain his own ends. And what was in the man's mind at the moment? What caused that gleam in his small, avaricious eyes? Hatred or—? But Slade could offer no certain alternative. He felt distrustful of the man, yet he knew very well that in Jenkins was his best chance of solving successfully this complicated mystery. If Ridley was the desperate killer Merrell had portrayed, then there was still danger. The cards were all in Ridley's hands now; he had but to lay them down, and the game was his, the prize his to scoop into his fingers.

Slade had to think fast, and he had to arrive at a quick decision. Characteristically he made up his mind and took the plunge.

"What are you willing to do, Jenkins?" he asked.

"Eh—what?" Jenkins looked blank for a moment, eyeing the Yard man with patent suspicion. "What're you driving at, guv'nor?"

"Suppose I said there was a way of making good——"

Jenkins was an artist in his own fashion. He interrupted with: "But I ain't done nothing! You ain't got nothing on me!"

Slade brushed the objection aside.

"We'll pass that over at the moment, Jenkins. That's something we can take up or drop—later. Understand? We can drop it if you're willing to do something to help us."

Just how competent an artist Jenkins was he showed by his sneering: "I ain't never split to the cops yet, guv'nor. You don't think I'm goin' to start now, do you?"

"I haven't asked you to ' split,' " Slade reminded him. He knew the crooks' code, and the status of the " squealer " in the underworld, and of what the " squealer's " life was worth if his perfidy became known to his criminal fraternity. "You can help in another way, Jenkins, and there may even be something in it for you."

"That's right," snorted the dowdy Miss Ankers, determined to enter the picture at all costs. "Bribe him! Get him to fix a frame-up. He'll probably be——"

"I'll fix you, Maud, if you don't shut your trap," growled Jenkins ferociously. "Well, let's 'ave it," he added turning to Slade.

The detective studied his man again for several seconds before replying. That vague feeling of uncertainty assailed him once more; yet he told himself there could be no danger. He would have them both watched. No, there couldn't be any risk.

"Keep with Ridley—don't let him get out of your sight—stay with him. That's all!"

Jenkins stared at the Yard man as though he thought he had taken leave of his senses.

"You mean it?" he exclaimed. "That's all you want me to do? Nothing more?"

"No—nothing more. Just make sure he doesn't get away from you."

Jenkins was about to spit, but recalled himself in time.

"It'll be a pleasure," he sneered. "I'll be 'is own blinkin' little shadow! But "—he paused and stared at the Yard man uncertainly—" where's the catch?"

"What do you mean?"

"Aw—come off it! When the police get a man this way there's a catch in it—always! Let's have it from the shoulder. No humbug."

Slade shook his head solemnly.

"I assure you, Jenkins—give you my word—there's not what you call a catch in this. It's all above-board. We want Ridley. With you close to him, watching him, he won't pull any fast ones —or he'll be clever. That's all I want. I'll have men on watch. But if you don't turn up he'll be suspicious. You go back and act normally, and keep your eye on him. That's all I want you to do— nothing more. You won't be sorry you fell in with this suggestion, I'll promise you that much."

Jenkins rose with a slight swagger.

"All right—it's a deal, guv'nor. I know when I'm on the right side of the fence, and when I ain't. But "—he glared round at the woman—" you hold her! If she gets out this'll all go straight to Ridley—an' what then?"

"Don't worry. We'll take care of Miss Ankers. She'll be escorted back to London——"

"But I didn't come from London!" cried the woman, in sudden desperation. "I want to go back to Manchester, where I came from!"

"To Manchester, then," amended Slade. "Satisfied, Jenkins?"

"Yes, I s'pose so. Though there's a catch in it—there's a catch in it," he reiterated. "Never knew the police to be pally without there being a snag somewhere."

"Well, you'd better wait outside now, Jenkins."

Slade signed to Rayner, who summoned the constable from the corridor.

"Take this man into the back room and wait with him till I come in," ordered Rayner.

When the two had gone Slade turned to the woman.

"I shall want you to sign a statement, so you'd better wait too."

Another constable conducted the woman away, and then Rayner swung round in his chair and got up.

"Now what?" he asked of the Yard man.

Slade picked up the telephone on the local inspector's desk.

"The Yard! I want a Flying Squad patrol down here!"

It took several minutes for him to make his connection, but

at last he was speaking to the person at Scotland Yard whom he wanted, and when he put down the phone he was smiling with satisfaction.

"Just lucky. Brawley himself will be down here within an hour. He was doing late patrol tonight, and he's expected back any time now. We'll let Jenkins kick his heels for another half-hour, and then turn him loose with Clinton and one of your men on his tail. It won't be a long wait. Brawley's men can take over. How d'you feel, Clinton?"

The sergeant grinned.

"Wideawake enough to keep one eye on friend Jenkins, sir. That bed at the ' Meridian ' was pretty comfy, considering. I got a good night last night."

Slade glanced at his watch. It was past two o'clock. He filled his pipe and lit it.

"Well, while we're waiting, Rayner, any questions?"

But the local inspector was too dazed by all that had happened to have any questions ready. If the truth were known this was long past what he considered his proper hour of retiring, and he was having considerable difficulty in not showing his sleepiness. The greater part of the half-hour passed with Clinton reading from his notes while Slade considered the evidence afresh.

In due course Jenkins was allowed to leave, and Clinton and one of Rayner's men set out together to follow him to Orton Lodge and take up stations outside the house. As soon as they were gone Miss Ankers, tearful-looking now, was ushered into the local inspector's private office, and the work of getting a signed statement from her begun. Slade himself undertook the task of scribe.

They were about half-way through the business when there was a sudden commotion outside in the corridor. Slade looked up from the sheet of foolscap before him, and the next moment the door was flung open, and a uniformed constable appeared, holding by the arm a dazed young man in spectacles.

"Good Lord!" exclaimed Slade. "Merrell! I wondered what had become of you. Thought you were keeping out of sight purposely, and——" He broke off. The constable had lowered Merrell into one of the vacant chairs, and Slade saw that his face was unnaturally white, and that a dried stream of blood streaked his face. "Why, whatever's happened?"

The constable straightened himself.

"Came upon him lying in the road not far from the Summerdale works, sir. He's taken a pretty smart cosh on the head. Hasn't properly come to yet."

CHAPTER XVII

A TERRIBLE DEVELOPMENT

As a matter of fact Merrell hadn't come to fully by the time Brawley's patrol car arrived outside the station. For half an hour Slade had been trying to get a coherent statement from him as to what had happened, but all he could learn was that the young man had followed his temporary housekeeper from the Cedars to the road that led to the lane which branched off to the brickworks. Somewhere along that road a great weight descended upon him, and he remembered no more. He did not even recall the policeman's rousing him and helping him back to the station. Slade, after examining the wound, told the young man that he was fortunate not to have been killed outright. The blow had struck the left side of his head; probably the aim had been misjudged in the darkness. Had the blow caught the young man fair and square on the back of the head he would have been killed instantly. But Merrell himself was too dazed to appreciate the narrowness of his escape. He lay on the floor of Rayner's office, an ambulance pillow under his head, groaning feebly and half delirious.

With Brawley's arrival Slade found himself called upon to make fresh explanations. Miss Ankers, half asleep, and yawning almost every other minute, was led into another office and allowed to make herself as comfortable as she could while the policemen busied themselves with this fresh complication. Rayner's sleepiness had left him. The advent of the wounded Merrell had stirred him to wide wakefulness. He rang through to his home, told his wife not to worry if he was not home till breakfast time, and gave himself up to consideration of the problems Brawley and Slade were discussing.

And for once Brawley was violently opposed to Slade's opinion.

"You should have held Jenkins," he repeated. "Can't see the sense in letting him go, Tony. In fact, it looks nothing short of madness to me. The chap's a crook all right, and he's in this neck-deep with Ridley. Now Ridley will be warned——"

"Or else," put in Rayner, "he might try to get that fortune for himself."

The Yard men stared at the local inspector. That was a possibility neither of them had considered. Brawley turned to Slade.

"What about it, Tony? Think there's a chance of that? Is he deep as that."

Slade considered.

"I shouldn't have thought so—though I admit there was something in the way he looked when I told him to go back that puzzled me. He looked as though something had just occurred to him——"

"And that's what it was!" exclaimed Rayner. "He didn't know till you told him that Ridley was after a fortune of that size; and you harped on Ridley's being a double-crosser. You've given him an idea, Slade: to play a fast hand and double-cross Ridley."

But the senior officer of Department X2 shook his head.

"I can't somehow subscribe to that theory, Rayner," he said. "Whoever gets that first certificate has first to go to the safe deposit; that's a trip to London. Well, we've enough men round the house to know if anyone leaves it. He'll be followed, and we shall be informed in time to arrive at the depository first."

Rayner shrugged.

"It sounds all right." He shook his head dubiously. "It certainly sounds all right. But I don't like it, all the same. There's something fishy in all this, something we haven't got the hang of yet."

"Well, I don't know about that, but I certainly think you did wrong, Tony, to let Jenkins go once you'd got him. He's only got to spill the word to Ridley, and you'll have the devil of a job——"

"But will he?" exclaimed Slade, rather heatedly, forced to defend his line of action. "That's the point—will he? I've played a gamble, Abe, if you call it that. Very well, then. But I didn't do it without some understanding of Jenkins. He's the sort that thinks ahead—but not far ahead. He's out to make what he can for himself, but with safety. That type of crook, who's used to being in and out of quod, isn't reckless. He knows the game he can play, and it's our luck that he always plays it in the same way."

"Yes," murmured Brawley. "Then what?"

It was plain he was far from convinced.

"Well, Jenkins now has an idea that he's been tricked. Ridley probably told him that he would get a good cut out of so much—nothing like a hundred and fifty thousand, anyway. You, Rayner, heard what Jenkins said Ridley had told him. I don't believe it; but I imagine it wasn't far from the truth. In my opinion Jenkins will go back and hang close to Ridley when the latter tries to get away. That's where we get a better chance—supposing Ridley's cleverer than we think. Two men are easier to keep track of than one.

And, too, Jenkins will have a job disguising that battered eye of his."

The other two did not reply immediately. They saw the force of Slade's contention.

" What is your own idea, Tony, as to what Ridley will do, what move he'll make?"

" I don't know," admitted the detective bluntly. " But it's obvious that he's got to get to London if all his trouble is to be fruitful. At the moment he's penned at Orton Lodge——"

" But is he?" demanded Brawley.

" What are you driving at, Abe?" frowned the C.I.D. man.

" Jenkins has been here some time. I mean, he's been away from the house a good while. Someone outed Merrell. Mightn't it have been Ridley?"

" You mean there's a possibility that Ridley has already moved off?"

" That's it," said Brawley. " You can bet he's got his car back from that lock-up garage at Twickenham by this time. For all you know he's in London by now!"

Slade frowned. He sat down, feeling suddenly tired. This new suggestion of Brawley's was certainly a possibility, and he had been so engrossed with his own angle of the case that he had not contemplated it before. He could give no reason why, but he felt that Brawley was wrong; he had nothing to base the feeling upon, and he was one of the first to distrust intuition. His fingers tapped his knee rapidly in jerky movements. He rose quickly and paced the office, staring at the still form of Merrell, who had now dropped into a heavy sleep.

" That's right, Abe, for all I know he's in London now. But if he is tell me why Jenkins hasn't phoned?"

Brawley shrugged.

" Why should he? He'll get nothing out of helping us."

" I gave him to understand he might."

" Pshaw! You know damned well, Tony, he didn't believe you. His breed have one confirmed idea of the police, and it's not of their being philanthropists!"

" Well, what would Jenkins gain out of keeping quiet?"

" Ridley may have left him a packet of money and a promise of more. That'd work with Jenkins, I'd say."

Slade turned to the local man.

" And you, Rayner. That your idea?"

Rayner shook his head.

" No! I've told you both what I think. Jenkins will try to get that hundred and fifty thousand for himself. You said, Slade, that he looked kind of queer when you mentioned the sum. When you told him that you gave him the notion of getting richer than he'd ever dreamed of being. *My* opinion is that Jenkins will go all out for himself. We all three think he's a gaolbird—we're certain of it. Very well, he knows what it is to be in and out of prison, what sort of life he's doomed to if he goes on in the same old way. Here's his grand chance to make his pile and clear out. Why, damn it!" he exploded, "if Ridley's prepared to commit murder for that amount—two murders or even more—why wouldn't Jenkins, a tough bird, try the same solution?"

Slade was silenced. He sat down again.

"Of course," he said at last, "your reasoning—both of you— is every bit as sound as mine, sounder if anything. But I still think we should wait until Ridley makes a move—or Jenkins," he added, glancing towards Rayner.

"But why," persisted the local man, "why wait?"

Slade glanced at Brawley. He saw the latter understood, and he turned again to the local man.

"Because, Rayner, we haven't a shred of evidence against Ridley. Remember, we're not out to stop that money being paid. It's nothing to do with us. It doesn't concern us. Gelder's affairs are finished with. Nothing can alter that mess. What we're out to get is a murderer, the man who slew Haunchwood and Ferriss. We've got to finish *that* job, and secure enough evidence to convict the man we arrest when he's tried. Very well, go to Orton Lodge now, arrest Ridley—and what have you got against him? Nothing! Absolutely nothing! You've less than nothing in fact. You've only got a number of conflicting theories and stories by witnesses who'd either turn you down flat or else flop the instant they took the stand for a cross-examination. Supposition and theory is the best we have——"

"But Merrell's story is direct evidence!" expostulated Rayner.

Slade smiled thinly. Rayner had plainly had no experience in working to secure evidence which would convict.

"Merrell's story wouldn't be of any use at all. He'd be asked why he didn't come forward voluntarily? And what could he say? Nothing if he didn't want to drag all that old Gelder Trust stuff into prominence again, and you can bet he wouldn't do that. He'd hesitate, and be told he had something to hide. It would be suggested that he was telling a fiction to hide his own guilt— possibly. You remember the Mason and Vivian case? Mason murdered the taxi-driver Dickey, but he's alive today because he had someone he could try putting the blame upon. This case would be worse than that, because it's a thousand times more involved, and an involved case is always a good one for the defence. Remember that. No, what we've got to do is get our man with that key and the other certificates on him——"

Brawley interrupted.

"But that won't be proof that he murdered Haunchwood and Ferriss. We believe he got those certificates from the safe in Cheviot Crescent, but we can't prove it. He could say he got those certificates anywhere—bought 'em—and get past with the yarn."

Slade smiled.

"True, Abe. But there's something else. Raymond Gelder drafted a letter of explanations with those certificates, and that letter was stolen. The chances are—in fact, it's certain—that either Haunchwood or Ferriss managed to get that letter, which would have been kept with the certificates. It was too valuable to lose, as, if its terms were forgotten, the certificates might become so much waste paper. Whoever has killed two men and done God knows what for that fortune will not have destroyed that letter. He'll keep it till the money is in his pocket, be sure of that. And, Abe, that letter will be our proof, not the certificates——"

"Still, I don't see how that's proof any more than the certificates themselves," muttered Rayner.

Slade regarded him tolerantly.

"The letter was addressed to Merrell—Merrell's name is on it," he pointed out.

"Well?" asked Rayner doggedly.

"It's plain then," said Slade, "that the letter is the one piece of concrete evidence required to substantiate Merrell's story—give a reason for it and everything else."

Rayner merely nodded. At last he saw. Slade was a clever tactician. He drove home his point finally.

"Arrest Ridley now, and you can be sure we shan't find the key, certificates, or that letter. He'll have seen to that. He's not such a fool as not to be prepared. I saw that the last time we were there, when we searched——"

"You mean," said Rayner incredulously, "that he *knew* Merrell was the one who burgled the house?"

"Of course he did! That was bluff, having us there, sheer bluff, to pretend he'd got nothing to conceal and was quite willing to have the police in the place. It didn't occur to him that he might be just too clever in making that move. I'm more cautious now than I should have been."

And, virtually, that is where the matter rested. They talked a deal more, but got no further; and Slade had his way. Fresh men went out to relieve the others watching the house, and Slade, Brawley and Rayner each took his turn. The new day dawned coldly clear, and the song of the few remaining birds was rather pathetic. Traffic appeared on the roads, and by eight o'clock Ploverton had shaken off sleep and was briskly stirring itself. By half-past eight Slade, Brawley, and Rayner were once more assembled; this time about the well-garnished table in the latter's dining-room, and Mrs. Rayner, a small body with a North Country accent and a very large dimple in her chin, bustled about frying bacon and brewing coffee, crooning a new dance-tune she had recently learned from the wireless. That was a pleasant dining-room, and the bowl of tawny chrysanthemums on the oak sideboard added a bright touch of colour that toned restfully with the browns and fawns of woodwork and wallpaper. Slade sat back in his chair restfully, listening to Mrs. Rayner's crooning in the kitchen, and pondering such trifles as whether the marmalade would be shop-bought or home made. Home made, he fancied, from what he had seen of the lady of the house.

He had just had time to learn that his surmise in this respect had been correct when there was a sharp ring of the front-door bell. The three men glanced at each other, and Rayner rose, his face grave. He had left instructions that he was to be disturbed only if the matter was really urgent.

He came back into the room with Clinton, and Slade took one glance at his assistant's face and realized that something important had transpired.

" What is it, Clinton?"

" Another murder, sir!"

Brawley half choked, and Rayner fell back a step. Only Slade remained motionless. But the expression in his eyes told of a new excitement pulsing within him.

" Well, go on, Clinton."

The sergeant glanced rather hesitantly at Mrs. Rayner.

" It's not pleasant," he said.

Rayner turned to his wife.

" Ethel, dear, would you mind?"

Mrs. Rayner nodded and rose.

" All right, Fred," she said, and patted her husband's arm as she moved towards the door.

" Now," said Rayner when his wife had gone. " Who is it?"

" Ridley!"

Slade sprang to his feet.

" You mean Ridley's been murdered, Clinton ! "

" Yes, sir. He's a terrible sight. His face was bashed in with a coal-hammer, and the murderer set light to the corpse. Poured some petrol over the body and lighted it. The head's badly charred, all the hair burned off, the hands and arms are burned, and the chest and one leg are pretty awful. Looks as though the job was done in a hurry, for the clothes are not all destroyed, and the flames didn't burn all the flesh."

There was a silence till Rayner moved forward and pounded a clenched fist in the palm of his other hand.

" Isn't that what I said would happen? " he said, addressing no one in particular " Jenkins! You gave him that idea of getting the money for himself, and, by God, he's taken it! He's off! Been gone goodness knows how long. Probably sneaked through the grounds; didn't stop for the car."

Brawley looked towards his friend and silently pitied him. Rayner had not realized the terrible accusation he had levelled at the Yard man. And, in truth, Slade looked beaten. He sat in his chair, his head bowed, his shoulders slack, his hands nerveless and still in his lap. Lines had appeared in his face, and there was a noticeable weakening of the line of his jaw.

Defeat!

That was the one word this fresh intelligence spelled. He had worked hard, night and day, for—defeat!

It was Brawley's heavy thump on his back that roused him.

" Come on, Tony, we aren't done yet, old man. You've taken 'em harder than this one, my boy, and never gone down for ten yet."

There was something more than sympathy in Brawley's glance and tone, and silently Slade's eyes thanked him. The Yard man glanced across at his assistant. Clinton's eyes were levelled on his face. There was still trust in Clinton's square, honest face. The sergeant was not doubting him. He was waiting for his superior's next words.

Slade rose, and his jaw tightened. The fighting light returned to his eyes. His lips worked, and gradually he gained control of himself.

" How was it discovered, Clinton? " he asked finally, in a quiet voice, but there was something about his tone, some undercurrent of swift purpose, that caused Rayner's eyes to flicker.

" Well, sir, it was about quarter past eight when one of the men crept round the back way behind a hedge and looked into the window of the kitchen. He saw that the blind was drawn, and, thinking it strange, he moved closer. As he couldn't make anything

G.M.N.—Y*

out—the blind covered all the window, which was fastened—he went round to the door. It was when he bent his nose to the keyhole that he smelled petrol and a——"

"All right, Clinton," broke in Slade. "You broke in, eh?"

"Yes, sir. The man fetched me, and I didn't hesitate. Busted in the window, as the door was locked and bolted, and there we found what I've told you."

"How did the murderer get out, if the door was bolted and the window fastened?"

Clinton had not wasted his time. His answer was forthcoming.

"Through the window of a rear bedroom on to the kitchen roof. When he jumped he struck soft earth. The deep prints are there."

"What else did you do?"

"Went down to the cottage at the bottom of the grounds and roused up the old woman, but she couldn't tell me anything. Been asleep since about eight o'clock, and hadn't waked till gone seven."

"That all?"

"That's all, sir. Your car's outside. I hopped along in it to save time."

"Good work, Clinton. I'll be with you in three minutes."

Clinton saluted and passed out of the room. Slade swung about, and there was decision in his voice when he spoke. Rayner and Brawley offered no word in argument.

"Brawley, I want you and two of your men to wait in the patrol car at the police station, in case the London road must be covered. Clinton and your other man can go to the railway station and make inquiries—and wait there if Jenkins hasn't been seen. Rayner and I'll go to the house before the doctor arrives. Oh, yes," he added suddenly, "don't forget the inquest on Haunchwood is at ten-thirty, Rayner. You'll have to cut along back to that!"

CHAPTER XVIII

THROUGH THE NET

THE remains of the body in the kitchen at Orton Lodge was indeed the "terrible sight" Clinton had described it. Slade, seasoned veteran that he was, who had viewed death in half a hundred grim guises, coming upon the grisly object suddenly, as the door of the kitchen opened under his hand, experienced a shock. The hairs on the back of his neck prickled, and he stood for a space staring with narrowed eyes wondering if he could really be held responsible. However, he did not remain holding the door-handle long. After taking a deep breath he knelt at the side of the gruesome corpse, thrusting away his distaste in his haste to grapple with this fresh problem.

But the horribly smelling and even more horrible looking thing over which he bent had little to offer him in the way of information. It was impossible to hazard the means of death, even, much less how long ago the murder had been committed. Slade rose to his feet not any more wiser than when he had hastened from Rayner's breakfast-table. He turned about, to find the local inspector standing in the doorway. Rayner's face, usually of a bright colour, was paler than Slade had seen it before. Obviously the man was shaken, and badly. They moved out into the hall, and Slade closed the kitchen door after him.

"We'll go down to the cottage," he said as he rejoined Rayner, and the latter nodded in silence.

Mrs. Hubbard, garbed in a bewildering array of drab-coloured clothes, opened the door to Slade's knock, and ushered the two policeman into her dark little sitting-room.

"You are the second callers I've had this morning," she mumbled gruffly. "Is something wrong at the Lodge, sirs? If it's about that man Jenkins you've come—like the first inquirer—I know nothing. Never saw him pass this place, and as far as I know he never has. Why should he go through the grounds this time? It'd be a longish way round to wherever he wanted to go."

"It was about Jenkins we called," said Slade, thankful that she did not recognize him as the stranger who had called upon her recently, inquiring about a red-haired man. But her eyesight was dim, and she had a way of peering through her old-fashioned steel rimmed spectacles that made her neck sag and rise like a turkey's.

"Well, I've told you all I can, gentlemen——"

Rayner interrupted. The local man was fast becoming excited. He considered that he had reason to doubt the wisdom of the Yard man's opinion now, and Slade suffered his interference in silence, knowing how the man felt.

"Do you sleep in the back bedroom of this cottage or the front one, Mrs. Hubbard?"

The old woman cackled.

"There's only one," she explained.

"Well, then," said Rayner patiently, "which way does its window face, towards the Lodge or to the road?"

"There's two windows, sir, one facing each way."

"I see. Now, did you see at any time during last night a flame behind any of the windows at the Lodge——"

"A flame!" she squeaked. "Goodness gracious me! Don't mean, sir, do 'ee, as there's bin a fire up at the Lodge, an' me slept a-through it all, while p'raps——"

Rayner endeavoured to stem the flood he had loosened.

"No, Mrs. Hubbard, there's been no fire. Only an accident. I merely want to know if you saw something that looked like flame——"

"An accident? A bad one was it, sir? Surely Mr. Ridley's not bad hurt, be he, sir?"

Rayner glanced at Slade in despair, and the Yard man came to the rescue.

"Were you awake at any time during the night, Mrs. Hubbard?" he asked.

The old woman shook her head decisively.

"No! I told the other caller that. But who are you gentlemen? I don't know what this is all about," she complained.

"We're from the police, Mrs. Hubbard——"

"Goodness gracious! You don't say! Why, there was a man here only day afore yesterday asking after a red-haired man. Might he a bin from the police too? I've bin a-wondering to meself several times since, I have."

"Quite possibly," said Slade, hiding a smile. "But tell me, Mrs. Hubbard, do you know Jenkins well?"

"No! Me know him!" She sounded slightly indignant at the suggestion. "Why, I wouldn't have that good-for-nothing cross my doorstep, that I wouldn't!"

"What do you know *about* him?" asked Slade hopefully.

"Precious little!" she snapped, and commenced a round of wheezy coughing. "He once tried to borrow five shillings from me, and when I told him to spend less on beer and cigarettes he turned quite nasty. It was the very idea of the thing, and his way. That man's no good, gentlemen, take it from me."

Slade tried one last angle.

"Do you know if Jenkins has any relations or friends in Ploverton, Mrs. Hubbard?" he inquired.

"No, he's a dirty little Cockney. Got no friends in Ploverton or anywhere else if you ask me, sir. Wonder Mr. Ridley kept him so long." All at once she peered at Slade more closely, her head held sideways, the wrinkled features almost grey in the dim light of the small room. "But why are you so interested in Jenkins? What's he done?"

"Oh, you'll read it in the papers——" began Slade, when she interrupted with a terse, "Never buy one. All lies! And I've heard enough of those in my life."

They left her after that, having wasted valuable time. Rayner's mouth was twitching.

"That's the answer all right," he stated dogmatically. "Jenkins got out of that window, climbed down, and made off through the grounds down the path leading by the cottage. She never saw or heard a thing—not likely to at her age. She's almost bed-ridden, only she doesn't know it. Waste of time going to her."

Slade made no rejoinder, and they were half-way back to the house when they encountered one of Rayner's men hurrying towards them. He saluted and addressed Slade.

"Sergeant Clinton's just been on the phone, sir, and he wishes you to know that no one answering the description of Jenkins has left by train this morning."

Slade turned to Rayner.

"And the car's still in the garage. So there's only one answer."

"What?"

"He's in the town somewhere, waiting a chance to get clear. He was clever enough not to leave by train because he knows that with his disfigured face he'd be remembered easily enough—especially if he went early, by a train with only a few passengers from this station."

"How do you think he'll try to get away, then?"

"Maybe by train later, when there are more people travelling—or by river. Take a boat and go downstream some way."

"But he could only get a boat from Baltch's."

"Very well. If we don't hear anything from Brawley or Clinton within an hour I'll call on Baltch while you go on to the inquest. Meantime, we'll have the grounds searched. They're wide, and he could easily hide away in them for a day—or even longer if he had food."

But by the time Rayner had to leave to attend the inquest the greater part of the more thickly wooded region of the grounds had been thoroughly searched, and no trace discovered of the wanted man. Nor had any further word been received from Brawley or Clinton. Slade was feeling acutely disappointed, and Rayner's pessimistic mumblings were getting on his mind. He was grateful when the time came round for the local inspector to leave. Declining

Rayner's offer of a lift back into the town, he said he would remain until the search of the grounds had been completed.

One by one the searchers returned to the Lodge and reported. And when they were all reassembled only one had observed someone not of their party; that was old Mrs. Hubbard setting out with large shopping-bag on arm and tall umbrella held stiffly vertical before her. She had gone down the road which ran past the cottage gate, evidently to take a bus.

Slade got through on the Orton Lodge phone to Mrs. Merrell, and learned that her husband was feeling much better that morning. He still had a bad headache, and there was a large swelling on his scalp, but the pain had desisted largely, and he was troubled now only with a slight throbbing.

After that call Slade got through to the Yard, and arranged for one of his own men, Polton, the man who had taken the photographs of Tangles upon Slade's first arrival, to go to the safe depository and watch the comers and those leaving. He was given a brief but graphic description of two people to look for, and when Slade heard Polton's brisk " Very good, sir," and the click of the receiver at the other end he breathed a sigh of relief.

During the time of the search of the grounds he had not been idle. He had been puzzling out the last moves in this desperate game. At first he had been frankly bewildered by the sudden turn of events. Another visit to the kitchen when the Ploverton police surgeon was engaged upon his examination produced little light upon the mystery. The doctor could say nothing—in fact, was afraid to commit himself upon such a strange case. He asserted that only a post-mortem could afford any satisfactory results of the nature Slade required; and even then, he added, he was distinctly doubtful, yes, distinctly doubtful. The corpse had been removed in the Ploverton Cottage Hospital ambulance, and someone had then opened wide the kitchen window to let out the fumes.

Try as he might, Slade had not been able to reconcile the obvious with his own idea of the case and his own summation of the rival interests. If Rayner were right, then he had made a grave—a very serious—blunder; a blunder which would discredit years of splendid work he had performed. But he could not bring himself to think he had been so wildly wrong as appeared. Jenkins . . . Jenkins? What was the riddle—and its answer?

It was while he was staring at the deeply imprinted footprint in front of the scullery that an idea occurred to him, an idea which resulted in his setting Polton to work miles away from Ploverton.

After ringing up the Yard Slade put through another local call—

to Baltch's. The cheerful bellow of Mr. Baltch himself replied to the detective's ring, and he told the Yard man that he was perfectly willing to check up his boats there and then. He would ring through in a quarter of an hour and let Mr. Slade know the result of the check if the detective would leave the number he was calling from. Slade gave Mr. Baltch the number of Orton Lodge, and twenty minutes later was summoned to the phone by the latter who reported that every one of his boats had been accounted for; he added, with a gargantuan chuckle, that none of those on the beach or moored at the pier showed any fresh signs of having been borrowed. Slade ruefully joined in the joke, and rang off.

There remained only Brawley's patrol, and the Flying Squad leader had not reported. It was certain that since the time Brawley's patrol had taken up its station Jenkins had not got by in a car London-bound.

Had the wanted man escaped before the discovery by Rayner's man of the corpse in the kitchen, or had he made off in some other direction, across the fields, perhaps, prepared to take a wide detour on the chance of not being accosted?

Slade weighed the prospects carefully, and decided that if by eleven o'clock no word of the wanted man was received he would get through to the Yard again and instigate a nation-wide broadcast. Another hour was just about as long as he dare allow himself to wait without acting.

As a matter of fact, Slade was pacing the drawing-room of Orton Lodge, three-quarters of that precious hour almost gone, when once more the telephone bell rang with shrill insistence. He rushed to the instrument, and thrilled when he recognized Clinton's deep tones at the other end of the wire; and Clinton, as Slade noted immediately, sounded excited. He had news.

He had!

He said that Jenkins had just walked into the station, mingling with a group of other people, and had purchased a third-class single ticket to Paddington!

The train left in four minutes' time. What were Slade's instructions?

They were brief. Clinton must miss the train, and wait for him, Slade. They would travel up to London by car. But for security's sake Brawley's man could take the train.

Clinton was about to ring off when a sudden question from Slade stayed him.

There was no mistake—about Jenkins.

None, Slade was informed. Of course, Clinton hadn't got

too close to the man; he might recognize the detective. But the discoloured bruise under his eye was unmistakable, despite the fact that the man was wearing a thick scarf well wrapped up round his chin.

Had he any luggage? Slade inquired.

Only one brown-paper parcel, tied with a piece of knotted string, Clinton informed him, and——

At that point the sergeant rang off, breaking the conversation abruptly. However, when Slade replaced the receiver he was frowning more perplexedly than ever. A fresh doubt had seized his mind at Clinton's words.

"It can't be!" he muttered to himself. "No, it can't be!"

CHAPTER XIX

THE MAN WITH RED HAIR

ON the London road Slade and Clinton, in the former's car, came upon Brawley's patrol, and it did not take Slade long to acquaint the Flying Squad leader with the latest development. Brawley was frankly amazed.

"Why, Tony, it's sheer madness!" he exclaimed. "Nothing else. How can he hope to get clear with that face? There's not a chance in a million."

"There is—just one," said Slade, in a tone that made Brawley glance at him swiftly.

"Eh? What's your idea now, Tony?"

"A clever man will often take a great risk—because he's clever, Abe. That's why our man is counting on that one chance in a million. He believes he'll make it, and have the laugh of us."

"You're holding something back," threatened Brawley darkly, "and I don't like it, Tony."

"I'm holding nothing back, Abe. You know the facts. Figure out the answer."

Brawley scratched his head.

"There's a catch in it somewhere. I can guess that. But I can't see it. Jenkins has hooked it—Clinton saw him. The man killed Ridley for what he'd got, and, having killed a man, he lost his nerve and tried to destroy the body, probably with some vague notion of ruining the evidence against him. You know what crooks of Jenkins's type are capable of after they've killed a man. They're

' trunk ' murderers frequently. But there's no catch in that much, is there?"

Slade smiled wearily.

" It sounds pretty straightforward, Abe, doesn't it?" he asked quietly, not willing to be drawn.

Brawley grunted and turned to Clinton.

" What were your arrangements with my man, Clinton?"

" He's to follow Jenkins when he leaves the train—hang on to him . . . but Inspector Slade has already got a man covering the safe depository."

Brawley's brows raised.

" Quick work, Tony," he approved, and turned to Clinton again. " That all, Clinton?"

" Yes, sir. Except that, should he miss his man, he will ring the Yard at once."

Brawley chuckled.

" That's a good one. You've got my best shadower, and make arrangements for his falling down on the job. Why, I've never known Brooks to slip up when shadowing a man. I believe he's capable of dissolving into thin air at times."

" It was my fault, Abe," confessed Slade mildly. " You see, I thought——"

Brawley's expression had changed. He was scowling with mock annoyance.

" I'm just beginning to, Tony. There's something mighty deep about all this. I'm just tumbling to it—and that's why Clinton didn't go with Brooks."

" Clinton didn't go because he might have been recognized. That would have ruined my scheme."

" Oh, so you've got one, have you? Fine! Well, we'd best be shifting or we'll be too late to see Brooks turn him in."

It was nearly an hour and a quarter after Slade left Orton Lodge that the two cars turned into Parliament Street. The traffic policeman at the top of Derby Street caught a glimpse of them as they approached, and swung out a right arm. Buses, taxis, private cars, and commercial vehicles all pulled up short to allow the two police cars to turn. The traffic policeman's white-sleeved arm dropped after a smart salute, and the traffic resumed its flow.

" Not bad going," said Brawley as he climbed out of the patrol car.

" No, not bad," assented Slade. " I should imagine we're ahead of any report."

Followed by Brawley and Clinton, he made his way to the office of Department X2, to find Farrar seated at Clinton's desk attending to routine correspondence.

"Well, Farrar, anything to report?"

The sergeant shook his head.

"Not a thing. Report of the inquest's in the papers, but it's not very long. We're still in the possession of important information," he grinned.

Slade sat down, and Brawley pulled himself up a chair, and lit a cigarette.

"Been any phone calls lately?" asked Slade.

"No. Pretty quiet so far this morning," said Farrar, making way for Clinton. "Ferriss hasn't roused much interest in City circles from what I can make out."

"I wasn't thinking of Ferriss," replied Slade, and commenced filling his pipe. "Oh," he added, after he had dropped his match into an ash-tray, "you might make a note, Farrar, to return this photograph to Mr. Sunliss. The address is on the photo. I——"

The phone bell rang.

As Slade stretched out a hand to pick up the receiver his glance met Brawley's. He smiled faintly.

"Hallo! Yes. All right—put him through." He looked at Brawley over his shoulder. "It's Brooks. I wonder what he wants to say?"

Brawley cleared his throat with a rattle. He was about to say something when Slade was speaking again.

"That you, Brooks? Yes. What's that? He never got off the train—at any station? But of course he did. How do I know? Well, it's a guess—but it's right! He got off at Paddington——"

The man at the other end of the wire was wearing an anxious face. He interrupted Slade quickly, shaking his head from side to side.

"But I saw every one off that train at Paddington, sir. He wasn't on it—he didn't get off. Am I sure? Well, as sure as I am that he's not here in this box with me."

When Slade replaced his receiver he eyed Brawley archly, and his grin was mocking.

"Well, every sleuth has to have his first failure some time, Abe."

Brawley made an exasperated gesture.

"Stop that stuff, Tony. You knew Brooks wasn't going to find his man at Paddington. Why? How did you figure it out?"

"Simple. A disguise."

Brawley frowned.

"Still I don't see, Tony, and I'm not particularly obtuse——"

"No, not particularly," agreed Slade, grinning.

Brawley crushed out his cigarette and grinned in turn.

"Feeling better, eh, Tony? Things breaking right again?"

"Well, I shouldn't be too sure, Abe. But I have an idea." Slade wasn't giving too much away just then.

"All right, voluble. But you haven't explained the finer points of the disguise. Know what kind it'll be?"

"Again, Abe, I have a very good idea. But it's only an idea. I'm placing my trust in the fact that Polton won't slip up——"

"Well, let's hope it's not misplaced."

Farrar went out soon after that, and Clinton dug himself into a mass of routine work, the details of which had accumulated on his desk. Slade took out his case-book from the drawer of his desk, and began slowly going over several points upon which he was not altogether clear. He read aloud from the book, and at intervals Brawley would interrupt with a short question, which Slade would pause to answer.

Half an hour went by, and then the phone rang again. This time when Slade lifted the receiver he and Brawley were no longer engaged in friendly bantering. Both men wore serious faces, and for an instant, as his hand was held out to lift the instrument, Slade hesitated. In that instant the last dark doubt crossed his mind and vanished.

"Yes?" he asked into the mouthpiece, and Brawley leaned forward, so as not to miss a word, while Clinton put down his pen and swivelled round in his chair. "Oh, it's you, Polton. . . . Yes, I understand. Good man. We'll wait for your next call."

He replaced the receiver and sat back with a smile on his face. Brawley banged his fist in his other palm.

"This is all very well!" he exploded. "But, Tony, how the devil, if Jenkins is disguised, did Polton recognize him? Answer me that one."

"I'd hate to disappoint you, Abe——"

"Well, don't!"

"But you see, I gave him a description of what our man would look like."

Brawley stared.

"You gave him a description! You mean to say you knew what disguise he would have!"

"Well, I had a notion. To be on the safe side I gave him a couple of descriptions. One actual, the other a disguise."

"Tony, you've been holding something back from us——" accused the Flying Squad leader.

"I haven't, Abe." And suddenly Slade's voice was serious again. "I haven't," he repeated. "It was a chance shot. I had to make it. Thank God I was right!"

There was another silence in the office while Slade jotted some notes down on the desk-pad by his blotter; Clinton resumed his work upon the correspondence piled at his elbow. Brawley lit another cigarette and rose.

"Know how long it'll be before Polton rings you again, Tony?" he asked.

"No. Maybe in fifteen minutes, maybe in ninety. I'm waiting here till that call comes through, Abe."

Brawley nodded.

"Well, I'll trot along downstairs and see what's fresh in my line, Tony. When you get Polton's call give me a buzz. If I can make it I'd like to cut along with you—be in at the death."

"Right, Abe. Though I certainly want it to be anything but the death!"

The door swung to after the broad figure of the Flying Squad leader and Slade turned to his notes once more. For nearly an hour he sat there in his swivel-chair, reading and digesting what he had written. He became engrossed in the task, and did not note the passage of time. Several times Clinton rose and went out of the office, and returned again, without Slade being aware of it. From time to time he pulled down from a row of books above his desk a black-bound file, and his eye would travel up and down the red finger-tabs at the edge of the leaves then he would immerse himself in what he was looking up. It was ten minutes past one when Polton got through a second time.

He was phoning from a public call-box at the end of the road in which he had run his man to earth—Sylvester Street, Shoreditch.

"One thing, Polton," said Slade hurriedly. "Has he still got red hair?"

"No—black now!"

"Right! I'll be along as soon as I can get there, Polton."

Brawley came up in answer to Slade's buzz on the house-phone.

"I've been tracing our friend Miss Ankers, Tony," he said. "I got her trail at last. It's right—she's from Manchester. But she's got a crooked sister, who married a jailbird named Jennings. The couple live in Sylvester Street, Shoreditch. Now, where are we going?"

Slade looked at Brawley queerly.

"Sylvester Street, Shoreditch," he said in a strangely husky voice.

CHAPTER XX

UNMASKED

SLADE, Clinton, and Brawley left their car in the yard of the police station in Old Street, and proceeded the rest of the way on foot, after assuring the inspector at the station that they required no reinforcements. Sylvester Street proved to be one of those mean thoroughfares bounded at one end by a barrier in the form of several iron posts. Beyond the posts stretched the confines of a narrow lane, consisting, apparently, of tumbledown cottages that had long been empty, for in place of windows boards bridged the openings, and on the boards of the ground floor were pasted posters of many shades, generally advertising some speedway or greyhound track.

Leaning against one of the iron posts, his jacket collar turned up, a thin cigarette pasted to his lower lip, was Polton. When he caught sight of the three approaching he turned and shuffled off down the lane. The others, without quickening their pace, followed. Where the lane turned abruptly Polton lingered.

" It's number fifteen," he said as soon as Slade caught up with him.

" All right, Polton, let's have it. What did he do? Oh, just a minute. Clinton, keep an eye on the street. Now, then," Slade added, addressing Polton again as Clinton retraced his steps.

" He arrived at the safe depository, as you said, sir," recounted Polton, sinking his voice to a conspiratorial whisper, " and he was in there about twenty minutes. When he came out he walked along till he came to a post-office. He went in. I followed. I saw him take a telegraph form and fill it in and hand it to a girl at one of the counters with a coin that looked like half a crown. He got a sixpence and some coppers change, so I gathered he'd sent a fairly long message. But I hadn't time to tackle the girl, because he went out directly he pocketed the money. And he led me to a cheap restaurant, where he had a meal, over which he took his time."

Slade nodded understandingly.

" Gave the message time to arrive."

" You think then, Tony, that he sent the message here?" queried Brawley.

" I'm sure of it," said Slade. " Now, Polton, what did he look like when he entered the safe depository?"

"Well, he'd got a darkish overcoat on and a dark grey felt hat, with the brim turned down all round. I could see that his hair was reddish, and he had a red moustache——"

"But——" began Brawley, only to be stopped by Slade's hand on his arm.

"Just a minute, Abe. Let's hear Polton through first. I want to know where he changed."

"In a public convenience," said the plain-clothes man quickly. "He went there immediately he'd left the eating-house. I can tell you, sir, I had a shock when he came out changed that way. I wasn't certain at first that he was the right man, but there was something in his walk that settled it. He walked as though he was tired, and he swung his arms in a way that isn't what you might call exactly common. His hands turned a bit, if you know what I mean, sir, every time his arms swung forward."

Slade's eyes were shining.

"I know what you mean all right, Polton. Smart work, man, twigging that. Go on."

"Well, sir, I followed him from the public convenience to a bus stop. He got on a bus that took him to the Bank, and there he changed on to one going to Old Street. I was off that second bus within half a minute of his walking away. He didn't seem to know his way about, and asked several people. At last he came to the top of Sylvester Street. I saw him stand and look round for the name, as though to make sure of where he was, and then he began walking down, looking at the numbers on the doors. I pulled up behind the telephone-box at the other end of the street and watched. I saw him pause before one door, hesitate, as though not certain whether to knock or walk away, and then finally lift the knocker. A few seconds after that the door opened, and he stood there talking to the person who opened it; then he went inside. I walked up the street to the house, noted its number, and went back and got through to you, sir."

"That all, Polton?"

"That's all, sir. I never took my eyes off that house till I saw you coming down the other street. He's still in there, and nobody else has come out."

"Right. Now, what did he look like after that change?"

Polton pursed his lips and trod his heel on the stump of his cigarette.

"He'd got a black wig on, and he'd taken off the moustache, and was clean-shaven. But he'd rubbed something into his cheeks that made 'em look darker than I thought they were at first. Having turned up the brim of his hat at the back made a difference, too. But he hadn't changed his walk, and, apart from the clothes, that was what gave him away."

Slade nodded thoughtfully as Polton came to another halt.

"Sure he didn't make a telephone call anywhere, Polton? Not while he was in the restaurant?"

Polton's head-shake was positive.

"No, sir. He couldn't have done so without my seeing; and he didn't make a call from the time he left the safe depository."

"Very good. We'll go and tackle number fifteen now, then, and —well, we'll see what we shall see."

"Damned mysterious all of a sudden, aren't you?" grumbled Brawley, as they turned back down the lane.

"I've got the idea you've said that more than once this morning, Abe," smiled Slade.

"Well, what's the mystery? You've got Jenkins—or Jennings, if that's his name—cornered. Why beat about the bush?"

Clinton approached.

"All clear, sir."

"Right, Clinton. Come on. . . . No, Abe," Slade resumed, talking to the Flying Squad leader, though he did not turn to him, "I'm not beating about the bush. It's just that I shan't be absolutely positive until I get inside number fifteen—and we may be running into danger."

"Well, we're armed. Though you'd have been crazy enough to have come without a gun if I hadn't insisted."

"This is it, sir," whispered Polton as they drew abreast of a house half-way down the street.

The company of four men paused, and Slade lifted the knocker and rapped loudly with it. There was a space of silence, and then footsteps could be heard along the passage-way inside. The door opened, and the head of a woman who was no longer young regarded them.

"What is it?" she demanded brusquely, eyeing them with suspicion.

"Jim in?" inquired Slade.

"No, 'e ain't. What d'you want with 'im, any'ow? An 'oo are you? Coppers?"

"I'm from Scotland Yard," explained Slade.

The woman sneered.

"Well, gorblimey! there's enough of you, ain't there? This is Sylvester Street—not Sidney Street." Her sneer changed to a leer. "An' I don't know where Jim is, so if you'll be excusin' me——"

Slade's gentle manner dropped like a discarded cloak.

"That'll do, Mrs. Jennings!" he said gruffly. "If you don't want to make things worse for your sister you'll drop that attitude and answer our questions civilly."

The woman's expression changed. Fear crossed her face, greying it.

"Why, good gawd! what's Maud bin up to now?"

"That can wait. I've some questions to ask you——"

"Well?" The woman's truculence was returning.

"This isn't the place to say them—on your doorstep!"

Out of the corner of his eye Slade had noticed a number of tousled heads appearing at neighbouring windows. Mrs. Jennings stood back grudgingly.

"Aw' righ'. Better come in, though I don't trust coppers."

The four of them entered, crowding the narrow little passage, which smelled musty and faintly fetid. She led them into a front parlour, bare save for the few rickety sticks of cheap and ugly furniture. A dark cobweb graced one corner by the window, and on the opposite wall was a large stain, relic of a festive occasion when Mrs. Jennings had had a bottle of beer thrown at her head.

"Now, what's it all about?" she asked, when they were all assembled in the small room.

Slade nodded to Clinton, and the sergeant closed the door and remained with his back to it. The woman eyed the manœuvre sullenly.

"Who is the man you've got in this house?" demanded Slade, coming straight to the point.

"Man?" queried Mrs. Jennings, raising her voice. "Why, there ain't no——"

"Stop!" exclaimed Slade. "Speak softer. Don't think you can warn him that way."

The woman wiped her mouth on the sleeve of her filthy blouse. As she looked up at the detective he saw that there was something in her features similar to her sister, though the likeness was not strong.

"Who is he?" Slade repeated.

"There ain't no man 'ere!"

She stuck to her point stubbornly.

"Very well," said Slade. "Let me see the telegram you received this morning."

"I ain't never 'ad no telegram this mornin'," she muttered, but her look revealed that she was lying.

"Remember, we can check up with the postal people."

"Check up what you like. I ain't 'ad no telegram this mornin'."

Slade swallowed hard and pressed his lips tightly together. The woman was a fool, and she was trying his patience sorely.

"Mrs. Jennings," he said severely, "do you want to find yourself and your sister involved in a murder case——"

"What?"

The woman's face had blanched beneath its coating of grime. She appeared momentarily dazed by the word "murder." She was about to say something further when Slade's sharp ear caught the creak of a stair. Without another word the Yard man quickly pushed Clinton to one side and wrenched open the door. He rushed into the passage in time to hear the kitchen door slammed shut and a key turn.

Slade did not hesitate. He drew a heavy service automatic from his overcoat pocket and fired at the flimsy lock, which burst. The detective rushed into the kitchen, to find the door into the scullery beyond secured against him. He crossed to the window, smashed at the frail frame with the heavy butt of his gun, and forced an opening. Stepping on to a chair, he crouched through the opening he had made, the jagged pieces of glass ripping at his clothes. One piece tore the back of his right hand, and blood trickled into his palm, but he did not notice it.

He was scanning the small backyard. At the end was a ramshackle shed, half supported by and supporting a scaffold pole used as an aerial mast. The pole was swaying to and fro violently, as though someone had been clinging to it. Slade dropped to the ground and, ducking, ran to the shed. He had almost reached it when a bullet flattened its nose against the wall of the scullery, sending brickdust flying. That bullet had winged perilously near to Slade's head.

He paused to shout back a warning to the next man following him—Polton—and then dived into the shed. A loose board had been torn from its back, and through the opening was revealed a section of the backyard of the house opposite in the next street. A line of washed bed-linen and under-garments hung flaccid from a cord slung between two whitewashed walls. The centre sheet bulged suddenly, and Slade sent a bullet through it.

A shot rang out in reply, and the man being pursued took a flying jump at the farther wall. His hands caught the top, clawed wildly, and he heaved himself up on one knee. For a moment he clung there, swaying, fumbling, breathing hard.

Slade called in a sharp voice to him. The man half turned, snarled, and raised his right arm. But Slade's gun spoke a fraction of an instant sooner. The man's head jerked up, and his body stiffened; he slipped down to the ground.

When Brawley and Clinton came up Slade had taken off the black wig and had wiped the perspiring face, revealing the blond hair and pale features of John Ridley.

"It was either him or me," he said simply, in answer to Brawley's amazed stare.

CHAPTER XXI

SLADE PAYS A CALL

CLAIRE MERRELL, bright in a new dress of Nile green satin, her eyes alight with fresh happiness, opened the door of her flat in Stanthorpe Mansions. She smiled up at the man who stood outside, and held out her hand in a friendly gesture.

"I'm glad you came, inspector," she said.

"So am I," said Slade as he entered. "You know, this is rather a different call from my previous one."

"Nicer?" she asked, a trifle coquettishly.

"Much," he smiled, and passed into the drawing-room, where Merrell, who had been seated on the divan reading a magazine, rose. His head was bandaged, and he tapped the bandage with a finger.

"Can't do too much reading, inspector," he said. "Makes the old top spin, you know."

His face was pale, and the anxious lines had not all disappeared from under his eyes, but behind the lenses of his glasses the eyes themselves twinkled more boyishly. Merrell looked younger than Slade had seen him looking before.

"You're lucky to be reading at all after that cosh," said the Yard man. "Mind if I smoke, Mr. Merrell?"

"No, not at all. Make yourself at home. Here, take this chair. It's a favourite with me, and seems to get you where your back wants getting."

The woman came in, and they sat round the bright fire, chatting lightly, until Merrell eased himself back on the divan and threw the end of his cigarette into the heart of the blaze.

"Everything finished about Ridley?" he asked quietly, not meeting the detective's glance.

"Yes—everything!"

Claire Merrell looked up quickly.

" You mean——? "

Slade tapped down the ash in the bowl of his pipe.

" He passed out about six o'clock this morning."

" And he said——? " Merrell was staring at the fire intently, his lips closely pressed.

" Nothing. Not a syllable. He was a beaten man, and he took it hard. His spirit was broken. Ruthless himself, he took his defeat for what it meant—the end."

In the short silence that followed a blazing coal slipped from the grate and fell into the hearth. The woman picked up the tongs and threw it back into the red heart of the fire.

" We were astounded when we read the truth," she said. " About his many disguises, I mean."

" To think that *he* was that old woman!" murmured her husband. " What did he call himself, Old Mother Hubbard? A great sense of humour!"

" You're right," agreed Slade. " A great sense of humour for such an unscrupulous crook. His cupboard was absolutely bare!"

" That was the motive for Jenkins's—or Jennings's, rather—murder, because the man knew his secret, I take it?"

" Yes, Jennings knew far too much for Ridley's peace of mind. He could have blackmailed him ever after. But, as a matter of fact, Ridley did not trust Jennings. He followed him out that night he met his sister-in-law, saw you following the man, and—well, you got that thump across the head. He also saw us take Jennings and the woman to the station, and that decided him. He couldn't be sure how much Jennings would tell us, and he couldn't afford to take any risk. As I understand what happened, Jennings went back to the Lodge intending to tell Ridley what we had found out, and to extort a good sum from him. Jennings wasn't after that hundred and fifty thousand, as Rayner thought. I'm sure of that. He wanted some spot cash—and Ridley didn't see eye to eye with him. Jennings was killed almost as soon as he got back, and the corpse treated—you know how. It was fiendish, but it was clever. Then all he had to do was assume the *rôle* of Mrs. Hubbard and pack up some other disguises in a shopping-basket. But——"

" He must have been a superb actor!" exclaimed Claire Merrell.

Slade smiled thinly.

" We know now that he started his career as an actor. His first change was when he directed a company, and his first known piece of crooked work was when he ran the General Provincial Touring Company into bankruptcy. He came out of that richer by several thousand pounds, and from that time never turned back to the footlights. He eventually ran into Haunchwood and Ferriss, two clever swindling rogues, and worsted them at their own game. The Summerdale firm he bought when it was on the verge of going into liquidation. By drastic cuts he made it just about pay its way, and ever after it offered a splendid background for him. What really puzzles me is how you yourself ever got into the firm, Mr. Merrell."

The younger man stirred on the divan.

"I told you, inspector, it was through Claire. She knows the wives of lots of people who can pull strings; and you should know that Ridley got himself mixed up with a lot of strings."

Slade laughed.

"All right. I won't press you too much upon that point." Mrs. Merrell was blushing prettily. "There was one thing, however, that made me suspicious of Ridley from the beginning, even before you told me what you saw on the night of the murder at Tangles."

"What was that, inspector?"

Slade knocked out his pipe and put it back in his pocket.

"I asked him for the name of the company Ferriss represented —a Continental company, remember?—and he was careful not to give it to me. Turned the talk to something else, and appeared to forget. But he didn't forget. He was purposely keeping back that name. That made me suspicious. Of course there wasn't a name?"

"Why, no, of course not! Ferriss wasn't on the books. We didn't do any trading with Continental firms."

"No, I thought not. All that bunk about good materials being exported despite tariffs didn't quite go down. By the way, what's going to happen to the Summerdale works?"

"A Peterborough firm are taking over the plant."

"I see."

"Oh, I say, inspector!" broke in the woman, turning to Slade. "Tell me now what happened that day you followed Ridley to Ploverton. How do you think it all worked out?"

"Well, you see, Mrs. Merrell, there can be little doubt now that Ridley thought he'd killed you. But he wanted to make sure, and he thought the surest way was to call at the shop in Shaftesbury Avenue. I'm not sure that he was right, but it was a smart move, anyway. What's more, it was a lucky one for me. However, when he turned into the gate at the cottage he was smarter than I thought. He knew he was being followed, and the quarter of an hour I hung about outside, being careful "—Slade smiled ruefully—" gave him more time than he wanted to make his change. When I knocked Mrs. Hubbard was there to meet me and invite the poor fly into her parlour. It was too great a change for me to detect, and the little rooms were dark, closely curtained; added to which, he acted the part splendidly. I was completely taken in. Of course, when I arrived at the Lodge Jennings had his tale ready. I was sent off to the works. It was easy for Ridley to get there first, and I wasn't to know when I arrived that he had got there not many minutes before me. Quick work, but every move of it was calculated, and there was very little chance of a slip-up anywhere."

After a pause Claire Merrell turned to Slade with another question.

"How did Jenkins—no, I suppose I must call him Jennings—fit into it all? Neither of us suspected anything like the truth, and when that horrid man appeared at Canterbury Road——"

She shuddered.

"I'm not sure yet, but I believe that Ridley had employed Jennings on and off for years to do numerous dirty jobs for him. He had a slight hold over him and over his wife too. That's how he came to send the telegram to Sylvester Street. He knew the woman dare not squeal, and he thought the corpse had been officially identified as his own. There were the clothes, you know. So there seemed no reason why Mrs. Jennings should learn of her husband's death, and for a few pounds she'd be willing to hide him for a day or so—until his yacht was ready. He had been careful to see that Jennings got nothing on him. Jennings might have guessed at the truth of the murders—indeed, when we questioned him he took it calmly enough—but Ridley was careful to see that Jennings was armed with no proof. That was the clever part of Ridley's great scheme. No one had any real proof. In fact, the only proof there could be was his gun—and the certificates. As we've the gun we shan't want the certificates."

He smiled at her, and impulsively she stretched out a hand and caught his arm.

"You've been very sweet about it all, Mr. Slade," she said softly, the firelight making pretty play with her hair and features. "I was rather stubborn at first, and I owe you a lot. I—I shan't forget that night at Tangles. . . ."

Her eyes were very soft and expressive then. Hastily Slade thought of something to say.

"That reminds me, Mrs. Merrell, what's happening about Tangles? You know we found the old safe down in the cellar? That's where the certificates were hidden."

Her hand came away from his arm. She glanced at her husband, and then stared at the fire.

" Yes, Sergeant Clinton told us that when he called for some further particulars. But Sid's thinking of selling the place."

Merrell nodded.

" Yes, we've both had enough of Ploverton, I think. Neither of us will feel the same again towards the old place. It's as though it has a bogy of its own, and one we don't want to raise—if you understand me."

" I understand you, Mr. Merrell," nodded the detective.

Merrell twisted himself round on the divan and patted the bandage on his head.

" I'm afraid this is a bit tight, Claire. Ah, that's better! I say, Slade," he added, as though something had just occurred to him, " what's happened to our substitute housekeeper? Ankers, wasn't her name?"

" Yes, Maud Ankers, Jennings's sister-in-law. Oh, we let her go. No point in holding her or charging her with anything. And with Jennings dead——"

" What's the wife doing now?" interrupted Claire Merrell.

" I heard from Brawley that she's got a job in a factory. There's a boy about fourteen, just leaving school. Rotten for the youngster."

" Well," said Merrell hesitantly, " if there's anything we can do, Slade. We've got plenty now, and—well, to tell the truth, both the wife and I have been wondering about the woman. We didn't know, of course, if there was any family; and, in a way, we're a bit responsible."

Slade took out his pipe again and slowly filled it.

" Right, Mr. Merrell, I'll let you know. Very good of you. But you know what East Enders are. No good giving them a lump sum. It'd be blued in a month. But the boy will want a job. A good, steady job with a prospect might be the making of him; and I seem to remember that Mrs. Merrell is rather fortunate at securing positions for people!"

The woman laughed lightly.

" Yes, probably I shall be able to do something, inspector. But isn't there something else—surely?"

" Well, I'll get Clinton to go along and make a few soundings, as it were." Slade glanced at his watch. " I'm afraid I'll have to be going——"

" Oh!" protested Claire Merrell, " but you're staying to dinner —isn't he, Sid?"

Merrell looked at Slade, and a smile spread across his face.

" Rather! Now we've a friend at court—or, rather, the Yard— we're not forgetting it readily. And that reminds me, Slade, there's one other thing I've been wanting to ask you. It's about Jennings's call at Canterbury Road. How the devil did he know Claire was going there?"

"Simple," replied Slade. "Maud Ankers heard you and your wife mention your wife's aunt, and she heard you discuss what had better be done with the key. She knew just as soon as you when you'd made up your mind for Mrs. Merrell to go to her aunt's. We pumped her of a good deal, you know; and, if you remember, you also discussed the best way of getting there. That's how she knew where the place was. She reported faithfully to Jennings as soon as you'd both left the house, and when the news was passed on to Ridley he knew what to do."

Merrell nodded glumly.

"What fools we were—Claire and I—really! My Lord, if I'd known then what I know now we'd have let the whole thing rip——"

His wife turned on him.

"We wouldn't!" she decided, her pretty mouth set grimly. "We were out to get what was ours—legally and in every way— and we wouldn't have been downed by a crook of Ridley's stamp!"

Slade smiled to himself and felt for his matches.

"You know," he said, "that's one of the truest things I've heard about this affair. It was your taking the offensive that speeded things up——"

She laughed.

"Really, inspector, I believe you're trying to flatter me in some subtle way!"

"Far otherwise," countered Slade. "I'm beginning to understand why Lorette's is a success."

Both the Merrells stared at him.

"Why, surely you don't believe that!" exclaimed the woman. "The truth is Lorette's is hardly paying its way. I've considered selling out heaps of times. I had an offer, too, once. From someone you've heard of."

Slade succeeded in mastering his surprise.

"Don't tell me it was Ridley."

"I won't—because it was Ferriss, calling himself Haunchwood!"

"What was the idea?" asked Slade, frowning, for he did not understand what she was driving at.

"A bluff, I suspect. I don't really think he meant to sink money into the firm, but he was scouting round to find out what he could about me. He'd got something from Ridley, I believe, and wanted to find out for himself. As you know, he was double-crossing every one except himself. He'd got the certificates in the safe in Cheviot Crescent, and to think I refused to go to see him there! I might have offered that snap I took of him in the grounds of Tangles for them! I wonder if he would have exchanged!"

"He probably would have had you accepted the invitation to tea," said Slade.

She frowned prettily.

"Am I to hunt for more subtle flattery, inspector?"

"No, Claire, you're to hunt up that dinner," said her husband, laughing. "Then we'll see if our policeman friend can flatter your prowess as a cook. I've always understood the police are partial to cooks. Any truth in that, Slade?"

The Yard man closed one eye and appeared to ruminate.

"It depends upon whether the menu includes"—he sniffed—"a well-cooked chicken."

Claire Merrell started.

"Why, how——" she began, and stopped suddenly as Slade sniffed again.

She glanced uneasily at her husband. They both sniffed.

"Oh, Sid!" she wailed. "It's probably a cinder by now!"

And she fled from the room.